THE MUMMY OF MONTE CRISTO

ADAPTED FROM *THE COUNT OF MONTE CRISTO* BY ALEXANDRE DUMAS

J TREVOR ROBINSON

Immortal Works LLC
1505 Glenrose Drive
Salt Lake City, Utah 84104
Tel: (385) 202-0116

Cover Art by Megan King
http://www.approximatelymeganndesign.com/

Stock Photos by Samantha Strathy

ISBN 978-1-953491-03-9 (Paperback)
ASIN B08JPQHWSS (Kindle Edition)

Dedicated to Nan who taught me to take no guff, Mom who taught me to read, Katrina who never lets me give up, and Penny who finds new ways to teach me patience every day.

BOOK ONE

THE DEATH AND LIFE OF
EDMOND DANTES

CHAPTER 1
ARRIVAL IN MARSEILLE

As Edmond Dantes was mummified alive in the darkness beneath Monte Cristo, he reflected on the events which had brought him there.

The look-out at the Marseille docks spotted the Michaeleon pulling in from sea on the 24th of February, 1815. The big three-mast ship came from Tunisia with untold exotic goods nestled in the hold. Spectators gathered to watch the Michaeleon sail into the harbour, past the rocky islands in the bay and the imposing walls of the prison of the Chateau d'If. The locals took a sense of pride in seeing the Marseille-built Michaeleon return to port.

A massive grey appendage emerged from the water just outside of the harbour and interrupted the spectacle. The slithering tentacle covered in razor-sharp ringed cups rose twenty feet straight up into the air before slamming down onto the deck of the Michaeleon. The ship's pilot sounded the warning bell; the bell of the old fort on shore answered it. The sailors sprang into action with pistols and swords to dislodge the tentacle before it could pull them under.

Another incoming ship, the Pharaon, increased their sails to pick up more speed. A young man next to the pilot directed the deckhands to man the ship's harpoon guns. They fired the large metal hooks into the blubbery sides of the kraken surfacing next to the imperiled Michaeleon. The beast's ivory beak breached the surface, surrounded by smaller tendrils. One of them wrapped around the leg of an unfortunate seaman, dragging him closer to the beak to be torn in half.

The Pharaon drew closer. As a defensive measure against just this sort of creature, it had an extendable steel spike beneath the water line. The young man ordered it deployed, and their course allowed them to ram the kraken at full speed. The wounded creature screeched and flailed, withdrawing from its attack on the Michaeleon to focus on removing itself from the spike as the crew brought four-pounder cannons to the deck. With the tentacle clear of the Michaeleon's deck, the sailors on that vessel brought their own cannons to bear as well. Fired upon on both flanks, the kraken decided to submerge and flee in search of an easier meal.

Monsieur Pierre Morrel, owner of the shipping company Morrel & Son and of the Pharaon, stood on the dock with great agitation. The Michaeleon was not one of his ships, but a kraken attack was never an easy thing to witness, especially when lives were lost. He made a mental note to check in with the ship's owner later and see if the dead man had any family.

Another concern for him stood aboard the Pharaon itself; or rather, not aboard it. The young man giving orders was certainly not Captain LeClere. Furthermore, the ship was several days late in returning to Marseille.

Whoever the acting captain was, he had handled the kraken and now threw tow lines to the injured vessel. Morrel's wooden leg beat an uneven rhythm against the dock as he rushed to a small skiff and paid the oarsman to bring him out to the Pharaon.

"Did you see that, monsieur?" the oarsman asked. "I've never seen a kraken so big in the harbour in all my days! Isn't the coast guard supposed to keep them at bay?"

"Some ambassadors are returning from abroad and requested an escort, from what I hear," Morrel said. "It seems that kept them busy."

When Morrel came alongside, a rope ladder waited for him, and the young man stood at the top of it. A tall and slim young fellow of about eighteen or twenty, with hazel eyes and hair as black as a raven, and as pale as a hardy life under the Mediterranean sun allowed. His demeanour, even in the wake of battle, radiated a sort of calm peculiar to men who are equipped to deal with danger. Nevertheless, he looked worried.

"Edmond Dantes? Is that you, then?" Morrel asked as he climbed. "Where is Captain LeClere? Why did he leave you in command?"

"M. Morrel, I regret to tell you that Captain LeClere has died,"

Edmond said as he helped to pull Morrel up onto the deck. "We lost him when we made port at Naples."

"Lost him?" Morrel asked, devastated to hear such news about his best captain. Morrel's wife and LeClere's were bridge partners, and their children played together. "Was it pirates?"

"Just a moment, sir," Edmond said. He gave new orders for a course correction to bring themselves and the Michaeleon into the docks. The pilot and eight other seamen sprang into action to respond. It impressed Morrel despite the terrible news.

"Ah, M. Morrel!" called another voice behind him. Morrel recognized the accent at once and was not surprised to see M. Danglars approaching.

Danglars was the ship's supercargo, responsible for buying and selling as Morrel's representative in foreign ports. His curly brown hair, receding already at twenty-five, resisted any attempt to tame it. It framed a round and rubbery face, with a large gap between the front teeth. Danglars pushed his way past the deckhands to reach Morrel without bothering to excuse himself, and his beady eyes kept tabs on Edmond as he did so.

"All of our transactions have been processed as directed, sir," Danglars said when he reached Morrel. His voice was somehow both deep and nasal at the same time, a combination that Morrel found both unique and unpleasant. "I have a summary of the ledger here if you'd care to review it."

"I'll look at it shortly, Danglars," Morrel said. Danglars was adept with figures, but his logs had a history of irregularities that worried Morrel. Every inconsistency had an explanation, and there had never been any trouble, but Morrel would not be surprised to learn Danglars was embezzling. Still, he had never been able to find any proof of it. "Tell me, what happened to Captain LeClere?"

"Ah, I see young Edmond has told you about our entirely avoidable misfortune," Danglars said with a sniff. "We were ashore in Naples having supper, and LeClere heard a commotion in the street. A *loup-garou* was running loose in the street, and the captain put himself in harm's way to draw the beast's attention from some young women. It was elaborate suicide, really."

"Werewolves! Foul creatures, the lot of them," Morrel said. "Was the captain at least suitably equipped?"

"Not in the least," Danglars said. "A jeweler arrived with silver bullets and put the wolf down, but it had already mauled the captain beyond hope of rescue. All we could do was bring him back to his cabin; he wanted to breathe his last aboard the Pharaon."

"*Mon dieu*," Morrel said, making the sign of the cross. "It will be a small comfort to his widow that he died a hero, but small comfort is better than none. Did he have any last words?"

"Ask Edmond; he was alone with the captain when he died and took it upon himself to give the crew new orders immediately," Danglars said, staring at Morrel with intent. He pressed his thin lips together and stretched his cheeks, an expression which Morrel had learned served as a smile on Danglars' face. "While you're at it, I would suggest asking him about the unscheduled stop which not only delayed us but also brings us into port under the Hunger Moon. It's a bad omen, sir."

"I doubt very much that the moon cares about your date of arrival, M. Danglars, and Edmond was, after all, the first mate," Morrel said, frowning. Danglars' superstitions could be tiresome, but if Edmond had ordered the delay he would need to learn why. "See to it that everything is ready for customs to come aboard. I will check in with you before I leave the ship."

Morrel hobbled across the deck on his wooden leg, grateful that the harbour was calm. He had lost the leg twelve years earlier, during the darkest period of Europe's history: the Dead Plague.

Beginning in late 1787 in Eastern Europe, a mysterious event set in motion a terrible perversion of nature. The source of it was a tightly-guarded secret, but something spread across the continent which turned men, women, and children into walking corpses, hungry for human flesh. People called the creatures many names: undead, revenants, ghouls, zombies. Whatever the label, the Plague spread like fire and raged for seventeen years. One bite from an undead transmitted the infection; if the victim could avoid being devoured completely, they were doomed to become a zombie themselves.

Morrel had just avoided that fate in 1803, when a zombie concealed itself in the shadows beneath his front porch. Cold hands had clamped onto his ankle, and the zombie's teeth passed through his boot to tear off a chunk of the flesh and tendons beneath. Morrel had only just been able to put a bullet through the zombie's head when he fell. The quick action of his neighbour, a doctor, resulted in his losing the leg beneath the knee soon enough to prevent total infection.

He found Edmond supervising the crew from the upper deck. The crew responded as well to him as they ever had to Captain LeClere, and he handled the responsibility well. Morrel had seen many young men in their first command position turn to arrogance, but Edmond gave his orders respectfully. LeClere seemed to have taught him well. Morrel beckoned for Edmond to follow him to the captain's office and waited for Edmond to close the door.

"M. Danglars tells me that there was an unscheduled stop," Morrel said. "Can you explain it, please?"

"Of course, but it is a delicate matter," Edmond said, standing at attention. "I wasn't certain whether to log it before talking to you first. It has to do with Captain LeClere."

"LeClere ordered the detour?" Morrel asked.

"In a way, sir. When he was dying on his bed, he sent everyone else away. His last request was that we deliver a letter to Marshal Bertrand at the island of Elba," Edmond said. "The crew were allowed to come ashore as far as the beach, and I was taken to see the marshal alone."

Morrel stroked his chin, surprised by the young man's words. Omitting the visit from the logbook was prudent; Elba was the prison of Napoleon Bonaparte.

When the Dead Plague reached France in the summer of 1788, King Louis XVI and his court showed little concern for the commoners and instead focused on protecting themselves. The people revolted against this indifference in 1789 and overthrew the monarchy in a grand Revolution. Napoleon, a Corsican commander in the French army, organized his troops to subdue the worst of the undead uprising within France and earned the country's adoration. The revolutionary government made him first a general and later their highest rank of First Consul.

Seeing an opportunity to increase French power, Napoleon led the army across Europe. Wherever he went, he wiped out the undead and demanded that the countries he liberated become vassals of France. Weakened by the Plague, they submitted to French rule. Finally, in

1804, he found something in a region of Eastern Europe which would one day become Ukraine. Napoleon never publicized his actions there, but because of what he did, every zombie in the world was destroyed in the same instant. He returned to Paris and gave himself a new title: Emperor.

All was not well for Napoleon, however. Royalist aristocrats who had survived the Revolution remained in exile, working among the new vassal states to stir up resentment against Napoleon and reclaim their former positions. The end of the Dead Plague did not end Napoleon's ambitions, and he continued to expand his empire; in 1812, he overextended himself with a disastrous attempt to invade Russia and gave the Royalists their opportunity. Humiliated by his Russian defeat, Napoleon returned to Paris to find a coalition of Royalist-backed rebel forces waiting for him. He was forced to abdicate his throne, and the monarchy was restored with King Louis XVIII. Napoleon was exiled to Elba with his marshal and six-hundred men in his personal guard, and allowed to rule the native population there as a king.

"Sir?" Edmond said, bringing Morrel's thoughts back to the present. Morrel realized he hadn't spoken for several minutes.

"You should be alright," Morrel said carefully. "As you said, the landing was made at LeClere's request; no judge in the country would convict you for a dying man's last wishes. As for the letter, I would not expect trouble. The postal service already carries news to and from the island, and what's good for the goose is good for the gander."

"Thank goodness, sir," Edmond said, relaxing his shoulders. "I had half-convinced myself of the same thing, but it's good to hear you say it."

"Yes yes, that's often the way of things," Morrel said with a smile. He checked for eavesdroppers at the cabin door, then returned to Edmond. "Did you see the emperor? How is he doing?"

"He entered the marshal's apartment while I was there and seemed quite well. In fact, he spoke to me, sir," Edmond said.

"And what did he say to you?" Morrel asked.

"He asked me questions about the Pharaon, our trip from Marseille, and what was our cargo. He seemed pleased to have someone new to talk to, if only for a few minutes," Edmond said. "I told him that she belonged to you; he told me he knew the firm and that a Morrel had served in his regiment many years ago."

"Imagine that, the emperor remembers the name Morrel! That was my uncle, Policar. He would love to hear that, but..." Morrel stopped his joyful exclamations and laid a hand on Edmond's shoulder. "Edmond, you did well to follow Captain LeClere's last wishes. Regardless, I think it would be best if you tell nobody else about your visit to Elba."

Edmond nodded, and then they heard a clamour outside signaling that they had reached the docks. Men shouted to each other as they lowered the gangway for the customs officers and health inspectors to come aboard.

"Excuse me sir, but as acting captain I should be out there," Edmond said.

"True enough, true enough. Go!" Morrel said, watching Edmond leave before following him out onto the deck.

The health inspectors came aboard first, wearing thick leather overcoats and masks of fine mesh to avoid any possible contagion. The uniforms made Morrel imagine Hell's own fencing team. They verified the ship's logbook and compared the entries to a list of recent known outbreaks. With everything in order, they presented their bill to Edmond and left to admit the customs officers.

The customs officers wore ordinary suits and cravats and were accompanied by several pairs of uniformed gendarmes. Each pair brought with them a drake on a leash, a four-legged reptilian creature the size of a wolf. The gendarmes and their drakes inspected the cargo hold for any smuggled contraband. Meanwhile, the customs officers went to the supercargo's office with Danglars' assistant to inspect the books and determine what taxes would be excised from Morrel's profits.

"I take it that young Edmond has given a satisfactory explanation for the landing at Elba?" Danglars asked, unhappy to see Morrel smiling after meeting with Edmond.

"He did," Morrel said.

"Ah, very good," Danglars said with a frown. "Speaking of the late Captain LeClere, did Edmond give you his letter? I think the captain entrusted him with one."

"You're awfully knowledgeable about a private meeting between Edmond and the dying captain, M. Danglars," Morrel said, his eyes narrowing.

"I may have passed the door of the captain's cabin as they were talking," Danglars said, blushing. "It must have slipped my mind."

Edmond soon returned and Danglars took the opportunity to retreat, though he remained close enough to keep an ear on their conversation.

"The customs details are taken care of, sir," Edmond reported, "and the Michaeleon is safely at dock as well. The voyage is over!"

"Expertly handled, Edmond," Morrel said. "When you're done, I insist you join me for lunch. We should talk about the late captain, the journey at large, and perhaps your career as well."

"It would be my honour, M. Morrel," Edmond said, not bothering to hide his brilliant grin. "But I've been away for three months and need to see my father. How has his health been? Have you seen him lately?"

Morrel chuckled and rapped his knuckles against his wooden leg. "Us old cripples need to stick together! Your father has been fine, although you know how he likes to keep to himself. I expect a certain someone else will be receiving a visit soon after? A certain girl in the Catalan village?"

"Well, sir, that reminds me of something," Edmond said, a flush creeping up to his high cheekbones. "Mercedes, that is the Catalan girl, agreed to marry me once I returned; I'd like to request a few days leave, sir."

"For your wedding? Of course, dear boy! Consider it done," Morrel said.

"The wedding, yes, but also an important errand I need to conduct in Paris. I'll be back as soon as possible," Edmond said.

"Not to worry," Morrel said. "Take the time you need. It will take six weeks to unload the cargo, and three months to prepare for the next voyage. Just be back by then; after all, the Pharaon cannot sail without her captain!"

"Sir? I told you, Captain LeClere has..." Edmond trailed off, his eyes growing wide as he realized what Morrel had said. "If this is a joke, it's a cruel one. I've dreamt of being captain of this ship since I first saw her and learned every inch of every job on her to prepare for it."

"No joke, Edmond," Morrel said. "Mind you, I still need to confer with my business partner before it can be official. But it's a formality; he leaves the staffing decisions largely in my hands."

"M. Morrel, I swear that I won't let you down," Edmond said with tears in his eyes as he shook Morrel's hand.

"You can thank me once it's official. Now go see your father! Go see your blushing bride!" Morrel said.

Edmond saluted Morrel and sprinted down the gangway, dashing towards the famous street of La Canebiere. From dawn to midnight, people swarmed La Canebiere's many markets and restaurants and social clubs; the saying went that if Paris had La Canebiere, Paris would be a second Marseille. Morrel felt a large measure of paternal pride. He had a son of his own, only eight years old, but he couldn't help seeing Edmond as a *de facto* godson.

Lurking by a mast, Danglars held a distinctly different attitude.

"Captain? At only nineteen?" he muttered with a scowl, too low for anyone to hear.

CHAPTER 2
THE ASSISTANT PROSECUTOR

Late the following afternoon, a most unusual wedding ceremony began on the outskirts of Marseille. Though Marseillais weddings were often colourful, no common citizen of the town would recognize these rites as traditional.

This wedding took place deep in a grotto by the coast. Instead of jubilant guests in their Sunday best, the solemn attendees wore dark cloaks and hoods. Instead of dancing, all but three stood in a circle at the very rear of the grotto where the afternoon sunlight did not reach, and the only light came from candles and large brazier. Instead of laughter and singing, a Latin chant and the crashing of waves on the rocks outside mingled with the muffled protests of a man gagged and bound to a stone chair in the middle of the circle.

Three cloaked figures remained apart in the center of the circle behind the stone chair. One of them stood, while the other two knelt on the stone floor.

"We uphold the ancient tradition of the divine right of kings," the standing figure proclaimed in a deep baritone. A diamond pendant hung on a chain from his neck. "As we serve our monarch on earth, so do the merciless and inscrutable angels serve God in heaven. As the angels are brutal in persecuting the forces of hell, so must we be brutal in persecuting those forces as they exist on earth."

"Amen," the two kneeling figures said. The circle around them echoed this response.

"All of life flows to us from God through the crown," the standing figure continued. "To trespass against the crown is to trespass against life itself."

"Amen," the kneeling figures repeated, followed again by the circle.

"Brothers and sisters, we gather here today to witness an ascension within our ranks. Our Stone Brother Gerard de Villefort rises to the rank of Silver Brother, with the responsibilities and hidden knowledge which accompany the position," the standing figure said. "If he can demonstrate his dedication, then his ascension and marriage to Sister Renee will be complete. Brother Gerard, Sister Renee, lower your hoods."

The kneeling figures looked at each other and nodded. Once lowered, the hoods revealed a man of about twenty-seven and a woman just turned eighteen. The young man had ice-blue eyes, tightly curled brown hair, and soft features to the point of being feminine. The young woman was a vision of Venus, with a heart-shaped face and delicate nose, and chestnut hair that gleamed red in the firelight. A stone pendant hung from the young man's neck, and a square steel pendant hung from hers.

"Brother Gerard de Villefort, do you solemnly swear to use your life and influence to uphold the position and authority of the king, and to do whatever is necessary in service to the king's embodiment of the greater good?" the standing figure asked.

"I do so swear, Diamond Brother," the young man said.

"Sister Renee de Villefort, born Saint-Meran, do you solemnly swear to use your life and influence to uphold the position and authority of the king, and to do whatever is necessary in service to the king's embodiment of the greater good?" Diamond Brother asked.

The young woman swallowed and glanced back at the stone chair behind her only for a moment. "I do so swear," she said.

"The Revolution and the usurper forced those of us loyal to the crown to desperate measures," Diamond Brother said. "In the light, we worked with the rulers of other lands to overthrow the usurper. In darkness, like today, we made offerings to the forces of heaven to restore our beloved monarchy. In keeping with that tradition, it is time to extract the tax."

Diamond Brother beckoned to members of the circle. One stepped forward to hand Renee two silver chalices. A second figure handed Villefort a weathered, bloodstained axe; a headsman's blade used in executions before the Revolution, when the guillotine had come into vogue and replaced it.

The guillotine, capable of more rapid and reliable beheadings than an axe, had become popular during the Dead Plague as a quick method to dispatch bitten victims before their turning. Once decapitated, a body could not reanimate. During the Revolution, it took on a new primary purpose: the separation of aristocratic heads from their shoulders.

Villefort took a position next to the chair and hefted the axe. Once Renee knelt in front of the chair with the silver chalices ready, Diamond Brother's hood bobbed in a nod. Villefort brought the blade down to sever the prisoner's wrist in one stroke.

The victim screamed against the gag. Renee winced, but caught the falling hand in one of the chalices without looking away. She held the second beneath the stump, catching the spray of blood. Villefort handed the axe away and reached into the prisoner's pocket. He retrieved a handful of coins and dropped them into the blood-filled chalice. Together he and Renee carried the chalices to the brazier.

"A tax of blood for the crown," Villefort and Renee said together. Renee eased the blood onto the coals, producing a hiss of steam.

"A tax of gold for the crown," they added. Renee upended her chalice and allowed the coins to fall into the flames.

"A tax of flesh and bone for the crown," they finished, and Villefort dumped the hand into the fire. An aroma like roasting pork filled the cave, and the circle resumed their chanting until the prisoner in the chair stopped struggling. Diamond Brother raised his arms.

"Via the power granted to me by the monarchy, I now pronounce you man and wife, and members in good standing of the Silver tier of the Eternal Royalist League. Long live the king!" he declared and drew back his hood as the circle repeated the cheer.

Diamond Brother's hood revealed Marquis Alphonse de Saint-Meran, Renee's father and the Minister of Finance to King Louis XVIII. Driven into hiding by the Revolution, the Saint-Merans could only return to France after Napoleon had been dethroned. He shook his new son-in-law's hand while two other members of the circle stepped forward to present Villefort and Renee with new silver pendants to replace those they already wore.

With the ritual complete, the other cloaked figures lowered their own hoods to talk amongst themselves as the circle dissolved into small groups. Servants removed the corpse from the chair, threw it into the sea, and worked to scrub away the fresh bloodstains.

"You both did very well," Saint-Meran said with a smile.

"Father, you know I love the king with all my heart," Renee said, her face pale. "But doesn't it seem...extreme, to kill a man this way?"

"Renee my dear, you mustn't think of him as a man. He was a criminal and worse, a Bonapartist," Villefort said. "I verified everything myself."

"How good it is to have an assistant prosecutor in the order!" Saint-Meran said with a chuckle. "Between your position and your dedication, you'll soon reach the rank of Inquisitor."

"It is nothing more than my duty, sir," Villefort said in a deep bow. "All Bonapartists are traitors, and however distasteful it may be, exterminating them is the price we pay for a civilized society."

Saint-Meran put his arm around Villefort's shoulder. "I'm glad to hear you say that. I must admit, considering your father's history, I was wary when you applied to become a member of the League."

"My father is dead to me, sir. I haven't spoken to him in years," Villefort said with a scowl. "I don't share his convictions, beliefs, or even his name; Villefort was my loyal mother's maiden name."

"Quite right," Saint-Meran said. "I was going to say, once you paid the ascension fee to graduate from Wooden to Stone Brother and I learned of your record as a prosecutor, it soothed my doubts considerably. You'll be a fine husband to my dear Renee."

"Thank you, sir," Villefort said.

A fat balding man, Minister of Health M. Chastain, approached them with a glass of wine in his hand and a deep flush in his jowls.

"Did someone mention young Villefort's law career?" Chastain said. "Gerard, you must invite me to the trial of that Provencal man, the one accused of killing his father. My gut tells me it will be a show not to miss, especially after seeing you swing that axe, and you can imagine how loudly my gut can speak!" He chuckled and patted his expansive stomach.

Renee spoke up again. "You see, there is a case I can support! A man who would kill his own father obviously deserves no mercy at all."

"Then you're halfway to understanding why stamping out Bonapartism is so necessary," Villefort said, laying a hand on Renee's shoulder. "Think of it this way: the king is the father of the entire nation. Rebelling against him is like conspiring in millions of counts of patricide at once, and so they are guilty of a far worse offence than murdering one man. Do you see, my love?"

"I suppose so," Renee replied, her brow furrowed. "I cannot help but think sometimes that I would rest easier if you had chosen a different profession, like medicine, rather than the role of avenging angel that you have taken on."

Villefort smiled. "If I do my job well, you may consider me one of the moral physicians of our nation."

"Indeed, let us hope so," said the Count de Salvieux, a narrow man who had sidled up to the conversation. His gold pendant shone in the candlelight; rumours said that he had reached the rank of Gold Brother for his role in securing military support from England for the returning king. "You know, I visited the Tuileries just the other day to advise His Majesty. I spoke to his chief aide while waiting for my appointment, and the subject of this very marriage came about. News of the union of a Bonapartist's son and a Minister's daughter travels far, it would seem. The King himself overheard our conversation and gave his royal opinion on our young friend."

"What did he say?" Villefort asked, spellbound.

Salvieux took a long inhalation from a slim cigarette, savouring the smoke before replying. "His Majesty's view was that Villefort—notice that he used your new name—is a young man of great discretion and loyalty, and sure to become a great figure in the legal profession. Those were his very words."

Villefort was so elated to hear this that his legs shook beneath him. Renee passed him a cup of wine, and the smooth warmth of it soon restored his strength to stand.

"If only another of the usurper's supporters were in front of me, so I could demonstrate loyalty worthy of this praise!" Villefort muttered. "I almost feel as if I could swim to Elba and execute the ogre himself!"

As if Villefort's words had manifested into reality, a grotto servant approached to whisper in his ear. Villefort's eyes widened, and he retreated with the servant to a quiet corner to confirm the details. When Villefort returned to Renee and the ministers, an exuberant joy illuminated his face.

"My dear, you were wishing that I was a doctor instead of a lawyer," Villefort said. "Well, the two professions share one quality: my time is not my own, not even on the day of my wedding. I've been called away for a serious matter that may yet make work for the executioner."

"How dreadful!" Renee exclaimed, once again turning pale. "What happened?"

"If my information is correct," Villefort said, "a Bonapartist conspiracy has been uncovered. I've just been given the letter of accusation."

The letter had been addressed to Villefort's direct superior, M. Desmarais, but a bout of illness had bedridden Desmarais for several days. In his absence, his secretary opened all incoming mail and determined which matters needed to be forwarded to Villefort.

"The letter is anonymous, but given the nature of the accusation I must take it seriously," Villefort said.

"And the accused person," M. Chastain asked, "are they in custody?"

"The gendarmes have brought him to my house, under close guard. Please excuse me, but duty calls," Villefort said. "I must find out if this Edmond Dantes is truly a traitor to his country."

"By all means, Brother Gerard, make haste!" Saint-Meran said. "You are the king's servant, after all."

As Villefort shed his cloak, Renee grabbed his arm.

"My dear husband, please be merciful on our wedding day," Renee said with her deep brown eyes wide.

"All I can promise is to be fair. If M. Dantes is innocent, I shall be as gentle as a dove and set him free," Villefort said, smoothing her hair as he kissed her forehead.

With that, he dashed up the cliffside path to a waiting coach. It wasn't until he had set off that he noticed a spot of blood drying on the leather of his boot.

CHAPTER 3
THE EXAMINATION

On the way to his home, Villefort made great effort to assume the detached air that was vital for examinations. Though he could command his features like a seasoned actor, his joy risked overpowering the need to appear stern. Even the bitter reminder of his father in the grotto couldn't spoil how everything in his life was aligning.

Not yet thirty, Villefort already held a high official position and the salary which came with it. As Saint-Meran had said, his influence would help him to rise within the Eternal Royalist League. He had also just married a young and charming woman, whose family possessed considerable political clout which could also further bolster his career.

Renee's mother had escaped the guillotine, only to be dragged from a carriage by the undead and devoured. When the Marquis died, Renee would inherit a fortune and increase Villefort's own fortune even further. The fees paid to the League for his initial Wooden status and elevation to Stone would be recouped soon enough, and the world would be at his feet through the connections he would make in the League.

Far from Villefort being heartless, he did enjoy Renee's company in a reasonable sort of manner. He intended to be kind to her and keep her happy, and to help her if she needed it, but in a heart so full of love for the king little room remained to truly love anyone else.

Villefort arrived in front of his house, next door to the Marseille Palais de Justice. Magistrate Berger waited on the front step, which brought Villefort's happy daydreams down to earth and reminded him of the solemn work to be done.

"Berger, good evening. I've seen the letter, good work arresting this man," Villefort said with his features composed. "Have you discovered anything since then?"

"Nothing new, monsieur. The special order from M. Desmarais' secretary said only to arrest him and await your directions," Berger said. "All papers related to the suspect are sealed and on your desk. The prisoner is named Edmond Dantes, quite young, but the new captain of a ship belonging to Morrel & Son of Marseille."

"M. de Villefort! Thank goodness." Another man approached, hobbling at speed on a wooden leg. "Your men have committed a dreadful mistake and arrested one of my captains."

"M. Morrel, I presume?" Villefort asked. "I am about to examine your M. Dantes."

"Excellent, excellent," said Morrel. "You do not know him, but I am sure that you will see straight away that he is one of the most trustworthy people you will ever meet. Your secretary told me the charge is treason; this must be a mistake!"

Villefort stood looking down on Morrel. He knew of Morrel by reputation, but not his well-earned reputation of being an honest businessman. Instead, Villefort knew of Morrel's connection through family and business associates to known Bonapartists. Morrel's professional reputation did him no favours in Villefort's mind either; Villefort considered businessmen to be a vulgar class, interested more in their customers and ledgers than in the king's good name or the smooth operation of the bureaucracy.

"You must be well aware, M. Morrel, that a man can seem quite trustworthy while still being the vilest sort of political criminal. Is that not true?" Villefort said.

His tone chilled Morrel and made him remember Edmond's account of Napoleon's kind words regarding serving with a Morrel.

"Monsieur," Villefort added, "I will perform my duty as impartially as ever. If your man is innocent, he will be released. If he is guilty, leniency would set a dangerous example in the current climate."

Without waiting for another reply from Morrel, Villefort entered his house and shut the door. Police filled the antechamber, and chained drakes guarded the prisoner. Edmond stood steady against a wall, taking in his surroundings with interest. Villefort gave Edmond a sidelong glance as he passed to his office, where his secretary Mariane waited with a packet of documents.

Villefort still found it odd to be working with a woman even after so many years. Necessity had driven adaptation after the Dead Plague ended. So many skilled and able-bodied men had died fighting the horde, either in the army abroad or defending the women and children in their communities at home, that many women faced no choice but to leave the home and find work. The alternative was to starve.

"Bring in the prisoner," Villefort said as he entered his office. He compartmentalized his first impression of a courageous and bright young man, quite unlike the cowards and dullards who tended to get caught up in revolutionary activities.

The office was kept dark aside from a fire in the hearth and a candle on the desk when prisoners were brought in, as an intimidation tactic. Guards led Edmond to a chair which was positioned to keep his features illuminated while Villefort could remain in shadow. Edmond remained as calm as could be expected and took his seat with as much ease as he could manage. As soon as his wrists touched the arms of the chair, manacles sprang out from beneath and clamped shut, locking him in place.

"Monsieur, are these necessary?" Edmond asked, staring at the cuffs. "There must be some mistake; I need to get back to my wedding, right away."

Edmond felt the first stirrings of panic as officers returned, wheeling a large contraption between them. The device consisted of an arched frame which fit on either side of the interrogation chair, and two pale dagger-sharp crystals of aquamarine as narrow as tapers.

"If you have nothing to hide, then you have nothing to fear," Villefort said.

The officers adjusted the pointed crystals on the frame to be level with Edmond's temples without quite touching his flesh. A third crystal, colourless and the size of a man's head, sat on a pedestal in front of Edmond connected to the frame with a thick cable. Their task complete, the officers returned to the hall.

"Before we begin," Villefort said, "we must calibrate this device. Answer honestly: what colour are my eyes?"

"Your eyes?" Edmond asked, quite bewildered by the experience. "I would say a very pale blue."

As Edmond spoke, the large crystal glowed with a soft white light. It reminded him of Mercedes, and he felt a pang in his heart at the thought of her anguish. The light dimmed after a few seconds.

"Good," Villefort said. "Next, I need you to tell a lie. Large or small, as long as it's untrue."

Edmond frowned in silence for a few moments. He turned his head the barest fraction but straightened again at the prick of the crystals.

"Your eyes are dark brown," Edmond said. He had struggled to think of something appropriate to say; dishonesty was not in his nature.

The large crystal darkened to black, but still managed to emit a glow. Like before, it remained in this state for only a few seconds before returning to the colourless default.

"An uninspired lie, but good enough," Villefort said, fighting not to smirk. He read aloud from his papers. "Edmond Dantes, nineteen years old, already captain of a merchant vessel. Accused of conspiracy against the crown."

Villefort glanced at Edmond but Edmond said nothing, afraid of what the crystal device would do if he spoke out of turn.

"What were you doing at the time of your arrest?" Villefort asked.

"I was celebrating my wedding day, monsieur," Edmond said. A crack in his voice was the only sign of his emotions as the crystal glowed white again. "I was about to marry the love of my life; in fact, we were just about to leave for the town hall to make it official."

Despite his professional impassiveness, Villefort could not help but be moved. His own marriage was only an hour old, and Edmond had been perhaps that far away from marriage himself. Villefort had heard of the lively wedding celebrations of the lower class and imagined the contrast between that ceremony and Edmond's present circumstances. Villefort allowed Edmond to wait as the light from the crystal dimmed again, already composing a speech about this juxtaposition to impress the Marquis de Saint-Meran with later. Finally, he returned to the task at hand.

"Have you ever served under the usurper?" Villefort asked.

"No, monsieur," Edmond said. The crystal cast its white glow upon his face.

"It is reported that you hold extremist views," Villefort said. No such report existed, but he found that he could learn a great deal about a man from his reaction to a blatant lie.

"Sir, I hardly hold any views at all," Edmond said. "I'm only nineteen, I have no experience of the world besides my journeys aboard the Pharaon, and certainly no worthwhile opinions on how it should be run. The only extreme feelings in my life are my gratitude and affection towards my father, Mercedes, and M. Morrel. The three of them have enabled me to create everything good that exists in my life."

As Edmond spoke, the crystal's light remained steady. Villefort wasn't pleased that Edmond neglected to give the king due credit in his fortunes but admitted that the omission could be due to ignorance. After all, Edmond was eight years younger than Villefort, and that was very little time to learn how the world worked.

More importantly, Villefort grew convinced that the accusation was false. He was not interviewing some radical plotting against the crown; he was interviewing the victim of a cruel prank. It was a blessing in disguise for Villefort; he could return to Renee and tell her that he had shown mercy to Edmond and obeyed her first request as his wife. It would be a simple way to make her happy and start their marriage on a good footing. Villefort summoned the guards, who took away the interrogation device and unfastened Edmond's shackles.

"M. Dantes," Villefort said, stepping around his desk to sit on the edge of it, "do you have any enemies?"

"Enemies?" Edmond replied. He rubbed at his wrists, already red from their brief time in restraints. "None that I can imagine. The crew seem to like and respect me and were happy enough to see me made captain; I haven't been in contact with anyone else for months."

"Your career is moving quickly, and you're about to be married; someone could have had their eye on your position, or your betrothed, or is simply jealous of you having them," Villefort said. "Can you think of anyone like that?"

"I should hope not! I'm not sure I would want to know if such people were in my life, since I would be forced to hate them," Edmond said.

For just a moment, a face came to his mind of a new acquaintance from the day before. He dismissed it just as quickly; he believed

Mercedes when she said Fernand was happy for them and couldn't imagine that anyone she called a friend could be capable of such a thing.

"Take my advice, Edmond: a man should always be aware of those who wish him harm," Villefort said, convinced that Edmond lacked a malicious impulse in his entire being. "It's clear to me that someone is attempting to ruin you. Here is the letter that was sent to me, do you recognize the writing?"

Villefort presented the letter of accusation to Edmond. A cloud passed over Edmond's brow as he read the note.

The crown prosecutor is informed by a friend of the throne, that one Edmond Dantes, first mate of the ship Pharaon, arrived this morning after stopping at the Island of Elba. There, he delivered a letter to the usurper and was given one to deliver to the Bonapartist faction in Paris. Proof of this crime will be found on arresting him, for the letter will be found upon him, or at his father's room, or in his cabin on board the Pharaon.

"Sadly, I cannot guess who wrote this," Edmond said, returning the letter.

"You seem like an honest fellow," Villefort said. "So tell me, not as prisoner to prosecutor but man to man, is there any truth at all to this anonymous letter?"

"Well, yes, in the strictest sense," Edmond admitted. "I was given a letter to be taken to Elba and given one there to take to Paris. But I only undertook the errand because it was the dying wish of my captain, Jean-Michel LeClere."

Edmond then told Villefort the entire story which he had already told to Morrel, of the loup-garou and LeClere's death, meeting Marshal Bertrand and Napoleon, and the planned journey to Paris.

"I swore to my captain that I would do as he asked, without knowing what it was, and here we are," Edmond said.

Villefort considered the tale, no longer needing the crystal device to be assured of the other man's honesty.

"If you are guilty of anything, it is nothing worse than failing to ask questions before giving your word. Thankfully, imprudence is not a crime," Villefort said. "I will need to fine you for landing on Elba without authorization, and also for carrying mail without a permit, but it's clear that the charge of treason is baseless."

"Oh, thank you monsieur!" Edmond said, laughing aloud with relief. "I knew this would turn out to be a misunderstanding. When I tell Mercedes, she'll be so happy!"

"I'm sure she will," Villefort said with a smile. "There's no reason to keep you from her any longer. Just give me the letter from Elba, and your word that you will be available for further questions if needed."

"Of course, the letter," Edmond said. "I had it in my breast pocket for safekeeping, but the officers took it when they searched me. Is it among the papers on your desk already? It was a cream-coloured envelope, addressed to M. Noirtier."

Only Villefort's skill prevented him from showing his shock at hearing the name Noirtier. He shuffled through the stack of documents and soon found the envelope, addressed to M. Jules Noirtier at No. 13 Rue Coq-Heron in Paris. If a cockatrice had burst into the room at that very moment and turned Villefort to stone, he could not have been more stupefied.

"Do you know M. Noirtier? Have you ever met, or heard his name before?" Villefort asked, still staring at the envelope. "Who knows you were sent to deliver this to him?"

"I don't know him, sir; I've heard wartime stories about Bonaparte's senator Jules Noirtier, but it couldn't be the same man, could it?" Edmond said, alarmed at the change in Villefort's tone when freedom had seemed so close. "I haven't told anybody about the letter, not even Mercedes. Marshal Bertrand gave it to me, obviously he knows, but I can't say who else he may have told."

"Three people know, and that's already too many," Villefort muttered through clenched teeth. He broke the envelope's seal and read the contents twice.

"Have you read this?" he asked aloud.

"No sir; you broke the seal yourself," Edmond said.

"Letters can be re-sealed," Villefort said absently, reading it a third time. He discarded all impressions of Edmond's character in the face of the danger Villefort held in his hands. If Edmond was lying and knew the contents of the letter, it would be the end of Villefort's career. Nobody could ignore the connection between the names Villefort and Noirtier if the existence of the letter came to light.

"M. Dantes," Villefort said, surprising himself when his voice came out almost at the level of a yell. He regulated his volume before continuing. "Unfortunately, I spoke hastily before and cannot release you tonight. I need to speak to M. Desmarais, the crown prosecutor, and see what he thinks. It's a formality, but an important one which must be observed."

"I've dealt with enough customs officers to understand formalities," Edmond said, relaxing by a fraction. "May I say, you've been more of a friend than a judge during this awful joke."

"Yes, well," Villefort said without anything in mind to finish the sentence. He walked in a circle around the desk, committing Noirtier's letter to memory. "I will do what I can to keep you detained for as short a time as possible. Meanwhile, the only evidence supporting the accusations against you is this letter from Elba."

Villefort crumpled the paper into a ball and cast it into the fireplace. Neither man spoke, but both heaved a great sigh when the last of it crumbled to ash.

"Now, it is important that you understand what will happen next," Villefort said. "You will be detained until the evening in the Palais de Justice next door. Keep this in mind: if anyone else comes to question you, tell them exactly what you told me except for any mention of this letter. Don't tell anyone else that you were given anything when you stopped at Elba. Do you understand?"

"Yes, of course," Edmond said.

Villefort summoned the guards once more and gave them instructions in a low voice, to which they nodded.

"Follow them," he said to Edmond.

Edmond saluted Villefort and left. Villefort half-threw himself into a chair once the door closed behind them.

"By the king's own grace!" he muttered. "If Desmarais had been at his desk and seen this, I would have been ruined. This cursed letter and my poisonous father would have destroyed all my prospects."

Life returned to his ashen features and a smile revived his thin lips.

He realized that, while the letter could have ruined him, the near miss with disaster could catapult him to even greater fortune. With a plan in mind and Edmond safe in a holding cell, Villefort gave orders to his valet to prepare for an immediate trip to Paris.

"But first, I need to return to the Marquis!" he said.

CHAPTER 4
FATHER AND SON

In order to understand the depravity of the letter of accusation which brought Edmond to Villefort's office, one must understand what had happened after Edmond left the Pharaon to see his father the day before.

Edmond entered a small house on the Allees de Meillan and ascended four flights of a dark staircase. He took the stairs two at a time, one hand on the railing and the other on his heart. He paused before a half-open door and looked into the small room beyond.

Thin and grey from several bouts of ill health, Louis Dantes kept himself amused by running his trembling hand through the creeping plants he tended at the windowsill. His other hand, and the forearm it belonged to, had been lost many years before. Like M. Morrel and many others of their generation, Louis carried the scars of having lived through the dark days of the Dead Plague.

The news of the Pharaon's arrival had not yet reached Louis' room, or rather he did not know it had until Edmond cleared his throat at the door. Louis jumped from his chair to see who his visitor was; his look of worry turned to cries of joy when Edmond rushed forward for a long-awaited embrace.

"Father, are you ill again?" Edmond asked when he pulled back. "You're so pale!"

"No, no, fear not. I just wasn't expecting you today, and your surprise appearance nearly shocked me to death!" Louis said with a chuckle. "Sit and tell me all about your journey; it will be all too soon that the sea calls you away again."

Edmond guided Louis back to his chair and sat at the edge of the bed himself.

"Father, I have excellent and terrible news," Edmond said. "The bad news is that Captain LeClere has died, God rest his soul. But a bit of good has come out of it; M. Morrel has been very clear that he wants to give me command of the Pharaon!"

"My boy, a captain before he's twenty! What a stroke of luck!" Louis said, beaming with pride. "You'll have new responsibilities, a crew of your own, a new salary, a share of the profits!"

Edmond laughed. "It's more than I could ever have hoped for! And with the first pay I get, I'll buy you a house and garden of your own," he said. "You won't have to pass any more time in this one small room!"

"Oh, my dear son. You're so good to your old...to your old father..." Louis said. His pallor worsened as his voice trailed off.

"Father?" Edmond asked, worried.

"I'm fine, I'm fine, don't worry," Louis breathed, leaning his head against the back of his chair.

Edmond dashed around the room opening cupboards, searching for a glass of wine to revive his father's spirits, but found nothing; no wine, and also no food.

"Father, what happened? I gave you two hundred francs before I left," Edmond asked, noticing now that Louis' cheeks were not so full as he remembered. He knew his father drank modestly, ate simply, and never gambled. Two hundred should have kept him fed and content.

"You did, but you remember our neighbour, Caderousse?" Louis said. "He came around and reminded me of some money we owed him; what else could I do but pay?"

"But that was a hundred and forty francs!" Edmond said in shock. "You've lived on sixty francs for three months? I'll send for food and wine immediately; we need to get your strength up!"

Edmond emptied his pockets onto the small wooden table, revealing a dozen gold pieces and some smaller coins. The jingling of metal attracted attention, and footsteps in the hall brought a round face with a thick beard to the door. The black whiskers parted in a grin.

"Caderousse, how nice to see you," Edmond said, straining to sound polite.

Caderousse was a slippery character but could engage in fits of kindness when the mood struck him. In any case he was their neighbour, and the Pharaon's chaplain had said often enough to love thy neighbour.

"Dear Edmond, our world traveler, you're home at last!" Caderousse said, spreading his arms wide in a melodramatic greeting. He still held a scrap of cloth and a stitching needle, the tools of a tailor. Caderousse specialized in protective garments to ward off creatures of the night. Runes covered his own vest which he had embroidered himself, to ward off gnomes and fairies and other such things.

"Home and at your service," Edmond replied, forcing a smile.

"Oh, not at all, not at all. I'm a fortunate man, I have generous neighbours and all that I need," Caderousse said.

"Of course, and thank you again for that loan," Edmond said, making an effort not to grit his teeth. "And for being so generous with my father about the terms of repayment."

"What is done is done. Let's talk about your journey and happy return, young man!" Caderousse said with a smile, ignoring or missing the barb. "I had gone to the quay to match a piece of mulberry cloth, when I met our friend Danglars. Well, I knew then that the Pharaoh must have returned!"

"The Pharaon," Edmond said.

"Yes, that very ship," Caderousse said. "Of course, I asked Danglars where our little Edmond was, and he told me he expected you would go to see your father, and so I came as fast as I could for the pleasure of shaking hands with a friend." He grasped Edmond's hand for a brief pump before Edmond could react.

"You're very kind, Caderousse," Louis said.

'I suppose so, but only because I love you both so dearly, as honest folks are so rare. But it seems you have come back in a wealthy way, my boy," Caderousse continued, stealing a glance at the handful of gold and silver which still sat on the table.

"Oh, this money isn't mine," Edmond said in an offhand way, having noticed the greed shining in Caderousse's dark eyes. He swept the coins into a nearby box. 'I was worried that my father had been in need of money while I was gone, and he showed me that my fears were unfounded. I'll put these away again for you, Father. Unless our dear neighbour is in need of some assistance, of course?"

"Thanks be to God; I live within my means and am in no need at all. But I am as much obliged in refusing your offer as if I'd taken advantage of it." Caderousse bowed his head in a pantomime of graciousness.

Edmond had almost forgotten about Caderousse's flowery way of speaking, and it was beginning to give him a headache.

"Is there anything else, Caderousse? I was about to go and get a bottle of wine to celebrate coming home," Edmond said.

"Yes, and to celebrate becoming captain!" Louis said, smiling despite his weakness.

"That hasn't been made official yet, Father," Edmond said. "Let's celebrate once we know that it's true."

"No no, nothing at all. I only wanted to welcome you back. Besides, I wouldn't want to keep you from visiting a certain other someone who's been awaiting your return!" Caderousse said, waggling his bushy eyebrows.

Louis laughed. "Of course, he'll want to see Mercedes, won't he?" he said, nudging Edmond in the ribs. "Such a sweet girl. You know, she visited while you were gone."

"Oh, and what a light she brought to this old house when she did!" Caderousse said, pretending to swoon. "She really is a lovely young woman, and we're not the only ones who know it."

"What are you implying, Caderousse?" Edmond asked, his gut turning over.

"Merely that Mercedes is a very fine girl, and fine girls attract followers and offers by the dozens! Of course, the rumour mill says that you're soon to be a captain, so what better offer could she have received in three months than yours?" Caderousse said.

"I have every faith in Mercedes that she has been faithful to me in return," Edmond said, sweat breaking out along his back.

"Glad to hear it!" Caderousse said. "When one is to be married, there is nothing like implicit confidence; but never mind that, my boy, go announce your arrival, and let her know all your hopes and prospects."

Edmond kissed Louis upon the head and nodded to Caderousse before leaving the apartment with haste; first to find food for Louis, then to find Mercedes. Caderousse lingered for a moment, then left as well. He went downstairs to find Danglars waiting for him at the street corner.

"Well, did you see him?" Danglars asked with his typical sour expression. He retrieved a throwing knife from a nearby tree; he often passed the time aboard the Pharaon by tossing the blade.

"I just did," Caderousse replied. "It seems you were right, and our young friend is indeed moving rapidly up in the world! A captain's post at his age, and the hand of a lovely woman as well; if only my own life would go as smoothly!"

"Indeed, very rapidly," Danglars said. "Too rapidly, I say."

"He did admit that it is not yet a certain thing, that he becomes a captain," Caderousse added. "I almost hope that it falls apart in some way; if he were to reach such a lofty perch, there would really be no speaking to him anymore."

"Perhaps it could fall apart, and he would remain what he is," Danglars muttered, "and perhaps become even less than that. After all, the full moon is right for strength and productivity, and causes wounds to bleed more freely."

"Hmm?" Caderousse grunted, distracted by a woman walking past.

"Nothing, I was simply thinking out loud," Danglars said. "Is he still with that Catalan girl?"

Caderousse chuckled. "Oh yes, head over heels it would seem! He will be quite annoyed when he reaches their village. Every time I have seen Mercedes come to the city, she has been accompanied by a man."

"Go on," Danglars said with an evil grin.

"He is another Catalan for certain, but not a particularly impressive specimen. His name is Fernand, I believe, though she calls him her cousin." He laughed again. "What he lacks in looks or charm, he makes up for in persistence and self-assurance, although I can't imagine how he comes by it."

Danglars took Caderousse by the arm. "Come, let's go down to the Catalans as well. We can wait for Dantes at the inn, have a glass of wine, and then hear whatever news he has."

Caderousse hesitated to make the journey until Danglars offered to pay. They made good time to La Reserve and called for a bottle. The waiter confirmed that Edmond had entered the village gate ten minutes earlier. Danglars and Caderousse sat under the budding trees and listened to the birds singing a welcome to an early spring.

CHAPTER 5
THE CATALAN VILLAGE

At the edge of Marseille, near where Danglars and Caderousse drank their wine, sat a bare and weather-worn wall. A wide gate stood open in the middle of it at the head of a hillside path down to the coastal village of the mysterious people known as Catalans.

Three or four hundred years ago, a dozen ships had run ashore there. The boat people spoke an odd dialect of Spanish and had the dark colouring of that region, but dressed in robes more similar to ancient Roman clothing. The Marseillais people were curious about the newcomers, enough of whom spoke French that they could communicate.

The group had introduced themselves as Catalan refugees, looking for somewhere to live and work. They convinced the locals to let them build a village; soon it bustled with life as a fishing port, trading fish and handmade crafts to the Frenchmen up the hill. The Catalans were not all that they seemed, however.

It soon became common knowledge that many of them possessed supernatural gifts, such as the ability to control water or move objects without touching them. Men and women who could control fire were held in high regard, and much of their folklore exalted the great deeds of past Flamekeepers. Rumours swirled that Spain had driven out the refugees for witchcraft, and even that they hadn't come from Catalonia at all. Regardless, the Catalans proved to be honest people, God-fearing people, and good neighbours.

As the decades passed, Marseille and the Catalan village grew together peacefully. Their fashion changed with the times, incorporating some exotic traditional flourishes into the French styles. While the custom of the villagers was to intermarry, they remained on good terms with the larger population of Marseille. It became common by 1815 to see Catalans and Marseillais drinking together in taverns and working side-by-side in the shipyards.

In a hut along the main street of the village waited a beautiful young woman, about nineteen with jet-black hair and velvet brown eyes. She sat against a wall running her dark hands along her large black braid and the beads woven into it made from polished wood and seashells. She jittered a shapely leg against the earthen floor.

Balancing his chair on two legs, a young man of about twenty rested his elbow on a rough and scarred table nearby. He was a small man, short and thin without the commanding presence that many Catalan men had. His features could have been noble if they belonged to a pirate king on the high seas or a revolutionary fighting for freedom, but seemed out of place on this sulking young man. His colouring was dark as well, with an unkempt mop of black hair.

"It's an early spring this year, Mercedes," the young man said in the peculiar Catalan tongue. "It is the perfect season for weddings."

Mercedes huffed. "Fernand, you've proposed to me a hundred times and I've always given you one answer. Are you really so stupid to ask me again?" she said. "My heart belongs to Edmond, and you know that."

Fernand threw his head back. "Maybe I need a hundred and one refusals to believe that you would rather marry a Frenchman than be the wife of a Flamekeeper!" he groaned.

To prove his point, he held his hand over a row of unlit candles on the table. One wick sprang to life, and Fernand made that flame jump between that candle and the others with deft movements of his fingers. The fire danced and stretched in unnatural patterns for a few moments before Fernand clenched his fist, snuffing it. Fernand looked at Mercedes, expecting a reaction to his display, but she hadn't bothered to watch.

"Why throw away centuries of sacred tradition?" Fernand said. He placed his hand on his narrow chest. "Only radicals take husbands from outside, and you know what my gift means for my destiny! I can think of nothing greater than to have you, who I've longed for these past ten years, as my wife."

"Whose fault is it that you've been pining for me, Fernand?" Mercedes asked. "I've never led you on; I've told you honestly that my love for you as a friend and cousin is very different than my love for Edmond."

"Any other Catalan woman would jump at the chance to marry a Flamekeeper," Fernand said with his arms crossed.

"Then marry one of them," Mercedes said.

Fernand answered by flicking a walnut at her. She scowled for a moment before bursting into a laugh, which soon infected Fernand as well. The brief merriment faded to silence while Mercedes continued to fidget with her braid at the window. Unable to let it go, Fernand tried another tactic.

"This ungifted Frenchman that you say you love: how certain are you that he loves you in return?" Fernand said. "He has been away for three months, and is late returning. That's a long time to avoid giving in to loneliness in some foreign port, if he's even still alive."

Mercedes spun to face Fernand. "Fernand Mondego! I thought you still had a good heart underneath that jealousy and arrogance, but then how could you say something so cruel?" she demanded with anger and restless grief. "If Edmond has died, then I know in my heart he died loving nobody else but me."

"That could be arranged," Fernand said, just loud enough to make sure Mercedes could hear.

"Really? You'd duel him for the prize of my hand? Challenging a man is a poor way to please the woman who loves him," Mercedes said with a scornful laugh. "You would either lose, or win only to see me hate you."

Fernand growled and paced through the small hut.

"Fernand," Mercedes said, more gently. "In spite of your petulant behaviour today, I would dearly miss your friendship. As you said, Edmond has been gone for a long time and the seas are treacherous."

Fernand tried to ignore Mercedes' tears, despite being willing to die to prevent even one of them from falling. "Your answer is no, once and for all?" he asked softly.

"I love Edmond Dantes, and nobody else. And I always will, for as long as I live," Mercedes replied steadily. "If he's dead, so be it; I will die too."

Fernand hung his head. "Then we wait as friends to see if he returns."

They did not wait long. Over the noise of the village outside, a joyous voice came closer crying, "Mercedes! Mercedes!"

"He's alive!" Mercedes exclaimed.

Her blush became a glow, not just the glow of a girl in love but her Catalan gift radiating from her with joy. She rushed to the door, calling Edmond's name and illuminated like a lighthouse guiding him to shore.

Fernand recoiled like a horse catching sight of a snake and fell into a chair. Oblivious to Fernand's melodrama and everything else, Edmond and Mercedes held each other close. Mercedes' light cast wild shadows throughout the hut and made it impossible for Fernand to ignore them as they murmured to each other in the relief of being reunited.

As Mercedes brought her excitement under control and her glow faded, Edmond noticed at last the gloomy figure seated in the corner. Fernand gripped the arms of his chair to prevent his trembling hands from doing anything rash, though small tongues of dim blue flame licked at his knuckles.

"My apologies, I did not realize that Mercedes had company," Edmond said with both cordiality and caution. "Edmond Dantes, at your service."

"This is Fernand Mondego, my cousin and a dear friend, and the man who I love most in the world after you," Mercedes said quickly.

Edmond smiled and extended a hand to Fernand while keeping one arm around Mercedes. Fernand stared at it without responding to the gesture of friendship. Edmond glanced between Fernand's thin face and Mercedes' embarrassed grimace, and he remembered Caderousse's jokes. While Edmond was a virtuous young man, he was still a young man, and could feel icy jealousy creeping into his bowels.

"I didn't realize when I rushed here that I was on my way to meet an enemy," Edmond said.

"Absolutely not," said Mercedes, glaring at Fernand. "I was just telling Fernand about our coming wedding, and he was about to congratulate us. Weren't you, Fernand?"

Fernand could only nod at the steel in Mercedes' voice, numb with the flesh-and-blood reality of Edmond Dantes standing before him. Edmond was taller than him, more muscular, more confident. Fernand looked at his own scrawny forearm and compared it to Edmond's toned sailor's muscles. Despite being a fisherman himself, Fernand never managed to build the sort of mass that other men of the village had; he had been thin for as long as he could remember.

"I was also telling Fernand that if any misfortune were to befall you, I would throw myself off the highest cliff," Mercedes continued, with a look that told Fernand she knew the dark thoughts swirling in his mind.

"Of course," Fernand croaked. "Pardon me; I must have eaten some bad fish."

"You see?" Mercedes said, smiling. "There is no enemy here, and Fernand will be happy to take your hand in friendship."

Fernand stood on shaking legs and offered his hand to Edmond. His hatred was tempered by his reluctance to have Mercedes disappear from his life entirely, but his hand gripped Edmond's for only a moment before his willpower broke and he ran into the street.

His guts churning with grief and rage, Fernand sprinted up the hill into the streets of Marseille. This took him past La Reserve, where Caderousse and Danglars still sat with their wine. Caderousse waved his arm to catch Fernand's attention.

"Hello there, Catalan! Frederick, Fyodor, Ferdinand, whatever your name was! Where are you running to?" Caderousse said. "Come, join us! Are you really in such a hurry that you have no time to pass with your friends?"

"Particularly friends with a bottle in front of them," Danglars added, stretching his lips wide in what should have been a smile.

Fernand wiped sweat from his brow and sank into a chair at their table. The shade of the trees over the patio calmed him enough to accept a glass of wine from Danglars with a silent nod of thanks.

"Hello Caderousse, Danglars," Fernand said after a fortifying sip. Fernand only knew either of them in passing; he and Danglars both spent time around the port, and Caderousse often came to the village for fabric and thread. Marseille was by no means a small enough town for everyone to know everyone else, even after the decimation of the Dead Plague. "You called me over?"

"Well, you were running like a madman towards the sea, and I feared you would throw yourself in," Caderousse said, laughing with a sound like a startled mule. "I thought you would prefer to swallow some wine than three or four pints of saltwater!"

Caderousse sat back with a smile, satisfied at what he considered a most witty remark, and had another swallow of wine. What little of his face that showed between his thick beard and shaggy dark hair already began to turn pink. Fernand gave a groan that was nearly a sob and rested his face on the table.

"Fernand, I must say," Caderousse said with the brutal honesty of drink, "you look uncommonly like a rejected lover. I thought you Catalans were all wizards; can't you magic young Dantes away?"

"I will sit here until I die," Fernand said, his nose flattened against the wood. "Just let me starve."

"Caderousse," Danglars scolded, "stop mocking the boy. Fernand, what has you so troubled?"

"Surely you can guess?" Caderousse said with a wink, not noticing Fernand's fists clenching. "Our friend, the brave Catalan, one of the best fishermen in Marseille, has been in love for years with a very fine girl. But she loves the first mate of the Pharaon, which has arrived in port today. You should know, as you were on it!"

Caderousse brayed again at his little joke, then affected a look of sadness. "And so our friend has been dismissed," he said, poking the top of Fernand's head.

Fernand looked up to glare at Caderousse. The drunken tailor began to look like a prime target for venting his anger and likely wouldn't laugh so much with the beard singed off of his face.

"Mercedes is her own woman, free to make her own mistakes," Fernand said. "If she's short-sighted enough to choose a sailor over a Flamekeeper, that's her decision."

"Your rudeness aside, I feel great sympathy for our friend," Danglars said to Caderousse, making a great show of pity as he turned to face Fernand. "Caderousse tells me that you were born under the sign of Cancer, correct? Cancer never handles romantic loss very well, something to do with the position of Venus. You couldn't have expected Dantes to return so suddenly, if he returned at all!"

"Dantes has returned!" Caderousse shouted suddenly, raising his empty glass. Danglars refilled it for him without asking for the eighth or perhaps ninth time. In contrast, Danglars still sipped from his first glass; he also topped up the half-ounce or so that Fernand had drunk.

"You should have seen how happy old Louis was earlier," Caderousse continued, drinking more wine. "Edmond is home, he's a hero and soon a captain, he's to be married. Fortune is bringing him gifts by the armful! Next week, he'll be Emperor of France."

"Quite right, and the boy could stand to come by some bad luck," Danglars said. He watched Fernand squirm and suppressed his own shudder at the thought of being ordered about by Edmond.

Enduring Edmond as acting captain after LeClere's death was humiliation enough, and the prospect of it being permanent made his blood boil. Danglars had no illusions of becoming captain himself, but the thought of being subordinate to someone six years younger was an insult. Besides, there was something about Edmond which set Danglars' teeth on edge. He was too energetic, too vibrant, too well-liked for Danglars' taste.

One moment in particular had solidified Danglars' hatred for Edmond. On Edmond's first day aboard the Pharaon as a new sailor, he had both brought his belongings in a black bag and looked back when they left port. Either one of those would have been a bad omen, and Danglars had spent the journey in a fuming rage about the bad luck Edmond had risked bringing to the ship. Danglars had never confronted Edmond about it, but he also never forgave Edmond for the danger he could have put the ship in that day.

Danglars forced a smile and raised his glass. "Gentlemen, a toast to Captain Edmond Dantes and his beautiful wife Mercedes!" He watched Fernand.

Caderousse emptied his glass again with a smile and only a slight wobble. Fernand gripped his glass and stared at it until the wine boiled inside it and the glass itself started to bubble. Danglars knocked it from his hand before the fuming alcohol could burst into flame and waved for a fresh glass.

"Oh look, there are the lovebirds now!" Caderousse cried with delight. "How sweet, they're walking arm in arm. Dantes! Hello, Dantes! Hello, come over!"

The haze of wine prevented Caderousse from seeing the look of murder upon Fernand's face or the gathering heat shimmering around him as the couple approached. Fernand's anger only dissipated when Mercedes turned her bright eyes toward him, reminding him of his earlier promise not to harm Edmond.

Danglars looked between his companions. "I sit between an envious drunkard and a self-entitled coward," he muttered too low to hear, "who ought to be nursing their wrath instead of complaining. Dantes is on his way to a charmed life where he will look down on us all and laugh. Unless I take matters into my own hands."

Caderousse pestered Edmond and Mercedes for wedding details, and Fernand had found a spot on the table to focus all of his attention on; nobody noticed the sinister uptick of Danglars' mouth.

"We still have to go to the town hall for the documents, but tomorrow or the day after will be the wedding feast. We hope to have it here at La Reserve, upstairs! As soon as possible after that, we go back to the town hall to make it official," Edmond said.

In France at the time, a decree of the king after the Restoration required all official marriage ceremonies to take place at the town hall in front of a judge; any religious rites would be performed afterward.

"All of our friends are invited, of course. M. Caderousse, M. Danglars, we would be delighted if you could come," Mercedes said, her head on Edmond's shoulder.

"And Fernand! Anyone so important to Mercedes simply must be there!" Edmond added.

Fernand sat with his back to them and neither saw him wince at the prospect. He nodded without a word.

"You are certainly in a hurry, Edmond. Didn't Morrel tell you, we don't set sail again for three months?" Danglars asked.

"Yes, but I have another commitment to take care of," Edmond said. "One final errand on the late Captain LeClere's behalf, which will take me to Paris, and we want to be married before having to spend any more time apart."

Danglars nodded while his devious mind raced. He knew LeClere's last request had involved diverting the Pharaon to Elba and delivering a letter to Napoleon's marshal. Reason suggested a purpose for Edmond's trip to Paris: he must have been given another letter on Elba and told to deliver it in order to fulfill LeClere's obligations.

"This gives me a capital idea," Danglars muttered while Edmond and Mercedes said goodbye and walked away together with all the calm and joy of young love. "Enjoy your happiness while you can, Dantes."

CHAPTER 6
THE ACCUSATION

Danglars turned to Fernand, who sat pale and trembling again, once Edmond and Mercedes left. Caderousse, meanwhile, murmured the words of an old drinking song to himself.

"Well," Danglars said, "it seems like this marriage won't be such a happy occasion for everybody. You clearly love the girl."

"Ever since I was old enough to notice the charms of women," Fernand said. "I can't understand why she would reject my gift for a commoner like Dantes."

"Yes, your gift; flame is a rare omen among the Catalans, isn't it?" Danglars pushed another full glass of wine in front of Fernand. "It entitles you to greatness, yet you sit here moping rather than remedying your situation."

"I would burn Dantes to ash in a heartbeat," Fernand said, sulking as he nursed his glass. "But Mercedes has said that she'll throw herself into the sea if any harm comes to him."

"Women! They mean less than half of what they say," Danglars said, waving a hand with a chuckle. Caderousse laughed with him and hiccupped.

"Mercedes doesn't play those sorts of games," Fernand insisted.

Danglars rolled his eyes. He needed to convince Fernand that Mercedes would not kill herself; the truth of that didn't matter.

"Fernand, I'd like to help you, but—Caderousse!" Danglars said, feigning indignance as Caderousse nudged him with the bottle. "My friend, if I were to cut you, I expect that I would find more wine than blood."

"Me, drunk? Me? Drunk?" Caderousse said, eyes squinted. "What a joker you are! These bottles are no larger than a thimble, I could drink four more and never have a trouble with, er..."

Caderousse lost the thread of his thoughts and contented himself with refilling his glass. The task appeared to require great focus. Fernand fidgeted and drank more of his own wine during this exchange, then rounded on Danglars.

"You were saying?" Fernand demanded. "You would like to help me, you said, but how?"

"Hmm?" Danglars pretended to concentrate. "Ah, yes, I remember. Dantes doesn't need to die; for your purposes, we only need to stop the wedding."

Fernand huffed and crossed his arms. "Nothing but death would keep them from marrying. You're a fool."

"You talk like a noodle, Fernand," Caderousse said. "Danglars is a very clever fellow! It would of course be a pity for Dantes to die. If Danglars says he does not need to die, then so much the better! I like Dantes, Dantes is a good fellow. Dantes, your health!" And he took another deep drink.

Fernand rose, but Danglars pulled him back into his seat. "Ignore him,and think. Why should Dantes need to die? Absence accomplishes the same goal. The walls of a prison would separate the lovebirds just as effectively as six feet of grave dirt."

"One gets out of prison, don't forget," said Caderousse, pointing a wavering finger somewhere between Danglars and Fernand. "And when one gets out of prison and one's name is Edmond Dantes, one seeks revenge, wouldn't one? Why should Dantes go to prison? He's not the sort to rob or murder, after all. He's an honest sort. I like Dantes. Dantes, your health!"

Fernand gripped Danglars' arm. "Do you mean to say that you have the means to have Dantes arrested?" He grinned at the look in Danglars' eyes. "You hate him as well, don't you? I recognize it well enough. I wonder, what has he done to you?"

"Hate Dantes? You wound me!" Danglars put a hand over his heart in a pantomime of umbrage. "My only motive is securing your happiness. If you think that my offer of charity is tainted by self-interest, then I'll leave and you can find your own solution."

"No!" cried Fernand. Danglars felt a pulse of heat coming from the hand on his arm and worried he had pushed too far. "I hate Dantes, I confess! He took what's rightfully mine and I hate him with every flame I can muster! I don't care about your motives. If you know how to remove him, I'll do anything I can to help. If I could, I would kill him."

Caderousse lifted his head, hiccupped again, and gaped at Fernand.

"Kill Dantes! Why are we speaking of killing Dantes? I won't stand for it, I tell you, not at all," he said. "He is a good neighbour, he offered to share his money with me this morning. I will not stand for him being killed! His father is such a sweet old man."

"Nobody is speaking of killing Dantes, you're too drunk to follow our joke." Danglars filled Caderousse's glass once more.

Fernand tore at his hair. "The means, damn it, the means!"

Danglars sighed and called the waiter for pen, ink, and paper. He also requested yet another bottle of wine. When the paper arrived, Caderousse laid his arm across it.

"Pen and paper are frightening things, aren't they? They can wound a man in as many ways as a blade or a pistol," Caderousse said with a woozy sort of fear. "I have always been more afraid of a man with paper than any other weapon. Let's drink to Edmond's health again."

Danglars maneuvered a glass into Caderousse's hand, and Caderousse took another swallow as if by reflex. When he made no more effort to interfere, Danglars continued.

"Let's say, hypothetically, that Dantes has returned home from a voyage during which he landed at the island of Elba," Danglars said. "Let's say as well that someone could use that fact to denounce him to the crown prosecutor."

"The Pharaon landed at Elba?" Fernand asked, astonished.

"Hypothetically," Danglars said with his queer smile.

His plan was simple. If Edmond had been tasked with delivering a second letter from the island, it would serve as evidence for the accusation. Edmond would tell the truth about LeClere's dying request, but it would be his word against the accusation. The Elba letter would condemn Edmond to prison and maybe even time as a galley-slave. At the very least, he would be arrested and questioned. Even if the prosecutor dismissed the entire thing, the letter would be confiscated. Edmond's errand would be a failure, and his wedding day would be ruined. If Danglars spent the rest of his career on the Pharaon answering to Captain Dantes, he could at least treasure that memory to endure the humiliation.

"I'll do it now, just tell me what to write." Fernand reached for the pen.

"You could, but you would need to sign your letter, and they would have you confront Dantes in person. Mercedes can't know that you had denounced him, can she?" Danglars said.

Fernand's eyes widened, and he leaned back in his chair to finish his wine. Danglars refilled it for him before taking the pen back and transferring it to his left hand.

"Hypothetically, if someone wrote a letter left-handed to disguise their penmanship, it would be untraceable and anonymous," Danglars said. "With enough detail, the authorities are duty-bound to investigate."

He set to writing and showed the letter to Fernand who read it in a low voice.

The crown prosecutor is informed by a friend of the throne, that one Edmond Dantes, first mate of the ship Pharaon, arrived this morning after stopping at the Island of Elba. There, he delivered a letter to the usurper and was given one to deliver to the Bonapartist faction in Paris. Proof of this crime will be found on arresting him, for the letter will be found upon him, or at his father's room, or in his cabin on board the Pharaon.

"Not one word in the letter is untrue, and it cannot be connected to you to distress Mercedes. All we need to do is fold the letter and address it," Danglars said, doing exactly that.

Fernand stared at the letter, but Caderousse lunged forward and laid his hand across it. The last shreds of sobriety in Caderousse's mind had followed the reading of the letter and by instinct grasped the misery it could cause.

"Yes, and an excellent joke it is!" Caderousse exclaimed, slurring his words. "We shall laugh about this for years and years."

"We shall indeed," Danglars agreed. He took the letter from beneath Caderousse's limp hand with ease and moved it beyond reach. "Of course, this is all just a joke. I would be heartbroken if anything happened to our good friend Dantes. The responsible thing to do is destroy this silly letter."

Danglars squeezed the paper in his hand, barely even wrinkling it, and tossed it into a corner of the patio. Fernand drained his wine glass again and followed the path of the paper with his dark eyes.

"Very good!" Caderousse said, relieved that the letter was gone. "I like Dantes. He's a good man. Dantes, your health!"

Caderousse lifted his glass, but it and the final bottle were both empty.

"Caderousse, at this point I believe that you are more grape than man," Danglars said. "If you drink any more, you'll have to sleep at this table. I refuse to carry you home; let's depart while you can still stand up."

Caderousse grumbled but agreed and invited Fernand to join them on their walk.

"No, thank you," Fernand replied, eyes still locked to the patio corner. "It's been a trying day; I just want some sleep."

Danglars and Caderousse left him, but Danglars stopped at the bend in the road to look back. Sure enough, Fernand left the inn with a piece of paper in his hand; instead of passing through the gate to the Catalan village, Fernand made haste to the city centre.

"In search of a post box, I hope! The thing is at work and will take care of itself," Danglars muttered.

CHAPTER 7
THE MARRIAGE FEAST

The next morning, February 25th, the sun shone down on Marseille and turned the waves into a network of dazzling light. La Reserve was a hive of activity with the wedding feast set for that very afternoon. All of Edmond's and Mercedes' documents were in order—Morrel had used what influence he had to expedite the paperwork—and they remained unaware that Edmond would be in a cell by sundown.

The feast was to take place in a second-floor room overlooking the patio. Over each of the many windows was written the name of one of the principal cities of France, for reasons that the owners of La Reserve had long forgotten. A wooden balcony ran around the perimeter of the building, where guests could choose to holler happy greetings at passers-by and mingle with guests of other functions. Many of the Pharaon's crew elected to do exactly that.

Edmond and Mercedes' friends filled the room wearing their finest clothes. An orphan, Mercedes' only living relative was Fernand—her third or perhaps fourth cousin. The Dantes family had always been small, and the Dead Plague had spared only Edmond and Louis. The guests drank, laughed, and discussed the upcoming ceremony: the feast scheduled to begin at twelve o'clock, with everyone proceeding to the town hall to witness the legalities at two. With that completed, they would return to La Reserve for music, wine, and dancing well into the night to celebrate the newlyweds.

When Morrel entered the room, a chorus of cheers rose from the Pharaon's crew. Gossip had long been a favourite hobby of the French, and it was expected that Edmond was soon to be made captain. Morrel's appearance at the wedding suggested that the promotion had been approved and made official by his partner M. Clairmont.

The crowd called for the bride and groom, and they soon made their entrance. Mercedes was flanked by Edmond and Louis, with her bridesmaid behind. Fernand entered next, as the closest family available to give away the bride. He wore the colourful garments that served as formal wear among the Catalans. Danglars and Caderousse also slipped into the room, almost late but unnoticed.

Danglars made the correct faces and repeated the correct sounds to hide his dark mood. If Fernand had sent the letter, Danglars would have expected the postal service to see the prosecutor's address and give it highest priority. Instead, Edmond was still a free man. Danglars wondered if Fernand had experienced a change of heart. The window to send another accusation was slim if there would be any hope of catching Edmond with the incriminating Elba letter in his possession.

Oblivious to Danglars' scheming, Edmond wore the formal uniform of Morrel & Son with a sword at his side, his fine features alive with joy on what he expected to be the finest day of his young life. With Mercedes beside him, her radiant glow lit him as well. Her simple white dress and magical illumination gave the impression of an angel. They took their seats at the head table with Louis sitting at Edmond's right as the best man.

Louis wore the best finery he still owned, with shining steel buttons and a walking stick carved with mermaids; Edmond had made it from a solid piece of driftwood after sighting the creatures on a previous voyage. An embroidered silk cloth, a long-ago gift from Caderousse, wrapped the stump of his left arm.

Caderousse himself had oiled and combed his beard, and wore a fashionable coat of his own craftsmanship. Much happier than Danglars, his opinion of the Dantes family was swayed for the better by the prospect of food, drink, and a party. All that tainted his fun was a vague sense of doom, as if he were troubled by a dream. Danglars wore the same uniform as Edmond with minor differences particular to their posts. Instead of a sword, he had a pair of daggers.

Fernand's face alternated between a deep flush and a sweaty pallor as he found a seat for the feast, his mouth flitting between a rictus smile and a preoccupied frown. Nobody else appeared to notice, with their attention focused on Edmond and Mercedes.

"The fool could not act more suspicious if he tried," Danglars muttered. "But is it from guilt or only jealousy?"

Morrel approached Edmond and laid a hand on his shoulder before paying his respects to the radiant bride. Turning back to Edmond, Morrel reached into his coat.

"If I may," Morrel said as he withdrew an envelope, "this is a wedding present which I insist that you open right away."

Edmond accepted it with thanks and opened it to find a captain's badge bearing the arms of Morrel & Son. Tears rose in his eyes as Morrel pinned the badge to his coat.

"I think you can guess what M. Clairmont said," Morrel said with a wink. He turned to address the room. "Without further ado, I want to officially congratulate the next captain of the Pharaon on his imminent marriage!"

Danglars pantomimed along with the applause of the other guests and kept his face composed and neutral.

Nobody at the wedding could say they had ever attended a grander feast. Diot sausages, lobsters in dazzling red shells, plump prawns and other delicacies of the sea, and many other delights passed from hand to hand and table to table. Louis chuckled as he raised a glass of topaz-coloured wine.

"Listen to this silence!" Louis said, smiling. "How would anyone know if we were enjoying our food?"

Indeed, conversation had almost ceased as everyone savoured their meal. Unnoticed, Fernand stared at the door without eating or drinking. Quite without warning, a blur of red entered through one of the windows, and a woman's scream rose from the corner.

"*Un lutin!*" she cried.

One of the vicious dwarf-like creatures had smelled the feast and come to investigate. It wore a blood-red travelling coat the same shade as its skin, and matching trousers with black fur boots. Red eyes glared from under a white powdered wig resting on a head the shape of a crescent moon. The forehead and chin both reached wicked points which snagged, pulled, and tore at tablecloths and women's dresses. It lashed out with long and rotten teeth, sharp as razors, at anyone who drew too close. The guests gave it a wide berth as the troublemaking creature roamed the room. Chortling and snarling at the wedding guests, it knocked over furniture and snatched food off of the floor.

Edmond drew his sword and advanced towards the foul creature that dared to disturb his wedding day. Lutins were a more common pest in the countryside, but on occasion some made their way into the larger towns. Seeing the possible danger to Mercedes, Fernand could not stand back and let the beast go unchallenged. He ran to Edmond's side, flames dancing across his fingers.

"What rotten luck, I have a waistcoat at home embroidered with just the right symbols to repel lutins!" Caderousse said. "I need a pen and paper!"

Caderousse reminded himself of further murky recollections from the night before but disregarded them in the moment to trace the runes he needed.

"Lutins are known to be harbingers of doom," Danglars muttered. To keep up appearances, he drew one of his daggers and approached the lutin as well. "Perhaps today shall take a favourable turn after all."

"There are no vacancies at the inn today, friend," Edmond said, thrusting at the lutin with his sword.

The lutin threw aside a plate of sausages and hissed at Edmond, clenching its tiny fists. It faked a dodge to the left and lunged from the right, swinging the daggerlike points on its bizarre head. A lucky slash caught Edmond on the back of the hand, but he kept hold of his sword.

Thinking of Mercedes' happiness, Fernand gritted his teeth and conjured a ball of flame to defend the man he hated most in the world. Though the lutin sidestepped the fireball, flame caught the hem of its coat. Screaming almost too high to hear, the beast flailed across the room until it found a flagon of water and doused itself.

Edmond and Fernand moved toward the lutin again, but Edmond flinched when it hurled the empty flagon at his head. It used the distraction to leap at Fernand and land a punch on his chin. Lutins have great strength for their size, and the blow staggered him. Fernand landed on his tailbone with a crash, another ball of flame fizzling out in his hand.

The lutin searched for another target to torment, but a burst of light dazzled it. Mercedes stepped forward, glowing with fury like the July sun and directing it at the lutin's eyes in a tight beam. Danglars took the opportunity to throw his knife, which caught the lutin in the shoulder. Black blood welled up from the wound, and another awful scream came from its throat.

Edmond lifted his sword again. The lutin pulled the knife from its flesh and tossed it at him, but he batted it aside with his blade. Like an animal in a trap, the Lutin snapped its head left and right as Edmond advanced on it.

From the hall came heavy footsteps and the snarling of drakes, distracting Edmond. The lutin bolted for the nearest window and leaped into the street below; it rolled when it hit the cobblestones and scurried into a convenient sewer. Caderousse ran to the window after it, yelling and waving a piece of paper covered in symbols.

Edmond took Mercedes into his arms to ensure she was unhurt. Danglars helped Fernand, nursing a bruise on his jaw but otherwise unhurt, to his feet. Among the guests, the worst harm consisted of scratches and bumps and a few torn clothes.

"I must say, Fernand, you and Dantes are quite gallant fellows. Rushing in to distract that creature until I could ward it off, you looked like brothers in arms!" Caderousse said. The wine and excitement had for the moment erased any feelings of envy or jealousy from his heart.

Fernand nodded, staring at nothing, as a fist pounded on the door. It was no tapping of a lutin or some other gnome, but a measured pounding that could only mean one thing. The guests fell silent in confusion.

"I demand admittance, in the name of the king!" said a voice from the hall.

A magistrate forced the door open and entered, wearing his official scarf of office. Behind him stood four soldiers in black plate mail with two drakes on chains. The drakes tasted the air with their forked tongues and scanned the room. Unease gave way to dread among the guests.

"Magistrate Berger!" Morrel shouted, pushing forward. "If someone has complained about the noise, we had an unexpected visit by a violent lutin. It's under control now."

Even as he spoke, Morrel knew the police would not send so much force for a noise complaint. Morrel also knew Magistrate Berger and could see on Berger's face that the matter was dire.

"No, M. Morrel," Berger said. "As reluctant as I am to intrude upon a wedding, we are here with an arrest warrant. Who here answers to the name Edmond Dantes?"

Nobody moved, terrified to even glance at the groom and give him away, but Edmond himself stepped forward with dignity.

"I am Edmond Dantes," he said with a steady voice. "May I ask why you're here?"

"Edmond Dantes," Berger replied, "I arrest you in the name of the king."

"Why?" demanded Mercedes. "Why are you arresting him?"

"I cannot say, because I was not told. The charges will be explained to M. Dantes soon enough," Berger said, his expression solemn and regretful. Moved by the anguish on her face, he continued. "He arrived yesterday on a ship, correct? Perhaps it's an issue with the vessel's paperwork, some matter of health or customs."

Louis struggled to his feet with his walking stick, but Edmond steadied him with some quiet words and stepped forward to surrender to the officers. Berger removed his scarf and whistled, bringing the fabric to life. The animated scarf bound Edmond's hands behind his back while he reassured Mercedes that everything would be resolved soon. Meanwhile, Caderousse glared at Danglars.

"What did you do?" Caderousse asked.

"Nothing," Danglars said, feigning surprise. "I'm as bewildered as you are."

The events of the night before, previously a blurry recollection, rushed to the forefront of Caderousse's mind with utmost clarity. The veil of drunkenness obscuring his memory fell away, and his throat went dry. Caderousse turned to question Fernand, but he had disappeared.

"This is all part of that dreadful trick you were devising yesterday," Caderousse said in a hoarse voice. "If so, I can only say that it is a distasteful joke indeed, and double the evil will rightfully fall on you when your part is found out."

"Nonsense," Danglars replied. "I had nothing to do with this. Besides, you saw with your own eyes that I tore the letter to pieces."

"Liar!" Caderousse hissed. "I know what I saw: you crumpled the paper and threw it away, unharmed, into the corner."

"You drunken fool," said Danglars, "you couldn't see past your own nose!"

The officers led Edmond down the stairs to a carriage. Two of the gendarmes accompanied Edmond into the carriage, one rode on the back with the drakes in their cages, and the last drove from the front with Berger next to him.

"Adieu, adieu, dearest Edmond!" Mercedes cried, stretching her arms out to him from the balcony, radiating her light as if the touch of it could set him free.

Edmond heard this cry like the sob of a broken heart and leaned from the window of the carriage to look back at her.

"This is not goodbye, Mercedes!" Edmond shouted. "I will see you again!"

The carriage turned a corner where Mercedes could no longer see it. Louis stood by her side and did his best to comfort her, both of them victims of the same blow. Morrel took a cab to the prosecutor's office, hoping to find a friendly ear there but doomed to find only Villefort.

Meanwhile, Fernand reappeared. He poured a glass of water with a trembling hand, swallowed it in one long drink, and poured another.

"He's the origin of this misery, I'm certain," Caderousse whispered to Danglars. "Fernand and whoever put this foul idea into his head to begin with!"

"It is a terrible shame," Danglars said.

The other guests clustered around the various crew members of the Pharaon, having taken Berger's suggestion to heart and asking everything they could think of about the voyage. Danglars offered some vague ideas, all of which he knew were false. With no satisfactory answers, everyone returned to their seats to drown their discomfort with food and wine.

"Morrel is returning!" a lookout called from the balcony some time later.

Mercedes rushed to greet Morrel at the door, but the look on his face dismayed her even further.

"What happened?" Mercedes asked. "What were the charges?"

"It's, ah, it's more serious than we thought," Morrel said quietly and took a moment to compose himself. "They've charged Edmond with treason as a Bonapartist agent."

"This is your fault!" Caderousse hissed, dragging Danglars into a corner. "Your trick has gone too far, too far! That innocent girl and that poor old man will die of grief, Danglars. I am determined to tell them all about it."

"You simpleton!" Danglars whispered back. "Here are the facts: the Pharaon made landfall at Elba, and Dantes went ashore. If there's no letter from the island, then he'll be found innocent. If the letter exists, then what do you expect will happen to people who defend him? Taken in as accomplices, most likely."

With the instinct for self-preservation that runs deep in drunks and moochers, Caderousse saw the sense in this reasoning; or at least, he saw the danger to himself and how to avoid it. He considered the grieving bride, but caution defeated generosity in the end.

"I suppose," Caderousse mumbled, "that we could wait and see what becomes of it."

CHAPTER 8
THE CHATEAU D'IF

What became of it was Villefort's interrogation of Edmond, when Edmond read the anonymous accusation and gave Villefort the letter from Elba. The officers then escorted Edmond out of the house through a side exit to the Palais de Justice next door. The gloomy corridors of the imposing courthouse could make the boldest criminals in Marseille shudder, but Edmond held his nerve admirably. When one of his guards knocked upon the iron jail door, Edmond focused on Villefort's promise to set him free even as that same door slammed behind him. From there they escorted him to a tolerably neat chamber with bars across the door and window; there was no denying that he was a prisoner. Even the quality of the air seemed different, thicker and somehow wrong.

Edmond entered the holding cell at four o'clock in the afternoon, two hours past the time of his intended marriage. The sun vanished quickly, leaving him in darkness for hours. Without vision, his hearing seemed to sharpen, and the slightest sound sparked the hope of release.

Finally, when the first claws of despair began to grip him around ten o'clock, Edmond heard unmistakable footsteps approaching. A key turned in the lock, the hinges creaked, and torches flooded the cell with light. Dazzled, Edmond tried to leave but the gleam of metal stopped him. Four gendarmes waited for him with swords and carbines.

"Are you here for me?" Edmond asked, dumbfounded at the display of force.

"You're the only one here. What do you think?" one gendarme replied. The others snickered.

"By the orders of M. de Villefort?" Edmond asked.

The gendarme nodded, relieving Edmond. He followed them out of the prison to a carriage in a back street, where another officer sat with the coachman.

Edmond wanted to ask their destination, but the gendarmes pushed him forward; without the power nor intention to resist, he found himself seated between two of the guards and across from the others. The carriage pulled away, rolling over the stones with a heavy grinding. As the city passed on the other side of the grated window, Edmond was aware that he had only traded one prison for another. One familiar street after another passed him by until they stopped at the port.

The officer dismounted from his place by the coachman and approached the guardhouse. A dozen soldiers emerged in ranks, creating a corridor from the carriage to the water.

"This can't possibly all be on my account!" Edmond muttered as they pushed him along this corridor to a boat near the quay.

The soldiers watched with cold curiosity as Edmond sat in the boat facing behind, with the gendarmes taking positions around him once again. The boat pushed off, and the oarsmen propelled it toward the mouth of the harbour.

Edmond's lungs and spirits took welcome comfort in the pure sea air after so long in a cell, but the sight of La Reserve and the Catalan village passing, tempered his relief. Sounds of revelry drifted over the water from the inn as the night's customers enjoyed themselves, reminding Edmond of happier times from just that morning. A woman stood on the beach looking out, and he wanted to believe it was Mercedes and call out to her. Edmond restrained himself, unsure of how his guards would respond to him shouting like a madman, and wished in silence if it were Mercedes that she would release her light for him.

The boat continued on, with only the slap of oars against the water and lapping of waves against the hull to break the silence. Their course made no sense to Edmond. The boat was too small for a long voyage, and there was no reason for them to take him to a ship outside the harbour. Perhaps they planned to leave him on some remote point to swim back to shore as a petty joke.

Edmond shook his head to banish these unhelpful thoughts and took his lack of restraints or handcuffs as a good sign. He clung to Villefort's destruction of the Elba letter and promise of release, so long as he did not say the name of Noirtier, but soon his resolve broke.

"Where are we going?" he asked.

"You'll know soon," the guard on his left said.

"Then what harm is there in telling me now?" Edmond replied.

"Your broken nose, if you don't shut up," the guard in front of him said.

"Sir," Edmond said, "I implore you as a fellow loyal Frenchman to tell me where we're going."

The guards ahead of him looked at each other, and one shrugged.

"You're a Marseillais sailor, and you can't guess where we're going?" a guard said.

"Not at all. Obviously I can't escape, and I'll find out in ten minutes or an hour anyway; why not tell me sooner?" Edmond asked.

"We're ordered not to tell you," the guard said, "but we have no orders to stop you from turning around."

Edmond twisted to look. A hundred yards away in the darkness rose the black and frowning rock which hosted the infamous prison of the Chateau d'If. The island sat on the water like a scab, near enough to shore to see Marseille but too far to permit escape. A prisoner who got loose from his cell would be noticed before he reached the edge of the island and either caught before he reached the water or shot as he swam away. The gloomy fortress loomed atop the island like a scaffold waiting for a condemned man.

"The Chateau d'If?" Edmond cried. "This is a mistake; we need to go back to M. de Villefort."

The guards only smiled, immune to such pleading.

"Is there a magistrate at the prison?" Edmond asked, eyes wide. "I need to clear this up!"

"There is only a governor and the garrison, a few turnkeys, good thick walls, and the sea," the guard in front said.

"But I haven't been charged or tried!" Edmond protested. "Villefort promised I could go free!"

"I don't know what M. de Villefort has or hasn't promised, and I don't care," the guard said. "I just have orders to follow."

In desperation, Edmond lunged for the edge of the boat. He was a strong swimmer and reckoned he could make it to shore, and from there he could get passage on a ship. Captains were always happy to acquire the services of an experienced seaman, and he could escape Marseille until there was a chance to clear his name.

Before Edmond could get over the side, the guards pulled him back into the bottom of the boat. Edmond cursed with panic as four carbines pointed at his head, but he held still. A brief temptation gripped him to fight back and end the nightmare he found himself in, but he recognized the impulse as cowardice and resisted it.

Edmond remained in that position until the boat ran aground on the island. The guards grabbed him by the arms and coat collar and hauled him to his feet. Edmond made no further resistance, feeling like a man in a dream. He allowed himself to be led until he found himself in a courtyard surrounded by high walls.

The garrison patrolled the walls and the courtyard: suits of plate armour, eight feet tall, and animated from within by some combination of magic and machinery. Edmond had heard rumours about these things, the forged. Created centuries ago to replace soldiers on the battlefield, they had unfortunately lacked initiative and the essential creative drive of human beings. They had found use in less demanding positions, such as guarding prisoners.

Soon a disheveled grey-haired woman with a large ring of keys emerged from the prison's central tower. A forged followed behind her, the number nine daubed on its dented breastplate in red paint. After exchanging formalities with the guards, she beckoned at Edmond.

"Prisoner! With me, Neuf and I will take you to your cell," she said.

The guards pushed Edmond to follow the turnkey, who called the forge's number in a rough bark. The forged fell into step behind Edmond, and this strange parade made their way to a room below ground. The bare stone walls seemed to reek with all the misery that had ever occurred between them, and the only illumination came from a lamp on a stool.

"This is your cell for tonight," the turnkey said. "It's late, and the governor is asleep. Tomorrow, maybe he'll move you. For now, there is bread and water and fresh straw to sleep on; all a prisoner can wish for. Good night."

Before Edmond could open his mouth, or even notice where the food was, the turnkey left with the lamp and closed the door. Edmond stood alone in silent and timeless darkness, still wearing his dress uniform.

The turnkey returned at dawn with orders from the governor to leave Edmond where he was. She found Edmond still standing in the same place, eyes swollen from crying. Edmond had not slept or even moved, unable to process the rapid change in his fortunes. The turnkey tapped him on the shoulder with a long stick she carried for such purposes, at last catching Edmond's attention.

"Are you hungry?" the turnkey asked.

"I don't know," Edmond said once he remembered how to speak.

"Do you want anything?" the turnkey replied without a trace of compassion.

"I want to see the governor, this is all a terrible error," Edmond said. "Madame, what is your name?"

"Leblanc," the turnkey said, scratching a wart on her nose.

"Mme. Leblanc, this is all a misunderstanding. I have to get back to Marseille right away!" Edmond insisted.

Leblanc only shrugged and left. The door closed before Edmond could force enough movement into his stiffened legs to attempt escape. His bottled emotions spilled over again; he fell to the ground and wept bitterly, yelling at the walls to know what crime he had committed.

This was how Edmond spent his first day at the Chateau d'If. Forged patrolled the halls, each with their own number, and sometimes brought him food. None of them answered when he spoke to them. Whether they could speak at all or had orders not to, he couldn't say. He ate his meals without tasting them and paced his cell like a zoo animal.

The memory of his escape attempt in the boat tormented him; if he had distracted the guards somehow, or acted sooner, he could have secured his freedom. Instead, he was confined in an impregnable fortress and ignorant of how his father or Mercedes fared. He could only wait for Villefort to correct the situation. He threw himself onto his straw in a fury and chewed at these maddening thoughts until Leblanc returned the next morning.

"Are you feeling more reasonable today?" Leblanc asked. Edmond made no reply. "Stop pouting. Is there anything I can do for you?"

"I want to see the governor," Edmond said again.

"Not possible," Leblanc said. "That's against prison rules."

"Then what can you do for me?" Edmond asked.

"Bring you better food, if you pay for it, or books, or exercise time in the courtyard," Leblanc said.

"I don't care about that," Edmond said. "All I want is to see the governor."

"I just said that isn't allowed," Leblanc said. "If you annoy me by asking for things you can't have, I may forget to send you any food."

"Then I'll die of hunger," Edmond said, glaring at Leblanc.

Edmond's resolve worried Leblanc. Her salary depended on the number of prisoners kept in the Chateau, so she replied in a softer tone.

"What you ask is impossible, but you'll be allowed to walk in the courtyard if you behave," Leblanc said. "If you see the governor there, you can try to address him, and he might reply. That's the best I can do."

"I need to see him now, I don't belong here!" Edmond said.

"You shouldn't brood on what is impossible, or you'll be mad in a fortnight," Leblanc said. "The banker who lived in this cell before you lost his mind and began offering the governor a million francs for his freedom."

"I don't have a million francs to offer, but I can pay you one hundred if you take a message to a girl named Mercedes in the Catalan village," Edmond said, rubbing his hands across his face. "Can you at least do that, and tell her where I am?"

"And risk losing my job? I think not," Leblanc said.

Rage flared deep within Edmond's heart. He had never had the opportunity to be truly ground beneath the wheels of bureaucracy before and could not understand Leblanc's uncaring attitude. He stood, picked up the stool and swung it like a bludgeon in front of him.

"Then maybe I have to kill you where you stand and take my freedom that way!" Edmond cried, advancing on Leblanc with panic dancing in his eyes.

The threat still echoed in the cell when Leblanc whistled and stepped aside; a forged, this one numbered twelve, stepped into the room and grabbed Edmond by the throat. It lifted him to the ceiling, cutting off his air as his feet dangled and kicked. Edmond pried at the forged's fingers, but they held firm. Black spots swam in front of his vision.

When his arms fell to his sides, he heard Leblanc say something as if from the top of a crow's nest, and the metal hand released him. Edmond crashed to the cold flagstone floor.

"I will talk to the governor about you after all," Leblanc said. "Douze, hold him."

Leblanc left, not bothering to close the door. Edmond was too busy struggling for air to attempt escape, and the forged lifted him to his feet like a sack of laundry. With Edmond upright, it stood behind him and took hold of his wrists, restraining him as effectively as any shackles. Edmond remained this way long enough to catch his breath and for the aches of his fall to set in, when Leblanc came back with a second forged which grabbed Edmond by the ankles.

"Douze, Quatorze, *allons-y!*" Leblanc commanded, and they carried Edmond down the hall.

"What is the meaning of this?" Edmond demanded. His voice came out in a rasp.

"By the governor's orders, you are transferred to the dungeon," Leblanc said. "We keep madmen with the madmen."

It was useless for Edmond to struggle; the forged were too strong and they held his wrists and ankles like the ends of a stretcher. They descended to a cell on an even lower level of the fortress, dumped Edmond onto the floor, and locked him in.

Edmond felt around the walls of the dark room and sat down in the corner until his eyes grew accustomed to it. Leblanc's prediction seemed to be coming true; Edmond felt that he was going mad.

CHAPTER 9
THE AFTERMATH

Back in Marseille as Edmond waited in the holding cell at the Palais de Justice, Villefort made haste to the home of his new father-in-law the Marquis de Saint-Meran in the fashionable Place du Grand Cours in Marseille. The guests of Villefort's wedding ritual laughed and mingled over coffee in the salon, and Renee waited for her husband with great anticipation. Their ritual robes were gone, replaced by finery more befitting the setting. Villefort's entrance spurred a general exclamation.

"Here's the great Guardian of the State now!" cried one guest.

"Are we threatened with a fresh Reign of Terror?" asked another.

"Has the Corsican ogre escaped?" shouted another with a drunken laugh.

Villefort ignored them, instead approaching Renee and the marquis.

"Alphonse," Villefort said, "can we speak privately?"

"A serious matter, then?" Saint-Meran asked, adjusting his monocle and observing the cloud over Villefort's face.

"So serious that I must leave for a few days, I'm afraid," Villefort said, looking to Renee.

"Must you leave on our wedding night?" Renee asked. "Where are you going?"

"Yes Villefort, where are you going in such a hurry?" asked another government official who had overheard, drawing even more attention.

"That, madames and monsieurs, is an official secret," Villefort said to his audience. "But if anyone has a letter that needs to be taken to Paris, a friend is going there tonight with great haste."

The guests murmured to each other about Paris and intrigue and Bonapartist plots. Meanwhile, Saint-Meran and Villefort excused themselves to the library.

Alone in the library, Villefort spoke. "Forgive my indiscretion, but do you own any land? It is vitally important."

"Yes, seven or eight hundred thousand francs worth," Saint-Meran said. "We reclaimed it from some ungrateful commoners after the Restoration."

"Sell it all, right away, or risk losing every franc all over again," Villefort said. "It may already be too late."

"Are you joking?" Saint-Meran said, peering at Villefort's face. The grave seriousness he saw there convinced him that whatever had called Villefort away presented a genuine and imminent danger.

"Alright. You said you—or your supposed friend—are going to Paris," Saint-Meran continued. "I'll write a letter for you to bring to my broker right now."

"I need another letter as well." Villefort put Saint-Meran's order into his pocketbook. "Send for the Count de Salvieux and get him to write a letter for direct admission to see the king. I have news that must be brought directly to him without delay."

"Of course, of course. I'll call for Salvieux immediately," Saint-Meran said.

Villefort had another motive for wanting the admittance letter from an influential man like Salvieux. If he told what he knew to the keeper of the seals, who regulated the king's visitors, the keeper would take all the glory for himself. On the other hand, if Villefort could deliver the news in person, he would hold the king's favour for life.

Villefort returned to his coach with the second letter after saying a regretful goodbye to Renee. Back at his house, his valet had prepared all the required supplies for the three-day drive to Paris.

A woman's call interrupted Villefort before he could enter the house. He turned, aggravated that this was becoming a repeat occurrence.

The woman approaching him, with thick black hair and fierce eyes that drilled into his soul, could only be Mercedes who Edmond had spoken of. She still wore her wedding dress, but Villefort recognized her from Edmond's description regardless. Villefort understood at once why someone would envy Edmond for holding her heart; Mercedes' unique beauty could inspire any man to extremes. No further news had reached her of Edmond since Morrel's return to the aborted wedding feast, and she had decided to take matters into her own hands.

"Are you M. de Villefort, the prosecutor? I'm here to ask about Edmond Dantes." Even in grief she held her head high, seeming to challenge Villefort rather than grovel before his authority.

"The man is a criminal and beyond help," Villefort said, caught off-guard by such noble bearing in a commoner. "I examined the evidence myself, and it speaks for itself against him."

"At least tell me where he is!" Mercedes demanded, tears escaping from her defiant eyes. She grasped the sleeve of his jacket. "I don't know where he's been taken or if he's been executed and thrown into the sea!"

Villefort felt the first twinge of doubt. Dismissing Edmond Dantes as just one man, and a necessary sacrifice to the greater good of public order, was simple. But in front of him stood a reminder that Edmond did not exist in a vacuum and was not a faceless unit of humanity which could be removed from the world without consequences. People loved him and would miss him. His absence would ripple outward causing pain and suffering which Villefort could not foresee.

Time still remained to reverse his decision, Villefort realized. He could send word to the prison governor that there had been an error, to release Edmond and return him to the mainland, and accept what came of it. Perhaps the matter would blow over while Villefort was in Paris warning the king of what his father's letter said transpired on Elba.

The thought of his father gave him pause. Despite Edmond's promise to keep quiet about the name Noirtier, he would doubtless tell everyone in revenge for his treatment if he returned to Marseille. Villefort's career, his prospects, and his standing in the Eternal Royalist League would be ruined. The knowledge of Villefort's actions for the sake of self-preservation would surely stain the authority of the crown; it may even be enough to spark another Revolution.

"I do not know where he is, nor do I care as long as he has been removed from society," Villefort said, the barest tremble in his voice. "He's no longer any of my concern."

Villefort pushed Mercedes away, closing and locking the door behind him.

Mercedes stood in a daze on the steps. She understood in a way that a great miscarriage of justice had befallen her and Edmond, but could not articulate the nature of it or how to fix it. She had no education in the law and had grown to womanhood during political turmoil. For as long as she could remember, the things that the government were allowed to do and the things they did anyway varied from one week to the next. Having been rebuffed by Villefort, Mercedes simply had no idea where to begin fighting for Edmond's freedom.

Her feet brought her back to the Catalan village and her hut by the beach, and she collapsed upon her simple couch. Fernand stayed by her side, though Mercedes could not say for how long; he murmured words of comfort that she did not hear, laid kisses upon her hand that she did not feel, and lit candles that she did not see. Gradually, she became aware of the light of dawn streaming through her window. Fernand slept on the floor by her couch, and she could not say whether or not she herself had slept.

Meanwhile, in the silence of his house just after refusing to help Mercedes, Villefort found that remorse could not be banished by locking a door. He uttered a sigh that was almost a sob and sank into a chair in his salon.

A vice compressed his heart as he considered the innocent man he had sacrificed to his own ambition on the altar of his father's faults. He could almost see Edmond with him in the salon, staring with the silent question: why?

Villefort had always believed in capital punishment for criminals, to remove guilty men from the earth for the sake of the greater good. He had condemned many himself with his irresistible eloquence without ever a moment's regret. They had been guilty of trespasses against the crown and its subjects, or at least had insufficient proof of their innocence.

But Edmond Dantes had convinced Villefort that he was no Bonapartist, just an unlucky messenger. Destroying a man guilty of violating the social order was one thing; destroying an innocent man to protect himself was another. His collar felt far too tight.

"It was the only way. The only way to uphold my duty," Villefort muttered. "The king needed me to act, and I did."

By some miracle, the words soothed his conscience by a fraction. Villefort rose to his feet and paced the salon floor.

"I am a loyal servant of the king. He rules by divine right, above the law; loyal service to him can sometimes be expected to stray outside the law as well," Villefort continued, speaking with greater confidence to the empty room.

For several minutes his ranting became less coherent as he ran his hands through his hair. He fell silent when he caught sight of himself in the mirror, distracted by his pale and disheveled reflection. He lowered his shaking hands and stared at them.

An epiphany struck Villefort. A still small voice deep inside of him spoke a single word: penance. Having whipped himself up into royal fervour and still dwelling on his marriage ceremony, a remedy occurred to him.

"A tax of blood," he whispered. He closed his eyes and bit down onto the web of flesh between his thumb and forefinger.

At the first taste of blood in his mouth, he drank from his wound. He composed feverish silent heretical prayers in half-sentences, not addressed to God but rather to the merciless angels who served Him. Villefort sought not His wisdom, but their brutal strength to continue on the path he had committed to.

By the time Villefort's valet announced that the coach waited for the long trip to Paris, Villefort felt much calmer. He stepped into the coach with a clean handkerchief wrapped around his hand and commanded the driver in a steady voice.

Villefort and Mercedes were not the only individuals to be busy that afternoon and evening. After learning of Edmond's charges and imprisonment, M. Morrel was determined not to give up. He attempted to rally his friends and the most influential people in Marseille to petition for Edmond's release, but his pleas bore no fruit.

Rumours spread faster than disease in France, and everyone already knew about Edmond's arrest for treason. With the political climate as it was, most wanted to remain neutral for fear of drawing the government's attention. Morrel soon realized that he couldn't help Edmond, and his attempts would only hurt himself and his family.

In his room down the hall from Louis Dantes, Caderousse lay uneasy on his bed that night. He shut himself away with wine and the intent of drowning both his sorrow and the memory of his own role in Edmond's arrest. He succeeded only in becoming too drunk to fetch more wine and not drunk enough to ignore his own failings. He stared at the ceiling all night in a spiral of sombre reflections.

Louis Dantes sat by his window, hoping for news of Edmond which never came. Fatigue caught him unawares while he tended to his plants, and he fell asleep in his chair.

Only Danglars was content. When the Pharaon set sail in three months, his orders would come from a more suitable candidate for captain, with more seniority and less ostentatious good fortune. Perhaps the new captain may even be amenable to suggestion.

During the visit to Elba, Danglars had gone ashore and spoken with a drunken old soldier in Napoleon's guard who had shared astonishing stories about the Dead Plague. It would take time, and money, and a great deal of searching, but what Danglars had learned on Elba may well be the key to making his fortune. Captain Dantes would never have made the necessary diversions for Danglars to seek out what he needed, but another captain, one more open to a spot of bribery, may be just the ticket.

Danglars slept well that night and awoke refreshed the next morning.

CHAPTER 10
THE KING'S HUNT

The capital of France always has been and always would be Paris. Honoured as a major global centre of culture, society, and art, Paris had earned the name of the City of Light. However, beneath the city ran a network of tunnels filled with the remains of the dead. Residents of the city knew these tunnels as the Catacombs.

The Catacombs were a consequence of Parisian history. Rich veins of limestone ran beneath the city at its founding, which were mined out over centuries to leave behind tunnels and chambers which would become the oldest stages of the Catacombs.

By the year 1200, Paris also faced a dilemma of overcrowded cemeteries. To make room for new burials, the people of the city exhumed any graves older than a century and relocated the occupants to ossuaries in the walls of a large crypt adjacent to the church of Saints Innocents.

In 1780 multiple forgotten mines caved in and damaged the city above. When a basement wall collapsed beneath a neighbour of Saints Innocents, King Louis XVI stepped in. He commissioned a combined response to the problems of the cave-ins and the overcrowding.

Thus were the Catacombs born. Teams of engineers reinforced the abandoned mine tunnels, and workmen followed them to build more ossuaries. Church officials trailed behind the workmen to inter the city's bones in the walls. The increased capacity allowed more people, not just the oldest graves, to be exhumed and placed in the Catacombs. When the Dead Plague took France by surprise in 1788, the Catacombs proved to have an unexpected additional benefit.

The dead had more ways than just their teeth to spread the Plague: if a dozen or more of them congregated in any particular place, any corpse still intact enough to rise would do so. Few were brave enough to research the effect to learn how it worked or how to counteract it; those who survived the attempt never did reach a satisfactory answer.

By the time the Plague reached them, the graveyards of Paris were depopulated and the occupants of the Catacombs disassembled to bare bones. Thus when the dead came to Paris, they did not raise nearly so many corpses as they had in other major cities. In later years, after the Revolution, some historians speculated that this may have led the Parisian elites to underestimate the magnitude of the problem, leading eventually to the Revolution.

But in late February of 1815, while Edmond Dantes and his loved ones tried to comprehend their misfortune, the worst danger in the Catacombs was that of losing your way. The tunnels were accessible from many well-known points around the city and many more secret ones. People sometimes ventured into them to find a private place to bring a companion, others wanted bragging rights, and some never came back. A man named Philibert Aspairt entered the Catacombs on a dare in 1804. His body was not found until January 1815, mere feet away from an exit.

Past that very spot in the vast grave tunnels of Paris strode King Louis XVIII of France, known as Louis the Desired to his supporters for his position as the first post-Restoration monarch. In a departure from the usual courtly costume, he and his entourage wore dark leather and high boots with tricorn hats. A jovial look shaped the tiny features in the centre of Louis' meaty head, unusual for a person so deep in the Catacombs. He and most of his party carried carbines while servants carried torches. The entourage included guards and two chained drakes, trained to navigate the tunnels and return to the surface.

As they passed row after row of grinning skulls in the walls, the king spoke at length. King Louis XVIII was prone to taking an interest in obscure subjects and regurgitating the trivia he learned to a captive audience.

"The mummies of Egypt are not the only expression of the art," Louis said, continuing a lecture which had begun an hour earlier about the burial methods of the world. "Examples of mummification have been found in cultures all over the world, including Europe. Of course, I don't mean those drunken Irish who fall into bogs and accidentally preserve their own remains, which were likely half-pickled to begin with!"

Louis chuckled, with his courtiers taking the signal to laugh with him to remain in his good graces. Movement caught his eye and he swung his carbine up to fire, but it was only a rat. He continued his speech.

"The Guanche savages of the Canary Islands made mummification their primary form of burial, with a caste of people devoted to the task, and varying levels of ritual depending on the status of the deceased," Louis said. "This was all prior to the arrival of our Spanish friends and their efforts to settle the region. Closer to civilization, the Capuchin monastery in Palermo had a custom of mummifying monks after they passed. Some even say that the incorruptibility of saintly relics is a form of mummification."

The Duke de Blacas, keeper of the seals, followed the hunting party. A messenger had arrived just prior to the king's excursion into the Catacombs and shared just enough with Blacas to worry him.

"Sire, could we cut this short and return to the palace?" Blacas said, only to be scoffed at again by the king. "There is an urgent matter which concerns the usurper."

"Yes, you've mentioned. Did you read the latest report on the usurper from my Minister of Police? I have," Louis said. "The men watching the usurper on Elba report that he remains there, bored out of his treacherous little mind. He has directed the miners of the island to dig to the centre of the earth, presumably to conquer some hidden country there. He has a full-time guard posted at the beach to warn of any further uprisings of the undead, despite destroying the source of their rising himself. I believe that he is quite close to going mad."

"Of course, sire," Blacas said. The report the king cited was a week old, with the latest update due to arrive at the palace any minute. "Far be it for me to suggest that the Minister of Police is mistaken, as you selected that worthy personage yourself. It is more likely that my messenger has been misled. However, sire, may I advise that your majesty interrogate him yourself, to eliminate all possible doubt. He has, after all, made the two-hundred-league journey from Marseille in barely three days."

"When the semaphore would have conveyed the same message in

three hours? He must believe the message to be important indeed," Louis said with a laugh.

The king began to speak again but stopped himself and pointed silently. The party all raised their carbines and crept towards a perpendicular intersection. An aide lifted a bullseye lantern to dispel the shadows in the gloomy cross-tunnel. The light revealed a dirty man in rags fleeing for a ladder, his escape cut down with a bullet from the king's rifle. The entourage cheered and applauded the shot.

"An excellent hunt! Truly excellent!" exclaimed the king. "I daresay, they get craftier every year. It's astounding, really, the bargains that the rabble will strike for a chance at having their crimes pardoned."

Servants rushed forward to wrap the body in a sack and carry it out on a stretcher as the group followed the drakes back to the nearest exit. The king returned to his earlier train of thought as they walked, determined to show off his knowledge about the handling of the dead.

"If the Guanche were to mummify this man, they would begin by washing the body and eviscerating it. Heaven only knows what they did with the organs, but they would stuff the cavity with a mixture of mud, bark, and moss," Louis recited.

Blacas' stomach rolled over, but he said nothing.

"The outer part of the body would be preserved with a resin made of minerals, plants, and animal fat. They would dry out the body, either out in the sun or by actually smoking the poor devil like a sausage," Louis continued, licking his lips. "Lastly, they would wrap the remains in animal skins. A commoner like this would be wrapped in only one skin, but men of higher status would have more."

"Sire, the messenger at the palace?" Blacas asked.

"Blacas, you are like a drake with a bone!" Louis said, rolling his eyes. "Who is this messenger, that you must annoy me so?"

"His name is Villefort, sire; he is the assistant prosecutor from Marseille. He has a letter of entry from the Count de Salvieux," said Blacas.

"Salvieux?" the king said. "Why did you not say so sooner?"

King Louis XVIII signaled to his entourage to make all haste back to the palace. Blacas decided not to remind the king that he had been trying to deliver this news for over an hour.

"And his name is Villefort, you say?" Louis asked. "You know who his father is, of course. Noirtier, the former senator."

"The son of Noirtier?" Blacas said, flabbergasted. "What could qualify such a man for a position in your majesty's government?"

"Because Villefort is loyal and ambitious," the king said, "and with his father's treason looming over him, he will spend his entire career looking to prove that loyalty in pursuit of his ambitions. Such a man can always be counted on to go to extremes, if need be, in service to the crown."

Back at the palace of the Tuileries, there was a little room with an arched window. This room had a reputation of being the favoured parlour of many past kings, Louis XVIII included. Napoleon himself had loved it as well, but reminding the king of this fact was not a wise endeavour.

Blacas admitted Villefort two hours after he had secured the king's attention at last. Louis sat at a beautiful walnut table, having changed from his black leather hunting ensemble into a more fitting outfit for receiving visitors: a navy-blue jacket with gold epaulets, black linen trousers, and an immaculate white cravat.

Dust coated Villefort's travelling clothes, which were also not the proper cut for court and especially not when contrasted with the king's attire. He noted this difference with chagrin and reminded himself that the urgent circumstances forgave such deviation from protocol. He dropped to one knee in a deep bow.

"Rise, M. de Villefort," intoned the king. "Tell me what you know. The Duke de Blacas assures me that you have information of interest."

It was an effort for Villefort to get his tongue to form the words he needed to say, and his legs shook in the presence of what he saw as divinity. The king's thick head, rather than seeming disproportionate, appeared as large as required to contain a mind which must dwell on the continued existence of a nation. Louis' compact features appeared to Villefort as delicate and refined, with the high forehead and receding white hair signaling the king's obvious and endless wisdom. The gravity of his message just overcame his excitement.

"The news is bad, incredibly bad, but I hope that it is not yet irreparably bad," Villefort said, fidgeting with his bandaged hand as he spoke. He took a deep breath, as if preparing to deliver a closing argument in a trial. "Sire, I have come to Paris as rapidly as possible to inform your majesty of a conspiracy; not some impulsive and insignificant plot dreamed up by angry commoners, but an actual conspiracy that menaces your majesty's throne. Sire, the usurper has armed ships."

The king remained silent, but his shrewd eyes widened.

"However mad his plan is, he has by now left his exile on Elba to land at a destination I could not discover," Villefort said. "I only hope that there is enough time to raise the army and prepare a defense."

"How did you learn these details?" the king asked.

"Sire, they are the result of an in-depth investigation into the affairs of a sailor. I have been watching him for some time on suspicion of Bonapartist activities and arrested him on the day of my departure," Villefort said. "This man had secretly, or so he thought, visited Elba and was given a message to deliver to a conspirator in Paris, whose name I could not learn."

"One of the Bonapartist clubs in the Rue Saint-Jacques, no doubt. What about the message, did you secure a document?" the king asked.

"Regrettably not, sire. The message was oral, committed to his memory. I was able to extract the contents from him," Villefort said.

"And where is this man now?" asked the king.

"In prison, sire. The matter seemed serious enough to warrant it and to warrant me leaving my wife on the day of our wedding to bring the news directly to you," Villefort replied. His hand throbbed for a moment, then subsided.

"Ah yes, your marriage. You wedded the daughter of my Minister of Finance; I remember. Congratulations," the king said. He considered the message and indulged Villefort with a smile.

"M. de Villefort, while I appreciate the haste you made to bring this to my attention, I fear that you have been taken in by exactly the sort of lower-order plot you yourself dismissed. Having been so recently restored to the throne of my ancestors, I have watched the usurper vigilantly," the king said. "If he moved, I would know. However, do not think you have travelled all this way in vain. I recognize your devotion and the lengths you have gone to in order to warn me of what you thought was a credible threat, and I extend to you my royal gratitude."

A bell sounded and servants entered with a covered dish. They set it before the king and revealed a mouth-watering meal of what appeared to be large pork medallions served with mushroom sauce and delicate greens.

"Have you ever had the pleasure of eating a beast which you have brought down yourself? It is magnificently satisfying, I must say," King Louis XVIII said, smiling. "I make a deal with every creature I hunt: if you escape me, you have earned your freedom. Otherwise, you have earned a place on my table."

Small noises of delight escaped the king's lips between bites as Villefort stood crestfallen before him. Before Blacas could escort Villefort out, the Minister of Police, Baron Dandre, burst into the room pale and trembling, on the verge of fainting.

"Sire," Dandre said in between gasps for breath, "it is the usurper. He has escaped Elba."

CHAPTER 11
THE CORSICAN OGRE

King Louis XVIII set down his knife and fork with care.

"Dandre, you shall have to repeat yourself," Louis said. "I was hunting earlier, and the gunshots may have damaged my hearing. I thought I heard you say that Napoleon Bonaparte has escaped from Elba, but that cannot be true. If it were, it would mean that my Minister of Police has failed in his single most vital role!"

Baron Dandre shuffled beneath the king's stare but said nothing. Villefort felt a curious mix of dread and hope; Bonaparte's return spelled disaster, but it also meant that Villefort's frantic trip to Paris had not been in vain.

"Monsieur, I command you to speak!" the king shouted, red in the face.

"I am indeed to be pitied, sire. I can never forgive myself!" Dandre said. "Sire, the usurper landed three days ago at a small port near Antibes."

"Three days!" the king exclaimed. "The Corsican ogre has had his filthy boots upon French soil for three days and I only find out now? Antibes is only two hundred and fifty leagues from here. Why, that is just up the coast from Marseille, and this man has just made that journey in three days! How did you come by this news?"

Dandre hesitated before answering. "I received it by semaphore, sire."

"The semaphore!" the king roared. "A provincial prosecutor is able to uncover this plot by his own initiative, but meanwhile my own Minister of Police learns of my impending overthrow by the clacking slats of the semaphore!"

The king hefted the silver domed plate-cover and hurled it at Dandre, missing by an inch.

"I am surrounded by traitors and imbeciles, heathens who would see a return to the Reign of Terror and the end of the House of Bourbon!" the king screamed. "At least tell me how many men he has with him!"

Dandre's silence told the king all he needed to know. He paced, fuming.

"After twenty-five years in exile, it took seven allied armies and the efforts of the League combined to overthrow that man and restore me to the throne of my forefathers," the king said. "So many sacrifices and so much blood, only for it all to be undone by that filthy commoner and his rebellious upstarts! Dethroned again!"

He kicked over a nearby chair, then hefted it over his head and hurled it against the nearest wall.

"We have learned nothing from being overthrown, and our subjects are the same treacherous and capricious fools they have always been! They don't understand that their very lives are owed to my lineage, that they would be nothing without the greatness of me and my House!" the king roared, reminding Villefort of the righteous wrath which destroyed Sodom and Gomorrah. "They care nothing about their proper role in the universe—to support and nourish their rightful rulers! The usurper will make them flowery promises, and they will flock to support him, and he will once again take up residence in these hallowed halls!"

After this tirade, the king stood silent, catching his breath. After a few moments he wiped the perspiration from his brow with a handkerchief and smoothed back his thin hair. He speared another morsel of meat from the plate and chewed it while staring at the table. Finally he laid a hand on Villefort's shoulder and turned him to face the Minister of Police, pointing at the esteemed baron with his fork.

"M. de Villefort, tell Baron Dandre how you learned the crucial news which caught him by utter slack-jawed surprise," Louis said.

Hatred smoldered in Dandre's eyes, and Villefort realized his peril. Dandre's career was over; if Villefort did not choose his words carefully, Dandre may use his last remaining influence to question Edmond himself. If the truth of the matter came out, it would ruin Villefort as well.

"Sire," Villefort said, "the usurper is one of the most devious and aberrant minds in the world. If he were to accept your authority, imagine what he could accomplish on the side of light! But instead, that intellect was bent toward concealing this secret from the entire world. It is impossible for anyone to have seen this coming."

"Impossible, and yet here you stand warning me of exactly what the ogre has done!" the king said. "Such a grand word, impossible. It was impossible for a man with an office and spies and a budget of fifteen thousand francs!"

Dandre flinched at the king's sarcasm. Villefort tried again to ensure his own safety by helping the minister recover his pride.

"Sire, the suddenness of this event must prove that the issue is in the hands of chance. It is by chance that I found this plot, and I've profited from this chance as a good and devoted servant; that is all. My arrest of the conspirator could have happened yesterday or tomorrow just as easily, and my report would be too late," Villefort said. "If your majesty gives me more credit than I deserve, I fear that your opinion of me will suffer when I cannot continue to deliver at such a level."

Dandre's look of hatred softened, and Villefort understood that he had succeeded in avoiding the creation of a powerful enemy without sacrificing the king's gratitude. This display of humility also softened the king's temper.

"Very well. Dandre, get out," the king said. "This is no longer a matter for the Minister of Police but one for the Minister of War."

"At least we can rely on the army," Blacas offered. "Every report confirms their loyalty."

"Yes, and we have just learned how much faith we can place in reports," the king said, giving Blacas a withering look.

"Sire, I am afraid there is one more report I must deliver," Dandre said. "An update on the affair in the Rue Saint-Jacques and the death of General Quesnel. With this new information in mind, it may be that this was connected to the usurper's return."

"An affair in the Rue Saint-Jacques," muttered Villefort, eyes wide. The location held a grave significance in his mind, and he called on the skills of his profession to maintain a neutral expression.

"We've concluded that the General's death was not suicide, but assassination," Dandre said. "Quesnel had just left a Bonapartist club in the Rue when he disappeared, and was not seen again until he was found face-down in the river Seine. According to the general's valet, he was seen with an unknown man in the morning and had an appointment with him again in the afternoon, though the valet did not know the street number."

Villefort stared at Dandre as if his very life hung on the words coming through the man's lips. The king turned to face him, having decided that Villefort now warranted consultation on such matters.

"M. de Villefort, do you agree that General Quesnel, who had been infiltrating the Bonapartists at my command, was discovered by these men and ambushed to silence him?" the king asked.

"It is probable, sire," Villefort replied. His mouth felt as dry as sand. "Do we know anything else about this stranger?"

"The valet has given his description; we will find him. The man is in his early fifties, with black eyes and shaggy brows, also a thick mustache," Dandre said. The description was all too familiar to Villefort. "He was dressed in a blue frock coat. A man was followed yesterday matching this description but was lost sight of at the corner of the Rue de la Jussienne and the Rue Coq-Heron."

"Continue searching," the king said. "General Quesnel would be indispensable to us at this pivotal moment, and his assassins must be brutally dealt with. It has been too long since the royal drakes were allowed to run a man to the ground."

The conversational tone in which he pronounced such a terrible fate struck Villefort with awe and terror. God must have commanded the great flood in the days of Noah with the same demeanour.

"I shall not rest until the man is caught, sire," Dandre said with his fist over his heart.

"We shall see," the king said. With the heat of the moment gone, he returned to his abandoned meal. "M. de Villefort, I will no longer detain you. You must be fatigued after so long a journey, go and rest. I expect you are staying with your father?"

"No, sire," Villefort replied, light-headed. "I am staying at a hotel in the Rue de Tournon. I have not seen my father, nor do I plan to; I came straight here when I arrived in Paris."

"Ah, I forgot," the king said with a smile that revealed he had forgotten nothing, "you and M. Noirtier are not on the best terms. Another sacrifice you have made to the royal cause; another display of loyalty and fealty which should be rewarded."

"Sire, your kindness in granting an audience is reward enough. I can think of nothing else to request." Villefort bowed once more.

"In any case," Louis said, detaching the cross of the Legion of Honour from his own coat, "take this as a token of my gratitude, so that neither of us will forget it."

"Sire," Villefort said, flabbergasted, "this is an officer's cross and one of the highest honours in the land."

The king pressed it into his hand, and Villefort kissed it with tears in his eyes.

"You're correct, but I haven't time to procure you a civilian one. Blacas, see to it that the proper documentation for the award is made out." The king took another bite and dabbed his lips with a silk napkin. "Now, take what rest you require. Do you have any further news of earth-shattering events to convey, the hammer of heaven coming down to crush the English perhaps?"

"I have no other important news, sire," Villefort said, bowing again.

"In that case, you may be of greatest service to me in Marseille upholding your prosecutorial duties," the king replied.

"Sire, I will be on the road again within an hour," Villefort said.

The king sent Dandre to fetch the Minister of War, and so Dandre and Villefort exited together.

"Young man, you entered the palace today by luck's own door," Dandre said as they stepped out into the street. "Your fortune is made."

These words reverberated in the back of Villefort's mind as he climbed into a coach and let dreams of ambition spiral in his imagination.

Ten minutes later, Villefort reached his hotel. He ordered a meal and fresh horses, and gave the clerk a parcel of letters from the Marquis de Saint-Meran's salon. The hotel's bell rang sharp and loud as he ate, and someone mentioned his name to the valet. Curious about who could know of his presence, Villefort instructed the valet to send the guest in.

Villefort turned pale as the visitor entered, a man of about fifty wearing a blue frock-coat, about Villefort's height, with black eyes and bushy brows.

"Good grief," said the very man who Dandre sought for General Quesnel's murder, "what a great deal of ceremony for visiting a guest in a hotel! Is that the custom now back in Marseille?"

"Hello Father," Villefort said with regret. He waved for the valet to leave them in privacy.

CHAPTER 12
PATERNAL LOYALTY

M. Jules Noirtier waited a moment after the valet left, his mustache elevated on one side in a smirk. He opened the door again to see the valet scurry away from where he had waited to eavesdrop. Noirtier reached into his coat and produced a small lump of grey stone about the size of a fist.

"Barrois," Noirtier said, "keep watch."

The stone unfolded itself, revealing arms and legs as well as batlike wings. It flew in a lurching manner to the outside of the door, where it found handholds in the wood and faced the hallway like an unattractive knocker. Noirtier bolted the door, satisfied in their privacy.

"A gargoyle?" Villefort asked, still surprised that his father could find him so quickly. "I suppose for a man of your hobbies, it's quite a useful pet."

"Oh yes," Noirtier said happily. "I've come to own Barrois only recently, but he has already saved my plans and my life many times over. Now, my dear Gerard, I must say that you don't seem very glad to see me."

"I'm delighted," Villefort said without discernible enthusiasm. "Your visit is just unexpected, Father."

"I could say the same to you, here in Paris so soon after marrying in Marseille," Noirtier said, taking a seat.

"I was hardly expecting to be here either. You shouldn't complain; my arrival has surely spared you from a firing squad," Villefort said with a chilling gaze.

Noirtier raised one bushy eyebrow and leaned back in his chair to clean his nails with a pocketknife. He had gone through many ordeals during the Revolution and Bonaparte's coup, including escaping Paris in a hay-cart and fleeing from bloodhounds over the plains of Bordeaux. Villefort needed to elaborate in order to penetrate Noirtier's calm demeanour.

"Father, you are aware of a certain Bonapartist club in the Rue Saint-Jacques?" Villefort asked.

Noirtier gestured with the knife. "Yes, at No. 53. I am president there, what of it?"

"It may surprise you, Father, but I had an audience with the king himself today. It would seem that General Quesnel went to visit your club and was found face-down in the Seine the next day." Villefort stared at his father. "Would you know anything about this?"

"That's a fine story, son," Noirtier said. "Now let me tell you a far more interesting one."

"I suspect I already know the story you want to tell. Is it about the usurper escaping Elba?" Villefort asked.

Noirtier's hand slipped and nicked his finger. He put the small cut to his mouth, and Villefort felt a twinge in both his stomach and his own hand.

"Surprised?" Villefort said. "Believe me, nothing less important would bring me such a long way from home on the evening of my own wedding."

"Impossible." Noirtier watched Villefort carefully. "On the night of your wedding, he had not yet landed. How could you have known?"

"By intercepting a letter from Elba, addressed to you, still in the pocketbook of the messenger!" Villefort said, almost shouting. "If that letter had fallen into anyone else's hands, you would have been shot and I would be ruined."

"Shot!" Noirtier scoffed. "Hardly. Do you have the letter with you? It is mine, after all, and I should like to read it. I knew the escape was coming, but that letter was to contain vital details."

"I burned it immediately," Villefort said. "We have a more pressing matter to attend to: specifically, saving your life."

Noirtier rolled his eyes. "Your profession has made you overly dramatic, but go on."

"The general, as I said, was found in the river," Villefort said, gritting his teeth at his father's refusal to take matters seriously.

"Regardless of whether the rightful king or your godless pretender sit on the throne, such a thing is still murder."

"Murder! A fine choice of words," Noirtier exclaimed. "When I think of murder, I think of the counts who lounged in their fenced-off estates while demons feasted on Parisian flesh. They ignored the apocalypse and continued to rule us and tax us as we were slaughtered. I call that murder."

"Father, this is no time to talk politics," Villefort said. "I'm trying to tell you that the police are on your trail and you want to discuss fiscal policy?"

"Do you know what I saw under the Bourbons before the Revolution? I saw honest men torn apart in their shop fronts, because if they did not brave the Plague in order to have their due for the tax collector, they would be shot," Noirtier said. "When the emperor was on his throne, the taxman came far less frequently."

"Only because the government's money came from looting the aristocracy's homes and plundering the nations he conquered," Villefort said. "And let's not forget the blunder of selling Louisiana to the Americans!"

"Those homes were furnished by ill-gotten funds; it was only fair to reclaim it," Noirtier said. "We sold war bonds, as well. People were happy to buy them."

"He tried—you tried—to reform the Senate to allow any common peasant to join the House of Peers," Villefort said, disgusted.

"We had to, after your side's reforms to the creation of barons and counts," Noirtier replied. "And what are these whispers I hear about that League you've joined supposedly profaning the name of God?"

Villefort stopped himself from saying any more. Regardless of how their conversations began on the rare occasions when he saw Noirtier, it always returned to politics. It was exhausting, and he wished they could interact any other way.

"Father, the police know about your involvement in General Quesnel's death," Villefort said, making the effort to keep his voice low and calm. "They don't have your name yet, but they have your description, right down to your coat."

"When the emperor reaches Paris, he'll remember my name and pardon me," Noirtier said.

"That is your entire plan of self-preservation? The usurper will not make it two leagues into the interior without being caught like a wild beast and sent back to his rock in the middle of the sea or one even more remote," Villefort said. "The people will rise up. They remember what he did after he wiped out the Plague."

"Mistakes were made; nobody is entirely immune to corruption. It won't happen again," Noirtier said, frowning. "The people will rise, you're correct; they'll rise to go and meet him and escort him here to Paris."

"What makes you think that?" Villefort asked.

"We have our own police and intelligence, son, more than a match for yours. If you want proof, consider my presence now. How did I know where and when to find you?" Noirtier said.

"No matter how stupid you think the royal police are, you need to be careful," Villefort said. "They know the exact description of the man they're looking for, and there will be no mistaking you."

"I see!" said Noirtier, looking around the room. His eyes settled on Villefort's toiletry kit by the sink. "If this man were not on his guard, they may catch him yet! It would be wise for him to alter his appearance."

Without another word, Noirtier took Villefort's toiletry kit and used lather and razor to cut away his mustache and shave his head bald. He replaced his black cravat with a red neckerchief from Villefort's suitcase and took a brown coat to replace his blue one. He admired his handiwork in the mirror.

"There! Now I look nothing like the man they're trying to find," Noirtier proclaimed. "You know, son, you likely have saved my life. I will return the favour when the emperor is restored to his proper place."

Villefort shook his head, exasperated with Noirtier.

"You still doubt me. Well, never mind. Just remember this: when the emperor is back on his throne, keep your head down," Noirtier said. "Don't boast of what you did today and remain inoffensive. I'll use my position to help you as you have used yours to help me."

"And I suppose that when the political tide turns back," Villefort asked, "you'll expect me to protect you again?"

Noirtier smiled gently. "Not expect, but perhaps hope. Adieu, dear

Gerard! When you come to Paris next, do remember to visit your dear old father. Barrois, to me!"

Villefort sat pale and agitated at the window as his disguised father strolled past a group of police officers on patrol. They never gave Noirtier a second look, seeing only a bald and clean-shaven stranger. Villefort hurried about the room to dispose of the evidence Noirtier had left behind and to prepare for the return to Marseille. On the road, he learned in Lyons that Napoleon had entered Grenoble, only eighteen leagues away. There was tumult on the road home as the countryside reacted to their former emperor's return, but Villefort reached Marseille unmolested.

As he entered his home, his heart swelled with all the hopes and fears of an ambitious man who stood on the edge of losing everything once more. Villefort needed solace and remembered the peace he had felt when he had first left Marseille. He sent his valet away and unwound the bandage from his hand. He reopened the wound with a penknife and drank deep of his own blood once more to chase that sense of calm.

CHAPTER 13
THE HUNDRED DAYS

Napoleon blew into Paris like a spring storm, and the Royalist resistance was as effective as a man trying to buy more favourable weather. True to Noirtier's prediction, the French working class rallied to Napoleon's banner. The memory of prosperity from his first reign stood fresh in their minds, rather than his excesses of power after the Dead Plague had been eliminated, and Napoleon found himself in charge of an army without a purpose. The exiled emperor recaptured the throne on March 20, 1815.

For his efforts in racing to Paris, Villefort gained little else besides the king's gratitude, more of a liability than an asset in the new climate with the king himself in hiding once more. Duke de Blacas forwarded him the paperwork for his cross of the Legion of Honour, though Villefort had the prudence not to wear or display the medal.

M. Desmarais lost his position as crown prosecutor of Marseille for his Royalist sympathies. Only Noirtier's influence stopped Villefort from losing his office as well. Being the son of a Bonapartist senator, once the albatross around Villefort's neck, became his greatest advantage. He both gained Desmarais' vacated job and continued to stifle the secret of Edmond Dantes.

Villefort did not miss the irony that he had imprisoned Edmond for what was now harmless information under the emperor's regime. It was no longer the letter but Edmond's imprisonment itself that was the secret.

Renee was no longer as profitable of a match as she had once been, which somewhat cooled Villefort's feelings for her. Renee noticed him become distant but had patience and took it to be a stress reaction to political currents. On long and dark nights Villefort considered petitioning for a divorce, but he held on to hope that the winds would shift again if only he waited, making his marriage a suitable one again. Besides, more than just the law bound them together. Villefort found himself thinking often of the nameless commoner in the grotto and the smell of his hand roasting on the brazier.

Meanwhile, Napoleon's return emboldened M. Morrel to make a new plea on Edmond's behalf. He made an appointment to see Villefort in early April, who recognized the danger as soon as he saw who Mariane had put into his datebook.

Morrel entered the office expecting to find a chastened man at the mercy of a new leader. Instead, he came face to face with the same insurmountable barrier of calm and glacial manners. The only noticeable difference in Villefort was a distinct pallor which Morrel did not remember seeing before. Villefort pretended not to remember Morrel and made a show of checking the datebook again.

"M. Morrel, is it?" Villefort said. "To what circumstance do I owe the honour of this visit?"

Villefort waved a patronizing hand at the seat near his desk. His keen eyes noticed a pulsing vein near the surface of Morrel's skin, and he considered activating the hidden shackles. Villefort's arms had become host to a score of nicks and cuts from his new habit of seeking comfort in the taste of his own blood. The impulse to sample another's blood passed without Morrel even realizing the danger.

"Monsieur," Morrel said, "you may recall that I came to speak on a prisoner's behalf before the landing of the emperor. He was the new captain of my ship and accused of being in league with the emperor on Elba. Well, what used to be a crime is today a service to society. Therefore, I've returned to ask what has become of Edmond Dantes."

Villefort would rather have faced Morrel with pistols at five paces than to hear that name, but remained calm. He walked to the large register of prisoners across the room and took his time searching for the name Dantes. If Morrel had been less anxious, he may have realized that the crown prosecutor normally delegated such tasks to subordinates.

"Here he is," Villefort said. "Edmond Dantes, a sailor, charged with treason against King Louis XVIII. He was carried off to Fenestrelles, or Pignerol, or some such place."

"Indeed!" Morrel said, hopeful at last. "But as you say, he was charged with treason against the old monarch. The same act demonstrates his loyalty to our current ruler. Surely the first task of the new government should be releasing the prisoners who were found guilty of supporting it?"

"If only it were so simple," Villefort said, feigning a sigh. "The order for imprisonment came from a very high authority, and any pardon must come from no less lofty a height. Napoleon has hardly been back for a fortnight, and I cannot imagine the letters have been sent yet."

"Can't we expedite the process?" Morrel asked. "The poor soul has been locked away for over a month already! Your secretary recommended I petition the Minister of Prisons, but I know that he receives two hundred petitions a day and may decide to read three of them."

"True, he's a busy man," Villefort said, improvising, "but if I countersigned and presented yours, he would certainly consider it. My duty dictates that justice must be done. I'll deliver the petition to the Minister's hand myself."

Morrel's entire body relaxed at this news that the machine of government would for once work towards Edmond's happiness rather than against it. Villefort gave up his place at the table to Morrel and gave him a pen and paper.

"It's important that you write exactly what I say," Villefort instructed. "I know the language of the law and which phrases will open doors for M. Dantes."

Morrel wrote what Villefort dictated, which spelled out Edmond's patriotic actions in no uncertain terms. Morrel accepted all of Villefort's embellishments, thinking them Edmond's best chance at freedom. Well-intentioned exaggerations painted Edmond as an active agent in Napoleon's return to increase the odds of the minister granting this release. Villefort read the completed petition aloud and added his name to the bottom.

"There; now it should be clear to anyone that this statement is the verified truth," Villefort told Morrel with a cold smile. "The rest of it is in my hands. I'll see to it that this petition is seen by the Minister of Prisons."

Morrel breathed a sigh. The strokes of Villefort's pen looked like a key unlocking the unknown cell in which Edmond languished. He hastened to tell Louis Dantes that his son would soon be free.

Alone, Villefort folded the petition and locked it in his desk drawer for safekeeping in the hope of another Restoration. The Eternal Royalist League continued to meet in secret, sacrificing men and women loyal to the new regime to encourage the angels they revered to intervene on behalf of the House of Bourbon again. If such a miracle came to pass, Villefort would enter the petition into Edmond's file to prevent any other prosecutor from ever thinking to release him.

Villefort did not need to wait long. At the fields of Waterloo on June 18, 1815, Napoleon suffered his final defeat. His short second reign would go down in history as the Hundred Days, a mere interruption of King Louis XVIII's tenure as a monarch. Louis took no chances after his return; on the advice of the Eternal Royalist League, he ordered an Inquisition to stamp out treason in his kingdom and make the prospect of supporting any more usurpers too horrifying to contemplate.

The second Restoration dashed Morrel's hopes for Edmond. Petitioning any further would not help Edmond's case and would only serve to bring the wrath of the Inquisition to Morrel's own doorstep. Morrel himself only escaped the brutality of it by becoming a recluse for over a year, managing the affairs of Morrel & Son from hiding.

Edmond Dantes remained in his dungeon, oblivious to history unfolding on the mainland. He knew nothing of Waterloo, the Inquisition, or even the Hundred Days.

Villefort found new happiness in his marriage. The Marquis de Saint-Meran was rewarded for his loyalty with more land and a higher position in court than before, brightening Villefort's own prospects. He became eager to escape Marseille; every street-corner and familiar face served to remind him of Edmond, and he fell back on the comfort of blood more and more often. He requested a transfer to the crown prosecutor's position at Nimes, and he and Renee left Marseille behind.

Danglars spent the Hundred Days in a state of dread. Like Morrel, he realized that the new ruler could mean a new lease on life for Edmond. Nightmares tormented him of Edmond walking out of the sea, his waterlogged flesh covered in barnacles like the undead from the terrifying nights of his youth. In these dreams, Edmond pursued Danglars without resting, finding him no matter where he hid. Every dream ended with Edmond dragging him beneath the water to drown.

During the three months leading up to the Pharaon's next departure, Danglars obsessed in finding every possible good omen. He had never been so happy to set out to sea, reasoning that it would be harder for Edmond to find him if he were released.

The new captain was a man named Orgon, who was glad to accept a few gold pieces for the detours and diversions Danglars wanted. Danglars soon learned that the drunken soldier from Elba had told him the truth, when he found a single shard of putrid green crystal buried in a Tuscan churchyard. On that same day, he first heard about Waterloo. To the superstitious Danglars, it was a clear sign that the cosmos approved of his plan.

Though he was conscripted into the king's army to combat Bonaparte's return, Fernand cared nothing about the Hundred Days or their implications. He only cared that Edmond was absent and that as far as Mercedes knew, his own hands were clean. Edmond's imprisonment gave Fernand time to ingratiate himself further into Mercedes' life. He comforted her, distracted her, and wormed into the void in her life which Edmond had left behind. He hoped his love would someday wear away her resolve like the ocean worked to erode the seaside cliffs.

In moments of respite after returning home, however, Fernand sat motionless on the summit of those same cliffs. Overlooking Marseille and the Catalan village, he watched the beach; like Danglars, fearful that some messenger of vengeance would arrive there. Fernand's mind was set. If Edmond returned, they would duel. Fernand would incinerate him with every shred of flame he could create as revenge for stealing Mercedes' heart, and then take his own life.

Oblivious to his role in her heartbreak, Mercedes' familial love for Fernand remained intact. She wept at the sight of his thin arms swimming in the sleeves of his standard-issue uniform the day he left for war. When Fernand was preparing to leave, Mercedes placed his knapsack onto his thin shoulders and touched a hand to his cheek.

"Be careful," Mercedes said. "If you die, I'll be alone in the world."

These words allowed Fernand to carry a ray of hope in his heart that Mercedes really would belong to him if he returned and Edmond did not. The possibility that Edmond would return, and while Fernand was away at war, nevertheless settled in to wage a war of its own against that hope.

Mercedes was left to face the vast sea on her own. She wandered the Catalan village with her eyes almost always shrouded in tears, or stood like a statue on the cliffs to stare at Marseille. Many times, she considered throwing herself into the sea to end her misery, but her upbringing was a religious one, and she had no desire to substitute one hell for another. Little by little, she learned to deal with the pain.

Caderousse was drafted into the army as well, though he and Fernand were not stationed together. He welcomed the distraction from his role in the dreadful fate of Edmond Dantes.

Edmond's father Louis, whose only hope to see his son rested in Napoleon, was crushed by the emperor's downfall. He died after the second Restoration, under conditions too horrible to recount here. Despite the political danger of doing so, M. Morrel paid for the expenses of Louis' funeral and what small debts he had accrued at the end of his life.

CHAPTER 14
THE RAVING PRISONER
AND THE MAD ONE

A year after Waterloo, the new inspector-general of prisons, M. de Boville, came to inspect the Chateau d'If for the first time. Edmond could hear the preparations from his cell, his hearing having sharpened from spending long hours in darkness and having nothing to look at during the day. He knew it signified something uncommon, but decided that it was an affair of the living; in his dungeon, Edmond considered himself one of the dead. He concerned himself with memories of his father and Mercedes.

Inspector de Boville visited each cell in the Chateau, inquiring how the occupants were fed and if they had any request to make. The response from every prisoner was that the food was vile, and their only request was the basest requirement of civilized life: their liberty. Boville and the governor of the Chateau d'If, M. Jacquard, discussed the inspection over a glass of wine in Jacquard's residence.

"I shouldn't complain, because it lines my pockets, but the government must understand that these visits are pointless," Boville said with a rueful smile. "One prisoner is the same as the next: they're all ill-fed and innocent. Still, I must be able to say that I was thorough. Are there any others?"

"Only the dangerous and mad prisoners in the dungeons," Jacquard replied. "We have one of each: Prisoner 14 and Prisoner 45."

"Let's play out this farce to the end, then," Boville said with a sigh.

Two clanking forged guards and Leblanc the turnkey accompanied them to the dungeons. Leblanc led them down a stairway so dark, foul, and humid as to be loathsome to all of the senses at once. Inspector Boville marveled that anyone could live in such a place and remembered

Jacquard's warning: one was a dangerous conspirator against the crown, and the other was quite simply mad.

"The dangerous one, 45, how long has he been here?" Boville asked.

"Just over a year," Leblanc said. "He had an ordinary cell at first but tried to kill me at mealtime."

Boville observed Leblanc's bitter features and hunched shoulders. It troubled him to consider what kind of woman would choose to live as one of the few human beings on an isolated island populated by inmates and silent automatons.

"Thankfully, he is nearly mad already," Jacquard said. "When you visit again next year, he should be more docile."

"So much the better, he will suffer less in such a state," Boville said, demonstrating the natural philanthropy and charitable spirit of bureaucrats which made him such a fit for his office.

"In another cell about fifty feet away, we have the mad banker," Jacquard said. "An Italian who has been here since 1811, he went mad sometime in 1813, and the change is astonishing. He used to weep, now he laughs. His madness is entertaining and should lift your spirits if the first prisoner is in a mood."

Edmond heard their conversation but did not raise his head until the key turned in his lock. Crouched in a corner of his dungeon, he deduced that the stranger to whom Jacquard spoke with hat in hand held a position of authority. Edmond sprang forward with clasped hands.

A forged lurched forward and wrapped one large metal hand around both of Edmond's wrists. Boville recoiled from the display of force, but was fascinated nonetheless. The forged could crush every bone in Edmond's hands with a single squeeze.

"Monsieur," Edmond said. It had been so long since he'd spoken to another human being, along with the trauma of being lifted by the throat when he had first arrived, that his voice rasped like unfamiliar gravel in his own ears. "I know that many men must plead with you, but I truly am innocent. Tell me what crime I have supposedly committed, and give me a trial. If I really am guilty, then please shoot me."

Edmond had no way to be certain of why he had been sent to the Chateau d'If. Villefort had promised that the letter from Elba would mean no more than a fine, and the unsigned letter denouncing Edmond contained no other accusations. He remembered every word of it and obsessed for hours over each syllable to find any hidden meaning in them.

"Are you well fed?" Boville asked, adhering to his script.

"Perhaps, I don't know," Edmond said with a shrug. "All that matters is I'm innocent, rotting in prison for what might be a clerical mistake, and I could die here cursing my anonymous executioners."

"He's humbler than you led me to expect," Boville whispered to Jacquard. "Later, show me the evidence against him."

"Certainly," Jacquard said. "You'll see how severe the charges are."

"Monsieur," Edmond continued, "I know it isn't in your power to release me, but you can have me tried; that's all I ask. I was sent here with no trial or verdict, or even knowing my charges. Uncertainty makes this wretched fate even harder to bear."

"I shall see," Boville said, surprised at Edmond's touching display. "All I can promise is that I'll examine the evidence in your case. Who was it that arrested you?"

Edmond uttered a barking noise that nobody in the dungeon, himself included, recognized as a laugh.

"Saved at last! I was arrested by M. de Villefort of Marseille," he said. "He'll be able to clear up this mistake."

"M. de Villefort has left Marseille and is now the crown prosecutor in Nimes. Did he have some cause to personally dislike you?" Boville asked. "Should I expect some bias against you in his case notes?"

"We never met before my arrest, I don't think. He was very kind to me, once I explained the situation," Edmond said.

"You have my word then, I'll read your file and see what can be done," Boville said.

While Edmond babbled his thanks, Jacquard gave an order to the forged to release his hands. They left Edmond alone again with a new hope to obsess over in the darkness, a hope which could finally signal his reunion with Mercedes.

"That was certainly unsettling, but not for the reasons you said," Boville said. "I hope that your madman is as amusing as you say."

"Oh, I can guarantee he is," Jacquard said. "Prisoner 14 fancies that he possesses an immense treasure and the secret to unimaginable power. His first year here, he offered me one million francs to release him; two million the second year, then three, and so on. Mark my words, he will ask to speak to you in private and offer you five million."

Leblanc led the way through a corridor sloping down further into the fortress.

"Why are the cells so irregularly spaced down here?" Boville asked. "It seems you could easily fit more cells along this expanse."

"You'd have to ask the builders," Jacquard said. "My understanding is that we walk next to one of the large support columns of the Chateau, a pile of rubble and mortar that serves some structural purpose or other. Ah, here we are."

Leblanc opened the door to Number 14's dungeon. An old man in tattered garments sat in the middle of a circle traced on the floor. He drew geometric lines within it with a piece of plaster pried loose from the wall. He ignored the door and continued in his calculations until the torch lit the walls of his cell. Astonished to see so many visitors, he wrapped himself in the tattered coverlet of his bed like a sort of toga.

"I am here to visit the prison and hear the requests of the prisoners," Boville explained, reciting the same script he performed for each prisoner. "Are you well-fed? Do you want for anything?"

The man who they called the mad banker smiled. "It is excellent that you have come! I hope that we shall understand each other," he said. "I am Gianmarco Faria, investment advisor to kings, noblemen, and cardinals."

"I am pleased to make your acquaintance," Boville said, already concealing a smile. "Now, have you anything to ask for or to complain of?"

"The food is the same as in other prisons: terrible. The lodgings are unhealthful, but expected for a dungeon," Faria said. "However, I have a more important matter to discuss with you. Could we have a few words in private?"

Jacquard and Boville shared an amused look.

"What you ask is impossible, monsieur," Boville said. "Regulations prohibit my remaining alone with any of the prisoners."

"Even if I wished to speak to you of a large sum of money, amounting to five million francs?" Faria asked. Reading the look on Boville's face, Faria held up a hand in supplication. His gaze could have convinced anyone else of Faria's sanity, were it not for the setting of their conversation. "We needn't be alone after all, the governor has heard my offer as well."

"Monsieur, I can tell you the story as well as he can. It concerns his treasures, of course," Jacquard said. "The government has a rich tax base, M. Faria. Keep your treasure until you are liberated."

"But what if I am not liberated, and stay here until my death?" Faria cried. "You would miss out on money acquired honestly, rather than by the piecemeal plunder of the nation. I will offer you six million and content myself with the rest, if you only grant me my freedom."

Faria grew exasperated at Boville and Jacquard's disbelieving faces and Leblanc's snickering in the hall.

"I am not mad! The treasure exists! I will sign a contract: I will lead you to the treasure, and if it is not there, I will come back without resistance," Faria said. "If that's not good enough, I'll stay here! Just swear that you will release me if you find the treasure at the appointed place, and I'll wait here in my cell."

"Are you well fed?" Boville said. "You have not replied to my question."

"Nor you to mine!" Faria said. "You refuse my gold and refuse me my liberty; I will keep one and God will grant me the other. Good day!"

Faria cast away his improvised toga and resumed his place on the floor, continuing his calculations.

"What are you doing there?" Jacquard asked, laughing. "Counting your treasure?"

Faria did not respond to this sarcasm. With no further entertainment and convinced of Faria's lunacy, Boville and Jacquard left. Boville's impression of Faria locked the door of his cell with more permanence than any turnkey.

The French government had no interest in allowing men who lost their minds in prison to rejoin the living. The people could not be allowed to see the bureaucracy as the vast machine it was, or to believe it was in the business of grinding human beings into paste and extruding them as unrecognizable wretches. These horrors would be too similar to the callousness in the face of the Dead Plague which had sparked the Revolution of 1789. The public had made an exception for the public tortures and executions of the Inquisition, but those were understood to represent a sort of vengeful madness on the part of the king and had been, in so many ways, a deviation from the norm.

Inspector Boville kept his word to Edmond and examined the register of prisoners. He found a copy of the petition written by Morrel and countersigned by Villefort, with all the embellished details of Edmond's loyalty to the emperor. A note in Villefort's hand summarized the contents: "Edmond Dantes. Violent Bonapartist, took an active part in the return from Elba." Boville concluded that nothing could, or should, be done for Edmond.

Unaware of this, the visit brought new vigor to Edmond. He had long since lost track of the date, but now he took a fragment of plaster and recorded the date which he had heard Boville say: June 20, 1816. From then on, he made a mark every day in order to not forget again. Days, then weeks, then months passed without any news. After ten and a half months, Edmond doubted if the inspector existed as anything but a figment of his imagination.

In the summer of 1817, the government transferred Governor Jacquard to oversee another prison. He brought Leblanc, his sole human subordinate, with him. The new governor and turnkey found it too tedious to learn the names of their prisoners and only learned their numbers instead. The unhappy young man in the dungeon was no longer called Edmond Dantes; he was now only Number 45.

CHAPTER 15
NUMBER 45 AND NUMBER 14

Edmond endured the hardships common to prisoners in isolation. He doubted his memories, his innocence, and even his sanity. Edmond made requests at every mealtime of the new turnkey, a man named Dufresne: to be moved to a different dungeon or a proper cell, permission to walk outdoors or to have books, visitors, specific meals, a bottle of wine.

Edmond never expected his requests to be granted, and they weren't; his vain pleas to Dufresne were his only opportunity for human interaction. He tried speaking to the forged as they patrolled, but the desperate sound of his own voice at such times frightened him too much to continue.

One of the many methods by which France punished lawbreakers was to sentence them as slaves pulling oars on massive galleys, and before his own captivity Edmond had seen several of them on the sea. Edmond had found the notion revolting at the time, but in the darkness of his dungeon he wished for that life of slavery. Having activity and company during his captivity would make all the difference. In his present circumstances he was denied even the company of rats and the possibility that he might catch one and keep it as a pet.

Without education beyond his profession, Edmond lacked the option to imagine nations of the past or far-off lands of the present to distract himself. His past was short, his present melancholy, and his future doubtful. His childhood in Marseille and his brief sailing career constituted his entire pool of memory to draw from, nineteen years of life to reflect upon in eternal darkness. His energetic spirit was like an eagle caught in a sparrow's cage. When thoughts of his father or Mercedes became too painful, Edmond dwelled on the cause of his predicament. The anonymous letter which had destroyed his life consumed him.

Recalling the letter never failed to fill Edmond with rage. He uttered blasphemies that terrified Dufresne, threw himself against the walls in fits, and screamed at the forged in the hallway. The accusation letter stood out in his mind with every word written in flame. Though his imagination was limited by inexperience, Edmond subjected his unknown enemy to the most horrible tortures he could invent and found them all lacking. After all, torture is followed by death, and death by rest, or at least the boon of unconsciousness.

It should not have been a surprise that this line of reasoning brought him to consider suicide. Contemplating the yawning abyss of death and the obscurity beyond was a morbid comfort and less terrifying than the prospect of his future existence. He reflected on times at sea, when water and wind or magic and monsters had tried to destroy the Pharaon and all aboard, and he had used all of his skill and intelligence as a man and a sailor to avoid such a fate. But he had been happy then, with reasons to live.

Two methods of suicide sat at his disposal. He could hang himself with his sheet tied to the iron grate of his window, but he refused such a death. On the sea that fate was reserved for pirates, and they had the benefit of a sudden drop to break their necks. This left him the second option: starvation. It was 1821, though Edmond had once again lost track; nearly six years had passed since his arrest when he first refused his food.

To avoid suspicion, Edmond waited for Dufresne to leave and threw his twice-daily meals out the window. An easy task at first, as time passed the repugnant food started to look like a grand feast. Only the dread of his own future gave him strength to continue.

The natural yearning for life still tormented him; he was still young and could still have fifty or sixty years ahead of him. Fifty years could hold many opportunities for a miracle to open his cell door and set him free. Nevertheless, Edmond persisted in his determination to die until he lacked the strength to stand up and throw away his food. The next day he could not see, and Dufresne suspected he was dangerously ill.

As Edmond lay dying, a delirious contentment washed over him. Lights danced before his eyes in strange patterns that defied sense, spirals that folded in on themselves and grew larger as they shrank. They were a welcome alternative to staring at the walls of his dungeon, but then a surprise late in the evening: a sound within the wall he leaned against. A persistent scratching noise, like some iron tool attacking the stones.

Edmond's weakened hopes awoke and seized on the idea at the forefront of every prisoner's mind: freedom! Whether blind chance or the forces of heaven had seen fit to take pity on him, the noise drew him back from the abyss. It continued for hours but ceased once Dufresne's footsteps descended the dungeon stairs.

Despite participating as a cog in the mechanism of the prison system, Dufresne still experienced fits of compassion which his career had not yet stamped out. Like Leblanc before him, Dufresne was paid in proportion to the number of inmates he managed. Seeing that Edmond was ill, Dufresne secured broth and white bread in place of the standard meal. With the renewed purpose of investigating the noise, Edmond accepted the food and recovered his strength. Simple as it was, it tasted better than even the sausages and lobster of his wedding feast.

With food in his belly, he could think clearly. The noise could have two possible sources: a fellow prisoner seeking freedom, or workmen maintaining the prison. He resolved to dig toward the noise himself. If he met another prisoner, they could combine their efforts and be free even sooner. If he found workmen instead, he had nothing to lose if he were caught tunneling.

As all men eat, all men must deal with the consequences of digestion. In the Chateau d'If each prisoner was left a metal pail for that purpose, which was emptied once a week. The pail in Edmond's cell had an iron handle, easy to remove from the loops and reattach later. With this thin piece of iron in his hands, he chose a stone that he judged to be in the direct path of the noise and attacked the plaster holding it in place.

The cell was always damp, and that dampness had weakened the plaster. Edmond could break it off in chunks, which he tossed out his window. He chided himself for spending so long floundering in inactivity, wondering how far he could have dug if he had begun this project when he was first imprisoned.

After three days of work and listening for Dufresne to avoid discovery, Edmond had removed all of the plaster. Using the handle as a lever, he pried the stone from its place a quarter-inch at a time. With an hour of labour, he created a cavity large enough to fit his shoulders through. Seeing no reason to stop, he continued working behind it.

The wall was a mix of more large stone blocks and smaller pieces of rubble, the spaces between filled with more plaster. As he rested, he heard the sound of his mysterious companion digging as well. Whenever he heard Dufresne returning, he replaced the stone and moved his bed against it.

After several days, Edmond encountered the first obstacle in his project: a stout wooden beam set horizontally into the stones, blocking his short tunnel. He would have to dig under or over it to proceed.

"Blast and damnation!" Edmond said aloud, forgetting his fear of speaking to an empty room. "Is my every attempt at liberty from this cursed place to be thwarted?"

"Blasting powder would be useful, certainly," said a voice from below him, "but we already live in damnation."

Edmond's hair stood on end. He had not heard another human voice but Dufresne's in four or five years. "Who are you?"

The voice hesitated. "You first," it said.

"My name is Edmond Dantes, a sailor before I was thrown in here to be forgotten," Edmond said, his happiness at having someone to speak to overruling any caution. "I've been here since February of 1815."

"What was your crime?" asked the voice.

"I am entirely innocent, but some anonymous devil accused me of conspiring to get the emperor to return from exile," Edmond said.

"Return? Exile?" asked the voice. "Then Napoleon is no longer on the throne? My, the outside has changed. I was imprisoned in 1811, and at that time he still ruled the world."

Edmond shuddered, realizing that the other man had been in prison four years longer than he.

"Listen," the voice continued, "do not dig any further, but continue speaking so I may follow your voice. Describe your cell, and how it is oriented to the outside world."

"My tunnel is level with the floor, and concealed by my bed. To my left is the door, which opens onto a corridor. To my right is the window, which faces a small courtyard," Edmond said.

As the sounds of digging resumed, he continued describing the cell in more minute detail. He gave measurements as best as he could define them, and told all he could remember about the route from his first arrival on the island to his dungeon. Though his long confinement had given him cause to doubt it, Edmond possessed an excellent capacity for memory. His mental picture of the prison was quite correct, at least in this respect; though his dungeon sat below ground level relative to the main courtyard, the geography of the island left him in a built-up section along a cliff, overlooking another part of the fortress.

"Alas!" the voice said. The digging stopped. "It seems I've miscalculated my angle. I expected to see open air and the sea below when I broke through your wall, where I could dive in and swim for one of the nearby islands. Instead, I find another cell."

"Not just another cell, but human company!" Edmond said, frantic that this mysterious person might get discouraged and stop. "You must be as starved for contact and conversation as I am. Please, don't give up when we are so near to each other! I swear that I would never breathe a word of your tunnel to our jailer, not even under torture!"

"How old are you?" asked the voice after another moment's hesitation. "You sound like a young man."

"I was only nineteen when I was arrested," Edmond said, "and I have lost track of what year it is now."

"Not quite twenty-six!" said the voice. "Too young to be a traitor. Very well, it is about time for M. Dufresne to return, and I must sleep; I will return tomorrow."

"Yes! Please!" Edmond said. "We can talk about anything; the people we loved and were forced to leave behind, our lives before this terrible place, anything at all. If you are young, I will be your comrade. If you are old, I will be your son. Just don't abandon me."

"You have my word," said the voice. "I will return."

Edmond proceeded with his routine of cleaning up the evidence of his day's labour and concealing the tunnel, then lay on his bed in the nearest state to contentment that his circumstances could allow. He would no longer be alone and perhaps even have an accomplice with which to regain liberty. At worst, he would have a companion, and captivity that is shared is but half captivity.

As Edmond waited for the sound of his neighbour again, the

pressing madness of solitude returned to make him doubt his senses. Had he imagined the voice in the tunnel? Had he imagined the tunnel itself? He fought the urge to pry the stone from the mouth of the tunnel again just to prove to himself it existed.

Finally, after Dufresne's final visit of the night, Edmond heard three knocks from the tunnel. He exposed the opening, and the floor of the tunnel gave way under a mass of stones and earth disappearing down the hole. From this passage appeared the head and shoulders of a man, who, with a helping hand, sprang into Edmond's cell.

CHAPTER 16
AN ITALIAN SCHOLAR

E dmond pulled his visitor up from the tunnel, ushering him into the scant moonlight from the window to view him better. The man stood shorter than Edmond, with deep lines in his face and brittle white hair, though his eyebrows and beard were black. He appeared to be in his sixties, but with a vigor that suggested prison had aged him more than time.

He smiled at Edmond's enthusiastic greetings, his moist eyes suggesting that he shared Edmond's enthusiasm to have someone to talk to. Despite the disappointment of finding another dungeon rather than his expected freedom, he thanked Edmond for the warm welcome and looked around to examine the cell tunnel.

"Your removal of the stone was crude, but effective. What sort of tool did you use?" he asked.

"Only this pail handle," Edmond said.

"Only that? Extraordinary," the man said, raising his eyebrows. He spotted the simple wooden bed frame on which Edmond slept. "Ah, that makes sense. I was left an iron bed in my cell, and some careful disassembly allowed me to make a rudimentary chisel and a lever. Those let me dig the fifty feet between my cell and yours."

"Fifty feet!" Edmond said.

"Yes, although if I could have better measured my angle, it would have only been forty. A few degrees were the difference between breaking through to the sea and breaking through to you. And here I find that the wall of your cell overlooks a courtyard full of those dreadful metal men." The man sighed and leaned against the wall.

"Tell me, who are you? What was your life before you came to this place?" Edmond asked, determined to distract his new friend from this setback. "I've never met someone with such determination that they could tunnel through fifty feet of rock with only homemade tools, after all."

The stranger smiled but his eyes remained sorrowful. "My name is Gianmarco Faria; as I told you, I was imprisoned in the year 1811. Prior to that, I was one of the finest investment advisors in all of Europe."

"Investment advisor?" Edmond asked. He had never heard of such a profession. "What did you do?"

"The marvelous thing about wealth is that, like a living thing, it can reproduce and create more of itself," Faria said. "However, to do so, it requires wise investment. A vault full of hoarded gold will never produce an additional penny. But if some of that gold is lent to a businessman, to be paid back with interest, your wealth can create more wealth. Not only for you; the businessman who borrows the money grows wealthier from the opportunity you helped him pursue, his employees benefit with their wages, and his customers benefit from what he sells them. That's investment."

Edmond nodded. He had never been involved with the finances of Morrel & Son, but he had heard Morrel refer to his business partner M. Clairmont as an investor.

"How can one man possibly know what is best to invest in?" Edmond asked.

"By keeping track of as many world events as possible, and market forces, and changes to the political landscape," Faria said. "One must also keep in mind unintended consequences. Consider a tariff—as a sailor, you must know about tariffs."

Edmond nodded, having overheard Danglars and Captain LeClere discussing those import fees often enough.

"A king declares a tariff on foreign steel to make it artificially more costly. Investing in that country's steel industry may seem wise, since it's now protected," Faria said. "The trouble is, the protected steel must necessarily be inferior steel. Otherwise, businesses would buy local instead of imported even without the tariff. Eventually, the protected steel industry would collapse, and you would lose your investment."

The idea fascinated Edmond. He had never considered the implications of trade beyond his own role in transporting the goods.

"Speaking of political changes," Faria said, "you said that the emperor is no longer on the throne. Who rules France, his son?"

"No, the monarchy returned in 1814. Louis XVIII is King," Edmond said. He didn't know that the Hundred Days had ever happened or how close he had come to freedom.

"Then the Bourbons have returned!" Faria said with a sigh. "The cycle of dynasties continues, briefly interrupted by upstarts like a Cromwell or a Napoleon, while ordinary people continue being crushed underfoot. But every so often, as was seen across the Atlantic in 1776, those people rise up and chart their own destiny. You are young; with luck, you will see it happen again."

"If I ever get out of prison," Edmond said. "I have told you what brought me here; what was it that doomed you?"

"Like I said, I advised men and women on how to grow their wealth. One of the simplest ways to help your wealth grow is to keep it safe from those who want to take it, which I helped many people do in many countries," Faria said. "Of course, when people wish to take wealth from others, they have a tendency to band together and call themselves governments in order to do it."

"You committed tax fraud?" Edmond asked.

"Some call it that; I call it defending my clients' natural rights of self-ownership against a mob with guns," Faria replied with a rueful smile. "Unfortunately, I was found out, and now here I sit in a French prison."

Edmond recalled something he overheard the previous turnkey say years before.

"You worked with money; are you the banker who they say is, well, ill?" Edmond said, before considering how his new friend may respond. To his relief, Faria chuckled.

"Mad, you mean? Yes, I am the poor mad banker of the Chateau d'If; nobody understood my profession well enough when I was locked up to give me the proper epithet." Faria danced in place like an organ-grinder's monkey. "Jacquard sometimes brought visitors to my cell to laugh at my insanity. If children were ever unfortunate enough to be found on this island, I'm certain I would be promoted to entertaining them too."

A deep sigh ran through Faria. "At any rate, it would give me something to do, now that my attempt at escape is thwarted."

Edmond stood quiet for a time. At last an idea formed, so simple that it shocked him. He dragged his bed frame over to the window to confirm his theory.

"Your tunnel connects our cells, and my cell overlooks the courtyard," Edmond said. "If we started in the middle and dug outward, we could reach the courtyard wall and follow that to get nearer the sea."

Faria shook his head. "It took me years just to dig this far. There is more than rubble and plaster under these stones, you know; there is cement that's become as hard as granite. If I can remove a cubic inch of it in a day, it's an accomplishment.""So much work, only to find that a simple mistake has led me here instead! I am happy to have someone to talk to, but a friend is still a poor substitute for freedom."

"Come here and look at how close you are to your goal," Edmond said, refusing to be dissuaded.

Faria looked but saw only the flaws in Edmond's idea. "Yes, look! The wall around the courtyard is patrolled by forged. They would catch us and drag us back to our cells," he said. "We would both be tortured and the tunnel blocked up."

As Faria spoke, a pair of prisoners walked past in the courtyard grass. Deep in conversation, they paid little attention to their path and one man collided with the back of a forged. The two men scrambled away before the forged could turn around, and it did not pursue them.

"Look!" Edmond said. "The forged may be strong and inscrutable, but they are not very observant, are they?"

"It seems that way," Faria said carefully. "It would explain why their use on the battlefield was curtailed, and such a weakness would not deter them much from their task here. After all, what sane prisoner would try to escape by the sea?"

Faria and Edmond shared a chuckle at that, and Edmond nearly wept from the simple enjoyment of having someone to laugh with.

"What if we could tunnel under the courtyard wall, and come up from underneath?" Edmond said once he regained his composure. He pointed at a forged on patrol on the courtyard wall. "We could listen for those footsteps, then follow close behind it. If we don't touch it or make a noise, it won't know we're there. When we reach the edge, we can use our sheets as a rope to climb down the cliff. From there, we can swim for freedom after all!"

"You understand that this is madness," Faria said, stroking his beard as he considered it. Finally, a broad grin broke through the mass of whiskers. "Thankfully, I have a reputation for being mad."

With a new sense of life, Faria plotted aloud about where in the tunnel to branch off from while Edmond listened with rapt attention. Escape had never occurred to him; some things seem so impossible that the mind refuses to dwell on them. Faria's devotion to mining away fifty feet of rock astounded him, especially when success meant flinging oneself into the sea and possibly to a watery grave. And then, to swim for the nearest island, at least three miles away!

Faria decided to start the branch from a disused chimney which he used as a dumping ground for large pieces of rubble. The rubble could be moved, saving them some of the effort of tunneling downward. Seeing Faria regain his enthusiasm for the project, Edmond knew he could do no less. Faria had dug fifty feet; Edmond was younger and stronger and could dig a hundred. Faria was willing to swim three miles despite no experience on the sea; Edmond, who had often dived to the sea floor to bring up bright seashells for Mercedes, could swim the distance and help buoy Faria as well. He guessed he could make the distance in an hour and had often spent twice as long in the water.

"It's settled, then!" Edmond cried, grasping Faria's thin shoulders. "We escape together, return to our families, and discover what strange new developments we've missed in the world."

"And with us both working, we'll be able to dig with half as many delays!" Faria said. "I've lost half of each day just recovering from the work."

"How did you pass the time?" Edmond asked. "I would find it torture to take any break from progress at all."

"I keep my mind occupied by writing or studying while my aching muscles recover," Faria said.

"You're allowed books and paper?" Edmond asked, surprised.

"Oh no, they never bring such luxuries to the dungeons," Faria said. "I only have what I made for myself, like that chisel. When you visit my cell, I can show you my book: thoughts and meditations from a career of observing the world's markets, the result of all my studies so far. When I escape, I will have it published and title it 'Free Markets, Free Men: The Possibility of Liberty'."

"You've written a book without paper?" Edmond asked.

"I've used every scrap of cloth I could spare, in the smallest script I can manage," Faria said. Indeed, the rags he wore provided for modesty but not much else. "Thankfully, I was arrested in winter and thus had a surplus of clothing when I arrived here. With some chemistry and remnants from mealtime, I can make linen as easy to write on as parchment."

"You are a chemist as well as a banker?" Edmond said, already in awe of his new companion's breadth of knowledge.

"To be successful in the world of finance, one must know a little of everything; for instance, I can speak five languages almost fluently, and Greek well enough to get by," Faria said. "You can consult experts on nearly anything, of course, but some opportunities require quick action. A man should be able to take advantage of them without waiting weeks for a reply."

"I'm still astonished that you wrote a book in here. How on earth did you do it without a library?" Edmond asked. Even without formal education, he had overheard academics in taverns and inns. It seemed to him that writing a scholarly book involved a great deal of writing about the contents of other books.

"I have had access to many vast libraries throughout my life, but my experience is that certain books are so influential as to be referenced by other authors again and again," Faria said. "I tracked the knowledge most useful to me to its sources in about one hundred and fifty well-chosen books and spent long hours memorizing them. Now I can remember them with a minor effort and be transported through history, philosophy, and science."

Edmond had an active memory himself, but his mind reeled at the idea of holding so much in his head. Faria continued to speak about the things he had made during his imprisonment. The prison served fish once a week, and Faria used the bones to make pens. He made a penknife from a scrap of his iron bed frame. A disused fireplace in his cell provided old soot, which he mixed with his own urine to make ink. Edmond could sit still no more.

"Please, show me the workshop where you've created and hidden all these things!" Edmond exclaimed. "When may I visit your cell?"

"Right away, if you like." Faria led Edmond back through the tunnel. For the first time in six years, Edmond left the four walls of his dungeon.

CHAPTER 17
THE BANKER'S CELL

The tunnel was not quite large enough to stand upright. Edmond emerged at the far end in Faria's cell, coming up through the floor. Edmond looked around in hopes of spotting the marvels Faria had described, but none were visible. Aside from the ancient fireplace, it looked like his own cell.

"M. Dufresne won't return for a long while, it's just a quarter past twelve now," Faria said.

There was no clock, only a series of lines on the wall opposite the window. Sure enough, the moonlight coming in sat just beneath a line labelled with the number twelve.

"How did you know where to draw the lines?" Edmond asked.

"Mme. Leblanc happened to tell Jacquard the time once during a visit, which informed me where to make the first mark," Faria said.

Faria gave a brief explanation of the movement of the earth around the sun, and how the lines allowed him to keep time better than with a watch. Edmond had seen the sun rise behind the mountains and set in the Mediterranean and assumed it was the sun which moved. Every word that came from Faria's lips seemed to hold all the mysteries of the world.

Next, Faria used his chisel to raise a stone from the old fireplace. This exposed a gap that served as a safe hiding place for his treasures.

"What would you like to see first?" Faria asked with a smile, enjoying Edmond's youthful enthusiasm.

"Your book, of course!" Edmond said, excited.

Faria pulled several rolls of linen from the hole, consisting of strips of cloth four inches wide and eighteen long. The page numbers and tight Italian print were meticulous. Edmond could understand Italian almost as well as his native French and had no trouble reading it.

"I wrote the final word at the end of the sixty-eighth strip about a week ago. If our escape is successful, I just need to find a publisher brave enough to print it," Faria said. "Of course, it won't be necessary to bring these scraps with us; now that it is written, I am committed to memorizing this book as well."

"You've done all of this and the tunnel as well. There can't be enough hours of light in a day," Edmond said.

Faria reached into the hiding place and took out a lamp fashioned from a fish skull and other odd materials with a wick emerging from the mouth.

"I pretend to have a skin disorder and use the sulphur they give me to make matches. The lamp oil is the fat left behind from my meals," Faria said.

Edmond found the ingenuity required to build such tools in the depths of their prison overwhelming. Faria reached into the hiding place yet again, this time bringing out a ladder woven from cords of cloth and a fishbone sewing needle.

"This was part of my original escape plan," Faria explained. "I intended to get as close to the water as possible before jumping. When we reach the wall, it can serve the same purpose."

Edmond's thoughts drifted from Faria's inventions to his evident intelligence. Perhaps someone so ingenious and clear-sighted could shed light on the dark mystery of his own misfortunes. Together they could at last reach an answer to the question that had gnawed at him for so many years.

"Is something troubling you?" Faria asked, fearful of the dark look brewing on Edmond's face.

"I was thinking that you've been so kind as to tell me about your past life and show me all your fine creations, without me offering any details about myself," Edmond said.

"It's no trouble at all," Faria said. "We have plenty of time to get acquainted, and I confess that I enjoy showing off."

"My past life wasn't a long one, with no time for any events important enough to mention," Edmond said. "The most significant one is the misfortune that led to my arrest. If I could discover the source of that evil, then I could stop raging at random chance."

"You don't even know why you were charged?" Faria said, surprised.

Edmond shook his head. "I don't know that I've been charged at all. I was interrogated over a misunderstanding, and was told that I could go free," he said. "Instead, I was brought here."

"Come, let me hear your story," Faria said. He put his creations away into the hole beneath the fireplace and invited Edmond to sit beside him on the bed.

Edmond recounted his history, focusing on the events of his last mission on the Pharaon. Captain LeClere's death, the package for the grand marshal on Elba, the letter to a Monsieur Noirtier; and how this trail of breadcrumbs led to the unfinished wedding, his arrest and interrogation, and his hope torn away by his arrival at the Chateau d'If. He even recited the anonymous letter that accused him of treason.

An active listener, Faria absorbed Edmond's story with intent and interjected only to better understand the sequence of events. When Edmond finished, Faria sat considering the tale in silence.

"In my experience," Faria said at last, "the average person is hesitant to hurt another. Assaulting the life or property of a fellow human being is an idea that most moral people just never seriously consider. On the other hand, there have always been a percentage of people to whom others are not living and thinking beings. They see other people as means to an end or obstacles to their own happiness. To them there is nothing wrong with robbing a man or destroying his life to benefit themselves."

Edmond felt a creeping sense of dread locking up his guts. With his answers within reach, he doubted if he wanted to hear Faria's insight after all.

"This was a very targeted and very personal attack. The author of that letter had information about your life and knew things only someone near you could know. This narrows the pool of suspects," Faria said. "We must look at the people in your past life and ask the question *cui bono*—who benefits?"

"I'm quite certain that I knew nobody at all who could be so vile as to do this even if they could gain from it," Edmond said.

Faria nodded. "I believe you, or rather, I believe that you believe it," he said. "But humour an old man and consider who could benefit from your disappearance?"

Edmond's trusting nature and belief in his own insignificance came together and failed to produce an answer. "Who could see anything important enough in my life to warrant removing me from it?" he asked at last.

"You may be thinking in too grand a scope," Faria said. "Envy can start somewhere quite simple, perhaps even too obvious to notice. Focus on your life: you were made captain of the Pharaon and about to marry a lovely woman?"

Edmond nodded, not trusting his voice as he remembered who and what he had lost.

"We can search for clues there," Faria said. "Who could benefit from keeping you away from the Pharaon? Did you have a rival for Mercedes' hand?"

"I suppose there was a young man, Fernand. A Catalan from the village," Edmond said, his stomach churning. "But he would never have written such a letter; I met him, and he would prefer to get rid of me with the point of a knife rather than the point of a pen."

"Still, he has a motive," Faria said. "Could Fernand have known about your visit to Elba?"

"I don't think so... Wait," Edmond said. "We saw Fernand again the night before the wedding. He was on the patio of the inn with a neighbour of mine who was extremely drunk, and another man, Danglars."

"You mentioned Danglars was the supercargo on the Pharaon, correct?" Faria said. "Would he have known about the visit?"

"Well, yes; he came ashore with me, but stayed on the beach," Edmond said. "He couldn't have known about the other letter that I was to carry to Paris."

"It would be simple enough to guess that you had been given a message on Elba," Faria said. "So Fernand had a motive and Danglars had the information. What other suspects do we have with both?"

"Nobody," Edmond said, his face falling. "But I know Danglars' handwriting from paperwork on the Pharaon, and I saw Fernand's in the guest register for the wedding. Neither matches the accusation, and Caderousse was too drunk to write anything."

Faria stood and fetched his iron penknife. With his left hand, he scratched out the first few words of the accusation on the wall. Edmond recoiled at the sight.

"That's the same writing!" Edmond said.

"Indeed." Faria nodded. "It's curious; when a right-handed man writes with his left, it differs little from person to person. The same is true of a left-handed man using his right."

Edmond turned quite pale.

"Are you alright?" Faria asked.

"They had pens and paper at their table that day," Edmond said, pressing his hands to his temples. "Oh, those heartless, soulless, wretched demons!"

Edmond's mind reeled with all the missed opportunities to divert his fate; he could have dueled Fernand the moment they met, he could have thrown Danglars off the ship in the open ocean, he could have broken into Caderousse's room some dark night and smothered him in his sleep.

"Dwelling on what you may have done won't help, nor on what preemptive strike you may have made," Faria said gently, guessing the content of Edmond's thoughts from the look on his face. "No man can know the future."

"Tell me," Edmond said frantically, "since you see the clues and details that I missed: how was I sent here without charges, trial, or sentence?"

"That is more difficult; the justice system of any sufficiently bureaucratized nation is indistinguishable from a maze of thorns." Faria stroked his beard. "There are so many laws, contradictory and selectively enforced, that nobody can hope to uphold the law; they can only interpret it. Any inconvenient problem a lawman may find has a loophole in which it can disappear. Who was the official who examined you and how old?"

"He was the deputy prosecutor, a man named Villefort," Edmond said. "I would guess he was twenty-six or twenty-seven at the time?"

"Old enough to be ambitious, but too young to be thoroughly corrupt," Faria said. "His name sounds familiar. How did he treat you? Did his demeanour change at any time?"

"After I explained the circumstances of visiting Elba, he was very helpful," Edmond said. "He became distraught when he read the letter from Elba, but then he did me the favour of burning it."

"You asked him to do this?" Faria said.

"No. He took it upon himself, saying it was the only proof against me," Edmond said. "He asked that I swear never to utter the name it was addressed to. There's no point in keeping that vow anymore; the prison inspector told me Villefort no longer even lives in Marseille."

"You said the intended recipient was, if I recall, a M. Noirtier?" Faria asked. His eyes lit up. "I know that name! When the emperor was in power, I spent several months in Paris working for one of his ministers. There was a senator named Noirtier at court who was very curious about my profession."

Suddenly, Faria burst out in laughter. Edmond gawked at him until the outburst of mirth passed.

"I am sorry, my friend," Faria said, wiping his eyes. "It is most rude of me to laugh at your misfortune, but with so little humour to be found between these walls, it caught me quite off guard."

"I think that I've missed the joke," Edmond said.

"It is only that Noirtier had a very bright young son who I met a time or two," Faria said. "They disagreed on nearly everything. When I met him, he had already begun to use his mother's surname to distance himself from Senator Noirtier; that name was Villefort."

Edmond groaned and fell back on the bed as everything fell into place. Villefort's shift in attitude during the examination made sense, even with Edmond's lack of political experience. For a member of the king's justice system, it would be a scandal for one's father to be revealed to still be involved with Napoleon.

A noise like a wounded animal crept from Edmond's throat as he paced the cell. In a desperate attempt to return to his senses, he balled up his fist and slammed it against the unyielding stone wall. The pain cut through his fog of distress enough that he could speak again.

"I must be alone to think this over," Edmond said. He hurried through the tunnel back to his own cell and moved the stone back into place to conceal it.

Dufresne found him hours later, sitting upright in bed with a fixed stare. Edmond did not acknowledge the food Dufresne brought, but a muscle beneath his eye twitched in a most unsettling way. During this period of contemplation, he settled on a goal for his life after the escape and swore a solemn oath to its completion.

Faria's voice from the covered tunnel roused Edmond some time later; he had come to invite Edmond to join him for supper. Faria's reputation for amusing madness afforded him a certain improvement in his food, such as a small amount of wine and better bread on Sundays. As it was a Sunday, he was happy to share these luxuries with Edmond.

The look on Edmond's face concerned Faria at once; Edmond carried himself like a man with a distasteful mission ahead of him. It gave Faria cause to regret helping him in his inquiries.

Faria's happiness at having someone to speak to overruled this trepidation when Edmond urged him to speak of other matters. The demands of his profession, where charisma and tact mattered as much as mathematical skill, had molded Faria into a fine orator. Edmond listened for hours with admiring attention. Some of what Faria said related to things Edmond already knew, or applied to the sort of knowledge he'd acquired on the sea, but others were entirely new to him. In these uncharted waters, Edmond had only to ask for guidance, and Faria clarified the matter like a lighthouse cutting through fog.

"Please," Edmond said at last, "teach me some small part of what you know. If nothing else, it will prevent you from growing weary of my ignorance if I can learn enough to keep up in your conversation."

Faria smiled. "We have time enough while we dig, I suppose. However, my knowledge is rather confined; once I have taught you math, science, history, and what languages I can speak, you will know as much as I do."

To Edmond's ears those confines sounded like a vast ocean. He and Faria devised a plan of education as they ate, to begin alongside the tunnel improvements the following day.

In addition to Faria's lessons, Edmond learned something about himself: he was a natural student. There was a mathematical bent in his mind which he had never had opportunity to discover, and his romantic nature found an artistic quality even in dry equations. He spoke Italian already and some Romaic learned on eastern journeys; these helped him to learn Spanish, English, and German.

Lessons did not stop even for digging, and digging stopped only when their muscles failed them. Then Faria would draw some diagram and continue teaching, or recite from the books in his mental library. Without other distractions, Edmond memorized them as Faria had with ease; together they committed Faria's book about freedom in Italy to memory as well.

Edmond allowed himself to dwell on his oath only when alone in his own cell for meals or sleep. He swore to escape from the Chateau d'If and ensure that the men who had put him there suffered as much as he had within its walls. Focusing on Danglars, Fernand, and Villefort, he remembered Mercedes less and less frequently.

After a year of this, Edmond was a new man: more educated, erudite, and resilient than the boy he had been in 1815. Less and less of each day needed to be devoted to education, freeing more time to plan the escape itself. They devoted rest periods to watching the forged on the courtyard wall and learning their schedule. Edmond and Faria switched from one language to the next in conversation, both to give Edmond practice and to keep themselves entertained.

Faria told Edmond grand tales of historical men earning fame and glory by their wits and achievements. A worldly man, Faria had acquired a dignified air of melancholy in his travels and associations. As human nature is to imitate those whom they admire, Edmond grew to wear that demeanour like a cloak. Faria's courtly polish and politeness from dealing with gentry and aristocrats wore off on Edmond as well.

Finally, the extension of the tunnel was complete. The heavy tread of the forged as they patrolled on the surface was unmistakable. They only needed a sufficiently dark night, to eliminate the possibility of the new governor or Dufresne spotting their escape. Even a fellow prisoner seeing the escape from a window could doom them.

A loosened flagstone served as the exit point from their tunnel, and Edmond built supports beneath it to avoid a cave-in and early discovery. Faria's cries of pain in his cell interrupted this installation. Edmond rushed back with as much speed as the tunnel allowed.

Faria sat in Edmond's cell to carve wooden pegs from the bedframe to secure the ladder, and Edmond found him in the centre of the room. Deep purple circles grew beneath Faria's eyes, his lips were white, and his hair stood on end.

"Listen closely! Help me to my cell while I can still move, then find a small bottle of purple liquid in the remains of my old coat," Faria forced through clenched teeth. Edmond rushed to follow these instructions while Faria continued.

"I am about to suffer a seizure; this has happened once before, and I know what to expect. I will convulse, then appear to be dead," Faria said. "When this happens, open the bottle and pour eight to ten drops down my throat. If I am lucky, it will revive me."

In Faria's cell, Edmond set him down on the bed and rummaged through the hiding place in the hearth until he found the bottle.

"You'll need to hold me down," Faria urged as his breathing quickened and his body quaked. "Don't let me cry out or make any noise. If Dufresne finds us, the escape is ruined."

The shaking worsened. "I must tell you..." Faria's words trailed off into gibberish as his body spasmed violently.

Edmond climbed atop and straddled Faria to keep his limbs from hitting the wall and covered Faria's mouth when the mumble became a loud groan. When the seizure subsided, Faria lay as cold as marble with his mouth drooping on the right side. Edmond took only a moment to catch his breath before retrieving the bottle.

Edmond took great care to open Faria's jaw and measured out the prescribed ten drops. He listened for footsteps approaching the dungeons while he waited for the medicine to take effect, but heard nothing. A long and anxious hour passed before colour returned to Faria's cheeks. Though his mouth continued to droop, Faria uttered a sigh and made an effort to move. Edmond helped him to get comfortable.

"I did not expect to see you again," Faria said in a whisper. "The tunnel is done; you could have escaped after giving my medicine."

"And leave you behind?" Edmond insisted. "I'll wait until you regain your strength, and we'll escape together as planned."

Faria shook his head and reached across his body with his left hand. He took his own right wrist and lifted the arm off the bed, then released it; the entire arm fell back lifelessly.

"The first attack was brief, and I could stand up without help afterward. Now my arm is useless, and I can't feel my right leg either," Faria said, his speech slurred by the deformation of his mouth. "My brain is bleeding, Edmond. Another attack will come, though I can't predict when, and it will kill me."

"You will not die, because this third attack will not occur until after we are free," Edmond said, holding Faria's good hand. "We'll be able to get you the care that you need."

"Edmond, I cannot escape with you," Faria said. "I cannot stand, let alone swim. All I could do is cling to you with my remaining arm and drag you to the bottom of the sea. The disease is a family curse, I'm afraid. My great-grandfather offended a *strega*—that is, a practitioner of witchcraft—in Sicily when he was a young man. She laid a curse upon him that his sons and their sons without end would bear this fate."

A deep coughing fit took him, phlegm spraying from the slack side of his mouth. It was difficult for Edmond to look at the state of his friend, his teacher, the man who had given him his best chance to escape despair.

"Then I'll stay with you until then. I owe you so much, I couldn't forgive myself if I left you here," Edmond said.

Faria squeezed Edmond's fingers with his good hand.

"You're a good man, Edmond Dantes," Faria said. "Finish shoring up the flagstone so that nobody discovers it. Return here tomorrow after Dufresne makes his rounds, I have something of utmost importance to tell you."

Edmond set to his task immediately and took the extra precaution of blocking off the tunnel near the exit. He hoped that if the flagstone did collapse, the space beneath would be dismissed as an innocent sinkhole.

CHAPTER 18
THE TREASURE

W hen Edmond returned the next morning, Faria sat upright in bed. He had a brief hope that Faria's illness had passed, but Faria's mouth still drooped. With his good hand, Faria patted the bed to invite Edmond to sit.

"Edmond," Faria said, "you have been a true friend. I hadn't planned to tell you like this, but circumstance requires it; it is time for me to share the secret of my treasure."

"Your treasure?" Edmond asked, uneasy.

Throughout their friendship, Edmond refrained from asking Faria about the treasure at the root of his reputation for madness. Faria had never brought it up, and Edmond hadn't wanted to offend or agitate him. He had come to think that Faria's delusions stemmed from his isolation; with Faria bringing up the topic after such a traumatic episode, Edmond feared that he had suffered a relapse.

"Your worries are written all over your face," Faria said with a smile. "No, I'm not mad. The treasure is very real and now forever beyond my reach. But you've been like a son to me during our time together; consider it your inheritance from a loving father, and put it to good use."

Edmond interrupted, but Faria spoke over him.

"It's crucial that I tell you everything now; the next attack will come without warning and silence me," Faria continued. "Once you escape, I'd rather that you have the treasure instead of rebuilding your life from nothing while it remains hidden forever."

To humour a loved one at death's door, Edmond listened while Faria told him of a man in Italy named Leonardo Spada. He struggled to tell the story without feeling in half of his face, but Edmond hung on to every word.

"I worked with Leonardo just before I was arrested, helping to build his meager portfolio," Faria explained.

Leonardo had inherited a very old name but very little wealth. A well-appointed home had been passed down through his family, of which he was the last living descendant. It had belonged to his older brother, but that entire branch of the Spada family died badly during the Dead Plague. The Spada family had once been renowned for great wealth, but it had disappeared around the end of the 15th century.

Leonardo passed hours in the family library whenever he could, poring over old manuscripts for any clue to the fate of the family fortune. He found no record of a spending spree or any large investment to account for the missing gold, nor of any robbery.

"One day, I found him celebrating," Faria said. "Leonardo showed me an account in a volume about the history of the City of Rome."

Around 1496, Pope Alexander VI and his son Cesare Borgia were desperate for gold to fund their plans and pay off debts. Italy was impoverished at the time, and the pope thought to raise money by creating two new cardinals. He selected two of the richest men in Rome and sold them the appointments.

"Of course," Faria said, "it was not an entirely voluntary purchase. When the most powerful man in the world sends armed men to your home to demand money, and feels generous enough to bestow something on you in return, it's more similar to extortion with a gift attached."

Despite the aggressive tactics, the two wealthy men were honoured by the opportunity. One of the new cardinals was a man named Rospigliosi and the other was Cesare Spada.

"And this is how the Spada family fortune was lost?" Edmond asked, suspecting Faria may have gotten sidetracked from the story he wanted to tell.

"Indirectly, yes," Faria said. "But there was another stage to the pope's plan."

Faria explained how the pope arranged favours and attention for the two new cardinals so they would feel welcome in Rome and move to the city. As they had done with so many others, the pope and Borgia planned to murder the new cardinals. In the confusion of their deaths,

Borgia's men would seize the wealth the new cardinals had brought to Rome.

The pope invited them to dinner at his vineyard. Rospigliosi suspected nothing, but Spada was prudent and cautious enough to write his will. At dinner, Spada and Rospigliosi were urged to taste a specially-selected bottle of wine presented by the pope's butler. By the end of the day, they were dead.

"The cause was determined to be bad mushrooms," Faria added. "Eaten after leaving the pope's vineyard, of course."

The pope and Borgia rushed to claim their plunder, but they found no money or jewels at Spada's home to meet their expectations. Spada's will bequeathed the house with all its books to his nephew and a breviary with gold corners. That nephew became the ancestor of Leonardo Spada.

"Breviary?" Edmond asked, unfamiliar with the word.

"A book of the psalms, hymns, prayers, and so forth which are required for a cardinal's duty," Faria explained. "This one was custom-made for Cesare Spada, and Borgia didn't see it as worth taking."

Cesare Spada's heirs searched the house themselves, with no more luck than Borgia's men. History moved on, the pope and Borgia died, and it was assumed that the Spada family would bring their wealth out of hiding. This was not the case. Somehow, the fortune had been completely hidden. The family went from fame to obscurity, culminating in the childless Leonardo Spada of 1807.

"As I said, Leonardo hired me to help with his portfolio, and I doubled his income quite handily," Faria said. "The breviary with the gold corners had remained in the library and become a family relic, the circumstances around it forgotten until Leonardo found the account I just told you. It was a beautiful book regardless, and the family enjoyed the reminder of their long-ago status."

Faria had read a great deal about the Borgias, and worked with Leonardo to continue the investigation into his family history. Rospigliosi's stolen fortune was easy to trace as it made its way into the coffers of the Borgias, but the Spada fortune remained unaccounted for.

"I calculated and recalculated three hundred years' worth of family finances, and did not find a single clue. Leonardo Spada died with no family, and left his library and the famous breviary to me. We had become friends in our time together, much as you and I have," Faria said with a smile that touched only one side of his face.

Two weeks after Leonardo's death and a month before Faria's arrest, Faria stayed late into the night rereading a set of papers for the thousandth time. The house was to be sold, and Faria was going to leave for Florence. He fell asleep at the desk and woke up in utter darkness. Groggy, he stumbled to his feet and knocked the breviary to the floor. Unable to see where it was, Faria opened the curtains to get enough moonlight to find a candle.

"By moonlight I saw the breviary open on the floor, and I picked it up to assess any damage. As I examined the pages, I was shocked to see flowing silver on the flyleaf," Faria said. "The message revealed why Cesare Spada had put the breviary in his will. Spada's only option had been to use secret ink to write the note and hope his family would find it. There was no other moon-script in the book, so I peeled away the flyleaf and kept it with me."

With his good hand, Faria held up a cylinder of paper rolled so tight and for so long that it resisted smoothing out. Edmond read it aloud.

"This 25th day of April, 1498, I have been invited to dine with his Holiness Alexander VI. I fear that he is not content with the money already raised by my appointment as cardinal and intends to kill me. I therefore declare to my nephew and heir, Guido Spada, that I have buried the family fortune and my greatest treasure of all in the caves of the small island of Monte Cristo; I pray that he will recall our visits there," Edmond read.

The message was followed by directions and landmarks to guide the nephew to the correct spot. At the end was another note.

"Guido, I pray also that you may use what you find there in pursuit of noble goals. There is power in that cave to make a man great or make him a terror the world has seldom seen. It may be too terrible for anyone to wield, but I have not the strength to destroy it. Be wise, and be careful," it said.

Edmond was incredulous. For the first time, he had evidence that a kernel of truth sat within Faria's madness, or that it may not be madness at all.

"What did you do next?" Edmond asked.

"I resolved to set out and find the treasure, of course!" Faria said.

"The Spada line had ended with Leonardo, and I intended to use the treasure to nurture my ideas of liberty in Italy. My sudden departure aroused the suspicion of the police, who were watching me already for the financial self-defense I told you about. I was arrested, and eventually transferred here."

Faria took a deep breath to steady himself.

"And now, here we are. If by some miracle we escape from this place together, half of the treasure is yours. If I die here and you escape alone, I bequeath it all to you with my blessing," Faria said.

Edmond read the flyleaf note again, memorizing it by habit. A detail caught his attention that he had not noticed on the first reading.

"Cardinal Spada refers to the family fortune and his 'greatest treasure' as if they are separate things," Edmond said. "And the warning at the end, about being wise and careful, seems like an odd note to add if he were only speaking of money."

"Indeed!" Faria said, pleased that Edmond had noticed this. "It is a very strange warning. There is power to be had in wealth and cowards who insist that money is the root of all evil. But history suggests the cardinal was too clever to fall for that sort of envious thinking. What can we infer?"

Edmond grasped the point immediately. "There is something else in the cave, some other source of power. A weapon perhaps, or some magical device?"

In the rear of Edmond's mind, a dark idea was already taking shape. He imagined venturing into the caves of Monte Cristo and finding a sword that glowed with supernatural light or a suit of impenetrable armour, bringing it home to Marseille and laying waste to the men who had stolen his life.

"There were many rumours about Cesare Spada in his time; he was renowned as a great explorer," Faria said. "He ventured to far-off lands and found many relics from ancient cultures, most of which found their way into museums. One rumour said that he had found the secret to eternal life in his travels, and that this was the pope's true goal in acquiring the Spada fortune. The only other piece of evidence is this."

Reaching under his tattered rags, Faria revealed a pendant on a fine chain and handed it to Edmond. It was an eight-sided piece of tarnished silver, hammered thin and inscribed with intricate designs.

"This amulet and a note hid behind the flyleaf on the inner cover, written in ordinary ink. It said that this was 'the key to the power of Monte Cristo,' in those exact words," Faria said.

Edmond put the pendant on over his head and concealed it beneath his own ragged garments. "Do you know how much the treasure amounts to?"

"The family ledgers showed two million Roman crowns going missing; in French coin today, perhaps thirteen million francs. The Spadas were great believers in holding their wealth in gold, jewels, and ingots which would stand the test of time," Faria said, enjoying the mingled shock and joy on Edmond's face.

"I withheld this secret from you as long as I could in order to test your character and then surprise you. If we had escaped before, well, this," Faria said, inclining his head toward his useless right arm, "I would have waited to tell you until we stood on the shores of Monte Cristo together. But, as the generals say, no plan survives first contact with the enemy."

Edmond struggled to find the right words to express his gratitude.

"I have no claim on this treasure. It belongs to you and you alone," he said.

"You are my son, Edmond Dantes," Faria said with a tear rolling from his eye, "the only son this life has granted to me. My profession kept me too busy to marry, the curse on my family dissuaded me from fathering children, and you have been as kind to me as any man can hope his sons will be in his old age. Get out of this place, find the island of Monte Cristo, and make the most of your life in memory of me."

Moved to tears himself, Edmond threw his arms around Faria's neck and wept.

CHAPTER 19
THE THIRD ATTACK

With the story of the treasure out in the open, it became all the more real and valuable in Faria's mind. He spoke at length about all the good a man could do with thirteen million francs, to which Edmond listened with a twinge of guilt; his thoughts focused on the harm he could inflict on Danglars, Fernand, and Villefort. They also speculated about the mysterious power Spada hid on the island, but nothing they thought of seemed more or less plausible than anything else.

Faria did not know the island of Monte Cristo, but Edmond had often passed it en route home to Marseille aboard the Pharaon and even landed there once. An unforgiving lump of rock in the water between Corsica and mainland Italy, home mostly to birds and goats, covered in shrubs and bushes but with very few trees.

Edmond drew a map of the island, and Faria advised him on how best to find and recover the treasure. Edmond struggled to match his enthusiasm, since the treasure had first been hidden over three hundred years earlier. For all that he or Faria could know, someone may have found it by chance the day Spada buried it. Faria insisted that if someone had uncovered the power Spada had hidden, it would have gone down in history as a momentous event; Edmond argued that many momentous things had happened between Spada's day and their own. They debated in circles, never reaching a conclusion. They agreed, at least, that Edmond would make for the island as soon as he was free.

To add insult to injury, fate snatched that possibility of freedom from Edmond's grasp. The new governor ordered that the wall they tunneled under be rebuilt. Edmond's precautions prevented discovery of the tunnel, but the repairs used stronger masonry than the previous crumbling stone. Their simple iron tools were inadequate to dig any further.

"So much time and effort, wasted by the whim of a bureaucrat!" Faria moaned.

"Don't despair for me," Edmond said. "If I'm stuck here, so be it; I am no worse off than I was. I don't consider the time wasted. Forget the gold; you've given me the treasure of an education and friendship in this terrible place. Even if I live out the rest of my days in this prison, I will always be grateful for what you taught me. Perhaps I will become a teacher and friend to the next occupant of your dungeon, the way you have been to me."

Edmond did not give up on restoring the tunnel but had greatly diminished progress. Faria remained paralyzed on his right side and spent his days brainstorming new ideas for Edmond's escape. He compelled Edmond to memorize the directions on the flyleaf note for when he could reach Monte Cristo. When Edmond could recite it word for word, Faria burned the paper to avoid any chance of the governor or Dufresne finding it. Faria knew he would die before Edmond saw another chance at freedom and delivered a dire warning for that day.

"When I die, you must return to your dungeon and close the tunnel behind you," Faria said. "The curse of the *strega* lashes out at mourners after death as well. My great-grandfather released a cloud of poisonous gas when he died, my grandfather's body dissolved into a swarm of locusts, and my father's corpse burst into flame. It nearly killed everyone who had come to his funeral. I cannot predict what will happen with me, but you must get to safety."

Life went on, until one night Edmond awoke suddenly. He heard Faria calling to him in the darkness, and a cold sweat broke out on his brow.

"Can it be that time?" Edmond muttered as he pulled up the stone and rushed through the tunnel. By the light of their fish-skull lamp, he found Faria sitting upright in bed. His features writhed, his functioning hand clenched, and blood filled his eyes.

"My friend," Faria said, resigned to his fate, "you understand?"

Edmond nodded, holding back tears. Every instinct in his body told him to scream for help, to have Dufresne call a doctor, but that would spell ruin for them both.

"Remember what you said, Edmond. If you cannot be free today, then be a friend to whoever takes my place here. Perhaps he will be young and strong like yourself and be able to help you escape," Faria said. "And remember your promise! You must not be here when I die, or who knows what the curse will do."

Edmond rushed forward to hug Faria one last time, and his eye caught the hearthstone hiding place. He murmured reassurances to him, anything he could think of to give Faria some peace. Faria grew cold and shivered with such force his teeth rattled. Convulsions flung bloody foam from his lips, and Edmond held Faria's limbs in place as best he could until the fit subsided. Faria lay twisted, still, and unblinking.

Edmond rushed to the hearthstone, digging through the contents of the banker's hiding place to find the bottle of purple medicine. It was only one-third full; Edmond hoped it would be enough. He gave Faria the same amount as before and waited. The previous dose had revived him after an hour, but two hours passed with no change. With nothing to lose, Edmond emptied the bottle down Faria's throat before returning to his own cell. Edmond left the lamp in the tunnel with a match to relight it and waited in darkness.

Edmond did not know how long he waited there before he heard faint movement again at the far end of the tunnel. His heart soared.

"The medicine did better than was expected!" Edmond muttered. "It not only revived him, but he can walk again!"

Edmond opened the tunnel again, lit the lamp, and hurried to the other end with a smile on his face. Faria stood in the middle of the dungeon, facing away from the tunnel.

"My friend!" Edmond cried.

Faria turned, but Edmond could see by the flickering light of the lamp that he was no longer Faria. The bloody eyes in his ashen face had clouded over in death. One side of his mouth still hung slack, but the other side bared his teeth in a snarl. The thing that used to be Faria took a single shambling step toward Edmond, dragging the right leg but otherwise unimpeded.

Panic clawed at Edmond's gut. Born during the worst of the Dead Plague, Edmond grew up among the constant threat of walking corpses. They had burned the long grass of the plains within a mile of Marseille to prevent the possibility of an undead lurker lying in wait to bite an unwary foot. A constant guard stood along the coast, watching for the zombies which rose sometimes out of the water to feast upon the living.

Rogue zombies sometimes slipped through the perimeter and crept into the town, shrouding the population in fear until they could be found and destroyed. Other times, unlucky souls stumbled over immobilized zombies in the forest and were turned themselves, then shambled back to Marseille. If enough undead gathered, the dead in the hospital and the cemetery rose to meet them despite not being bitten themselves. They lived under the constant fear that a victim had gone unnoticed and risen up to prey upon unsuspecting civilians.

As a child, Edmond's greatest fear was turning a corner, opening a closet, or reaching into a barrel just to find rotten jaws sinking into his flesh. His young mind couldn't conceive of a worse fate than becoming such a scourge on his family and neighbours. The fear and uncertainty of those long-gone days crashed upon Edmond in an instant at the realization that his teacher and friend had become a zombie and was locked in a dungeon with him.

The creature swung at Edmond, who scrambled back into the tunnel with the sole aim of retreat. Fear made him clumsy, and the zombie closed one cold hand around his ankle. Edmond kicked with his other foot as it dragged him back, aiming for the pallid fingers. He heard Faria's bones crack and joints pop out of place. As the creature bent low to bring its teeth closer to his captive foot, Edmond put all of his strength into one final kick. For one terrifying moment there was no give in the grip on his ankle, but then the ruined hand loosened, and Edmond could crawl to his own cell.

Edmond had nowhere to hide and no weapons to put Faria to rest. He could summon Dufresne, but that would result in discovery of the tunnel and an end to any chance of escape. Even worse, Faria's corpse could overtake them both. If it were capable of spreading its vile taint, the Chateau d'If would soon be the epicentre of a new undead uprising. Edmond needed to deal with this himself.

"If only the chisel weren't still in the hearth!" he muttered as he heard the zombie enter the tunnel, but through his despair, this sparked an idea.

Edmond picked up his latrine bucket, by good fortune cleaned that morning, and threw it into the corner of his cell farthest from the tunnel mouth. The bucket was no use as a weapon, but it clattered against the stone wall. The zombie groaned as it emerged from the tunnel, visible only as an outline in the dark. Edmond hoped it was no more capable of seeing him.

Edmond moved along the wall to the tunnel with care not to make a noise. Heart pounding, he guessed he could see the zombie approaching the corner where the bucket had landed. Edmond lowered himself into the tunnel and returned to Faria's cell where the light still burned. He went to the hearth and pried up the secret stone, intending to take the chisel. He made his decision, hefted the stone, and braced himself for the consequences.

"Gianmarco Faria!" he called. It grunted at the noise and dragging footsteps drew closer. Edmond stood by the tunnel, and as soon as the face which used to belong to Faria appeared, he swung the stone in a wide arc.

The forehead broke and bent inward, stunning the creature, but it still flailed to grab him. Edmond reared back for another swing, adding his upper body strength to the pull of gravity in order to cave in the zombie's skull. The arms stopped grasping for his flesh, but the snarling mouth continued to move. One final swing finished the thing for good, and Faria lay at rest.

Edmond's grief welled to the surface. Sobbing, he moved Faria's body to the bed, arranging the limbs in a peaceful pose. He was about to return to his own cell when he realized the scene would make no sense to Dufresne in the morning. As always, he had to protect the tunnel. With reluctance, Edmond moved Faria to a position by the hearth to tell what he hoped was a likely story. The hearthstone sat in its proper place; the blood and brains stuck to it would set the scene when Dufresne came with breakfast. Edmond stroked Faria's brittle hair one last time and returned to his own cell.

Edmond waited for dawn without sleeping. Dufresne brought the meagre breakfast at the usual time, and Edmond listened to his footsteps trail down the hall. His saucepan clattered to the floor, the noise carrying through the tunnel, and his footsteps hurried back up the corridor. Hours later, three sets of footsteps returned. Edmond returned to the tunnel and crawled to the other end to eavesdrop on the proceedings in Faria's cell.

"What the devil happened to Number 14?" the new governor said. Edmond remembered the man's name was Regnault, or perhaps Renaudin.

"Looks like he bashed his brains out against the stone," Dufresne said. The bed creaked as someone set Faria's body there. "It's a shame, really. He was mad, but well-behaved."

More movement in the cell, and a new third voice described Faria's injuries in medical terms. Edmond did not understand them all, but he now understood the delay in Dufresne's return; they had sent to the mainland for a doctor.

"As unlikely as it seems," the doctor concluded, "Dufresne's guess appears to be correct."

"Ghastly!" Regnault exclaimed. "Imagine doing that to yourself, clubbing your head on a stone until you died."

The doctor chuckled. "Men can do drastic things in the grip of madness. I once saw a grieving father lift a horse above his head when his son lay crushed beneath it," he said. Edmond heard a soft click.

"Is the knife really needed?" Dufresne asked. "He is clearly as dead as the bed he lays on!"

"We are in the employ of his majesty's department of prisons, Dufresne," the doctor replied in a dispassionate tone. "No matter how clearly dead he is, I must follow the formalities and ensure he is not faking."

Edmond could not guess what the doctor did, but he heard Dufresne gag.

"There!" the doctor said. "If he were faking, that would have ended the charade."

The three men discussed the paperwork for the death of a prisoner, and Edmond bit his tongue; they never once referred to Faria by name or gave any acknowledgement to the great mind that had burned out in the filthy confines of their prison. He wanted to spring from hiding and force them to realize what a brilliant and singular human being Faria had been, but to do so would have been lunacy. Dufresne grunted as he forced Faria's body into a sack meant to be his burial shroud. The hour of burial was set for ten or eleven o'clock that evening.

"Shall I stand watch over the corpse?" Dufresne asked.

"What for?" Regnault asked. "Simply lock the door as if he were alive."

Edmond heard all three men leave and the solid clunk of the lock turning. After that, a silence fell over the dungeon which chilled Edmond to the core. When he was certain the cell was empty, he raised the flagstone and emerged from the tunnel.

CHAPTER 20
THE CEMETERY OF THE CHATEAU D'IF

Faria's crude winding-sheet lay illuminated by the pale moonlight. A simple canvas sack concealed the body of the man who had taught Edmond so much, waiting for him to be buried. A barrier far more solid than canvas or stone now separated Edmond from the only friend he had known during his captivity, a barrier he could not dig through. Edmond sat on the edge of the bed and wallowed in grief.

Alone again, condemned to silence and loneliness, with no company but his own thoughts. Facing a return to the solitude of before Faria had entered his world, Faria's fate appeared kinder than his own. Faria's suffering was over, while Edmond's had just been renewed. The months or years of work required to complete the tunnel again would be even more arduous with nobody to talk to. Like an old enemy thought long dead, the idea of suicide crept once again into Edmond's thoughts.

"It would be so easy," Edmond muttered, face stretching into a desperate grin. "I have Faria's penknife; it would be enough."

It comforted him for a moment, presenting an escape at last from the confines of prison, but like a summer storm it expended itself quickly. The horrible mystery of what lay on the other side of that blade knocked the wind out of him.

"No!" Edmond said. "I will not die now, after suffering so long. When I gave up once before, God sent me Gianmarco Faria and gave me a reason to hope for life and liberty again. I will not throw that away now. I must escape, win back the happiness that was stolen from me, and bury my executioners."

Their faces floated in front of his vision, laughing at him: Danglars, Fernand, and Villefort. His own words echoed back to him with a ring of clarity, and he looked again at Faria's shroud. The canvas reduced the body within to an anonymous lump. Edmond paced the dungeon, filled with a giddy energy. He stopped by the bedside, looked again at the canvas, and laughed.

"In death, my dearest friend, you've given me one last gift!" Edmond said to the corpse. He went to the hiding place under the hearth and took the penknife, the fishbone needle, and thread. He cut the sack open, taking a moment to cross himself at the reminder of what he had been forced to do to Faria's body.

"He's not here," Edmond reminded himself. "This body is nothing more than a set of clothes that he's no longer wearing."

Edmond dragged the body through the tunnel and arranged it on the bed in his cell. He often slept with a rag wrapped around his head and eyes and remained asleep when Dufresne brought his meals. He disguised Faria's body the same way, hoping Dufresne would assume the shape beneath the blanket was Edmond. He stripped off his tattered clothes, the remains of his wedding attire, and left them in the tunnel as he returned to Faria's cell. Edmond climbed into the empty sack and used the needle and thread to sew himself inside.

Nothing remained but to wait until nightfall. Edmond worried that his exhilarated heartbeat would give him away if Dufresne returned at that moment. From inside the sack, Edmond could not see the clock marks on the wall. As he waited, Edmond reviewed his hastily-formed plan.

A forged would likely carry him to the cemetery and wouldn't notice or care that it carried a live body rather than a dead one. Then Edmond would have to allow himself to be buried. As an experienced swimmer, he could hold his breath for long periods; he hoped long enough to wait until the gravediggers left. In the dead of night, he could emerge unseen from the ground and run to the coast so he could swim for freedom.

On the other hand, if he were discovered or if the weight of the dirt was too much for him, at least his captivity would still come to an end. He could worry about finding clothes when he reached land; his prison rags would only weigh him down during his swim, and serve no purpose at all afterward. He wore only the thin silver pendant from Spada's breviary.

His thoughts returned again and again over the hours to his brief battle against the walking horror of Faria's corpse. The zombie had been stopped, but Edmond could not guarantee that it would remain dead. Before the Dead Plague, nobody believed it possible for the dead to walk in the first place. After Napoleon destroyed the source of it, nobody believed the world would ever see another zombie. There was no guarantee that Faria's zombie followed the same rules as the Dead Plague, either. If the *strega's* curse allowed, Faria's limbs could once again twitch. The zombie could rise from Edmond's bed, uncover the tunnel, and find him helpless and blind. He tried not to imagine Faria's teeth, slick with spittle, tearing through the canvas and sinking deep into the flesh of his belly.

It took all of Edmond's willpower to fight through that dread. He pressed one hand against his chest to still his racing heart and wiped sweat from his face with the other. As time passed without the scraping of stone to signify death coming to devour him, it became easier to believe that the danger was past. Finally, he heard footsteps once again approaching the dungeon. The door opened, and dim light spilled across the fabric in front of Edmond's eyes.

"Troix, *allons-y,*" Dufresne said.

Clanking footsteps approached and cold metal hands thrust under Edmond's body to scoop him up. Edmond remembered the strength of those hands, one of which had held him aloft by the throat during his first days at the prison. What had been the number of that forged? It carried Edmond out of the dungeon like a groom carrying his bride across the threshold.

It took Edmond a moment to register a simple fact which astounded him once he realized: he was no longer in the dungeon. He had lost track of how long his entire world had consisted of only his and Faria's cells or the tunnel. Edmond had not been on the far side of those doors since he was first brought to the island.

The forged carried him up the stairs, Edmond heard another door open, and fresh cold air wafted through the fabric of the sack. They walked a ways further, and the forged set Edmond on the ground. He took the opportunity to release the breath he had held since the dungeon. The fresh air biting into his lungs was ecstasy, chilling him from the inside out. The salty cold was a welcome change from the unmoving damp of his cell. He struggled not to weep with joy.

Dufresne busied himself with metal hitting against metal. Edmond assumed he was taking spades and tools from a chest. Something heavy landed next to Edmond with a thump, and Dufresne wound a cord around Edmond's feet and lashed it tight.

While Edmond tried to guess what was happening, Dufresne gave more orders to the forged which lifted Edmond again with a weight bound to his feet. They passed through another door and continued walking. The noise of the crashing waves grew louder.

"Bad weather tonight!" Dufresne shouted. "I am afraid, M. 14, that you stand a good chance of getting wet."

Dufresne chuckled, but Edmond did not understand the joke. Uneasy, he questioned the soundness of his plan.

"Troix, stop! Two steps forward," Dufresne commanded. The forged shuffled into position. "Last time you started too far back, and the poor fellow burst apart on the rocks. The governor gave me an earful then! Farewell, M. 14. Now, Troix, *allons-y!*"

The forged shifted its grip to hold Edmond by the ankles and whirled in a circle like a hammer-thrower in the ancient Olympic games. After four or five revolutions, the forge released Edmond. He sailed through the air, falling so fast his stomach threatened to rise up and out of his chest. Despite his speed, the descent seemed to take an eternity.

Edmond realized too late his dreadful mistake. The rocky island of the Chateau d'If had only the thinnest layer of soil, where even the hardiest grass struggled to grow. Even if the ground could be dug, the scarcity of land made it impractical for the prison to maintain a cemetery.

Edmond had been flung into the water with a thirty-six-pound weight tied to his feet. The sea was the cemetery of the Chateau d'If.

CHAPTER 21
THE ISLAND OF TIBOULEN

Stunned but alive, Edmond kept his wits enough to hold his breath as he hit the water. The rough canvas soaked through almost immediately, and the shock of cold water disoriented him. He thought he had lost his knife, only to find it in his other hand. Battling his muddled perception in the black water, he ripped the sack open with the blade. He pushed his upper body through the hole, but the iron bound to his legs continued to drag him down. Lightheaded, he contorted himself in the water and sawed at the cord. Finally, the weight pulled free of his feet and he kicked to the surface for a life-giving breath.

Edmond could not rest. Though he had escaped the island, he risked being seen if anyone looked to the sea. He may have screamed as he flew through the air, or Regnault could have been watching just the right patch of water through his window from simple bad luck. Edmond had no way to know.

He risked a look back at the dark shape, blacker than the sea or sky, his entire world for so long. With a shudder, he put the prison behind him and dove again. By swimming beneath the surface until his lungs ached, he swam until he could no longer see the looming shape of the island when he came up for air.

Edmond needed to get his bearings. Treading water and reading the stars, he determined the correct direction to reach the Frioul Archipelago. This chain of barren islands sat further out to sea than the Chateau itself, but they were the nearest uninhabited land he could reach. A nude man emerging from the sea in the night would arouse suspicion if anyone saw. After resting at Tiboulen or one of the other empty islands, he could make the effort to swim towards the mainland.

He continued to use the sky to keep his course, remembering his short life as a sailor.

In spite of his peril and the risk of becoming an appetizer to a kraken, Edmond savoured the kiss of the water against his skin and the simple joy of movement. His only exercise for years had been to pace his cell or to dig, and his muscles rejoiced at being used to propel himself through the sea. He might have laughed if he did not need every breath he could get or if fear did not pursue him through the waves.

Every splash sounded like a pursuit boat from the Chateau d'If. If they found him he would be shot and either returned to the prison or left to drown. The sky darkened even further in tune with these thoughts, and the clouds burst open. While rain pummeled Edmond from above, a sharp pain hit his knee beneath the water, and he thought his escape was over. He reached forward in another stroke, refusing to surrender, but his hand touched solid rock. He had reached the shore of Tiboulen.

The island was an ugly pile of stone, even less hospitable than the island of the Chateau d'If. Edmond crawled out of the water, his arms and legs burning, and spread his hands wide to let the rain wash over him. Exhaustion soon overtook the joy of reaching land, and he stretched himself out on the granite to rest.

A roar of thunder woke him from a deep sleep. He drank from a pool of rainwater and considered swimming for the larger island of Lemaire nearby. As he weighed his options, lightning illuminated a fishing boat in the distance. The wind and waves drove it on a relentless course towards Tiboulen, and Edmond cried as loud as he could to warn them of the danger.

The lightning revealed the boat's progress toward the rock in frozen moments. Between two flashes, the storm tore away the mainsail; in the darkness that followed, a violent crash roared through the night. Edmond ran as fast as he dared across the rain-slick rocks to offer help, but no cries of distress reached his ears. When the sun rose, he found only broken wood and dead men.

The red streak on the horizon captivated Edmond's attention. During his captivity, he had forgotten that such a thing as sunrise existed. As the flaming disc of the sun rose above water, golden light played across the whitecaps of the waves. The beauty of it brought tears to his eyes, eyes beholding a riot of colour for the first time after long years of grey.

If the prison did not already know that Edmond was gone, he guessed they would find out in two or three hours. Dufresne would bring breakfast, see that the dinner in Edmond's cell was untouched, and discover Faria's body. The tunnel would be found, and they'd sound the alarm. Police on land and soldiers at sea would be hunting for a fugitive. Time was running out for Edmond to stay ahead of their pursuit.

He formed and discarded one plan after another in his mind as he deliberated on the best place to make landfall. Before he could decide, a small vessel on the horizon caught his attention. It was a single-masted tartan flying the Genoese flag and heading out from Marseille. For a ship to be leaving at such an early hour, Edmond guessed they wanted to keep their trade hidden from the customs officers.

"I could swim out to them," Edmond muttered. "But if they're who I think they are, what's to stop them from turning me in for the reward? I should wait, restore my strength, and swim for the mainland alone."

His growling stomach revealed the flaw in that plan; he had last eaten before Faria's death. Indecisive, his gaze landed on the wreckage of the fishing boat from the night before, and inspiration struck him.

He ran to the wreckage and took a sailor's cap from one of the dead men, put it on, and seized one of the broken timbers. Using it for buoyancy, he kicked with all of his strength toward the tartan. This latest alteration to his escape plan still left him uneasy, however. If the tartan continued sailing close to the coast, he stood a chance of reaching it. If it picked up speed and went out to sea instead, he was doomed to drown.

Edmond made painful progress closer to the tartan, waving and calling for help at the top of each swell. It took half an hour for anyone on board to take notice. A figure on the deck pointed to him and waved for the attention of others. They launched their rowboat, and Edmond propelled himself away from the timber to meet them.

His enthusiasm was ill-timed, and he had underestimated his own fatigue. Edmond struggled to stay afloat. A voice called out "Courage!" in Italian before his ears sunk beneath the surface, and he felt as if the iron weight were tied to his legs again. A hand grasped him by the hair, but his strength failed and he lost consciousness.

Edmond awoke coughing up saltwater onto the planks of the deck. Someone helped him to his feet, revealing the Chateau d'If receding into the distance. His shout of joy triggered a fresh round of coughing. One of the crew handed him a gourd of rum, and an older man who he assumed to be the captain scrutinized him as he drank.

"Who are you?" the captain asked in bad French once Edmond could stand on his own.

"I am a Maltese sailor. We came from Syracuse when the storm overtook us last night and wrecked us against the rocks," Edmond replied, affecting clumsy Italian. He pointed back towards Tiboulen and the visible wreckage. Nobody survived to dispute his story, and his skills as a sailor would give plausibility to the lie. "I had the good fortune to survive the crash and cling to the rocks until I saw your vessel. My crewmates and the captain were not so lucky. Thank you for saving my life."

"That was Jacopo you have to thank; he spotted you, and pulled you out of the water," the captain said. He pointed to the stout and swarthy man who had given Edmond the rum. Edmond shook Jacopo's hand and offered his sincere thanks.

"I nearly hesitated," Jacopo said. "Your hair's two feet long and your beard nearly that, you look like a madman."

"I once owed a debt to a holy man," Edmond said, thinking quickly, "and as part of my repayment to him agreed to live by his faith's rules for ten years, which included not cutting my hair. The vow expires soon, and I will be very happy to visit a barber!"

The sailors around him chuckled at the story. Men who live on the sea lead colourful lives, and none of them found the story far-fetched.

"Well, you are alive," the captain said, stroking his chin. "Now what are we to do with you?"

"Anything you please; I am in your debt," Edmond said. "If you prefer, I can leave at the next port you reach. I'm a good sailor, I'll certainly find a position."

"Do you know the harbours of the Mediterranean?" the captain asked.

"I've been sailing it since I was a child, there are few ports that I could not enter or leave blindfolded," Edmond said.

"A bold claim!" the captain said with a thin smile. "I've heard many desperate men spin tall tales, so let's see you prove your mettle. We're heading to Leghorn; take the helm and get us there."

Edmond did as he was told, and the other sailors took their positions. Jacopo returned shortly with trousers and a jacket. The clothes were sturdy rough-spun garments designed to hold up to seafaring life. To Edmond, who had spent his confinement wearing nothing but the rags of his wedding suit, they felt like fresh silk.

Properly dressed, he tested the rudder, found it responsive, and issued his first orders. With a nod from the captain, the other sailors followed his directions. Edmond was taken back to his last time in command of a vessel, so long ago, when happiness was so close to his reach. Under Edmond's direction, they reached Leghorn ahead of schedule.

"Perhaps we'll keep you on after all, if you're agreeable," the captain said.

Edmond opened negotiations with the captain to serve on the ship, which was called the Young Amelia. In his past life, he had little experience in bargaining for his wage. Faria's tutelage had included lessons in managing money, and Edmond understood what needed to be done.

When hiring a new sailor, a captain is looking for a man with skills and motivation to increase the overall usefulness of his ship and crew. Someone who slows the ship down or encourages laziness is a liability. Someone who provides only an extra pair of hands to move cargo is an asset. Meanwhile, a man who can get them from one port to another at greater speed is an even more valuable asset.

The captain has an interest in paying beneficial men accordingly, to keep them happy and keep their services, while not hiring the liability at all. At the same time, he must pay a rate which doesn't cancel out the profit brought by the new man's skills. The sailor himself has an obvious interest in securing himself as high a wage as he can get. It was a delicate dance, one performed by uncountable players throughout history.

In this instance, Edmond was happy to allow the captain to dictate his price. If the treasure hidden at Monte Cristo were real, his wages would be immaterial. Even if the treasure had already been plundered long ago, the job had an additional benefit for Edmond. It would provide cover to hide from the gendarmes searching for him, and he could leave as a free man at the end of his employment at any port he pleased. In the end, they agreed upon a wage for a term of three months and shook hands to seal it.

They decided Edmond's work would not begin until they finished at Leghorn, to allow him to recover from the shipwreck. He sat enjoying some bread and another helping of rum, but froze when he heard the faint report of a cannon. A small white cloud of smoke rose above the distant speck of the Chateau d'If.

"It seems that the Chateau d'If has had an escape!" the captain said. He glanced at Edmond, but Edmond drank his rum with calm composure.

When Jacopo sat down by him for a rest, Edmond took the opportunity to ask a question that had been on his mind since he had awoken on deck.

"If you would be so kind, Jacopo, what is today?" he asked.

"It is the 28th of February," Jacopo said.

"And the year?" Edmond asked. In response to Jacopo's incredulous look, he smiled sheepishly. "My head is still rather scrambled from nearly dying twice."

Jacopo nodded, having seen men behave in all manner of ways after a brush with death.

"The year is 1829, my friend." Jacopo clapped him on the shoulder.

The words landed in Edmond's heart like stones dropped into a well. Three days prior had been the fourteenth anniversary of his arrest. He had been thrown into the Chateau d'If as a boy of nineteen and had escaped as a man of thirty-three. What had become of Mercedes, who certainly must think he was dead? His heart filled with hatred as the faces of Danglars and Fernand and Villefort arose in his mind. The oath of vengeance he had sworn in his cell was no longer merely a whim of anger, contained within the stone walls of the Chateau d'If. He was free and could begin planning the downfall of his enemies.

CHAPTER 22
THE SMUGGLERS

Within his first week aboard the Young Amelia, Edmond confirmed his suspicions about his new companions. The crew traded often with other small ships outside of established ports, beyond the watchful eye of customs officials. When they did come into port, they did so at night and made their exit before sunrise. Edmond had fallen in with smugglers.

Though the captain didn't suspect Edmond (or "the Maltese" as they had begun calling him) of being the fugitive from the Chateau d'If, he remained wary. He worried that the Maltese may be a spy planted aboard his ship by officials seeking to stop practitioners of unregulated trade. Edmond eased these suspicions by handling his duties too well to have been anything but a lifelong sailor. Edmond also stuck to his story no matter what was asked; he knew Malta almost as well as he knew Marseille and could give any account needed to back up his claims.

The next time they entered a port legitimately, Edmond had a new milestone to look forward to: he had not seen his reflection in fourteen years. He brought his first wages to a barber, who was shocked by Edmond's appearance. Edmond had brushed and cleaned his hair to a point aboard the ship, but such a wild beard was still quite out of fashion at the time.

The barber's scissors cut away the weight of Edmond's years in captivity as well as the physical weight of his accumulated hair. He soon sat clean-shaven with a more contemporary hairstyle, just reaching his chin, and asked for a looking-glass at once.

Edmond had entered prison with the round and smiling face of a young man who loved his career and expected happiness ahead. That face had lengthened and bore the lines of his suffering. Despite days under the Mediterranean sun, he was still pale from long deprivation of sunlight. If he didn't know it was his reflection, Edmond would think he was looking at some intellectual from the far north. Together with the changes to his voice, nobody from his old life would be able to recognize him. He hardly recognized himself.

His crewmates were incredulous when he returned in a new set of sailor's clothes to replace what Jacopo had lent him. Captain Russo insisted that Edmond recite his story again to prove he was the same man they had rescued days earlier.

The crew of the ship were very efficient and lost little time wherever they went. Goods and merchandise filled the ship's hold as quick as magic and were unloaded as if they had never existed at all. Russo valued punctuality and always paid the men their share of the profits before the next nightfall. Textiles at one port, contraband cotton in another, English snuff, untaxed tobacco, exotic and potent medicines not approved by any health inspector, liquor, and even banned books all spent time in the Young Amelia's cargo hold. At first, Edmond could not understand why they smuggled such innocent items as linen and wine. Russo explained it to him in the cargo hold.

"Our business is bringing people what they want when they're forbidden from having it. Consider this fabric," Russo said, holding up some floral-printed damask. There were several crates of the fabric stacked in the hold. "This was woven in France, where they have the equipment and expertise to produce good damask quickly and cheaply. In Greece, quality damask is hard to find from local weavers, and that scarcity makes it more expensive than French damask even after the cost of shipping the latter. But the Greek damask-makers guild wants to protect their trade and had a tariff put on French damask to raise the price. Instead of being allowed to buy better damask cheaply, the Greek people can only get poor damask at a high cost and good damask at even higher cost."

Edmond nodded along. Between his life on the Pharaon and Faria's lessons, he knew a thing or two about tariffs.

"This creates opportunity for enterprising men to smuggle the superior French damask into Greece. Then the Greek people can still have what they want at a reasonable rate," Russo added with a smile. "There are such restrictions everywhere which keep us in business.

Some goods are forbidden, others simply restricted. We carry them all, within reason."

Every morning, Edmond woke early to take in the sunrise on deck. After the Chateau d'If, any time spent outdoors was a gift. On one such morning, the rosy dawn light painted the peak of Monte Cristo, rising from the ocean not quite a league away. It was near enough for Edmond to jump overboard and swim there. But what then? He had no tools to recover his treasure—if nobody else had found it in the three hundred years since it was hidden. Even if he found it, he had no boat to leave the island.

He needed to wait for a better opportunity, but his years at the Chateau d'If had taught him how to wait. After waiting fourteen years for liberty, he could wait six months for wealth. Still, he recited under his breath Cesare Spada's note describing the location where the treasure had been hidden. When the time came, if it did not exist, at least he was free.

That freedom still carried risks. The act of carrying goods which governments do not want to be carried brings with it, by nature, the threat of violence. Every pickup and delivery were made under the watchful eyes of cannons and pistols from both sides, and any chance encounter with the authorities could result in drawn steel. Jacopo explained it to Edmond once over breakfast.

"Imagine that you're a shoemaker," Jacopo said. "A man steals the shoes you've made and escapes. You can tell the police or the guard to try and recover your property. But what if instead of shoes, you sell untaxed medicine? Then nobody will help if you are robbed. You must take matters into your own hands and make an example of what happens to people who cross you."

Edmond saw a practical demonstration of this lesson when customs officers discovered the Young Amelia unloading a shipment of dried mandrake leaves near Corsica. The leaves were an effective remedy for a painful skin epidemic on the island, but they were banned from public use. The official justification for the ban was side-effects from overuse of the treatment. The only legal remedy was an ointment, the chief ingredient of which was grown on farms owned by the brother of the Minister of Foreign Affairs.

These customs officers were diligent in upholding their duty to keep the leaves out of Corsica, and one of them died in the subsequent battle. Edmond was also wounded by a musket ball to the shoulder. Jacopo rushed to Edmond's aid with all the concern he would show to his own brother; meanwhile Edmond took an odd satisfaction to his own stoic response to the injury. He was also encouraged and disquieted by how little the sight of the dying officer affected him; it boded well for his future plans.

Edmond's heart was not entirely cold, and he noticed Jacopo tending to his wound with care. Jacopo reacted to a kind of nobility he saw in Edmond's character, treating him with deference by instinct. Edmond resolved to follow Faria's example and become Jacopo's teacher, if he wanted one. When he made the offer, Jacopo was eager to agree.

"Who knows," Edmond said with a smile. "One day, you may command your own vessel."

Two and a half months passed with Edmond learning the smuggler's trade and passing on his own knowledge to Jacopo. He made contacts and friendships among all the people they dealt with and learned the secret signals of smuggling as another language.

They passed Monte Cristo a dozen times without landing, and Edmond formed another plan. With his saved wages, he would hire a boat once his term on the Young Amelia ended. It was an imperfect plan, bringing the owner of that boat into his secret, but he had no other ideas for reaching—and just as important, leaving—the island.

In any spare moments between working or focusing on the problem of transportation, he dwelled on the power that Spada had written about. The frustrating lack of clues in the note made it impossible to guess what he would find. Without stone walls confining him, his imagination roamed farther in search of other interpretations. In prison, he had pictured the power as a flaming sword; on the open sea, the sword became a crystal that could sway men's minds. That crystal became a ship that could soar through the clouds and rain death from above. What set his teeth on edge was the fact that he could not build his future plans without knowing what, if anything, waited for him on the island.

One night on shore, Captain Russo brought Edmond to a tavern which was a common meeting-place for smugglers. The commotion and conversations of men from all corners of the world provided good cover for secret discussions. On this occasion they discussed a delivery of kraken blubber which needed to change hands several times en route from Turkey to France. The blubber made for exceptional lamp oil, burning bright and slow with a clean flame. Most ports paid a bounty for krakens killed near their waters, so the blubber was cheap to acquire for anyone willing to shoulder the risk. The candlemakers of France, however, had banded together and lobbied for a law banning its use.

Russo's contact stressed the importance of a neutral landing site for the exchange, so that the Young Amelia could carry the cargo the final leg of the journey. Edmond smelled opportunity, and he drew Russo aside to suggest Monte Cristo as the ideal location. The deserted island was remote enough to avoid scrutiny and near enough to France to complete the delivery with ease. Russo agreed, having used the island for this exact purpose in the past. When the plan was finalized with the other party, it took great effort for Edmond to conceal his excitement.

CHAPTER 23
THE ISLAND OF MONTE CRISTO

The night before sailing to Monte Cristo, Edmond obsessed over every step of the directions in Spada's note. Whenever he closed his eyes he dreamed of descending into a grotto paved with precious stones and emerging prepared to rain righteous fire upon his enemies. His misgivings about whether the treasure still waited for him melted into the night.

Daylight brought a sense of sobriety, but the excitement remained. Monte Cristo appeared before them at sunset, the highest peak blazing red. Edmond sought any detail that could aid him in his search, but the effort was in vain from such a distance. No gambler was ever as nervous as Edmond then, steering the ship to weigh anchor off the shore. He was given a fright when Jacopo spoke of spending the night on the ship.

"Wouldn't we rather shelter in one of the caves on the island, sleeping in the fresh air?" Edmond asked. He had landed on the island before as part of his old life aboard the Pharaon but never strayed beyond the beach.

"There are no caves on the island," Jacopo replied, chuckling. "Who told you that there were?"

Edmond restrained himself from panic. Three hundred years was long enough for an accident to seal Spada's cave, or Spada himself could have concealed it. Regardless, Edmond's plan needed to wait until the kraken blubber had been taken aboard.

The exchange was smooth and swift, and morning found the Young Amelia with a hold full of valuable goods. Edmond set off into the brush of the island, claiming that he intended to kill a goat for their lunch to celebrate. Jacopo insisted on coming along, but soon returned to the others with a fresh kill while Edmond continued to explore.

He climbed to a rocky peak, a thousand feet above his companions, and looked down on them with a gentle smile. He considered the amount of money they each stood to earn from this venture and how they would soon risk their lives again for a similar sum. Sooner or later they would return to some port town with six hundred francs each, to spend it on frivolity and women. Edmond mused about how paltry six hundred francs looked next to his potential treasure, if only it still existed.

He continued wandering and found a cleft between two walls of rock. A creek ran through it, meeting the sea with a mouth wide enough to admit a small boat. Despite the passage of time, he could make out certain faint marks on rocks following the creek. The marks veered off into another branch of the cleft which left the water behind. Edmond could picture Spada scratching them into the stones to serve as guideposts for his nephew. In the secluded valley, Edmond had renewed hope that the dark and wondrous island still kept Spada's secret after all.

The trail ended at a clearing in the valley, with no sign of any cave or grotto until Edmond noticed a large boulder resting against the rock wall to one side. None of the scattered granite chunks even approached the boulder's size, itself twice as large as Edmond. It was unlikely to have fallen from the cliffs and landed just where it was. Edmond smiled, realizing it must be the gateway to Spada's treasure trove. If it was true, then the treasure was certainly untouched; what treasure-hunter would find such riches and then take the time to seal the cave again when they left?

While Edmond explored, the Young Amelia's crew prepared the goat he had killed alongside some other provisions for a commendable lunch. They fired a pistol shot into the air to signal to Edmond that the food was ready and watched his athletic form spring from rock to rock on a path back towards them until his foot slipped. He staggered on the edge of a rock and disappeared. Edmond had become well-loved among the crew, and they raced to his aid.

They found him bleeding and senseless and revived him with some rum. The diagnosis was not good; he had twisted his ankle and broken several ribs and could not even be carried closer to shore without screaming in agony. When he recovered enough to speak, he convinced the crew to leave him on the island to rest; with water and food nearby, and a pistol in case of animals, he could wait for them to complete the blubber delivery and return. The drop-off point was not far, and they could be back for him in a week.

"By then," Edmond assured them, "I'm certain that I'll have recovered enough to move."

Captain Russo was not convinced but relented after Edmond added a pickaxe to his request.

"So that I may build a shelter if customs or weather delay you," Edmond said.

Despite Edmond's words, Jacopo insisted on remaining behind with Edmond to watch over him, even offering to give up his share of the delivery to do it.

"You are a good-hearted fellow, and I'm certain God will reward you for it," Edmond said with a peculiar smile. "I cannot ask you to stay with me. All I need is a day or two of rest, then I can gather some herbs I saw among the hills which will aid my recovery even further. It's not worth your missing out on the payment for this venture."

In the end, nothing the crew said could shake Edmond's determination. They left what he had asked for along with more rum, and after much turning back to say farewell, they set sail. Edmond waited where he was for an hour to be certain they would not turn back. He dragged himself to a rock where he could watch the Young Amelia until she sailed out of sight.

"If anyone had told me fifteen years ago that I would find such friendship and devotion among smugglers, I'd have called them a liar," he said to the empty island with a smile.

Edmond sprang to his feet and wiped away the goat's blood he had painted himself with. He stretched his limbs wide, twisting at the waist to limber his muscles, and took up the gun and pickaxe. Soon, he stood again before the boulder he had found earlier and greeted it with open arms.

"Now," he exclaimed, remembering the tale of the Arabian fisherman which Faria had told him, "now, open sesame!"

CHAPTER 24
THE SECRET CAVE

The sun warmed the island with a sonorous heat. Insects droned, green lizards scattered before Edmond with every step, and goats leaped across rocks in the distance. Aside from such animal life, Edmond was utterly alone. An incredible excitement built in the pit of his stomach, reminding him of his escape from the Chateau d'If. It overwhelmed him enough that he needed to lay down his tools in front of the boulder and fortify himself with rum before continuing.

With the pickaxe, Edmond dug a small trench around the base of the boulder. He hoped to make room to lever the stone away from the wall and reveal the cave entrance behind it. The earth was easy enough to dig away compared to the masonry of the tunnel. Soon Edmond had created a ledge to tip the rock over and a ditch for it to land in.

The rock wall posed more of a problem. The joint between the boulder and the wall had been cemented by the hand of time or perhaps by some trick of Spada's. Edmond managed to create a small hole in the wall and then stripped a stout branch away from one of the island's olive trees to use as a lever. The rock was so well joined to the wall that the hard olivewood lever snapped in two.

Frustrated, Edmond sat down to a small meal from his supplies and glared at the rock. Some greater force than leverage would be required, but what? His eyes fell on the full horn of gunpowder Jacopo had left for him. Edmond took up his pick again and extended his lever-hole downward so he could pour the powder into a cranny behind the rock. He tore a piece from his handkerchief to make a fuse, then packed the hole with wet clay from the creek. He lit the fuse and ran around the bend of the valley, hoping the granite walls would protect him from the blast.

The explosion echoed across the island like a cannon shot, and the seabirds who roosted there took wing en masse to escape it. Edmond returned to behold the results of his work. All but the lower third of the rock was pulverized, exposing a rough triangular opening just large enough for him to enter.

When he stepped into this granite closet, his foot caught against an iron ring in the ground. Edmond cleared away the dirt and found that the small cave was paved with flagstone, and the ring marked the edge of a trapdoor. He ignored the racing of his heart to grasp the ring with both hands and heave the trapdoor upwards. A staircase beneath it disappeared down into the earth.

Contradictory thoughts of what to expect at the bottom of those stairs roared in his mind. Faria was mad, and Spada buried no treasure here; the hidden masonry was an unused vault built for some other purpose. Faria was right, but the treasure had been found before he was even born. Faria had been entirely correct, and the treasure waited for Edmond to claim it himself. The mysterious power was both a figment of Spada's own imagination, as well as a concrete reality which Edmond could use to take back the reins of his life. All of these possibilities and more seemed equally true all at once, and he needed to catch his breath before he could proceed with a smile on his lips and hope in his heart.

Rather than a stale and gloomy grotto, Edmond found that the air in the cavern below the stairs was as fresh as outdoors, admitted along with dim sunlight by cracks and fissures. The cavern was warm, dry, and spacious. Other chambers branched off from it with no way to guess the full extent. It was also quite empty.

Not daring to give up yet, Edmond recalled Spada's instructions: to look in the farthest angle of the second opening to the west. The cavern showed no passage in that direction and so Edmond roamed along the walls, tapping them with his pickaxe and finding nothing but the dull sound of solid rock.

As disappointment began to caress his neck, one section gave a hollow noise. Without hesitating, he plunged the pickaxe with all force through a wall built of stucco and painted to resemble the rocks around it. Behind the stucco stood another wall of loose white stone, which collapsed under his blows and revealed a new chamber.

A great stone table, carved with symbols Edmond could not identify, dominated the centre of this new chamber. Runnels along the surface and down either side would carry away any liquid spilled onto the table. In an antique oak cabinet, Edmond found an assortment of mysterious silver instruments alongside gleaming blades of all shapes. A drawer contained rolls of linen and large vials of oil and other substances.

Near the cabinet stood a man-shaped form made of wood with metal joints, which Edmond only glanced at. The wooden statue was also covered in carvings, but there were more fascinating things in the cave than a tailor's dummy. Another cabinet stood nearby filled with old yet pristine books.

"The curse of the pharaohs," Edmond read aloud from the spine of one book. Next to it was a treatise on the mummification of Egyptian kings and beside that a Spanish book about preserved remains in other cultures.

His circuit of the room brought him around to the door again, where he found a recessed shelf in the wall which he had overlooked. A wooden chest bound with iron sat there, three feet long and two feet wide, with the crest of the house of Spada emblazoned across the lid. Edmond held his breath as he lifted the box out onto the floor and pried the ancient lock apart with the pickaxe. He hesitated, then raised the lid with eyes half-shut against the possibility of disappointment.

When Edmond opened his eyes, he saw that the chest was divided into three compartments. Gold filled two of them, both coins and bars of bullion. The final compartment was filled to the brim with precious stones: diamonds, pearls, and rubies—some of them set in finely-worked rings to further increase their value. His mouth fell open at the scope of riches before him.

Edmond heard laughter and realized it was his own. He ran his hands through his hair and sprang to his feet, adrenaline and joy compelling him to move however he could. His mirth was cut short when a cold hand gripped his shoulder and spun him around, forcing him to face the carved wooden tailor's dummy.

On closer inspection, Edmond realized it was similar to the forged from the Chateau d'If. Instead of plate armour, this one was clad in dark wood and carved in the rich Renaissance style from the neck down. The blank head carried only the barest suggestion of human features, and the body was decorated with curling leaves, cherubs, and the faces of saints. The head tilted to one side.

"Present your key or be removed," it said in stilted Italian. The timbre of the voice was bizarre and made Edmond think of a copper sheet being struck with a hammer.

Edmond grabbed the thing's fingers to loosen its grip, not wanting to discover what it meant by removal, but they did not budge. It repeated the request as it walked forward, pushing Edmond towards the door.

"Present your key or be removed," it said again.

Edmond managed to contort his body to slip out of his loose sailor's shirt and slide to the floor. He rose to his feet again, still with no way to fight the forged guardian but at least free from its grip. The head swiveled to face him, still clutching the empty shirt, but it did not move.

"Key detected," it said in the same strange voice. Edmond realized he had never heard any forged speak. "Welcome, master. Have you come to claim the power?"

Edmond looked around for the supposed key, then remembered the eight-sided amulet Faria had given him which still hung against his bare chest. Edmond straightened his back and gave the wooden forged what he hoped was an authoritative look.

"I am the master of the island of Monte Cristo, here to claim the treasure and power hidden by Cardinal Spada," he said. "What are you?"

"Cardinal Spada instructed this one to guard the treasure and the power," the forged said. "Cardinal Spada gave this one a name: Baptistan."

It pointed to its own chest with one wooden finger, drawing attention to the name carved in small relief on the left breast between a pair of doves bearing olive branches.

"Tell me, Baptistan," Edmond repeated, "what is the nature of the power hidden here?"

"Life and death," Baptistan said.

It pointed to the books, then the cabinet of instruments, and finally the stone table. An idea took hold in Edmond's head, too outlandish to be true.

"What does that mean?" he asked.

"This one does not understand the question," Baptistan said. "Cardinal Spada told this one that the power was life and death."

Edmond took another look at the books. Faria had told him what he knew about the mummies of Egypt, bodies preserved against the ravages of time. Faria had also spoken about the legends surrounding these mummies. Under the right circumstances, rumour had it that a mummy could rise and seek vengeance against anyone who disturbed it, wielding incredible power to do so. There were stories of men undergoing the process to seek these powers, but these claims were never backed up by solid proof. If the stories were true, then none of them had survived.

"Did the Cardinal tell you how the power would be given to the master of the island?" Edmond asked.

"Yes," Baptistan said. "This one has been given every instruction to successfully confer the power to the master of the island. Warning from Cardinal Spada: the procedure will include severe pain. Are you ready to begin?"

Pain was familiar to Edmond, but doubt nagged at him regarding this decision. The gold and jewels would be easy enough to use to further his goals, but he wondered if he was ready to risk this transformation for revenge. Baptistan waited for an answer, indifferent if Edmond took a minute or a lifetime to reach a decision. To settle his mind and buy some time, he returned to the chest to count his new fortune.

The bullion amounted to a thousand ingots of gold, each one between two and three pounds. Edmond measured out what he guessed was two million francs of gold coins, and even that was fewer than half of them. The gems and rings were plentiful enough to fill ten double handfuls. Faria had estimated the treasure at thirteen million francs; Edmond thought that it may be even more. Sitting on his haunches before this wealth, Edmond reached a decision.

"I'll return to the world," he said aloud, "and ascertain the state of affairs. If I have no other choice, I'll return and claim the power that Spada has left for me."

He saw Danglars, Fernand, and Villefort in his mind again, laughing at him; under no circumstances would he allow their crime to go unpunished, even if it meant leaving his humanity on the floor of Spada's cavern.

CHAPTER 25
THE STRANGER

The Young Amelia returned six days later, and the crew was overjoyed to find Edmond alive and mobile. He feigned some lingering signs of his falsified injuries to keep up the lie. The delivery of the kraken blubber had been a success, though they had a near miss with the coast guard on their way out of port.

Edmond brought some coins and gems with him from the grotto, and in the next port he found a jeweler who kept his questions to himself. Edmond sold four of his smallest diamonds for five thousand francs each. The next day, he gifted Jacopo with a modest ship and money to hire a crew and begin the next stage of his smuggling career. The only condition he gave the stunned Jacopo was an errand: sail to Marseille and inquire about an old man named Louis Dantes and a Catalan woman named Mercedes Herrera, and then to meet Edmond at the island of Monte Cristo.

This sudden show of wealth brought a slew of questions from his crewmates. Edmond spun a story of being heir to a wealthy family who became a sailor to spite his father after an argument. He said he had come into possession of an inheritance from an uncle when they arrived at Leghorn. Faria's education provided enough support for the story that none probed further. With his three months of service complete, Edmond took his leave of the Young Amelia despite Captain Russo's offer to promote him to first mate.

Edmond's next stop was Genoa, which has long held a well-deserved reputation as the ship-building capital of the Mediterranean. Soon he had purchased a fine yacht, after giving the former owner a handful of fine gems. The seller offered his services to find a crew for the vessel, but Edmond declined in favour of sailing it himself. Before he left

Genoa, he commissioned the building of a secret compartment with three divisions in the cabin. After some maneuvers in the harbour to get the feel of the yacht, he set sail for Monte Cristo and landed in the hidden creek.

The treasure still sat present and accounted for, and Baptistan asked Edmond again if he would accept the power of Monte Cristo. Edmond again deferred but commanded Baptistan to help him carry the chest to the yacht. They loaded the treasure into the hidden compartment.

Over the next week, Edmond practiced navigating the yacht and asked Baptistan every question he could think of to draw out more information about what would be done to him if he consented to be mummified. He learned far more than he wanted to know about the process of mummification itself, but Baptistan did not know which steps, if any, would preserve Edmond's mind or grant him the strange abilities associated with the mummy's curse. When Jacopo arrived at the end of that week, the answers he brought were of no comfort either.

Louis Dantes had died, though Jacopo did not know how, and Mercedes Herrera had disappeared from Marseille. Edmond received this news as he had endured taking a musket-ball to the shoulder. He was not surprised to learn his father had died, as he had been an old man and in ill health even when Edmond had been arrested, but Mercedes' disappearance perplexed him. Jacopo did not know Edmond's real name or his connection to Louis Dantes, but offered his condolences regardless. It was not until sunset, after Jacopo had departed, that Edmond allowed himself to grieve in the privacy of solitude.

Still, Edmond needed more information than Jacopo could provide. His mirror convinced him he would not be recognized in Marseille, and his new wealth could furnish any possible disguise. He left Baptistan to guard the grotto once again, and his swift yacht soon entered the port of Marseille.

Edmond weighed anchor just opposite the place where gendarmes had forced him into a boat fourteen years ago to be taken to the Chateau d'If. His confidence in his changed appearance was tested when a gendarme and customs officer approached to see his bill of health and other documents.

Edmond was prepared and had secured an English passport under the name of Lord Wilmore along with a fine suit of clothes to match the role. The prestige of a foreign passport and the transfer of a small bribe sufficed for the bureaucrats to overlook his missing papers, and they allowed him through without further incident.

The first person to catch Edmond's attention as his boots struck French soil was a man named Dalton who he had served with aboard the Pharaon. Edmond interrupted Dalton in the midst of hauling crates and asked about some minor subjects as a travelling Englishman: recent events, the weather, the best inn for a glass of wine, and so forth. Dalton never showed any sign he knew who Edmond was. As a final test, Edmond asked him for news of the Pharaon herself.

"Pharaon? I used to sail aboard her, before the hard times hit M. Morrel," Dalton said. "He lost all his other ships, then had to make layoffs from the Pharaon too, and now she's late returning from Calcutta."

"What happened to the other ships?" Edmond asked.

"Two were seized during the Inquisition," Dalton said. "That left him with the Pharaon and the Oracle, but then the Oracle was lost at sea. We still don't know if it was a storm, pirates, or sea monsters."

"The Inquisition, of course," Edmond said. He had no idea what Inquisition Dalton meant, and it had never been mentioned aboard the Young Amelia.

Not wanting to take up any more of Dalton's time, Edmond handed the man a gold coin and left. He resolved to check on M. Morrel at the earliest opportunity, but had other matters to attend to first. As his feet carried him through the streets of Marseille, the sights carried him back to his childhood. Memories good and bad flew at him from every angle. He passed the home of the woman who had taught him to read and the general store where he had worked his first job as a stock boy. He passed a deserted lot where an inn had once stood; the men of the town had corralled two dozen undead in the building and burned them when he was just a small boy.

Even the ghastliest memories of the Dead Plague brought a tear to his eye, for no reason but that they were his memories and he was back in the only home he'd ever known. Reminders of vicious zombie assaults brought fresh questions. If he allowed Baptistan to mummify him, he would become a creature not so different than those in his childhood nightmares. Was revenge worth such a drastic cost? He had no clear answer by the time he reached the Allees de Meillan where his father had lived.

The plants Louis had loved so dearly were gone from the front of the shabby little house, and he learned that newlyweds had moved in to the street-facing apartment on the fifth floor. Edmond sighed, finding small consolation in knowing that new life carried on where the old man had spent his time.

When Edmond recovered his composure, he asked after Caderousse and learned that he had encountered some difficulties several years ago. Caderousse had left Marseille to manage a small inn on a country route. Edmond thanked the concierge of the house and left.

A few days later, the inhabitants of the house learned that the dwelling had been purchased by a Lord Wilmore. Wilmore's letter reassured them that he would not be vacating any of them, except for the couple in the fifth-floor apartment facing the street. They were told they could choose any other vacant apartment in the building and live there rent-free, as long as they moved immediately.

This strange event remained the source of many rumours in the neighbourhood for months thereafter. The facts were few and far between, but one truth was that the same well-dressed stranger also roamed the Catalan village that evening. He met with a poor fisherman there and spent over an hour inquiring about people who had been dead or gone away for years. The fisherman woke up the next day to find the handsome gift of a new fishing-boat, but no further sign of the stranger.

CHAPTER 26
THE INN

A circle of screaming men stamped their feet in the basement of a run-down inn, midway between the towns of Beaucaire and Bellegarde. In the middle of the circle, two scaled and emaciated creatures pecked and slashed at each other. With the heads of roosters and wings of bats, they were a disgusting sight to behold.

The innkeeper hoped to cater to more upscale clientele than these men, but a nearby canal had revolutionized transportation in the area, and carriages seldom took the dusty road across the sunbaked plain. For this reason, the innkeeper took what customers he could and oversaw the collecting of money and recording of bets in his basement.

A lucky blow from one of the beasts drew blood and a shriek from the other, and the wounded animal's flesh turned to stone. Half of the circle erupted into mad cheering and rushed to the stocky, bearded innkeeper to claim their winnings. A man with heavy gloves herded the winner back into its cage.

"Caderousse!" a hoarse voice cried from upstairs. "A guest is here!"

The innkeeper completed his transactions and hurried upstairs, closing the heavy door behind him to muffle the noise of the cockatrice fights in the basement. Caderousse and his wife had run the establishment for seven or eight years and fared as well as the stunted fig trees in what passed for a garden outside. His teeth were still white and even, and only a few silver threads in his thick black beard betrayed his age.

Caderousse's clothes were still festooned with the wards and sigils he had once made a living from. In his advancing years he was wary of possible attacks from any variety of the night's strange creatures at his remote inn. Before the canal, he had bolstered his income by sewing elaborate costumes for the townspeople at either end of the road to wear to festivals and feast days. Those days and the costumes were gone, and Caderousse had just the inn.

His wife, Madeleine, was a sickly specimen. Beautiful once, she had withered under the unforgiving sun to match her disagreeable nature. Every day she found some event or non-event to complain of or an opportunity to rant against the fate that had taken her from her pleasant country village to the middle of nowhere.

"It is God's will that life be this way," Caderousse would say with a mournful look whenever she complained.

On this day, he found Madeleine waiting on a solemn-faced man dressed in a close black frock in spite of the heat.

"*Mon dieu!*" Caderousse exclaimed. "You offer our guest nothing but water? Woman, we have better hospitality than that! Our honoured guest must have wine!"

Madeleine cleared her throat and nodded towards the man, and Caderousse noticed the white collar he wore.

"*Mon dieu!*" Caderousse said again. "Madeleine, what are you thinking to serve wine to a man of the cloth? Bring cold water, at once!"

The pale, dark-haired priest gave Caderousse a critical look through his modest iron-rimmed spectacles.

"*Buongiorno, signor*. My name is Busoni, an abbe travelling through your country," the priest said in a strong Italian accent. "I was just speaking to your wife. You are Gaspard Caderousse, formerly a tailor from Marseille?"

"I am he," Caderousse said. "The tailoring trade has rather declined in Marseille. It is so hot there, I expect the residents will soon decide to go without clothing altogether!"

Caderousse chuckled at his joke until Madeleine cleared her throat again, and he remembered his guest's profession.

"I wanted to provide weary travelers with rest and refreshment, but alas, the canal has ruined that," Caderousse said. "I pride myself on being an honest man, but honesty will not make one rich!"

Abbe Busoni gave him a curious look at this statement, and Caderousse had a fleeting impression of something familiar in Busoni's eyes.

"Honesty is a rare virtue. Sooner or later, God always rewards the good and punishes the wicked," Busoni said. He withdrew a piece of paper from his black frock and checked the details written there. "This brings me to why I have come here. Did you, around 1814 or 1815, know a young sailor named Dantes?"

"Dantes? Edmond Dantes?" Caderousse said, his face flushed. "Of course I knew him! We were close friends, such close friends! Oh, I miss him dearly. Do you know what has become of him? Is he alive, is he prosperous, is he happy?"

"Quite the opposite. He died in prison, wretched and heart-broken," Busoni said. "Edmond took his own life by dashing his brains against a flagstone, able to bear captivity no longer."

The flush on Caderousse's face turned even darker as tears rose to his eyes, and he turned away to mop his face with a handkerchief.

"That poor fellow, that unfortunate boy!" Caderousse said when he regained his voice. "Father, I fear that this young man's fate is proof against your claim: the good are not rewarded in this life, but rather the wicked."

Caderousse stood to pace, speaking more to himself than to the priest.

"Did I sometimes envy Edmond his good fortune? Of course, I am only human, we all grapple with such feelings!" Caderousse said. "But ever since he was taken away, I have lamented deeply and sincerely his unhappy fate! Edmond! You knew him, then?"

"I met him only briefly. His suicide was not successful right away, and he had sense enough to ask for a priest in his last hours," Busoni said. "I could be of limited help, as he had already doomed his immortal soul, but he took comfort in speaking to anyone who was not his jailer."

"*Mon dieu,*" Caderousse breathed again, picturing Edmond dying of a gruesome wound on a prison bed.

"The strange thing is that Edmond insisted to the end that he did not know why he had been arrested," Busoni said, indifferent to the tailor's distress. "He beseeched me to clear his name, if I could, and to take care of one other matter."

"Ignorant! Ignorant of the cause of his woe! Of course he was, the dear boy. Anyone who knew him must surely know he could never harm a soul," Caderousse said. "What was the other matter?"

"In prison, Edmond had a wealthy cellmate; an Englishman who had the good fortune to be released. He had been arrested while in possession of a valuable diamond," Busoni said. "The Englishman gifted the diamond to Edmond as thanks after Edmond nursed him back to health from a severe fever. Edmond kept it safe, hoping that he would be released and could sell it to make his fortune. Here, I have it with me."

Abbe Busoni placed a box on the table. Inside lay a dazzling jewel set into a finely-worked ring. Caderousse's beady eyes locked onto the gemstone like a compass needle swinging to true north.

"Such a beauty! Surely, that must be worth ten thousand francs!" Caderousse said.

"Fifty thousand at least; I had it appraised. Edmond wanted me to sell the ring and divide the money in Marseille amongst his father Louis and four others," Busoni said, checking his paper for the names. "Danglars, Fernand, Mercedes, and you. I have been to Marseille, but Louis Dantes is dead and the others have moved on. You are the first of his friends that I've been able to find."

"Louis! Oh, that poor old man. Yes, indeed he did die. Starved to death, the poor soul," Caderousse said.

Busoni's nostrils flared, but he remained silent. Caderousse noticed nothing, as he kept his eyes on the diamond instead of on his guest.

"I had left Marseille already, but the news reached me all the same. There was no escape from the gruesome stories of the Inquisition, after all," Caderousse said.

"My monastery must be the exception," Busoni said. "I have heard this Inquisition mentioned in passing, but heard no details. Pity an ignorant foreigner and explain what happened, *per favore*. It seems impossible to me that a man could starve to death in such a prosperous place as Marseille."

"Oh, those were tumultuous times, M. Busoni," Caderousse said. "First the dead roamed the land and the king was dethroned, then a Republic rose up, then that became an Empire. The Empire fell, then returned, then fell again. There were horrible acts of violence on all sides. When the king was restored the second time, he was furious."

"Go on," Busoni said.

"Rulers are capricious people, I find, especially when they fight each other. One comes to power and uses it to hurt the people who opposed him," Caderousse said. "Then another takes power and hurts the people who supported his predecessor."

"You're saying that Louis Dantes supported Napoleon?" Busoni said. Louis had been a kindly old man, happy to tend to his plants and let the affairs of the world pass him by.

"Well, he was thought to, and that was enough," Caderousse said. "The king wanted a show of force, to shock and awe the people of France enough to wipe out any ideas of removing the monarchy again. And so the Inquisition started. Bonapartists and those suspected of being Bonapartists were rounded up, questioned, sometimes tortured and executed in public places. The lucky ones were able to avoid that fate by signing over assets to the crown."

"What happened to—" Busoni began, catching himself before he could ruin his disguise. "What precisely happened to Louis Dantes?"

"With Edmond arrested for aiding Napoleon's return, old Louis was declared guilty by association," Caderousse said. "He became one of the unlucky victims of the Inquisition. They locked him in an iron cage and hoisted him twelve feet above the town square. From what I was told, they only brought the cage down when the crows began to swarm."

Busoni was silent for a long time after hearing this. He drained his water glass and motioned for Madeleine to refill it, then drained that as well.

"Edmond had mentioned his friends, Danglars and Fernand. Did they, or anybody, try to help Louis?" Busoni said at last.

"Those two were no friends to Edmond or to Louis," Caderousse said. "M. Morrel, Edmond's former employer, tried to give Louis money for food when Edmond was first arrested. Louis didn't want to be a bother, but Morrel gave him a red silk purse full of coins and kept visiting to top it up. I have that purse now, in fact, though it's been empty for some time."

"So Morrel at least had Louis' interests at heart?" Busoni asked.

"Oh yes. Morrel loved Edmond as much as his own children, even tried to have him pardoned from prison during the Hundred Days," Caderousse said. "Of course, doing so much to help a Bonapartist worked against him during the Inquisition. His business partner was arrested, two of his ships were impounded, and his business was nearly destroyed. By the time they took Louis, the fight had been beaten out of poor M. Morrel."

"Why didn't Danglars or Fernand help?" Busoni asked.

"Danglars had some sort of grudge against Edmond; I couldn't tell you where he came by it, but he hated the poor boy," Caderousse said. "And as for Fernand..."

"Mind your tongue, Gaspard!" Madeleine hissed at him, but he ignored her.

"Doesn't the Bible say, 'covet not thy neighbour's wife'? That skinny Catalan boy worshipped Mercedes, but she was engaged to marry Edmond," Caderousse said. "Fernand thought that he deserved her love more than Edmond did, but I think Edmond was too honourable to see Fernand's jealousy."

"Oh, I'm sure he saw it," Busoni said darkly. "But he never thought it would lead to betrayal."

Caderousse noticed Busoni's tone and with great effort averted his eyes from the diamond.

"Perhaps my darling wife is correct," he said. "If dear Edmond were still living and came here to ask me if any of his friends were false ones, I should tell him in a heartbeat. But what good is it to dig up the past for a dead man?"

"So I should follow his wishes and give the proceeds from the ring to men who hated him?" Busoni said. "Very well. Tell me where to find them, I will be on my way to sell the ring and return with your share."

"You make a true point, Father," Caderousse said. He licked his dry lips, captivated once again by the diamond. "Besides, to them even several thousand francs would be a drop in the ocean!"

"They are wealthy, then?" Busoni said.

"Oh yes, and powerful!" Caderousse said. "If either wanted to, they could descend upon this humble inn and crush me like a beetle. You really know nothing of their history? Well, it is a rather painful tale. I should like some wine before I tell it."

Caderousse rose and fetched a cheap bottle of red, filling a glass to the brim.

"Very well," he said. "It all begins with a wedding."

CHAPTER 27
THE STORY

"The wedding, yes," Busoni said. "Edmond told me that he was arrested minutes before he was to be married."

"Ah yes, La Reserve! Such a beautiful day, until that dark moment. Did he tell you about the lutin? One of the little beasts chose that day to cause trouble, and we made a fine show of driving it away together," Caderousse said, reminiscing. "Before I go further, you must swear never to tell anyone that I gave you this history. Danglars and Fernand are so powerful that either of them could shatter me like glass with the stroke of a pen."

"Confessions and confidentiality are my business," Busoni said. "I don't care for earthly scandals. My goal is to carry out the last request of a dying man. When this business is done, I will return to my monastery in Italy."

"Alright, as long as you're certain that this will not come back to me," Caderousse said.

"You have my word," Busoni said. "Now, tell me about Danglars and Fernand."

"Like I said, they each disliked Edmond for their own reasons." Caderousse took a deep drink from his glass. "One evening at La Reserve, they wrote a letter accusing Edmond of going to Elba and taking a secret mission from Napoleon. Danglars wrote it with disguised handwriting, and Fernand took it to the postbox."

"Faria, your reasoning was impeccable," Busoni muttered, too low for Caderousse to notice. "You were there, then. Why not stop them?"

Caderousse rocked backward. "There! Who said that I was there?"

"How could you know such details otherwise?" Busoni said. "Did you speak up against this foul plot, or were you a willing accomplice?"

Caderousse stammered defensive gibberish and then relented with a flourish of his hands.

"Very well! I was there! But you do not understand, they poisoned me!" Caderousse said. "Danglars gave me so much wine that I lost my wits. I could hardly understand the gravity of the situation, and when they told me that it was all a joke my drunken self believed them."

"Surely you were sober enough by the time Edmond was arrested, yet you said nothing," Busoni said.

"True, very true!" Caderousse bowed his head. He felt his very soul on display beneath Busoni's glare. "But Danglars convinced me that if Edmond really was guilty, any who defended him would be judged as accomplices. It was a politically dangerous day, you understand?"

"So you kept quiet out of fear," Busoni said.

"Yes, I held my tongue, and it was cowardly, but it was not criminal. To this day, that act of cowardice remains my only true regret in life," Caderousse said. "If I spoke out on Edmond's behalf, I may have been taken by the Inquisition, but I feel that I deserve no less. Every suffering since has been atonement for that day, and I tell my wife when she complains, 'it is the will of God.'"

They sat in silence for a while and Madeleine made a show of being too occupied with polishing the spotless bar to listen to their conversation.

"What became of Danglars after Edmond's arrest?" Busoni said at last. "All I know is that he no longer lives in Marseille."

"The miscreant is rolling in wealth, Father," Caderousse said. "He worked for Morrel & Son, like Edmond did, and stayed with them for a few years after the arrest. The job kept him away from Marseille frequently, but one day he left by land instead of by sea. It seems he had somehow earned or bought himself a barony and was on his way to Paris to sit in the House of Peers."

"Then Danglars is now Baron Danglars, eh?" Busoni said.

"Yes, and he was also appointed as Head of the Royal Bourbon Reserve Bank. He is quite literally in charge of printing the banknotes for all of France!" Caderousse said. "You would think he could spare some for an old friend! He still travels frequently, but for pleasure rather than the job of a supercargo. The old adage says that money cannot buy happiness, but Danglars is a happy man indeed."

Caderousse drank more wine while Busoni digested this information. He had hoped that the Spada fortune would be enough to crush his foes, but if they had wealth of their own it would be a more challenging task.

"What about the other man, Fernand, who coveted Edmond's fiancée and posted the fatal letter?" Busoni asked.

"The Catalan boy is now the Catalan general, also fabulously wealthy, but by a very strange path. His career is quite illustrious, from what I gather. I find it interesting to keep track of my old friends," Caderousse said. "He and I were both drafted into different regiments when Napoleon returned. When Napoleon took Paris and resumed control of the army, Fernand's regiment was sent to fight the English. On the night of Waterloo his general defected, and Fernand went with him."

"A risky move," Busoni said.

"Oh yes; if Napoleon had won the battle, Fernand would have been hanged!" Caderousse said. "But he and the general brought information to the English, which the Duke of Wellington used to trounce Napoleon. King Louis rewarded Fernand's betrayal with a promotion."

"Your king places a high value on honesty and integrity, it seems," Busoni said dryly.

"By 1823, Fernand was a captain and sent to Spain as a French spy," Caderousse continued. "He happened to meet Danglars there on one of the baron's vacations, and Danglars helped him make certain connections to aid his mission. That time, his reward was to be made a colonel and given a title. These days he is the Count de Morcerf."

"A baron and a count! The wicked rise to the top like cream in France," Busoni said. "They killed one man with despair and another with famine, and face no punishment."

"There's more still, and the strangest is yet to come," Caderousse said. "When Greece rose up against Turkey for independence, the king sent Fernand and some other military brass to Yanina to assist the Greek forces, which were led by Ali Pasha. The pasha was killed, and all the other men died or disappeared. Fernand returned home with a large sum left to him in the pasha's will. He returned to Paris, was promoted again to lieutenant-general, and bought a magnificent house."

"How generous of the pasha to do such a thing," Busoni said.

"War appears to have agreed with him, as well," Caderousse said. "Fernand was always a thin boy, some would even say sickly, but he has grown tall and broad-shouldered during his time away. There is almost no recognizing him; he went to war as a walking-stick and returned from Yanina as Hercules!"

"There was one final name: the fiancée, Mercedes," Busoni said. "Another Catalan?"

"She was once a humble fisher girl, this is true, but at this moment she is one of the greatest ladies in Paris," Caderousse said.

"How strange, that so many of Edmond's former friends would make their way to Paris!" Busoni replied.

"Not so strange on Mercedes' part, monsieur; she followed her husband there," Caderousse said, too occupied with draining his wine to notice the slight flush in Busoni's face. "Oh, she despaired when Edmond was arrested. She pleaded with M. de Villefort to release him, she looked after old Louis as much as he'd let her; anything to keep Edmond's memory alive. Fernand was her only source of comfort, but then he went to war. She prayed for Edmond and she prayed for Fernand, and in the end, one of them returned to her."

"And so she settled for her second choice?" Busoni said with a dry throat.

"I think it was more like a desperate woman seizing comfort where she could," Caderousse said. "When the heart has been deprived for so long, it takes what it can get. And Fernand, of course, saw her relief as love and saw that love as his entitlement, and happily nurtured it. Once Louis died, they married and left the unhappy memories of Marseille behind."

"Indeed," Busoni whispered.

"I saw her again with her son, in Spain; I was there too, as a soldier myself at the time," Caderousse said. "Little Albert is quite the image of his father. Let me see, I believe I have told you all I know about the persons Edmond named. How dreadful, that he thought so highly of people so hostile to him!"

"Do you know anything about a M. de Villefort? According to prison records, he interviewed Edmond the night of his arrest. What became of him?" Busoni asked.

"I heard that he was promoted and left Marseille as well; I never met him, but one hears about the deputy prosecutor in one's hometown," Caderousse said. "As he is not myself, I can only assume that he has had magnificent luck of his own, as rich as Danglars and as powerful as Fernand."

Busoni rose and paced, thinking at great length on what he had heard. Finally, he returned to Caderousse.

"Monsieur, thank you for relating such a long and painful tale. It's clear that Edmond was very much mistaken in who his friends were," Busoni said. "I cannot in good conscience carry out the letter of his request without betraying the spirit of it. You say that God has forsaken you for your role in Edmond's incarceration; perhaps today is your chance at redemption. The diamond is yours."

"What? You jest!" Caderousse said. "Do not toy with a poor old innkeeper, monsieur!"

"Louis is dead, and it seems you are the closest to a friend he had. Take the diamond and sell it; if you are wise and careful, and as honest as you say, the money will permit you a life of greater comfort," Busoni said, tapping the ring box on the table. "If I may, I'd like to take the purse that Morrel left on Louis' mantelpiece. Since the man is in such dire straits, such a memento may bring him comfort."

Distracted by the diamond, Caderousse waved an arm and instructed Madeleine on where to find the purse. Long and made of faded red silk, it bore the company arms of Morrel & Son stitched to the side.

"Very well," Busoni said. "Now to return this to Morrel and return to my monastery in Italy, away from where men injure each other in such inventive and despicable ways."

Caderousse and Madeleine waved from the door as Busoni mounted his horse and rode away along the dusty road. Madeleine gave Caderousse a strange look.

"Is it true, then?" she asked.

"That he has given us a fifty-thousand-franc diamond all to ourselves? Dear woman, it is as true as the beard on my face!" Caderousse replied gleefully.

"Not the diamond, you silly fool, the story! Did you really sit by, drunk, while your friend's life was casually ruined?" Madeleine asked

But her words fell on deaf ears, as Caderousse's hat already sat upon his head, and he stepped out the door to have the gem appraised.

CHAPTER 28
THE PRISON REGISTER

E dmond returned to Marseille the next day. Rather than the disguise of Abbe Busoni or Lord Wilmore, he wore a fake moustache with a bright blue frock coat and yellow trousers. He still affected an English accent, but one from the north country rather than the posh tones he used when pretending to be Wilmore. In this disguise, he visited several government officials around town.

"Good morning," Edmond said to each of them. "I am chief clerk of the banking house of Thomson & French of Rome. We've worked with Morrel & Son for some ten years now and have a sizeable amount loaned on their securities. Recent events require me to inquire about the firm. Could you provide any information?"

He repeated this script in front of the mayor, the postmaster, the director of land sales, the chief of police, several judges, the municipal minister of livestock, and finally M. de Boville, the inspector of prisons. Edmond could not restrain a gulp of surprise, which Boville did not notice. Boville certainly did not see any resemblance between the well-groomed Englishman before him and a raving prisoner who he had once visited at the Chateau d'If.

Since leaving Caderousse, Edmond had learned more from several sources about Morrel's misfortunes. M. Clairmont's arrest in the Inquisition had maimed the firm's finances, and the forced surrender of half their ships to the crown crippled their ability to rebuild. The loss of the Oracle at sea compounded the trouble and put all of Morrel's hopes into the Pharaon. Meanwhile, the Pharaon was late in returning from Calcutta with cargo. Creditors and investors in Morrel & Son called for repayment, hoping to recover at least some of their money before Morrel declared bankruptcy. One creditor who had not yet received his money was M. de Boville.

"Oh, your fears are quite well-grounded," Boville said with regret. "I have two hundred thousand francs lent to Morrel; it seemed quite a solid investment at the time. That money was going to be my daughter's dowry. He assured me that when the Pharaon returned, I would be paid; if the ship has been lost at sea, then the money is lost with her."

"My time in this lovely town has been filled with stories of Morrel's bad luck," Edmond said. "However, I can bring you a slice of good fortune. My employer has authorized me to buy Morrel's debt from you."

Boville jumped. "Buy it?" he asked. "Certainly, by all means! What rate of discount did you have in mind?"

"You misunderstand; I'm authorized to pay you your entire principal. Two hundred thousand francs, though I'm afraid I may not pay you interest," Edmond said.

"The entire principal!" Boville repeated. "Of course, of course, as soon as you wish!"

Edmond took a bundle of banknotes from his pocket and counted out Boville's sum.

"Your firm will likely lose out on this loan," Boville said as he signed a receipt for the transfer.

"Don't trouble yourself with that," Edmond said. "Thomson & French have their reasons, though I'm not privy to them. Perhaps they've invested in a competitor and wish to hasten Morrel's ruin. In any case, your daughter's dowry is back in your hands. I only ask a small fee."

"Of course, of course!" Boville said, happy to part with a percentage of his money when an hour ago he had expected to lose it all. "The commission is normally one and a half?"

"No no, good chap. I'm very well-compensated by my employer," Edmond said with a chuckle. "What I meant was, you are the inspector of prisons. When I was a boy, I was tutored by an Italian banker named Gianmarco Faria. He disappeared quite suddenly and I've since learned that he was confined to the Chateau d'If."

Edmond paused, watching Boville's face but finding no reaction except curiosity.

"I was hoping your registers may have some information about his arrest and whether he is alive or dead today," Edmond continued.

"You knew Gianmarco Faria, the mad banker?" Boville said, surprised. "The poor devil; if he wasn't mad when he went into the Chateau, he certainly was by the time I met him. He had a wild story about some fantastical treasure and offered it to anyone he saw if only they would release him."

"What an unlikely tale!" Edmond said with dry English irony. "He certainly wasn't crazy when I knew him, I can tell you that much. You speak of him in the past tense; he's dead, then?"

"Yes, I am sorry to say; five or six months ago, in February," Boville said.

It was Edmond's turn to be surprised. "Out of a whole country's prisons, you remember the date of one prisoner's death? Impressive."

"Not so impressive, really," Boville said. "Faria's death was accompanied by a very peculiar incident. His cell was about fifty feet away from that of a dangerous Bonapartist agent named Edmond Dantes—a man who had personally helped to bring about the Hundred Days. I met him as well, a dangerous fellow. I don't expect I shall ever forget his face!"

"He sounds formidable," Edmond said.

"Oh, very much so," Boville replied. "Dantes must have fashioned tools for himself somehow, because they discovered a tunnel connecting his dungeon to Faria's. Another branch headed towards the outer wall. They clearly planned to escape but then they must have argued."

"Argued? What makes you say so?" Edmond said.

"Well, Dantes murdered the banker. Took up a flagstone and bashed the poor man's head in!" Boville said, miming the action. "Then he took Faria's place in the burial sack. He must have thought dead prisoners of the Chateau were interred in an ordinary grave that he could free himself from."

Boville laughed, and Edmond feigned polite confusion until he explained the joke.

"Of course, you may not know: the Chateau d'If is an island," Boville said. "They simply tie a weight to the sack and throw the dead into the sea."

Edmond joined in the laughter this time. "Goodness! I should like to have seen the prisoner's face at that moment. So, both Faria and Dantes died on the same night?"

"Oh, yes," Boville replied. "It was a shame about the banker, he seemed a gentle soul aside from his madness. I took no pleasure in seeing his death certificate. Knowing Dantes is dead, though, brings me a small measure of relief."

"Then it is official! Edmond Dantes is, in the eyes of the law, a dead man," Edmond muttered as Boville added his francs to a pocketbook.

"Would it be alright if I saw Faria's entry in the register for myself? As long as I'm here, I should learn as much about his fate as I can," Edmond asked.

"Certainly, come to my study." Boville led the way to a room lined with books and presented Edmond the register for the Chateau d'If.

Edmond made a show of studying Faria's entry. When Boville turned away to count his money again, Edmond turned the pages to find his own name.

The accusation written in Danglars' disguised hand was there, along with notes from Villefort's examination, but there were omissions; the name Noirtier did not appear in Villefort's notes. Edmond folded up the accusation and slipped it into his pocket.

For the first time Edmond saw Morrel's petition, made with the best of intentions during the Hundred Days. Villefort had done an excellent job of ensuring Edmond would remain in prison in the event the king reclaimed the throne.

"Thank you, sir," Edmond said to Boville. "I have all I want, and you have your funds. Now I must take my leave; my business in Marseille is not yet done. *Au revoir*, monsieur."

Edmond's demeanour changed as he left the inspector's study behind and left the character of the English clerk with it. Seeing Boville again and speaking aloud about Faria and the Chateau d'If threw his mind backward through time. For the first time since his escape, Edmond allowed himself to remember the terror of having to kill Faria's zombie before it could kill him.

He forced a deep breath of the salty coastal air into his lungs and reminded himself he had learned some good news with the bad: as far as the world knew, Edmond Dantes was dead. No gendarmes searched for him, no court waited to hang him. He was, by all rights, a free man.

How long he could remain a man at all was another matter. A fraction of his wealth would be enough to grant a reprieve to Morrel, the only man alive who had remained upstanding and true through Edmond's ordeal; would the remainder be enough on its own to combat his foes? Fernand was a general and a count, Danglars a well-connected banker, and Villefort remained a mystery.

Until speaking to Caderousse, Edmond had overlooked the notion that his old antagonists may not occupy the same stations in life as in 1815. Edmond leaned his head back and closed his eyes, absorbing every detail of the sun's warm rays against his face. If he allowed Baptistan to mummify him, and if he survived, would he ever know that feeling again?

With no answers at hand, he again assumed the demeanour of the English clerk and strode off into the town. As he had said to Boville, his job in Marseille was not yet complete.

CHAPTER 29
MORREL & SON

The headquarters of Morrel & Son had undergone radical change between 1815 and 1829. Instead of the energy of industry, instead of the mingled aromas of exotic goods from around the world, it sat on the verge of dereliction. The warehouse once echoed with the good-natured shouts of workmen directing and joking with one another, but now the only echoes were of morose footfalls against the stone floor. Once a thriving business, it now resembled an abandoned beehive.

Of the many clerks who were once employed by Morrel & Son, only two remained. One was a young man named Emmanuel, about twenty-three years old, and smitten in love with Morrel's daughter Julie. The other was an old cashier with only one eye, who had been nicknamed Cocles for so long he would probably not recognize his real name if anyone addressed him by it.

Cocles was one of those individuals who can focus on one subject to the exclusion of all others; in his case, that one thing was arithmetic. The man's brain was an abacus, making him well-suited to his work but preventing him sometimes from noticing key details about the world around him. He could calculate the company's ledgers without a single error or transposition but was blind to the dire straits they had entered.

All of the other clerks had deserted Morrel, not from any malice, but from the practicality of feeding themselves and their families. Only the love-struck Emmanuel and oblivious Cocles were devoted enough in their own ways to stay.

On the day of June 5th, Cocles found fourteen extra sous in his register, and brought them to Morrel to be recorded. Morrel thanked him and forced a smile as he swept the coins into an empty drawer. This integrity, when Cocles could have been excused for pocketing the coins instead, was why Cocles held one of only three keys to Morrel's office. Morrel himself held one, and Julie held the other.

"Cocles," Morrel said, "any news of the Pharaon yet?"

"Hmm? I don't believe so," Cocles said.

Morrel sighed, wondering why he had bothered asking. The Pharaon was well overdue; it had left Calcutta on schedule with pigments and spices at the same time as a rival's ship called the Jacqueline. The Jacqueline had been in port in Marseille for two weeks already, with no sign or word from the Pharaon.

While Morrel brooded, Edmond presented himself at the warehouse door, introducing himself again as the chief clerk from Thomson & French. Emmanuel had learned to expect a request of payment from every new face. He did his best to shield Morrel from the visit, but Edmond would hear no refusal and was soon led to Morrel's office. On the stairs, they met a beautiful but anxious girl of eighteen or nineteen.

"Is M. Morrel in his office, Mlle. Julie?" Emmanuel asked with a flush of colour in his cheeks.

Julie's eyes darted about. "I believe so; I shall go and knock."

Julie hurried upstairs to give her father time to make himself presentable. Morrel received Edmond with every courtesy and an offer of brandy, which Edmond declined for a glass of water.

Fourteen hard years were written across Morrel's face in new lines and deepened the ones he already had. His hair was white at only fifty years old, and his direct gaze now wandered about in search of solutions to his problems. Morrel's wooden leg was gone, sold long ago, requiring him to lean on a crutch to get around.

"Thomson & French, of Rome," Morrel said. "I must apologize, I can't say that I remember doing business with your firm before."

"Nevertheless, we have taken it upon ourselves to consolidate your debts, as it were. We hold bills amounting to, let me see, four hundred thousand francs due payment from you," Edmond said, still speaking with the accent of northern England. He presented Morrel with the receipt from M. de Boville, which was the largest, and an assortment of others from around Marseille.

"Yes, I recognize those sums," Morrel said in a thin voice.

"Morrel & Son has an impeccable reputation; you have run it for twenty-four years, and your father before you for thirty-five, and in all that time you have never allowed a debt to go unpaid," Edmond said. "However, I also understand that you have been beset with recent difficulties. Your main investor was taken away in the Inquisition, it seems?"

"Sir, I promise, the moment my ship returns I shall be in perfect form to meet these liabilities," Morrel said in a rush of words. "I have indeed been the victim of accidents, politics, bad weather, and simple ill luck, but the Pharaon and her cargo will be able to set everything right, I swear on my life."

"And if the Pharaon doesn't return?" Edmond asked. Morrel's anguished silence was all the answer he needed.

"As I was on my way here, I saw a vessel entering port. Perhaps that is your ship?" Edmond asked.

"No, sadly not," Morrel said. "My clerk Emmanuel spends part of each day watching the port with a telescope for incoming ships. The vessel you saw is called La Gironde; a fine ship, also coming from India, but not mine. I can still hope that she brings word of the Pharaon, but at this point, could it possibly be good tidings?"

Both men started at the sound of footsteps on the stairs. Julie entered with tears in her eyes at the head of a group of desperate men.

"Sunk!" Julie wailed. "Father, the Pharaon is sunk! These men are the only survivors; they were rescued by the ship that came into the harbour today."

"Small fortune is better than no fortune, I suppose," Morrel said in a hoarse whisper. "Penelon, tell me, what happened?"

From the half-dozen haggard sailors, an older man with a thick beard and leathery face stepped to the head of the group.

"It was a storm, M. Morrel," the man said. "We did all we could, I swear, but it wasn't enough. I'm sorry."

"What did you do?" Edmond asked.

"Who are you to ask?" Penelon replied, eyeballing Edmond from his boots to his coiffed hair.

"I am a representative of Thomson & French, here to discuss financial matters with your employer," Edmond said, putting as much sneer into his voice as he dared to maintain his disguise. "As a stakeholder in the company, I have every right to ask: what did you do to save the ship?"

"Not that it's any business of some errand boy," Penelon said, puffing out his chest, "but I saw we were carrying too much canvas as soon as we spotted the storm. We took in the studding-sails, stowed the flying jib, but that was too little and too late. We tried lowering the mainsail, taking in two reefs in the topsails, let go the bowlings, hauled the brace, lowered the to-gallant sails, and hauled out the reef-tackles on the yards. It wasn't enough, and we sprung a leak when we hit the storm."

"I see," Edmond said. "Well, that certainly seems to be thorough. Thank you for the report."

Penelon turned his nose up, happy to have shown up an Englishman. For his part, Edmond sat back in his chair, satisfied Penelon appeared to be a conscientious sailor who really had done all he could.

"And nobody else survived?" Morrel asked.

"No, sir," Penelon replied. "Just the six of us. We wouldn't have made it ourselves if La Gironde hadn't picked us up."

Morrel crossed himself and lowered his head. After a moment of silence, he picked up his crutch again and opened the strongbox in the corner of the office.

"You're home now, praise God, and you've more than earned your pay," Morrel said. With his free hand, he took out six pre-measured stacks of banknotes and doled them out to the weary sailors. Some tried to refuse it, since the ship and cargo had sunk, but Morrel wouldn't allow it.

"Whatever comes, nobody will ever say that Morrel & Son reneged on paying their staff," he said.

The sailors murmured their thanks and left, unsure of what else they could say. Morrel sighed as Julie left with them and closed the door, then he returned his attention to Edmond.

"I'm sorry for the interruption; where were we?" Morrel asked.

"Your debts, monsieur," Edmond said. "It seems to me, looking at the sums, that my firm is currently your largest creditor. We are not heartless or cruel; given what I have just seen, I am authorized to extend your bills with no additional interest. How much of a delay do you require?"

"Two months," Morrel said after performing some mental

calculations. "I cannot impose upon your kindness, and two months is the minimum I would need to secure the funding to pay what I owe you."

"Let us be gentlemen and say three months," Edmond said. "Today is June fifth; on September fifth at eleven o'clock, I shall come to collect."

"I shall expect you, and I will pay you," Morrel said. They signed the required paperwork, and Edmond took his leave.

"I will pay you, or I will be dead," Morrel murmured to the empty office.

On the stairs, Edmond met Julie again. After making sure they were alone, he beckoned her to come closer.

"Mademoiselle," Edmond said, "one day within the next few months you will receive a letter from a man called Signor Dimonte. Do exactly what it says, no matter how strange it appears."

Seeing a look of fear on Julie's face, Edmond gave her a warm smile.

"You have nothing to fear, and I swear it will help your father," he said.

"Very well," Julie replied. "I promise."

"Good. Adieu, mademoiselle," Edmond said before taking his leave. He found Penelon and the other sailors in the street, discussing what they could do next.

"You there, Penelon," Edmond called. "You seem like a fine sailor. I have a proposition for you."

CHAPTER 30
THE FIFTH OF SEPTEMBER

Morrel rushed to tell Julie and his wife Sarah about the generosity of Thomson & French, their sole ray of hope in the wake of the loss of the Pharaon. The danger was not past, however. Other creditors still held claim to funds, and they were not so forgiving. It was only by the grace of the Englishman's extension that Morrel was able to meet these other debts at all.

Morrel & Son's only remaining income came from the sale of the dwindling supply of goods already in the warehouse and certain investments they had made in more prosperous years. Even these could not meet their obligations; when the warehouse was empty and the investments sold, the strongbox still did not hold nearly enough to pay the firm of Thomson & French.

The clerk had not appeared in Marseille since his meeting with Morrel, nor had the survivors of the Pharaon. Morrel assumed they had left to find other positions and couldn't fault them for it. After all, he had no other ships to employ them on and no money to buy one.

Throughout July and August Morrel tried anything he could to bring in the money he needed. He had some meagre success renting his warehouse space to other firms, but that only just kept food on his family's table. Sarah sold her services as a seamstress, and Julie earned a few coins scrubbing bedpans at the hospital. Matters reached such a point that even the single-minded Cocles saw in black and white that the company's balances trended into the negative if no new cash flow were realized. They owed four hundred thousand francs; they had perhaps fifteen thousand between them.

Morrel risked a reluctant trip to Paris in a desperate gambit. The Danglars fortune was renowned, and Morrel hoped as a last resort to talk to him. The money he owed to Thomson & French would be nothing to a man like Danglars, after all. Morrel had given Danglars his first job in the shipping industry and hoped that he could appeal to Danglars' sense of gratitude and pity. If that didn't work, he hoped to try to recover the money he suspected Danglars had embezzled from Morrel & Son over the years. Morrel returned from Paris with nothing but dust on his clothes and the humiliating memory of a flat refusal from Baron Danglars.

Despite this, his features bore a peculiar calm. He hugged Sarah and Julie, shook hands with Emmanuel and Cocles, and told them about what had transpired in Paris with a placid smile. His manner worried Sarah, who decided to write to their son Maximilien and tell him to come home. Only twenty-two years old, Maximilien was an enthusiastic and upright young man enrolled in the military college at Paris to become a medic in the army, and had earned a great deal of respect from his father. Whatever happened, Sarah prayed Max could help them through it.

Morrel continued his odd behaviour over the coming days. He ignored his usual routine, spending long hours locked in his office instead. Julie could hear the scratching of his pen through the keyhole and debated using her key to go in and discover what he was writing. When she told her mother, Sarah remembered with dread that he had taken up officially-stamped paper the day before, of the kind used for formal contracts and wills.

Their worry grew stronger when on the afternoon of September third Morrel held Julie close, stared long at Sarah's face, and asked Julie to give him her key to his office. Julie was bewildered and worried, as the key had only ever been taken from her in childhood as a punishment. She pretended she had left it in her room. Morrel did not press the issue.

On the morning of the fifth, the day when the clerk was due to return, Max arrived. While Sarah and Julie were relieved to see him, Morrel received him with a detached pleasantness. As Max and Morrel retired to the office to discuss matters, a stranger arrived with a letter addressed to Julie. In a thick Italian accent, he instructed her to read the letter immediately for the sake of her father. She tore the seal open and read:

Go at once to Number 15 in the Allees de Meillan, and ask the porter to admit you to the room on the fifth floor. There is a red silk purse on the mantel there. Bring it to your father; he must receive it before eleven o'clock.

Remember your promise - Signor Dimonte

With a joyful cry, Julie ran to get Emmanuel. Together they rushed to the Allees de Meillan.

Meanwhile, Morrel explained everything to Maximilien. Max knew that the business was in trouble, but not the extent of it. He met Morrel's eyes and saw the turmoil there, an expression he had seen in hospital patients nearing their breaking point from pain. Max wrapped his arms around his father in a supportive embrace, ignoring Morrel's protests, and noticed an object jabbing into his ribs. Max stepped back and opened his father's coat, revealing a pistol hidden there. For the first time, Morrel's façade of peace broke.

"Have you no respect for a dying man's privacy!" Morrel blurted.

"Father, why do you have that pistol?" Max said, fearing he knew the answer. "Can it really be that bad? Do you have no other options?"

"Of course I don't!" Morrel said. He waved the pistol around the room, and Max fought the urge to duck. "If I had any other option, I wouldn't require this! Cocles will tell me when the clerk from Thomson & French arrives. When he arrives, I shall leave, so to speak."

"But all you face is bankruptcy, Father," Max said in as soothing a tone as he could manage. "Many men have declared bankruptcy throughout history. You wouldn't be the first. Think of Mother and Julie, left here alone. Think of me."

"Declare bankruptcy? I would be the first Morrel to do so." Morrel placed the barrel of the pistol under his chin. "I may not be able to escape dishonour, but I can wash it out with blood."

Seeing that reason would have no impact, Max took a different tactic. He took out his own sidearm and held it up where his father could see.

"Very well. If you pull that trigger, then so will I," Max said. Keeping eye contact with Morrel, Max held his pistol to his own temple. "What will it be, father? Face bankruptcy with your family, or face eternity with me?"

"No!" Morrel shouted. "Maximilien, drop that pistol at once! I am your father, obey me!"

"I will not," Max said in the same even tone. "My fate is locked to yours, and my life is in your hands. What you do, I do."

They stood in a standoff, guns to their heads, Morrel sweating while Max stood dry and still as a statue. The clock in the hall ticked louder than ever before as the hands moved towards eleven o'clock. It rang once, four times, eleven, and the two men still stood in silence. Finally, there was a knock at the door.

"M. Morrel, the agent of Thomson—" Cocles began, oblivious to the peril and tension in the room.

"Father!" Julie cried, bursting into the room with a bundle of red in her hands. Morrel hurried to hide the pistol in his desk drawer and Max dropped his to his side. Julie failed to notice in her excitement.

"Father, you are saved! We are all saved!" Julie said.

"What are you talking about, my dear?" Morrel asked.

He looked closer at the item being presented in Julie's hands. Morrel had a vague remembrance of the red silk purse, and the monogram of his company stood out on the side. With trembling hands he opened the brass closures to find a bill for his entire debt to Thomson & French, marked as paid in full, as well as a diamond the size of a hazelnut and a note which only read "Julie's dowry."

The purse also contained a folded piece of paper, which turned out to be a contract of partnership. The terms were similar to Morrel's near-silent partnership with the late M. Clairmont, though this contract was even more favourable to Morrel himself. They detailed new investment from a man referred to only as Signor Dimonte, along with an address to write to with any questions. Altogether, the contents of the purse were enough not only to save Morrel & Son from bankruptcy, but also to keep it alive long enough to buy a new ship. Morrel felt as though he were waking up from a deep nightmare.

"Where did you find this?" he asked Julie.

"In a house in the Allees de Meillan, on the mantelpiece of a room on the fifth floor," Julie said. She explained the coming of the letter, though she left out that the clerk had told her to expect its arrival. If the man who had arranged their salvation wanted to remain hidden, she would respect his wishes. "Emmanuel came with me to the house, but when I came out he was gone."

"M. Morrel!" Emmanuel gasped as he burst into the office as well. He could get only enough air for a few syllables at a time. "The Pharaon! In harbour! It's impossible!"

Morrel hobbled as fast as he could out of the office and into the street. On the way, he met the clerk from Thomson & French in the vestibule. Before Morrel could say anything, the clerk plucked the receipt of full payment from the purse and gave it a perfunctory glance.

"Everything seems to be in order," Edmond said, stamping the document with a portable seal before tucking it back into the purse and leaving without another word.

Without time to interpret the bizarre scene, Morrel continued to the docks where a ship identical to the Pharaon in every detail weighed anchor. A crowd gathered on the pier to watch with mixed interest and apprehension. Not so long ago, they had faced the constant worry of dead men returning from the sea. An entire dead ship returning was a matter to keep a close eye upon.

The crew of this vessel, thankfully, were very much alive; rather than human flesh, they hungered for the simpler tastes of beer, meat, and cheese. In the hold was the same cargo the original Pharaon had been sent to Calcutta to retrieve, and at the helm was Penelon himself. He made a sign to Morrel to come aboard.

"What is this?" Morrel asked in the privacy of the captain's cabin while the customs officers conducted their inspection.

"Well, sir," Penelon said, "after the first Pharaon sank, me and the men were approached by a man calling himself Dimonte. He seemed to have a great interest in you, sir, and making sure the wrongs done to you were set right."

Overcome with gratitude to the mysterious Signor Dimonte, Morrel shook Penelon's hand with a smile on his face. Together they walked out to the bow and waved at the crowd. One man in particular observed the scene with delight from a secluded corner.

Edmond had learned much from Faria about the strategies and calculations involved in investment, and one of the chief lessons Faria had given him was to never invest based on who your friends were.

Money had a way of tainting friendships, and it should be done only with great caution.

Still, Edmond was confident he had done the right thing. Morrel & Son was a strong company before the Inquisition had crippled it, and he believed it would recover with the new Pharaon and a fresh investor. The trust he had set up to funnel money into Morrel & Son, and to reinvest the profits, represented only a small fraction of Spada's treasure, yet he knew it would be a saving grace for Morrel.

"My last friend in the world has been rewarded for his loyalty," Edmond muttered, unheard by anyone above the din of the port.

His heart resolute, he made his way unnoticed to his yacht moored several berths away and sprang into it with the grace and agility of a veteran sailor.

"Now, I bid farewell to kindness, humanity, and gratitude; I know not when or if I will see them again," he muttered. "The business of reward is done, and now I must begin the enterprise of vengeance."

The yacht set out to sea, bearing with all speed to the island of Monte Cristo. Edmond anchored the boat and ran to the hidden cave. He closed the trapdoor behind him, descended the stairs two at a time, and held the eight-sided amulet above his head as he walked through the grotto.

"Baptistan!" he called, his voice echoing off the dry stone walls. "I am here to claim the power of Monte Cristo!"

"At once, master," Baptistan said without excitement or concern. It beckoned to the stone table. "Please, disrobe and recline upon the work surface."

Edmond did so, discarding his clothing in a pile. In contrast to the warm air of the cave, the stone table stung like ice against his bare skin. Baptistan busied itself mixing a concoction of ingredients from the vials and bottles in one of the cabinets and brought it to Edmond's side.

"Master, this one is obliged to ask if you are certain," Baptistan asked. "Once you decide to undergo the process, it cannot be stopped."

"The dead do not change and neither will I," Edmond said. "Do it."

"Drink this," Baptistan said.

The potion was smooth but bitter, and a peculiar sensation of peace radiated through Edmond from his gut soon after he swallowed it. Baptistan massaged Edmond's skin with perfumed oils; Edmond noticed for the first time that its palms and fingertips were upholstered with supple leather. With a keen blade, Baptistan shaved every inch of Edmond's body hair away, except for that on his head. By the time the process was done, Edmond's body was comfortably numb.

"The elapsed time for the draught to take effect is over," Baptistan said. "The procedure may now begin. Master, this one reminds you that this will hurt."

Without further warning, Baptistan plunged the blade into Edmond's chest, carving deep incisions from each point of his clavicle and the bottom of his abdomen to meet at his sternum. Edmond felt only an unpleasant pressure and a deep itch as Baptistan folded back his flesh to allow access to his entrails. When the wooden hands lifted out a loop of Edmond's intestines to hang from a hook suspended above the table, he noticed a slight tugging sensation from his bowels.

It wasn't until Baptistan cracked his ribs open with a large silver lever that any pain filtered through the chemical haze. As scarab beetles poured out from unseen crevices beneath the table and crawled into his exposed body cavity, Edmond's mind dwelled for a moment on the events which had brought him to such a place. To withstand the worsening agony, he forced himself to focus once more on the faces of his enemies. He swore he would endure, he would survive, and he would bring Hell itself to their doorsteps.

BOOK TWO

THE COUNT OF MONTE CRISTO

CHAPTER 31
SINBAD THE SAILOR

Towards the beginning of 1838, two young men of high Paris society adventured in Italy. One was Franz de Quesnel, Baron d'Epinay, who had lived there for close to four years and agreed to be a guide to his friend Viscount Albert de Morcerf for the Carnival of Rome. Both were in their mid-twenties, a prime age for seeking adventure.

The son of the famous General Fernand de Morcerf, Albert had assumed that his father's name would suffice to secure lodgings during that grand event and left certain planning until the last minute. This left them with reservations for only two bedrooms and a parlour at the Hotel de Londres. The owner, Signor Pastrini, informed them with regret that he had no other accommodations available.

With a few days yet before their rooms would be available, Albert was seized by a whim to visit Naples. Bored of Naples, Franz left Albert to it and hired a boat for a trip to the island of Elba.

Franz made a fine figure standing at the prow of the boat as it glided across the waves, his short sandy hair blowing in the wind. His lineage as part of an old aristocratic family showed itself in his features, delicate almost to the point of being elven. Though he came from a staunch Royalist background, Franz found the usurper's military career and brief return to the throne fascinating.

Some of that interest stemmed from his ancestry. Franz's father, General du Quesnel, was murdered in Paris just before the start of the Hundred Days. The culprit was never apprehended, but everyone knew he was killed by Bonapartists trying to keep Napoleon's pending return a secret. Though Franz had been only two years old when his father died, he felt this pilgrimage was a necessary one.

Franz spent half the day spellbound, walking in the footsteps of that famous former inhabitant and talking to residents who had known him. But Elba was a small island, with only around six hundred inhabitants calling it home after the departure of Napoleon and his guards. Franz soon saw the entirety of it.

The captain Franz had hired, a man named Gaetano, was eager to earn a few more hours' worth of Franz's money. He recommended the hunting on several nearby islands, and Franz made simple work of several pheasants in the afternoon. When he remarked on his desire for a greater challenge, Gaetano suggested the nimble and crafty goats on the island of Monte Cristo.

"I enjoy the sound of these goats, and I'll enjoy the flavour of one even more," Franz said. "To Monte Cristo, then!"

Gaetano gave sign to the men to set a course, then turned back to Franz.

"Your excellency, I should mention that the island is sometimes a refuge for men hiding from the law," Gaetano said. "Smugglers are a decent enough sort of criminal and keep to themselves. But the pirates..."

"Yes, pirates do seem to be a rather different sort of game than goats," Franz said with a frown as the sails filled with wind. "I thought piracy was a problem of the past on the Mediterranean? At any rate, I have heard nobody complain about them."

Some of the nearby crew laughed, and Gaetano cracked a smile.

"They don't often leave anyone behind to complain. When they've taken what they wish from an unfortunate ship, they tie the crew to each other and chop a hole in the vessel's bottom," Gaetano said. "The doomed crew have to decide if they would rather throw themselves into the sea or wait for it to come to them. If they are particularly strong swimmers, they may be lucky for a while. But sooner or later, the sea claims them all, and nobody but God can see where they come to rest."

If he had known this sooner, Franz may have hesitated in visiting the island. Unlike many of his age and status, he wasn't prone to courting danger for a thrill. He was also not prone to displays of cowardice. When danger presented itself, Franz d'Epinay fancied himself a man who would face it and retreat only when necessary. After considering the situation, he waved his hand.

"I've been through Sicily and Calabria without falling prey to pirates. If trouble should appear, I trust in your skills to outrun it," Franz said.

With a favourable wind, the boat made six or seven knots an hour towards the inhospitable peak of Monte Cristo and approached it after dark. The sailors were on constant alert for unwanted visitors, though Franz couldn't tell how they could keep watch in the darkness when his hand was invisible in front of his face. He supposed one learned such things if it meant one's livelihood. In a peculiar way it reminded Franz of the financial tutoring his uncle had insisted he take.

"Seven of every ten great families lose their wealth in the second generation, thanks to the poor decisions of impulsive sons, and the name of d'Epinay will not suffer that fate," his old uncle had often said. Franz bore a great responsibility to his family name, as his father's assassination and his mother's death in childbirth left him as the last of the Quesnel line.

A spark of light in the darkness interrupted Franz's thoughts. Franz asked Gaetano about it and was shushed.

"Keep your voice down, excellency," Gaetano whispered. "The island is not so deserted as we thought tonight. If they are simple smugglers, they will bring us no harm. Patience."

The crew maneuvered the ship closer to land without a sound, and Gaetano lowered himself into the sea to swim for shore. Afraid and excited in equal measure, Franz took the time to examine his weapons: two double-barreled hunting guns and a rifle, along with his customary dagger. For half an hour nobody spoke, until soft splashing reached the boat and Gaetano returned.

"Spanish smugglers," Gaetano said with relief in his voice. "They have with them two Corsicans on the run from the law."

"I thought smugglers ferried goods from place to place, not people," Franz said.

"It's not so strange as you think," Gaetano explained. "A man on the run from the law often catches sight of a vessel with good fellows on board and comes to seek hospitality. It is bad form to refuse help to some poor hunted devil, and the vessel can carry them away to pursue their life and liberty for another day. Often they pay back the kindness by suggesting some safe spot for the good fellows to land unobserved."

"Indeed, and I suppose such good fellows have ways to recognized each other when they meet at a deserted island in the middle of the night?" Franz said with a smile, guessing that island tours were not Gaetano's only source of income. "No matter, we must all eat somehow. Will it be safe to land?"

"Very safe, excellency," Gaetano replied. "The outlaws, I think they are quite harmless as well. They broke some law in Greece against trading on a holy day, they say."

"That's hardly a reason to become a fugitive," Franz said.

"The difficulty came when they refused to pay the fine," Gaetano said. "In Greece, refusal to pay a fine is grounds for arrest. When the carabineers come to arrest you, they have license to kill you if you resist."

"Isn't that simply how any law works? How else would you enforce them?" Franz said. "I don't think that's unique to Greece, although I've never heard it spelled out that way before."

"As you say, excellency," Gaetano said, inclining his head.

Franz considered the situation. He knew very little about Gaetano, who could be luring him into a trap. Franz decided the situation was too elaborate to be a ruse; plus, he had come so far in his little adventure that to change course now would be silly.

The boat drew close enough to shore for Franz to see half a dozen men seated around a fire. Gaetano sang the chorus of a fishing shanty and the crew followed suit. The song appeared to be a signal, and the men on shore approached the beach.

The landing was made politely, both sides displaying their weaponry to ensure no misunderstandings. Gaetano introduced Franz only as a Frenchman travelling for pleasure. One of the smugglers left to bring this news further inland. Another led them not to their fire, but to another small clearing ringed by rocks cut to resemble low chairs.

A pile of cinders in the centre of the clearing told Franz the clearing must be a popular resting-place for visitors to the island. The sailors kindled their own fire to roast some of Franz's birds, while Franz could smell the smugglers cooking goat and considered offering a trade. Soon the smuggler who had gone inland returned.

"Our chief is quite excited to learn that a Frenchman visits our island," the smuggler said. "He invites you to dine with him. The only condition is that you consent to be blindfolded on the way."

"A house, on this rock? How peculiar," Franz said. "Gaetano, do you know anything about this chief? Is this wise?"

Gaetano and the crew were eager to offer rumours about the mysterious smuggler chief with the secret home on Monte Cristo. He was known only as Sinbad the Sailor, but lived a double life travelling the world disguised as a dandy. He used that disguise to take justice into his own hands, snatching criminals from under the nose of the law and deciding himself whether their lives deserved be saved or forfeit. One story went that Sinbad rescued a man from prison, only to pluck out the criminal's eyes in an unfamiliar land as a more fitting punishment. Another claimed Sinbad bought slaves from the Arabian chattel markets, only to set them free in more forward-thinking nations.

Some said Sinbad's house was a mansion camouflaged among the rocks, others said it was a subterranean palace dug out by a thousand blind servants. Some said he had a magnificent gentleman's yacht, others that he rode through the sea on the back of a giant tortoise. None of these wild and conflicting stories portrayed Sinbad as the sort to lure an innocent man into danger.

"Lead the way," Franz said to the smuggler.

With the blindfold secure around his eyes, the smugglers led Franz further inland. He kept his bearings for a time until his guides gave him several quick spins in each direction. A change in the air around him suggested that they entered a cave, and he heard the crackling of another fire. The air changed again, warm with a hint of perfume in the air. His feet trod upon plush carpet, and his guides released his arms.

"Welcome, monsieur. Please, you may remove your blindfold," said a rough but amicable voice in excellent French and a strange but pleasing accent.

CHAPTER 32
THE ENCHANTED GROTTO

F ranz saw before him a man in his late thirties or early forties. The man wore some costume of the middle East: yellow embroidered slippers with curled toes, white pantaloons billowed at the ankles and bound by a red sash at the waist. He wore a black vest, also embroidered, over a white silk shirt. On his head sat a red fez cap with a long blue tassel.

As his gaze reached the cap, Franz allowed himself a double-take at his host's face. The man's irises were a deep red, like firelight viewed through a glass of Bordeaux wine. While the features of his face were dignified, the skin was starkly white. This was not the ordinary paleness of a man who avoids the sun, but rather the pure white of talcum.

Franz had heard of albinos, men and women with stark white skin and hair along with red eyes, but the stranger's jet-black hair and goatee suggested otherwise. His skin had that sun-weathered texture of men who spend their lives on the sea, but without any of the colour which comes with that life. It almost seemed that his skin was made of fine white leather.

Aside from those oddities, the stranger was certainly a handsome man. His unusual eyes sparkled and his smile revealed brilliant white teeth. Despite the warmth of the cave, the man's face was the only skin exposed anywhere on his person. His shirt reached to his wrists, he wore delicate black gloves, and a red cravat matching his fez hid his throat.

The chamber around them was decorated in a tasteful blend of Eastern styles, with crimson brocade and Arabian swords in silver scabbards on the walls. A divan sat in a recess, and a fine Venetian-glass lamp cast its glow across the thick Turkish carpet on the floor. Egyptian tapestries portraying scarab beetles and their jackal-headed god hung at the far end of the room, among other tapestries from lands Franz couldn't identify.

"I apologize for the precautions. Much of the year, this island remains deserted. If the secret of my grotto were discovered, I would arrive one day to find it plundered to the bare walls," the stranger said with a laugh. "Let me repay you for that breach of etiquette with a good meal and a comfortable bed."

"Make no apologies, good sir," Franz said. "I understand the impulse to have a secret refuge where none can find you; I often think of renting an apartment in Naples and giving nobody the address. Besides, your home is so enchanting that I feel as though I've entered the tale of the Arabian Nights!"

The stranger nodded his thanks. "Secret though this place is, it is always gratifying to hear the praise of visitors. Now, Ali, is supper ready?"

One of the many tapestries moved aside, and a Nubian servant in a plain white tunic and trousers entered to beckon them into the dining room without a word.

"While I won't pry and ask your true name or title," the stranger asked, "it can be annoying to spend more than an hour in a man's company and not know what to call him. People generally refer to me as Sinbad the Sailor; what shall I call you?"

"Considering our surroundings, I see no reason why I shouldn't be called Aladdin!" Franz said with a smile.

"Excellent," Sinbad said. "Then, Monsieur Aladdin, let's adjourn to the dining room."

Franz followed Sinbad through the hidden door and beheld a splendidly-covered table laden with roasted goat, a ham with jelly, and a gigantic lobster on silver dishes. Smaller vessels held fruit from around the Mediterranean, sauces and gravies, and olives. Marble columns adorned with bas-reliefs stood around the room. Ali served them alone and did such a fine job of it that Franz needed to voice his compliments.

"Ah yes, faithful Ali," Sinbad remarked. "He is a poor devil quite devoted to me for saving, if not his life, at least much of it. In his homeland, he crossed a well-connected man. For this, he was sentenced to have his tongue cut out, then his hands cut off the next evening, and his manhood torn off on the third day at sundown."

"What barbarism!" Franz said.

"I discovered his plight and bought his freedom," Sinbad said. "Unfortunately, I didn't arrive until the morning of the second day."

Smiling, Ali juggled a pair of kumquats before making them dance across the backs of his knuckles. Franz was surprised by Sinbad's casual tone when he told this tale of cruelty and salvation and tried to return the conversation to a less grave track.

"I have heard rumours that, like that famous sailor whose name you use, you are an avid traveler?" Franz asked.

"Oh, yes. I made a vow long ago when it seemed unlikely that I could accomplish it, and have made some others which I hope to fulfill as well," Sinbad said. He continued to smile, but his red eyes flashed with a brief ferocity. "I come and go as I please, with devoted servants who love me for reasons beyond their salaries. Sometimes I deliver some wrongly-named criminal from the grasp of the law, other times I see that a punishment is not severe enough and correct that as well. It is the happiest existence I can imagine."

Franz noticed small glimpses of a quiet rage slip through Sinbad's relaxed calm and suspected that some dreadful persecution in his host's past prevented it from being such a happy life as he said. For the sake of politeness, he decided against pressing the matter and instead continued his meal.

"This food is superb, better than any restaurant in Paris," he said.

"Paris, the city of light! Someday I shall journey there myself," Sinbad said. "Soon, I hope. It all depends on circumstances, which depend on arrangements, which depend in no small part on chance."

"When you do come to Paris, I hope to see you there. Though I have no subterranean palace of my own, I can try to repay the hospitality you've shown me," Franz said. "I plan to stay in Rome a while longer, but I need to return to Paris at some point; I'm engaged to be married."

"Marriage? Congratulations, Aladdin. As for your invitation, I should enjoy nothing more," Sinbad said.

Though Franz ate with gusto, he noticed that Sinbad touched very little; hardly enough to say that he ate anything at all. When the meal was cleared away, Ali brought in a small covered silver cup. Franz lifted the cover to inspect the dish, and Sinbad watched him intently. A pale green paste sat within, like fruit preserves but with an unfamiliar aroma.

"Can you guess what it is?" Sinbad asked.

Franz shook his head.

"Nothing less than ambrosia from Olympus," Sinbad said. "One spoonful will take you to the ends of the earth. If you love money, it transports you to El Dorado. If you're a poet, it brings you to a land of inspiration like you've never seen. If you're ambitious, it will make you a king; religious, it will introduce you to God."

Sinbad took a teaspoonful of the magic paste and savoured it on his tongue before swallowing with eyes half shut. His miraculous description reminded Franz of some artists he had met in Venice, and he could guess what the paste really was.

"Hashish! I have heard tell of it, though never tried it," Franz said. "It is illegal in France and Italy, I thought."

"Highly illegal. This is the purest hashish from Alexandria," Sinbad said. "Bring it to any shore within a week's journey of here, and we'll have broken the law; in fact, as this island is technically a part of Tuscany, we're breaking it now."

A chill went up Franz's spine, but his resolution to see this adventure through stood firm.

"Well, I see no other option but to see for myself if this magical herb is as much as you say," Franz declared as he took a spoonful.

The bitter and astringent taste shocked him, reminding him of his first time tasting black chai tea as a child. Sinbad led him to another chamber, a round room encircled with a low divan where every surface was covered in animal pelts. Maned lions from the Serengeti, striped Bengal tigers, Siberian bears, and Norse foxes represented only a small portion of the menagerie. Elegant Turkish tobacco pipes lay within easy reach, prepared by Ali who began to prepare coffee as well.

The sweet aroma of burning tobacco, one of the great simple pleasures of civilized life, filled the room. Franz and Sinbad continued their conversation, returning to the topic of travel and places they had been. Despite Sinbad's clear advantage over Franz in terms of experience, he expressed genuine interest in Franz's perspective on the world. The coffee arrived as Franz's head swam from the hashish.

"Turkish coffee, Turkish pipes, Turkish tobacco," Sinbad said. "The Orientals are the only men who truly know how to live, I think. When I'm finished in Paris, I think I'll go and spend the rest of eternity in the

East. If you wish to find me again you would do well to start looking in Cairo or Shanghai."

"I could take you there myself this instant," Franz said, fascinated by the touch of a bearskin's fur. "I feel wings like an eagle spreading out from my shoulders, strong enough to carry us around the globe in a day."

"The hashish is taking effect! Worry not, my young friend," Sinbad laughed. "Ali and I will be your guides and watch over you. Fly as high as you like, and we will catch you if you fall."

Franz surrendered to the strange sensation which carried off all the physical fatigue of the day. His perception brightened, and he could count every hair on every animal skin in the room if he wished. Franz even imagined he saw a deep glow emerging from behind Sinbad's red eyes.

Sinbad continued to speak to him, soothing words with no sound in them, as Franz's mind left his body to sail upward through the stone above his head. In the sky, he spun and pirouetted above the peak of Monte Cristo, then sailed across the sea to Paris, to Florence, to Rome. He could see Albert, chasing women and smoking cigars.

Franz did not realize he was narrating his adventure as he flew, or that Sinbad listened to his every word. He did not notice Baptistan enter the room, nor the questions Sinbad asked about the Viscount Albert de Morcerf. Whether due to the hashish or the odd glow in Sinbad's eyes, these memories slipped away from Franz's mind as soon they occurred. This caused him no worry at all, and he sank into a restful sleep in a seamless transition from hallucination to dream.

CHAPTER 33
THE WAKING

Franz woke up to warm sunlight and the buzzing of grasshoppers rather than Sinbad's magnificent grotto. He found himself in a much smaller cavern, laying on a bed of fragrant heather and sheltered by a simple wooden door with a grated window. The door had no latch and opened with a gentle push.

His visions from the night before had become dim and indistinct, and even the fantastic dinner felt like a dream. Franz stepped out into the sun and saw Gaetano's ship still waiting where they had landed the previous night. A yacht pulled away from the island in the distance, near enough that Franz could use his pocket telescope to recognize Sinbad standing tall at the helm.

Franz held on to a vague memory of Ali presenting the cup of hashish and was surprised by how refreshed he felt. Unlike any of the times when he and his friends had drunk wine late into the night, his head was clear and his step was light. Gaetano relayed a message from Sinbad that he regretted not saying goodbye in person, but urgent business had called him away.

Of course, curiosity seized Franz and he insisted on searching the rocky space where he had awoken for any sign of a hidden door. The sailors humoured him, knowing that many had done exactly the same and never found the entrance to Sinbad's retreat. Like all those others, Franz found nothing.

"I wonder what the authorities think of Sinbad in the countries where he practices his hobby?" Franz said to Gaetano.

Gaetano laughed. "Why would he care what they think of him? That yacht of his is more like a bird that can beat any frigate on the open sea. Plus, a man like him can find friends at any coast and disappear anywhere he likes."

It was clear to Franz that the mysterious Sinbad was on excellent terms with smugglers across the length and breadth of the Mediterranean, with all the privileges that included. As for Franz, his fancy for goat-hunting had passed after his hashish experience. They returned to the mainland where Franz caught the mail-coach to meet Albert in Rome for Carnival.

Carnival was a long-standing tradition in the Catholic world, a week-long celebration culminating in a flurry of activity on Shrove Tuesday. Though Carnival was observed across the globe, the grandest by far was in Rome. During Carnival, Rome would discard its reputation of a sombre city of prayer and reflection. The week before Lent, Carnival was a last chance for physical indulgence before the fasting period meant to purify the soul. Men and women from all around wore costumes of all kinds to have fun and engage in grand misadventures. This made it no easy task for Franz to reach the Hotel de Londres.

When he arrived at last, he found Viscount Albert de Morcerf lounging in the hotel lobby reading a newspaper. Albert's Spanish complexion and wavy dark hair made him easy to spot. Albert made no sign that he saw Franz, but set the paper aside and lit one of his ever-present cigars.

Some of the other patrons took excited notice of him when they saw how he lit the tobacco. First he made a loose fist, then flicked his thumb upward and produced a small flame at the end of it. The novelty of this trick had worn off somewhat for Franz; Albert was descended from the Catalans of Marseille, and like many of them, had a talent for magic. Albert had inherited not just his father's strong chin, but also his gift of flame.

Albert could light his cigar with no spectacle if he chose, but he still found the flourish just as amusing as when he had first thought of it. Albert leaned back to puff smoke rings into the air and spotted Franz as he did so. Albert's jovial features lit up with a wide grin.

"Franz, my dear fellow, where have you been? It feels like I've been waiting in this lobby for a fortnight," Albert said. The skinny viscount gave Franz a tight hug. "Let's get to our rooms and get you unpacked, then see what Carnival has to offer!"

Their apartment consisted of two small bedrooms and a parlour which looked out over the street and the festivities below. By good fortune, the parade of *Mortirevolta* would pass beneath them.

The parade began with a group of Carnival-goers dressed in rags and grey face-paint assembling at one plaza and pretending to be the undead, grabbing bystanders who then were obligated to join their ranks as they spread out across the city.

At another plaza, a militia of people in French military costumes gathered around an actor portraying Napoleon. With pistols equipped to fire harmless paint, this army would march towards the undead to do battle. This loose re-enactment of Bonaparte's liberation of Rome had become one of the focal points of Carnival.

"Be careful Franz," Albert said with an elbow to his friend's ribs. "If the League catches wind of you enjoying the parade, they'll revoke your membership!"

"Very funny," Franz said, rolling his eyes. He touched the chain hanging from his waistcoat. At the end of it, next to his watch, was the pendant signifying him as a Steel Brother of the Eternal Royalist League; not the lowest rank for nobility in the League, but also not high enough to be privy to the private meetings and ceremonies of Silver members and above.

A girl in the hotel's red bellhop uniform brought Franz's bags, accompanied by Signor Pastrini. Pastrini apologized again about the meagre accommodations, but the rest of the floor was rented by a very rich gentleman who he guessed was either Sicilian or Maltese.

"Very fascinating," Albert said, "but we are both famished. We must have some supper immediately. Once that's sorted, secure us a carriage for the week."

"Supper will be available post-haste," Pastrini said, "but the carriage will be impossible to provide."

Albert rolled his eyes and puffed a small cloud of smoke.

"Alright, alright. What sum will remove the insurmountable barriers standing between us and our carriage?" Albert stuck his cigar between his teeth and pulled out a roll of banknotes.

If the carriage weren't vital for the Carnival experience, Franz would have laughed. Being a creature of Paris and not knowing Italy as Franz did, Albert had heard the word "impossible" and interpreted it as "requires a larger tip."

The carriage really was essential, and Franz regretted leaving Albert in charge of it. First, it would provide easy passage through the city as the crowd parted before their horses. Second, it would provide a vantage point where one could see everything and be seen by other Carnival-goers. Franz reminded himself that Albert was two years his junior and less experienced with the world in general.

Eventually, Pastrini convinced Albert he was not fishing for a gratuity and that getting a carriage or horses really was impossible. Albert sulked for a moment, then clapped his hands together.

"Right, well, this will work itself out. Everything always does! Let's eat!" he said.

Secure in the philosophy that the right connections and a full purse would always win the day, Albert ate a hearty meal and looked forward to Carnival.

CHAPTER 34
A TALE OF ROMAN BANDITS

Franz and Albert discovered over breakfast the next day that the matter of a carriage was not quite so bad as they feared. There were still no carriages available for the final three days of Carnival, which Albert remarked were the most important days to have a carriage. However, carriages in the preceding days would be merely difficult to find rather than impossible. Without giving Albert a chance to complain, Franz asked Pastrini to arrange whatever he could get.

"Well, this is a nice sort of place. No carriages when they are most needed, leaving us to scamper about on foot like law clerks! There ought to be a law," Albert said as he lit another cigar.

"Or perhaps you should have written ahead to make the proper arrangements when you said you would," Franz said.

"How could I know how ignorant Italians are to the fine art of bribery?" Albert asked. "If we were in Paris, this entire situation would have played out far differently."

Franz surrendered the possibility of Albert owning up to his mistake and accepted in his own mind that he was partly at fault as well. If he had wanted to be sure of having a carriage, he should have done it himself. While Albert made a fine companion for finding memorable entertainment and good food, he had a reputation for being fun rather than being reliable for good reason.

By mid-morning, Pastrini found them a carriage to rent for the day. The main festivities had yet to begin, so Franz escorted Albert around the city for sightseeing. The splendor of Saint Peter's Basilica took even Albert's breath away. Franz had read stories where the hero is said to have seen something so beautiful that it moved him to tears and had experienced the sensation himself in only two places: Westminster

Abbey in London and Saint Peter's in Rome. The scope of the place overwhelmed the senses, filling the visitor with an awareness of how much effort and planning and artistry were devoted to creating such a place. Franz doubted that even the staunchest atheist could visit such a place without a stirring in their heart.

They spent a contemplative day there, then returned to the hotel to dine and freshen up for the evening. Franz wanted to show Albert the Colosseum at night, when the ruined walls loomed and every corner held untold mysteries. His idea was to take a route outside the walls of Rome and back in again through the Porta San Giovanni, keeping them away from other famous ruins of the Empire to give the Colosseum opportunity to shine. Franz had never tried taking such a route before but was hopeful for its success. Despite his annoyance with Albert over the matter of the carriage, Franz was determined to give him a memorable first impression of Rome. As they discussed their plans, Pastrini entered.

"Excellencies, your carriage-driver told me the route you plan to take tonight," Pastrini said. "You absolutely cannot travel outside the walls of the city at night. It is not safe on account of the infamous bandit Luigi Vampa."

"If he is so infamous, why have I never heard of him?" Albert scoffed.

"Vampa is a notorious bandit chief at only twenty-two years old, feared all around Rome. His band attacks any well-appointed carriage they find after sunset and demands to know who the occupants are and how they made their fortune. If they dislike the answer, they are robbed or taken hostage," Pastrini explained. "Very few have ever convinced him they should be allowed to pass unharmed."

"How is he to know if his victims are lying?" Albert laughed. "My income originates from my father's fortune as a general and senator, but I could just as easily say that I'm a butcher."

"He travels with a woman who he calls his queen, named Teresa, who has the Sight of Cassandra," Pastrini said. "She can look at a man and know the truth in his heart, they say. And unlike poor Cassandra, Vampa believes every word she says."

"This story gets better and better!" Albert smiled. Before Pastrini could notice Albert's mockery, Franz prompted him to tell them more.

Vampa had grown up as a poor shepherd's boy, Pastrini revealed, and the beautiful Teresa also tended the sheep on the next farm over. A severe young man with ambition beyond sheep, Vampa decided to craft his own destiny. He paid the local priest to teach him to read and write and from there taught himself to draw. When he sold some drawings and bought a knife, he taught himself how to carve. When he sold his carvings, he had a considerable amount of gold for a shepherd's boy.

"How do you know all of this?" Albert said.

"I grew up in his village," Pastrini said. "He had few friends, but everyone knew him."

Pastrini continued with his tale. Vampa's employer gave him an old rifle to fend off a pack of wild drakes which had been attacking flocks in the area. With his usual intensity and practise, Vampa could soon fire from the hip and put a rifle-ball through a crow's eye at the very limit of the gun's range.

As intimidating as Vampa was, Teresa could always bring out his softer side. In love since childhood, Vampa did everything he could to bring her the finery he knew she deserved. She did not yet have the Sight; this came to her later.

When Vampa and Teresa were eighteen and hoping to be married, a gang of bandits roamed into the area. Their chief, a villain named Cucumetto, was rumoured to be a demon with unholy appetites. Horrible rumours swirled about what happened to the women he abducted in the time it took for their ransom to arrive, and many believed the ones who died were luckier for it.

One day, Vampa and Teresa were tending their flocks in the hills when a ruddy-faced man in fine clothes and a wide-brimmed hat hurried towards them. Knowing a secret place among the rocks, they allowed him to take shelter there just before a pair of *carabinieri* arrived on horseback asking about a fugitive bandit, none other than Cucumetto himself.

With no love for policemen and no knowledge yet of the rumours, Vampa claimed not to have seen the fugitive, and the carabinieri went on their way. Cucumetto emerged from hiding just after they left, thanked Vampa with words and gold, and went on his way with many backwards glances at the fair Teresa.

Life continued as normal for the two lovers for a while. One day,

Vampa completed an exquisite carving of an eagle which he sold to a census clerk passing through the village. He brought this money straight to the dressmaker's shop.

When he next saw Teresa, he carried a splendid gown in his arms—her wedding dress, if she would have him. Overjoyed, Teresa took the dress to their secret place in the rocks to change, and Vampa waited outside.

As Vampa waited, a well-dressed traveler passed by who seemed lost; seeing a chance to earn a fee, Vampa offered to guide him. Vampa walked alongside the man's horse for ten or fifteen minutes to make sure he stayed on the correct road, his rifle slung over his shoulder as a matter of cautious habit.

When no more chance for the traveler to mistake his way remained, he gave Vampa a gift of three jewels, far exceeding the value of the short work of guiding him. Vampa's honour wouldn't let him accept such overpayment, and he insisting the man take a fine dagger which Vampa had engraved himself. The traveler asked Vampa his name, and then introduced himself as Sinbad the Sailor.

Franz swallowed hard. "Sinbad the Sailor, did you say?"

"Yes, excellency," Pastrini said. "This part of the story I did not hear until very recently, when I had the misfortune to be accosted by Vampa myself; thankfully, he recognized me from our youth and sent me on my way unmolested."

"It's a fine name, I did enjoy the stories of that fabled figure's journeys in my youth," Albert said. "I should take on a nickname, Hercules or Mercury perhaps. Or Vulcan!"

Albert conjured a globe of fire the size of a tangerine and held it aloft for a moment, before clapping his hands together and extinguishing it to Pastrini's great relief.

"Proceed, please," Franz said.

After parting ways with Sinbad, Vampa returning to Teresa's makeshift changing-room. He heard a faint cry before he could reach it; listening carefully, he could distinguish his name.

Vampa cocked his rifle and ran to the top of the hill for a better vantage point. A man carried Teresa away towards the woods, too far for Vampa to hope to catch him. With only one option, Vampa steadied his rifle and took aim. The ball flew on a straight path into the kidnapper's back; the dying man collapsed on top of Teresa.

"The *strega* say that under certain conditions, when the planets align just so, and a woman locks eyes with a dying man who means her harm as he breathes his death rattle, the secrets of the world are revealed to her," Pastrini said. "Whether you believe that or not, it was then that Teresa's gift awoke."

When Vampa arrived to haul the corpse off of Teresa, he recognized the kidnapper as Cucumetto. In a moment of inspiration, Vampa stripped the body and took Cucumetto's gold, weapons, and wide-brim hat for himself. He and Teresa made their way into the woods to find the bandit camp, marched into it, and declared themselves the new king and queen of the group.

The bandits laughed at first, until they realized that Vampa had gotten the better of their chief. They soon recognized him as their superior in every respect that mattered. He reformed their practices immediately; the wanton ravaging and plunder of Cucumetto was replaced with the methodical raids of Luigi Vampa.

When Pastrini finished his story, Franz gave Albert a look.

"Well Albert, what do you think now of Luigi Vampa?" Franz asked.

"I think he makes for a marvelous tale, particularly with a good meal," Albert said through a cloud of sweet tobacco smoke. "And I think we had better be on our way to the Colosseum if we are to see it tonight at all."

"Will your excellencies be travelling there beyond the walls or through the streets?" Pastrini asked.

"*Mon dieu*, after that tale, by the streets of course!" Franz said. Albert rolled his eyes, but didn't protest.

Pastrini looked relieved. "Very good. I will give your carriage-driver a safer route which I believe will suit you."

As the young men climbed into their carriage, Albert permitted himself a chuckle.

"Really Franz, I thought you had more courage," Albert said. "You will never have any adventures if you don't take any risks!"

CHAPTER 35
THE COLOSSEUM

Pastrini's route was just as good as Franz hoped. They reached the Colosseum without passing any other ruins, keeping Albert's visual palate clean. The only sour note was a traffic jam caused by city guards dispersing revelers who'd started a mild panic by getting an early start on the *Mortirevolta*.

The delay allowed Franz time to think about the story of Luigi Vampa and the appearance in it of Sinbad the Sailor. Was it mere coincidence that the man from Monte Cristo appeared on that hillside by chance, at just the right time to distract Vampa and bring him into conflict with Cucumetto? Nothing seemed outside the realm of possibility for the enigmatic Sinbad. Franz's questions multiplied like rabbits, while the answers were as reluctant to reproduce as the giant pandas of the Orient.

The sight of the dark, frowning ruins of the Colosseum distracted Franz from these thoughts. Moonlight played through the surviving windows and crumbled openings, inviting the travelers to venture into a true relic of the ancient world. Crossing the threshold of the Colosseum appeared to be some sort of summoning ritual, causing a multitude of guides to emerge from the shadows.

Franz was happy to pay one of them to lead the way and explain the history and construction of the Colosseum. Franz had heard it all seven or eight times, but Albert was engrossed and unusually attentive. Franz slipped away from the chattering guide to find his own way and some reflective quiet.

He found a stairway opposite a large aperture which gave him an undisturbed view of the vastness of the building. Within a quarter-hour, he heard furtive footsteps approaching and withdrew further into the darkness to not be seen.

A man stepped into the moonlight wearing a thick brown mantle that hid the lower portion of his face and a wide hat which concealed the rest. His finely-cut trousers and black leather boots suggested a wealthy man, but offered no other clues.

Soon another noise drew both the stranger's and Franz's attention, heralding the arrival of another guest. This newcomer was dressed for the Carnival in purple Egyptian robes, with his hands and head wound tight in linen bandages, and a gold mask painted like the face on a pharaoh's coffin.

"I came here directly from the Castle of St. Angelo, your excellency," said the first stranger from beneath his wide hat, his accent revealing him as a native of Rome. "There was some difficulty in reaching Beppo, but his usual bribe produced the required information."

"Beppo is an informant of yours?" said the costumed man in a perfect Tuscan dialect.

"I always maintain contacts capable of reaching the prison, in case I ever find myself there," the Roman said. "Beppo told me that two executions are scheduled for the day after tomorrow at two o'clock. One is of a convicted murderer, sentenced to be *annegamento*. The other is Peppino, and if we do nothing he will be *decapitato*."

Franz recognized the word *decapitato* as beheading, but the word for the murderer's fate was not in his vocabulary.

"You've inspired the government of Rome with such extreme fear that they're happy to make an example," the Tuscan said, crossing his arms. "Peppino's only crime was providing your band with food, and they'll kill him for it. His death will be more merciful than yours would if they caught you; I suppose that with one *annegamento* already on the program, they wish to keep the entertainment varied."

"They'll have more entertainment than they bargained for," the Roman said with his hand on his dagger. "I would be a true coward if I stood by and allowed Peppino to die for helping me. I'll surround the scaffold with twenty of my best men, rush the guards when Peppino is brought out, and carry him away."

The Tuscan laughed. "My friend, I worry that you've grown too accustomed to overwhelming force being your only tool," he said. "When one only has a hammer, the world starts to look like a nail."

"And what does your excellency suggest?" the Roman asked.

"A more elegant solution. For two thousand piastres, I purchase a delay of execution for Peppino. During that time, another thousand piastres will see to it that he can escape," the Tuscan said. "Gold is not just a means to buy goods and services, my friend; it is also the most capable tool in the world to settle difficulties without violence."

"Forgive me, you know I am utterly devoted to your service," the Roman said, shifting his weight. "But I have never seen gold stop a rifle-ball or a blade. I'll feel better with my men ready in case your plan is unsuccessful."

The Tuscan waved one bandaged hand dismissively, the fingers wound with great care to hide the skin underneath. Franz thought Albert would find such dedication to a costume impressive in the extreme.

"Take whatever precautions you wish, but my solution will work. I've rented the three lower windows above the Cafe Rospoli, look for a signal there," the Tuscan said. "If I've secured Peppino's pardon, the windows will be hung with green curtains. Otherwise, if I fail, the curtains will be red and you may storm the scaffolding as you see fit."

The Roman began to speak, but the Tuscan raised a finger to silence him.

"Listen! Tourists are coming. It's better that you are not recognized and we are not seen together," the Tuscan said. "When one keeps their allies secret, it is easier to take one's enemies by surprise. Remember: the lower windows above the Cafe Rospoli."

The Tuscan stepped backward into a shadowed alcove and disappeared. The Roman pulled his mantle closer around his face and proceeded in the other direction. Franz dared not move in case either man remained near enough to hear him, but soon Albert and the guide approached in a circle of warm torchlight.

All the way back to the hotel, Albert entertained himself with reciting the facts and history the guide had told him. Franz let him speak, eager to be alone in his bedroom to think about what he had heard.

The Roman was an utter stranger to him. On the other hand, the bandaged Tuscan had made too strong of an impression on Franz for him to ever forget that voice. Though he had not used a Tuscan accent the first time they met, Franz recognized the voice of his host from Monte Cristo, Sinbad the Sailor.

Franz pursued sleep in vain that night. The stories of Sinbad's singular hobby, spiriting smugglers and outlaws from one shore to another, had been one thing. It was altogether different to hear him offer to spend three thousand piastres in bribes with armed bandits as a backup plan. Sinbad had presented himself as carefree and eccentric in the grotto, but Franz grew to believe the man may be dangerous. Sleep did not come to Franz until the early hours of the morning, and he slept late in turn.

Like a true born and bred Parisian, Albert spent his morning in arranging the evening's entertainment. Franz left him the carriage for the day while he wrote some necessary letters, and when Albert returned he had secured them a box at the Teatro Argentina for the opera that night.

Albert was quite satisfied as he lit a cigar, having left his calling card throughout the most fashionable parts of Rome and secured more invitations than they could possibly accept. He also claimed to have seen every remarkable sight in Rome; Franz didn't comment that the feat would have taken him at least two weeks. Albert had also neglected to learn a single detail about the opera to be performed that night; for him, the most important part of the opera was to be seen in a fashionable box and attract some cultured feminine attention.

Franz smirked. Though Albert made jokes to cover his embarrassment, Franz knew his friend hadn't yet secured a single romantic liaison during his European tour, and the failure grated at Albert's every nerve. Albert de Morcerf considered himself to be the finest modern example of Parisian manhood and found it baffling that the mere fact of being a wealthy viscount did not tempt the women of Italy to disregard their husbands and lovers for an affair with him.

Albert was even more baffled by their lack of interest in the Catalan Flamekeeper tradition; most Italian women he met either didn't believe him or care that it destined him for greatness. While his gift made for a fine party trick and had lured many young ladies to compromising situations in Paris, it was greeted with mere curiosity in Italy. Albert had therefore resolved he would rectify this situation during the Carnival and find some beautiful woman looking for a last indulgence before Lent. He was determined, in his words, to plant the flag of Morcerf in Italian soil.

Franz learned for himself that the opera to be played was Parisina performed by Coselli, Moiani, and La Specchia. Albert was oblivious to their good fortune, but they had an advantageous box from which to hear one of Italy's great composers sung by three of the country's finest vocalists. Franz marveled at how Albert could arrange such a thing by accident while still being capable of failing to arrange their carriage ahead of time. It was, he had to admit, part of Albert's charm.

Albert, for the most part, ignored the goings-on of the stage in favour of peering into the crowd with his opera-glasses and attempting to catch the attention of every attractive woman he saw, with no success. His antics did draw the eye of a countess whom Franz knew from Paris and who recognized him as well. She waved for them to come join her at the intermission.

"You know that beauty?" Albert said, flabbergasted. "My goodness, look at her! Is she French?"

"No, she is Venetian. Have you not met Countess Garzone?" Franz asked.

"Ah, I recognize the name but have never seen her face!" Albert said. "I was meant to meet her at Mother's winter ball, but I was indisposed with a lovely servant girl and missed her entirely."

Franz rolled his eyes. "Well, come along. She's invited us over, so you have no excuse to miss her again."

Albert seized his hat with excitement and passed his fingers through his hair. Franz led the way to Countess Garzone's box while Albert continued fussing with his collar and lapels. Franz presented Albert as one of the most distinguished young men in all of Parisian society. Franz did not exaggerate on behalf of his friend; back home, Albert really was cited as a model example of what a young man should be.

Countess Garzone gave them a gracious welcome and was soon engrossed in conversation with Albert about the latest developments in

Paris. Franz left them to it and took a chair on the other side of the box in order to watch the ballet when the curtain next rose. A common feature of Italian operas at the time, the ballet provided the singers an intermission to rest their voices between acts. While waiting for the curtain to rise, Franz took the opportunity to scan the other boxes. After all, it was still Carnival, and he was nothing if not a man.

CHAPTER 36
THE VAMPIRE

In a box opposite them, not far from Franz and Albert's original box, sat a dark-haired woman of exquisite beauty. Her colouring and the dress she wore suggested her heritage was Greek. Behind her, in shadow, Franz could just distinguish the figure of a man. Curious, he interrupted Albert to ask Garzone if she knew who the woman was.

"Oh, her. She comes to the opera often, but I'm afraid I don't know much about her," Garzone admitted. "She's been in Rome at least since the beginning of the season and hasn't missed a single performance. Sometimes she attends with that man there, other times with a large black servant."

The curtain rose on the ballet. Despite the superb arrangement and choreography, Franz's eye returned again and again to the stunning Greek. She was engrossed by the dancers with a look of eager delight, mesmerized by the music and the display of skill and grace. Her companion never moved or reacted, not even when the cymbals and trumpets crashed through the crescendo of the piece. He remained seated while the Greek beauty jumped to her feet in a standing ovation.

Having rested during the ballet, the opera performers returned to the stage. The second act opened with that famous duet where the titular Parisina lets slip to her husband Azzo the secret of her love for Ugo. The admission wounds Azzo to his core, who sings his progression from disbelief to despair and further still to rage, until he awakens Parisina in the night to threaten her with his vengeance.

Franz had heard the duet twice before and found himself just as moved the third time by the song of betrayal. When it completed, he rose to join the rest of the audience in raucous applause but froze with his hands apart and an unspoken bravo on his lips. As the Greek woman reacted with her customary enthusiasm, her shadowy companion also stood and moved forward into the light.

The full intensity of his gaze rested on the stage, where Azzo declared his thirst for revenge. Without smiling or blinking he brought his gloved hands together in a firm rhythm. His pale, yet weathered features were exposed in full to the light; that same light gleamed red off his eyes. Franz knew without a doubt that the man was Sinbad the Sailor.

Instead of any foreign costume, Sinbad wore an elegant suit of black and silver, the only colour being the red cravat tied around his throat. Countess Garzone burst into a fit of laughter at Franz's slack-jawed expression, and she insisted on knowing what had happened.

"That man with the Greek I asked about, do you know anything about him?" Franz asked, pointing at him.

Garzone's laughter died when her gaze followed Franz's finger. "I don't know a thing about him, aside from that I would never want to be alone with him. Look at his skin, like a fresh corpse risen from the grave!" she said. "If he were a vampire, I wouldn't be surprised at all."

It was Albert's turn to laugh. "A vampire? Countess, please, even when the dead roamed the earth there was no such thing as vampires," Albert said. "They're a ghost-story out of Romania, a peasant's tale to excuse some mad devils who chose cannibalism over starvation."

"Regardless, he looks as if he'd like to open my throat with his teeth and drink his fill; whether a vampire or a madman, it makes no difference," Garzone said with a shudder.

As comical as Albert found the situation, Countess Garzone became quite agitated by the sight of Sinbad and insisted that Franz escort her home. In her carriage, she told him of her friend, the late poet Lord Byron, and his steadfast belief before he died in the existence of vampires. Byron's belief was so sincere that he had convinced Garzone, even claiming to have seen one during a trip to Paris.

"He described an unnaturally pale man with dark hair, his mouth on the neck of a young woman in a dark alley. The man was muttering something about how she must 'pay with her blood'. Byron barely escaped and said the man's face looked dead and absent of any human feeling," Garzone insisted. "Tell me, doesn't that sound like your Sinbad?"

"We sat an entire theatre away from him," Franz replied. "Can you really be so sure in comparing a second-hand story to flesh-and-blood reality at such a distance?"

Garzone's fear remained beyond reason, and when Franz expressed an interest in learning more about Sinbad, she begged him to promise not to seek him out that night.

"By the light of day, whatever dark power and darker hunger he has will be diminished. Find him then, if you have to," Garzone insisted. "Oh, I'd feel better if you didn't go near him at all!"

Franz gave his word not to go looking for Sinbad until at least the morning, left Countess Garzone at her door, and returned to the hotel. Albert still did not comprehend the depth of Italian fidelity and was amazed to see Franz returned so soon. As it happened, Albert had gotten a closer look at Sinbad and the woman in the theatre lobby on the way out.

"They must have been speaking Greek; I couldn't understand a word. At any rate, I think my reputation must precede me!" Albert lit a pipe of English tobacco with his finger. "The man happened to glance my way, and I swear he recognized me; I even saw him mouth the name Morcerf. I must say, he has devilishly strange eyes."

More exciting to Albert than the question of Sinbad was an idea which had come to him on the journey back to the hotel.

"We don't need a carriage any more, Franz," Albert said, so pleased with himself that he bounced in his seat. "They're truly impossible to find for tomorrow or the rest of Carnival, but I checked with Pastrini. It turns out that carts and oxen are in ready supply. With just the right peasant costumes and tasteful ornamentation, we'll stand out even in Carnival! We'd still have our vantage point, and our creativity would surely get people talking. If your friend the countess was willing, she'd make quite a fetching milkmaid!"

Franz considered the idea, and a slow smile crept across his face. "Albert, I must give you credit. This time, you've really done it!"

"Don't look so shocked Franz, it has been known to happen," Albert said with a satisfied grin. "I've already sent Pastrini to find us a cart and two oxen, and I expect him back any minute."

Indeed, Signor Pastrini arrived in short order flanked by two servants. The servants were uniformed but not in the colours of the Hotel de Londres.

"Pastrini, what news of our cart?" Albert asked.

"Your excellencies, the cart is yours if you want it. However, you may wish to decline it in favour of another offer," Pastrini said, indicating the servants. They stepped forward and presented formal invitations to Albert and Franz.

"You're aware, of course, that the Count of Monte Cristo has rented the rest of this floor," Pastrini continued. Franz tried to conceal his surprise at the mention of the island, but Albert only waved a hand.

"Yes, yes, you told me this while I was waiting for Franz on our first day here. What about him?" Albert said.

"The count has heard of your dilemma regarding the carriage and has extended invitations to join him," Pastrini said.

Franz and Albert opened their invitations. The count offered to have breakfast with them in his rooms, give them seats in his carriage, and have them join him at his rented windows above the Cafe Rospoli. For the second time in under a minute, Franz was caught off guard. The Cafe was the same location where Sinbad was to leave the Roman stranger a signal about the stay of execution.

"Isn't a man slated to be killed on the plaza just outside the Cafe Rospoli tomorrow?" Franz asked.

"Indeed, the *tavolettas* were just brought to me," Pastrini said.

The *tavolettas* were slabs of wood inscribed with details of scheduled executions, much like a theatre program. It was the habit of Roman hoteliers to copy this information for their guests, and Pastrini handed one of those copies to Franz.

The Piazza del Popolo, the square outside Cafe Rospoli, was to host two executions the next day. One was Andrea Rondola, guilty of murdering a priest. The other was Rocca Priori, alias Peppino, found guilty of aiding and abetting the nefarious bandit Luigi Vampa. Just as Franz had overheard in the Colosseum, Rondola was to be *annegamento* and Peppino to be *decapitato*.

"Albert, I think we should take the count up on his offer," Franz said, eager to make Sinbad's acquaintance again. He knew that Albert would think of the carriage and window, and no further; meanwhile, his own curiosity burned to find out if Peppino's life would be spared. As expected, Albert agreed, and they sent word with the servants that they would call on the count in the morning.

Franz and Albert woke at an early hour, too excited for the day's events to remain in bed. With assurance from Pastrini that the count was an early riser and ready to receive them, they crossed the landing which separated their apartments from the count's.

A servant admitted them to luxurious rooms furnished very much like Sinbad's island retreat. Exotic influences permeated the decor, from Egypt to the Far East and from Madagascar to Mumbai. Splendid paintings by masters of the medium hung between Turkish tapestries and Zulu shields.

The servant passed into the next room to inform the count of their arrival. Franz and Albert were treated to the harmonies of a gusle, that stringed instrument of the mountain men, before the door once again muffled it.

"What do you make of all this?" Franz asked.

"Our generous neighbour must be a prince travelling incognito," Albert said. "Just look at these wall hangings!"

Before Franz could reply, the door opened again to reveal the owner of the riches around them.

"Gentlemen," he said in a husky, commanding, yet cordial voice which Franz recognized immediately, "welcome to my humble apartments. Breakfast will be ready presently."

There was no mistaking the man's tone, complexion, or features; particularly not his intriguing red eyes. Their host, the Count of Monte Cristo, was beyond a doubt the same man from the theatre, the same man from the Colosseum, and the same man who called himself Sinbad the Sailor.

CHAPTER 37
L'ANNEGAMENTO

"Franz and I must thank you, count," Albert said with a bow. "You've rescued us from a great dilemma, and we were on the point of inventing a makeshift vehicle when your generous invitation was delivered."

"If only Pastrini had told me of your circumstance sooner!" Monte Cristo said, motioning for Franz and Albert to sit. He wore a fashionable dark grey suit with white gloves and a deep blue cravat. "I travel alone, but seek every opportunity to meet my neighbours. My steward overheard his attempts to secure oxen for you."

Monte Cristo caught Franz's eye but said nothing of their previous meeting on his island.

"Count, your invitation mentioned windows above the Cafe Rospoli," Franz said, wondering if he could get some reaction from him. "Those would provide a view of the executions in the Piazza del Popolo, yes?"

"I thought I'd heard something about an execution. One moment, I should see if my steward has carried out some orders I gave him," Monte Cristo said, examining Albert's face. He extended his hand and rang a bell three times. "I've simplified the act of summoning my servants. One ring is for my valet, two for my majordomo, three for my steward. Bertuccio, are the windows at the Piazza del Popolo ready?"

Franz recognized the steward, a man of forty-five or fifty, as the same smuggler who had brought him Sinbad's invitation on the island and blindfolded him. His seaman's clothes had been replaced with a more appropriate uniform, but his face was unmistakable. Like Monte Cristo, he gave no sign that he recognized Franz.

"Your excellency, the windows have been secured and prepared. A

Russian prince had rented them, but I paid him a sufficient sum to turn the rental over to your use," Bertuccio said.

"Very good, Bertuccio. Give orders to the coachman. Oh, and secure the *tavoletta* from Signor Pastrini," Monte Cristo said.

"Actually, I have one here," Franz said. "Count, I fear that we abuse your kindness. This meal looks superb."

"Nonsense, you abuse nothing; I enjoy having company. I understand you men are from Paris. One day I'll visit that city, and perhaps you may extend your own hospitality then," Monte Cristo said. He read the *tavoletta*. "Interesting. I was at the cardinal's residence yesterday evening, and there was a rumour that one of these men was going to be pardoned. Perhaps the *tavoletta* was written out prior to that."

He set down the paper and looked from Franz to Albert.

"You may be deprived of the sight of *decapitato*, but the *annegamento* will be entertainment enough. The cardinal said that one of those remarkable Catalan people has joined the city's employment," Monte Cristo said, "and they've added executions to his duties to make full use of his gift."

"A gifted Catalan, you say?" Albert said, interested by any mention of his heritage. "What would his gift be, then?"

"The movement of water, of course. That's what the punishment of *annegamento* means: drowning," Monte Cristo said. "It's a surer method than the *mazzolato*, where the condemned is struck in the temple with a mace until he dies, since an ill-placed blow would simply extend the punishment. Yet it is also not so quick as the guillotine, and the victim has time to consider his crimes. I have never had the pleasure of watching an *annegamento* myself, so this is quite a happy coincidence."

Franz paused with his fork halfway to his mouth and set it down again. "You make it sound like you've studied the tortures of the world. Do you enjoy watching these spectacles?"

"There are few methods of punishment which I haven't seen," Monte Cristo said. "At first I watched them with horror, then with indifference, and now with curiosity. After all, our greatest preoccupation in life is death. Some people spend their entire lives doing nothing but avoiding death, with the result that they never truly live."

"Isn't that what living is: not dying?" Albert said.

"Ah, but there's a great difference between how you or I live and how a poor peasant farmer does. Think of our ancestors in the days when kings controlled all the world's wealth; every day for ordinary people was a struggle to acquire another twenty-four hours' worth of food, with no time for leisure or pleasure," Monte Cristo said. To illustrate the point, he savoured a crisp morsel of bacon. "Though we still have kings today, we also have entrepreneurs and employees rather than serfs. The average person's lot in life is greatly improved; they have time for activities beyond survival."

Franz and Albert chewed in silence for a moment. For the first time, Franz wondered what Signor Pastrini or the girl who had carried his bags did with their time when not occupied with the hotel.

"Pardon the diversion, I do have a habit of getting off track. I was telling you why I find the acts of torture and execution so fascinating," Monte Cristo said. "Mankind has invented as many ways to inflict pain as we have of sharing joy. Consider the scavenger's daughter, an ingenious device created by our English cousins. The victim's arms and legs are folded against his chest, and iron hoops tightened around him. As opposed to the rack, which tortures by extending and dislocating every joint, the daughter compresses the bones and lungs until every breath becomes not just agony, but a decision to be carefully weighed. Torture, not death, is the true way to punish a man."

"Explain your meaning, count," Albert said, forcing a chuckle in spite of the grim topic. "You've excited my curiosity."

No blood rose to colour Monte Cristo's face, but Franz glimpsed a deep hatred flash in his red eyes.

"Imagine if a man had irrevocably stolen something you held dear: your father, your betrothed, your livelihood, even your liberty. It leaves a wound in your heart that can never heal, yet some bureaucrat decides that separating the criminal's head from his shoulders will bring you reparations?" Monte Cristo said in a rush. He made a visible effort to calm himself and raised his cup to his lips. "It's almost a shame the *decapitato* is cancelled, or you could see how brief the punishment of decapitation is. In recompense for a victim's years of suffering, the criminal receives a moment of physical pain and then eternal rest."

"For such deeply personal crimes as you mention, I agree that the justice systems of the world are often lacking," Franz said. "But that's why dueling is permitted in Paris and so many other places."

"Dueling!" Monte Cristo said with delight. "A marvelous pastime. I've fought many duels, to first blood and sometimes to the death, and always won. Dueling is a pleasant enough method to avenge an insult or a blow, but the sort of crime that weighs heavy on the heart and prevents one from sleeping at night requires a slower punishment."

"Following such a course, you'd risk becoming a target of the law yourself," Franz said.

"I have learned in my travels that wealth and connections are all that one needs in order to avoid a courtroom and a cell," Monte Cristo said. "A simple bribe and the dropping of a name will cause nearly any cog in the bureaucracy to turn a blind eye as you walk away to freedom. My, but we've picked a strange topic of conversation for such a happy time as the Carnival! You must excuse me; by accident, we hit upon a subject which I am quite passionate about. How is your meal?"

"Superb!" Albert said. He held up a piece of his sliced ham and Swiss cheese sandwich on his fork. "This *croque-monsieur* is so rich, I love it."

"The trick is to use French toast as the bread," the count said. "I've decided to introduce it to the world under the name of my island: the Monte Cristo sandwich."

Franz cast several glances at Albert over the course of breakfast; his friend was as captivated by the count's intensity as if they were enjoying ghost stories around a fire rather than discussing torture. The conversation moved to lighter subjects, and Franz remembered that Albert had not seen the count at his island or in the Colosseum, and did not have those experiences to colour his impression. After the meal, of which the count ate very little, Franz rose and gave his sincere thanks.

"Where are you going?" Albert said. "Whatever you had planned today, reschedule it; the count has invited us to join him at his window, remember?"

"Yes, I'll see you there after the execution," Franz said.

"And miss the spectacle? The only public executions back home are by guillotine, and the count has just said those are as boring as can be," Albert said. "I can't return to Paris, tell them that I had a chance to witness an agrimony, and then admit that I passed it up! I insist that you come with me."

"I think you mean *annegamento*, not agrimony," Monte Cristo said with a smile. The count tapped the *tavoletta* paper. "The culprit to be drowned is a true scoundrel. A priest offered him food when he was begging, but no money, so he clubbed the priest to death with a log. Surely you can find the stomach to watch such a beast be put down."

Franz looked again at Albert, whose face was the model of eagerness, and gave in. Albert applauded and drained his coffee.

Before they could leave, a servant called the count away to speak to a messenger. Franz and Albert returned to the salon where Albert gave a cry of joy upon seeing a selection of cigars laid out upon the table for after-breakfast smoking.

"Well, what do you think of the Count of Monte Cristo?" Franz said while Albert passed cigars under his nose for appraisal.

"What do I think?" Albert said, surprised . "I think he is a fine and fascinating fellow, well-read, lays a magnificent table, and he has excellent taste in tobacco."

"But did you notice anything strange about him? Such as how intently he looked at you?" Franz asked.

"Yes, I know. It's my own fault, really," Albert said, shaking his head. "I have been away from Paris for more than a year, and my clothes must be quite out of fashion by now. Certainly my hair needs a trim! The count must think I'm some provincial putting on airs. Be a good chap and disavow him of the notion at the first opportunity."

Albert centered the cigar between his lips and conjured a flame on the tip of his forefinger to light it just as the count returned.

"My word!" Monte Cristo exclaimed. "How in the world are you doing that?"

"You mentioned the gifted Catalans earlier, remember?" Albert chuckled, fragrant smoke emerging from his nose. "My own parents are both of that mystical stock, and I inherited the gift of flame like my father. Perhaps you've heard of him: General Fernand de Morcerf?"

"I believe I've heard that name before, yes," Monte Cristo said. "Please, take more cigars for the day."

Without needing a second invitation, Albert filled his cigar case from the selection on the table.

"With all my heart, it's a fine thing to have a decent cigar again. The local fare is rather dreadful. When you come to Paris, I'll show you where to find the best tobacco in all of Europe," Albert said.

Together they departed in the carriage for the Plaza. Revelers filled the square, eager for the festivities of the Carnival even as they waited for the scaffolding to be erected for the executions. The *mandaia* was already in place, very similar to the guillotine except for the curve of the gleaming blade. Franz had never before seen this terrible instrument up close. Next to it, workmen raised a single stout post. An open iron hoop with a latch stood at about neck-height on the post, and shackles hung midway down.

"Which windows are yours?" Franz asked the count, his nerves trembling in anticipation of what they were about to see.

Monte Cristo pointed at the first level above the Cafe de Rospoli, and Franz saw he had kept his promise to the bandit king Luigi Vampa: the windows were hung with green drapes. The *mandaia* would not be used after all.

The view from the windows provided the perfect angle for seeing the execution platform, and Monte Cristo's rented rooms included a parlour and some side closets. Though Albert chattered away and Monte Cristo sat at ease, perspiration rolled down Franz's back at the prospect of the macabre entertainment which would begin their day and end all the days of another human being. The crowd below laughed and jeered, mocking the men they expected to see die.

A double line of soldiers filed out of a nearby church to clear a path to and perimeter around the scaffold. Next came the executioner, a slim man wearing the traditional black mask and black silk uniform of his trade. Two wineskins hung from his belt at one side and a knife at the other. He walked to the platform and stood several paces behind the *mandaia*.

Finally, the condemned men were brought out. The first man was slender and dark-haired, walking with a firm step and calm in his face. Behind him came a fat and fair-haired man who shuffled to the platform with slumped shoulders.

Franz felt Albert's hand upon his shoulder. Albert's face had taken on a green tinge to match the drapes, and his latest cigar smoldered forgotten between his fingers. Monte Cristo watched the proceedings with the same intensity as he had the duet of Parisina the night before.

The soldiers secured one of the fat man's wrists into the shackles which hung from the upright post. A monk pushed his way through the perimeter to deliver a sealed parchment to the captain. The captain read this message, spoke to the monk and the executioner, and announced to the crowd that Peppino had been pardoned, and there would be no *decapitato* today.

"What?" the fat man roared, who Franz took to be Andrea Rondola. "Why him and not me? I was told I would not die alone, I was promised!"

Rondola lunged forward to choke the life from Peppino himself, but his lone shackle stopped him short. This sudden change of demeanour mystified Franz, but Monte Cristo only chuckled.

"Some people, I may never understand why, are happy to suffer as long as they know others are suffering as well," Monte Cristo explained. "They're like children at the beach who lose their sand castles to the tides, and rather than learn from their mistakes they destroy another child's castle to ensure nobody can enjoy one."

The guards overpowered Rondola with ease and fastened the second cuff. He continued to scream and curse as the iron hoop tightened around his neck to immobilize his head, a process which Franz found difficult to watch. He and Albert each turned away from the window, but Monte Cristo touched their hands and implored them to watch. His tone was somehow soothing and commanding at once, reminding Franz of the dinner in the grotto. Both Franz and Albert returned their gaze to the platform.

Rondola could not move more than an inch in any direction due to the shackles and collar holding him upright against the post. The crowd continued to mock him; Peppino had since returned to the church under guard. Rondola's wide chest heaved with deep, panicked breaths as the executioner stepped forward and opened his wineskins.

The executioner made graceful flowing motions with his hands, coaxing twin streams of water up and out of the skins. The water danced in the air before the amazed crowd in figure eights and spirals. Franz was no stranger to the abilities of the Catalans, but the masked man put far more artistry into his task than Albert's cigar-lighting or showy bursts of flame.

After juggling the water for a time, the executioner held his hands together to form the liquid into a shimmering sphere encasing the entirety of Rondola's head. Rondola's chest stilled as he held his breath, but the water was patient. He could not fight the impulse to inhale forever, and the sphere shrank by a fraction as Rondola's body betrayed him by pulling it into his lungs. Rondola thrashed against his bonds, but his efforts soon weakened and his legs failed. Only the iron collar biting into his chin held him up.

The executioner kept one hand extended towards the sphere of water and reached for his knife with the other. He drove the blade once into each of Rondola's lungs, twisting the blade each time. A gush of water and blood poured from each wound, to the sound of raucous cheering from the crowd. With Rondola's death confirmed, the executioner allowed the sphere to collapse with a wave of his hand.

Franz could no longer contain himself and half-fainted back into his chair. Albert's eyes were closed in a nauseated grimace, and from the way he held the curtain Franz suspected it was all that kept him upright. Monte Cristo looked from Franz to Albert, judging their reactions, and turned again to face the plaza. Franz read something like triumph on the man's colourless face.

CHAPTER 38
THE CARNIVAL AT ROME

F ranz's senses returned to him in time, as a groggy and somewhat frantic Albert gulped at a glass of water. Down in the square, Rondola's soaked corpse was removed and the scaffolding disassembled in the time it took for Franz to come back to himself. Only the crowd remained, full of noise and excitement with a great church bell singing above it all.

"Gentlemen, as you can no doubt hear, the Carnival has begun!" the Count of Monte Cristo said, unaffected by the spectacle of Rondola's death. "Make haste, dress yourselves."

He opened a wardrobe to reveal harlequin costumes in various colours and sizes, but Franz did not move. Seeing the sombre look on his face, Monte Cristo beseeched him to find some perspective on what they had witnessed.

"Yes, you've seen a man executed," the count said, waving his hand. "You've also seen a man granted a second chance at life, which is by far a rarer spectacle. There, Albert sets the example!"

Franz was surprised to see Albert pulling on the boots of a harlequin costume in blue and white. "Albert, are you really going to join the revelry after that?"

"What I'd most like to do is to bring up my breakfast and sleep until that execution becomes a faded memory," Albert said with uncharacteristic crassness. "But as repulsive as the sight was, I must agree with the count. Rondola is dead, and I can't change that by being miserable. Peppino is alive and no doubt much happier than I feel right now, and what I can do is try to emulate that feeling."

"In addition, think of when you are an old man and reminiscing about your life," Monte Cristo said. "Will you want to remember having mourned a murderer, whose character was revealed at the moment of his death to be as ugly as his crime, or will you want to remember the excitement of Carnival?"

Franz relented and selected a costume in green and yellow for himself before stepping into the other room to dress. The count retired as well, emerging in a similar costume to what Franz had seen him wear at the Colosseum. A violet robe hanging to his knees and elbows revealed that once again he was wrapped head to foot in clean linen bandages. A round collar-piece of gold cloth with inlaid turquoise rested on his shoulders, and the same Egyptian pharaoh mask covered his face. The pupils of the exaggerated kohl-lined eyes were cut out, revealing the count's red irises. Above it rose a tall red crown with a feather emerging from the front.

"Good show, Monte Cristo! You cut quite the exotic figure in that getup!" Albert said. "How on earth did you wrap yourself so quickly; are those long gloves and breeches, or have you worn those bandages under your clothes all day?"

The count chuckled behind his mask. "I would be a poor master of disguise if I gave away all of my secrets."

Albert and Franz completed their costumes with masks of their own. The three of them descended to their carriage; the driver was dressed as an owlbear and the carriage had been equipped with rooftop seats for a better view. They were ready to join in the raucous energy of Carnival.

The amiable carnage of the city-wide party of Carnival is difficult to imagine for someone who has never attended. Revelers in costumes are everywhere, pushing their way through the melee on foot or flinging confetti and flowers into the crowd from carriages and windows. Clowns, harlequins, peasants, princes, dogs, cats, dragons, beasts, zombies, soldiers, knights, and sages mingled with thousands of other costumes.

A woman dressed as a werewolf dash from one person to the next, lifting each mask for a passionate kiss before running away again to find a new target as the subjects of her fleeting embrace laughed and readjusted their costumes. Albert cheered for a man dressed as a cabbage engaged in a fistfight with a man dressed as an ox. The cabbage bloodied the ox's nose, the two men shook hands, and they shared a drink from a bottle of wine.

After the spectacle of the *annegamento*, Franz and Albert felt like men drinking in order to drown a violent sorrow, except they drank in the Carnival instead. The image of bloody water pouring from Rondola's lungs hung in front of their eyes, pushing them to embrace the spirit of the festival. For every handful of confetti thrown at them, they threw double. For every flower that landed in their carriage, they responded with a bouquet.

The count in his splendid mummy costume participated as well, but with more restraint than Franz and Albert. Indeed, he spent as much time observing them as he did observing the Carnival. When the carriage came back around to the Cafe Rospoli, he excused himself.

"Gentlemen, the carriage and drivers are yours for as long as you like. If you grow tired of being actors in this scene and decide to spectate, you are welcome to return to my windows," Monte Cristo said.

Looking up, Franz noticed a woman in a blue domino mask watching the proceedings with a dazzling smile. His imagination supplied the features beneath the mask, forming the picture of Monte Cristo's beautiful Greek companion from the opera. While Franz thanked the count for his generosity, Albert threw flowers to a carriage full of women dressed as demons in shades of flame. Sadly, the carriage parted from theirs at the next turning.

"What a shame!" Albert said as they left. "I imagine those hellspawn would have made for heavenly company."

"Too bad they didn't know your situation," Franz said, intoxicated by the Carnival atmosphere and feeling more carefree than usual as he nudged Albert in the ribs, "or they'd know that you're nearly ready to sell your soul for an evening of comfort!"

Albert returned a friendly shove. "Hold your tongue, let's hope the Carnival doesn't pass without producing some tale I can bring home!"

"But of course there will be a silver lining," said Franz, fighting to maintain a straight face. "If nothing else, nobody will be able to disarm you in fencing when you return to Paris."

"Why is that?" Albert asked.

"Because by then you'll have the strongest grip in all of France!" Franz guffawed as Albert beat him about the face and neck with a bouquet in feigned outrage.

A chorus of feminine laughter caught Albert's attention; the carriage of demons had caught up to them again. They applauded the fine show of his play assault on Franz, and the two men bowed to their hellish admirers. Albert threw the battered bouquet to one who wore a dress the colour of fresh blood, and she blew him a kiss before the carriage pulled away again.

For the rest of the day, they encountered the devilish chariot at intervals. The girl in red kept Albert's beaten-up arrangement of flowers and later threw a small bunch of violets back to him. Albert placed it in his button-hole as the demons disappeared again.

"There you are, the beginning of the adventure you've been looking for," Franz said.

"You make jokes, but I really think you're right," Albert said. "I'll have to keep these violets so she can recognize me again tomorrow."

They encountered the demons only once more that day, and Albert's admirer clapped her hands in appreciation when she saw the violets on proud display.

They passed the Cafe Rospoli again, but Monte Cristo and the Greek woman were not at the window. The great bell rang again, as a generally-accepted signal to end the masquerade for the day. The costumes of Carnival were traded for the costumes of society, to attend the operas and ballets. Franz and Albert returned to their hotel, where they learned Monte Cristo had returned in a second carriage and ventured out again already. Pastrini told them the count had left them the key to his box at the Teatro Argentina, to use as they wished.

Albert had other matters on his mind and asked Pastrini to arrange a change of costume for the following day. He also preserved the bunch of violets, transferring them to the lapel of his jacket.

At the Argentina that night, where the performance was The Algerian Captive, they seated themselves in Monte Cristo's box to enjoy the show. Countess Garzone entered her box during the first act. When Franz and Albert waved at her from the count's box, her shock was so comical they knew it would be cruelty not to visit and satisfy her curiosity.

"You've wasted no time in becoming bosom chums with Lord Ruthven!" Garzone said, referencing the vampiric villain of a series of popular English novels.

"Well, I would hardly go so far," Franz said, "but I cannot deny that we've been enjoying his hospitality all day."

He explained to Garzone that her supposed vampire was the Count of Monte Cristo and their neighbour at the hotel, and the events of the day so far. When he mentioned the *annegamento*, his voice hitched and Albert's smile faltered. While the fun of the Carnival had dulled the edges on the gruesome experience, the images were still all too ready at hand.

Garzone pressed for more details about Monte Cristo, but Franz and Albert could supply little besides what they had already said.

"He is...a very intense personality," Albert said, struggling to articulate his impression of the count.

Their gossip turned to the count's Greek companion, though they could not say much on this topic either. Albert speculated that it was she they had heard playing the gusle in the count's suite that morning. Soon enough, new visitors arrived to see Garzone; custom dictated that Albert and Franz depart to allow them in.

Pastrini was busy fulfilling Albert's request while they were away; Franz and Albert returned to their rooms to find an assortment of devil costumes.

"When our lovely demonesses see us dressed like them tomorrow, and the woman in red recognizes her violets, it will be as clear a sign as anything!" Albert said.

Franz agreed that the idea was sound, and the costumes were quite fetching. The next morning he chose a yellow leotard with a snarling mask and pointed tail while Albert selected a red costume to match his would-be liaison. The Count of Monte Cristo entered their apartment as they put the last touches on their outfits. His mummy costume had been replaced again by a more conventional frock coat. As always, he wore gloves and a cravat.

Previous engagements left the count only a quarter of an hour to visit, but he spent the time conversing with Franz and Albert on a variety of subjects. A turn of phrase revealed him as a connoisseur of world literature, a remark told them he was an admirer of art, and a brief detour into the world of the sciences showcased his interest in chemistry. Albert was quite impressed by both the count's manners and his permission to keep the carriage. Albert had not been eager to return to his oxcart idea and lose equal footing with the laughing demonesses.

Franz and Albert descended to the street after breakfast, where the masquerade began anew. They carried on in much the same way as they had the previous day, though Albert was now preoccupied with scanning the crowd for his enticing demon.

Before long, a fresh bunch of violets flew into their carriage from a neighbouring vehicle full of harlequins. It seemed the women had had the same idea as Albert and changed their costumes to match what he had worn the day before. Unlike the puffy sleeves and baggy pants of Franz and Albert's harlequin costumes, the diamond patterns adorning the women clung to them in a manner that would defy decency at any time of year but Carnival.

The woman who had thrown the violets had even chosen an outfit in blue and white, as Albert had worn the day before. Albert replaced the faded bouquet on his lapel with the fresh one and raised his mask to touch the old bouquet to his lips before throwing it back to the blue harlequin. Her companions tittered amongst themselves as she caught it and pantomimed swooning into their arms, and then inspiration struck Albert.

With his devil's mask back in place, he raised one arm to the sky and sent a tight cone of flame straight up into the air, eliciting genuine shock and applause from the surrounding festival-goers; even the other carriage-driver took his eyes off the road to watch. Albert gave his best nefarious laugh to complete the display.

This flirtation continued throughout the day as the two carriages parted ways and found each other again and again. They even caught a brief glimpse of the count standing at his Rospoli window, once again wearing his superb Egyptian costume.

Albert had the carriage to himself the next day, as Franz had a previous engagement with an old friend, but they reunited at the hotel for dinner. Albert was overjoyed; his demoness had resumed her red costume and raised her mask to him that day, revealing as fair a face as he could have hoped for. Albert sat down at the writing desk to pen a letter which he planned to throw to her the following day.

Albert became almost bashful and asked Franz if he could use the carriage alone again the following day. Franz could guess Albert's goal in having the enclosed vehicle to himself and could not in good conscience stand in the way. They agreed that Albert would use the carriage and Franz would take advantage of the seats offered to them at the count's Rospoli windows.

Franz wore his harlequin costume again and spent the day with an ever-changing assortment of the count's other guests, including sporadic visits from Monte Cristo himself. In between tossing confetti into the maelstrom below or calling out to women passing by in the street, he played chess with an Albanian diplomat, arm-wrestled a Turkish banker dressed as a minotaur, and had a frank talk with Monte Cristo regarding his doubts about the arranged marriage waiting for him in Paris. In the street below, Franz caught glimpses of Albert travelling past, or the now-familiar carriage with Albert's *objet d'amour*, but never both at the same time.

Again, they reunited at the hotel; again, Albert was in ecstasy. He had not managed to coax the woman into his carriage, but she had thrown him a letter before he could throw his, having once again anticipated his plans. The letter was written in an elegant hand and invited Albert to meet her on the last day of the Carnival, during the candle-game of *moccoletti* which brings the grand event to a close.

Albert's instructions were to wear his harlequin costume with a knot of rose-coloured ribbon on the left shoulder, wait at the church of San Giacomo, and follow the demon who would steal his candle. Franz grinned at the subterfuge of it all and was glad for Albert finally having his long-awaited romantic adventure.

"Well, it looks like I will be attending the Duke of Bracciano's ball alone tomorrow evening!" Franz said.

"Never mind the duke, I may not leave Rome for a month if this woman is as good company as I hope she'll be," Albert said with a waggle of his eyebrows. "She's enticing, it's like she knows what I'm thinking before I do!"

The Count of Monte Cristo paid them another visit after dinner. Nothing piqued his eccentricities that evening; they spoke about the opera and society figures, horse-racing and pistol-shooting. The absence of the count's quirks gave Franz time to think about the man.

The count must have recognized Franz from his island and must have guessed that Franz recognized him as Sinbad, but he had said nothing about it even when they sat alone at the window the day before. As Franz studied the count's strange complexion and stranger eyes he considered the possibility that Countess Garzone could be even partly correct in her insistence that the count was a vampire.

His commanding presence made him a natural leader and could be mistaken as a vampire's power of compulsion. Such a ruby hue in the eyes could not be natural, nor the way the count's face appeared so much like fine-grained white leather. For the first time, Franz noticed that the count did not reveal so much as an inch of exposed skin below the jawline. The man was never seen without his cravat and gloves, except for when he wore the bandages of his Carnival costume.

Franz scolded himself. The rational explanation for the count's appearance was an illness, which would be rude to gawk at, but the possibility of the supernatural still lurked in his thoughts. Two things were certain: first, if the count visited Paris after all he would make a definitive splash when he arrived. Second, Franz was quite sure he did not want to be in Paris at the same time as the Count of Monte Cristo.

Fat Tuesday, which the French call Mardi Gras, was the final and most dramatic day of the Carnival. It presented the last opportunity for excess before the fasting and self-reflection of Lent, which would begin at eight o'clock that evening. Albert dressed as instructed, and Franz resumed his yellow devil's costume to avoid any confusion. If the days before had been chaotic, Mardi Gras was good-natured pandemonium, a human storm of merriment. As sunset approached, the candle-sellers ventured out into the crowd.

The candle-game of *moccoletti* is a simple one. One purchases a candle, which vary in size from mundane to comically large. Among the crowd, points of light bloom in the gathering dusk like stars and multiply like rabbits until the streets glow so bright it is as if the sun had returned. From that point everyone has two goals: keep their own candle alight, and extinguish those of everyone else. A man with a philosophical mind may speculate that the candles represent life itself, as mankind has only one way to spread it but so many varied ways of extinguishing it. This idea did not occur to many of the participants, however, who took part for the simple reason that it was a thing done during Carnival, and it was fun.

Albert was quite focused on his quest to reach the stairs of San

Giacomo by seven o'clock, with his candle intact. The route to the church was fraught with peril as revelers tried to knock his candle away or snuff it out, but Albert was something of a boxer and had the advantage of relighting his flame with the snap of his fingers.

From his vantage point, Franz could see Albert ascend the steps of the church. A small-waisted figure in a red dress and demon's mask stepped out from behind a pillar to snatch the candle from Albert's hand. They took their leave arm in arm, and when Franz lost sight of them he returned to the havoc of *moccoletti* with a smile on his face on behalf of Albert's success.

Time waits for no festivities, and all too soon the bell sounded eight o'clock. All of the candles extinguished at the same moment as if by some immense blast of enchanted wind. Utter darkness blanketed the streets, and the crowd fell silent except for the sound of carriage-wheels bringing revelers home. The Carnival had ended.

CHAPTER 39
THE RANSOM

Moonrise came late that night, and the streets remained in darkness as Franz returned to the hotel. Though the season of Lent had begun for the faithful, Pastrini had no intention of forcing the fast upon any of his guests and had dinner waiting for Franz.

Albert had made it quite clear that he wouldn't be rushing home that evening, so Franz changed into more acceptable clothes and ate alone. He chuckled at the idea of what Albert must be getting up to, but his mirth was tinged by a dark unease which he justified as being normal for the end of Carnival. There was still the Duke of Bracciano's ball to attend, and Franz took the opportunity to use the Count of Monte Cristo's carriage once again.

The duke's house had a well-earned reputation for being one of the finest in Rome, and his parties held a similar reputation for attracting the cream of society; Franz was therefore not surprised to see Countess Garzone. They gave each other warm greetings and traded Carnival stories; Franz laughed when Garzone told him about being accosted and kissed by a young woman in a werewolf costume.

"And where is your funny little friend, the viscount?" Garzone asked. "Did you lose track of him during the *moccoletti?*"

"Not precisely," Franz replied. "Albert met a woman and is at a rendezvous with her as we speak."

"Goodness, off in the night with a strange woman while a stranger to Rome himself! I hope he's armed, at least," Garzone said. "You hear so many tales of brigands and beasts in this city, and now we have vampires as well!"

Franz chuckled at the joke but could not suppress a shudder. It was too easy to imagine the count stalking Albert through darkened streets before tearing out his throat with his teeth in order to feast on the warm blood within.

"He hasn't got a gun or a knife, but Albert is never entirely disarmed," Franz said. "You've seen him demonstrate his little talent, of course?"

"Oh yes, the parlour trick with the flames," Garzone said. "I hope it's enough to protect him from the misfortunes that can meet a man in the night."

Franz accepted a glass of wine from a passing servant and took a deep drink to steady his worry. The servant soon returned and told Franz that a messenger waited for him at the hotel, with an urgent letter from Viscount Albert de Morcerf.

Franz rushed to the carriage. In front of the hotel stood a man wrapped in a cloak who approached Franz as soon as he descended.

"I bear a letter from the Viscount Albert de Morcerf," the cloaked man said from the shadows of his hood.

"I am Franz de Quesnel, Baron d'Epinay. I was told the letter is for me," Franz said.

The cloaked man handed over an envelope. It was indeed addressed to Franz and written in Albert's hand.

"Will you wait for an answer?" asked Franz.

"The viscount certainly hopes so," the cloaked man replied.

Certain he didn't want to waste any time, Franz moved closer to the hotel's lantern and opened the letter there. He read it twice to be sure he had not mistaken the words, as Albert's irreverent writing style almost obscured the gravity of the situation.

"Albert is the prisoner of Luigi Vampa?" Franz demanded.

"As you say," the cloaked man said.

"And Vampa will really kill him if I don't pay four thousand piastres in ransom?" Franz asked, the blood draining from his face.

"As you say, excellency," the cloaked man said again. Franz saw he had no choice.

"Wait here, I will go to my room and get the money," he said.

The cloaked man nodded and Franz ran inside taking the stairs two at a time. Franz knew where to find Albert's pocketbook, and Franz combined their money on the writing desk only to find that they were a thousand piastres short.

Franz asked himself who in Rome he could borrow the difference from. At the end of Carnival there was no guarantee any of his friends in the city would have the cash available. Then Franz remembered the Count of Monte Cristo. He looked back at the letter, countersigned by Luigi Vampa himself dictating the amount of the ransom and the time by which it was due, and rushed across the hall to knock on the count's door. Ali, the Nubian servant from the island grotto, opened it. Instead of his tunic, he wore more conventional livery.

"I must see the count, it is an emergency of life and death," Franz said.

Ali nodded and led Franz to a room surrounded with divans. Monte Cristo wore a similar outfit as their time on his island, with billowing white pantaloons and a silk shirt with an embroidered black vest. As always, he wore his gloves and cravat. When Franz entered in such an agitated state, Monte Cristo set aside his pipe.

"Franz, what brings you unannounced at such an hour? Look at the state of you; it must be dire news indeed," Monte Cristo said, a look of concern on his strange white face.

"Albert has been kidnapped by Luigi Vampa," Franz said. "With all our money, I'm a thousand short of his ransom and Albert is going to be killed."

Monte Cristo took the letter and read it to the bottom, then returned it to Franz and stepped to a nearby cabinet.

"Let's not waste time. Vampa is a legend in this country," Monte Cristo said. "I'll gladly pay Albert's ransom."

"Actually Sinbad, I was wondering if there's any need to send Vampa the money after all," Franz said, watching the count. "Particularly considering how Vampa is, as he said at the Colosseum, 'utterly devoted to your service'?"

Monte Cristo held Franz's gaze without speaking, giving Franz time to wonder if he had miscalculated. He tried not to imagine the count's teeth closing around his throat or meeting the more prosaic end of a dagger in the heart for his insolence. Franz felt as if the entire world were revolving forward like a wheel, with him as one of the spokes, as Monte Cristo's luminous red gaze probed into his soul. Finally, the unpleasant sensation ended when the count broke eye contact.

"The man who brought this must be waiting for your response," Monte Cristo said.

"In the street, wearing a hooded cloak," Franz replied. A cold sweat down his neck and back caught him by surprise.

Monte Cristo led Franz to a balcony overlooking the front door of the hotel, where the cloaked man still remained. Monte Cristo whistled sharply, drawing the cloaked man's attention and holding a candle to illuminate his own face. The cloaked man saluted and took a running leap to the front wall of the building. Finding handholds on ledges and decorations, he scaled the wall to kneel before the count with his hood down. It was none other than Peppino, the shepherd narrowly rescued from losing his head.

"Excellency, I didn't know that you stayed here," Peppino said in the tone most Roman men reserve for speaking to the Pope. He glanced at Franz before lowering his head again.

"Don't worry, you may speak in front of my friend," Monte Cristo said. "You may also stand and dispense with the ceremony. I didn't give you your life, I merely returned it to you. Now, what's happened to the Viscount de Morcerf?"

"Excellency, the Frenchman's carriage passed Teresa's carriage many times during the Carnival. Her Sight told her that he was a worthy target, and the chief declared him fair game," Peppino said. "She launched a flirtation with the Frenchman, under the chief's watchful eye of course."

"Luigi Vampa was there, at the Carnival?" Franz asked.

"Signor, he drove the carriage," Peppino said. Franz recalled the coach driver, who had dressed as a gargoyle when the women wore demon costumes and as a trained seal when they wore harlequin. "She drew him in, could See when he had been hooked, and arranged a rendezvous."

"Yes, I saw him meet her," Franz said.

Peppino chuckled. "You saw young Beppo, the chief's informant at the prison and the most slim-waisted young man you will find in all of Rome. Beppo led the Frenchman outside the walls to a coach, waited for him to become a tad too forward, and held a pistol to his head. The band arrived soon after," he said. "The Frenchman used some devilry to cover his hands in flame to try and fight, but the chief had seen him demonstrate this at the Carnival, and he was quickly doused with water and tied."

"Oh dear. To be a young man so close to love and have it snatched away! How sad," Monte Cristo said with the faintest touch of sarcasm. "Where is Vampa now?"

"The band has taken residence for the night in *la foro prigione* of San Sebastian, and the viscount is with them," Peppino said.

"Then we set off at once. Have you ever been?" Monte Cristo turned to Franz.

Franz shook his head; in all his time in Rome, he could never bring himself to visit such gruesome relics of the past. He no longer seemed to have any choice in the matter.

"I have a carriage standing ready at all hours in case the whim of travel takes me, and Ali can drive," Monte Cristo said. "Let's rescue Albert, and with any luck he'll emerge from this adventure with nothing worse than a good scare and a tale to tell."

As they drove beyond the city walls, the count explained the history of *la foro prigione* of San Sebastian.

CHAPTER 40
THE HOLE

During the Dead Plague, waves of undead assaulted Rome as they did cities throughout Europe, but Napoleon's armies hadn't yet reached Italy to respond to the threat. An architect named Enzo Spinazzola invented a new kind of defensive measure: *la foro prigione*, or hole prison.

The hole prisons were simple, yet elegant. A deep, wide pit would be dug, lined with stone, and concealed at the top. Underground chambers opened onto the pit; militia members would enter the chambers by hidden trap doors on the surface. At ground level, other soldiers lined up behind vast wooden mobile barricades. When a zombie horde approached, the soldiers would move the barricades in formation to funnel and push the zombies into the pits. There, they couldn't reach any possible victims while the militia in the chambers used pikes and torches to neutralize them.

As when the Dead Plague reached Paris, the city government of Rome didn't treat the situation with the seriousness it deserved. Spinazzola proposed a line of *foro prigiones* along the walls, but they allowed no construction without the proper permits and licenses. Frustrated, Spinazzola hired a crew himself and had the pits dug beyond the city limits while council debated his permit applications. Soon after completion, the pits proved instrumental in preventing a fresh wave of waterlogged undead from beneath the ocean from reaching the walls of Rome, and the Pope consecrated each pit in the name of a saint.

"When Napoleon defeated the dead, they cleaned the hole prisons as best they could. Still, there remain streaks of dried ichor soaked into the stone, and deep grooves where the zombies tried to claw their way out," Monte Cristo said.

"How do you know so much about so many things?" Franz asked, more from a need to keep his mind occupied than any expectation of a straight answer.

"Stories about the undead are a particular interest of mine," Monte Cristo said. "So many questions about them that remain unanswered. How did they move with no life in their hearts? Why was destroying the brain the only sure way to put one down? How could hordes of undead, but not individual zombies, raise formerly peaceful corpses who had never been bitten?"

Franz nodded absently. To him these questions were academic; Napoleon had wiped out the Dead Plague ten years before his birth, and he had never needed to fear the dragging step of a hungry corpse.

"Imagine if one of those inhumanly strong and nearly invulnerable horrors had retained their human intelligence? What would become of the world then?" Monte Cristo continued, gazing out the window. "Besides, I was a child toward the end of the uprising. Someone dear to me was maimed by them, but survived. Others did not. It seems only right that I learn everything about it."

Peppino exited the carriage several times to give passcodes to sentinels they met along the way until they reached the edge of the great pit. A final lookout waiting by the trap door allowed them entrance to subterranean corridors which followed the same curve as the round sides of the pit itself.

Franz guessed from the noises and laughter that the bandits used the side-chambers as dormitories and meeting-halls. The corridor they followed spiraled down; the defenders of Rome would have advanced up those stairs to kill new zombies as they filled the pit.

In one of the lowest rooms, a figure leaned against a rough-hewn table with a book in his hands while two guards played a quiet game of draughts. Franz couldn't see the title of the book but was curious about the kind of literature an outlaw would read.

Monte Cristo raised a finger to his lips to tell Franz to be silent and walked upright into the room. The guards noticed him first and sprang to their feet with admirable speed. The other man set aside his book and took up a carbine in one fluid motion.

"Luigi, you receive your friends with a peculiar ceremony indeed," the count said, unperturbed.

"Weapons down!" The bandit chief set aside his own gun. "I beg your pardon, excellency; I wasn't expecting your visit and did not immediately recognize you."

"Clearly I'm not the only one you failed to recognize; you're holding a friend of mine hostage. Does my memory fail me, or did we not agree that my friends would be allowed to visit Rome unmolested?" Monte Cristo asked in a tone that made Franz shudder. "Your prisoner has dined with me and ridden for hours through the streets of Rome in my carriage, yet you set a price on his life as if he were anyone else."

Vampa cursed his guards in Italian. *"Va fa Napoli!* You missed this in your surveillance and told me he was fair game? Do you expect Teresa to do all the work?" Vampa said. "I work with imbeciles! You're lucky not to spend the night in the pit yourselves!"

Vampa fought to regain his composure, then turned to face Monte Cristo in a deep bow.

"My humblest apologies, excellency; I didn't know the prisoner was a friend of yours. I'll take you to him at once," Vampa said.

Vampa opened a door at the far end of the room, and a blonde woman who Franz had not noticed paused in her meal to glance at the count.

"The man with no future returns," she said with a gentle smile.

"Queen Teresa, how do you do this evening?" Monte Cristo asked, favouring her with a small bow.

"I'm comfortable and free; all I need to be happy," Teresa answered. Nothing in her eyes declared to Franz her clairvoyant powers. "When the only man I've never been able to read comes to visit, I know the evening is about to become more interesting."

The door led to one of many alcoves overlooking the pit. Men with long spears would have stood there to break undead skulls from a safe distance. A rolled-up rope ladder sat in the alcove, and a figure wrapped in a cloak lay in the pit itself.

"Albert!" Franz shouted, fearing the worst.

Franz needn't have worried; Albert sat up, stretched his arms, and rubbed his eyes. In a peculiar display of courage in the face of impending doom, he had fallen asleep.

"Franz, you came! I knew you would," Albert shouted, waving an arm. "I'm alright, just in dire need of dry clothes. They soaked me nearly to the bone, can you believe it?"

"The prisoner is free to go, with my sincere apologies for the misunderstanding," Vampa said. He kicked the rope ladder into the pit, and Albert wasted no time in climbing up. He went into the next room as if in just another hotel and took a pear from a bowl he found. Franz admired his resilience; from his manner, nobody could guess that Albert had been mere hours from his own murder.

"Franz, I cannot thank you enough for coming so quickly," Albert said with his mouth full. "And I must assume thanks are due to the count as well?"

"I can refuse nothing to his excellency; he has secured your freedom without any ransom," Vampa said.

"Capital!" Albert said. "Then my dear Monte Cristo, from the very bottom of my heart, I'm forever in your debt. Anything you ask of me, if I have any earthly means of providing it, I will."

He offered his hand to the count and didn't notice when the smallest shudder ran through Monte Cristo's body or the shadow of a frown that touched his lips as they shook on it.

"Signor Luigi, is there any formality to fulfil before I take my leave?" he said.

The corner of Vampa's mustache twitched. He was accustomed to his prisoners quivering before him, not making polite inquiries if there would be anything else.

"None, sir. You're as free as the air, and I'll lead you back to the exit myself," Vampa said.

As they walked, Franz remembered a curious phrase he had heard twice already in regard to the kidnapping.

"Signor Luigi, if I may ask," Franz said, "what do you mean when you say that you thought Albert was 'fair game'?"

"Nothing else but the source of his money," Vampa said. "He was overheard bragging about his father, a general and senator in France. This means his fortune comes from the state. My darling Teresa Saw the truth of it, and so we abducted him. Unfortunately, she missed his friendship with the count. The Sight shows her so much, it can be overwhelming."

"Vampa is an interesting sort of humanitarian," Monte Cristo said.

"He robs from the rich, by which he means the government, and gives back in his own way to the poor."

"Do you ride around at night, secretly distributing bags of gold to the peasants?" Albert asked.

"Of course not; we buy from them," Vampa said. "The food we eat, the clothes we wear, the weapons we use and any other supplies we need; all bought honestly. The money that was stolen from the people is in this way returned to the people."

"I see a flaw in your plan, signor," Albert said, smirking. "Even if I agree with your premise that my fortune was stolen, it was from the people of France. Had the ransom been paid, you would be handing it over to the people of Rome."

"It's an imperfect system, I admit, but perhaps one day I'll expand my operation to other countries to try and correct it," Vampa said. "If I were to ransom an Italian senator while he visited Paris, it would help balance that score."

"You can't fairly call the government's revenue stolen, can you?" Franz asked. "After all, it must fund itself somehow. Would you have every road become a toll road?"

"Grocers and bakers fund themselves every day, through people buying their services willingly," Vampa said. "As for your roads, I propose this: at your hotel, ask if there is a toll for using the stairs and hallways."

By this time, they had returned to the exit. Vampa held the trapdoor open, led them to their carriage, and apologized again to Albert and Monte Cristo. Along the way, Monte Cristo gave Albert a fresh cigar; Albert tried several times in vain to summon fire from his wet fingers to light it.

"My dear Vampa, you compensate for your mistakes in such a gentlemanly fashion that I almost feel thankful that you committed them," Monte Cristo said. Albert followed him into the carriage, but Franz paused.

"One more thing, Signor Luigi: what were you reading when we arrived?" Franz asked.

"A book by a countryman of mine, Signor Gianmarco Faria, called The Possibility of Liberty," Vampa said. "I bought a copy from a travelling priest several years ago. It's one of my favourite works, though I'm sad to say it was published after the author's death."

His curiosity satisfied, Franz climbed into the carriage. Before they could leave, Albert leaned out the window. Still too soaked to create a flame, he lit his cigar off of Vampa's torch. They returned to the hotel with enough time for Albert to change into dry clothes and return with Franz to the Duke of Bracciano's ball, where he found Countess Garzone almost immediately for a dance. As they whirled away into the crowd, Franz replayed the events at *la foro prigione* again and again in his mind. He couldn't ignore how the count had shuddered when he had touched Albert's hand.

CHAPTER 41
THE ARRANGEMENT

Bright and early the next morning, Albert knocked on the count's door again with Franz standing behind him. Franz still found the count intriguing and terrifying, and the only thing clear to him in that confusion was that he did not want to send Albert into the count's domain alone.

"My friend, the trifling amount of effort to rescue you isn't worth mentioning," the count said when Albert thanked him yet again for his rescue. "Honestly, what did I do? I rode in my carriage to meet you, I reminded Luigi Vampa of his obligations, and together we rode back to the hotel. If anything, I should congratulate you on your bravery. Not many men can face death with such calm as to fall asleep!"

"I suppose I was determined to show those bandits that the French can smile—or sleep—in the face of eternity itself," Albert said. "Anyway, I don't care how simple it was for you to save my hide; I'm still thankful that you did so. If I can repay the favour at all, just name it. My father possesses considerable influence in both France and Madrid and I place it, through myself, at your service."

"Monsieur de Morcerf," Monte Cristo said, "I humbly accept. In fact, I had already made up my mind to ask you a favour. We three have spoken of my visiting you and Franz should I ever reach Paris. I would appreciate it if you would open the doors of that world to me, since I have no connections there yet."

"Someone as distinctive as you would require no introductions!" Albert said, delighted that the count's favour was something he was so well-suited to provide. "I will, and with pleasure. Your timing is excellent; I've received a letter today from my father summoning me home to Paris to be married. By the time you arrive, I'll have had a chance to make arrangements for you. Just promise me that you truly intend to visit Paris, and this isn't some passing fancy. I intend to tell my parents all about you, and they'll be eager to meet the man who saved their son."

"I pledge on my honour: this visit is no fancy," Monte Cristo said. "Besides my desire to see the finest capital in all of Europe, other matters of absolute necessity compel me to go to Paris."

These words, wrapped in an inscrutable sphinxlike smile, brought back dim recollections for Franz of his dinner in the grotto on the island. He tried to recall if the count had mentioned plans involving Paris; piercing the fog that time and excitement had built between him and the memories was a struggle.

Albert and Monte Cristo agreed that the count would give Albert three months to reach Paris and settle in at home before visiting. The count even insisted on setting the day and hour he'd arrive: the twenty-first of May at half past ten in the morning. Albert promised breakfast would be waiting in his apartment on the Morcerf estate.

"Your visit is well-timed," Monte Cristo said. "I must leave for Naples today and won't return before Sunday morning. I would have regretted not seeing you again before you left for Paris. Franz, are you departing tomorrow as well?"

The count's red eyes turned to Franz, setting his nerves on edge.

"I am, but not for France," Franz replied. "I go to Venice and plan to remain another year in Italy. Unless you plan to make your stay in Paris a long one, we likely won't meet there."

"Then this is *adieu*! I wish you each a safe and pleasant journey," Monte Cristo said.

He extended his hand to Albert once more, and Franz again noticed the barest shudder. Next, Monte Cristo took Franz's hand. It was the first time they had done so; even through the count's glove, Franz felt an icy grip.

In spite of the kindness the count had shown them, Franz found himself hoping he would never see those red eyes again. His apprehension must have shown on his face, since Albert brought it up while they packed their belongings.

"Albert, I can't help but think that becoming the count's friend is a dreadful mistake and that it will bring you nothing but misery," Franz said, taking his last chance to convey his misgivings.

"The count has been nothing but generous to us, two utter strangers to him before this week," Albert said as he lit a fresh cigar. "On the other hand, you've been increasingly cold toward him lately, bordering on rude. Do you know something about him that I don't?"

"Listen to me Albert, and don't repeat a word of what I tell you. I have met the count before, in a grotto beneath the island of Monte Cristo. He goes by the name Sinbad the Sailor; the same man from Pastrini's story about Vampa," Franz said.

Franz told Albert everything he could remember about the strange circumstances of his dinner with Sinbad and the hashish they consumed afterward. To his credit, Albert listened to Franz with profound attention and never once interjected with one of his typical jokes. His cigar smoldered out and needed to be re-lit before the story was through.

"He associates with smugglers and thieves," Franz said. "I overheard him and Vampa the night we went to the Colosseum. That's why I asked him to free you from the bandits; Vampa pledged his undying service to the count in front of me. There are too many coincidences for me to be comfortable with this. We don't even know his name, beyond his title."

"Let's examine what we do know about him," Albert said. "He travels the world on his own vessel. He bought an island and built a getaway there for privacy and bought a title for prestige. So far, he's merely eccentric and rich."

Albert paused for a deep inhale of the fragrant tobacco, one of the cigars offered by the count, and continued.

"A bandit king serves him out of gratitude for some reason," Albert said. "Considering that I currently owe my life to that friendship, I'm disinclined to examine the source of that gratitude too closely."

"But who is he?" Franz asked. "Where does he come from, how is he so rich, what happened to give him such a peculiar outlook? Why are his eyes and face such an unnatural colour, and why are his hands so freakishly cold?"

"Tell me this," Albert said. "When you asked the count for help rescuing me, did he reply by asking 'who is Albert de Morcerf, where is his money from, why does he look how he does'?"

"Well, no," Franz said. The count had asked no questions at all but immediately offered to pay the ransom.

"Precisely! He used his influence and had me, a nearly perfect stranger, freed," Albert said. "In return for that monumental favour, all he wants is that I make introductions for him back home. Meanwhile you seem ready to burn him at the stake for his deformities as if we were witch-hunters in the Colonies!"

Franz was not accustomed to hearing Albert make more effective arguments than he could. He doubted the foundations of his misgivings and admitted the chance he was being too harsh on the count.

"Please, at least be careful around him," Franz said. "There's so much about him we simply don't know."

Albert agreed to proceed with caution, and they set out together for a last luncheon before parting ways. When they returned to the hotel to settle their bill, Albert caught Signor Pastrini's attention while the bellhops brought their luggage out to the travelling coach.

"Signor Pastrini, I nearly forgot to ask: how do you pay for the upkeep of your stairs?" Albert asked, getting only a baffled look from Pastrini prompting him to elaborate. "Someone put the idea in my head last night. My bill has no stair-using fee, but so many people tromp up and down them that they must require repairs sometimes. How is it paid for?"

"Excellency, I'm not certain I understand," Pastrini said. "When I set the price of the room, I choose one that allows me to pay for any repairs the hotel may need."

Albert nodded, looking from the main staircase to the street outside.

CHAPTER 42
THREE MONTHS LATER

The metal tips of a lash passed within an inch of Albert's nose. He responded with a thrust of his rapier, but his opponent dodged to the side, anticipating the move. Frustration and admiration blended into a grim smile on Albert's face as he waited for an opening.

They dueled in the loft of a pavilion, at the edge of the grounds at 27 Rue de Helder in Paris, behind the main house and away from the road. The Count and Countess de Morcerf lived in the main house, but the pavilion held Albert's apartments. Scattered mementoes of Albert's past and present hobbies surrounded the dueling men. An eclectic mix of the implements of painting, music, and fighting mingled with treasures and furniture from around Europe. The late May sun streamed in through the skylights, illuminating the sheen of sweat on Albert's exposed chest and reflecting a glow from the other man's uncommonly pale skin.

Albert lunged around the side of an armchair which may once have been sat in by Henry VIII, but his opponent's strange eyes caught the move and he slid away to just beyond Albert's reach. The lash touched Albert's back without breaking the skin, as if his opponent were more interested in proving a point than in wounding Albert.

Albert growled, having received six or seven such blows already. His temper rising, he swung his sword in a wide arc, slashing at his opponent who moved like oil to avoid each one. The lash flicked out again to wrap around Albert's blade and yank it from his grip. Steel clattered on hardwood as the sword tumbled down the stairs.

The sword tumbled past the second-story bedroom and landed by the smoking room on the ground floor. In that smoking room, Albert had curated a selection of the world's tobaccos for his expected breakfast guests. The date was the twenty-first of May, and it was the day when the Count of Monte Cristo had promised to arrive.

Disarmed, Albert glanced around the room for a new weapon. Improvising, he held up a hand and flashed a bright flame at eye level to dazzle his opponent. The move gave Albert time to retrieve a long fighting-stick from across the room. His opponent rubbed the spots from his eyes but not in time to avoid catching the stick in the small of his back. Albert pressed the advantage with a series of rapid blows to the torso, then swept the stick in a low arc and knocked the pale man to the ground.

Albert planted his knee on his opponent's chest and held up a globe of fire the size of a grapefruit. If Albert brought it down, his opponent's hair would burn, his eyes would boil, his flesh would run like molten wax and his brain would cook inside his skull to a lump of useless jelly.

Facing this grim death, the pale man smirked. Albert laughed and extinguished the flame, helped his opponent to stand, and threw him a towel.

"A fine effort as always, Lucien!" Albert said as he dried off his own sweat. "Although it seems you've recently had a very different kind of scuffle; perhaps you narrowly escaped the jaws of my future mother-in-law?"

Lucien Debray, secretary to the Minister of Finance, looked down at himself. Like Albert, he was shirtless; unlike Albert with his parents' dark Spanish colouring, Lucien was peculiarly colourless. His blonde hair was among the fairest in France, and the eyes in his pale face were a light shade of grey. If not for the near-constant mischievous smile upon his face, Lucien would seem to have been drained of life itself. On this occasion, Lucien carried several spots of livid colour in a series of love-bites running from his neck down to his chest.

"I have no idea what you mean, Albert," Lucien said, pulling his shirt back on. "My visits to the baron's wife are to discuss investment opportunities. By the way, I've seen your betrothed; she sends her regards."

"Her very warmest, I'm sure," Albert said in a deadpan.

Eugenie Danglars, the daughter of Baron Danglars and Albert's arranged fiancée, was an unconventional woman and utterly disinterested in marrying him. As far as Albert could tell, she had no other man in her life; she simply did not care to be his wife. Albert was not too put out by this; after all, men had mistresses for a reason.

"In any case, I'm seeing both her and her mother tonight at the theatre," Albert said. "I think Eugenie is coming directly from her club meeting."

Dressed for breakfast once more, Albert and Lucien descended to the smoking room. The fragrance of toasted leaves hung thick in the air, intoxicating in and of itself, and Albert observed the assortment with pride. As was the custom in Paris, and in Albert's home particularly, the guests would retire to that palace of comfort after breakfast to sit and digest with the aid of the finest smoking available. Albert had taken care to find the most exquisite French-made cigars to sit in pride of place in the arrangement, among jars of loose-leaf from around the world.

"Remind me, who else are we expecting before we can eat?" Lucien said. He rummaged through the sideboard for a biscuit and a glass of sherry. "I enjoy a good sparring match, but it's driven my appetite absolutely mad. I was bored, and you've amused me; now I'm hungry, so feed me."

"It's nobody's fault but yours that you got the time wrong," Albert said. "We're waiting for four more people; it was going to be three, but Raoul invited a guest at the last minute. It's a good thing he told me, or one of us would have to go without."

"Without what?" Lucien asked, sinking into one of the armchairs scattered throughout the room. "You still haven't said what you're serving."

Albert smiled. "You'll see. Now, tell me about the turnings of the great ministerial machine."

"Oh, you know," Lucien said, tracing a lazy circle in the air with his biscuit, "a war here, a revolution there. Don Carlos in Spain was quite effectively ousted recently, that was an upset. It's a good thing the Royal Bourbon Reserve Bank liquidated their Spanish assets when they did. Rumour has it that Baron Danglars profited by a million francs on it."

"I can't say I know much about Spanish affairs, but that sounds as if it bodes well for my bride-to-be's dowry and inheritance," Albert said.

"Really, you're better off not knowing these things," Lucien said, sipping his sherry. "They're dreadfully dull most of the time, and take up so much room in the mind. I was up all night writing letters to people who must know the minister's opinions and orders on current events around Europe, and my brain feels like it's been spread across the continent with a butter knife. That's why I'm here so early, I was simply too discombobulated to sleep. You're very lucky to have nothing to do."

"Lucky! Imagine that, a man who's privy to great international intrigues telling me that I'm lucky to not be part of it!" Albert laughed. "If you still need amusement, I'll introduce you to an especially amusing man today when he arrives."

Lucien sighed. "I know so many men already. Couldn't you invite an amusing woman—or several? I hope this devil brings breakfast with him, I'm wasting away!" He laid a hand across his forehead and swooned. "I hardly remember my last solid meal, I've been so busy, but I think it was at M. de Villefort's. Lawyers give such horrible dinners, I don't know why they bother at all. And the look of him rather puts me off my food."

Voices murmured at the front door of the pavilion. Albert's valet soon admitted a young man with thick black hair and a thin dark mustache.

"Beauchamp!" Albert exclaimed. "So glad you could make it! I need to critique that horrible newspaper you work for. Why do you bury important matters like the theatre schedule on page seven while some claptrap about elections in Turkey makes the front page?"

"Don't lay too much blame on me, Albert," Beauchamp chuckled. His hangdog features, or perhaps just his career, made him look tired even when he smiled. "I write the stories, but I don't dictate the layout."

"In all seriousness, congratulations!" Albert said. He handed Beauchamp a glass of sherry and clinked the bottle against it. "Your first front-page headline! I don't see the excitement of the story, but it's exciting to see your name on it. Bravo!"

"You're becoming quite the Renaissance man, Beauchamp," Lucien said from his chair. "Last month it was science articles about some new steam engine, this month it's news from far-off Turkey. One day perhaps you'll even write a story I find interesting."

Beauchamp smiled and took a short pencil from the breast pocket of his jacket.

"Not every paper can be a yellow rag like the Nightly Assemblage that you're so fond of," Beauchamp said, flicking the pencil at Lucien.

"Journalistic integrity isn't quite dead yet, and The Independent prides itself on thorough fact-checking before printing a story."

"But that takes so long!" Lucien said, throwing his head back. "By the time you've done all that, whatever the story's about happened days or weeks ago. If there's a scandal to be outraged about, I want to know about it now."

"Gentlemen, enough about foreign affairs and journalism," Albert said, hoping to steer the conversation back towards some topic he could follow more easily. "I hear a carriage, more guests are coming."

"This breakfast is liable to be the highlight of my day," Beauchamp said. "Later, I'm going to the Senate Chamber at the House of Peers to cover your future father-in-law giving one of his interminable speeches."

"Don't sound so depressed about it," Albert said. "Baron Danglars is an important and influential man in both the sphere of finance and of human rights, and you're a journalist; you should be excited to hear him speak."

"I should, but I can't muster your enthusiasm," Beauchamp said. "All of his speeches are the same: a lecture about the past and platitudes for the future. I'd rather be writing about some important new discovery, but I must take the assignments I'm given."

The valet returned. "Baron Raoul de Chateau-Renaud, and Captain Maximilien Morrel," he announced.

A fit-looking and confident young man of thirty, Raoul was the consummate picture of a French military gentleman. He walked into the room as if he lived there and lifted Albert off his feet in a warm hug.

Raoul's companion, the same Maximilien Morrel who once stopped his father shooting himself in Marseille, stood with his shoulders rounded and his hands in his pockets. Where his gaze had been like green steel in 1829, now Max's eyes darted around as if assessing the threat presented by each of the other men. Like Beauchamp, his round face looked fatigued, though to a more severe degree.

Both Max and Raoul wore the dress uniform of French cavalry, and both still carried the bronzed complexions and thick beards of their time spent on campaign in Africa. With his typical enthusiasm, Raoul shook hands with everyone and clapped them each on the shoulder; he hadn't seen any of his friends since he'd left for his tour of duty a year before. He soon returned to Max's side.

"Gentlemen, I'd die of shame and embarrassment if I waited another second to introduce you to this man," Raoul said. "Captain Maximilien Morrel, distinguished field medic, my dear friend, and the man who saved my life. If the army had only four or five more men like him, the entire world would be speaking French within a fortnight."

Max shifted his weight and smiled without looking at anyone and gave a small jump when Albert approached him. He relaxed somewhat when Albert shook his hand with sincere warmth.

"What a ringing endorsement!" Albert said. "It's a pleasure to meet you, Captain Morrel. Will you be in Paris long before your next tour of duty?"

"Please, viscount, call me Max. M. de Chateau-Renaud exaggerates," Max said, avoiding Albert's question. "He makes himself sound helpless; he was in danger, yes, but I only helped."

"You're too humble!" Raoul said with a wide smile. "I'll set the scene: we were in the jungles of Algeria, in the dead of night. I was inspecting the watch, and heard weak cries of pain in the trees."

Raoul mimed drawing his sword and prowled through the smoking room. The other men, accustomed to but never tiring of his theatrics, settled in for another of Raoul's exuberant stories.

"I went to investigate and found a native laying against a tree, holding his stomach. I tried speaking to him in some of the local dialects, but he just shook his head muttering again and again," Raoul said. "Foolish me, I got closer to hear him better."

He turned and lunged at Beauchamp for dramatic effect. "Suddenly, the man's head spun in a half-circle!" Raoul said. "Where the back of his head should have been was a jackal's face, and it's jaws clamped on my arm like a bear trap!"

Raoul rolled back his sleeve to show a mangled scar, still fresh and pink. "Of course the creature had the luck to get my sword arm, and the way it squirmed I couldn't use my knife," he said. "I even tried to pry the teeth from my flesh, but it was like trying to split masonry with a toothpick."

He returned to Max, whose face betrayed both embarrassment and reluctant pride at the story.

"Naturally, I called for help, and our brave medic answered!" Raoul said. "He approached without a sound and shot the beast. It howled in pain, released my arm, and I drove my knife into its heart."

"Bravo!" Lucien said. "But tell me, Captain Max, how does one sneak up on a thing which literally has eyes on the back of its head?"

"Simply, sir: you approach from the side," Max said. When this elicited a hearty laugh from Lucien, Max smiled a little easier. "We learned later that these things are called *kishi*; they lure in victims with their human face before striking with their jackal's face. Thankfully, their condition is not contagious like lycanthropy."

"Well, I'll be certain to tell the men at the club that today I had breakfast with a pair of genuine monster-slayers," Lucien said. He looked at Albert. "Assuming, of course, that we ever actually eat."

"Patience, we're waiting for one more guest," Albert said. "Since he saved my life as surely as our new friend Max saved Raoul, I couldn't possibly begin without him."

Lucien groaned. "Do you mean to tell me that we're waiting for your mysterious Count of Monte Cristo? How do we know that your one-week friend from Rome will even arrive?"

"Our Albert required rescuing?" Raoul said, eyes wide. "My goodness, it must have been formidable danger indeed to have resisted your mighty flames!"

Raoul chuckled, and Lucien laughed aloud again.

"He never had a chance to use his fire, to hear him tell it," Lucien said. "They saw him coming and drenched him to the bone!"

"My monsters had no extra faces, but they were deadly nonetheless," Albert said. He explained to Raoul and Max the story of his capture and subsequent rescue by the count. Raoul listened with interest and declared it an adventure worthy of a song.

"But is it worthy of starving to death?" Lucien asked, pretending to faint. "I've never even heard of this count. Where does he come from?"

Raoul agreed that he'd never heard the name either, despite having studied aristocratic lineages as part of his education.

"Certainly not from Monte Cristo itself," Max said. "My father ran a shipping company, and some of his sailors knew that island as a spot to rest. The count may own the island, but nobody lives there. The main occupants are goats, which taste good but aren't much for titles. Some of the older sailors spin a tall tale about hidden caves, but I don't place much stock in them."

"At any rate, our guest of honour is the lord and master of those goats; he bought the title from Tuscany," Albert said.

"You told us he's a wealthy man, a world-traveler, and a hero. Countess Garzone says in her letters that he's a vampire," Lucien said. "I say that in another minute he'll be late, and we should eat without him."

Indeed, the clock struck half-past ten at that moment.

"Albert, just admit that you invented the whole story in a haze of sambuca and tainted Italian tobacco so that you may quit starving us," Lucien said.

The sound of the clock still rang through the house when a carriage door slammed outside. Nobody noticed Max jump again and half-turn to the door before the valet entered.

"His excellency, the Count of Monte Cristo," he announced.

Albert smirked when Lucien's mouth dropped open in a perfect "O" of surprise. He made a mental note to begin spreading the gossip of what it took to shake Lucien's cool demeanour. The shock on his friends' faces was a great satisfaction to Albert as the singular man made his entrance.

His clothes were simple enough but made by the finest tailors. His jet-black hair fell to his shoulders in a fashionable wave and provided an almost offensive contrast to the bloodless white of his finely-lined face, in which his red eyes shone like rubies. As always, he wore a cravat knotted about his throat and delicate gloves over his hands.

"Viscount Albert de Morcerf," said the Count of Monte Cristo in the same smoky timbre Albert remembered. "Thank you for inviting me to your home."

CHAPTER 43
THE BREAKFAST

"Please excuse the few seconds of tardiness," Monte Cristo said. "It would seem there's some unwritten law here forbidding anyone traveling faster than the post-horses."

"Don't apologize at all; I'm happy to introduce you to some of my friends, who were beginning to think you were too fantastic to be true," Albert said. "There is Baron Raoul de Chateau-Renaud, whose ancestor was said to have a place at the Round Table. Here is M. Lucien Debray, private secretary to the Minister of Finance, and across from him M. Beauchamp Fournier, who writes marvelous articles which I can't understand a word of."

Monte Cristo nodded to each guest in turn.

"Finally, a more recent acquaintance," Albert said. "An army medic and hero of men, Captain Maximilien Morrel."

The name rang like a gong in Monte Cristo's ears. Memories of a previous life tumbled through his mind—of a time he had vowed to set aside. Monte Cristo stared at Max, seeing a one-legged man standing to one side of him and a girl weeping with gratitude to the other. The count blinked twice and coughed, then extended his hand to Max.

"You wear the handsome uniform of the conquering French, monsieur. Their victories are becoming legendary," Monte Cristo said.

"And beneath that handsome uniform beats the heart of a hero," Albert said. "Max saved Raoul's life from a jungle beast on campaign, and that's enough for me to consider him a dear friend already."

"Then he has a noble heart," Monte Cristo muttered, unnoticed by anyone. He noted the bags under Max's eyes and the slump in his broad shoulders. "Well enough, but he seems changed."

As the valet entered again to speak to Albert, Raoul leaned in toward Max and Beauchamp.

"It seems that Albert has not deceived us after all," Raoul said. "What do you think, Max?"

"I can't say I care for how he was just staring at me," Max said, "but I almost feel like I've met him before, briefly even. Was he one of the dignitaries we guarded at the Embassy?"

"Gentlemen," Albert called, "breakfast is ready. Count, this way please. Since you've never been to Paris before, I was sure to select a particularly dignified French delicacy."

"Just remember, I'm also a stranger to French dining customs," Monte Cristo said. "If you find anything too Eastern or too Italian in my manners, please excuse me and correct my errors."

The dining table was laid with the usual assortment of jams, croissants, and clotted cream, but a silver covered dish at each place setting drew the eye. Next to each dome sat a pristine white napkin with elaborate gold embroidery.

"Albert, you dog! Are you serving what I think you're serving?" Raoul exclaimed. Grinning, he grabbed Max by the shoulders. "Max, you're in for a treat if my eyes don't deceive me."

Albert smiled as his friends took their seats. Only the count noticed Max's hesitation before approaching his chair; he seemed on the brink of speaking to it before he shook his head and sat down.

Servants stepped forward to withdraw the domes in unison. A cloud of steam issued from each plate, bringing with it the aromas of brandy and figs and the delicate smell of flambéed poultry. A single ramekin sat on each plate, and each ramekin contained a single plucked bird the size of a sparrow. The flesh had been roasted to golden brown, and to Max's surprise, the bird's head was still attached to the body.

Raoul rubbed his hands together and Lucien closed his eyes to breathe in the steam. Albert was quite proud of himself and looked to Monte Cristo for approval. The count looked at his bird with an expression that defied interpretation.

"Gentlemen, I have a confession to make," Beauchamp said. "While I've attended many society dinners in my role as a journalist, I've never seen this dish before and have no idea what it is. Could someone explain what this marvelous aroma is called?"

"Gentlemen, what you have before you is the great French delicacy of ortolan," Albert said. "The ortolan songbird is captured in the wild and kept in a dark cage where it thinks it's night and gorges itself. When the bird is fat enough, the chef drowns it in a barrel of Armagnac, killing and marinating the creature in one go. It's then plucked and flambéed in a delicate sauce and presented to be eaten whole."

The dish garnered mixed reactions around the table. Lucien and Raoul were eager to taste their birds, having experienced the dish before. Beauchamp eyed his plate with renewed curiosity, and Max had turned rather pale. Monte Cristo looked around the table, settling on Max.

"Captain Morrel, surely you've eaten stranger fare while abroad?" Monte Cristo said.

"Well, yes," Max said, "but at the risk of sounding rude, isn't there a more humane way to end the bird's life?"

"I've never seen this dish in person, but I have heard world-class chefs discuss it," Monte Cristo said. "You could break the bird's neck first, but the depth of flavour comes from the bird attempting to inhale the brandy and saturating its own blood with the alcohol. It really is essential to the finished product, I hear."

"I see your reasoning, from a culinary standpoint," Max said, "but I can't help thinking that if I were a bird, I'd hate to die that way."

"Drowning in brandy? I've always expected and hoped that's exactly how I'll meet my end," Lucien said, getting a raucous laugh from the other guests.

"I see that Albert wasn't exaggerating your nobility," Monte Cristo said. "Consider this: an animal is not a man, but property, and a wild animal is only property which no man has yet claimed. I find it a waste of energy to consider whether the property that became my breakfast was treated well or led a fulfilling life, whether we talk about the bird itself or the figs used in the sauce. My thinking is that when all of the injustices that men perpetrate against each other have been dealt with, then there will be time to worry about if animals have ambitions beyond their next meal or becoming ours."

Beauchamp produced a notepad and another pencil from his pocket midway through Monte Cristo's answer. "That was quite good —'whether my breakfast led a fulfilling life'—I may need to sit you down for an interview!" he said, copying the words to paper.

Monte Cristo nodded and indicated the bird on his plate again. "Our enjoying this meal today may have effects long into the future. If the hunters of these birds continue to do business, someone will think to farm them, and the bird's existence will be secured for all time," the count said. "After all, the American eagle's numbers are dwindling, but nobody has reason to worry that chickens or ducks will meet extinction."

"Very good, then our consumption of this morsel will feed not only our bodies, but our very souls," Lucien said. "May we please eat now?"

"Be my guest," Albert said with a grin. He unfolded his embroidered napkin and covered his head with it, to Max and Beauchamp's great surprise. Lucien and Raoul did the same, and Monte Cristo came to their aid with an explanation.

"The diner covers his head with the napkin while eating ortolan, because the dish is so indulgent that he must hide his gluttony from God," Monte Cristo said. He grinned, showing his straight white teeth. "Or, to accept another explanation, to hide the sauce and juices dripping down your chin. Simply hold the bird's head between your fingers, and place the body in your mouth."

Still unsure about the dish, Max followed Albert's example and covered his head anyway. He had to reposition it several times and hold up a corner to be able to see his plate, but he could soon pick up his bird as directed. He made himself ignore how much the morsel resembled a sleeping baby chick, and bit down.

Max was shocked to find that the bird had not been deboned and the delicate skeleton fell apart with a crunch between his teeth. Tiny shards of bone pricked the inside of his cheeks, and the miniscule cuts tingled and burned at the touch of brandy in the sauce. The flavour was as exquisite as Lucien and Raoul claimed, with complexities that the rustic home cooking of his youth and the rations of his military career had not prepared him for. He recognized the taste of hazelnut and the gamey character unique to a wild bird. Max's misgivings about the dish faltered in the face of a simple fact: it was delicious. Did Albert and Raoul dine like this every day in Paris?

True to Monte Cristo's word, Max's chin was smeared with evidence of his meal. The head-covering seemed too fancy for cleaning his face, so he groped instead for the plain napkin that lay beneath his fork. His fellow diners looked satisfied, and Monte Cristo dabbed his lips with his plain napkin as well. Morrel noticed that the ornate napkin meant to cover the count's head remained folded and untouched by his plate; he seemed to feel no need to hide any sins in his meal.

"*Mon dieu*, that was the most splendid ortolan I have ever eaten," Lucien said. "I could easily eat an entire meal of them, but sadly man cannot live on ortolan alone. Beauchamp, be a friend and pass the croissants."

CHAPTER 44
A SINGULAR GUEST

Max found the remainder of breakfast far more familiar. Eating a crumpet with apricot preserves, he noticed that the count took very little onto his plate.

"Count, are you feeling well?" Max asked.

"After such an *amuse-bouche*, how could I feel any other way?" Monte Cristo said. "Don't let my plate fool you; as Albert can attest, I eat everything from everywhere, but only a little at a time. This is a feast by my standards; I haven't eaten since yesterday morning."

"The devil you say!" Raoul said. "Why on earth not?"

"I made a detour to Nimes for some inquiries, and stopping for a meal would have made me quite late," Monte Cristo said. "Instead, I did what I generally do when I'm hungry and not inclined to eat; I slept."

"What a coincidence," Lucien said. "I dined with M. de Villefort recently, who used to be the prosecutor in Nimes."

"I can never sleep on such a long ride if I'm alone," Raoul said. "You never know when highwaymen could jump out of the bushes."

"Oh, I never travel unarmed," Monte Cristo said with a grin. "They would be in for quite a surprise."

"You have some recipe to sleep when you please, even when hungry?" Max asked. "That would be useful to our men in Africa, where food can be quite scarce."

"I can see why you'd think so, but my recipe would be quite perilous for an army," Monte Cristo said with a smile. "The recipe is simple: pure Cantonese opium and the best Indian hashish blended together. It can be eaten as a paste or pressed into pills. You may ask Baron Franz d'Epinay, he tasted it one day when we dined together."

"Do you have this drug with you now?" Beauchamp asked, his journalistic curiosity piqued.

"And may we try some?" Lucien added, motivated by a rather different impulse.

"I do, and you may not," Monte Cristo said. "I use a highly potent mixture for my own high tolerance of it, not to be shared. Though, if you call on me at home I may have a more recreational blend available. I am something of a chemist and make them myself."

Monte Cristo took out an emerald as large as the birds they had eaten. The gem was hollowed out into a pillbox with space for a dozen small pills, though only five sat inside. Raoul, a connoisseur of fine stones, remarked on how magnificent the emerald itself was.

"I used to have two others like it," Monte Cristo said. "I gave one to a sultan in exchange for a slave-woman's freedom. The other one I gave to the Pope recently to pardon a man from losing his head. My title does not carry much power or influence, but I am able to occasionally lease the influence of others."

Everyone stared with astonishment, aside from Albert. He suspected that Peppino, from the executions at Carnival, was the pardoned man in question. Meanwhile, Monte Cristo spoke in such a matter-of-fact way as to convince them that he must be either honest or mad, and the evidence of the emerald in front of them suggested the former. Albert felt vindicated that his friends believed at last the wild tales he had told them about the Count of Monte Cristo.

"Count, if you could," Beauchamp said, "we've heard of how you rescued our host from the Roman bandits. How did you manage that? The way Albert tells it, all you had to do was appear and this Vampa character nearly prostrated himself at your feet."

"I should have sworn Albert to secrecy," Monte Cristo said. "It is simple enough: I met Luigi Vampa when he was still a child. I gave him some gold to show me my way, and he gave me a dagger he had made. Several years later, he mistook my identity and tried to rob me on the road, but I was able to get the better of him and a dozen of his men. Rather than kill him or turn him in, I let them go."

"With the promise that they no longer patrol the roads?" Beauchamp asked.

"Certainly not," Monte Cristo said. "Only with an oath to respect myself and my friends. You see, Vampa has a particular *modus operandi* which I can find no fault in; he robs only those who he judges have acquired their wealth by robbing others. He had heard my title somewhere and did not know that my island has no human inhabitants at all; it was an honest mistake."

Lucien arched a single blond eyebrow in response to this reasoning.

"This proves the importance of connections," Albert said. "If I weren't your friend and you weren't Vampa's long-ago captor, my body would likely still lay in that dreadful pit. And it's in connections that I'll finally be able to repay you."

Albert spread his hands wide, indicating his friends.

"If your unique personality weren't enough to have you received anywhere, my friends and I will present you to all of Paris. Any questions of French habits, or where to find the best bazaars and finest women, just ask," Albert said. "The only thing I cannot provide is lodgings; these rooms of mine are quite full with just me here."

"Or quite empty, if you were looking for signs of a woman," Lucien said with a smirk.

"That reminds me, you said something about marriage before leaving Rome. Are congratulations in order yet?" Monte Cristo said.

"Not quite; it's still being arranged," Albert said. "Hopefully I can introduce you to my betrothed soon. Her name is Mademoiselle Eugenie Danglars."

"Danglars," Monte Cristo said. "That sounds familiar. Is she connected to Baron Danglars, who prints your country's money?"

"Yes, and it's a good thing that he does," Lucien said. "I swear, everything in France gets more expensive every year."

"Technically, Baron Danglars is the chairman of the Royal Bourbon Reserve Bank," Beauchamp offered. "Printing banknotes is one of the bank's mandates, as well as setting interest rates and setting the reserve requirements for the commercial banks."

"Didn't I tell you, count? Half of what Beauchamp says flies above my head," Albert said.

"It's quite simple; the reserve requirement is how much gold a commercial bank must hold in their vaults as a percentage of the money they owe to their customers in savings and interest. This allows them to protect against—" Beauchamp said, before Lucien silenced him by tossing a clementine at his head.

"Then I have two reasons to see Baron Danglars." Monte Cristo sipped at a cup of tea. "I have a letter of credit from Thomson & French and I imagine Danglars' bank will be as good as any to bring it to. And I must meet the man who will be your father-in-law!"

"Actually, it's not that kind of a bank. Baron Danglars does also own a commercial bank, but the Reserve—" Beauchamp cut himself short when Lucien hefted another clementine. Meanwhile, Max looked like a man electrified.

"Did you say Thomson & French?" Max said with an energy quite unlike the shyness which had surrounded him all morning. "Count, maybe you could help me with a search that my sister and I have carried on for years. Thomson & French did my family a great service ten years ago, and for some reason they've denied it to this day. They claim not to have ever sent the clerk who brought us our good fortune."

"I'll do what I can," Monte Cristo said.

Beauchamp asked Max to elaborate, and while the party adjourned to the smoking room Max told the tale of the nameless clerk who had saved Morrel & Son.

"My only clue is the name Dimonte," Max said, missing how intensely Monte Cristo listened. "The clerk never gave his name, but the purse of treasure and the bill forgiving our largest debts came with a document. In it, a man named Dimonte became the new silent partner of Morrel & Son. My father only ever dealt with him through intermediaries, but his investment and his gift of a new ship was timed too perfectly to be coincidence."

In the smoking room, Albert was in his element. He introduced his friends to the buffet of tobacco, making recommendations to each of them based on what he knew of their tastes in both leaf and smoking apparatus. When Albert learned that Max had only ever smoked army tobacco rations, he at once packed an elegant calabash with a sweet and mild leaf for him.

"They grow these calabash gourds in such a way that they naturally form a perfect shape for pipe-smoking," Albert explained. "The bowl is a stone called meerschaum, which pulls tar out of the smoke. A calabash pipe will give you the cleanest, crispest draw every time."

When Albert conjured a flame on his fingertip to light the pipe and then his own cigar, Max recognized it as a Catalan talent from his boyhood in Marseille. Albert was always happy to talk about himself and his gift, and Max relished the chance to smoke and listen without speaking for a few minutes. The large curved pipe was a far more pleasant smoking experience than any wrinkled army cigarette, just as Albert promised.

Suddenly, Albert brought his hand to his forehead. "I just remembered, we'd begun to talk about the count's lodgings, but got sidetracked!" he said. "We need to find him suitable accommodations. Gentlemen, ideas!"

Raoul suggested finding a hotel in the Faubourg Saint-Germain, which Lucien rejected as gloomy before recommending the Chaussee d'Antin. Beauchamp sang the praises of the Boulevard de l'Opera, and Max mentioned that his sister and her husband were very happy in the Rue Meslay.

"You have a sister?" Monte Cristo asked. "How long has she been married?"

"Nine years, to one of the kindest men I've ever known," Morrel said. "Emmanuel was a clerk at Morrel & Son, who was loyal to Julie and Father through their darkest hour. I stay with them when I'm on leave, and their home is as refreshing as a warm bath after being on campaign."

"I'd like to meet them, if I may," Monte Cristo said, smiling but with a furrowed brow. "Gentlemen, these are excellent suggestions but unnecessary. I sent servants ahead of me, and they've already purchased a house for me. By the time I arrive there, Ali will have furnished it to my liking."

"Ali? Isn't that the name of your mute Nubian?" Lucien said through a ring of smoke. "His appearance will absolutely be talked about in the papers for weeks, if anyone catches a glimpse of him."

"If you already have a house, then all you need is a mistress to keep it warm!" Raoul said, then raised his eyebrows when Albert chuckled and shook his head.

"I think Albert remembers seeing Haydee, my Greek companion, in Rome," Monte Cristo said. "Yes, she came with me to Paris. You may find your mistresses at the opera; I purchased mine in Constantinople."

"A slave?" Raoul said. "Goodness, your ways truly are exotic. Just don't let her speak to any French women; they'll tell her that French law says she was freed the moment she set foot here, and your arrangement will change dramatically."

"There is no worry of that; she's been free since the moment after I bought her," Monte Cristo said. "She stays with me of her own accord. Everyone around me is free to leave and they know that I'll remain their friend when they do."

The conversation continued a while longer, but after refilling and smoking through his pipe a second time, Lucien rose to leave.

"Albert, your guest is charming, but now I must leave the best company to go into the worst," Lucien said. "I return to the minister's office; I'll tell him all about the count, and we'll soon learn where his mysteries began."

"I wish you the best of luck," Monte Cristo said, grinning. "Many have tried and found the same thing: there is simply no more and no less to me than I decide to show."

Beauchamp rose as well and looked at the clock. "If I hurry, I'll just be able to reach the Chamber in time to record Baron Danglars' speech. But with what I've heard today, I think I have something far more exciting to share with my readers," he said with a bow.

Raoul and Max were the next to leave. Max left his card with the count and secured a promise that the count would visit soon. Finally, Albert found himself alone with the Count of Monte Cristo.

CHAPTER 45
THE PRESENTATION

The valet returned to tell Albert that Countess Morcerf would be ready in half an hour to receive his guest. They passed the time with a tour of the rest of Albert's house. When the tour reached the loft where Albert had sparred with Lucien and kept his treasures, Monte Cristo took quick appraisal of the contents.

There was a certain impulsive taste on display in the room, indicating some intelligence and wit about Albert, if not much maturity. Albert planned to guide Monte Cristo through the collection but wasn't surprised when Monte Cristo instead educated him on the history and significance of each piece. Only one painting gave the count pause.

It hung in a place of honour in the hall to receive the most complimentary light. When it caught Monte Cristo's eye, he took several rapid steps forward and stared at it in silence with a brief tremor running through his body. It was the portrait of a young woman with a dark complexion and lustrous eyes, dressed as a traditional Catalan fisherwoman. The painter had surrounded her with a subtle aura, as if she were glowing softly. Her gaze was turned to the sea, as though she waited for something to arrive on the waves.

"Is this Baron Danglars' daughter, Mlle. Eugenie?" Monte Cristo said at last in a calm and deliberate tone. "You have a charming fiancée, if so."

"Goodness, no!" Albert said with a laugh. "I'll forgive you the mistake, but this is my mother. She commissioned it years ago while my father was away. Lucky for me, he never cared for it, and so it found a home here. My father is one of France's most esteemed senators and a decorated general, but appreciating fine art has never been one of his strengths."

Albert checked the time. "Speaking of my parents, they should be ready to make your acquaintance. They've been eager to meet you and thank you since I wrote home from Italy about our bandit adventure," he said. "Consider it the first of my promised introductions, to a man and woman of real status."

Monte Cristo bowed without answering, accepted the offer without enthusiasm or regret, and followed Albert to the main house without comment. Above the antechamber door in the main house was a gold shield which Monte Cristo stopped to examine, with figures of birds arranged on either side of a diagonal band of blue.

"Azure seven merlets, gold, placed bender," Monte Cristo said, using the heraldic terms. "Quite impressive."

"Those are the arms of the family of Morcerf," Albert said. "It's a very old French family, with a more recent infusion of Spanish blood. My paternal grandfather was French nobility and married a Catalan woman, and then my father married another Catalan himself."

Monte Cristo studied Albert's face, but detected only the simplicity of conviction. There was no sign of Albert knowing his parents came from the humble Catalan village at Marseille.

"I can read the shields, but I'm largely rather ignorant of heraldry. My title is still quite fresh. I was surprised by how simple it was for the right craftsman to simply produce a coat for me on short order. One must have something on the carriage-panels to escape being searched by customs, after all," Monte Cristo added, continuing to watch Albert. Still, there was no reaction; Albert's belief in his family history appeared genuine.

Albert admitted Monte Cristo into the salon. At the same moment, the Count de Morcerf entered as well by another door. Morcerf was a man in his mid-forties, but carried himself with the vigour of a man ten years younger. His black goatee and eyebrows contrasted with his almost white hair, and though he wore civilian clothes, he wore the ribbons of his military decorations on his lapel.

While Morcerf advanced to meet Monte Cristo, Monte Cristo remained rooted to the spot by a fleeting moment of doubt. Fernand Mondego, he remembered, had been thin in the extreme, a boy who seemed to lack an ounce of muscle or fat. The Count de Morcerf was a powerful specimen of a man, six and a half feet tall with a fifty-inch chest, brawnier even than Monte Cristo's servant Ali. With Morcerf's muscle mass, obvious despite his custom-tailored suit, Monte Cristo guessed he weighed eighteen stone at least. This man had the same eyes, and Monte Cristo knew from Caderousse that Fernand had returned from war as a new physical specimen, but he still doubted his conviction for a moment.

"Father," Albert said, "I have the honour of presenting the Count of Monte Cristo, my generous friend and the saviour of whom I wrote to you."

"Anyone willing to confront murderous bandits to rescue my son is more than welcome in my home," Morcerf said. The voice erased all of Monte Cristo's doubts; it was unmistakably Fernand. "Please, have a seat. The countess will arrive shortly."

Monte Cristo selected a chair by the window which put the sun at his back, to better study Morcerf's face. Despite Morcerf's youthful energy, time had written its story on his dark features. With effort, Monte Cristo looked beneath the physical transformation and saw the scrawny young man who once sent a poison letter to eliminate a rival.

"I find myself greatly honoured," Monte Cristo said. "On my first day in Paris, I sit in the company of a man whose merit equals his reputation for honour. From everything I've heard of your record, I'm surprised you're not still on the battlefield with a marshal's staff!"

Morcerf reddened slightly, averting his eyes from the glare of the sun. "Oh, I left the service after reaching the rank of general, monsieur," Morcerf said. "I could have stayed on, but my battles would have been in the salons as a diplomat. I hung up my sword, entered politics here at home instead, and now study the useful arts. Industry, production, that sort of thing."

"The fact that you enlisted at all and rose so high attests to the French character, I think," Monte Cristo replied. "Albert just explained your family's history as I admired your coat of arms; rather than living comfortably off of the fortune of such an old lineage, but instead enlisted as a soldier and climbed a ladder of victories to your current place."

"Well, there was not much of a fortune left by the time I came along," Morcerf said. "Much of our wealth was stolen during the Revolution, so my enlistment was a matter of necessity."

"Still, you rebuilt your family name and could have retired in leisure, but decided instead to embark on a second career," Monte Cristo said, admiring Morcerf's easy manner of lying about his past. "What can I call you but a model of altruism? Bravo!"

"If I didn't fear boring you, I would bring you to the Chamber with me today," Morcerf said. "There are some debates scheduled today which may be fascinating to a world-traveler like yourself. Speaking of which, I must leave shortly to attend them. If I'm late once, that bastard Baron Givenchy will bring it up for months."

"If my home were as fashionable as yours, I doubt I should ever leave it," Monte Cristo said.

"We're very fortunate to call this place home. The only flaw against the property is its proximity to an entry into the Catacombs," Morcerf said with a shudder. "I've seen dreadful things in battle, but nothing so horrible as the shambling dead of my childhood. I'd prefer not to have such a reminder of the past so close to my bed, but it's a minor annoyance."

"I remember those days as well; the deceased were as hungry in my country as I'm sure they were here. Regarding the Chamber, I must admit my ignorance to French ways; what chamber do you mean?" Monte Cristo asked.

"The Senate Chamber, in the House of Peers," Morcerf said. "Any French nobleman with the rank of count or higher is eligible to become a senior senator, which I am. Lower nobles like barons can become junior senators. Any senator in the Chamber can propose a new law and participate in debates, but only the senior senators may vote on legislation."

"I was of the understanding that France once again has a king," Monte Cristo said. "How is it that he lets a chamber of counts make his laws?"

"Well, he has full veto power over any law we write and can impose his own whenever he chooses," Morcerf said with a laugh. "But outsourcing the day-to-day work to us allows him time to focus on other matters."

"It sounds like a fascinating place," Monte Cristo said. "I'd be more than happy to accept that invitation, if you renew it in the future. But today, as I've been flattered with the hope of meeting the countess, I will wait."

"Ah, here she is!" Albert said.

Monte Cristo's head snapped to the left, and he saw Countess Mercedes de Morcerf at the door. Her thick hair was still dark enough to get lost in, though the years had interwoven it with silver. She stood motionless, leaning on the gilded door-post and watching Monte Cristo. He rose and bowed to her.

"Mother, are you unwell?" Albert asked.

Mercedes waved away these concerns. "No, I'm simply overcome with emotion to meet the man who I can thank for the continued beating of my son's heart," she said, her face pale as she advanced with all the majesty she could manage.

"Madame," Monte Cristo said, "you and the count are too generous. It was a simple good deed done for a friend, as easy as breathing and with no more risk than asking the time."

"Then I thank God that my son found such a friend on his travels," Mercedes replied, raising her eyes to the ceiling with fervent gratitude.

Morcerf rose then and straightened his jacket. He kissed Mercedes on the cheek and left to go to the Chamber.

"M. de Monte Cristo and I will do our best in your absence," Mercedes told him as he left. "Your excellency, will you do Albert and I the honour of passing the day with us?"

"Nothing would please me more, but as I told Albert this morning, I'm still ignorant of my Parisian dwellings beyond knowing the address," Monte Cristo said. "My first stop in Paris was Albert's apartments for breakfast. I must find my house and discover if my instructions have been followed."

"Then I shall require your promise that we will have the pleasure another time," Mercedes said.

Monte Cristo bowed to the request, and Albert escorted him back to his carriage in the driveway.

"I won't invite you over today, as I can show you nothing but a house in the midst of arrangements," Monte Cristo said. "Give me a few days to prepare for the sake of my reputation, and you will not be disappointed."

"With that much time at your disposal, I know to expect a palace rather than a house," Albert said.

Monte Cristo said *adieu* and sprang into the carriage. He noticed as he left, the stirring of a curtain at the salon window. When Albert returned to his mother, he found the curtains drawn to create a deep gloom and her face hidden with a veil. Among the thick aromas of the various flowers in the salon, Albert could smell the sharp odour of his mother's smelling-salts.

"No no, I'm alright," Mercedes said in response to his concern, though a catch in her voice betrayed her. "It's the flowers, I think; their perfume can be overwhelming at times."

"Are you sure?" Albert asked. "After all, you were so pale when you came in to meet the count."

"Was I?" Mercedes asked, almost to herself, as Albert directed servants to remove the flowers to another room and open the windows for more air. "Tell me more about the count. Where does the name Monte Cristo come from? Is it a family name or that of an estate?"

"Just his estate, I believe; he purchased an island in the Tuscan archipelago and, aside from the title, has no pretension to nobility besides his manners," Albert said.

Mercedes remained quiet for a moment. "You've spent time with M. de Monte Cristo and have a better sense of men's hearts than most do at your age," she said. "Albert, I ask as your mother: do you think the count is the man of high distinction that he appears to be?"

Albert considered the question. "Everything about him seems so remarkable, it's like he stepped into our world from some novel," he said. "He's like one of Byron's heroes, where virtue is mixed with some great misery and life's misfortunes have to be overcome by uncommon genius."

"And how old would you say he is?" Mercedes asked.

"Thirty-five, maybe thirty-six?" Albert said. "Of course you noticed his skin condition; it complicates the guesswork and makes one skew older, but he's said to me during various conversations 'at such date I was five years old, at this date I was twenty,' and so on."

Mercedes took her son's hand. "Albert, there's no doubt that this man has done you and this family a great service," she said. "Even so, please be prudent around this man. I can't say why he brings me such unease, but he just does."

"Mother, you're as fussy as Franz!" Albert said with a laugh. "If the count wanted to hurt me, he could have left me to the bandits. If he wanted to swindle me, well, he's so wealthy that it would be a great joke indeed for him to borrow money from me. What else could I have to fear from him? I think some people are put off by his eyes; they are unsettling, but you must take the chance to get to know the man behind them."

"Perhaps you're right," Mercedes said, shaking her head. "How did your father receive the count? I know he can be so preoccupied sometimes, or standoffish."

"On the contrary, Father was the picture of politeness. They got along famously," Albert said. "The count paid him two or three choice compliments as if they'd known each other for years. Father even invited him to the Chamber to hear the debates."

Mercedes didn't reply but allowed her eyes to fall closed. Not wanting to disturb her rest, Albert crept from the salon and returned to his own house. When the door closed, Mercedes opened her eyes again and gazed into the air ahead of her.

"Could it be possible?" she muttered. "Could it be him?"

CHAPTER 46
THE BREAK-IN

M onte Cristo's carriage had arrived at his newly-purchased house. Ali had chosen a handsome house on the Champs Elysees, surrounded by a brick wall and masked in front by trees and shrubs.

The gates rolled open at the concierge's command without the carriage even needing to stop. In Paris, like anywhere else, the count was served almost with the speed of magic by people who understood that maintaining his favour would leave them set for life. Ali and Bertuccio presented themselves at the carriage; Ali wore an expression of expectant pride as he waited to see the count's reaction to his work, while Bertuccio offered his arm to aid the count down from the step.

"Thank you, M. Bertuccio. Ali, if the interior is half as handsome as the exterior, then you've done splendidly," Monte Cristo said. "Bertuccio, what about my agenda for today?"

"The notary is already here your excellency, and your cards were engraved as soon as I knew the number of the house," Bertuccio said. "As instructed, the first card went directly to Baron Danglars, and the rest wait in your bedroom."

Monte Cristo nodded, handing his hat and cane to a footman. As always, he kept his gloves. He passed through the house, complimenting and criticizing the decorative flairs of each room as he went. A short and round man with a receding hairline sprang to his feet and bowed as Monte Cristo entered the salon, and the two of them discussed the purchase of a country home.

"All seems in order, M. Deschamps; tell me, where is the house I am purchasing?" Monte Cristo asked as the notary looked in his portfolio for the bill of sale. "This is my first time setting in France; I saw an advertisement for a country house and enjoyed the description so much that I purchased it."

The question shocked Deschamps. "Does your excellency not know? Your house is in Auteuil, far enough from here to serve as a country retreat but not so far as to prevent entertaining."

"Excellency," Bertuccio blurted, the blood draining from his face. "Auteuil is so near to Paris, it will hardly be suitable for your relaxation. If you'll allow me, I will find you a better house at any of a dozen other locations."

"Never mind," Monte Cristo said with a wave, "Auteuil will do fine, and besides, the notary is already here. Bring the man his fee."

Monte Cristo signed the deed, and Bertuccio returned with an uneasy step to hand Deschamps a bundle of banknotes.

"Very good, your excellency. Your keys are with the caretaker of the house, and here is the deed to prove your ownership of it," Deschamps said before Bertuccio escorted him out.

Alone, Monte Cristo took a small clasped book from his pocket and unlocked it with a key that he wore around his neck. He arrived at a particular page.

"Auteuil, rue de la Fontaine, No. 28," the count read. "The address is the same; I'll let Bertuccio stew overnight."

When Bertuccio returned, Monte Cristo told him that he wished to visit his new country house the next morning and required Bertuccio's company. Bertuccio received the news with a fit of trembling most unusual to his temperament. But it would be inconceivable to defy the count's orders, and so he went to bed that night with a churning stomach and a heavy heart.

Like the Morcerf home, the Count of Monte Cristo's residence had a less conspicuous side-entrance. Near this gate to the Rue Ponthieu, a figure sprang over the wall in the night and crossed the lawn to the mansion. He pried open a lower window with a crowbar and admitted himself to the count's house.

This burglar had heard of some fop with more wealth than sense buying the house and filling it with treasures before he even arrived. The burglar, whose name was Broque, planned to take some of those riches for himself.

The first rooms Broque prowled through proved the stories; priceless Oriental vases caught his eye at every turn, but as beautiful as they were, he dared not toss them into his sack and risk breaking them. Small paintings, however, he plucked from the wall like ripe fruit as well as silverware and jeweled ornaments from display cabinets. Broque moved at random through the house, snatching valuables with all the discretion of a magpie and all the glee of a child at Christmas.

As Broque reached the second story, an enticing waft of perfume from behind a door caught his interest. With care not to make a sound, he turned the handle and found himself in a feminine sitting room which opened onto a bedchamber. There, a beam of moonlight through a glass panel in the ceiling fell across an exquisite specimen of beauty.

Her thick dark hair and olive skin were of the Greek type, with thick lashes laid across delicate cheeks. Sleep had parted her full lips, and she had thrown the covers off of herself enough to reveal the curve of her waist and a generous bosom, only just covered in silk nightclothes and moving with her breath.

Broque's greedy and vulgar mind realized he had found treasure of a different sort, likely the millionaire's mistress. To someone who has already decided they are entitled to what does not belong to them, one kind of plunder is not so different from another. Broque set his sack and crowbar on the floor and drew a dagger from his belt as he advanced on the bed.

A floorboard creaked behind him, and before Broque could react, a rough band wrapped around his throat and pulled him back into the hall. His feet never touched the ground as he flew around a corner and was released to slam against a distant wall.

Dazed, Broque looked around to find the source of this attack. He saw the slender figure of a man approaching. He coughed and groaned at a sharp pain in his ribs, and cursed his bad luck. Broque had known about the house for days, but had waited too long and the owner had arrived. He saw only one way out and waited hunched over on the floor with his dagger hidden against his breast.

"I may have let you leave," said the slender man without a trace of mercy in his voice. "I was willing to consider that you were not evil, but merely misguided. I was even in a charitable frame of mind after a chance encounter this morning, and may have offered you a job. After all, I have many plans in motion, and require many hands to do the work."

The slender man's footsteps drew closer, and Broque tightened his grip on the dagger. When the man stood above him, Broque struck. He lashed out with the dagger, carving a deep gash in the man's leg as he stood up, and buried it to the hilt in the man's chest. Breathing hard, Broque stepped back to watch the millionaire die; when that distasteful business was done, he could return to his loot and escape.

The millionaire did not so much as flinch, dumbfounding Broque. Instead, he pulled the dagger out of the wound as if shooing a fly before tossing it away. The blade remained dry and clean, and the wound did not weep even a single tear of blood.

Broque got his first clear look at the man whose home he burgled, the fabled Count of Monte Cristo. He wore dark trousers and a white silk shirt, open at the chest and marred only by the dagger-hole Broque had made. White bandages wrapped his hands and chest, also extending up to cover his head and neck. His face remained partly in shadow, but the moonlight reflected against red eyes burning with fury.

White tendrils crept out from under the count's sleeves and lashed forward. They entwined Broque's arms from wrist to shoulder with the same rough texture that had pulled him from Haydee's bedroom. As the bandages extended, they exposed patches of dry grey flesh. Broque stood helpless and restrained as another tendril emerged from the ragged hole where he had stabbed the count. This band of living cloth snaked forward to cover his mouth, stifling his panicked cries.

"I may have forgiven you just for stealing from me, but then you threatened someone under my protection," the count said. "I can't let that pass."

"What's happening?" a woman's voice asked. Haydee stood at her chamber door, rubbing sleep from her eyes.

"Just an unwanted visitor, my dear," the count said. "I was about to show him out."

A chorus of muffled clicking reached Broque's ears, and a glistening black beetle emerged from beneath the bandages on the count's collarbone. Another beetle emerged from his sleeve, and dozens more followed. They marched across the trail of bandages connecting Broque to the count and crawled beneath Broque's clothing wherever they found an opening. Broque screamed against the cloth enclosing his mouth as the beetles bit down and tore away chunks of his flesh.

"Some people have no manners," Haydee said, yawning and returning to her bedroom. "It's far too late for visitors."

CHAPTER 47
THE HOUSE AT AUTEUIL

In the morning, no sign remained that Broque had ever entered the house. Monte Cristo gave instructions to his servants to return the objects to their proper places and to take Broque's clothes to the nearest poor box.

Bertuccio crossed himself multiple times as he made preparations for the trip to Auteuil. An ordinary man may have seen his reluctance and taken pity on him. The count was no ordinary man and had a method to this apparent cruelty.

The drive to Auteuil took less than an hour, during which time Bertuccio's condition worsened. He even flinched when Monte Cristo gave the driver the precise address of the house.

Number 28 stood at the edge of the village, with nothing beyond it but countryside. A storm loomed on the horizon as they travelled, giving the scene the appearance of a play's painted backdrop. The count hopped to the ground in front of the house but had to reprimand Bertuccio to get him to follow. The caretaker was happy to relinquish the keys after seeing the deed.

"I hope you enjoy the house more than the previous owner did, excellency," the caretaker said. "It's been at least five years since the Marquis de Saint-Meran visited here; I've been wondering when he would sell it."

"Saint-Meran, you say?" Monte Cristo said, affecting surprise his face didn't reflect. "I've heard the name before. He was the previous owner?"

"Oh yes, an old-stock gentleman," the caretaker said. "He was a devout Royalist during the wars and married his daughter off to a man who became the king's attorney at Nimes for a while. It's a shame she died when she did; so young, and such a blow to the Marquis. Especially with the terrible way he lost his wife, bless her soul."

Bertuccio leaned on the wall for support, and the count judged that he required only another gentle nudge.

"Very well; Bertuccio, bring a light and let's tour my new retreat," Monte Cristo said.

Bertuccio obeyed silently as they traversed the large ground floor and well-appointed upper story. Monte Cristo didn't mention the trembling of the lantern's light as they discovered a winding stairway down from the larger bedroom.

"A private staircase!" Monte Cristo said. "How convenient! Come, I wish to see where it goes."

"Only to the garden, excellency." Bertuccio swallowed heavily.

"How could you know where it leads? We've just arrived," Monte Cristo said. "Regardless, I wish to see for myself."

Bertuccio heaved a great sigh and led the way. They made it as far as an oak tree looming over a stone bench when Bertuccio stopped and set down the lantern.

"I cannot go on!" he cried. "It's impossible, intolerable, a joke from the depths of hell!"

"*Mon dieu*, Bertuccio," Monte Cristo said. "What's the matter with you?"

"It isn't natural that this should happen," Bertuccio said. "That you should buy a house in Auteuil of all places, and that it's number 28, and then to force me to stand right where I killed him!"

Bertuccio sank onto the bench, his head in his hands.

"Bertuccio, don't give me cause to doubt Abbe Busoni's recommendation of your services," Monte Cristo said. "Continue babbling like this and I'll have no choice but to have you committed. If you have some secret to confess, I can guess the shape of it easily enough; you are Corsican after all, and the vendetta runs deep in your culture."

Bertuccio nodded. The vendetta was a sacred Corsican tradition, a blood feud sworn under very specific circumstances. If a Corsican was murdered, the killer could expect the victim's family to hound him until they saw justice done, often at the point of a knife.

"I've interceded with the law on your behalf before, will I need to do so again?" Monte Cristo asked. "When Busoni told me you had a matter on your conscience, I assumed he meant that you had stolen some money, not murdered a man."

"It wasn't murder!" Bertuccio said. "Only vengeance, the vendetta, like you said. I thought God was satisfied in the punishments I've already suffered, but it seems I'm not yet free. It was in this garden and on this very spot that I achieved my vengeance."

"Vengeance against whom? The Marquis de Saint-Meran?" the count asked. He put his hand to his heart. "Bertuccio, tell me that the death of his daughter was not your doing."

"No, not the Marquis or his daughter," Bertuccio said. "It was another man; he descended the same staircase you did and buried his child almost exactly where you stand. It was here that I drove my dagger into Gerard de Villefort's heart!"

"Villefort!" Monte Cristo exclaimed. "He was a prosecutor, reputed to be the most rigid defender of justice to ever enter a courtroom. You assassinated him?"

"Indeed, but he was no paragon of justice," Bertuccio said. "The man was a callous villain, only serving justice when it suited him."

"This is a revelation indeed," Monte Cristo said, recalling Lucien Debray's claim that he had seen Villefort recently. "Tell me everything, and I hope you can provide proof."

Bertuccio shook his head. "I had proof once, but lost it. With a careful search, it may be found again, but I've never wanted to try."

Bertuccio sat for a moment collecting his thoughts and braced himself to begin his story.

CHAPTER 48
THE VENDETTA

"Where to begin?" Bertuccio said. "I'm sure that Abbe Busoni told you what he knew."

"He may have given me some particulars, but that was at least seven years ago," Monte Cristo said. "I've forgotten most of it."

The story started with his brother Cristofano, a lieutenant in Napoleon's army and Bertuccio's dearest friend. Orphaned at a young age by the Dead Plague, they had only each other to rely on for years; Cristofano was more of a father than a brother to Bertuccio. He fought at the battle of Waterloo when Napoleon fell and survived taking a wound there.

At that time, Bertuccio lived with Cristofano's wife, Assunta, in the north Corsican village of Rogliano. Cristofano wrote to them explaining the events of the battle, his long recovery, and his pending return home. He would be passing through Nimes, where Bertuccio had contact with an innkeeper through his smuggling work. Cristofano asked his family to send him some money there so he could complete his journey home.

Bertuccio decided instead to take the money to Nimes himself and greet Cristofano in person. They had been separated for too long, and Bertuccio thought it would be a splendid surprise. An upcoming smuggling run would also bring him close to Nimes, so he left half of his money with Assunta and brought the rest.

The wind had other plans, delaying his arrival by a week. By this time, the Inquisition was in full swing. The king's men selected their Bonapartist targets strategically, torturing those who would attract attention and extorting those who could pay. This emboldened a group of furloughed Royalist soldiers to roam the south of France, conducting an Inquisition of their own and publicly murdering anyone they suspected of having fought for Napoleon.

"Ah yes, I recall hearing of those massacres. Many innocents died, thanks to the wisdom and justice of the mob," Monte Cristo said. "They did such things in America, too. The colonials would believe someone to be a witch, and that was all they needed to murder her in the name of the greater good. When emotions run high, it seems the need for evidence is the first thing to be discarded."

"I entered Nimes to find a town in chaos," Bertuccio said, staring at nothing like a man remembering war. "The streets ran so deep with blood in places that a man could literally wade in it, and bands of looters rushed through the alleys plundering and burning as they went."

Bertuccio worried that Cristofano may not have other clothes besides his Napoleonic uniform. He soon learned the answer when he found Cristofano's body sprawled in the street before the very inn where they intended to meet, his splendid blue coat soaked with blood.

"Finding him dead wasn't even the worst of it," Bertuccio said. "His neck was torn open, and the wound was surrounded by bloody lip-smears. One of those monsters had devolved into such an animalistic state as to drink Cristofano's blood!"

"How revolting," Monte Cristo said. "I'm not entirely ignorant of the men who compare my appearance to a vampire, but the thought of a man practicing their dietary habits is almost beyond belief."

"Of course, I wished to find the murderers myself," Bertuccio said, his chest heaving with the memory, "but the people of Nimes are cowards and gave me no clues. With no option for the natural justice of vendetta, I decided to appeal to the king's justice. I went to the crown prosecutor, M. de Villefort."

Villefort's career had flourished from his roots as the deputy prosecutor of Marseille, thanks in part to his reputation of being the man who first informed the king of Napoleon's return. Bertuccio went straight to Villefort's office to plead his case and asked him to avenge a man who his police had been unable to protect. Villefort had asked Bertuccio who his brother was, and Bertuccio answered that he had been one of Napoleon's soldiers. Villefort responded by dismissing the matter entirely.

"He said to me, 'your brother was smitten with the sword and died

by the sword.' I told him that Cristofano hadn't died to a sword,"
Bertuccio told the count, "but to a beast on two legs who drank his blood
and left him less dignity than a wolf leaves a sheep."

"And how did Villefort react to that?" Monte Cristo asked.

"He had a wild expression in his cold blue eyes, and said 'If he
fought for the usurper, then your brother was indeed a sheep. He
followed a wolf who wished to prey on the entire continent. If I found
his murderer, I would decorate him, not incarcerate him.' I was
stunned," Bertuccio said.

"Sadly, your story has again become familiar," Monte Cristo said. "It
seems that the abuse of power by bureaucrats is a universal language."

"I had no other option. I leaned in close enough that I could smell
his rank breath," Bertuccio said, "and I told him, 'you think it was a
service for someone to murder my brother for being a Bonapartist? Then
I'll be a Bonapartist as well, and I declare a vendetta against you.'"

"I've heard tales of Corsican passion, but I assumed they'd been
exaggerated," Monte Cristo said.

"That was not all. 'Protect yourself as best you can, monsieur; the
next time we meet, I'll stop your heart and watch the life drain out of
your cursed eyes,' I said to him, and spat in his face," Bertuccio said. "It
was his turn to be shocked, and I left the room before he could recover."

Villefort took the threat to heart. He shut himself away and left his
house only under guard. He even transferred, or rather fled, to
Versailles. Bertuccio followed him like a hunter stalking a deer. A
hundred opportunities presented themselves to kill Villefort, if only he
had a rifle or pistol, but he remembered Assunta waiting for him.

The trick was to strike without being apprehended. Bertuccio
watched Villefort as he went from his home to the courthouse, or to the
secretive meetings of his Royalist League, always with guards. Finally,
Bertuccio found an opening in his target's routine: Villefort began to
visit the house in Auteuil, always travelling alone.

Lying in wait at Auteuil, Bertuccio learned that the Marquis rented
the house to a young widow, a baroness. Nobody in the village knew her
name. Bertuccio saw her once, a woman with wavy blonde hair and a
pretty yet matronly face. He also saw that she was heavily pregnant.
When Villefort arrived and embraced her, it revealed the mystery. Still,
Bertuccio needed to wait for the right moment.

One night a servant left the house on horseback at full gallop. He returned hours later covered in dust and followed by Villefort himself. They rushed into the house, and instinct told Bertuccio to take his knife and spring over the garden wall.

Villefort's habit was to enter and leave by the garden gate, where Bertuccio could conceal himself in the gloom and bushes. Groans of agony could be heard from the house. Hours later, the door at the foot of the stairs opened and Villefort appeared with a spade and a box. Bertuccio's hatred mingled with curiosity as Villefort dug a shallow hole.

"When he had finished stamping down the earth to hide his treasure chest—or so I thought—I sprang out and stabbed him in the heart. 'Do you remember me, from Nimes?' I asked him. 'Do you remember my brother?'"

Villefort's blood gushed out over Bertuccio's hands and he fell to the ground without enough air to yell, on the very spot where he'd buried the box. Bertuccio pushed the body aside and dug up the box with haste. Blood seeped through the loose earth, leaking into the box through gaps in the wood. Bertuccio filled the hole again to prevent anyone suspecting the theft, then rushed out into the night.

"So your vendetta became a robbery as well?" Monte Cristo asked. "This is surprising, Bertuccio. I've heard of Corsicans poisoning their blades for a vendetta; did you do this as well?"

Bertuccio recoiled. "Poison! No self-respecting Corsican would use poison, I promise you," he said. "And it wasn't a robbery either, though I intended to take his treasure home to Assunta as a widow's pension."

Down at the river, Bertuccio had forced open the box with his knife. Instead of gold he found a silent newborn baby boy wrapped in fine linen. The boy's purple face was smeared with Villefort's blood, but he wasn't yet cold. Having worked as a hospital assistant in the past, Bertuccio blew into the infant's mouth to inflate the lungs. It gave a feeble cry and the awful purple colouring gave way to a healthy pink.

"I thought God was smiling on me, blessing my vengeance by allowing me to save a life the same night that I ended one," Bertuccio said.

"Then you are a father; I never knew. Congratulations, Bertuccio," Monte Cristo said. "It seems that your vendetta was successful. How, then, did you come to be in prison, giving confession to Abbe Busoni?"

"Don't congratulate me; that's not the end of it," Bertuccio said.

He had brought the infant to an orphanage, leaving half of the linen cloth with the boy and keeping the other half in case he could ever return. The cloth was monogrammed with the letters H and N inside a baron's seal and would serve as adequate proof for the nuns.

He couldn't return the child to his mother without explaining what he'd done and being arrested. At home he told Assunta the story of how he had avenged Cristofano. He returned to his life as a smuggler but insisted that his crew never land at Nimes again. The innkeeper they had an arrangement with decided to open a branch to his inn on the road from Bellegarde to Beaucaire.

The country's political unrest in those days meant steady work for the smugglers, and Bertuccio earned enough to keep Assunta comfortable. One day after a long voyage, he found her standing at the door with a bashful look. Inside their house sat a crib, and in the crib lay the baby from Auteuil. He had grown a thick mop of blonde hair, and his soft blue eyes were similar to and yet so unlike his father's. On the wall above the crib were the two halves of the linen cloth, stitched back together.

Bertuccio was overjoyed, having regretted abandoning the boy since that night. They named him Benedetto but soon learned that something was wrong. Benedetto's teeth grew in too soon and too sharp, and even as an infant he wailed until given meat to eat. As a toddler, he caught rats and bit off their tails. Then they noticed their neighbourhood had far fewer rats. He bit other children as well, and Assunta when he was upset. A local dog went missing when Benedetto was ten. By then, Benedetto had developed into a crafty little thief as well, stealing from everyone in the village and lying so skillfully about it that only Bertuccio could see through him.

"I never told him his origins. I tried to trick him into becoming a smuggler and learning discipline on the sea by tempting him with tales of adventure," Bertuccio said. "He laughed in my face and pointed out that he had everything he needed at home. Assunta loved the boy in spite of everything and wouldn't hear a word about sending him away."

Bertuccio's journeys became as much of an escape from Benedetto as a source of income; money which Benedetto was happy to spend as soon as it came in. Bertuccio counselled Assunta to hide their money, which even she admitted was wise.

"This was simply our lives, for a while," Bertuccio said. "I should have seen Benedetto's capability for depravity, and stopped him before... well, to tell that part of the story I must talk about my time in prison."

"Go on, then. I recall only the vaguest details from speaking to Abbe Busoni," Monte Cristo said.

In early June of 1829, a drop-off went sour and Bertuccio fled into the countryside, taking refuge at the inn between Bellegarde and Beaucaire. A hidden loft stood on the back of the building as part of their arrangement with the innkeeper from Nimes. By that time, Caderousse had come to manage the inn.

Through a spyhole, Bertuccio witnessed Caderousse greeting a jeweler who offered him fifty thousand francs for a large diamond. The jeweler insisted on hearing the story again of how Caderousse came to own it, and Bertuccio learned that an abbe named Busoni had given it to him as part of a dead man's will.

"Did you believe the story?" Monte Cristo asked.

Bertuccio shrugged. "I had never known M. Caderousse to be a liar, although I would not want to depend on his courage."

Caderousse and the jeweler argued over the price of the diamond, with Caderousse and his sickly wife taking offense at the jeweler's offer of forty-five thousand francs instead of the expected fifty. Caderousse relented in the end and accepted the forty-five thousand.

Bertuccio had half-expected violence, but the jeweler dissuaded that by showing the couple a pair of pistols he kept within his coat; after that, the conversation resumed a more civil tone. The jeweler was annoyed from the argument and Caderousse was sulking about gaining a sizeable sum of money lower than he had expected, but a storm obliged the jeweler to stay the night. He visited upstairs to select a room.

"As I heard the creaking floorboards of him getting comfortable, an evil look passed between Caderousse and his wife," Bertuccio said. "If only I had intervened!"

CHAPTER 49
THE RAIN OF BLOOD

"I fear I can guess what happened next," Monte Cristo said, disappointed but not with Bertuccio. "Some men cannot receive any good fortune gracefully without wanting even more."

Bertuccio resumed his gloomy tale. Caderousse's wife Madeleine poured glass after glass of wine for the jeweler at supper while he warmed himself by the fire. His gait was rather unsteady when he returned upstairs to sleep.

Caderousse looked anxious, while Madeleine's eyes gleamed with malicious intent as they whispered to each other for an hour. Bertuccio decided to get what rest he could and speak to Caderousse in the morning. The hidden room remained dry enough to wait out the storm and was furnished with cots as an overnight hiding-place. As odd as the scene had been, Bertuccio had no reason to suspect anything, and fell asleep.

A single pistol shot tore through the countryside quiet and woke him up at an unknowable hour. Bertuccio heard a struggle in the overhead room, with pained groans and panicked cries, and then a great weight hitting the floor. The ceiling was not as watertight as Bertuccio expected, and warm rain dripped upon his head.

Silence fell once more, broken only by a single set of footsteps. Through the peephole, Bertuccio saw Caderousse stagger down the stairs covered in blood. He held the diamond case in one hand and a fistful of banknotes in the other. Caderousse found a fresh shirt in a cupboard, pulled on a coat decorated with odd symbols, and disappeared into the night.

"I heard more groaning upstairs and thought that I maybe could help somehow," Bertuccio said.

He had forced open the hidden door in the partition and rushed up the stairs, tripping over Madeleine's body. A small hole pierced her throat, and the back of her head was a mess of ruined flesh. The pistol shot had taken her through the neck.

The jeweler's bedchamber sat in shambles, with sprays of blood across the walls. The unfortunate jeweler lay on the floor with three open gashes in his chest and a table knife protruding from a fourth. The second pistol lay discarded to one side with the hammer down, having misfired. Bertuccio arrived just in time to see the jeweler gasp his last breath.

He could do nothing for the man or Madeleine, so Bertuccio decided to flee. Before he could escape the inn, armed customs officers confronted him at the door. The pistol shot had attracted their attention during their search for the fugitive smugglers from Bertuccio's ship.

Bertuccio was still so appalled by what he had seen that he lost the power of speech. The officers found a babbling man covered in blood—which had dripped through the ceiling from the jeweler's room—in an inn with two corpses and took him as the murderer. They brought him before a judge in Nimes.

"My only hope was for them to find Abbe Busoni, who had given Caderousse the diamond," Bertuccio said. "His testimony would reveal Caderousse's motive for murder."

Months passed, and to the credit of the judge, he did make every effort to find Busoni. When Bertuccio had given up hope, Busoni himself came to visit the prison and testify to the story of the diamond. The wheels of justice grind slowly, and Bertuccio remained in custody, but he did ask Busoni to take his confession for the vendetta against Villefort.

"I made that confession to unload Villefort's murder from my soul," Bertuccio said. "Busoni also seemed to take it as proof that I hadn't killed Madeleine and the jeweler without motive."

Finally, they apprehended Caderousse abroad and brought him back to France. He made a full confession, though he tried to excuse his own guilt by stressing that the murder was Madeleine's idea. Caderousse was sentenced to hard labour for life, and Bertuccio was freed.

"Abbe Busoni approached me when I was released and suggested I leave my smuggling life behind. He said he took confession for a man who had need of a steward and gave me the letter of introduction which I eventually brought to you. Now my only smuggling is at your behest," Bertuccio said. He heaved a deep sigh. "The only promise he asked of me was that I never give himself or you cause to regret your kindness. And have I, excellency?"

"No, you've served me faithfully," Monte Cristo said. "I only wish you had taken me into your confidence sooner; I didn't know you had a sister or adopted son until now. Why did you not mention them?"

"Because I've seen neither of them since," Bertuccio said.

With his freedom secured, Bertuccio had returned home as soon as possible to rejoin Assunta. Instead, he found a scene of brutality so vile that it would remain a local legend for a hundred years.

Taking Bertuccio's advice, Assunta began to hide their money and refused to comply with Benedetto's unreasonable demands. Benedetto had grown into an imposing young man, thickset and round-shouldered. Though his hair was still blond, his beard had grown in bright ginger. He and his friends frequented the local taverns in search of women, who were taken in by his blue eyes and strong jaw.

One night, Benedetto returned home drunk with his thuggish friends. They demanded that Assunta give them some money to return to the tavern with, and she refused again. When Bertuccio found one of Benedetto's goons drunk in that same tavern, the man wept as he confessed what had happened.

Benedetto had suggested they "play Inquisition" and torture her until she told them where she hid the money. The goon who told Bertuccio the story had struck Assunta in the face and kicked her in the stomach. He had even obeyed, though with less enthusiasm, when Benedetto commanded him to hold her feet in the fire until she talked.

When she still didn't tell them where the money was, shocked that the boy she had raised was doing this, Benedetto bit off two of her fingers. The goon had described to Bertuccio the horrible crunching noise the bones had made as Benedetto chewed them; when he had swallowed, he went back at once for the thumb.

"The goon had more to say," Bertuccio said to the count, his face haunted. "But before he could describe anything else of that night, he vomited on the floor and blacked out on the table."

Assunta's remains looked as though wild dogs had savaged her by the time she was found; an unsettling echo of Cristofano's death in Nimes. Every possible hiding place in the house was broken and ransacked in search of the money, and Benedetto was never seen in the village again. For the first time, genuine shock registered on Monte Cristo's face.

"I see why you wouldn't mention this before," the count said. "Your adopted son, a fugitive and a monster, your sister so tragically deceased. I do regret causing you to relive these events, Bertuccio."

"I've never tried to find Benedetto since; God cursed me for my first vendetta, and I have no urge to start another. I hope he's already dead," Bertuccio said. "It's just so strange to be back in Auteuil. I imagine that Villefort's bones lie in the village cemetery, unless they took him to Versailles."

"Anything is possible," Monte Cristo muttered, remembering again what Lucien Debray had said about dining with Villefort. "Even that Villefort may have cheated death."

For a moment he observed Bertuccio's absolute dejection. The spectre of cannibalism looming over Bertuccio's story caught the count by surprise. The notion of a man eating human flesh had always been abhorrent, but in the wake of the Dead Plague, it was an insult to the memory of everyone who had ever been pulled down and devoured by the undead.

"I won't press you on the matter again," the count said at last, "but I hope you take some consolation in the value you have added to this garden. Knowing that such pain occurred here makes me appreciate the beauty that much more. I expected this to be a simple garden; now I have a stage on which ghosts perform their endless plays. I have no fear of ghosts; even when the dead roamed the countryside, some say they caused less harm in those years than the living are capable of in a single day."

Monte Cristo rested a gloved hand on Bertuccio's shoulder. Bertuccio looked up to find the count smiling at him; not a warm smile, but the warmest he had ever seen on those stark white features.

"I'll remain here in the garden a while longer before we return to Paris, but you may retire to the carriage if your nerves require it," the count said. "When we reach the city, take the rest of the day to yourself and return to my service in the morning. We will return, but knowing what I know now, I'll double your wages for any day that I need you in Auteuil."

Tears in his eyes again, Bertuccio nodded and walked with a heavy step to the front of the house. Alone again, Monte Cristo opened his locked book and took notes about Bertuccio's story. He also sketched the plan of the garden, marking Benedetto's temporary grave and the path from it to the staircase.

Back in Paris, Bertuccio took his leave and ventured off into the city. All of the other servants were likewise dismissed, save for Ali. Monte Cristo stripped off his gloves and untied his cravat, handing them to the mute Ali. The count stretched and flexed his bandaged fingers, still wrapped tight. The clean white bandages ended at a line along his exposed neck, where they seemed to disappear beneath his flesh.

Monte Cristo and Ali traversed the house, giving it a more thorough accounting than time had allowed the day before. A large crate stood upright in one of the parlours, and Monte Cristo asked what it was. Ali responded by holding his elbows akimbo and mimicking a stiff walk.

"Ah, then we had better let him out!" the count replied.

Without need for a crowbar, Monte Cristo put his hands out toward the box; tendrils of bandages emerged from his sleeves and worked into the cracks of the nearest side. With a motion like cracking a whip, the count tore the side off the crate in one motion. The wooden figure of a man covered in ornamental Renaissance carvings stood among a nest of padding.

"Present your key, or be removed," it said in stilted Italian.

The count pulled an eight-sided pendant from beneath his shirt, the same as he had shown the first time he and this construct had met.

"Master, what may this one do for you? Are you satisfied with the power?" Baptistan said.

"So far, yes," Monte Cristo said, flexing his tendrils in a thoughtful manner before retracting them again. "Although the true tests of it are yet to come. Baptistan, your task is to guard this house as you guarded the island of Monte Cristo. Do you understand?"

"Yes, master. Guard duties are well within this one's capabilities." Baptistan fell into step with Ali to continue the tour of the house.

As Monte Cristo noted the changes he wished to make, a carriage pulled up in front of the house. Ali held out the count's gloves and cravat to cover himself with, but relaxed when the new arrival rang the bell in a distinct pattern.

Bandages still exposed, the count walked to the foyer to meet a young woman with thick dark hair. A green silk mantle embroidered with gold hung around her shoulders, and she greeted the count in the language of Mount Olympus as he bowed and raised her dainty hand to his lips.

"Haydee, my dear," the count said, replying to her use of Greek in kind. "I trust your time in the city was agreeable?"

Any outsider would find the count's deferential demeanour towards Haydee astonishing. At the same time, anyone observing the warmth of the smile she returned to him would know at once they had been companions for some time.

"I hardly set foot off the carriage, contenting myself to drive around and learn where everything is," Haydee said. "This is a beautiful city; I hope our business here allows us to stay long enough for me to see it all."

She inclined her head to Baptistan and exchanged several quick hand gestures with Ali. The two of them often communicated in such a way, and Haydee claimed it was as though Ali still had the power of speech. She looked at the count's red eyes and colourless face.

"Count, you're rather overdressed considering present company. Would you not like to be more comfortable?" she asked.

She reached to the line of the count's neck where his skin overlapped his bandages, but he moved her hands gently away.

"I'm afraid that my comfort is short-lived; while the Count of Monte Cristo may spend the day at home, Lord Wilmore must venture out in search of information," Monte Cristo said. "I've given Ali my recommendations for changes in the house; don't hesitate to add your own."

Monte Cristo left Haydee to her own devices and entered his dressing-room. There he shed the costume of a foreign millionaire and donned a suit cut in the English fashion. He replaced his fine gloves and cravat with coarser leather gloves and a high collar to match the suit. Ali applied a false mustache to the count's upper lip, and powdered the count's face to resemble the complexion of the British Isles. A pair of spectacles with subtle smoked lenses completed the disguise, giving his piercing red eyes the illusion of an unremarkable brown shade. It was Lord Wilmore then, not the Count of Monte Cristo, who exited the house by the rear doors.

Rather than take a carriage, he crossed the Rue Ponthieu and entered a much smaller and humbler house, purchased in the name of Gianmarco Faria. A hidden door in the basement of this house opened into the famed Catacombs of Paris. In the dark tunnels, Wilmore melted into the shadows to find his way to another forgotten entrance. He emerged in an alley not far from a government office, and with the payment of a few minor fees, got access to the prison records to look for a man known only as Benedetto.

CHAPTER 50
UNLIMITED CREDIT

The next day, a small open-topped travelling carriage with the arms of a baron pulled up to Monte Cristo's home. A man stepped down wearing a blue coat and white waistcoat which strained to stay closed over his expansive gut, with a massive gold chain draped across the front. Ribbons decorated the coat and watchchain, not awarded by the crown or by Napoleon, but instead by various professional societies and interest groups as a reward for him championing their causes in the House of Peers.

The baron's free-flying curly hair was as white as fresh snow, wrinkles and liver spots decorated his round and rubbery face, and thick spectacles magnified his squinted eyes. He affixed a smile to his face as he approached the door; or rather, he stretched the corners of his mouth backward and bared his upper teeth, which was not entirely the same thing.

While his driver asked the concierge if the Count of Monte Cristo was receiving visitors, the baron surveyed the sky, checking whether the clouds still predicted an auspicious time for first impressions. His horoscope had been unclear on the matter, which upset his digestion but couldn't be helped.

With the clouds judged to be acceptable, the baron scrutinized the house and gardens through the gate with a closeness that defied manners. He whistled through his front teeth as he did so, observing that the count must be very wealthy indeed. The baron made a mental note to press Monte Cristo for political contributions when they met, wondering whether appealing to the count's sense of guilt or the mob's sense of envy would be the most effective tool.

"Well? Is he home?" the baron asked when his driver returned. His deep voice may have sounded pleasant if not for the clipped nasal consonants and general arrogance of his tone.

"My lord, the count is not accepting visitors today," the driver said.

"Not accepting visitors? Did you tell that glorified doorman that Baron Danglars is here to see his master and that I had come specifically out of my way en route to the Chamber?" the baron huffed. "No matter. He has a letter of credit to discuss; when he wants his money, he'll need to come to me."

As Baron Danglars yelled for his driver to take him to the Chamber, loud enough to be heard on the far side of the street, Monte Cristo observed him from his bedroom window with powerful opera-glasses.

"Age has not been kind to him," Monte Cristo said, half to himself and half to Ali. "He ought to be not quite fifty, yet he looks ten years older at least. I suppose it was only a matter of time before his inner ugliness spilled outward, since he makes no efforts to contain it. Ali, make me presentable."

Ali helped the count with his gloves, cravat, and everything else to cover his wrapped form and present the public image of the Count of Monte Cristo. Dressed for public visibility, the count rang his bell three times to summon Bertuccio.

"I recall that part of my instructions in setting up this household was that I have the finest horses in the city," Monte Cristo said. "Tell me why I just watched a pair of magnificent dappled greys leave my property bound to someone else's carriage."

"Your excellency," Bertuccio said with a deep bow, anxious to please after the events in Auteuil. "You refer to Baron Danglars' horses? I tried to buy them, but the baron paid sixteen thousand for the dappled greys and would not sell."

Monte Cristo waved a hand. "Offer him thirty-two. It's a rare banker indeed who would refuse to double his capital," he said. "I have a visit to make this evening, and desire that those dappled greys be pulling my carriage. Also, don't reveal that the horses are for me; buy them in your own name if needed. You may go."

When Monte Cristo arrived in the Rue de la Chaussee d'Antin, Danglars was occupied in a meeting. The men he spoke to represented groups with names like the Coalition for Fairness, the Order of Dignified Employment, and the League of Concerned Citizens.

Legislation was the topic of the meeting; the nation's prison guards had pooled their money and wanted to buy a law. If they could dictate mandatory minimum sentences for minor crimes, they hoped to maintain their own job security while watching over a smaller proportion of violent inmates. Baron Danglars was happy to accept their fee and already had a good notion of how to present the law as a matter of public safety and the greater good.

When his footman entered to announce the count, Danglars' oversized ears perked up. Danglars explained the circumstances to his guests with a chuckle as he concluded the meeting.

"A most ridiculous error has been made, which I must rectify," Danglars explained. "Thomson & French, the bankers of Rome, have sent me a stranger called the Count of Monte Cristo and given him unlimited credit. I fear someone is trying to pull a hoax on me, but I'll get to the bottom of this, and he who laughs last will laugh best!"

Danglars escorted the gentlemen to the door, pressing a small bundle of holly twigs into each man's hand as they left. "For luck in your travels."

With his guests dispatched, Danglars hurried to the lavish salon where he received only his most distinguished guests. As with every room in his house, a filigreed horseshoe of pure silver hung above the doorway for luck. The salon was an overdone conglomeration of white and gold furnishings arranged around copies of fine paintings that had been sold to Danglars as originals.

In front of one of these paintings he found the Count of Monte Cristo, standing straight-backed and calm. Danglars took a moment to catch his breath, smoothing his wild hair with a sweaty palm and straightening his thick spectacles. When the count turned, Danglars was taken aback by the man's chalk-white face and crimson eyes, but motioned for him to sit regardless. Danglars had assumed the rumours of the count's appearance were exaggerated and that it was an affectation he used to get the better of people. Danglars was sorry he hadn't thought of such a trick himself.

"I presume I have the honour of addressing M. de Monte Cristo?" Danglars said.

"And I have the pleasure of speaking to Baron Danglars, chevalier of the Legion of Honour, member of the House of Peers, chairman of the

Royal Bourbon Reserve Bank?" Monte Cristo said. The count didn't react to the deliberate omission of his title, but recited every one listed on Danglars' card. Danglars pressed his thin lips together in response to the irony.

"You'll excuse me for neglecting your title, monsieur, but you understand that times are changing and that I am a man of the common people. After all, it is 1838," Danglars said, spreading his hands as though the point were self-evident.

"Such a man of the common people that you call yourself "baron" while refusing to call others count." Monte Cristo glanced around the lavish parlour. "Will I be meeting any of the common people who share this palace with you? I assume there must be other families living here, the house could fit seven or eight quite comfortably."

"What? What an absurd—that is, that's not what supporting the common people means, monsieur," Danglars said, caught wrong-footed by the challenge.

"Of course, how silly of me; you must forgive me, I am new to French customs. Those other families must live at one of your other houses," Monte Cristo said. "I'm told you have three in total."

"Being a man of the common people," Danglars said, "is not about reaching out to them directly. It's about ensuring the correct laws are written, so others will take care of them."

"I see." Monte Cristo nodded. "The absolute model of philanthropy."

"Precisely!" Danglars stretched his lips again in what he still assumed constituted a smile. "Speaking of money, we've reached the reason I wished to see you. I've received a very unusual letter from Thomson & French of Rome, regarding yourself."

"Unusual how?" Monte Cristo said.

"Well, the letter gives you unlimited credit with the Danglars Bank. There must be some mistake," Danglars said with a chuckle.

"My apologies, baron, is the word unfamiliar? The men who wrote the letter are Anglo-German, I believe; perhaps something was lost in the translation to French?" Monte Cristo said.

"The wording is correct, but the directions cannot be," Danglars said.

"Can't they?" Monte Cristo asked, raising his eyebrows. The light caught his eyes from a new angle, bringing out a ruby glow. "The letter states that the house of Thomson & French will guarantee that any withdrawals I make from your bank will be paid back to you, without limit. Which do you lack confidence in, their ability to pay you back or their intentions of doing so?"

Eyes locked with the count, Danglars felt a headache pressing in, coupled with a queer sensation like cutlery scraping across the inside of his skull. The count patted the breast of his suit.

"If your trust in Thomson & French is the reason, I have identical letters from three other banking firms in Milan, Moscow, and Istanbul," the count said. "Or is your fear that my accounts with Thomson & French lack the income to cover the sum?"

"Of course that's not the issue," Danglars said slowly. Each word stretched from his mouth like taffy. "But if you tell me how much you think you'll need, I could judge my bank's fitness to fulfill your requests. For example, if you wanted as large a sum as a million, that would be a reasonable task."

Danglars' own words surprised him, as he never revealed the limits of his bank's resources to anyone. He didn't understand why he was offering this information or why it was such an effort to speak.

"The very purpose of unlimited credit is that one does not know how much one will need," the count explained, leaning forward.

Without blinking, he took a small case from his pocket and showed Danglars the contents: two treasury orders worth five hundred thousand each, a million francs of pocket money.

"Will you extend my credit, or will I take my letters to another institution?" Monte Cristo said. "It would be a shame if the Nightly Assemblage learned that the chair of the Reserve couldn't fulfill such a simple request from his own bank."

Danglars' headache worsened. To relieve the hellish scratching in his head, he heard himself agreeing.

"Whatever you say, count. I'm at your service," Danglars said. Immediately, the ache behind his eyes vanished. The count leaned back in his chair, his eyes no longer glowing.

"Are you quite certain?" Monte Cristo asked. "I would hate to think you had any lingering doubts."

Danglars removed his spectacles and rubbed the bridge of his nose, trying to sort out what had just happened. He hadn't planned on extending the credit, but then he had. The finer points of their conversation were already fading from his mind, leaving only his own word that he would honour the arrangement. He could not back out now without consequences.

"Of course, count. The resources of my bank are at your disposal," Danglars said.

"Excellent!" the count said. "Now, allow me to set your mind at ease. My current plans are to stay in France no longer than one year, and I expect the minimum that I'll need is six million; we shall see if I require more. Be so kind as to send me the first half-million tomorrow, half in gold and half in bank-notes. You may leave it with my steward if you don't find me at home."

"It will be at your house by ten o'clock in the morning," Danglars said, his mouth dry as he considered the strain of extending that much credit in so short a time. "I must admit, while I keep track of the great family fortunes of Europe, your own wealth is unknown to me."

"It's been in the family for a very long time, forbidden to be touched for generations," Monte Cristo said. "The accumulated interest has multiplied the capital in that time, and the moratorium on withdrawals ended only a short time ago. I'm certain you'll learn more about my fortune as we continue to do business together."

The count pronounced those latter words with the same smile which had so terrified Franz d'Epinay during the Carnival.

"Well, I suppose there's nothing left to do but to shake on it," Danglars said, heading to a small font at the side of the room. He dipped his right hand in, and approached the count. "If you may remove your glove, count? This is water from a spring outside of Paris blessed by Saint Matthew, and our handshake will be a good omen for our dealings together."

"I must decline; I suffered a burn many years ago which leaves the skin of my hand painfully tender to this day," the count said.

Danglars was taken aback, but wiped his hand dry on the lapel of his coat and shook with the count regardless.

"When I entered, I noticed you admiring some of my art collection," Danglars said. "I've carefully curated the pieces in this room according to the practices of *feng shui*; I understand you appreciate the Eastern cultures."

"Ah, the ancient art of Chinese geomancy, devoted to the flow of energy through a home," Monte Cristo said. He cast his eye around the parlour, cluttered with Rococo furniture at odd angles.

"I consulted the finest French expert of the art to arrange this room," Danglars said. "We stand in the centre of the house, where the greatest concentration of energy pools. The sofa and other seating are arranged to avoid any obvious pathways for the energy to escape. Even my artwork contributes to the *feng shui,* scenes of battle and struggle to facilitate lively discussion and vibrancy."

"Any Chinese master would be astonished at what you've done with this space," Monte Cristo said with a smirk that Danglars did not see.

"Sadly, my wife refuses to suitably arrange the energy in her boudoir. I think the baroness is home; you should meet her." Danglars rang for the footman.

"Baroness Danglars is with M. Debray at the moment, my lord," the footman said.

"I met M. Debray at a breakfast when I first arrived in Paris," Monte Cristo said. "He struck me as an upstanding young man."

Danglars led Monte Cristo through his home towards the chambers which his wife called her own, giving him some history of his wife's background.

"She somewhat lowered herself in marrying me, belonging as she did to one of the ancient families of France," Danglars said. "Her maiden name was De Servieres, and her first husband was the Marquis de Nargonne."

The conversation turned also to the count's connection to Danglars' future son-in-law, Albert de Morcerf, and their adventure in Rome; Albert had told the story multiple times for Danglars' amusement since returning home. At last, they were admitted to see the baroness.

CHAPTER 51
THE DAPPLED GREYS

After the eyesore of the baron's salon, Baroness Danglars' boudoir provided a relief for the senses. It was a small octagonal room decorated in soft pink satin and white Indian muslin, with well-kept antique chairs complemented by painted sketches of pastoral scenes. She had ensured the room was overlooked by Baron Danglars and his experts when they committed their crimes against good taste in the rest of the house.

Danglars blew on a preserved rabbit's-foot he wore on a chain and had the footman precede them to announce their presence. He carried himself as more of a visitor than the master of the house, knowing his reception depended on how agreeable Baroness Danglars found the count to be. In this case, she greeted them with a warm smile.

Monte Cristo had made a lively impression at Albert's breakfast, and Lucien briefed Baroness Danglars on everything he knew about the count. Having already heard fantastic stories from Albert, Baroness Danglars was quite eager to listen to all of Lucien's details and suppositions.

Baroness Hermine Danglars, no longer a young woman but still striking with wavy blonde hair and a pretty yet matronly face, sat at a magnificent piano when her husband and the count entered. Lucien stood at a small work-table making a show of turning the pages of an album, with an uncommon amount of colour in his pale features. Monte Cristo raised an eyebrow, but did not comment.

"Baroness, I present, if I may, the Count of Monte Cristo, who has been recommended in the highest capacity by my colleagues at Rome," Danglars said in a rambling manner. "One singular fact is all which the ladies of Paris need to know about this man in order to pique their interest, and it is this: though he plans only to stay in Paris for one year, he proposes to spend six million francs in that brief period. We can only hope that he remembers us in his use of it!"

Danglars bared his teeth again in what passed for his smile, his heavy breath audible through the gap in his teeth. The baroness rolled her eyes at the introduction.

"I assure you, Baron Danglars: I have a short list of people who will be always in my thoughts while I reside in Paris, and you occupy a well-deserved place upon it," the count said.

A chill ran down Lucien's spine when he heard this, but Danglars and his wife did not seem to notice anything untoward.

"When did you arrive in our fair city?" Baroness Danglars asked. "I can only assume that you arrived from the extreme end of the globe; that appears to be your custom, from the stories our friend Albert has told."

"I arrived yesterday, Baroness Danglars, and from no place more exotic than Spain," Monte Cristo said.

"Please, call me Hermine. You've selected a horrible time for your first visit to Paris; summer is most unfavourable. All of the best parties and balls are over, the Italian opera is in London, and the French opera is everywhere but Paris," Baroness Danglars said. "There is the Theatre Francais, but it may as well be nowhere, and that leaves only the horse races. Do you have an interest in horses?"

"I have spent most of my life in the East, where they value two things above all else: the fine breeding of their horses, and the beauty of their women," Monte Cristo said.

"It happens that I own the two finest horses in Paris, a pair of dappled greys," Hermine said.

Standing next to the count, Danglars smoothed his hair down again and fidgeted in place. Just then, one of Hermine's servants entered the boudoir with a look of worry. She exchanged distressed words with Hermine in hushed tones, and Hermine turned an evil look upon Danglars.

"Darling, I've just heard a very strange tale from my maid," Hermine said in a frigid tone that brought the smirk back to Lucien's face. "My coachman was about to harness my dappled greys, but he discovered they had been removed from the stables. Did you have anything to do with this?"

"Well, yes," Danglars said, "but it was for your own good! Those horses were too wild and fast to be safe, and it was my moral duty to remove them from this house before you got hurt."

"Am I then a child, who must have others decide for me what is for my own good?" Hermine demanded. "Tell me, what kind of profit did you make off of your 'moral duty' to sell my greys? I had promised to show them off for my friends."

"I fear that I must interrupt and take my leave," Monte Cristo said. "Other appointments demand my time. However, if Madame is a connoisseur of dappled greys, I would be honoured to hear her opinion on my own. I purchased them only this morning, in fact."

Monte Cristo sent a servant to instruct his coachman to drive past the boudoir window. Hermine remained seated where she was, glaring at Danglars, until Lucien looked outside and exclaimed for her to join him.

"Great heavens! Those are my horses!" Hermine cried. "I recognize every line of them!"

Danglars looked for himself and surrendered to his fate with a groan. Hermine whispered in Lucien's ear and fell back onto her chaise longue.

"The baroness wishes to know what you paid her husband for the horses," Lucien said. Though he maintained a straight face, it was plain he planned to laugh about this at his club for weeks.

"I don't accurately know, in fact. Somewhere in the neighbourhood of thirty thousand francs; my steward handled the purchase," Monte Cristo said. "I didn't even know he bought the horses from Baron Danglars."

Monte Cristo could see a fearsome storm brewing behind Hermine's eyes. Lucien reached the same conclusion and took his leave at the same time as the count; both of them could overhear from the hallway the beginnings of a tongue-lashing likely to last an hour or more.

The count's coach returned to the front of the house to retrieve him, where Baptistan waited for him. Its wooden form was concealed beneath a servant's livery, along with a muffler and wide hat, but there was no mistaking the artificial inflections of its speech.

"Did master's visit meet expectations?" Baptistan said.

"Definitively," Monte Cristo said. "The domestic peace of the household is in my hands. With a twitch of my finger, I'll gain the favour of both husband and wife. It would have suited me to be presented to Mlle Eugenie, but I have plenty of time in Paris. It will happen when it happens."

Two hours later, the dappled greys cantered up the carriageway to the Danglars estate. A note attached to the harnesses requested that Hermine receive them with the count's blessing. The note went on to say that the count could not bear to make his entry into Parisian society with the knowledge that a woman's regrets pulled his carriage. As a further peace offering, a gleaming diamond dangled from each horse's harness. Monte Cristo also wrote to Danglars, requesting forgiveness for any faux pas he may have made in the whimsical and Eastern fashion in which he returned the greys.

CHAPTER 52
FRENCH OPERA

Despite Hermine's dour predictions, it proved to be a fine week to visit the opera. The famous Levasseur, absent for weeks due to an illness, returned for one of his most celebrated roles with Theatre Francais. Levasseur's return and the subject of the performance, a popular opera called Love in Hell, attracted a fashionable audience which included Viscount Albert de Morcerf.

Love in Hell told the tale of a young man and woman in love during the Dead Plague. The young man was enlisted in Napoleon's Grand Army of the Living, called up to wage war against the undead across Europe. His lover, meanwhile, joined the militia at home to protect their rural village. At every opportunity, the young man returned home on furlough to visit her and steal what tender moments they could amidst the chaos.

Like most young society men, Albert reserved a seat in the orchestra section with the expectation that friends of higher standing would invite him to their private boxes. Raoul de Chateau-Renaud took the seat next to Albert, and they were joined by Beauchamp who had free reign of the theatre as a journalist. Circumstances granted Lucien the use of the minister's box, to which he had already invited the Danglars family.

With Danglars himself travelling abroad for confidential Reserve business, Hermine was happy to accept Lucien's offer, and her daughter Eugenie was eager to see the performance. Eugenie already sat in the box when Albert arrived in his orchestra seat, though Hermine and Lucien remained absent. Albert hoped and worried in equal measure that an invitation from elsewhere would arrive before receiving one to sit with his fiancée.

With rare exceptions like Albert and Eugenie, nobody in Paris dared arrive at a performance until it had already begun. The curtain always rose to a sparse audience no matter the performance, with the first act by and large ignored by spectators more interested in observing new arrivals. While engaged in that exact activity, a familiar face caught Albert's eye in a box on the first level. He nudged Raoul.

"Look, see the blonde woman in the box there!" Albert said. "That's Countess Garzone."

"Ah, yes! I remember her from your delightful story about the bandits," Raoul said. He studied Garzone through his opera glasses without any attempt at subtlety. "She's even more beautiful than I imagined! Well, will you do for me what Franz did for you?"

Some spectators around them, either unacquainted with the habits of the French opera or die-hard enthusiasts of the art, made vain efforts to shush the young men.

"With pleasure, once she notices us," Albert said. With luck, Garzone caught sight of them at once and waved.

"Your lovely Venetian countess was at the Champ-de-Mars races today," Raoul said. "It was a good set of runs, but the grand cup was won by a totally unknown jockey riding a horse nobody had ever heard of."

"Is the owner still a mystery, or did the secret come out after the race?" Albert asked.

"No!" Raoul replied. "All we know is that the horse was named Vampa, and the jockey's name is Job. It was a splendid horse, like one out of a painting, and Job looked about as big as your fist."

"Vampa, you say?" Albert smiled, already suspecting who had entered the horse.

"Shut up!" shouted a group of voices from behind them.

Raoul stood and turned around, scanning the crowd for anyone brave enough to own up to the demand. When they saw Raoul's military dress uniform and powerful frame, they fell silent. Raoul nodded and took his seat again with a smirk.

Hermine and Lucien took their seats in the minister's box. Albert could not see for certain if lipstick stained Lucien's collar, but he wouldn't bet against it. Eugenie showed no reaction when Lucien entered and continued watching the performance. When Hermine noticed Albert in the crowd, she fluttered her fan at him.

"My good fellow, I can't imagine how you could object to the lovely

Mademoiselle Eugenie," Raoul said. "She's everything you've pursued before: dark hair, captivating eyes, and money. Her ancestry and rank are slightly lacking, but I've seen you chase businessmen's daughters without so much as a title."

"Yes, but there is something...missing," Albert said. "A certain femininity, I think. Eugenie is made in the model of Diana the huntress, and I prefer a more demure presentation like the Venus de Milo."

Eugenie was as beautiful as Raoul said, but it was an intimidating beauty. Her raven-black hair fell in rebellious waves, her eyes as dark as unadulterated coffee, and the very shape of her face conveyed an unimpressed skepticism even at rest. She seemed to always ask the world at large "Yes? And?" without saying a word. Eugenie even elevated her hobbies to the level of professions, being an expert linguist and a fine composer. Her skills aside, having time to practice them was a mark of distinction.

The Dead Plague had claimed the lives of many brave men who died defending their homes and loved ones from the undead. This left yawning gaps in both the labour supply and in family incomes, driving more women to step into the workforce and become breadwinners; the alternative was starvation. The battles of the Hundred Days and the king's predations during the Inquisition multiplied the problem, claiming even more men for the grand purposes of deciding who would rule and soothing that ruler's ego.

Although the Danglars fortune was notable, it didn't occupy the same strata as the Morcerfs or the Chateau-Renauds. He was what some liked to call a "middle-class noble," the main difference between himself and ordinary people being his title. Danglars' ability to support his daughter without her finding a job, integral to his carefully-maintained image.

In Eugenie's musical pursuits, she had become very close with a schoolmate, Louise d'Armilly. Louise, a lively and nervous young woman with a cherubic face, had a powerful singing voice and spent long hours in Eugenie's company. Their most recent endeavour was to found the Parisian Ladies' Vampire-Hunting Club, inspired by Albert's tales of Countess Garzone's fear of the creatures. The club was a whimsically-named excuse for Eugenie and her friends to meet, read bloody vampire novels, and generally enjoy themselves.

Raoul, who had faced death and laughed, feared nothing in Paris and thought Eugenie to be a fine specimen. Albert, who had slept through his own rescue from bandits, found her self-assuredness to be a sour note.

Onstage the young soldier's lover completed her aria, where she pledged to wait for him and to keep their neighbours safe in his absence. The curtain fell on the first act and the orchestra left their stations for the typical half-hour intermission. This left the audience at liberty to visit one another. Albert and Raoul were among the first to leave their seats, disappointing Hermine when they appeared in Countess Garzone's box instead of hers.

"Albert, my globe-trotting friend!" Garzone said, extending her hand. "I hear that congratulations are in order, on account of you leaving Rome in one piece!"

"Yes, I had something of an adventure prior to returning home," Albert said with a chuckle. "But it was nothing compared to the altercations which my companion here has survived. Countess Garzone, I present Baron Raoul de Chateau-Renaud."

Raoul and Garzone made small talk which soon returned to the Champs-de-Mars races and the mysterious horse which had won the cup.

"If either of you know who owns that splendid beast, I insist that you tell me!" Garzone said. "It was the strangest thing; I was at the race, cheering my heart out for this mysterious new horse, and applauding like a madwoman when it won. Imagine my surprise when I returned home to find the very same jockey having a drink in the bar of my hotel! That would have been coincidence enough, but then I found in my room the gold cup which Job and Vampa had won. There was a slip of paper inside which read 'From Lord Ruthven to Countess Garzone.'"

"That seals it, then!" Albert said. "The owner must be the Count of Monte Cristo, who you were so convinced was a vampire."

"Is he here in Paris?" Garzone asked. Albert had to laugh as the colour drained from her face.

"He is, and I assure you that he is not at all what you think. The Count of Monte Cristo is a true gentleman and already a dear friend of mine," Albert said. "It was he who rescued me from the bandit, don't you recall? And that bandit's name, of course, was Vampa."

"But why would he send me the cup? And how would he know to call himself Ruthven?" Garzone asked.

"I imagine it is his sense of humour," Albert replied. "I told him some of our conversation about him, and this is probably his unconventional way of being friendly."

"It's a funny way of indicating that, if so," Garzone said. "In any case, my dreaded vampire is in Paris. What kind of effect has he produced?"

"He arrived with a grand splash, was talked about for a few days, and then the world moved on," Albert said with a shrug. "There was a coronation somewhere, England I think, and there was a diamond theft; those have since captured people's attentions."

"You sell your friend short, Albert. After all, the count was already a minor celebrity thanks to your little bandit story," Raoul said. "The rumour mill has continued to turn on the subject of Monte Cristo relentlessly, regardless of what happens in the rest of the world. He arrived in so dramatic a fashion; they say he bought and returned Baroness Danglars' horses in a single day, borrowed two million francs on unlimited credit, employs a goliath mute, and sleeps only two hours a night!"

"If he's been the centre of all this activity in less than a week, I can see why he is still such a hot topic of conversation," Garzone said. "Tell me, have there been any unusual disappearances lately? Perhaps murder victims found drained of their blood?"

"Countess, Paris is built upon a network of grave tunnels," Albert said. "We have no shortage of rumours about things preying on the slums in the night; you'll find that most of the perpetrators are simply men with grudges and debts to settle."

"Personally, I wonder if the count ever intends to slow down," Raoul said. "I suspect that this level of activity is simply commonplace for him, and he'll continue to generate news and gossip until such time as he quits Paris."

Their conversation continued until the bell rang to alert patrons to return to their seats for the second act. Garzone invited Albert and Raoul to visit her any Saturday evening while she was in Paris. By the time they returned to their former places, the entire audience had paused to stare at the Russian ambassador's box.

CHAPTER 53
LOVE IN HELL

Midway between Countess Garzone and the Danglars women, the ambassador's box had sat empty until the current occupant captured everyone's attention. A young, dark-haired woman dressed in a snug crimson Eastern-style wraparound dress, her graceful movements clear even from the orchestra section, took her seat at the front of the box. A man dressed all in black but for a red cravat at his throat, followed her. The pure white tone of his face made him unmistakable.

Occupants of the surrounding boxes leaned forward to scrutinize the new arrivals and the magnificent diamonds which glittered at Haydee's throat and in her hair, piled high behind her head. The audience ignored the second act completely, all their attention on Haydee and the count; Lavasseur sang his lament about returning home and not finding his lover anywhere, but he sang it to the backs of everyone's heads. Very few saw the young soldier make the decision to abandon the army to find his lover and make certain she was safe.

When the curtain fell, Hermine Danglars once again waved her fan at Albert to invite him over. Manners wouldn't allow him to avoid her any longer, and he proceeded to the minister's box while Raoul stayed behind to wait for a more tempting offer.

Lucien and Hermine welcomed Albert most graciously, while Eugenie offered only a polite hello before returning her attention to Haydee and the Count. Of course, only one topic of conversation occupied anyone's mind.

"Albert, the baroness is overwhelming me with questions about your mysterious count," Lucien said. As Albert expected, a small pink stain sat on his collar. "What is his birthplace? Where was he educated? Who was his family? Everything short of to which side he dresses."

Hermine gave a shocked laugh and batted at Lucien with her fan.

"To her I said that if she wishes to know these things," Lucien said, "she should invite the leading Parisian expert in Monte Cristology to the box, and here you are."

"With your connections, Lucien, I would have expected that you could commandeer some secret agents to learn these things for me," Hermine said. "This count buys my horses for over thirty thousand, then sends them back as a gift wearing twenty thousand francs of diamonds! Naturally I'm curious about him."

"Perhaps he has a diamond mine, it would explain his unlimited credit with Father's bank. Also consider how he decorates his lovely companion," Eugenie said to nobody in particular as she continued watching Haydee.

"Sadly, I know nothing about the source of his fortune," Albert said. "A diamond mine is as likely as anything else. As for his birthplace, he has not said for certain but I think he's Roman or maybe Sicilian. Of course his colouring makes it hard to guess, and for all I know he could have been born in deepest China."

"What I'd like to know is who the count has brought to the opera tonight," Eugenie said. "She looks like a marble statue which has come to life and left the museum behind."

"Eugenie, I've never known a woman to be so complimentary to the charms of her peers," Lucien remarked. "So many women are interested only in putting each other down, it's refreshing to hear some positivity for a change. I must agree, she's a magnificent example of the female form."

"Now here's a matter where I can shed some light!" Albert said. "Her name, if I remember correctly, is Haydee. She is a Greek who travels with the count; he described her as his mistress, though also made the arrangement sound less than permanent. Beyond that, I know she's a musician, and heard her playing from another room once."

"A musician!" Eugenie said, her eyes sparkling. "I must send her my card, she may be interested in playing with myself and Louise sometime."

"This is useful information; the count entertains visitors, then!" Hermine said. "My husband must invite him to a ball, so he'll feel obligated to invite us in return."

"Fishing for an invitation to the home of a mysterious and handsome stranger, who is rich as a nabob and apparently a bachelor?" Lucien said, raising his hands as if to deflect a blow. "Goodness, what will people think?"

"Is he handsome?" Eugenie asked, noticing the count for the first time. She glanced at him before returning her attention to Haydee. "He is dreadfully pale."

"That same pallor led Countess Garzone to think he was a vampire," Albert said, attempting to find at least some common ground with Eugenie.

"I thought I saw the Countess enter," Eugenie said. "Her lovely blonde hair is difficult to miss. Morcerf, you should introduce me to her sometime. Perhaps she's a musician as well."

"Indeed!" Hermine said, happy to see Eugenie take an interest in expanding her social circle above her own status. "But first, go to the Count's box and invite him here."

"I don't expect I'll have to; see, he's already noticed you," Albert said.

Hermine turned to find the count bowing in her direction and returned it with a wave. Albert left the box, as requested, to ensure Monte Cristo's attendance, but found the count exiting the box just as he reached it. Ali stood in front of the door with his arms crossed to form an enormous ebony barrier.

"Haydee prefers not to receive visitors while seeing the opera," Monte Cristo said. He chuckled at the crowd of curious spectators gawking at Ali.

"My word, you Parisians are a singular people!" Monte Cristo said to Albert. He addressed the crowd with a laugh. "Have none of you ever seen a Nubian before?"

Albert recognized one of the gawkers as M. Edouard, a man about Albert's age with a long nose and tousled hair, who knew the stories and characters of every popular opera to a fanatical degree. Edouard heard the count's question and raised his hand in greeting.

"Excuse me, monsieur? What's a Nubian?" Edouard asked.

Monte Cristo chuckled again and turned away, proceeding towards the minister's box with Albert.

"I expect Ali's novelty comes less from his background and more from his status as your attendant," Albert offered. "The crowd back there will start questioning him about you any minute, either forgetting or not believing he's mute. Your entrance into our little pond is still making quite a few ripples, it seems."

The count showed his teeth in a grin that made Albert uneasy in a way he couldn't identify. To cover his sudden nervousness, he took a cigar from his pocket and conjured a flame at the tip of his thumb to light it. The bite of the smoke in his lungs cleared his head almost immediately, and the count's smile appeared no more threatening than any other.

"My bride's mother is greatly anxious to see you," Albert said, "or at least to have you seen seeing her. By the way, if your motive in the races at Champs-de-Mars was to remain anonymous, naming the horse Vampa was a miscalculation. You've managed to scare Countess Garzone half to death!"

"Ah, how remiss of me," the count said. "Of course, they must know about your bandit adventure from Brest to Cannes by now. How are your parents? I would have thought that on such a fashionable night to be seen at the opera, your father would be here."

"Mother is well, keeping busy with her societies and committees. Father spends much of his time at the Chamber, of course," Albert said. "Madame Danglars invited him to join her here tonight, and he intends to come."

"Excellent," the count said. His red eyes glinted.

The two men made some brief small talk about the music thus far, reaching the conclusion that only the novelty of Levasseur's return prevented the audience from filing out. They reached the minister's box in time for the third act to begin, with Levasseur questioning the villagers in a panic to learn what had happened to his beloved. While Hermine fawned over the count and made every effort to get Eugenie to notice him, the Count de Morcerf admitted himself with a perfunctory knock.

Unlike Monte Cristo or even a less exotic figure like the Countess Garzone, Morcerf's arrival excited very little interest in anyone beyond his present company. Monte Cristo maintained a cordial expression while he made the appropriate pleasantries, but glanced in Haydee's direction. Engrossed in the performance, she hadn't looked their way. Monte Cristo positioned himself to block her view of Morcerf.

"I've heard that you're making a habit of saving lives," Morcerf said to him. "In Rome, my son says you had a man's execution cancelled. Then you rescued Albert, and there's a rumour that you single-handedly stopped some runaway horses here in Paris."

"Don't believe everything you hear about me; people have begun inventing their own facts about me in the absence of genuine ones," Monte Cristo said. "But if I'm in the right place at the right time to safeguard a deserving life, I consider it a privilege to do so."

"Perhaps you could tell us something about your companion," Eugenie said. "I hear she is your mistress; you're not married, then?"

"We're certainly not married, though I suppose mistress isn't entirely accurate either. I like your term, 'companion'," Monte Cristo said. "Haydee is an unfortunate exile of Greece who travels with me."

"A Greek? Named Haydee?" Morcerf said, tugging at his goatee.

"Of course, Morcerf knows Greece quite well!" Hermine exclaimed. "You served at Yanina protecting the pasha, didn't you?"

"While you were there, did you ever see another woman like Haydee?" Eugenie asked.

"Well, I was inspector-general of the pasha's troops. I owe my fortune to that post," Morcerf said, shifting in his seat. Unable to find a comfortable position, he stood. "Perhaps I should get a view of this beauty you're all so taken with?"

"Oh, but wait! The best part of the performance is about to begin, do you see?" Monte Cristo sprang up and put his arm around Morcerf's shoulder.

Monte Cristo pointed at the stage as they leaned out over the edge of the box together. Levasseur's character discovered his beloved, turned into one of the shambling undead. He sang of heartbreak in a soliloquy about whether he had the strength to put a musket-ball through her head to put her to rest. The reveal of a young girl hiding behind a barrel settled the matter, and Levasseur shot his former lover to prevent her from biting the child.

In the Russian ambassador's box, the sudden white flash of the count's face in the darkness caught Haydee's eye. When she saw Morcerf next to the count, all the blood drained from her face. She sat as rigid as any victim of Medusa, then snatched the opera glasses to better scrutinize Morcerf's face. When she assured herself of his identity, it was too much for her to handle. She uttered a cry that could be heard from the surrounding boxes and fell backward into her seat.

"Count, something has happened to Haydee! I think she's ill!" Eugenie said.

"Look, Ali is already reviving her. Don't be too alarmed; though she is strong in a great many ways, in others she is quite delicate. There are certain flowers which can cause her to faint with just their odour. Still, I should go," Monte Cristo said.

He found Haydee awake but still very pale. Her hands, normally so warm compared to his, were clammy and cold.

"Who were you speaking to in that box?" Haydee demanded with fire in her eyes.

"That was the Count de Morcerf, one of the men I have business with here," Monte Cristo said. "He says that he served your father and owes the Morcerf fortune to him."

Haydee laughed in hysterics for a moment, a demented sound where mirth had been replaced by rage.

"That wretch! That conniving, backstabbing, filthy wretch! He says he owes his fortune to my father?" Haydee said. "He calls himself Morcerf now? He was Fernand then, Fernand Mondego. He was meant to protect us. Instead, he sold my father to the Turks, sold my mother and I into slavery, and stole the Eye!"

"Are you certain it was him?" Monte Cristo said.

"There is no doubt in my heart, and if I am mistaken, let the gods strike me blind!" Haydee said. "From the looks of him, that is not all he has stolen. When he came to Yanina, he was a scrawny thing with hardly any meat on his bones. Now he's built like Hercules! My father would be sick if he saw how the Eye of Asclepius was being misused, and by such a cowardly traitor at that. Please, let's leave."

"Of course. Ali, go prepare the carriage at once," Monte Cristo said.

The count helped Haydee to her feet and led her to the lobby. As the carriage rolled, he stroked her cheek with his gloved hand.

"Rest easy, my dear. Together, we will ensure that justice finds Fernand de Morcerf," he said. "I said I have business with him, didn't I?"

"Yes, and I wish..." Haydee began, but stopped and grinned at the look on the count's face. "Oh, I see. He's one of the three, then?"

"He's one of the three," the count said. Haydee breathed a sigh of relief and lay against his chest, soon falling asleep for the remainder of the ride home.

Back in the minister's box, Morcerf continued to fidget with his goatee. He continued watching the Russian ambassador's box. He hadn't heard their conversation or gotten a clear look at her, but the incident left him uneasy. He took a cigar from albert and lit it off a small flame in his palm, reminiscing as he smoked.

On stage, Levasseur sang his finale. With no other purpose in life but hunting the undead, he returned to the army. For abandoning his post without leave, they shot him as a deserter before the curtain fell one last time.

CHAPTER 54
THE PARISIAN LADIES'
VAMPIRE-HUNTING CLUB

There was a hotel in the Rue Saint-Germain-des-Pres which was famous in some circles for the discretion of their staff and well-known in other circles for how comfortable their suites were for club meetings. It was in this capacity the Parisian Ladies' Vampire-Hunting Club met each Saturday, with a standing reservation for a fourth-floor suite.

Eugenie Danglars, founder of the club, sat sideways in an armchair listening to Louise d'Armilly play scales and chopsticks on the piano. Their other friends lounged around the room laughing over the latest horror fiction from England or playing cards. The Club was open to anyone whose company Eugenie and Louise enjoyed; debutantes from Eugenie's social circles pretended to be vampires and feast on penniless artists who lived in the crowded boarding-house which Louise called home.

A knock at the door caught Eugenie's attention, a coded series of sharp raps and measured pauses. Eugenie placed a gentle kiss atop Louise's head and went to answer the door.

"Valentine! You made it!" Eugenie said with a wide smile which neither her parents nor Albert ever witnessed. "I was starting to think you wouldn't."

"Oh, well, I was reading the newspaper with Grandpapa and lost track of time. Honestly, I would still be there now if he hadn't insisted I come," Valentine said. She brushed her shoulder-length red hair behind one ear, then her ears caught up to her words. Her large blue eyes grew even wider.

"Relax, Valentine, I know what you meant," Eugenie said, laughing.

"It's touching how devoted you are to your grandfather, really. I wish I had family that deserved half as much love as you show him."

"That's kind of you to say, Eugenie," Valentine said. "It's nice to be around friends again after spending all week surrounded by clucking hens!"

Coming from a well-positioned but middle-class family, Valentine worked as a legal secretary at the law firm of Dubois & Renard. Her father had secured the position for her, escorted her to the door on her first day, and made it clear he expected her to move into practising law herself. He was a difficult man to oppose, and it was simpler to go along with his plan.

"I constantly need to be on my guard there," Valentine said, grateful to accept a glass of white wine from Eugenie. "Any innocent thing I say could be twisted into something poisonous by the women I work with, and anything they say to me might have double and triple meanings; it's exhausting."

"Well, thank heaven you're off today." Eugenie clinked her glass against Valentine's.

Sipping her wine, Valentine went around the room to say hello to Louise and the other girls. Eugenie settled in on the piano bench next to Louise, brushing a finger against Louise's hand and joining her in a duet on the keys.

After some time to unwind, Valentine settled into the relaxed atmosphere of the Society. She found herself chatting with Marie, a girl Louise knew from the boarding-house who had found a book of American short stories. Together they became engrossed in a story called Young Goodman Brown, and both nearly jumped out of their skins when another knock came at the door.

"Are we expecting anyone else?" Valentine asked, trying to still her racing heart.

"Have you heard of the flamboyant Count of Monte Cristo?" Louise asked. "We invited Haydee, his Greek travelling companion."

"Pigeon, you've given away the surprise," Eugenie said, giving Louise a gentle smack on the shoulder and leaving her hand to linger a moment. When Valentine opened the door, Eugenie played a brief flourish on the piano. "Ladies, may I introduce a newcomer to our grand city, Countess Haydee de Monte Cristo!"

"Thank you, you're too kind. But I have to correct you; I'm not a countess. I'm just Haydee," she said with a smile as the other girls applauded. "I only hope you didn't invite me as part of some plan to attack the count with a stake. I promise you, he's many things, but not a vampire."

This drew some laughter from the room while Haydee took a seat.

"Of course, vampires aren't real," Valentine said. "But so many clubs have such impressive names; the Ancient Order of Caribou, the Stonemasons, even my father is a member of the Eternal Royalist League. It's fun to have a grand name of our own."

"Well, any excuse to enjoy some time away from the world is a good one," Haydee said. "I'm sorry, I didn't catch your name?"

"Oh! I'm sorry, my name is Valentine." she extended her hand. "Valentine de Villefort."

"Don't worry, she's nowhere near as dour as her stodgy old father," Louise said from the piano, misinterpreting the surprise on Haydee's face. "Her temperament must come from the Saint-Meran side of the family."

"Father is strict, yes, but he has a softer side if you know where to look," Valentine said. "He allows Grandpapa to live with us when he could just as easily have been sent to a sanatorium, after all. Haydee, do you have any family in France?"

"None at all," Haydee said. Only Valentine noticed the flash of darkness and pain across Haydee's delicate features, but she said nothing about it. "Ladies, don't let my arrival interrupt your activities. What were you doing before I arrived?"

"Well, Marie and I were reading a horror story from America," Valentine said. "You're welcome to join us."

"My customers bring me little gifts sometimes, and one in particular likes to give me foreign books," Marie explained.

"Oh, what kind of work are you in?" Haydee asked.

Marie giggled and lifted the hem of her dress to mid-calf. "Let's just say our Valentine is not the only working girl in the Club, Mlle. Haydee."

Despite Haydee's insistence that they resume where they left off, Valentine and Marie returned to the beginning of Young Goodman Brown for her benefit. The three of them made quite a tableau in the corner, huddled together and looking wide-eyed at the page while Marie read aloud. When they had nearly reached the climax of the story, Louise—prompted by Eugenie—tossed a plum at them and scared them witless all over again. Eugenie guffawed at the sight of it and wiped a tear from her eye.

"I suppose you think you're so brave?" Haydee asked with a smirk, tossing the plum back. "What do you think you'd do if you met a real vampire, with bloodstained fangs and his eyes on your pretty neck?"

"Why, I'd kill it," Eugenie said. She stood up from the piano and puffed out her chest. "As soon as I heard the first rumour of blood-drained victims, I'd start carrying a sharpened stake with me always. If any vampire tried to feast on me, he'd taste only his own death."

"What if I told you those victims already existed?" Haydee asked. She smiled when the other girls gave her their full attention. "Whenever I come to a new city, I make sure to learn the juiciest gossip. Not the sort of stories you see in the society column of the Nightly Assemblage; the gritty rumours from the pubs and street corners."

"And a man in a pub told you that Paris has a vampire?" Eugenie asked.

"Not precisely. But I did learn that every so often, people disappear. People who hardly anyone misses," Haydee said. "Sometimes they're never seen again; other times, their bodies turn up in the Seine or the morgue, with their necks torn open."

"It could be wild animals," Eugenie said. "Sometimes the police drakes get loose."

"I saw one of the victims myself. The bite wound was far too small to have come from a drake," Haydee said. "I've heard stories like this from all over the country, dating back to the Inquisition. The earliest one I've found was a Corsican soldier, murdered in Nimes."

The girls sat in silence, enjoying the thrill of Haydee's words. When Eugenie clapped her hands together with a single sharp sound, they all jumped.

"Well, never say that I'm not a woman of my word," she said, grinning. "Girls, we have a craft project for next week. Everyone bring in some wood; we're carving stakes."

Louise bounced in her seat. "Are we going to pretend to hunt vampires, like that zombie parade in Rome?"

"That could be fun," Eugenie said. "Even if we don't, it's never a bad idea to be armed for our own safety."

While the other girls laughed about what they assumed to be a ghost story, Marie leaned closer to Haydee.

"You know, I have heard some stories myself, but I never gave them much credit," Marie said. "I know this is all fun and games, but maybe I could ask some questions the next time I'm at my corner?"

"Maybe you could." Haydee stole a glance at Valentine.

CHAPTER 55
IDEOLOGY

On Sunday, yet another carriage pulled up to Monte Cristo's home in the Champs-Elysees. Unlike Danglars' carriage, no coat of arms and no insignia of rank decorated it. One of the most illustrious and dreaded figures in Paris stepped down from the carriage: Gerard de Villefort, the king's attorney and crown prosecutor of the nation's capital.

Through kings and emperors and governments in diametric opposition to one another, Villefort's upward mobility had been relentless. His permanence and reputation fed on each other in an endless cycle: he was respected for maintaining his trajectory through so many changes, and that respect fueled that very trajectory.

Although respected as a formidable and merciless force in the courtroom, it couldn't be said that anyone particularly liked him. He carried the same energy in his personal life as in his courtroom, with unbending scruples and rigid etiquette. He was set in his ways in every sense but his ambition and always alert for opportunities to serve the king in some greater capacity.

If his late wife Renee were still alive to see Villefort, she would have trouble recognizing the man she'd married. His brown hair still clung in tight curls to his head, untouched by the grey threads of time. His features still carried the same unusual softness despite the unforgiving expression which was his default. Age and his profession had worn deep frown lines around his mouth and a prominent crease into his forehead. He wore a long black coat, almost a cassock, with the red ribbon of the Legion of Honour on his lapel.

The most striking change was impossible to ignore. Though Villefort's eyes remained a glacial blue, the sclera around them were a bilious yellow. This unnatural shade tainted his skin as well. This severe and permanent jaundice had been a part of his appearance since before his elevation to Paris.

M. de Villefort made very few social visits as a rule. He didn't appear at the theatre, the opera, the races, or society balls. He belonged to no social clubs besides the Eternal League of Royalists, to which he was a major contributor. To his few friends he was a powerful ally; to his enemies he was an opponent as bitter and implacable as time itself; to everyone else he was a living statue of the law.

The concierge admitted Villefort, and a footman led him to the library. The Count of Monte Cristo pored over a large map with tracing paper, sketching possible routes from Guangzhou in China to St Petersburg in Russia. The count greeted Villefort with courtesy but took careful note of Villefort's unhealthy appearance.

"Sir, it has come to my attention that my daughter and your... companion, have become friends." Villefort spoke in the same tone with which he would address a jury, his default speaking voice for over a decade. "I felt it was my duty to come introduce myself."

"Monsieur, it's my pleasure to be able to meet the grand king's attorney of France without having committed a crime," Monte Cristo replied. "Besides, I understand that a social call from you is a rare gift indeed."

Villefort curled his lip at the count's sarcasm. It seemed to him that no gentleman as highborn as the count claimed to be could be so coarse as to speak to him in that way. Still, etiquette demanded he remain for an appropriate length of time.

"You're a student of geography, then?" Villefort indicated the map. "Given your reputation as a traveler, I would be surprised if there was any place on the globe you haven't yet visited."

"Believe it or not, there are many countries where I have yet to plant my feet," Monte Cristo said. He pointed to a gathering of chairs by the window and sat in one which put the sun at his back. "When I'm done in Paris, I may take respite in the East again before venturing into the frozen north to see what lessons in the human condition I may find there."

Villefort settled into the opposite seat, bracing himself like a wrestler who faces a powerful opponent.

"It's important to me that my daughter associates with the correct sort of people, and so I came here to learn about yourself and Haydee," Villefort said. He had made careful mental inventory of the details Valentine had told him at dinner. "Tell me, what king do you serve?"

"I beg your pardon?" Monte Cristo asked.

"You are visiting Paris, but you must be a citizen of somewhere. What king do you serve?" Villefort asked. "Or are you from one of those dreadful republics, flailing about on the world stage like slaughtered chickens who can't see their own wounds?"

"M. de Villefort, your steadfastness is the stuff of legend in Paris, but they said nothing of your skills at poetry," Monte Cristo said. The light at his back made it difficult for Villefort to see his expression. "My title comes from Tuscany, but the simple fact is that I am a citizen of nowhere."

"Impossible," Villefort said, on the verge of laughing. "You must be beholden to someone."

"Why must I?" Monte Cristo asked.

"You have a reputation as a philosopher; surely you understand the divine right of kings," Villefort said. "Romans 13:1 says, 'Let every soul be subject unto the higher powers. For there is no power but of God: the powers that be are ordained of God.' God created all the land and water necessary for life, and the monarchs he anointed created the nations necessary for society."

"The scripture certainly says that, according to my friend Abbe Busoni. And you're correct that the lines we draw between countries exist only because kings say they do," Monte Cristo said. "But I fail to see how that leads to my requirement to be anyone's subject."

"Everything that makes civilized life possible exists by grace of the king," Villefort said. "If you travel in France, you do so on the king's road. If you can read, you owe that to the king's schools. If you eat, you owe the food in your belly to the king for granting land to a farmer to grow the crops and livestock which made your meal."

"That's one way to look at it. I've always seen it a different way," Monte Cristo said. "When I travel, I can do so because men were hired to flatten a piece of ground. When I read, it's because it was useful for me to learn how. When I eat bread, it's because a farmer found it profitable to grow more wheat than his family needed and a baker found it profitable to bake more bread than he could eat. I cannot recall ever buying a meal from a king."

"You should give more respect where it's due," Villefort's teeth clenched. "We owe everything to the king; he provides for us and owns us, like a father owns his children."

"There I disagree with you categorically. I own myself, as everyone does," Monte Cristo said. "No king controls my actions. In fact, I've never had much need for any sort of king or emperor."

"Are you some kind of anarchist, then?" Villefort said, nauseated by the prospect. "You would have society fall apart into warring tribes, murdering each other to pillage their livelihoods?"

"What else would you call any war between nations?" Monte Cristo said. "Anarchy is a tricky label. Many think it means an absence of rules, when really it means an absence of rulers. And as I've said, I believe that every man is himself the ruler of a kingdom of one: himself."

"You cannot be serious. This is some foreign humour which has gone over my head," Villefort said. "Society couldn't possibly function as it does without kings and would be impossible if everyone followed your radical beliefs."

"Are they radical? I find them quite logical," Monte Cristo said. "Look at it this way: you tried to convince me that I don't own myself. If that were true, believing your arguments wouldn't be my choice; you would need to address them to my owner so that he may force me to believe them. Instead you addressed me, admitting your own unspoken belief that I'm in control of my thoughts and actions and that I alone am capable of deciding to change them."

Villefort flushed a deep orange colour as blood filled his yellow cheeks and his eyelids twitched. He formulated and discarded several replies without speaking. The count's views sat so far outside of the Royalist/Bonapartist dichotomy that Villefort struggled to fit them into his model of the world. Monte Cristo had the gratifying knowledge that the finest orator in Paris sat before him speechless.

"Does Haydee share these delusions of yours?" Villefort said at last.

"She spent many years in slavery and has developed a deep love of liberty since becoming a free woman," Monte Cristo said. "The truth of owning her own life, her own time, and the fruits thereof has been very appealing to her."

"I must confess to being caught off-guard," Villefort said after a deep breath. He delivered even this admission in his sonorous tone of courtroom authority. "I came here expecting to find a nouveau-riche playboy with a head full of little else but whims. Instead I found a scholar with a fortune or else a jester devoted to his craft. Our conversation has turned to dissertation quite unintentionally."

"That's alright, I find it refreshing to be challenged," Monte Cristo said. Despite the backlighting and gloom, Villefort caught a red twinkle in the count's eyes. "There is nothing quite like me. I go where I wish and when, and do what I alone judge to be right. My only two obstacles are time and distance."

"You forget a third obstacle, count: your mortality," Villefort said.

Monte Cristo only chuckled, seeming to find Villefort's comment amusing.

"This pursuit of yours, this study of humanity, it must be in service of some end," Villefort said. "You must have some ambition."

"You quoted scripture earlier; let me reference the Bible as well. The Gospels tell the story of Satan taking Jesus up to the highest mountain and showing him the entire world, asking what it would take to tempt him to sell his soul," Monte Cristo said. "I faced my own test of faith a long time ago and made my choice. That mission is my only ambition now, and I partake in it whenever I have the opportunity. If you seek examples, you may ask Albert de Morcerf about our time in Rome."

Villefort watched Monte Cristo in silence for a moment. The only credible possibility in his mind remained that this was a joke he did not understand or appreciate.

"Though I find your sense of civic duty lacking, no man could say the same of your pride," Villefort said. "However, there is another obstacle which may block your path: ill health. You should meet my father, M. Noirtier. He was once an audacious firebrand, very similar to you in many respects. He waded deep in blood and gore during the marches of the undead, the rise of the usurper, and the subsequent struggles for the throne. In the end, God punished him for disrespecting the crown."

"How so?" the count asked.

"The doctors tell me a blood vessel burst within his brain. This man who had defied death was instantly reduced to a sort of zombie himself, able to do little else but silently decay while still breathing," Villefort said. "Now he lives with me, attended only by a gargoyle and Valentine. He's been in this state for six years. Such a fate could still befall you, forever ending your mission."

"I'm no stranger to the condition you speak of; apoplexy, it is called. I may take you up on this offer to meet your father, as I once witnessed a man suffer two such attacks. The second attack killed him," the count said. "It fascinated me so much that I decided to learn more about the workings of the human body; I'm something of an amateur physician."

"Indeed?" asked Villefort.

"Indeed. For example," the count said, "jaundice like yours would typically come from a surplus of iron in the diet or a disease of the liver. Have you been to a doctor?"

"Not that it is any business of yours, but yes," Villefort said with a frown. "In 1817 I was attacked by a Bonapartist with delusions of revenge. The coward struck me with a poisoned knife and left me to die. I was permanently disfigured, and my breast still bears the scar, but I survived."

As Villefort recalled that dreadful night in Auteuil, he unconsciously licked his upper lip. Memories flooded back, of dragging himself to the house from the garden and ringing for a servant to help. The servant had bent low to help lift Villefort up, and he had seen vital blood pulsing in a vein in the servant's neck.

"Since you mention scars, I've noticed a great many on your hands," Monte Cristo said, referring to the pale network of faded and crisscrossing lines. "Mine bear old wounds as well; an incident left them badly burned, hence why I refrain from removing my gloves in company."

"Falconry," Villefort offered as his only explanation. He shook his head to clear it of old recollections. Monte Cristo declined to press the issue, though his gaze settled for a moment on a crescent-shaped scar between Villefort's thumb and forefinger.

"As long as we are on the topic of our physical irregularities, I could as easily ask you about your colouring," Villefort said. "It's at least as peculiar as my own; were you poisoned as well?"

"Nothing so dramatic, I'm afraid," Monte Cristo said, gesturing to his own face. "A simple case of albinism, nothing more. I've traced the affliction through my family tree back to the fourteenth century. As a younger man, I was ashamed of my skin colour and attempted to hide it. Now, like yourself, I wear it without shame or pride as just an immutable aesthetic characteristic."

A clock tolled the hour, and Villefort rose from his seat.

"This has been an enlightening visit," Villefort said.

"One last question, if you don't mind," the count said. "I understand that you're both the king's attorney and the crown prosecutor; would you be so kind as to explain these titles to a foreigner?"

"It is a difference of jurisdiction; being crown prosecutor means that I try any criminal within the bounds of Paris," Villefort said, always proud to explain his dual role. "Being king's attorney means that I prosecute the most heinous crimes from across France as well."

Monte Cristo escorted him to the door, maintaining a smile only until Villefort's carriage reached the end of his drive. His mask of civility dropped, revealing the burning embers of hatred. He rang for Baptistan.

"What are master's orders?" Baptistan asked.

"I've spent too long in the company of poison and require the antidote," Monte Cristo said. "Have the carriage prepared to visit the Morrels at the Rue Meslay in two hours. You'll find me in Madame's chamber."

"Advisement: this is a deviation from the established plan," Baptistan said. "No provisions were made for interacting with the Morrel family at this stage."

"It is my plan, and I'll alter it as I see fit," Monte Cristo said. "Prepare the carriage. Two hours."

Villefort sat in his carriage, uncertain what to make of the count. He replayed their discussion again and again, trying to find any indication that Monte Cristo had been joking beyond the inherent lunacy of the words themselves. The answers evaded him, compelling him to chase them more vigorously, until it felt as though his head would burst.

Villefort drew every curtain to block the outside world. He unfolded the penknife he always carried, found a suitable patch of skin on the back of his forearm, and made a small incision.

"Gabriel, Samuel, Azrael, give me strength," he whispered, invoking the names of the angels he had learned from the Eternal Royalist League. "Accept this tax of blood."

He brought his arm up and drank from the cut, feeling the calm of the ritual almost immediately. The clarity it brought reassured him that Monte Cristo was a harmless eccentric, some fop with a head full of Oriental whims. He had no need to forbid Valentine from associating with the count's woman, at least not yet.

As was often the case, Villefort's offering to the angels came with a revelation about the source of his anxiety. It was not Monte Cristo's nonsensical ramblings which had upset him but instead an article in the previous day's Nightly Assemblage. Someone on their staff had received a tip about Villefort himself and decided to raise the question of what brought him to Auteuil on the night of September 17 1817; the night he had been attacked by the Corsican.

This was not the first time the question had been raised, nor the first time he had used his influence to suppress it. It was, however, the first time that anyone had connected his presence there to the disappearance of several Auteuil residents who had worked as servants in that house. Typical to the style of the Nightly Assemblage's articles, it offered no new facts; it simply asked the question and left the reader to insinuate their own narrative, with a vague promise of further details which they may or may not ever fulfill.

As his carriage rolled towards home, Villefort recalled the reporter's name: Jordan Caillat. He would be sure to have some gendarmes pay M. Caillat a visit and help him decide if he wanted to pursue his story any further.

CHAPTER 56
HAYDEE'S ROOM

Monte Cristo ascended the stairs to Haydee's chambers, knocked on the door, and waited for his invitation to enter. When he stepped inside, his boiling rage was soothed almost immediately. These rooms were set aside for Haydee's exclusive use, though she had free reign of the house as well.

With the freedom to decorate her rooms in any fashion she desired, she had chosen to continue the themes prevalent in the rest of the house and the island grotto. Thick Turkish carpets covered the floor, marvelous works of silk hung from the walls, and luxurious divans piled with cushions provided the seating.

Haydee's maids attended to her when Monte Cristo entered, but vacated upon seeing him. Their strict orders stated not to be present when the count was allowed into the suite.

Haydee herself lounged on the divan nearest the window, stretched across the upholstery with all the contentment and flexibility of a satisfied cat. In one hand she held the ivory mouthpiece of a filigreed hookah, resting the tip of it against the full bow of her lips in between deep draws of the fragrant smoke. She held a book in her other hand, likely either a volume of philosophy borrowed from the count's library or the biography of some composer from her own collection.

She wore a white vest trimmed with silver and a bodice fastened with diamonds which left her throat and décolletage on casual display, with harem pants clinging to her generous hips. Deeper within the suite could be found the tools of her artistic pursuits: oils, canvas, clay, and several stringed instruments. Deeper still lay her boudoir, where her bed was situated beneath a skylight of rose-coloured glass.

Her long hair, so dark the highlights were tinged with blue, fell in waves around her delicate olive shoulders and framed a face which, like her famous countrywoman Helen of Troy, could launch a thousand ships if she desired. When she heard Monte Cristo's footsteps, she turned her deep brown eyes away from her reading and favoured him with the sort of smile men have fought duels over.

"Good morning, my love," Haydee said, resting her book on her thigh. "Are you still entertaining the pretense that you need permission to come in?"

"I promised when we first met to never intrude on your freedom or your privacy," Monte Cristo said with a smile. "If you told me to leave, what else could I do but comply?"

Haydee stretched, rolling her shoulders as she did so and watching for any reaction from the count. Anyone else could miss the slight glint in his red eyes and the subtle flare of his nostrils. She grinned at him. "I overheard some of your conversation in the library. That was Villefort, then? It must have been vexing to speak to him."

"I think I managed to perturb him as much as seeing him did to me," Monte Cristo said. "He may think us insane, but he doesn't yet think we're criminals."

"Still, you must need some relaxation. Come, make yourself more comfortable." Haydee patted the divan next to her.

Monte Cristo smiled, with a genuine look of contentment the likes of which nobody else in Paris had ever seen him display. He pulled off his white gloves and his silk cravat, exposing that strange line where the bandages of his neck seemed to disappear beneath his skin. Haydee moved over to make room on the divan for him and stretched her legs across his lap.

"There, isn't that better?" she asked, mischief in her dark eyes. "Master, you push yourself too hard. Your enemies aren't going anywhere."

"You know that you don't need to call me that," Monte Cristo said. "Your time as a slave is over; you've been a free woman for four years."

"Do you think I forgot? I can go where I please and do what I want in one of the most prosperous cities in the world," Haydee said. "I call you 'master' because it's fun, and it reminds me of how much my life has improved since you came into it. Nothing holds you back or stands in your way; you've even bested death, my love. Rather than ask why I call you 'master', you should ask why no one else does."

"Don't be so sure about that," Monte Cristo said. "Even I don't know my limits. I can be stabbed without blinking, and beaten without pain, but can I drown? Can I burn? If I were sent to the guillotine, would my body pick up my head and walk away?"

Haydee shuffled forward to rest all her weight in the count's lap and ran her fingers through his black hair.

"How much danger are you in, now that you've set these things in motion?" she asked him.

"I honestly can't say," Monte Cristo said. "My enemies are cruel, brutal, and powerful in their own ways. If I overplay my hand, they could retaliate. They may come after you, or find my heart and guess its importance."

Haydee nodded. She knew an ornate Egyptian cabinet stood in the count's bedchamber. It contained bottles of fragrant oils, yards of linen bandages, and four golden jars with carved heads from Egyptian mythology in a row on the top shelf: a baboon, a falcon, a jackal, and a human. The traditional canopic jars of mummification, these held the count's lungs and abdominal organs. In the middle of these four jars stood a fifth, made of black stone with an unadorned lid. Inside that jar, preserved by Baptistan during the ritual, rested the count's heart.

"The one way I know to claim the sleep of death is to destroy my heart," Monte Cristo said.

"Then I'll just have to do my best to safeguard it," Haydee said with a smile. Her fingers crept through the count's hair to the back of his neck. "Now, I thought we agreed you would get more comfortable."

Haydee found the seam hidden beneath the count's hair and finessed the delicate clasps there. She held Monte Cristo's red gaze as she peeled away the white mask of his former face to reveal what lay beneath and laid one hand against his bandaged cheek.

"Master of life and death," Haydee murmured. She set the mask aside and picked up the mouthpiece of the hookah again. "Relax with me. The world can wait; after all, it is yours."

Monte Cristo took the mouthpiece, resting it against his lips—not the smirking white mouth he showed to the world, but his true flesh. His wrappings exposed only the skin around his eyes and mouth, which was grey and lined like the bark of a young silver maple. He breathed the fragrant smoke deeply; not for the first time, he wished he knew what magic allowed him to do so when his lungs sat in a sealed golden jar.

"Enough of my business; tell me about yours," Monte Cristo said. "How was your time at the club yesterday?"

"It was fun," Haydee said. "The Danglars girl was actually fairly pleasant. Arrogant, but still amiable in a way. The Morcerf brat is quite right: she definitely does not want to marry him."

"Well, then it's a good thing I came to Paris," Monte Cristo said with a grin. Haydee laughed and toyed with the buttons of his shirt.

"The other girls were better company. One of them, Marie, was so taken by my vampire rumour that she'll look into it herself," Haydee said. "And speaking of vampires, I met Valentine de Villefort."

"If only Morcerf had a daughter, you could have all three dancing to your tune," Monte Cristo said. "What is Villefort's girl like?"

"Honest," Haydee said. "Kind. Clumsy, especially with her words, but I liked her. If there's room for it, we should try to spare her."

"I'll consider it," the count said, staring at nothing as he took another draw of smoke and returned the hookah mouthpiece to Haydee. "Of course you kept your secret, yes?"

"Of course," Haydee said, feigning offense and batting the count's chest with her fist. "Nobody knows who my family was, and nobody will. Not until we're ready."

"Perfect," the count said, smiling again. He stroked Haydee's cheek, and she nuzzled into the touch of his wrappings against her skin.

When the two hours had elapsed, Baptistan arrived at Haydee's door to inform the count his carriage awaited him. Monte Cristo dressed himself again, ensuring his mask sat square and the fastenings were secure. He checked in the mirror by Haydee's door that his cravat and gloves hid his bandages, and nodded.

Just as he had hoped, the time with Haydee cleansed his spiritual palate and rid it of the bitterness left over from speaking to Villefort. He stepped outside to his carriage in order to visit the Morrels.

CHAPTER 57
THE MORREL FAMILY

No. 7 in the Rue Meslay, home of the Morrel family, was a modest two-story building of white stone with a small courtyard and beds of beautiful flowers. A concierge opened the gate for the carriage, and Monte Cristo recognized him as old one-eyed Cocles, the clerk from Morrel & Son.

At the sight of Cocles, Monte Cristo's mind reeled backward through a dark haze of years and pain. This haze, illuminated in patches by sunbeams full of glittering dust-motes like the grotto under Monte Cristo, was where the count could go to retrieve the memories of his old life as Edmond Dantes.

The count could bring up dates and facts with ease: the years of Edmond Dantes' employment with M. Morrel, what he had done to save the Morrel family, or the sight of the rebuilt Pharaon returning to port. The emotional details which coloured those memories were faded and dim, belonging to a different man than the one who recalled them. He felt protective of the Morrel family, to be sure, but it felt like a promise made to somebody else that he would look after them.

To distract himself from these reflections on his old life, Monte Cristo recalled what Max had told him at Albert's breakfast. Max's sister Julie and her husband Emmanuel owned the estate and leased out the two small guest-houses and some space in the gardens to tenants. The Morrels lived in the main house with rooms set aside for Max.

That afternoon, Max stood grooming his horse when the carriage approached. His thick campaign beard had been trimmed down to just a wide mustache. He wore simple overalls and a sleeveless shirt under the warm summer sun, and enjoyed the ritual of brushing the horse almost as much as the horse did. Baptistan climbed down from the carriage, still wearing a servant's uniform, and approached to ask if Monsieur and Madame Herbault would receive the Count of Monte Cristo.

"The count? Of course!" Max said, surprised by Baptistan's voice and appearance but pleased that the count had remembered his promise to visit. Max opened the carriage door himself and greeted the count with a firm handshake.

"You employ some curious help," Max said. "He reminds me of a forged, but I've never seen one so small or made of wood. We had some of the typical variety as guards on campaign; they're also rather..."

Max meant to say that the tall, wide-chested plate-armour forged were useful as mobile cover against rifle fire, but stopped. His own words reminded him of an ambush attack one night in Algiers and the unspeakable violence that followed. His throat closed up and refused to cooperate.

The look of distress on Max's face troubled Monte Cristo, so unlike the hopeful idealism he remembered from when Edmond Dantes had rescued the Morrel family from ruin. Whatever the cause of the problem, the count felt a need to defuse it.

"I doubt Baptistan would be much use in battle," the count said, forcing a chuckle. "It's a prototype of a new sort of servant, invented by an American I met while travelling. I helped him escape some overzealous Luddites, and he offered Baptistan as a token of his gratitude. I send him reports every month, wherever I am, of how effective Baptistan's service is."

"Wonders never cease, do they?" Max said, his voice unfrozen by the change of topic. "Please, come this way. My sister is in the garden."

Max led the count and Baptistan past the horse to another part of the garden where every colour of bloom had been cultivated and arranged with care. A woman in her late twenties knelt trimming a rose bush when they entered. She jumped to her feet when a stranger and a man made of wood approached, but Max calmed her with an outstretched hand.

"Julie, don't be alarmed. May I present the Count of Monte Cristo, world-traveler and our guest this afternoon," Max said.

"Maximilien!" Julie chided, brushing dirt from her front. "You could have warned me! I'm wearing my gardening clothes, this is no state in which to greet a count!"

"Madame, don't be embarrassed on my account," Monte Cristo said. "I have great respect for those who can coax life from the earth; though I've learned many things in my travels, one thing I've never had any skill for is gardening."

"Well, alright then," Julie said, the blush in her cheeks receding. "Welcome to our home, count. Any friend of Max is a friend of ours. I'll get some refreshments."

Julie glanced at Baptistan, uncertainty written on her face as she considered how to phrase the question on her mind.

"My servant does not eat or drink," Monte Cristo said, anticipating her concern.

Julie smiled and retired into the house.

"Maximilien, you seem tongue-tied. Is something wrong?" Monte Cristo said.

"I'm sorry count, I invited you to come and now that you're here, I'm rather poor company," Max said, shuffling in place. "Sleep didn't come easily last night; perhaps that's the reason."

"Yes, perhaps," Monte Cristo said.

More dim recollections from the life of Edmond Dantes came to the count: nights spent wrestling with sleep on a bed of straw in a stone dungeon, mornings where he awoke on his yacht from nightmares of imprisonment. He wondered what memories disturbed Max's slumber.

Before he could ask any further questions, Julie returned with a pitcher of lemonade and several glasses. Behind her came her husband Emmanuel, carrying a tray of finger sandwiches.

"It seems that my visit is causing no end of disturbance," Monte Cristo said to Max as they approached. "Your sister is interrupted from her gardening, and her husband is interrupted from his afternoon activities. Still, your family appears to be a happy one."

"They really are," Max said, a smile breaking through his gloom for the first time. "Julie and Emmanuel are two of the kindest, most patient people I've ever met. They'd have to be, to let me live with them."

"Your excellency, welcome to our humble home," Emmanuel said. "Emmanuel Herbault, at your service, and you've met my wife Julie."

"It's a pleasure to meet you both," the count said. "Max told me the other day at breakfast that your shipping business is doing quite well. Morrel & Son, was it called?"

"Technically, the name has been Morrel & Dimonte for many years," Emmanuel said. "Julie's father renamed it when an investor by the name of Signor Dimonte took an interest in the firm."

"Yes, I heard about the mysterious Dimonte as well," the count said with an unreadable smile.

"In our darkest hour, he offered the funding we needed in exchange for a reasonable share of the profits, and it saved the business," Emmanuel said. "Ever since, we've done so well that we could expand to Paris to take advantage of the shipping hub this city has become. Someday, I hope to open another warehouse on the west coast and start a trade route to America. We've never even met the man; he's a notorious Italian recluse and only deals with us through intermediaries."

"You may not have met him, but Julie did," Max said.

Emmanuel shook his head with a sad smile. "Max, we've been over this. You're confused again," he said softly.

"I don't think so at all," Max replied. "That clerk, the one from Thomson & French; he was Dimonte, I'm sure of it. It can't be a coincidence; the clerk forgave our debts without any payment by notarizing a receipt Julie found in one of Father's old purses. In that same purse we received our first letter from Dimonte, and the new Pharaon arrived the same hour. There's no way they can't be the same man."

"This is all utterly fascinating. I always enjoy hearing the tales of how people make their fortunes," Monte Cristo said. "If the fortune was made honestly, it is an inspiration. If it was made dishonestly, the story can educate in other ways. Yours is truly a story of success snatched from the jaws of ruin."

"Oh, it was hard work even with Signor Dimonte's investment," Julie said. "After losing half of our ships to the Inquisition and the other half to the sea, it was a fight to restore the Morrel reputation and rebuild the fleet. But after years of long, tireless effort, here we are."

They enjoyed their sandwiches and lemonade at a small patio with a view of the gardens. The earliest hints of summer crept into the air, the birds sang, and the garden presented a portrait of tranquility itself. The count basked in it, taking a certain satisfaction in the very existence of this happy home. For one surreal moment, he wished Edmond was still alive to see the results of his actions.

Monte Cristo realized he had indulged his reverie for too long and was expected to resume the conversation. His hosts were too polite to draw attention to it and seemed distracted by the silent figure of Baptistan standing behind the count's chair.

"Pardon my lapse," the count said, "but contentment such as yours is a novel sight to me. My travels take me to places of such conflict and drama that a genuinely happy home becomes a rare treasure to be examined and appreciated."

"That's very kind of you to say," Julie replied, raising her glass to her lips with a smirk aimed at her brother. "Perhaps it will be even happier when Max brings his secret sweetheart around to meet us."

"Julie! Now I think *you're* confused," Max said, blushing furiously. "Speaking of treasure, count, would you like to see the famous purse for yourself? We still have it."

The offer caught Monte Cristo by surprise in the midst of enjoying Max's reaction to Julie's remark.

"A relic from a time of real calamity, how could I refuse?" Monte Cristo said.

Max led the count into the house, decorated in a tasteful pastoral style. In the drawing room, a glass display case housed a faded red silk purse and a piece of yellowed paper. The writing on it was still legible despite the ink fading from the original black to a dull blue. It was a receipt from Thomson & French for a large sum of money marked as being paid in full.

"Emmanuel is a good man, but he can be very unimaginative sometimes," Max said. "The clerk gave Julie clear instructions on where to find this purse and when, with no apparent motive. That bill wiped out the majority of Father's debts, and the large diamond that accompanied it paid off the rest with money to spare."

"And the bank denies ever sending this clerk to see your father?" the count asked.

"Precisely! But Emmanuel seems happy to discard the pieces of the story that don't fit, rather than try to see the larger picture they hint at," Max said. "It gets stranger: this is the exact purse Father gave to a friend to help him through a desperate time. The friend was the father of a sailor named Dantes, who worked for Morrel & Son until he was arrested for treason. The poor man died in prison."

"That is interesting. How could the clerk, whether he was Dimonte or not, possibly get his hands on such a thing?" Monte Cristo asked.

"Exactly!" Max said. "In his later years, Father became convinced that Edmond Dantes returned from the grave somehow to help him, out of gratitude for my father's kindness to his. The clerk and Dimonte were certainly the same man, but I think that somehow, Signore Dimonte is also the ghost of Edmond Dantes."

"That's a bold claim to make. You may be too young, but I remember a time when men rose from the grave," the count said. If any blood remained in his body, it would have rushed to his face; if his heart still resided in his chest, it would have raced. He realized he was unsure if he still had the capacity to cry. "My experience is that when a man returns from beyond the veil of death, mercy does not accompany him."

"Well, as I say, it's only one possibility. My father also doubted the official government report of Dantes' death which claimed he drowned trying to escape," Max said. "If only we could find some proof!"

"Did you see this clerk yourself?" Monte Cristo said.

"I did, but only briefly when he verified the receipt," Max replied.

The count nodded. "Was he about my height, perhaps a bit taller? An Englishman who wore spectacles, with a habit of licking the tip of his pencil?"

"You've described him exactly!" Max said, amazed.

"I had a feeling it may have been him. An acquaintance of mine, Lord Wilmore, is constantly doing good deeds of this sort. He's an eccentric fellow, but a pleasant enough travelling companion for short trips," the count said.

"This is wonderful! Since you know him, would you please help us finally thank him properly for his generosity?" Max asked, beaming.

The count shrugged. "I can try, but the last I heard he was preparing for an expedition to the furthest reaches of the Arctic. His whims are often unpredictable, and I cannot guarantee when he intends to return to civilization."

He softened his tone in response to the crestfallen look on Max's face. "Max, I promise that if Lord Wilmore knew what your family has done with his help—assuming it was him—it would keep him warm no matter how far into the frigid north he travelled," Monte Cristo said.

Max and the count returned to the garden, where they resumed conversation with Julie and her husband until Baptistan gave them a gentle reminder of the hour. Monte Cristo shook hands with the men and bowed to Julie.

"Madame, being in your home and the presence of your family has reminded me of a great many things I had forgotten. If you'll allow it, I would greatly enjoy visiting here again as a friend," the count said. Without waiting for an answer, he hastened to his carriage with Baptistan following behind.

"What an odd man," Emmanuel said as the carriage pulled away. "Pleasant, but very odd. What did you make of him, my love?"

"He seems sincere enough in his offer of friendship," Julie said. "It's just, I feel as though I've heard his voice before. For the life of me, I cannot imagine where."

In the carriage, Monte Cristo struggled to reconcile this intrusion of his old life into his new existence. He remembered Edmond Dantes standing on his yacht and bidding farewell to kindness, humanity, and gratitude before his transformation. He had not expected to meet them again in the form of Max and the Herbaults and didn't entirely understand his own decision to visit them.

To clear his head, he turned his focus to the next stages of his plan. Arrangements needed to be made for Villefort and Danglars which would require careful finesse. Finesse, he reminded himself, and another withdrawal from his unlimited credit with the Danglars bank.

CHAPTER 58
L'EPICURE

After the count's Sunday visit, Max slept better than usual. He guessed that credit was due to telling the count about his family's good fortune and learning that this Lord Wilmore may have had a role. That sense of hope had likely set him enough at ease to get some rest.

In any case, he woke on Monday morning refreshed and more confident than he had felt since returning to France. Instead of pulling on his overalls for the day, an idea struck him.

Shortly after the breakfast at Albert's house, Albert and Raoul had invited Max out with them for the afternoon. It turned out to be something of an ambush; Raoul insisted that Max have some fine clothes besides his dress uniform, and had enlisted Albert for his sense of style. Like Julie, Raoul enjoyed ribbing Max about the secret woman who had written him love letters throughout their campaign.

"Any woman would be swept off her feet by a handsome man like you in full dress," Raoul said, "but you need a middle-ground between that and dressing like a stable-boy. Are you going to strap on your sword and pin up your medals every time you take her to dinner?"

Max had spent the better part of three hours being escorted from one tailor's shop to the next, measured and prodded by no fewer than five old men who looked exactly alike, listening to Albert's advice about which colours did or didn't bring out his eyes. Orders were made and the clothes sent to Max's address; Raoul paid the entire bill and wouldn't hear a word of argument. All in all, Max couldn't deny the clothes looked and felt good. He had ended up with three jackets, three waistcoats, and three sets of trousers.

"The beauty of these pieces is that they'll work together in any combination," Albert had told him. "I've done the heavy lifting for you, as it were. You'll develop your own eye for these things as you go, but this will get you started."

Max chuckled to himself. He hadn't known what to expect when Raoul had insisted on introducing him around as thanks for Max saving him from the *kishi*, but Albert and the others proved interesting friends to have. Their unfamiliar society manners confused him at times, but when it came down to it, they were good company whether they were enjoying a smoke or dressing Max up like a doll.

Max selected a jacket he thought of as rust-coloured, though Albert insisted the shade was called "tawny," along with a green waistcoat and brown trousers. His reflection reinforced his uncommon good mood, and when he found Julie in the dining room, he scooped her up into an improvised waltz.

"Maximilien Morrel, put me down!" she cried, laughing. "What's seized you today?"

Max gave her a firm kiss on the cheek before letting her go.

"It's just a beautiful morning, Julie!" A grin lit up his face.

Julie put her hands on her hips with a knowing look.

"You're going to see her, aren't you?" she asked. "That mystery woman you won't tell us about?"

"Perhaps, perhaps not." Max took an apple from the table and headed for the door. "And perhaps I'll tell you about her, someday. *A bientot, ma puce!*"

Max savoured the sunshine on his face on his way to the Rue Frochot. The walk took him about half an hour, during which time he made the mistake of examining why he could feel so confident this morning when the day before he had been miserable and restless. By the time he reached L'Epicure Cafe, uncertainty threatened to chase away his high spirits again.

L'Epicure was a charming establishment, narrow but bright with a large front window and roomy patio. They served the usual cafe fare of coffee, pastries, and light sandwiches, but they did it well. The hospital where Max had received his medical training was nearby, and L'Epicure stayed open all through the night to cater to the hospital staff. He was pleased to see they were still around and going strong after his time abroad, though not only because he missed their coffee.

From across the street, Max could already see her on the patio.

There was no mistaking her wide blue eyes, though her red hair was shorter than in the photograph he had carried with him in Africa. She wore a sensible straight skirt and jacket, the unofficial uniform of office girls, sitting alone with a book and sipping on what Max knew would be a cup of sweetened tea without milk. She worked in one of the law offices nearby, a firm called Dubois & Renard, and came to L'Epicure every day for her morning break.

His heart raced and goosebumps raised themselves all up and down his arms. Doubt gnawed at him; writing letters to someone on another continent was one thing, but seeing them in person again would be quite another. Was he even the same man she remembered—or even worth her attention?

Max's legs made their own decision and he found himself walking across the Rue Frochot regardless. She didn't look up, engrossed in her book, when Max stood above her with only the low patio fence between them.

A young man sat at the window counter inside L'Epicure, watching Max without blinking. His blonde hair was combed and waxed into place and his creased military uniform was spotless. He caught Max's eye and smiled, but then a look of horror dawned on his mousey features. A dozen bloodstains grew and soaked through his uniform shirt, and a laceration an inch wide crept out of his hairline from his left temple. It traversed across his face, eliminating his eye and most of his nose before coming to an end on the right side of his jaw.

Max wrenched his eyes shut and took a deep breath to steady himself, clenching his fist so hard that his nails bit into his palm. He reminded himself that Hugo was dead and buried in a grave in Algiers, just as he had when Hugo had made a brief appearance at Albert's breakfast table. When he looked again, the wounded man's seat was empty with no indication that anyone else had seen him.

The woman, still captivated by her reading, didn't notice the struggle occurring next to her. She remained oblivious to Max until he placed a shining green apple on the table in front of her.

"Would you care for a snack with your tea, mademoiselle?" Max said, his voice shaking.

Valentine de Villefort looked up. The voice was familiar, but she didn't recognize the man in front of her by his clothes. She gasped when her eyes reached his square jaw and those green eyes she had dreamt of for the past eighteen months.

"Maximilien!" she screamed, leaping from her chair and half-throwing herself across the fence to wrap her arms around him. She stood half a foot shorter than him, and he could rest his chin on the top of her head. "You're alive, you're home, I can't believe it..."

Max returned the embrace as Valentine continued stammering. He breathed in her floral perfume like it was the first oxygen he'd had in months. She broke away from him with an abrupt push and a deep frown, picked up her book and swatted him across the chest with it.

"You never answered my last letter!" she said, switching focus to hit his arm. "I thought you were dead, or lying senseless in a field hospital, or naked in the arms of some tribal chief's daughter!"

"I'm sorry!" Max said, laughing under the attack. "I've been in Paris for two weeks and wanted to see you in person!"

"Two weeks?" Valentine asked, disbelieving.

"Well, I would have come sooner, but..." Max said, trailing off. The truth was that the monster of doubt on his back had made him struggle to justify bringing his dull and damaged self back into her life, but he couldn't bring himself to tell her that. "I suppose I don't have a reason."

Valentine sniffed and tucked a lock of hair behind her ear. She put her book back onto the table, picked up the apple, and inhaled the smell of it. Max got his first clear look at the title of her book, a history of a country called the Comoros. He had never heard of them before, but Valentine had a knack for finding unusual topics.

"Lucky for you, I forgot to bring a snack for later," she said, smiling again. "So I suppose you're forgiven."

Valentine looked all around to see if anyone was watching, but the other cafe patrons had stopped paying attention after she quit hitting Max with her book. She looked him in the eye and kissed the bright green skin of the apple. The sight lit a hopeful fire in Max's heart.

"Are you still worried about your father finding out?" Max asked.

"Of course I am!" Valentine said. "Why else would I have you address your letters to the office all this time?"

"I understand," Max said, his doubt creeping in again. "You don't want me to meet your family."

"What? Max, of course I want you to meet Grandpapa," Valentine said, confused by the change in his mood. "I've dreamed of introducing you. But you know how Father is."

"Would he really think I'm a Bonapartist?" Max said. As a rule, he did not follow politics; he found it disappointing that politics was determined to follow him. "That's ludicrous; Napoleon died, what, seventeen years ago? How many people are alive today who remember his reign at all, never mind fondly?"

"It's your family history, Max," Valentine said. "While you were on tour, there was an article in the newspaper about you saving a baron from some creature. When he read it, Father recognized the name Morrel and started ranting about your father being a Bonapartist troublemaker in Marseille. And even if he didn't hate you for that..."

Max winced, remembering the fact he had spent so much effort blocking out. He also recalled a maxim from his father: the road to hell was paved with the bodies of lawyers, and if it wasn't, then it ought to be.

"The engagement," he said through clenched teeth.

"It's still moving forward," Valentine said. "Franz d'Epinay is already on his way to Paris for the wedding, Father moved the date forward only last month."

"This doesn't kill us, Valentine," Max said. "I could ask Raoul, he's the baron from the news article, if he'd talk to your father on my behalf."

"Father never changes his mind," Valentine said. "Part of his goal is to tie our name into an old Royalist family. Franz's father died trying to prevent the Hundred Days, and Franz is a League member already."

"Raoul could sponsor my membership; surely a baron's word could help me join their club," Max offered.

"It's not the sort of club you join on a whim, Max," Valentine said. She touched the small stone pendant that hung beneath her clothes, next to her skin.

Her father had made the necessary donations to the League to ensure that his daughter would become a Stone Sister without the usual formalities, and she knew Franz was a Steel Brother. They would ascend to Silver status at their wedding, in a secretive ceremony like when her parents had married. Her father had never told her the details of it, and her mother had died too early for Valentine to ever ask.

"If only Grandpapa were in any state to help," Valentine said.

"Help!" Max said, an idea occurring to him. "You know, Raoul is not the only new friend I've made here in Paris. I've met an extraordinary man, the Count of Monte Cristo, who lives by rules entirely of his own. He visited Julie's house yesterday, and... Valentine, I can't explain why, but I'm convinced he would help us if we asked."

"Monte Cristo? Father was speaking about him at dinner last night," Valentine said. "He thinks the count is a harmless fop taking a Grand Tour of Europe. Asking M. de Monte Cristo for help may result in nothing but attracting Father's attention."

Max shuddered. Villefort's displeasure, with his proximity to the king and such direct access to the machinery of power, could manifest as anything from a stern lecture to a meeting with the executioner.

"I won't tell the count; not unless I have no other option," Max said. "We'll think of something, my love. Rome is a long way away; we have time before Franz gets to Paris."

A nearby church bell rang the half hour.

"I have to get back to the office," Valentine said, looking at Max with a helpless expression of love.

She gathered up her book and apple and took her handkerchief from her pocket. She held the fabric to her lips and kissed it, then set it folded on the table. With one last look at Max, she ran off.

Max took the handkerchief and held it to his own lips as she left. No good solutions to their dilemma came to mind. Franz couldn't marry Valentine if he were dead, but Max discarded the notion of murder. He had seen combat, but couldn't imagine killing a man in cold blood. Franz meant him no harm and likely didn't know Max even existed. Max sighed and wished he could reclaim the confidence he had felt when he woke up.

CHAPTER 59
MORTITE

While Valentine de Villefort fretted about how the man she loved wasn't the man she was engaged to, Gerard de Villefort arrived at Baron Danglars' home. Another man waited at the door already whom Villefort didn't know personally but could not fail to recognize.

"Count de Morcerf, is it?" Villefort asked, taking in Morcerf's expansive musculature.

"Yes, and you're the king's attorney aren't you?" Morcerf said, noting the sickly yellow shade of Villefort's face. He chuckled and held his hands in front of him. "I'm not under arrest, am I? I was framed, I swear!"

"Quite," Villefort said, arching his eyebrow. "Baron Danglars invited me. He said it was important, though he was annoyingly vague about why."

"That's what brings me here as well," Morcerf said.

A footman escorted them to Danglars' garish parlour, where Danglars himself waited for an appreciable pause before rising from his chair to greet them.

"Gentlemen, welcome!" Danglars said, stretching his lips wide. "Have you had a chance to meet? Count Fernand de Morcerf, our crown prosecutor Gerard de Villefort. M. de Villefort, the Count de Morcerf."

"We met at the door," Villefort said.

"Marvelous. Morcerf and I are old friends, back to our days in Marseille, and we've maintained our professional relationship since," Danglars said. "Gerard, you got your start in Marseille as well, correct?"

Villefort pinched the bridge of his nose, wondering if it would be necessary to excuse himself for a bloodletting before the visit was through. The officers he sent to visit the Nightly Assemblage printing-house had learned that M. Caillat, author of the editorial about his attack, was a correspondence writer and the editor didn't know where to find him.

"Gerard has been a great help in securing support for some of my legislation over the years," Danglars said to Morcerf. "I have an exciting proposition for the three of us to embark upon together, gentlemen. Before I can tell you about it, I have something to show you. Go ahead of me, and I'll join you shortly."

Danglars clapped his hands twice and the footman returned. He escorted Villefort and Morcerf to a staircase leading down into the wine cellar. The footman left them alone in the gloomy stone chamber, surrounded by wooden casks and racks of bottles.

"I can hardly see anything," Villefort said. "That simpleton should have left us a light."

"No need," Morcerf said. He raised his left hand to eye-level and brought forth a ball of flame the size of a torch to read the labels on Danglars' bottle collection.

"Impressive. That's a Catalan gift, isn't it?" Villefort asked. "In Marseille we had all manner of countermeasures ready at the prosecutor's offices to neutralize their powers when we needed to detain them. Once we arrested a woman who could move the air and had murdered a man by pulling all the breath from his lungs with a gesture. We needed to bury her to the neck in sand to prevent her from killing us in an escape attempt."

"That's...fascinating," Morcerf said, glancing at Villefort as he continued perusing the wine. "You know, I remember there being a deputy in Marseille named Villefort when I lived there. I never suspected that the feared M. de Villefort of Paris was the same man."

"Generally, very few people have reason to know the chief prosecutor's name," Villefort said. "Only those involved in upholding the law and those determined to break it."

A groan in the darkness caught their attention and Morcerf straightened up immediately.

"Tell me that you made that noise," Morcerf said, as another groan came from a different direction.

"That would be a lie." Villefort hefted his walking-stick like a rapier.

A stranger stepped into the firelight, wheezing from the ragged bite wound in his neck. The flesh of his face hung slack and pale, and the unmistakable film of death covered his unblinking eyes. The man's mouth hung open and his lower jaw twitched in anticipation of warm flesh.

Morcerf didn't hesitate, throwing a lance of flame from his other hand to incinerate the zombie's head in an instant. The light of his attack revealed a half-dozen more zombies approaching them from the same direction, but they could hear more groans and shuffling from all around them.

Another zombie lurched toward Villefort, a chunk of flesh missing from her shoulder. Villefort swatted her hands away with the end of his walking stick until he could reverse his grip on it and drive the metal point through her forehead and into the brain. The zombie's flailing stilled, but the stick remained lodged tight in the skull.

Villefort had grown up surrounded by this threat; the Dead Plague had reached France the same year he was born and was not put down until he was sixteen years old. Unlike Morcerf, who had only been a boy when the Plague ended and was hurling fire everywhere in a panic, Villefort took a moment to assess his surroundings. He found a new weapon near a wine barrel, a splitting maul with an axe blade on one side and a hammer's head on the other for driving taps into casks.

"You foolish witch!" Villefort yelled as one of Morcerf's fireballs missed him by inches. "You'll burn the entire house down with us inside! Maybe you can't burn, Catalan, but I can. Use your sword, like a gentleman!"

Morcerf drew his officer's sabre, made with a custom hilt to accommodate his enormous hand. With the full force of his strength behind each blow, he cleaved the skulls of the undead like overripe pumpkins and knocked their heads clean off their shoulders. Despite this prowess, zombies soon backed him and Villefort into a corner, more zombies than they could hope to fend off. Morcerf dropped his saber and coated his hands with flame to immolate the entire swarm, regardless of the consequences.

Every zombie approaching them dropped to the floor. Not a sound came from any of them, and their cold limbs didn't so much as twitch. By all appearances, they were simply dead.

"Bravo, bravo!" Danglars called from the darkness.

He approached Villefort and Morcerf with a team of servants. Two held torches to light the way and others came dragging metal cages on wheeled dollies. The servants piled the fallen zombies into the two cages like rags. Danglars stood with his hands behind his back until the task was complete, then dismissed them all. They left the torches in wall sconces and departed, leaving Danglars, Villefort, and Morcerf alone with the corpses.

"Danglars, what is the meaning of this?" Villefort demanded, hefting the blood-streaked maul. His ghoulish yellow face was also splattered with dark red.

"Relax, Gerard. You were never in any real danger," Danglars said. "Observe."

Danglars took his hands from behind his back. He held a banded wooden chest two feet long and nine inches in each other direction, which he unlatched. Indentations in the velvet inlay held shards of green crystal. The shards emitted a nauseous green glow, difficult to look at. The peculiar shade of chartreuse reminded Morcerf of the only time he had ever been seasick as a child and being made to clean up the pea soup he had regurgitated into the bottom of the boat.

When the box opened, the dead men and women in the cages reanimated. Those slain by Villefort and Morcerf remained still, but the rest thrashed against the bars of the cages and the weight of their comrades. Villefort raised his hatchet again as a precaution, and Morcerf conjured another flame, but when Danglars closed the box again the zombies fell still once more.

"What have you done?" Morcerf asked, breathless.

"Fernand, you and I have helped each other many times over the years," Danglars said. "Consider your information regarding that recent Don Carlos affair in Spain. That let me sell off the Reserve's Spanish assets and my own before the Don's overthrow made them worthless, and I profited by over two million francs from it."

Danglars turned to Villefort. "And you, Gerard. Your influence has been indispensable. My political career simply wouldn't be where it is today without your friendship."

"This seems like a strange way to repay me," Villefort said through clenched teeth.

"*Au contraire,* I have a magnificent way to repay you," Danglars said.

"Let me tell you a story. Over twenty years ago, I was a humble supercargo aboard a merchant vessel. One day, our dying captain sent us on a detour to Elba so he could carry out a mission for Bonaparte; we'd never suspected him as a traitor, and were bound by honour to fulfill his dying request."

Villefort and Morcerf each felt their blood run cold. Neither realized the other's involvement in the fallout of that visit to Elba, or the other's connection to the subsequent fate of a sailor named Edmond Dantes.

"I made landfall with the acting captain for the sake of taking some rest. On the beach I met a drunk named Balbiani who was desperate for someone new to talk to. He had a very interesting tale to tell," Danglars said.

"A tale about what?" Morcerf asked.

"A tale about the Dead Plague," Danglars replied.

Balbiani, as he had told Danglars on that fateful day in 1815, was an officer in Bonaparte's Grand Army of the Living. His regiment was the Third Expeditionary, one of many seeking the source of the Dead Plague with orders to destroy it. Their forces consisted not just of fighting men but also scholars, historians, linguists, and doctors.

Their research directed them to Ukraine, where they found a breakthrough: human beings. Few survivors remained in Plague-ravaged Eastern Europe, which had suffered for years before the Plague attracted Napoleon's attention, but those who the Third Expeditionary could find all had the same story to tell. According to them, the dead began to walk after a great explosion in the forest near Kharkiv on the night of October 12, 1787.

The regiment combed the undead-infested forest for weeks. When they found what they were looking for, there was no mistaking it.

"They found this, what Balbiani called mortite," Danglars said, holding up the box. "A chunk of crystal the size of a man stood in a deep crater, glowing just like the pieces you saw."

The regiment had attacked the mortite with picks, sledgehammers, even explosives while still fending off zombies from all sides. Parts of the crystal crumbled to dust easily; the mortite dust stopped glowing with that horrible light as soon as it fell away from the main crystal. Other parts broke off into shards, which the regiment was unable or unwilling to pulverize further in their haste to destroy the main crystal. They carted these shards away in boxes lined with lead.

"On November 2, 1804, one final swing of the pickaxe broke the core of the crystal into a shower of green dust," Danglars said. "All around them, the zombies in the forest fell to the ground. They didn't know it, but all across Europe and Asia the hordes of undead had all collapsed as well. A month later, Napoleon coronated himself on this victory."

"And that crystal, that mortite, was what gave unholy life to the dead?" Villefort asked.

"Oh, yes," Danglars answered with his peculiar smile. "Balbiani was quite wretched from drink by the time I found him; his regiment was decimated twice over in Kharkiv by the undead, and his only comfort on Elba was grain alcohol. But he told me they scattered the shards across Europe, hoping that if they never spoke of it again then the horror would simply fade away. Of course, drunks are always happy to talk."

"I fail to see how this explains the presence of zombies in your basement," Morcerf said.

"Commerce never stopped during the days of the Dead Plague. People still needed food, trade goods, gold, and most importantly they needed weapons," Danglars said. "By the time the Plague ended, the major weapon and steel manufacturers of Europe had become economic titans; even with the deep discounts they gave to help deal with the undead menace, their profits skyrocketed during those years."

Villefort's lip curled. His distaste of businessmen had not faded with time, and he still considered discussions of profit and loss to be vulgar distractions from the glory of the monarchy. Such matters distracted people and tricked them into thinking that the goods and services they enjoyed were created by common men rather than by the grace of God through the king.

"Gentlemen, I've put decades of work and experimentation into this plan. We invest in defense industries, use my mortite to raise a second Dead Plague, and watch our money grow in the ensuing panic," Danglars said. "Whenever we wish, we put an end to it ourselves and enjoy the benefits."

Danglars pointed at Villefort. "Not only will you be richer than you know what to do with, but you can be the man who 'discovers' the crucial clue to the source of the new Plague. You can tell the king about it and bask in royal favour when your information results in the end of the undead."

The idea caught Villefort off guard. Napoleon's memory had always claimed one triumph over the monarchy: no amount of political debate could erase the fact that Emperor Napoleon ended the Dead Plague after King Louis XVI failed to take it seriously. If Villefort could put the monarchy on equal footing in that regard, there was no telling how the king and God himself would reward him. That demonstration of loyalty, along with the money Danglars promised, could facilitate his ascent to Diamond Brother in the League.

"And Fernand," Danglars said, "when did you last lead an army to victory? Wouldn't you like to reclaim that rush and add another ribbon to your collection? Once Gerard tells the king about the source of the new Plague, you can volunteer to lead a regiment to destroy it. When you reach the appropriate place, we'll arrange some activity for your troops to make them think it was them who ended it."

Morcerf thought about it, and the flames dancing across his hands smoldered to nothing.

"It would be entirely under our control?" Morcerf asked. "We would be in no danger?"

"The starting and ending of it would be ours to dictate," Danglars said. "The zombies themselves will shamble around of their own devices as they ever did, driving up the demand for steel and the value of our investment. It won't be entirely without personal risk, but we can stay safe if we're careful."

In Morcerf's role as a senator, he had given out many military medals in recent years but received precious few himself. The money had an appeal for certain, but his mind came to rest on a vision of Mercedes. He remembered how concerned she had been for his safety when he had first been drafted and called to war. She was so thankful when he returned that she agreed to marry him, and another dangerous ride into battle could be just what he needed to reignite that flame of love.

"Alright, I'll join you," Morcerf said, sheathing his sabre.

"I'll consider it," Villefort added. "I can't ignore that you've clearly murdered multiple people to orchestrate this little demonstration."

"What, them?" Danglars asked, nodding towards the cages. "I thought you'd take issue with that, so I had the membership of the Rue de Lorraine Bonapartist Club abducted for this purpose."

Danglars opened the box again, prompting a flurry of activity in the cages as the dead reanimated once more. Danglars swung the lid back and forth to block and restore the dark connection between the crystals and the corpses, taking a sort of childish delight in the exercise.

"That's enough, you've made your point," Villefort said. "What makes that box so special?"

"It's an ordinary lead-lined box; as effective as Balbiani said it would be," Danglars said. "It gives us a lever to pull to end our new Plague whenever we wish."

Danglars opened the box once more.

"I've carefully calibrated the amount of mortite required. It needs to be in the vicinity of a corpse to raise it, but then the dead can travel as far as they like to spread the Plague. As long as the crystals are intact and not blocked, they could remain in France while still powering a zombie in the Americas," Danglars said. He gave one of the smaller shards to Villefort and another to Morcerf as the dead woke up again. "But without those pieces, my supply of mortite alone is not enough to reanimate so much as a mouse. I offer you these shards as a gesture of goodwill; we do this together, or not at all."

Villefort and Morcerf tucked their shards into their jackets to keep the diseased glow out of view. Danglars clapped for his servants again, who entered bringing three coconuts.

"In India, breaking a coconut at the start of a new business venture brings good fortune. Shall we?" Danglars asked.

Villefort shrugged and split his coconut open with the hatchet he still carried. Danglars threw his against the ground, shattering the shell. Morcerf crushed his between his palms like an egg. Danglars escorted them to the door, where they parted ways with assurances they would speak further about the plan.

Villefort left with his head swimming, convinced it would take more than his own blood to calm his nerves after the experience. Morcerf likewise left needing sustenance, but of a different kind.

Morcerf didn't think Danglars or Villefort had noticed, but his custom-tailored jacket hung too loose when he left their meeting. He had expended too much energy too quickly in the fight and through his flames, and needed to replenish it to maintain the frame he'd built around the scrawny fisherman he had once been.

He directed his carriage driver to the river docks, where an ever-present group of idle labourers waited to be hired. Morcerf opened his carriage door and whistled, admitting the first man to reach him into the carriage.

"Good afternoon, your excellency," the man said, taking off his hat in deference. "How may I be of service?"

"Don't speak," Morcerf said, drawing all the curtains closed.

Morcerf reached to the assortment of military ribbons he wore even on his civilian jackets and touched a round silver medal. His fingers found a hidden clasp and revealed a magnificent clear gemstone behind the false silver front. With remorse in his eyes, Morcerf held the gem.

Nothing but a brief glimpse of bright and cold white light seeping through the joints in the doors could be seen from outside of the carriage. When Morcerf returned home, his jacket fit as intended once again. That night, a shriveled corpse wearing the dockworker's clothes was brought to the riverside under cover of darkness. Morcerf's servants, dressed in black, weighed it down with chains and threw it into the Seine.

CHAPTER 60
DINNER PLANS

A few days later at the end of May, the Count of Monte Cristo was at home preparing for some very important visitors. He consulted the book which hung from his neck to ensure that everything proceeded in order and to organize anything else which needed doing. When Albert and Lucien came to visit, Monte Cristo tucked the book away once more and told the footman to admit them.

As they exchanged pleasantries, Albert could not help but marvel at the state of the house. Even having seen the count's apartments in Rome, Albert thought he had outdone himself with this more permanent habitat. The blend of Eastern and Western art which filled the space never managed to overwhelm the senses, as Danglars' salon did, but instead conveyed the presence of a mind which took the time to learn what worked together in harmony.

Lucien claimed to have accompanied Albert out of boredom and curiosity, and wandered about scrutinizing the decor. Monte Cristo guessed that while the boredom was Lucien's own, the curiosity originated from Hermine Danglars' boudoir. Anything Lucien heard would be repeated into Hermine's ear to be sure, which suited the count fine.

Lucien, like everyone else, would be allowed to see only what Monte Cristo wanted him to see. Monte Cristo also held the advantage that Hermine had no reason yet to suspect that the count needed watching. She was, he guessed, merely curious about how he spent the enormous sum he had borrowed from her husband.

"Oh yes, it is still proceeding very much as planned. Some things just have a way of getting themselves sorted when you're not paying attention," Albert said with no great enthusiasm, speaking about his upcoming marriage. "My father and Baron Danglars worked closely together in Spain many years ago, you know."

"Now that you mention it, I do recall hearing about Baron Danglars travelling all across Europe," the count said. "You're a lucky man indeed, marrying into that family; Mlle Eugenie is a beauty, and you'll do well with such a famously well-connected father-in-law."

"Eugenie's certainly pretty enough, I'll give her that. Like a graceful lioness, lounging in the sun and contemplating whether she'd like to eat me or not," Albert said.

"You seem to have misgivings about this arrangement," Monte Cristo observed.

Albert looked around for Lucien and leaned closer to the count while Lucien examined a gilded frame on the far side of the room.

"She's an intimidating woman, which isn't a trait I much care for," Albert said in a low voice. "But not all of the misgivings are mine; Mother doesn't approve of the match at all. She seems to dislike the entire Danglars clan for some reason."

"Why could that be?" the count asked, suppressing any emotion in his voice. "Perhaps Countess Morcerf, the very picture of aristocracy and refinement, merely dislikes the idea of your ancient lineage joining such a new one. I wouldn't worry too much about that; your legacy will ennoble Eugenie's, and her legacy will enrich yours."

As he said these empty words, Monte Cristo recalled Mercedes' strange behaviour when they had met at the Morcerf home. Mercedes was a clever woman; how much did she know, or suspect? If she had reason to think that Danglars played a role in the disappearance of Edmond Dantes, it would explain her hesitance to marry Albert to Eugenie.

The count's meticulous plans were crafted with an attention to detail and level of patience only possible to one who had shed the requirements of nature and did not need to eat, sleep, or even breathe. Still there was a wildcard, and its name was Countess Mercedes de Morcerf.

"Our families are having a meeting about the wedding next week," Albert said. "I feel as though I'm being pulled apart. My father clearly wants me to marry Eugenie."

"Then marry her," the count said with a shrug.

"But if I do, I worry it will plunge Mother into a fit of grief," Albert said.

"Then don't marry her," the count said. "My friend, I worry that you worry too much about what others will think of your actions. You cannot please everyone, so sometimes you must decide who you'd rather displease."

Albert considered the matter. "If it came down to it, and I saw the opportunity, I'd rather risk the disapproval of the count than the tears of my mother," he finally said.

Monte Cristo found himself moved by the simple remark and turned away from Albert. Lucien lounged in an armchair, with a pencil in his right hand and a notebook in his left.

"I see you've found something to keep yourself busy, M. Debray," the count said. "Are you sketching my humble salon for when Beauchamp writes an article about me?"

"Heavens, no. I'm too fond of art to inflict my clumsy hands upon it," Lucien said. "I'm figuring out a sum, one which may interest Albert."

"Oh?" Albert said. "I don't suppose it's to do with how long I can postpone my wedding day?"

"Not quite, though it does pertain to your bride," Lucien said. "The latest report from the Royal Bourbon Reserve stated that they'll be loosening the reserve requirements for commercial banks. Those banks will be allowed to hold smaller amounts of precious metal to back the paper money they loan out and pay in withdrawals."

"Lucien, you're coming dangerously close to boring me," Albert said with a groan. "What's the result?"

"Nothing less than an effective profit to the Danglars Bank of over three hundred thousand francs," Lucien said, smirking.

"What a fine position Baron Danglars has; as chair of the Reserve and also owner of the Danglars Bank, he can manufacture his own profits!" Monte Cristo said. "That reminds me, I've exhausted my supply of cash sooner than anticipated. I'll have to pay his bank a visit tomorrow."

"That's hardly anything compared to the million he made in English pistol manufacturing last year," Albert said. "That was a stroke of luck; he sold those shares the day before a bill was proposed to outlaw private ownership of firearms in the entire United Kingdom."

"Oh yes, luck indeed. Although that wasn't the baron, but the baroness who made that sale. Where she gets her information, I'd love to know," Lucien said.

"I'm certain you would," Albert replied with a grin, "particularly as you sit at the fountainhead of all news that would impact the markets. Yet you never seem to have a tip for any of us!"

Lucien shrugged. "You know Madame Danglars; she learns what she wants to know, and any man is powerless to stop her."

"If I were you, I might humble the baroness as a favour to her future son-in-law," Albert laughed. "A few words from you could influence the price of a stock in either direction. Cause her to lose a hundred thousand or so on a false tip and see if she learns some prudence."

Monte Cristo had to suppress a smile at Albert's artless joke and hoped Albert would remember saying it in a few weeks' time. Lucien didn't find it amusing and soon found a reason to cut his visit short.

"Listen, Albert; I find myself in a delicate position of my own," the count said when he returned. "M. Danglars is my banker, and I fear I got started on a bad foot with M. de Villefort. I'd like to try and improve my relationship with them both, particularly as Haydee is becoming such close friends with their daughters. Would it be considered good Parisian manners to invite them to dinner at my country-house?"

"Definitely, although I've heard that trying to be bosom chums with M. de Villefort is a losing game," Albert said.

"Good, then a dinner party it is; I had June 2 in mind. But that presents another problem," Monte Cristo said.

"What could that be?" Albert asked.

"Given what you've told me, I wouldn't want to risk offending your mother by forcing her into conversation with Baroness Danglars. The baroness would surely start pestering her with wedding matters which you've told me she'd rather avoid," the count said. "At the same time, it's well-known that we are friends and your absence would result in raised eyebrows. Baroness Danglars may think I meant to offend her by denying her that very conversation."

"If you're worried about Mother's opinion of you, don't be; she already holds you in an unusually high level of esteem for someone she just recently met," Albert said. "After all, you did save the life of her only son."

"Remind me to never save the life of another Frenchman," the count said with a chuckle. "They never seem to stop wanting to remind me of it!"

Albert laughed with him. "In any case, I think I can fix this," he said. "Mother has wanted to go to the seaside; I'll organize the trip so we can't possibly make it to dinner. You may send us an invitation for appearance's sake, and we may regretfully decline with a flawless excuse."

"And we keep the peace. Bravo, viscount," the count said. A small tumbler clicked into place in the vast machinery of his mind.

"Well, with that settled, perhaps I can convince you to dine with us tonight?" Albert asked. "My father is indisposed, so it would only be ourselves and Mother. She's a remarkable woman, and you've had no chance to properly speak with her. If only there were another woman like her but twenty years younger!"

"Impossible, I'm afraid," Monte Cristo said, ignoring Albert's unfortunate choice of words. "I have preparations to make for the dinner party and have another appointment tonight besides."

"When we've just arranged the subterfuge of avoiding dinner with a fake engagement, do you expect me to believe that?" Albert laughed. "Reconsider, it will be fun. We can speak Italian and Spanish, and you can tell us about the Greek slave who you treat like a queen. Where are my manners; bring her as well!"

"As much as I'd like to introduce Haydee to the upstanding Morcerf family, my appointment is genuine," the count said.

"Ha! Perhaps I should demand proof," Albert said, lighting a cigar.

In response, the count rang his bell and Baptistan soon entered.

"I'll ask you to be careful with your gift around my valet, he's more flammable than most," the count said. "Baptistan, tell the viscount about my appointment this evening."

"Of course, master," Baptistan said. Albert jumped at the sound of the construct's voice. "Major Bartolomeo Cavalcanti and his son Viscount Andrea Cavalcanti are expected tonight, at approximately seven o'clock."

"You're full of surprises," Albert said, shaking his head when the count dismissed Baptistan. "If I may ask, who are the Cavalcantis?"

"The major is from an old and wealthy Italian family and a veteran of the war against the dead. His son Andrea is about your age and with your same title, entering Parisian society with the help of his father's fortune," the count said, and shrugged. "Honestly, I barely know the major. We met travelling, had some passably interesting conversations, and have kept in touch in a casual fashion. He's asked me to help his son, in much the same way you've helped me, and that will be that."

"If you like, I can introduce the viscount to my friends when he's settled in Paris," Albert said. The count nodded his thanks. "Speaking of Italy, I've heard from Franz. Though he still finds you intimidating, he admits that Rome has become unbearably dull without you."

"Ah, Baron d'Epinay. Am I mistaken, or did he say he was the son of General du Quesnel?" the count asked.

"Yes, but he was assassinated when Franz was a very small boy," Albert said. "They never found out precisely who orchestrated the murder."

"A tragedy. Still, Franz is a clever young man and good company. He's engaged to be married as well, isn't he?" Monte Cristo asked.

"Oh, yes. He is to marry Mlle. de Villefort, though I suspect he's as enthusiastic about it as I am for my own upcoming marriage. M. de Villefort moved the wedding date up ahead of schedule as well," Albert said. "If your friend the major asks you to find his son a suitable wife, perhaps with money from her father and a barony title besides, I'd be happy to help in the search."

Monte Cristo laughed. When Albert left, the count rang for Bertuccio. He gave orders to arrange the house at Auteuil, ignoring Bertuccio's discomfort at being sent back there.

"It's at your discretion, with two exceptions: do not touch the garden, nor the bedroom with the red damask hangings. Leave them exactly as they are," Monte Cristo commanded. "Do what you like with the yard; in fact, I'd prefer it if the house were unrecognizable from the front."

"Of course, your excellency," Bertuccio said with a frown and a bow. "May I ask who you are expecting there?"

"You may not," the count said, cutting off further questions. "You'll remain at the house to coordinate a dinner I'm hosting there on Saturday."

Bertuccio left to execute the count's orders. Monte Cristo took a moment to enjoy the refreshing silence of the salon. As the aggravation of maintaining a cordial facade toward Fernand's son drained away from him, he centred himself and rose to prepare the drawing rooms for the Cavalcantis.

CHAPTER 61
MAJOR CAVALCANTI

The first carriage to arrive at seven o'clock was one of the small vehicles-for-hire which the Parisians called a cabriolet, or simply a cab; essentially, a covered bench with wheels and just enough space for two passengers plus a driver.

The sole occupant on this occasion was a man of about sixty with a thick grey mustache connecting to his sideburns. He wore a green military coat with black embroidered fastenings, boots in need of a good polish, and a hat resembling the kind worn by gendarmes. The left sleeve of his coat was folded and pinned just above where the elbow would have been, and he bore four ragged scars on that side of his face.

This man confirmed the address with the concierge at the gate and asked if it was the residence of the Count of Monte Cristo. Having been given an exact description of the man and his scars, the concierge opened the gate.

The one-armed man stared at Baptistan but said nothing as it led him to one of the drawing rooms. Monte Cristo waited there and rose to greet him with a smile.

"Major Cavalcanti, welcome! Please, have a seat. Would you care for a refreshment?" the count said.

Major Cavalcanti adjusted his collar, gawking at the count's astonishingly white complexion and blood-red eyes.

"You were expecting me, then?" Cavalcanti asked in Italian.

"Of course I was; Abbe Busoni told me you would arrive, so we could discuss the..." the count said, trailing off. He looked at Cavalcanti to allow him to finish the sentence.

"Discuss...the letter I received from him," Cavalcanti said, almost turning the statement into a question.

The count's smile faltered. "Yes, but also to discuss reuniting you with your son. Did you read the letter the Abbe sent you? Did you understand it?"

"Of course." Cavalcanti glanced around the simple yet elegant room.

"Then since we have a mutual friend in the Abbe, but have not met before, please tell me about yourself. And about your son," the count said, sitting and waving for Cavalcanti to do the same.

"Of course," Cavalcanti repeated, his eyes still wandering. "I am Major Castellano, here to meet my long-lost son Alberto, after his long absence from being, I think, lost at sea?"

The count frowned, sighed, and glared at Cavalcanti. He had hoped not to resort to this, but the plan was too important to be jeopardized by a poor thespian.

"Look at me," Monte Cristo commanded.

The tone in his voice did not allow disobedience, and Cavalcanti looked into the bright glow of the count's eyes. A light too intense to be reflected from the lamps probed into Cavalcanti's head, and he became aware of a headache he attributed to his long journey.

"The Abbe told me that you are Major Bartolomeo *Cavalcanti*, here to meet your long-lost son *Andrea*, who was *kidnapped by his tutor* as a boy." The count punctuated each correction by tapping a gloved finger against the armrest of his chair.

Cavalcanti nodded, never breaking contact with the count's eyes.

"He also said he gave you a generous sum of money for travelling expenses," Monte Cristo said. "This was a mere courtesy, as you have an income of half a million."

"Half a million," Cavalcanti muttered in a monotone. His face had gone slack, and his lips hung parted like a baby fallen asleep during a feeding. "Yes, half a million."

"Andrea was taken away at the age of five," Monte Cristo said. "He's now twenty years old and entitled to be a viscount; you are a count, as well as a major."

"I am a count, as well as a major," Cavalcanti said. The light in the count's eyes demanded that he accept it as the truth.

"Do you remember the wars you fought in? If anyone asks you for details, you must have them," Monte Cristo asked with another push into his guest's mind.

"I don't recall my battles, signor," Cavalcanti said. A brief look of confusion passed over his face.

The count sighed again. Cavalcanti presented an unavoidable weak link in this stage of the plan. Still, this obstacle was not insurmountable. He used the eldritch link with the other man's mind to skim through memories as he would skim a newspaper, looking for the scenes of violence which, by default, belonged to every European man of the major's age. He soon found them: images of the undead hordes, old echoes of the omnipresent terror from every direction in those dark times.

"You served in the only war which matters, between the living and the dead," Monte Cristo said. "You commanded men to build barricades and arm themselves to defend the women and children."

Monte Cristo built new images using pieces of real memories, leaving them in Cavalcanti's mind. In the real memory, Cavalcanti was pulled into an impromptu militia force to hold back the ravenous corpses. The count painted over it and left behind a memory of standing proud in uniform to direct other men to do those same tasks. With their basis in reality, Cavalcanti accepted these new memories without much struggle.

Satisfied that Cavalcanti was prepared, the count left one final instruction behind: that Cavalcanti would recall the false memories in lieu of his true ones only so long as he remained in France. With this done, he released the link.

"Now, the final matter from the Abbe's letter," Monte Cristo said, handing a wallet to the major. "Forty-eight thousand francs in bearer bonds, redeemable at any bank, which I owe Abbe Busoni for past debts and he has instructed me to pay to you instead."

Cavalcanti's eyes dilated. Though he remembered having a sizeable income, he also understood the wallet's contents as a vast treasure. Monte Cristo rang for Ali to bring wine and biscuits, and in the course of casual conversation quizzed Cavalcanti again on the finer points of the role he was to play. Cavalcanti's answers came far more readily.

Satisfied, the count left Cavalcanti alone with the money and wine to find Baptistan waiting in the hall. Baptistan informed Monte Cristo that his second visitor awaited him in the other drawing room. The count nodded and returned to Cavalcanti.

They continued on the subject of the major's son, Andrea. Cavalcanti did not have the documentation proving Andrea's lineage and legitimacy and was overjoyed to learn that the count had copies of those vital documents.

"After all," the count said, "he would do well to have these in the event that some suitable marriage prospect arose. What good fortune that Busoni sent these ahead of time. Give them to your son, when you see him; he'll take good care of them."

"When I see him?" Cavalcanti asked, wiping his brow with a checked handkerchief.

"I'm sure you suspected I had a surprise waiting for you; your son is here, in Paris, in this very house," Monte Cristo said with a smile. "I'll leave you here to compose yourself before I send him in. I wouldn't want to come between your reunion, and I imagine you have things to speak about in private."

"Yes, of course. How gracious of you, your excellency," Cavalcanti said.

"One other thing: whatever may be in style in Italy, your clothes have fallen quite out of fashion here in Paris," the count added as he walked to the door, pointing at Cavalcanti's clothes. "Thankfully your luggage also arrived before you and is in your suite at the Hotel de Paris."

"My luggage? Of course, my luggage," Cavalcanti said, still half-dazed. "And inside, I'll find everything I need?"

"Your valet at home will have packed your plain clothes and the uniform you wear on grand occasions; state functions, dinner parties with counts and barons, and so on," Monte Cristo said. He glanced at the major's left arm. "All tailored for your unique needs, of course."

"Yes, my valet. Lovely man. Loyal," muttered Cavalcanti, certain that he had a valet and equally certain that he couldn't recall the man's name or face.

"Now that those details are settled, prepare yourself to meet your son," the count said. "Please continue to enjoy the refreshments in my absence."

Monte Cristo bowed and moved a tapestry to reveal the door to the adjoining room on his way to meet and coach the young man slated to play the role of Andrea Cavalcanti.

CHAPTER 62
ANDREA CAVALCANTI

In the connected second drawing room, a young, well-dressed man stretched across a sofa and toyed with a gold-headed cane. He had straight sandy hair and a red beard cut into a fashionable goatee. His heavy eyelids gave him a permanent squint, allowing only brief glimpses of frigid blue eyes. He had the colouring of a recently faded sunburn, and his build was more powerful than most society men of his age. When the count entered, he sprang to his feet.

"The Count of Monte Cristo, I presume?" he asked with a bow.

"I am he, and you are?" the count replied.

"Viscount Andrea Cavalcanti, of the Florentine Cavalcantis," the young man said easily.

The count nodded. "I was told you would have a letter of introduction to me.".

Andrea offered a folded paper to the count, who perused it immediately.

"I hope everything is in order, your excellency. I admit, the signature confuses me; I've never met anyone by the name of Sinbad and only know the name from the Thousand and One Nights," Andrea said.

"The author of the letter is a friend of mine and one of Sinbad's descendants with an eccentric sense of humour; he's a very rich Englishman called Lord Wilmore, who often uses his ancestor's name," the count explained without taking his eyes from the letter.

"Ah, Wilmore! That was the man I met at—" Andrea muttered, but stopped himself.

Monte Cristo folded the letter again. "So, Andrea, tell me about yourself and your family."

"Certainly," Andrea said. His eyes never wavered, indicating either honesty or a talent for invention which ran so deep as to be pathological. "I am, as I said, Viscount Andrea Cavalcanti, son of Major Bartolomeo Cavalcanti of Florence. Though our family is still rich, with my father's income amounting half a million, we have suffered tragedy; I lost my mother when I was barely old enough to walk and was stolen by my tutor not long after. As soon as I came of age and was able to escape, I began seeking my father without success. Finally, I received that letter from your friend, Lord Wilmore, claiming that my father is here in Paris and that you would have further information."

"Very good," the count said, pleased that Andrea had learned his part better than his erstwhile father, and that powers of compulsion wouldn't be required. "Wilmore's instructions were sound, and I'm pleased to tell you that your father himself is in the very next room."

At those words, Andrea's eyes widened and a faint tremor shook him.

"My father is here?" he asked, but regained his composure. "That is, of course you mean that my father the Major is here, not that—well, I'm so eager to see him again that I forget my words. I long to feel the embrace of his arms again!"

"I believe you meant to say the embrace of his arm," the count said. "Remember that he lost his left one before you were born, and you've never known him without that wound."

"Of course, excuse me. The excitement of the moment, I'm sure you understand," Andrea said, taking the correction in stride.

"Your father is most excited to see you as well, though of course it's been so long that he may not recognize you," the count said. "He's also quite anxious to know how you fared during your long years as a hostage and if you were fortunate enough to escape the poor moral influence of your captors."

"Your excellency, I hope that no false rumours have reached you about me," Andrea protested, discomfort returning to his otherwise confident face.

"All I know is what Wilmore has told me. It seems he found you in an unpleasant spot after your escape, but didn't elaborate; I didn't ask for the particulars, as they don't interest me," Monte Cristo said. "Wilmore decided you were worth helping, and I trust his judgement. He found you, he found your father, he arranged for you to meet here. I have only one question for you, one which I'm certain concerns your father as well: have your misfortunes left you an ill-prepared stranger to the world which your fortune and your rank entitle you to?"

"Your excellency, rest easy on that score," Andrea said, his calm returning. "My captors knew it would behoove them to maintain my education if they wanted to ransom me back to my father someday. I've learned the ways of society well enough to conduct myself, I hope. Besides, if some defect in my manners is detected, it will surely be excusable by the circumstances of my upbringing."

Monte Cristo smiled, satisfied that Andrea required less coaching than the major, and pleased that he had already deduced one of the count's prepared suggestions.

"Still, I'd avoid making too public a story of your misadventures. Not everyone enjoys the kind of scrutiny which comes with being the latest gossip," Monte Cristo said.

The idea of such scrutiny and its consequences caused Andrea to turn a shade paler.

"Focus on blending in with your peers and forging aristocratic friendships with those around you," Monte Cristo said. "My friend, Viscount Albert de Morcerf, has already offered to make introductions for you."

"Anyone in my position would do well to blend in rather than to stand out," Andrea said, half to himself.

"As long as you don't deviate too far from acceptable norms, you'll have quite an agreeable position," the count said. "Your father will allow you an income of fifty thousand livres per year during your stay in Paris."

"Regardless of how long I stay?" Andrea asked, surprised joy sneaking into his voice. His smile revealed very white and even teeth in a rather wide mouth.

"Yes, although your father can only remain in Paris for a few days before he returns to Florence," the count said. "He has the money placed in a trust which is available for you at the Danglars Bank with a monthly withdrawal limit of six thousand francs."

"Ah, my dear father!" Andrea said. "I feel the warmth of paternal love already."

Without further ado, the count ushered Andrea through the

adjoining door to meet Major Cavalcanti. He closed the door, then moved aside a small painting which hung on the wall. Hidden behind it was an opening invisible from the other side that allowed him to observe the happy reunion.

When Andrea entered, Major Cavalcanti had already finished two or three glasses of the excellent wine and was happy enough to greet him.

"Hello! Are you here to visit the count as well?" Major Cavalcanti asked.

Andrea looked back at the door he had come through, cleared his throat, and addressed the major almost at a shout. The volume was unnecessary, as Monte Cristo could see and hear everything.

"My dear father! Don't you recognize me, Andrea, after all these years?" Andrea said.

"Pleased to meet you, Andrea," Major Cavalcanti said. An odd look passed over his face and his eyes unfocused for a moment, then he peered at the younger man.

"Andrea!" Major Cavalcanti rose from his chair and strode forward to wrap his one arm around his son. The wine left him unsteady on his feet. "My dear son, it's been so long! Let me look at you. Did those monsters feed you? Did they keep you warm?"

"Father, I'm in perfect health; like a zoo animal, my captors took good care of me and denied me only my liberty," Andrea said, still making sure to be heard through the walls. "It's a shame we have only these short days together before you leave again for home."

"And that you, having been kept your whole life in France, know it as more of your home than Italy ever could be," Major Cavalcanti agreed, tears brimming in his eyes. "Still, I'll return home with the pleasure of knowing you're alive and free."

"It will have to do," Andrea said gravely. "Now, I was told you have my documents?"

Major Cavalcanti handed the papers over without a word, still overcome with happiness at seeing his only son and heir again. Andrea read them and grinned like a hyena upon reaching the end. He glanced over his shoulder again.

"These forgeries are excellent," Andrea said to Major Cavalcanti in a conspiratorial mutter, speaking excellent Italian. "The count's keen ears, despite Andrea's efforts, missed nothing and knew the language as well as any other. "Do they sentence men to the galleys in Italy? False documents like these would fetch a man two and a half years each of fresh air and exercise at an oar."

Major Cavalcanti raised an eyebrow. "My son, what on earth do you mean? True, the originals were lost, but these are copies provided by a friend of the count's."

"Of course they are, of course," Andrea said. "Signor Cavalcanti, how much are you being paid to be my father? I am curious by nature."

Shocked, Major Cavalcanti struggled to form words, but Andrea held up a hand.

"As a show of good faith, I'll tell you my payment: fifty thousand francs to play the part of your son," Andrea said.

Major Cavalcanti's eyes unfocused again. "Yes, as your father I'm giving you an income for your time in Paris."

"Admirable commitment to your part, Father. Very well, we'll drop the matter," Andrea said, chuckling. He took another look at the major. "I seem to have forgotten the story in my absence; how did you lose your arm?"

"The Dead Plague!" Major Cavalcanti said. "My unit was disposing of quieted corpses, but one of the enemy was lurking in the pile. It sprang into action and bit deep into my forearm. Thankfully, my lieutenant was close at hand to destroy the creature and sever the infected limb."

"And you were a strapping young man of about twenty or thirty then, yes?" Andrea asked, looking at the stump. "That would have been good muscle, what a shame to have wasted it."

Andrea tapped a fingernail against his teeth without thinking, then caught himself and folded both hands behind his back.

Having seen enough, Monte Cristo closed the panel and made a production of making heavy footfalls to the door, knocking upon it, and rattling the knob before entering. The warning gave Andrea ample time to grasp Major Cavalcanti in an embrace again.

"It appears the reunion has not been a disappointment," the count said with a benevolent smile. "I invite you both to a dinner I'm hosting at my country house on Saturday. Among the other guests is your banker, M. Danglars, who it would be most beneficial for Andrea to meet."

"Of course," Andrea said, taking the hint at once. "My father and I will be there. What will the dress code be?"

"Your father should wear his dress uniform," the count said. "You should dress simply, and my servant will provide you with a list and the addresses of some shops. Also, some extra money from your father to settle your initial expenses in Paris."

"Thank you very much, Father," Andrea said, grinning as Monte Cristo pressed a roll of banknotes into Andrea's hand.

On their way out of the house, Ali provided them with the promised list as well as a paper with the address and time of the count's dinner. Monte Cristo's satisfaction at putting two more pieces into play mingled with his disgust at Andrea's nature as they left arm in arm.

He searched the house for Haydee for some happier company, but she had gone out somewhere to explore the city. Instead, he decided to pay a call to the Morrels.

CHAPTER 63
NOIRTIER

The next day was the first of June, and Valentine was eager to leave the law offices of Dubois & Renard at the end of the day. When she returned to her father's house on the Rue de Faubourg Saint-Honore, she took the stairs two at a time to her grandfather's room.

Villefort kept the old Bonapartist senator, Jules Noirtier, in a back room on the second floor, away from his own chambers. Noirtier sat in an armchair which could be moved on casters. The gargoyle Barrois, having grown over the years to the size of a large cat, held a book in front of Noirtier and waited for his wink to signal it to turn the page.

As Villefort told the count, an apoplexy had struck Noirtier in the autumn of 1832 and left him paralyzed. He could not walk, nor even stand. Speech was impossible, and the act of eating was an effort. Of all his body he only retained any control over his eyes, into which he focused all of his considerable will.

Valentine and Barrois often knew what Noirtier meant from only a glance. Villefort shared this aptitude, though he often pretended not to understand out of convenience. For anything more complex, Noirtier and Valentine had developed a code.

Noirtier's hair had grown long and white since the day Villefort brought news to the king of Napoleon's return, and his lean frame had atrophied. One side of his face hung slack, like a wax figure forgotten too close to a hearth.

Mirrors lined the room, on stands and hanging on the walls, so that Noirtier could see any corner of it regardless of his position. Though he could not smile, his eyes lit up when Valentine entered the room. His joy was as obvious to her as if he could stand up and sing her a welcome. Villefort's custom was to treat Noirtier like inconvenient furniture, providing the necessities of life but no warmth or companionship. While Barrois could speak in short sentences, it was not much more than a well-trained dog. Valentine was his only true friend, and he took real delight in listening to her stories about life outside the house.

"Good evening, Grandpapa!" Valentine kissed Noirtier on his wrinkled forehead. She sat nearby where she could face him directly, and took one of his immobile hands in hers. "Have you had a good day?"

Noirtier blinked his eyes slowly, the signal for "yes." If he wanted to disagree, he would flutter his eyelids at a faster pace. He followed this by winking his right eye, his usual signal to ask anyone in the room to fetch Valentine.

"Me? Oh, how was my day?" Valentine asked.

Noirtier blinked yes again, and Valentine told him all she could without breaking the legal code of client privilege. She had to admit there were parts of her job she enjoyed. Hunting through case law to find just the right precedent to support an argument was a dreary chore to many of her co-workers, but Valentine found it to be an exciting puzzle. Taking dictation for the senior partners didn't bother her either, as recording events in shorthand came easily to her. If it weren't for the vindictive ways in which people used the legal system against one another, the work itself would be even more enjoyable.

Valentine sighed while recounting all of this to Noirtier. She knew her skills would serve her well as a journalist, but a change of career was out of the question.

"Father has decided that I'll practice law, and that's that," she said. "He even organized my position at Dubois & Renard so I could learn the tricks of defense attorneys before taking a job with the government as a prosecutor."

Noirtier gazed at the floor for a moment, his signal for referring to his son. He followed this with a roll of his eyes, which meant the same coming from him as from any other man in Paris. Valentine laughed, happy to commiserate with someone who understood how impossible Villefort could be.

The main drawback to Valentine's work, as she had explained to Noirtier on many occasions, was her colleagues. She wasn't sure if the legal profession attracted disagreeable people or created them, but everyone in her office was quick to criticize and to pounce on any perceived flaw. The other women in the lunchroom said such awful things about each other in front of her that she sometimes worried what they said behind her back.

"That's why I eat at L'Epicure so often, to avoid the lunchroom," Valentine said. "And that's where... Grandpapa, I have a secret to confess to you."

Noirtier's gaze intensified, inviting her to share more.

"Grandpapa, I'm in love," Valentine said.

To Valentine's surprise, anger blazed in Noirtier's eyes.

"Why would that make you angry?" she asked, puzzled, before a guess came to her. "Do you think I mean that I'm in love with Franz d'Epinay?"

Noirtier blinked, and Valentine better understood his reaction. As a little girl, before his stroke, Noirtier had told her many stories about the Revolution and Bonaparte's reign; his political leanings had never been a secret, and he was as unhappy about the coming marriage as Valentine was.

"You can rest easy; it's not Franz. I'm still doomed to marry him, but I'm in love with someone else," Valentine said, smiling as Noirtier's anger dissipated into joy. "I feel like I can't even say his name in this house or Father would swoop down like a great yellow bat and destroy him. Oh, you'd like him. He's clever, and dashing, and kind; a gentle soul in a soldier's body."

Valentine reminded herself of a strange moment earlier that day. She had seen Max at the cafe during her morning break, wearing the dark uniform of the Hospital Saint-Bertrand. Saint-Bertrand was the same hospital where Max had trained to treat wounded soldiers in the field. Max had explained how, given that his tour was done and he hadn't signed up for another yet, he was in need of a job.

"It's refreshing to put my training to work without anyone trying to shoot me, stab me, or eat me," was how Max had phrased it, but then his eyes had taken on a faraway look.

He had opened his mouth to say more, but no words came out. Frustrated at the refusal of his voice to cooperate, Max had begun to growl and tug at the collar of his uniform. Unsure what else to do, Valentine just held his hand until his breathing steadied and he could speak again.

"He hasn't been entirely himself since he came home, Grandpapa," Valentine said. "He hasn't been sleeping, and he sometimes has these moments; he seems to get stuck, I suppose, or become depressed. I'm worried for him."

Noirtier's eyes widened and he raised them to the ceiling; a signal that he wanted something.

"Food or water?" she asked. Noirtier rapidly blinked for no.

"The dictionary, then?" Valentine said.

This time Noirtier blinked once for yes, and Barrois flapped on stone wings to get the book.

"Common, or alphabetical?" she asked, holding it on her lap. Noirtier looked to the left. "Common, then. E? S? A?"

Valentine recited her list of the most commonly-used letters in the French language. Noirtier blinked once when she reached the letter F, and again when she reached A while reciting the vowels. She continued repeating the series of letters until she could narrow down which word Noirtier wanted.

Noirtier knew he had been blessed with a devoted and inventive granddaughter. It hadn't taken her long after his stroke to think of using the dictionary, and the innovation of listing the most common letters first came soon after. His old heart swelled with pride when he recalled how she had visited a printing press and observed the typesetters at their work to see which letters they used most frequently.

"Familiar?" Valentine asked at last, having assembled enough letters to make a guess. Noirtier blinked yes, and she began the work of figuring out what he meant.

"You can't mean that he is familiar; I haven't said his name," she said. "Do you mean his behaviour? You've seen other men act like this?"

Noirtier blinked yes again.

"What kind of men, was it doctors? No, soldiers?" she asked, stopping when Noirtier blinked yes again. "Then it may be something to do with his time at war. Oh, I should have guessed that myself!"

Valentine set the dictionary aside and rested her head in her hands.

"Grandpapa, I don't know what to do," she said. "I've got no way out of marrying Franz, no way into the career I want, and no way to be with the man I love. Must I live out my days unhappy, unfaithful, and unfulfilled?"

Noirtier considered the problem and then fluttered his eyes rapidly. A determination in his look gave Valentine courage.

"You have an idea?" Valentine asked.

Noirtier blinked a very deliberate yes and stared at the bookshelf behind her. Valentine walked over to it and pointed at titles, watching Noirtier to find the right one. Her search ended with the New Testament of the Holy Bible.

"Of course I've been praying—" Valentine began, but Noirtier blinked rapidly and stared at the book itself. Valentine opened the book, unsure where her grandfather could be leading her. "Which book do you want? Is it the Gospels? Acts? Epistles?"

Noirtier blinked no to each of them until a grim satisfaction filled his gaze when Valentine listed the final book: Revelations.

In the next room, Villefort stepped away from the listening-hole which allowed him to snoop on Noirtier. It was irksome enough that Valentine was so ungrateful for the career path he'd given her and the husband he'd arranged for her, but the idea of her falling in love with some commoner was an insult all its own.

Villefort stalked through the house to return to his study and reflected on what a nuisance his father had always been. The old man was a contrary, stubborn heretic who worshipped false gods even after his emperor died of stomach cancer on a forgotten island. The very idea of an emperor was blasphemous; putting oneself on a pedestal above kings was like declaring something could be above God.

He remembered a night in September of 1832, after Noirtier had been arrested again and Villefort had needed to expend considerable influence to free him. The stress of it had driven Villefort to drink, and as the hot tang of a beggar's blood rushed down his throat, he had prayed in the pouring rain for the archangel Sealtiel to strike his father down. A week later, Noirtier had suffered his stroke and lost his ability to interfere with Villefort's ambitions. Or so Villefort had thought; it seemed a few final tricks still rattled in the old man's locked-away mind. Villefort resolved to be vigilant and not to let anything disturb the wedding.

To make matters worse, there was trouble in the slums as well. A street whore had decided to start asking questions about missing criminals and lowlifes. Some of the people she was speaking to were Villefort's informants, and it had gotten back to him.

He wouldn't care about disappearances in the slums as a rule, but the whore was blundering close to the trail of several degenerates that Villefort himself had offered up as sacrifices to the archangels. It was simplicity itself for him to bury the official investigations and cover up the deaths, but there was nothing to stop them from being reopened by an ambitious gendarme who caught wind of her questions. Villefort feared he would need to take matters into his own hands.

A footman interrupted him outside his study, bearing an envelope with the Count of Monte Cristo's mark. He would normally ignore the count's dinner invitation, but the address caught his eye: No. 28 in the Rue de la Fontaine, in Auteuil. His fingers went without thinking to his left breast where he carried the scar from his would-be assassination twenty-one years earlier.

Villefort sent his reply to the count, graciously accepting the invitation.

CHAPTER 64
GHOSTS

From the front, the Count of Monte Cristo's house in Auteuil looked like a brand new building, with cleaned brick and new topiaries. Bertuccio had followed his orders with the same care he gave to all of the count's requests, and it was unrecognizable as the former Saint-Meran house.

Within the house could be found the count's trademark splendor. Bertuccio had replaced every decoration and stick of furniture, leaving no trace of the previous owner and no doubt that Monte Cristo, with his love of Egypt and the Far East, had taken ownership. Like in his Paris home, the sensibilities of those far-off lands formed a tasteful blend with French habits to provide a mix of exoticism and comfort.

Flowers adorned every hallway to refresh what had so recently been a dim and dingy relic. Bertuccio himself was relieved to hardly recognize the house despite his history with it, aside from the back garden and the single bedroom which the count had ordered to remain untouched.

The count arrived with Ali at the stroke of five o'clock on Saturday. Bertuccio waited with impatience and unease, hoping for the count's approval and hoping even more to be dismissed back to Paris. The count did not dismiss him, but complimented his efforts with the house, which did help somewhat to soothe Bertuccio's nerves.

An hour later the clatter of hooves brought Max to the door, and Monte Cristo stood there to greet him. He wore one of the suits Albert had picked for him and already felt more comfortable in the fashionable clothes.

Behind Max rode Raoul and Lucien, and following behind came the Danglars carriage. Lucien offered Hermine his hand at the carriage door; Monte Cristo's keen eyes noted the passing of a folded note from

Hermine's hand to Lucien's. Hermine appraised the quality of the landscaping in the rearranged courtyard, but puzzlement soon took hold on her face. Danglars himself came down next.

Even if it had not been plastered across the newspapers the day before, Monte Cristo could have guessed Danglars' recent misfortune from one look at his slack jowls and thousand-yard stare. As the architect of that misfortune, the count already knew every detail.

Earlier that week, Monte Cristo had entered the Catacombs by the basement of the little house on the Rue Ponthieu. The shadows of the Catacombs enveloped him, and the darkness brought him to the basement beneath a telegraph tower in the countryside. A sack of gold and some mild persuasion convinced the operator to broadcast a false message. This message reached Lucien's desk, who conveyed it to Hermine at once.

Hermine had, of course, relayed the news to Danglars: that a workers' revolution had murdered the czar in Russia and taken control of the government. Danglars had rushed to sell all of his bank's Russian bonds and those belonging to the Reserve, taking a loss of over a million francs to avoid losing the entire investment. Beauchamp's paper, the Independent, confirmed the next morning that the telegraph message was a fake, there had been no revolution, and the operator responsible had fled the country.

Monte Cristo suppressed a grin when Danglars' driver approached his own doorman with a thick envelope. The count had included a note with Danglars' invitation requesting another withdrawal of several thousand against his unlimited credit, and to please bring it to dinner. He hoped Danglars felt the loss of each franc like a cut.

Monte Cristo led them all into the open two-story foyer and told them about the histories behind the paintings and *objets d'art* there. Max and Lucien were a rapt audience while Danglars only grunted in distracted response to any questions. Hermine also found herself preoccupied, looking around as if trying to remember something vital.

As the count explained the craftsmanship of a marvelous gold sarcophagus in the drawing-room, Andrea and the Major Cavalcanti arrived. Major Cavalcanti was the very picture of a veteran soldier, his impeccable black dress uniform tailored to accommodate his missing arm without detracting from the lines of the jacket. Viscount Andrea

Cavalcanti wore the height of men's fashion and a comfortable smile, staying close to his father as any dutiful son would.

"Cavalcanti!" Raoul whispered to Max and Lucien. "It's a fine old Italian name, isn't it?"

"The name may be old, but those clothes are suspiciously new," Lucien remarked with his usual smirk. "The viscount walks as though he's never been well-dressed before in his life!"

"Even if he's acting oddly, we should give him a chance," Max said. "You all gave me one, and I'm new to these fancy clothes myself."

"Oh, of course we will!" Raoul said, clapping Max on the shoulder. "We're just measuring him up first."

While the young men criticized Andrea from afar, Danglars approached the count.

"I've heard the name, but I'm unfamiliar with Italian nobility. Who are they?" Danglars asked.

"The descendants of princes and holders of a considerable fortune," Monte Cristo replied, guessing Danglars' motive. "The major mentioned they have an account with your bank, in fact."

"They speak excellent French," Hermine said, having shared a few words with Andrea.

"The major told me that Andrea was educated in the south, near Marseille," the count said. "I suspect he had something of an ulterior motive in learning the language, though; he's quite keen on finding a Parisian wife."

"He should be careful with that, sometimes they are more trouble than they are worth," Danglars said, watching Andrea and making a point to ignore his wife's raised eyebrows.

The servant returned to announce Monsieur de Villefort. Villefort spoke fewer than a dozen words as he entered the house and struggled to keep his emotions in check as he shook the count's hand.

"Why here?" Villefort muttered while Hermine stared at him. "Why here?"

A platter crashed to the ground in an adjacent room, and the count caught a glimpse of Bertuccio retreating as the door swung shut.

"Pardon me a moment, I need a word with my steward," Monte Cristo said. When he found Bertuccio, the man was almost as pale as the count himself.

"Come now, is it really so horrible just being in this house?" Monte Cristo said. "I thought restoring it would at least partly cure you of your aversion."

"It's not that, your excellency," Bertuccio said. "You didn't tell me that you planned to dine with ghosts and dead men!"

"What the devil are you talking about?" the count asked, feigning surprise.

"Follow me and I'll show you, but I must not be seen," Bertuccio said. They went to the second floor and stood at a balcony overlooking the guests. "There, that woman in the white dress with so many diamonds. She was the pregnant woman who waited for Villefort!"

"You must be mistaken," the count said, "you're pointing at Baroness Danglars."

"Every detail of that night is ingrained in my memory," Bertuccio said. His chest heaved, on the verge of a breakdown. "I'm certain I struck true, excellency, I pierced his heart and I saw him fall, but there he stands looking more demonic than ever!"

"Ah, yes, I forgot to tell you," the count said with a shrug. "You are a much better steward than you are an assassin. We've lived in Paris for nearly a fortnight, you really didn't know he was alive and the crown prosecutor?"

"Your excellency, I spend my days serving you faithfully and my nights reading in my quarters," Bertuccio said, wiping sweat from his brow. "You've never needed me to know who the prosecutor is, and I've never had reason to find out."

"Well, you've found out now," Monte Cristo said. "I suppose you should stay out of sight for the remainder of the evening, lest he have you arrested for attempted murder."

"I'll give instructions to the servants to complete my duties, starting with the setting of plates." He counted the guests.

Hermine was speaking to Villefort, Danglars was deep in conversation with Major Cavalcanti, and Andrea faced away to admire a limestone jar carved with hieroglyphics. Max, Lucien, and Raoul approached Andrea to introduce themselves, and a high-pitched keening leaked from Bertuccio's throat when Andrea turned to face them.

"*Mostro! Diavolo!*" Bertuccio said. "Benedetto!"

"Your adopted son?" the count asked. "The bastard child, you claim, of Villefort and Baroness Danglars? The one who murdered and ate your sister-in-law?"

"The same," Bertuccio said. "I would recognize his eyes and that predatory smile anywhere."

"Really, I think you may need a vacation; perhaps the shock of seeing Villefort alive has rattled your mind," the count said. "Now you're pointing at Viscount Andrea Cavalcanti from an old and respectable Italian family. Pull yourself together; the dinner hour is fast approaching and I don't want my guests to wait."

The count clapped his hands twice, and a shaking Bertuccio set to his work. Monte Cristo returned to his guests, and soon the clock struck six-thirty and servants threw the parlour doors open.

CHAPTER 65
THE DINNER

The place cards sat Villefort and Hermine next to each other, amplifying their mutual discomfort. Debray sat between Andrea Cavalcanti and the major, who seemed unsure where to rest his hand or his gaze. Andrea asked a passing servant if meat would be served and if he could have his served blue-rare. Danglars conducted an odd ritual of rapping his knuckles against the back of each chair twice before taking his seat next to the count.

Max was determined to look anywhere but at Villefort. When Max had told Valentine about the count inviting him to the same dinner as her father, she had been quick to advise caution so as not to arouse his suspicions. Max had promised to be careful, but still took it as a sign that the count could help them after all.

Monte Cristo intended to feed their curiosity as much as their appetites, and so his servants brought out a feast even more varied than that served to Franz in the island grotto. Fruit from every corner of the world came out as an appetizer in porcelain vessels from the furthest reaches of the Orient. Fish and fowl which some of the guests thought were only myths came in on silver dishes. Not a drop of French wine was served. Instead, bottles of Hungarian tokaji and Greek retsina shared the table with Japanese sake and a pumpkin wine from America. The Parisians and Italians at the table sat stunned by the variety.

Monte Cristo allowed the general astonishment to sit for a minute until plating was complete, then laughed and clapped Danglars on the shoulder.

"We live in a world full of wonders. In my travels, I've seen things that only our adventurous servicemen would believe," he said, indicating Max and Raoul. "A phoenix rising from the ashes of a burnt tower, a forest alight with glittering faeries, and even glimpses beyond the known edge of creation. Since not everyone is free to drift across the surface of the globe in search of the impossible and the unknowable, I sometimes feel it is my duty to bring some small measure of those wonders to my friends."

"Well, you should be commended for your efforts!" Raoul said, raising his glass. "A toast, to our gracious host!"

The other guests raised their glasses in turn, but when Andrea followed suit Danglars cried out.

"Young man, never toast with water!" Danglars said, leaning as far across the table as his belly allowed. "You're inviting your spirit to forget the land of the living and drift off into the underworld!"

Surprised by this outburst, Andrea set his water glass back on the table and instead raised a cup of tokaji.

"You're very kind, Raoul. To be honest, I put as much diligence into arranging this meal as M. de Villefort would put into building a criminal case, or that you would put into pleasing a woman," Monte Cristo said, prompting a guffaw from Raoul. "For example, this platter of eels; half of them are common river eels from the Korean peninsula, and the other half are hatchlings of a ferocious beast which dwells in the lakes of Scotland. They may taste no better than anything caught in French waters, but the impossibility of having them share a platter on this table was a challenge I couldn't pass up."

"But how could you bring them such a distance and still have them fresh when they arrived?" Hermine asked.

"They were brought here in specially-designed watertight casks filled with aquatic plants from their home environments," the count said. "The water was changed every two days, and they were still very much alive this evening when my chef laid his hands on them."

"That's impossible," Villefort said. "You're lying, or it's one of your little jokes."

The count rang his bell and Ali brought in a cart with two glass tanks. Several slithering eels coiled through the waters within, and the guests could see for themselves that they were the same breeds as what sat upon the table. Max was so impressed that he applauded, and after a brief snicker from Lucien, the other guests joined in with that applause.

"It's all very well to have money, but as a representative of the common people I must point out that this whim of yours must have come at great expense," Danglars said. "I gave a speech about this kind of profligacy in the Chamber just last week. We could just as easily be eating chicken tonight, and you could have given that money away to people who need it."

"My dear baron, where do you think the money went? I didn't burn a pile of francs in a magic circle and summon these eels from the netherworld," Monte Cristo said.

Villefort's eyes widened when the count mentioned magic circles and swallowed his third or fourth glass of wine. The count's keen eyes noted that discomfort as he continued.

"I paid men to catch the fish, and build the casks, and transport the casks while changing the water. With the great distances involved, I also paid men to transmit my orders to those far-away places," Monte Cristo said. "The wagon-drivers had travelling expenses like food and drink which they bought from inns along the way. The men who built the casks had to buy wood from lumberjacks. There are a hundred or a thousand other people who received some amount of my gold in order to bring this meal to our table, and that's only for the eels."

"That's entirely different," Danglars said. "You've paid men to do a series of jobs for you; I'm referring to donating your money and getting nothing in return but satisfaction."

"You mean that paying a man for nothing is nobler than paying him to use his time and skills to produce something?" the count asked.

"Yes, precisely!" Danglars said with a grin.

"Why?" the count asked.

Danglars' grin faded immediately. People did not challenge the content of his speeches; he was accustomed to cornering others into a position where they could either surrender to his point or accept the implication that they hated the poor. His mouth formed several shapes as he tried to build an answer, but nothing came.

"I for one appreciate the effort you've gone to," Raoul said, "not just with this dinner but with your entire house. If the gossip is true, you've owned it for less than a week. The previous owners had paved over the front courtyard, yet you've brought in a magnificent lawn."

"I'm fond of grass and shade, so I had it brought to the house. Paying several workmen a handsome sum to do it, of course," Monte Cristo added with a look at Danglars. "You've visited before?"

"Once, when the Marquis de Saint-Meran first advertised it for sale several years ago," Raoul said. "It was a truly melancholy place, with all the blinds closed and a smell of must in every room. If it had belonged to anyone but the Marquis, I would have thought a terrible scandal had happened here!"

Raoul laughed at his little joke, and nobody but the count and Hermine noticed Villefort's wince.

"Did it belong to the Marquis?" the count asked. "What a coincidence, as he is M. de Villefort's father-in-law from his first marriage, if I recall correctly."

"You do," Villefort said. "Did you honestly not know who you bought the house from?"

"My steward handles these things," Monte Cristo said indifferently. "I tell him to find me a country-house, and he does so admirably. But I do share the young baron's suspicion about there being a secret in these walls."

"For what reason?" Villefort asked, swallowing a fifth glass of wine in one go.

Hermine sipped her own wine and said nothing. Her husband, however, decided to chime in.

"Now that you mention it, Auteuil is getting something of a reputation for dark events. I read about it in the Nightly Assemblage," Danglars said. "We can't be far from the house where you were attacked by that Corsican, isn't that right Gerard? It was in that Caillat article."

"Yes, and thank you for mentioning it," Villefort said through clenched teeth. If Jordan Caillat had been present, Villefort would have sank those teeth into his neck with a smile.

"That's right, and he released a second article in yesterday's edition," Danglars said. "You were attacked there, a servant disappeared soon after, and the new article says that some mystery woman was renting the property at the time."

"Why, Monsieur Crown Prosecutor!" Lucien said as Hermine turned pale. "Do the gossips of Paris finally have something of yours to talk about?"

"Come on, Villefort," Danglars said with a grin, ignoring Hermine staring intently into the depths of her wine. "Who was she, and why were you visiting her?"

"Your question is impertinent, Baron Danglars," Villefort said, his sonorous voice wiping the smile off of even Lucien's face, "and you've interrupted our host. I suggest we drop this topic of conversation."

"Really, it's no trouble. But I was going to say that most of this house was simply neglected, the natural result of not being lived in, with the exception of one room," Monte Cristo said. "If you may indulge an eccentricity of mine, I think it may be haunted."

"Haunted?" Villefort asked, almost choking on his wine.

"Yes, haunted. It's a plain enough bedroom upstairs with red hangings, but the walls seem to exhale a deep sadness. I left it untouched when the rest of the house was restored, specifically to show you all tonight," the count said. "If you're done, we have some time before dessert."

When Monte Cristo rose, all but Villefort and Hermine followed him at once. They remained rooted to their seats for a moment, staring at each other. Finally, Villefort stood and offered Hermine his arm.

"We must go," was all he said.

The count concealed his glee at their discomfort as they passed him, instead maintaining the careful pleasantness expected of a host. With a lamp in hand he directed his guests up the stairs and through a series of rooms outfitted in his typical mix of Eastern styles with divans instead of couches and embroidered silk drapes in exotic colours.

When they arrived at the infamous bedroom, the difference was remarkable. Only the count's single oil lamp lit the room, and the furniture remained untouched from twenty years before.

"Positively frightful," Lucien said.

"It certainly is," Monte Cristo agreed. "The enormous mahogany bed, the grim blood-coloured curtains, the faded portraits on the wall with their staring eyes. What tales could their dour faces tell?"

Hermine fell into an antique armchair by the door.

"My dear, are you really brave enough to sit where the mysterious crime may have been committed?" Danglars said.

"But there's more!" Monte Cristo said.

The count moved to the corner of the room and pulled one of the red hangings aside, revealing the hidden staircase. Raoul stuck his head in to see it for himself.

"Oh, this is very well-done! Every proper haunted house must have secret passages! Where does it lead?" he asked.

"Down to the garden," Monte Cristo said. "Imagine some figure on a dark and stormy night, muffled in a cloak to hide his identity and the dreadful burden he carried from God himself, descending step by step. Maybe he carries the proceeds of robbery, or the evidence of a murder. It's a powerful image."

"Madame, are you well?" Lucien asked, noticing Hermine's pallor.

"I'm alright," she said, "ghost stories have always had a strong effect on me, that's all."

"By all means, let's get you some air," the count said.

He led his guests down the crooked stairs and out to the back garden. Villefort brought up the rear and could only step off the threshold to the garden path with great effort.

"Pardon my theatrics," the count continued, "but that bedroom captures my imagination to such a degree that I needed to share my mental picture of the event with you. It would be simple to imagine that room as the apartment of a loving mother, with the nurse using the stairs to avoid disturbing the rest of the house. That is, if not for the discovery my workmen made."

He took Hermine's arm and gathered everyone closer to him in the deeper darkness beneath a particular tree. He pointed to the ground.

"They were here, aerating the soil to refresh these old trees, when their tools struck something. They began to dig and found the ironwork and rotted wood of a box—and the bones of an infant," the count said. Instantly Hermine's arm stiffened. "The size of the bones suggested a newborn, and though it could have been a stillbirth, why bury it here and not the village cemetery?"

"Perhaps the child needed to be kept secret to prevent a scandal?" Andrea asked, listening with rapt attention since they had first reached the bedroom, his interest piqued by any suggestion of the macabre.

"I think so, and worse," the count said. "If one were burying a corpse, there would be no need for a padlock like the one the workmen found among the rusted ironwork. That would only be necessary if you were burying a living thing."

"Infanticide! How chilling," Raoul said. "The punishment for that is beheading, isn't it?"

Villefort nodded, breathing heavily. Monte Cristo looked around at his guests, satisfied that the two for whom the entire scene had been prepared were at the limits of their endurance.

"Enough grim tales and wild imaginings, we've forgotten our coffee and dessert. No need to use the stairs again, we may enter by the door here," the count said.

Everyone followed him, with Villefort and Hermine lagging behind.

"I must speak to you. Come to my office tomorrow," Villefort whispered in her ear.

CHAPTER 66
THE BEGGAR

The moment that etiquette allowed it, Villefort summoned his driver. Danglars was busy speaking with Major Cavalcanti and ignoring Hermine's hints that she wanted to leave as well, and she was grateful to accept Villefort's terse invitation to join him. When his wife left for a silent journey in the company of Villefort and his driver, Danglars shrugged and offered Major Cavalcanti her seat in his carriage.

Having learned that the major would return soon to Italy, Danglars was keen to know what connections he may have there which could further Danglars' own interests. Max, Raoul, and Lucien said their goodbyes to Andrea with promises to call on him. This left Andrea to ride alone in the small carriage he and the major arrived in.

Andrea spoke little during dinner. Though he had no formal education, he was shrewd and studious enough on topics that caught his interest. Therefore he chose to listen and observe the manners and habits of the other guests. He also took careful note of what they chose to speak about, to better learn about them himself.

The presence of the crown prosecutor had been an unwelcome surprise, and at first Andrea had worried that the dinner was some elaborate trap. However, Villefort had, by and large, ignored him during dinner and the tour of the house.

On the other hand, Baron Danglars showed quite an interest in Andrea after learning the Cavalcantis held accounts with the Danglars Bank. Andrea made sure to receive Danglars with warmth, listen to his questions, and laugh at his banal jokes. Before Danglars and the major departed, Danglars had given Andrea his card and an invitation to dinner at his home.

Andrea's carriage was a two-seater cabriolet like the cabs available for hire in any street, but without a driver. As he stepped up into it to take the reins, a hand rested on his shoulder.

Andrea turned, thinking it may be the count, but instead, a sunburnt face half-hidden by a thick black beard greeted him. A red handkerchief held back wild grey hair, and beady eyes glinted at him. The man wore filthy garments which an optimistic person could call rags, held together by patches on which he had drawn odd symbols with charcoal. He was a large man, but his bony limbs protruded in the manner of a man who had eaten only bare sustenance for a year or more.

"Caderousse," Andrea said, looking around to ensure they were alone. "How did you get here?"

"I should ask you the same thing, old friend," Caderousse said. "I'm glad I found you, as you seem to be in fine health, and such fine clothes too."

"What do you want?" Andrea asked, shifting his weight. Caderousse stroked his beard to make a show of considering his answer.

"Well, I haven't had such a good dinner as you, so right now I'd like you to spare me the walk back to Paris," Caderousse said. Seeing Andrea's reluctance, he smiled more broadly. "Come now, I'm so tired I can barely stand, and we have business to discuss. Would you be so cruel as to leave me stranded here, Master Benedetto?"

Andrea huffed through his nose and gave Caderousse a look of pure hatred.

"Not so loud, you fool!" he said. "You'll ruin everything! Get in the carriage then, and not a word until we're out of the village."

Grinning, Caderousse climbed onto the plush seat and hummed to himself as Andrea drove them past the other houses. Once he was certain nobody could hear them, Andrea spoke again.

"Out with it, old man. Why are you bothering me?"

"Why, Benedetto old friend, I'm wounded that you would talk to me this way!" Caderousse said. He put his hands to his heart and pouted. "Especially considering how you lied to me. When we last parted ways, you told me you were going to Tuscany to find work as a porter or a brewer, but instead I find you in Paris playing the part of a viscount!"

"You're spying on me? Hardly a very friendly thing to do," Andrea said.

"Who's spying? I wanted to congratulate you on your good fortune,"

Caderousse said. "Of course, I'm not properly dressed, so I waited until an opportune moment to speak to you alone."

"With you, there's no such thing as an opportune moment. Don't try my patience, you know how Corsicans can be," Andrea said.

"Come now! You were raised in Corsica, but you don't know if you're a Corsican any more than I know the feel of a queen's breast." Caderousse said. "You want to speak to me in a kinder tone, or I could become quite troublesome."

Andrea clenched his teeth. He could see where Caderousse was leading him and considered silencing the old man on a permanent basis. If he hadn't been full from the count's magnificent dinner and reluctant to get questionable stains on his new clothes, he very well may have.

Caderousse could guess the tone of Andrea's thoughts as well and lifted the hem of his shirt to reveal the handle of an old and rusted but serviceable pistol.

"A marvelous thing, the pistol," Caderousse said. "I'm but a frail old man, easy prey for anyone or anything that may choose to harm me. But with a pistol, I level the playing field and give myself a chance to survive against even the strongest brute."

"How much do you want?" Andrea asked, not eager to learn whether the pistol was loaded or a bluff.

"Benedetto! Have you forgotten how I used to divide my soup and beans with you when you were still hungry? You always did have a strong appetite," Caderousse said.

"How much, Caderousse?" Andrea asked again.

"Who is that prince you were dining with? Is he your benefactor or the mark of your next scheme?" Caderousse replied.

"How much?" Andrea shouted.

"To the point then." Caderousse huffed and rolled his eyes. "I think I could live quite comfortably on a hundred, no, a hundred and fifty francs per month. Yes, that would buy quite a bit of silence from me."

Andrea didn't let his relief show on his face. His part in the count's game, whatever it was, came with an income of six thousand francs each month. Caderousse's demand amounted to next to nothing, and if he spoke to the wrong person he would ruin everything. His silence came at a bargain. Andrea grumbled for a moment to make Caderousse feel like he'd won, then handed him the reins so he could retrieve some banknotes from his coat.

"Here," Andrea said, "take two hundred if it stops you increasing the price further, and you'll get the same each month as long as I keep my own income. Where can I find you to send the rest?"

"Do you really think I'm stupid enough to tell you where I sleep?" Caderousse said with a laugh. "You think I don't know what you did to that postman whose horses we stole? Why do you think I waited until after your dinner to speak with you?"

"You're full of questions, old man," Andrea said, clenching his teeth.

"I'll find you sometime each month, and let's leave it at that," Caderousse said. "So, how did you come by this good fortune? You still haven't told me."

"I've found my father," Andrea said. "Not my real one, but good enough for as long as he pays me."

As he said those words, Andrea considered they may be truer than he knew. The Count of Monte Cristo came across as ageless, but Andrea guessed him to be at least in his late thirties. The eerie white face and red eyes made it clear he stood apart from the rest of humanity, as did Andrea's rather unique urges. Perhaps the endgame of the count's charade was to acknowledge Andrea—or rather, Benedetto—as his own son.

"If he's in the market to hire a son, see if you can find me a position as grandfather," Caderousse said. "Although with you taking care of me, I may not need it. First thing in the morning I shall buy myself a proper coat, go and read the papers, and pretend I'm a retired baker. That sounds like a good life for an old man, yes?"

They rode in silence the rest of the way into Paris until Andrea stopped the horse at a cross-street. Caderousse jumped down and spun to give an exaggerated bow.

"Au revoir, Viscount Benedetto!" Caderousse said before disappearing into a courtyard.

Andrea sat fuming in his carriage, then took several deep breaths to steady himself.

"All is well," he muttered. "Two hundred francs is not so much, and sooner or later he'll let his guard down. I only hope he fattens up a bit first."

CHAPTER 67
A CONJUGAL SCENE

While Max and Raoul returned to their homes, Lucien parted ways with them once they reached Paris. He galloped to the Danglars mansion just as Villefort's carriage deposited Hermine at her door. With perfect familiarity, Lucien threw his horse's reins to a servant and rushed to offer Hermine his arm.

"Hermine, what happened back there?" Lucien asked, his usual sardonic manner dropped in the absence of an audience. "The count's little ghost story wasn't that fearsome."

"I'm just feeling unwell Lucien, that's all," Hermine said.

"I don't believe that," Lucien said. "You were in fine spirits when you arrived at the count's house, and I know your husband's disagreeable attitude wasn't enough to bother you."

Despite his inquiries, Lucien couldn't get any clear answer from Hermine about the source of her agitation. Finally, as a man experienced in the world of romance, he determined that it must be a quirk of womanhood; that sublime irrationality which sometimes possesses the fairer sex and overrides their reason.

They proceeded through the garish mansion until they reached the oasis of her boudoir, where Lucien lounged across the couch while the maid undressed Hermine. Wearing only her shift, Hermine stood staring at herself in the looking glass with deep melancholy. Lucien's smirk returned, as he knew a foolproof way to disperse that particular mood.

Lucien stood behind Hermine and brushed his fingers against her bare arms. He lowered his head to within an inch of her neck and breathed in the smell of her, an act which never failed to elicit a grateful shudder from Hermine as she felt the gentle movement of the air.

"Oh, Lucien," Hermine whispered. "Make me forget the stress of this evening."

"As you wish," Lucien murmured against her skin.

Their lovemaking on the sofa left them oblivious to the rest of the world. Debray steadied himself against the wall with his left hand while his right was otherwise occupied. For a few glorious moments, Hermine closed her eyes and forgot about the looming spectre of her awful secret.

The sound of an object striking the wall broke the spell. Frustrated, Hermine opened her eyes to find Lucien staring in disbelief at his left hand. The blade and handle of a double-edged throwing knife protruded from the exact middle of the hand in perfect vertical alignment. Between and below the knuckles of his middle and ring fingers, it pinned Lucien to the wall. In the time it took Hermine to notice this, Lucien's brain received the first signals of pain from his wounded appendage, and he responded with a disbelieving scream.

Hermine recognized the shape of the knife well enough, having found them in walls and furniture all over the house whenever her husband was in a mood, and looked past Lucien's shoulder. Danglars stood at the door. He held his coat open with one hand, revealing four more knives in the brace he often concealed on his person. No fury coloured his rubbery face, only the satisfaction of a well-placed throw.

"Good evening, madame. Good evening, M. Debray," Danglars said. "You know, the old saying really is true. If you can perfect your throw on a rolling ship, you'll never miss a target again. Thank you for the opportunity to demonstrate that, Lucien."

All of Lucien's attention remained focused on his hand and the trail of blood oozing down the pink wallpaper. Hermine gawked at her husband, thinking that perhaps God had chosen murder by a jealous husband to punish her for what she and Villefort had done. Rather than propel a knife into her exposed breast, Danglars instead pulled a folded newspaper from his pocket.

"I have here the end-of-day values for the Russian bonds which you two convinced me to sell," Danglars said evenly. "I won't bore you with the details, but suffice it to say they've risen even further since we sold, compounding our original loss."

Danglars found Lucien's jacket laying on the floor, finer than the young man's secretarial salary could afford, and used it to clean the dirt from his boots.

"M. Debray, I don't resent you for pleasuring my wife. The wealthy should share their wealth, and the beautiful should share their beauty," Danglars said. "Nor do I resent you giving her inside information to aid her gambling with my money, since I've indirectly benefited from it for so long."

Lucien didn't answer with more than a whimper, and tried to steady his legs beneath him so gravity wouldn't make the wound worse. His other hand wavered near the handle as he considered whether he could handle the pain of pulling it out.

"What I do resent you for," Danglars continued, "is passing along this unverified claptrap about the Russians that has caused me to lose over one million francs for nothing. Or perhaps not for nothing; your employer, the Minister, and I are on opposite sides of the Chamber, after all. Perhaps this was all an attempt to discredit me on the political stage."

Danglars walked over to Lucien, giving him a deliberate nudge with his expansive belly and prompting a small yelp of pain as the movement jostled Lucien's hand. Lucien could smell eels and exotic wine on Danglars' breath.

"For a proper throwing knife, the shape of the blade is nearly as important as the balance," Danglars said in a cheerful tone that didn't match his face. "The knife must be double-edged to ensure that it passes easily into the target. This feature also facilitates easy removal."

Danglars grasped Lucien's forearm and pulled down with all of his weight. The motion pulled Lucien's hand against the knife, or more accurately, pulled the knife through Lucien's hand. Lucien shrieked at the long gash bifurcating his hand from the centre of his palm to what was no longer the webbing between his second and third fingers. Danglars rang for the maid.

"Take M. Debray to the kitchen and bandage his injury. You may take him to the hospital, but don't clothe him if you hope to keep your job," Danglars said when she arrived.

Too frightened to question the order, the maid led a sobbing and nude Lucien from the room. Danglars turned to Hermine and spoke to a space several inches above her head.

"I know all about your dalliance with M. Debray," Danglars said. "I know about all of the young men you've laid with during our marriage. Truth be told, I've found it thrilling. There's a certain delightful ache in knowing that a younger and more handsome man is taking my place, and I relish it the way one relishes poking at a tender bruise."

Hermine was too stunned at this change from Danglar's usual submissive attitude towards her to reply.

"Up until now, your tips from M. Debray have been profitable ones. And your various charades about where you found your information were amusing," Danglars said. "Of course, it was obvious from the start that your hunches came directly from his desk. As I've grown rich off your suggestions, I've dutifully given you one-fourth of the earnings as a courtesy. Well, it's only fair that you reimburse me for one-fourth of the loss I took thanks to this fake news from Russia."

The ultimatum shook Hermine loose from her surprise.

"Reimburse you for a quarter of a million? How absurd!" she proclaimed.

To reclaim her dignity, Hermine snatched Lucien's abandoned shirt from the arm of the couch. As Lucien was a very slim man and Hermine a rather well-proportioned woman, the buttons refused to close. In the end she settled on holding the garment in place to cover her nudity.

"Oh, it's not so absurd at all. I suspect that between yourself and M. Debray you'll be able to acquire the necessary funds, and until you do, I had better not find the little secretary in my house again," Danglars said.

He grasped the handle of the bloody knife in the wall and worked it up and down to pull it free.

"Recall that I am a well-connected man. The association of dockworkers and stevedores bought a law from me that benefitted them greatly, and would happily do anything I asked," he said. "I could easily have a pair of suspicious crates transported from here to Marseille and thrown into the sea without a word being breathed to anyone. If your absence were noticed, I could say 'Alas, poor me! My wife has run off with the minister's secretary!' Do you see my point, madame?"

Staring at the very literal point of his knife, Hermine nodded. Danglars glared at her for a moment, then snatched Lucien's shirt to clean the blade. He threw the shirt across the room and turned to leave but stopped at the door.

"Oh, and about your little outbursts of ill health tonight; I presume they were regarding your secret love-child by way of M. de Villefort?" Danglars asked.

Hermine recoiled as if she'd been slapped.

"I'm not so ignorant as your first husband, M. de Nargonne. He killed himself when he learned the reason for your year-long disappearance, whereas I held that secret close to my breast for the correct time to wave it in front of you," Danglars said. "I wonder if that reporter, Caillat, knows this as well, and if he'll reveal it for all of Paris to read. Good evening, madame."

He left, not bothering to close the door behind him. Alone and naked, Hermine remained rooted to the couch where she had embraced her lover such a short time before.

She reflected on the odd set of misfortunes falling onto her house. Several of the Danglars Bank's investments had soured lately, exacerbated by Lucien's recent misinformation. The dinner party had frayed her nerves further, and her husband's abrupt change in manner was disorienting in the extreme. An unbearable pressure built up in her chest, and she held a pillow against her mouth to muffle her own screams.

CHAPTER 68
MATRIMONIAL PROJECTS

For Danglars, the next day was for the most part an ordinary one. He went to the Chamber and spoke out in favour of a tax increase, then returned home and dealt with his correspondence. He also took an appointment with Major Cavalcanti to finalize matters for Andrea before the major returned to Italy.

Danglars presented the calm yet brutal manner which everyone expected from him, but his agitation increased throughout the day. His losses from the Russian deception tormented him, just one example of many recent misfortunes.

A ship's captain and a faithful customer of his for many years, Jacopo Manfredi, had declared bankruptcy while still owing Danglars over six hundred thousand francs. A silver mine he bought in Peru turned out to be a worthless hole in the ground, and he couldn't find the previous owner to sue him for fraud. There had been many such cases, placing a severe drain on his reserves.

Danglars recalled his grand plan to bring back the Dead Plague. The lead-lined box of mortite sat secure in his study, the shards inside waiting for the right moment to reach into a corpse with their energy and start the machinery of astounding profits.

Villefort and Morcerf had each bought into the plan since his demonstration, but events had forced Danglars to funnel that money into his bank to recover his other losses. If he didn't find another source of funds to make up the difference, he knew he would have to face the wrath of a flamekeeping Catalan general and a merciless crown prosecutor. The idea of paying their shares out of his own never occurred to him as an acceptable alternative.

At the forefront of Danglars' mind, plots brewed to recover his financial standing. He obsessed over how his various assets were being used. Through his position as the Reserve chairman he had already lowered the reserve requirements on commercial banks, in effect printing more money for his bank, but that was a temporary measure. Danglars needed more. He could call the Count of Monte Cristo's withdrawal receipts in for repayment, but doing so would shake confidence in the Danglars Bank if word got out; he could only do that as a last resort. During Cavalcanti's visit, Danglars realized that one particular resource he controlled was about to be sold off, and he may have a chance to fetch a higher price for it. He ordered his carriage to Monte Cristo's house.

By good chance, the count was at home and receiving visitors. Danglars oozed graciousness when he entered the study, in the hopes that his request found the count in a favourable mood. Danglars did not suspect that the count already knew every detail of Jacopo Manfredi's bankruptcy as well as every other misfortune that had struck him. In fact, Manfredi was the same Jacopo who had long ago pulled a drowning Maltese sailor from the sea. The count had arranged an agreeable retirement for Jacopo in exchange for the bankruptcy.

"I understand you've had some difficulties lately," the count said. "They must be troubling you, but then I expect that's one of the pitfalls of holding a third-rate fortune."

Seeing the shock on Danglars' face, Monte Cristo hurried to correct himself.

"Don't think that was a judgement on you! My rating of people's fortunes only refers to where the money comes from," the count said. "A first-rate fortune is one with foundations in land and mines, which could only be erased by the most foolhardy mismanagement. A second-rate fortune is based in manufacturing, like the great American industrialists, and is only as secure as the owners' ability to adapt to changing technology and customer demands."

"And a third-rate fortune?" Danglars asked, struggling to keep the acid out of his voice. He doubted how sensible Monte Cristo's definitions were, considering what had happened with his Peruvian mine.

"I call any fortune third-rate that's based on speculation," Monte

Cristo said. "Someone lends out their money, hoping the interest will be profitable and those profits can be lent out again."

Danglars chuckled. "You've just described every bank in France."

"Third-rate fortunes can be quite large and impressive," Monte Cristo said. "But they can be destroyed with just a handful of bad decisions or a few months of bad luck."

"A fascinating system, to be sure," Danglars said. He mentally multiplied his recent losses by six months, paling when he realized his wealth could be wiped out long before that if his luck continued.

"If I may be so forward, are your current misfortunes the reason behind your visit?" the count asked. "Do you need me to lend you some money?"

"No, heavens no, my losses are trivial," Danglars said, sweating. "I came to ask for your help in another matter. Major Cavalcanti came to see me today. Did you know he only allows the boy five thousand francs a month? He's a gentleman, but a stingy fellow."

"That's the mindset of Italian millionaires for you," Monte Cristo agreed.

"You mentioned at dinner, or someone did, that the major brought his son to Paris to find a wife," Danglars said. "I imagine he'll want to find some grand old bloodline to unite the Cavalcanti fortune with, what do you think?"

"It's hard to say with Italians. The gentry there often mix with ordinary people, whether from curiosity or to keep from stagnating the blood I couldn't say," Monte Cristo shrugged. "But if Andrea is anything like other Italian nobles, he's as likely to marry a miner's daughter as he is to marry a princess. Or a banker's, as it were."

"And where would the Cavalcanti fortune fall on your scale of fortunes, do you think?" Danglars asked.

"Really, I don't know," Monte Cristo said, waving a hand. "I barely know the major, we have a mutual friend in Abbe Busoni. Busoni cares little for earthly matters like money, so has never told me anything about Cavalcanti's. Based on how old their name is and the major's income, I would guess they own some land in Naples or Florence."

"A guess is better than nothing," Danglars said. "Since you know so much of Italian customs, what kind of money do they give their sons when marrying them off?"

"It depends on if the major likes the match. If Andrea chooses a girl he disapproves of, the major may give him thirty francs a month. If he chooses a girl from a family the major has favourable dealings with, there may be millions involved," the count said. "All this talk of Andrea and marriage; are you planning to leave your wife, baron? Or are you thinking of Mlle. Danglars—and setting up Andrea and Albert for a quarrel?"

Danglars laughed. "M. de Morcerf and I have talked about the marriage, but I think both Albert and his mother would be pleased if it were called off.""Besides, I'm beginning to think Eugenie may do better as a Cavalcanti than as a Morcerf. Why weren't the Morcerfs invited to your dinner party?"

"They were, but they had a prior engagement to go to Cannes and take the sea air," Monte Cristo said.

"That's fitting, it's the air they both breathed in their youth," Danglars chuckled. "A nobility going back five hundred years is better than one that doesn't go back a single generation, which is why I find myself preferring young Andrea to young Albert. I thought that since you are introducing Andrea to Paris, you may be able to help arrange things."

"What do you mean about Morcerf's nobility?" Monte Cristo asked. "Albert told me it was a name with deep French roots."

Danglars laughed again. "My title and Morcerf's are the same age, but my name is older simply by virtue of being my real one," he said. "I was born Danglars and remain Danglars. He was born Fernand Mondego, a fisherman in Marseille. I grew up there as well, as did the Countess Morcerf. We've all known each other for over thirty years."

"How peculiar," Monte Cristo said, steepling his fingers. His chalk-white face betrayed no sign of his turmoil at the thoughts of Mercedes and Marseille. "If you knew that Morcerf was lying about his origins, why were you ready to join your houses?"

"Simply because we have known each other and have roughly equivalent prestige. But if a chance to marry into the Cavalcantis is on the table, it would be a much better investment," Danglars said. "After all, things have been said about Morcerf—that is, Mondego—which I'd rather not have follow my daughter if possible."

Monte Cristo snapped his fingers, his ever-present gloves muffling the sound.

"You've reminded me why the name Fernand Mondego sounds so familiar," the count said. "I recall hearing rumours years ago, perhaps the same ones you refer to, connecting him to the fall of Pasha Ali. Morcerf admitted to me himself that he served with the pasha's troops."

"The maddening thing is how incomplete the rumours are. All I can say for sure is that Greek food agreed with him; he was built like a stick prior to deploying there," Danglars said.

"So, you have the twin unknowns of Morcerf's past and Cavalcanti's present to investigate before making your decision; you bankers call it 'due diligence,' I think." Monte Cristo said. "Do you have contacts in Greece?"

"I do," Danglars said.

"Then get them to look into the matter properly, to make sure there isn't some scandal hidden like a zombie lurking in tall grass to bite your daughter's ankle," Monte Cristo said. "In the meantime, I'll inquire in Italy to get the truth of the Cavalcanti fortune."

"A marvelous idea, thank you!" Danglars said. He rose from his chair to leave, but paused when the count raised his hand.

"Before you go, I fear I must make a request," the count said. "The friend I mentioned, Abbe Busoni, visited today as a surprise. I felt obligated to repay him some money while I had the opportunity."

"Oh?" Danglars said.

"If I may impose, since you are my banker, do you have any francs on you at the moment?" the count asked. "My payment to Busoni has left me without a single banknote on hand. You'll be repaid from my credit with Thomson & French, of course."

"Er, well," Danglars said, thinking of the thousand francs he carried with him for pocket-money.

Parting with even that small sum was painful, but he didn't dare refuse. If word spread that the head of the Danglars Bank hesitated to pay a customer, it could spark a run on the bank as account-holders rushed to withdraw their own funds before a calamity struck. Ironically, that would provoke that very calamity due to the same reserve requirements Danglars himself had loosened; the loosening meant there was not enough money or gold in the bank's vault to cover every

442 | J. TREVOR ROBINSON

withdrawal. Suppressing a sigh, he handed Monte Cristo the money before returning to his carriage.

After Danglars left, the count rang for Bertuccio.

"What did you find?" the count asked.

"She went to the Palais, then returned home without stopping," Bertuccio said.

"Good. I have a new task for you: make sure my other house in Normandy is ready," the count said. "The Morcerfs have gone to the seaside, and a similar whim may strike me soon."

Happy to go anywhere but Auteuil, Bertuccio bowed and exited. Alone again, Monte Cristo stripped off his gloves and stretched his bandaged fingers.

"You condemned me to darkness for fourteen years, Fernand," the count muttered. "Let's see how you like Danglars dragging your secrets into the light."

CHAPTER 69
AT THE OFFICE OF THE
KING'S ATTORNEY

While Danglars schemed to auction Eugenie to the Cavalcantis, Hermine left to keep an appointment . She took her carriage to the Passage du Pont-Neuf, then walked to the Rue Guenegaud where she donned a thick black veil. She called a cab from there to the Rue de Harlay, and at last her roundabout route brought her to the Palais de Justice.

It was Sunday, and hardly a soul was to be found at the Palais. Only the most devoted lawyers had arrived to build cases against men and women afoul of the law, and only the most desperate people visited to try and secure help from the prosecutors.

Villefort's secretary, Mariane, recognized the veiled woman as the crucial—and only—appointment on his calendar for the day. Villefort sat writing in an armchair by the cold fireplace with his back to the door when Mariane showed Hermine in, and didn't move until Mariane excused herself.

He sprang to his feet once the door closed, drew all the blinds, and bolted the door. Hermine pretended for a moment that Villefort's sallow complexion was only the result of the lamplight, and remembered how handsome he had been before the assassination attempt. After that awful night, his jaundice had crept in and grown for years until attaining his present colouring of rancid butter.

"Thank you for your punctuality, madame. We haven't spoken privately in too long, and I regret that it happens now under such painful circumstances," Villefort said, holding her gaze just a moment too long before drawing out a chair.

The two former lovers stared at each other across the expanse of Villefort's desk, then he coughed and averted his eyes.

"Our past misdeeds left some indelible stains on the world," Villefort said. "Somehow, the Count of Monte Cristo has found what we hoped would remain hidden until our dying days."

"Don't call them misdeeds, Gerard," Hermine said. "Our time together was illicit, but I don't regret it, except for..."

"Except for our son; he was the dark mark of our affair," Villefort said. He did not add that the night of their son's birth was one of the many blows which had gradually pummeled his heart to stone.

"His birth, and his death, and the assault on your life all in one night. It's almost too horrible to bear thinking about," Hermine said. "The bones of our son, exhumed by some common ditch-digger, all while that dreadful Caillat man stumbles towards revealing it all in the press."

"I have men combing the country to find Jordan Caillat and silence him," Villefort said. He took a deep breath. "Madame, there is more about that night which I never told you. Understand, you were in such a state that I feared the truth would be the death of you. Hermine, the count lied to us."

"What do you mean, Gerard?" Hermine asked.

"The boy was born half-dead with his cord wrapped around his neck. Rather than question God's will, we wrapped him in your handkerchief and put him in a box, and I took him out to the garden for burial," Villefort said. "That is when that damned Corsican from Nimes leapt from the bushes and tried to kill me."

"Yes, you told me that. It was coated with that dreadful poison which marked you for life," Hermine said.

"The poison, yes." Villefort glanced down at his desk for a moment. "Only the barest chance spared me, the medical fluke that causes my heart to beat on the right side rather than the left. His blade missed his target, and I survived to watch his next actions."

Villefort had never told any living soul about that night, but he told Hermine there in his office. After he fell on the very spot the box was buried, the Corsican shoved him aside. Villefort didn't dare move for fear of alerting the Corsican the job remained unfinished, in case the assassin cut his throat to be certain. The Corsican dug up the box, filled the hole back in, and escaped with his loot.

"He must have thought he could sell the contents," Villefort said.

"Corsicans are small-minded people, obsessed with money. It's why so many become smugglers and criminals."

"I don't understand," Hermine said. "If the Corsican stole our son's coffin, then what did the count's landscaper find?"

"He can't have found anything. I returned to the house months later to erase any evidence of our having been there and dug up half the garden looking for the box," Villefort said. "I thought perhaps that when the Corsican discovered what he had stolen, he would have the decency to return and re-inter the child. But there was nothing."

Hermine blanched and fanned herself. The room had grown stuffy past the point she could bear.

"The box was nowhere in the garden, or in the street, or anywhere in Auteuil. I searched until I feared and half-hoped that I would go mad," Villefort said. "Unless someone buried another stillbirth there after I left, then Monte Cristo lied about ever finding the box. And..."

"And what?" Hermine asked, her wide white eyes visible through the veil she wore.

"And think, Hermine. Why would a man keep an infant's corpse rather than bringing it to a magistrate? The Corsican thought I was dead, but they are a spiteful people; he could have left the box anonymously at the courts and implicated you in the child's premature burial," Villefort said. Hermine uttered a piercing cry when she realized his meaning.

"Then the boy didn't die. Your assassin saved him, and our son may be out there somewhere, alive and well!" Hermine said. She paced the room, throwing her veil aside and tugging at her hair. "We gave up on him too soon, too soon! We're monsters, Gerard! God forgive us, we abandoned our flesh and blood to suffocate in a box!"

Villefort weathered this silently; though a new revelation to her, he had chastised himself for decades with the same words. He knew she needed to grieve, but he also feared that she missed an important point.

"Hermine," Villefort said, "you need to focus. His birth is the past; his continued existence is what we need to concern ourselves with. The Corsican knew who I was and had opportunity to learn your identity, too. He rescued our child, who may still be alive today. And he told someone this secret, or else it would never have reached the Count of Monte Cristo."

"Who cares about the Count of Monte Cristo?" Hermine wailed.

"You very well should!" Villefort said. "Why would the count tell us he found a box which cannot exist? He knows our secret and is using it to torment us. He may even know if our child is still alive and who or where he is; something I have never been able to learn despite my considerable resources."

"Why would he do such a thing?" Hermine asked.

"I don't know, but I do know that the man has no respect for civil society regardless of how well he imitates it," Villefort said. "A man who doesn't recognize the supreme authority of the crown is a man capable of anything. Have you observed the look in his eye when he speaks to us?"

"I try not to; his appearance is so fearsome," Hermine said. "Do you recall how little he ate at the dinner? Could he have poisoned us?"

"Impossible to say; we won't know until either something happens or nothing does," Villefort said. "I had been content to leave the count alone, thinking him a harmless nabob with ludicrous ideas. Now I see I must learn who he is, where he came from, and why he invites us to his house just to taunt us with our sin."

After Hermine departed, Villefort sat alone with his thoughts. Despite his promise, he had not told her the full truth of that fateful night in Auteuil.

When the Corsican left, Villefort had dragged himself back to the house, only daring to call for help once he was inside behind a locked door. A servant had answered him and stitched his wound in the kitchen, then asked Villefort if he needed anything else.

"They can help me," Villefort had muttered, half-dead and delirious. "The angels can help me. But they require their due. The tax of blood."

The servant had leaned in closer to hear him better, and Villefort lunged with the last of his strength. Clamping his jaws onto the servant's neck, he tore open the artery and filled his mouth with the copper flavour of fresh blood. Villefort called out in his mind to the archangel Raphael with every eager gulp, his energy returning and forging a stronger connection to the world of the living.

In the morning, there was no evidence to be found of this bizarre sacrifice. A heavy trunk concealed the body, destined for the king's kitchens. The spilled blood was explained as coming from Villefort's own wound, and Villefort told Hermine that the missing man had deserted them in the commotion of the birth and the attack.

Standing alone in his office, memories and stress collaborated to produce a splitting headache. Villefort knew only one remedy. He needed the grace of the archangels to sustain himself, and their price for such was blood. Ordinarily, an offering from his own flesh made with his folding knife would suffice. In this case, he needed not only relief, but also the wisdom to see why Monte Cristo toyed with him and the strength to punish the count for it. He needed a larger sacrifice, and he had an idea of who it should be.

The Palais de Justice stood on an island in the Seine, accessible by a series of bridges. One of those bridges lead to the unofficial slums of Paris. Villefort's informants told him that the inquisitive whore, a repeat offender named Marie Brouillard, worked her trade at a particular set of street corners; she would be easy to find, and easy prey to get alone.

Villefort dismissed his secretary and waited for darkness to fall. Only then did he unlock the bottom drawer of his desk with a key which hung from his neck. In a velvet-lined case sat an opera mask of fine white porcelain which covered his entire face except for his mouth and chin. He tightened the buckled strap around his head and put on a wide-brimmed hat and thick gloves before heading down a hidden back stair to the street. Villefort had ordered the secondary exit to be installed under utmost secrecy, and even his own secretary didn't know it existed.

The mask hid Villefort's face, and the shadow of the hat hid his mask. He kept a sharp watch for the whore as he made his way into the slums. When he found her, he caught her attention with a handful of banknotes.

For Marie, the evening's business had been slow so far. Any customer provided a welcome break from the monotony, even one dressed eccentrically. It wasn't so unusual for men to disguise themselves when they came to find a woman; many of them were high-ranking counts and barons who gave frequent speeches in the House denouncing prostitution and proclaiming it a sin.

Marie gave him a smile and led him by hand to a secluded alley she preferred. It couldn't be seen from the street, but the boarding-house where Marie lived overlooked it. Louise d'Armilly lived there as well, along with a host of other artists and working girls. The proximity to home made her feel safe in the alley.

She hiked up her skirt to give her customer the access he needed, but her mind was elsewhere. During the previous day's meeting of the Parisian Ladies' Vampire-Hunting Club, the girls had been thrilled when she told them all about what she'd learned so far. The new girl, Haydee, had been especially pleased to hear that her grisly rumours had at least some truth to them.

The man drew close to Marie, and she noticed his white mask for the first time. The touch of it against her neck as he sniffed and kissed her skin gave her a surprising chill she couldn't help but enjoy. It wasn't until he straightened up and faced her that she noticed the bright yellow of his exposed skin and the chill in his blue eyes.

Marie and Valentine had been friends long enough that, though Marie had never met M. de Villefort, she could recognize him from Valentine's description despite his mask. His breathing was heavy and his eyes were manic, and Marie thought it must be his first time visiting a prostitute. She remembered Valentine's mother had passed away long ago, and Villefort had never remarried or even courted another woman.

"You don't need to be shy, monsieur," she said. "I'll be gentle."

She offered M. de Villefort some more encouragement, but before she could say anything else, he forced all four fingers of his gloved hand into her mouth. Surprised, she bit down but her jaw only closed on thick padded leather. Marie's scream came out as only a muffled squeal. She thrashed and struggled, but Villefort had the advantage in size and strength and she accomplished nothing but knocking away his hat. For a fleeting moment, she thought of other girls who carried pistols in their bodices for this exact scenario.

"A tax of blood," Villefort whispered, more to himself than to her. "Michael, bring me strength. Gabriel, show me the way."

Before Marie could wonder what Villefort meant, he sank his teeth deep into her neck. Her frantic cries could not be heard through Villefort's glove as she felt the burning agony of the bite followed by rolling nausea as he sucked her blood out of the wound. Marie's struggles slowed as her limbs grew heavier and the alley grew darker. When he had drunk his fill, Villefort pushed the empty corpse into a pile of refuse.

Above this grim scene, on the third floor of Marie's boarding house, Louise d'Armilly sat sketching the view from her window. Eyes wide and too far away to recognize her friend, she flipped to a blank page to draw the grotesque white face of the man she had just seen murder an innocent woman.

CHAPTER 70
A WEEK IN EARLY JUNE

Villefort woke up the next morning with a renewed sense of purpose and the peace he needed to form a plan, thanks to the whore's blood. The one thing Villefort knew for certain about the Count of Monte Cristo was just that: the name of his county. The Italian government kept records of landed titles, and thus the count's true name. Once he knew that, there would be nowhere for M. de Monte Cristo to hide.

It didn't take Louise long to learn of Marie's fate when Marie didn't return home to the boarding house. She shrieked and became insensible when she realized whose murder she had witnessed. When she recovered herself, she ran all the way to the Rue de la Chaussee d'Antin to hammer on the door of the Danglars mansion. The servants, accustomed to seeing Louise, led her to Eugenie's rooms.

"Pigeon, what's the matter?" Eugenie said, her aloof mannerisms evaporating in privacy and the face of Louise's distress.

Louise threw herself into Eugenie's arms and sobbed. Eugenie could only stroke Louise's hair until she calmed down enough to speak.

"Marie is dead!" Louise said. "I saw it, I saw the whole thing!"

"Are you sure of what you saw?" Eugenie asked, cradling Louise's face and looking her straight in the eye. She made great efforts to hide her own shock for Louise's sake. "Could you be mistaken?"

"No, no, it was terrible. There was so much blood," Louise said, tears flowing again. "I was drawing at my window, and I saw Marie bring a man into the alley. You know how high up my window is, I didn't know it was her. I could have yelled, I could have stopped him..."

Again, Eugenie coaxed Louise back to a condition where she could continue speaking. Finally, Eugenie rang for a servant and resumed the imperious face everybody expected when they heard the name Eugenie Danglars. She commanded him to bring a bottle of brandy to steady Mlle. d'Armilly's nerves.

"Marie brought a man into the alley, and I thought he was just an ordinary customer," Louise said, holding the glass of brandy like a lifeline and staring past Eugenie. "I looked away to sharpen my pencil, and then he had his mouth on her neck. It all seemed normal, but then I noticed his hand was in her mouth."

"In her mouth?" Eugenie said, confused.

"Men have odd tastes sometimes, I thought he'd paid her to let him do that," Louise said. "But then he pulled away from her, and her throat was torn apart! He...he threw her into a trash heap like she was nothing, Eugenie. And when he turned..."

"What did you see?" Eugenie asked.

"He wore a dreadful white mask, shining like glass in the moonlight," Louise said. "The only part of his face that wasn't that awful glossy white was his mouth and chin, smeared with Marie's blood."

Eugenie took it upon herself to write to the rest of the Parisian Ladies' Vampire-Hunting Club to inform them of the tragedy, and that the next meeting would proceed as scheduled that coming Saturday.

Haydee received this letter on Tuesday. The count sat in his study finalizing the details of Baron Danglars' next financial calamity when the postman arrived. While his persona of Signor Dimonte invested in promising enterprises to multiply the fortune left behind by Cardinal Spada, the documents on his desk would establish a business venture doomed to fail: a riverboat ferry company in Upper Canada, whose only route was a river which would soon be dried up by a government dam.

Danglars would receive a tip about the ferry company, while the count blocked him in secret from learning about the plan to dam the river. Desperate for a lucrative investment, the count estimated that Danglars would commit at least half a million to it. When the dam was built, the ferry would lose every franc. Monte Cristo would lose a substantial sum as well, but his fortune could sustain the loss while it crippled Danglars even further.

In another room, Baptistan brought Haydee the morning's letters. Rustling papers, inaudible to anyone else, reached his ears. His sharpened hearing from Edmond Dantes' long years in a dark cell was not required to detect Haydee's cry of alarm. She burst into the room, flushed with anger, even as her eyes filled with tears.

"He killed her!" she cried. "Villefort, he killed Marie!"

Monte Cristo rushed to put his arm around Haydee's shoulder and read the letter himself. Eugenie hadn't held back when she wrote her letter, sharing every detail of Louise's account.

"This is my fault," Haydee said. "It can't be coincidence that she died after I nudged her to investigate the rumours."

The count glowered and crumpled the letter in his fist. He knew about Villefort killing before; the twin influences of gold and the red glow in Monte Cristo's eyes granted him access to records across France. Those records revealed dozens of murder investigations covered up by Villefort over the years, all following the same pattern of exsanguination. Each murder had occurred during Edmond's incarceration, or while the count gathered the information he needed to destroy Villefort. The count had no involvement in them, and no way to prevent them.

Marie's murder, on the other hand, was a direct casualty of his plan being put into action. By telling the Club about the vampiric murders, he intended to prompt them into spreading gossip to undermine Villefort in the public eye over time, as a small facet of the larger plan. The count recognized that somewhere he had made a miscalculation, one which had gotten Marie killed. How would Edmond Dantes have felt about this collateral damage? The count only felt outrage and a deep urge to somehow correct Villefort's injustice.

"We clearly can't encourage the Club to do any more," he said, holding Haydee as her silent tears dampened his linen shirt. "Don't blame yourself for Villefort's actions. We'll make sure he pays for what he's done."

Haydee retired to her room and a mournful melody soon filled the house. Monte Cristo returned to his desk, sealed up the ferry company documents to be sent out, and picked up a fresh piece of paper.

At the top of the page he wrote "Who killed Marie Brouillard?" Underneath, he retold the murder with enough salacious speculation to guarantee the Nightly Assemblage couldn't resist printing it. At the bottom he signed it as Jordan Caillat.

On Wednesday afternoon, Mercedes and Albert returned from their seaside retreat at Cannes to find the entire city talking about Marie's gruesome death. Fernand returned later, having taken a detour to Marseille; the Catalan community wanted to honour him and his accomplishments with a banquet, which he couldn't refuse. Mercedes refused to set foot in Marseille, insisting that she needed to get back to Paris, and Albert offered to accompany her.

Fernand tried for several days to reach out to Danglars to meet regarding Albert and Eugenie's upcoming wedding, but they couldn't settle on a date. Danglars was determined to avoid Fernand until his agents in Greece reported back to him

The Parisian Ladies' Vampire-Hunting Club met again on Saturday, under a sombre atmosphere. Louise was a sensitive soul and cried at a moment's notice over Marie. Valentine kept catching herself watching the door, waiting for Marie to enter and tell them what a comical misunderstanding it all was. Haydee pleaded with the other girls not to pursue the vampire rumours anymore; it was a silly whim that ended in disaster, and they should all go back to reading their horror stories and playing the piano.

"No. When you first came to this Club, you asked me what I'd do if a real vampire came to Paris. I said I would kill it," Eugenie said, standing up straight. She reached into her shawl and took out one of the sharp wooden stakes they had made the week before. "Whether Marie's killer is a real vampire or a mortal man with unholy appetites, it's clear what we have to do."

"Eugenie, Haydee's right," Valentine said. "Marie only asked questions, and this vampire killed her for it. What would he do if he found out we were actually trying to hunt him?"

"He won't find out. Because we're going to be careful," Eugenie said. "We just need to figure out how."

Mercedes knew nothing of the Club's mourning, but she felt a darkness gathering over the city of Paris. She couldn't identify the source of it, but her unease couldn't be shaken. In order to feel like she was taking some action about it, she reached a decision: in a week's time, to lighten everyone's spirits, she would host a ball.

CHAPTER 71
THE BALL

June 16, the day of the ball, proved to be the warmest day yet in the summer of 1838. The guests at the Morcerf estate represented a class of their own within French society; as the saying goes, anyone who remains in Paris during the summer is a die-hard Parisian.

Regardless of why they remained in Paris, they shared a single reason for attending the ball. The Count de Morcerf's company was nowhere near as attractive as the promise of Mercedes' hospitality and the decorating ideas they could borrow for themselves.

The ground floor of the main house thrummed with the rhythm of the waltz. Busy servants put the finishing touches on the garden on Mercedes' orders: coloured lamps and wax lights, creating an enchanted scene worthy of Oberon's court. Keeping with custom at the time, the garden remained off-limits until Mercedes herself proceeded there as the lady of the house.

Albert stood at the door greeting guests. Hermine put on a brave face when she extended her hand to him after descending from her carriage. She hadn't wanted to come, but heeded Villefort's suggestion to maintain appearances.

"Baroness, you look as lovely as ever," Albert said. "Your charming daughter arrived not long ago, and if I didn't know better I would swear you were sisters."

"You do have a gilded tongue, Albert," Hermine said, forcing a chuckle. "Where is my daughter?"

"Over there, speaking to Valentine de Villefort," Albert said.

Eugenie and Valentine stood in heated conversation, though Hermine couldn't guess their topic. When Hermine opened her mouth again, Albert held up a finger.

"Before you speak, I'll guess your next two questions," Albert said. "You were going to ask if the Count of Monte Cristo was invited, and next you would ask when he will arrive. Am I right?"

"How did you guess?" she said, glad her makeup hid her sudden flush.

"Because you're the seventeenth person to ask me those same two questions," Albert said with a laugh. "The first answer is that he was invited, although he only accepted when I told him my mother insisted. The second answer is that I can't predict his arrival any better than I can predict the weather a hundred years from now."

Hermine forced herself to laugh along with him.

"And for your third question, I don't expect his lovely Greek Haydee to come," Albert said. "His companion, as he calls her, is a free spirit. Speaking of spirit, I see the most courageous spirit I know coming up the path. Max, hello!"

Captain Maximilien Morrel approached in his dress uniform, his shoulders squared and determination in his eyes. He shook Albert's hand and bowed to Hermine, who returned a shallow curtsy.

Max caught Valentine's eye across the room. When his scan of the ball didn't reveal Villefort himself, he met Valentine's gaze again. A grin growing on his face, he walked past Albert without another word.

"Good to see you too, Max," Albert said. "Ah, there's the man of the hour now!"

Without noticing the look on Hermine's face, Albert walked down the path to meet the Count of Monte Cristo. As usual, the count smiled and made the briefest contact with Albert's hand.

"Count, so good to see you. It's a shame Franz couldn't be here; he arrived in Paris this morning, but he's weary from travel. I imagine he's asleep at his aunt's house right now," Albert said.

When the count stepped into the ballroom, all conversation stopped. Those who had met him waited with excitement to see what he would do, while those who had only heard about his behaviour and riches gawked at his appearance. His red eyes took in the room with a bored expression, until they locked upon Mercedes. The moment spun out into eternity before he gave her a respectful bow.

Meanwhile the Count de Morcerf engaged in animated

conversation with three men: one so frail and grey that a strong wind might destroy him, one in a blue coat with mismatched green piping, and the third wearing canary yellow on a rather rotund frame. Albert pointed them out in turn.

"First, that dry old stick discovered a new kind of salamander which breathes fire a single degree hotter than any other species. The discovery earned him a knighthood," Albert said.

"If he finds another degree, will they make him a baron?" Monte Cristo asked.

"Then there's that fashion victim," Albert continued, pointing at the second man. "Every year, he publishes a new study that mankind is a blight on the planet and everything we do is evil. He's awful to talk to but highly-regarded at the French Academy for his highly progressive thinking."

"Who knew that the Academy offered doctorates for hopelessness," Monte Cristo said. "With such a low opinion of his fellow man, one would expect him to start slaughtering them en masse for the greater good. That, or throw himself into the Seine with a cannonball tied to his feet."

"Lastly, the walking lemon there is a back-bencher in the House who's voted with the government five or six times and is almost always involved in some lawsuit or another," Albert said.

"Doing great honour to the peerage, I see," Monte Cristo said. "Do me a favour Albert, and don't introduce me to any of these men. If they ask for introductions to me, warn me so that I may run."

Albert guffawed, and Baron Danglars appeared at their shoulders.

"Have I missed a joke?" Danglars asked, wine in hand.

"Three of them, Baron Danglars," Monte Cristo said. "They're all over there, speaking to Morcerf."

"Please, you don't need to use my title. You know that as a representative of the common man, I prefer not to use it," Danglars said. He rubbed his sleeve against the diamond pin in his lapel to polish it.

"Indeed, but there's no title to go with your status as a millionaire," Monte Cristo said. "Besides, one is a baron for life while no such guarantee can be made for millionaires. Just think of Frank & Poulmann in Frankfurt, who went bankrupt yesterday."

"Bankrupt?" Danglars' mouth fell open. "That can't be, I had two hundred thousand deposited with them!"

"I'm sorry, that must be a heavy blow," Monte Cristo said, holding a hand to his breast. Frank & Poulmann had sold all of their assets to him in secret a month ago. The count had paid every other customer their account balance, given the employees a generous severance, and destroyed the firm all to hurt Danglars. "If I'd known, I would have been more delicate on the matter."

"Certainly don't speak of it so near to Viscount Cavalcanti," Danglars said.

Andrea scandalized some society ladies with a bawdy joke a few yards away. Danglars left to talk to him, and Albert excused himself to find Mercedes. He found her on an upper balcony watching the ballroom below. She embraced her son, then pointed down over the rail.

"Albert, have you noticed that the Count of Monte Cristo has eaten nothing?" Mercedes asked.

Waiters circulated with trays of fruit and flavoured ice, which most of the sweating occupants partook of with relish. Monte Cristo didn't sample any food or drink and also appeared to be dry of perspiration.

"Do you think he has a reason for not eating under our roof?" Albert said. "Don't forget that he ate breakfast at my apartments when he first arrived."

"Sharing your food is quite different than sharing your father's and mine," Mercedes muttered. "Why did you return? What is your intent? Are you even who I think you are, or am I mad?"

"Maybe he's just affected by the air in here; it's getting rather stifling," Albert said, not hearing her musings.

Mercedes nodded and went to find Morcerf.

"My dear, I fear our guests are wilting in this heat. The garden is ready, and I think I'll open it," Mercedes said to Morcerf.

"A capital idea!" Morcerf declared, having had a fair amount of wine already. "Lead the way, my love!"

Mercedes approached the Count of Monte Cristo. "Would the man who saved my son honour me with his arm as we go outside?"

Monte Cristo's eyes widened, giving Mercedes a look of such intensity she wished she could read the meaning behind his crimson gaze. He offered his arm without a word, and Mercedes laid a gentle hand on it as they proceeded through the garden door. The cold muscle beneath his sleeve felt like stone.

The other guests let out a cheer and hurried outdoors, filling their hungry lungs with crisp and clean night air.

CHAPTER 72
BREAD AND SALT

L eaving the party behind them, Mercedes led the count through an archway of trees toward the family greenhouse. Her hand trembled against his arm.

"Are you cold, madame? I've lived in so many extreme climates that temperature has no hold on me, but you lack even a scarf," Monte Cristo said.

Mercedes didn't answer him. In the greenhouse they stood surrounded by all manner of magnificent fruits and vegetables, ripened by the heat trapped within the glass. She reached into a vine and gathered a handful of white grapes.

"I'm certain you've had better in Sicily and Cyprus, but our French grapes do the best they can with unreliable sun. Please, try some," Mercedes said, holding the bunch out to Monte Cristo.

"I must refuse," Monte Cristo said. He held up a gloved hand. "Don't think me rude, madame. I never eat muscat grapes, they give me indigestion."

"I see," Mercedes said, letting the grapes fall to the sand beneath their feet. She selected a replacement from a nearby tree. "Try this peach, then."

Again the count held up a hand, the fine lines of his face emotionless, but he offered no explanation and the peach joined the grapes on the sand. Mercedes and Monte Cristo stared at each other in silence.

"Count, you pain me," Mercedes said, stifling a sob and brushing away tears. "I've heard of a beautiful custom in Arabia, surely you have too, which promises eternal friendship to a guest and host who share bread and salt."

"I know the custom," Monte Cristo said. "But we are in France, where neither bread and salt nor eternal friendship are observed."

"Then we're not friends?" Mercedes asked.

"Oh, shut up!" said an unfamiliar voice. "If I have to listen to any more of this, I'll turn this on myself."

A man stepped out from the wide leaves of an exotic plant, with a pistol aimed halfway between Monte Cristo and Mercedes. Clean-shaven with stringy red hair, he wore dirty clothes and a makeshift black mask. In his other hand he held a burlap sack.

"I'm sure you can guess where this is going," the man said. "Valuables in the bag, and nobody has to get hurt."

"I think you're mistaken," the count said in a tone that frightened Mercedes worse than the weapon. He moved between her and the robber, facing away from her. "I think you don't want to do this at all."

"What?" the man asked, but his pistol moved upward of its own accord. In the glass behind him, Mercedes could see twin pinpoints of red light reflected against the darkness outside.

"Your first plan sounded better," the count said. "Turn the pistol on yourself."

With terror in his eyes, the robber craned his neck forward to rest his chin on the end of his pistol. He bent his arm to point the weapon on an angle back through his own head.

"Stop!" Mercedes cried. "Stop, Edmond, spare him!"

The count jerked as if stabbed in the heart. For a terrible moment, nothing else happened. The robber made the first move, dropping his pistol and the burlap bag. He backed away silently, opened the rear door to the greenhouse, and waited. The count clapped his hands once and the man sprinted away into the darkness.

Mercedes kept a close eye on the count as he turned around, but his expression gave nothing away, and the points of red light in his eyes were nowhere to be seen.

"Edmond, what happened to you?" she asked.

The count considered his answer before replying.

"Whoever you think I am, you're mistaken. If I ever knew a man named Edmond, he left my company long ago," the count said. "I have seen much, travelled far, and suffered deeply; I have lost many people along the way."

Mercedes closed her eyes in pain. "Are you happy, at least?"

"Nobody hears me complain," the count said.

"I've heard that you attend the opera with a woman. Is she your wife?" Mercedes asked.

"No. She has nobody else in the world and neither do I. We are companions, for lack of a better word," the count replied. "Today we travel together; tomorrow we may not."

"Then you have nobody to keep you anchored to life?" she said.

"Not by choice," Monte Cristo said. His strange gaze locked on hers with a fearsome intensity, but she felt no danger in it. "As a young man, far from here, I loved a girl intensely and we were going to marry. Fate separated us before we could wed, and when I came back, she had married another man."

"I see," Mercedes said. Her legs shook so forcefully her entire body vibrated. "This woman made you suffer, surely. But can you find it in your heart to forgive her? She may have thought you were dead, or gone forever."

"My heart has no part in it anymore," Monte Cristo said, "but yes, she has been forgiven."

"And what about those who played a part in separating you?" Mercedes said, remembering a skinny Catalan fisherman and his deep jealousy of Edmond Dantes. She retrieved the bundle of grapes from the ground and held them out again. "Would you take bread and salt in their homes, if you could?"

Monte Cristo held up his hand. "Excuse me, madame. I never eat muscat grapes, they don't agree with me," he said again.

The grapes fell to the ground once more as Mercedes realized the futility of changing the count's mind. Before they could speak any further, four gendarmes burst into the greenhouse, led by a magistrate wearing his official scarf.

"Gentlemen, if you're looking for a robber, he just left," the count said. "He left his sack and pistol over there."

"Be quiet," the magistrate said. "Count Gianmarco Zaccone of Monte Cristo, you are under arrest. Will you come peacefully or under duress?"

"Well, how novel," the count said, curious to see where this led. "It appears that I am to be kidnapped."

"Not kidnapped; arrested," the magistrate said.

"I fail to see a meaningful distinction," the count replied. "But very well, I'll come along for now. Lead the way."

A look of puzzlement crossed the magistrate's face. He had arrested many people in his career, but never one who went along so casually. The count seemed to think he could leave whenever it suited him. The magistrate took the lead, followed by two gendarmes in front of the count and two behind.

As they left the greenhouse, Mercedes noticed that a single grape lay crushed in the sand. She couldn't say whether the count or the gendarmes had crushed it.

CHAPTER 73
THE INTERROGATION

Monte Cristo allowed the magistrate to escort him to a carriage like the one that took Edmond Dantes away so long ago. As they passed beneath the shadow of an overhanging tree, he decided against stepping into the shadow and travelling elsewhere through the darkness. Such a public display would ruin the plan and could only be used as a last resort.

They led the count to a small room deep within the Palais de Justice, with two chairs and a desk as the only furniture. Villefort already sat in the chair facing the door, his fingers steepled.

"Take a seat, Signor Zaccone," Villefort said.

"How could I refuse such a polite request?" the count said.

Without rushing, the count sat in the remaining chair with his own fingers steepled, mimicking Villefort's posture and avoiding touching his wrists to the arms of the chair. Villefort's frown deepened.

"Please, get more comfortable," Villefort said.

"I would be more comfortable at home," the count said. "But I can guess your meaning."

The count laid one deliberate hand on the arm of the chair, where an iron manacle sprang out to lock him in place. Without breaking eye contact with Villefort, Monte Cristo did the same with his other arm.

Villefort nodded and the gendarmes at the door brought in a familiar apparatus on wheels. In a few moments the arched metal frame sat in place above the count's chair. They adjusted the twin aquamarine crystals with their dagger points to the sides of the count's head, and placed the colourless indicator crystal on the desk in front of Villefort.

"We must calibrate the device," Villefort said. "Tell me a truthful statement."

"I've seen these devices before; interesting that the design has changed so little," the count said.

"There is no need to change what works," Villefort said, watching the crystal. It remained colourless and lightless. "Another true statement."

"Is the machine broken?" the count said with a smile. "I thought your crystal there was supposed to glow."

Villefort growled and waved for the apparatus to be taken away again. The gendarmes remained in the room to witness the remainder of the questioning, as Villefort took a deep breath to calm himself.

"Signor Gianmarco Zaccone," he said. "Born in Malta, raised in Syracuse. No criminal record, left Italy as a young man to fight the English in India."

"Really, M. de Villefort, I'm impressed," the count said. "I never tell anyone but my very closest friends about my upbringing, and you've managed to learn this on your own?"

"Even you can't hide from the building blocks of society: paperwork and bureaucracy," Villefort said. "Your title is registered to your real name, which led me to your birth records and military service."

"You've gone to a great deal of effort just to learn my name," the count said. "So why am I here?"

"Where did you go after the war in India?" Villefort asked.

"To the galleys," Monte Cristo said. "I was taken prisoner, endured for a time, then escaped by jumping into the water."

"And then?" Villefort said.

"Then I travelled," Monte Cristo said. "My family fortune was locked away in a trust, so I had to earn a living. If you'd like an account of every journey, we'll be here some time."

It took considerable effort for Villefort to maintain his composure. His search for information in Italy had returned very little beyond what he had already confronted the count with. In Zaccone's paper trail, a maddening gap of decades existed between leaving for India and taking ownership of some silver mines, his island, and his title.

Villefort's interrogation relied on the count reacting to his usual techniques like anyone else. When someone thinks the law already knows everything, they are more likely to offer up additional information in a desperate bid to save themselves. The count, however, seemed unperturbed and even disinterested in the proceedings.

Villefort found himself in a bind. With his tactics failing, he had only one secret in reserve: that he knew the count never found any infant beneath the garden in Auteuil. Villefort couldn't give up that leverage yet, reasoning that it may still prove useful.

"Are you now, or have you ever been, a Bonapartist?" Villefort asked at last.

"A Bonapartist, in 1838? How droll. I thought I was very clear about my politics, M. de Villefort: I have no more love for Napoleon than for any other man who uses force against peaceful people," the count said. "Of course, I'm thankful that he ended the Dead Plague. But beyond that, he was not meaningfully different from your king or any other."

"What would you know about the Dead Plague?" Villefort half-shouted, a nervous panic overtaking him for a moment.

"Nothing more than anyone else," the count said, surprised by the outburst.

Villefort steadied himself once more, running a yellow hand through his hair. "One more question, Signor Zaccone. What is your connection to Jordan Caillat?"

Monte Cristo grasped the point of the interview at last. His articles as Caillat were having the desired effect of disrupting Villefort's thoughts and undermining his reputation. Villefort must have reached the conclusion, due possibly to Auteuil, that the count and Caillat were somehow connected with one another. That conclusion led him to uncover Zaccone's paper trail, every word of which a fiction the count purchased with simple gold.

For a moment, the count considered using his compelling gaze to make Villefort tell him what he knew or suspected. The gendarmes in the room complicated that notion; if they noticed the link while the count devoted his attention to Villefort, he risked exposure.

"I've heard the name somewhere, but never met the man," the count said. "M. de Villefort, am I being charged with anything?"

Villefort released a slow exhale through his nose. He could have the count locked in a cell and forgotten, quietly removed from society as many others had been. It would, however, be the first time he did so with a person of influence and means. Putting a commoner into an oubliette was a trivial matter, but doing so to someone with money and a title would be another matter entirely.

If the count went missing, his servants and his Greek companion would notice. They could appeal to the Italian government and spark a diplomatic incident. The international scandal which would erupt from an Italian count disappearing in Paris chilled Villefort's blood. He could not possibly stifle or hide an investigation of that scale.

The count could guess what occupied Villefort's thoughts, even without his abilities. He remembered the outcome when Edmond Dantes sat down in a similar chair for a discussion with Villefort. If such a thing happened again, Villefort would find it quite difficult to keep the Count of Monte Cristo confined to a cell.

"There are no charges, Signor Zaccone," Villefort said, pressing a button to release the manacles. "You are free to go."

Monte Cristo rose, gave a deep bow, and exited the Palais de Justice to leave Villefort stewing in his frustration. Two days later, Villefort saw an infuriating new article by Jordan Caillat in the Nightly Assemblage.

Claiming an anonymous source within the Palais de Justice, Caillat accused Villefort of abusing his power to harass and interrogate a foreign national without cause. At the end of the piece, Caillat spent a paragraph in open speculation about whether this behaviour had anything to do with the incident in Auteuil in 1817.

"We know that M. de Villefort was married, in Auteuil with a woman who was certainly not his wife, and in the house when Gaston Piaget went missing," Villefort read aloud to his empty study. "What else could this man be hiding from us? Perhaps his mystery mistress has answers."

Villefort ground his teeth as he tore the newspaper to shreds, then reached for his penknife and rolled up his sleeve. He needed blood.

CHAPTER 74
LOVE AND WAR

The remainder of the week passed quietly. Wednesday's edition of the Nightly Assemblage brought yet another Jordan Caillat article to the public, titled "Who killed Jeremy Daucourt?" Like his previous pieces about Marie Brouillard and Pascal Verley, Caillat gave extraordinary detail about the crime scene and the curious exsanguination of Daucourt's body.

This time, Caillat raised the explicit question of how so many similar murders could go uninvestigated. To Villefort's horror, journalists from more reputable papers started to congregate outside the doors of the Palais de Justice, hurling questions at him every time he entered or left the building. Even worse, they asked him about details which could only have come from police documents he thought he had suppressed long ago.

The Count of Monte Cristo spent early Friday evening penning the next Caillat article about Lambert Jacquier, the son of a Bonapartist senator killed several years ago. Jacquier's father was killed in the Royal Inquisition which followed the Hundred Days, and Jacquier was in the midst of writing a book about the terror when he disappeared. Authorities found Jacquier's drained body in an alley off the Rue Pecquay, and the investigation stopped cold two days later.

A knock at the study door interrupted the count's writing. Baptistan entered, bringing the count's gloves and mask on a silver tray.

"Master, the Baron Chateau-Renaud and Captain Morrel have arrived without an appointment," Baptistan said. "Shall this one admit them?"

"Yes, send them into the parlour," Monte Cristo said, donning his gloves and covering the bandages which wrapped his true face. "I'll be there as soon as I'm properly dressed."

When Monte Cristo entered the parlour, mask fastened in place, he found Raoul pacing by the sideboard and Max half-sprawled across the settee.

"The count! Raoul, it's the Count of Montenegro!" Max said. If the smell of cheap wine wasn't sufficient evidence, his slurred speech made his present state clear.

"I found him about to start a fistfight with a gendarme," Raoul said. "It's a lucky thing I passed by when I did, or he'd be in a cell by now. He insisted on coming here."

"It's alright, Raoul," the count said. "Max, isn't it rather early to be drinking alone?"

"No no, it's fine. I wasn't alone," Max said. "Hugo was with me. We were talking about Franz."

Monte Cristo looked at Raoul, who raised an eyebrow.

"Do you mean Hugo Duval?" Raoul asked. "Max, Hugo died eight months ago. You were there."

"Yes, but sometimes he comes back," Max said. With difficulty, he pointed to his eye. "I can see him. Not now. But sometimes."

"Who was Hugo Duval?" Monte Cristo asked.

"He was in our unit in Algeria," Raoul said, keeping a careful eye on Max. "Young fellow, only about sixteen. During the siege of Constantine, he was badly wounded. Died in the medical tent nearly two days later."

"And Max was on duty, I take it?" the count asked.

The count could imagine the scene. An idealistic young man like Max, watching a friend who was little more than a boy die under his watch; that explained a great deal. It reminded the count of a young man he once knew who withstood a great trauma and suffered alone for years, before someone came along to share his pain.

"It's alright Raoul, I can take care of this," the count said.

"Are you certain?" Raoul asked. "I can stay if you need me. Franz is expecting me at the Villefort house, but he'll understand."

"No, go keep your appointment. Max and I will stay here and talk," the count said.

Raoul left, and the count sat in an armchair facing Max and considering his next words.

"Have I ever told you that I've been a prisoner?" he said at last.

"Prison? You?" Max said. "Impossible!"

"Possible and true," the count said, preparing a careful blend of truth and fiction. "I was captured at the outbreak of a war and thrown into a deep dungeon. There I had a cellmate who had lived alone in the dark for six years without even knowing his crime."

"How horrible," Max said, running his finger against the embroidered upholstery of the settee.

"My cellmate had lost everything; his wife, his family, his livelihood, and his freedom," the count continued. "He was on the verge of giving up before the turnkey brought us together and had actually begun starving himself. He saw death as the only escape available to him."

Max stopped fidgeting and listened to the count with rapt attention.

"Somehow, my presence helped him recover a sense of himself. He took comfort in telling me about his life, and asking about mine; there is a power in human companionship that makes trauma easier to bear, I think," the count said.

Monte Cristo dipped into Edmond's memories and retrieved the simple wonder of the first time he heard Faria's voice through the wall. It became a sort of rebirth for Edmond, having someone to share the pain of imprisonment and happy memories of the outside world. His rebirth in the cave under Monte Cristo had been a more harrowing experience. The agony of transformation had been a special kind of hell, and a pure and burning hatred for his enemies was the life raft Edmond had clung to while being mummified. In many ways, what walked out of that cave had been a raw and newborn thing.

"When I found freedom, my new life was difficult to adjust to," the count said. "I had entered that cell as one person and left it as an entirely different man."

"Yes, exactly!" Max blurted, sitting upright. "It's like there was a Maximilien Morrel who lived in my body up until October of last year, and then he died, and I've been living in his place ever since."

"Precisely," the count said, surprised that in the eloquence of drink Max found almost the exact words to describe his own relationship to the memory of Edmond Dantes. "It took me five years to come to terms with that feeling."

The count had drifted through the world for those first few years of undeath as more of a ghost than a mummy, laying the groundwork for his plan without feeling or experiencing the world around him. Then his work had brought him to Turkey. The count went there to find a witness to Fernand's crimes and a pawn in his plan, and instead found a damaged but still vibrant young woman. The captivity she had endured spoke to his own, and together they had brought each other closer to the land of the living.

"Like my former cellmate, I found it helpful to confide in someone. For me, that someone was Haydee," the count said. An echo of Edmond Dantes' deep love for the Morrel family passed through him like a breeze. "If you need someone to talk to, when you're ready to talk, my door is always open to you."

Max sat in silence for several long minutes. To relieve some of the tension, the count rang for a servant to bring bread and cheese to help Max sober up. When Max spoke, the words came in a slow drip.

"Hugo was a new recruit," Max said. "Just like me, it was his first tour of duty. He was so proud to serve his country and so happy to see the world outside France. He told me once that he'd never left Vouvant before."

The count nodded. So far, Hugo reminded him of any number of new sailors from the Pharaon.

"Hugo was wounded in an explosion while we sieged Constantine," Max said. "I had the bleeding controlled in the infirmary, but he was in bad shape. His face... He asked for a mirror, but I knew better than to give him one."

Unwilling to speak and break Max's momentum, Monte Cristo nodded as Max caught his breath.

"I'd been awake and tending to the wounded for three days straight," Max said. "I thought Hugo was alright; I thought they were all alright. Other medics came on shift and mine ended. I went to sleep. Hugo died when a blood clot came loose from his leg and got trapped in his heart."

"Were you close with Hugo?" Monte Cristo asked.

"The strange thing is, no," Max said. "Until he came to the

infirmary, we hardly spoke to each other. I can't think of why it's Hugo, out of all the men we lost, who keeps coming back."

A sort of curtain came down behind Max's eyes. It was a sensation the count knew well, having felt that same curtain descend when he spent too much time in the company of Danglars or Villefort, or even Albert de Morcerf.

"I thought serving my country would be noble," Max said, staring at nothing in particular. "It seems like such a strange notion now. It's wrong to kill a man in the street, but if the king tells you to go kill a man over a thousand miles away, it becomes virtuous."

Seeing that thoughts of war were having a toll on Max, Monte Cristo decided to change the subject.

"You mentioned Franz earlier," the count said, taking a piece of bread with a small lump of cheese. "Did you mean Franz d'Epinay?"

"I mentioned Franz?" Max said, his eyes wide. "I shouldn't—well you see—you've heard he's back in France, yes?"

"Yes, he arrived around the time of Countess Morcerf's ball," the count said. "I should make a point of visiting him and congratulating him on his coming wedding."

"The wedding is exactly the problem," Max said. "He's engaged to Valentine de Villefort, and I couldn't think of how to stop the wedding. Now it's the day of the contract signing, and it's too late."

"Why on earth would you want to stop Franz's wedding?" Monte Cristo said.

"Because, may she forgive me for telling you," Max said, "Valentine and I are in love. We have been ever since we met a year and a half ago."

Max told the count everything; the words spilled out freely. It had been February of 1837, and Max had gone to L'Epicure with a group of other recruits from his combat medicine course at Saint-Bertrand. His friends ordered much-needed coffee at the counter at the end of a grueling night shift, but a red-haired woman at the window with her nose in a book caught Max's eye instead.

"She reads everything she can get her hands on," Max said to the count. "That day, it was comparative anatomy of humans and centaurs."

Max had walked over to her, without any clear idea of how best to say hello but knowing he needed to try. He had pointed at a diagram of a human liver.

"I held one of those in my hands about four hours ago," he had said. "Don't worry, I've washed them since."

The girl had stared at him for a moment before bursting out laughing. It wasn't a cruel laugh but a cheerful one.

"Why on earth did you feel the need to tell me that?" she had said when she recovered.

"Because it was the best conversation-starter I could think of after a night shift with no sleep," Max had said. "My name is Maximilien, but everyone calls me Max."

"I'm Valentine," she had said. "Would you like to join me?"

They met in the cafe almost every day from then until Max was deployed to Africa, and wrote letters to each other throughout his tour.

Monte Cristo listened intently, thinking also of Haydee's request to make room in the plan to spare Villefort's daughter. By all accounts, she was an upstanding young woman. Helping the two young lovers find a life together may even make up in some small way for Marie Brouillard's death. Besides, hurting Valentine would solve nothing; she hadn't even been born when Villefort condemned Edmond Dantes to the Chateau d'If. She was blameless.

The count clenched his teeth for a moment as a possible contradiction occurred to him, in the sense of what he had in store for Albert de Morcerf. Valentine was an innocent bystander; Albert was a key component of destroying Fernand's life.

"If I can do anything to assist you and Valentine, I will," the count said, enjoying the smile which lit up Max's face. "We need only to figure out a strategy."

CHAPTER 75
A DRINKING PROBLEM

While Max poured his heart out, Villefort sat in his study fuming. Many men named Jordan Caillat lived in France, but Villefort's officers could pin down none of them as the same man who wrote for the Nightly Assemblage.

His investigation into Gianmarco Zaccone proved just as fruitless. Villefort lacked a single clue as to how his own path and Zaccone's could have crossed in the past, or what drove Zaccone to torment him with the knowledge of his secret child.

Villefort walked over to the fireplace. Like the staircase in his office at the Palais, it held a secret; when one pressed a carved oak leaf and twisted a lion's head in the correct way, a hidden panel revealed a compartment.

When the compartment opened, nauseous green light spilled out into the room. Although the servants feared Villefort too much to ever enter the study without permission, Villefort felt safer hiding Danglars' shard of mortite. The repulsive crystal was difficult to look at, but it also rippled at the edges of his vision, so he preferred to keep it out of sight.

Behind the mortite shard lay a tight paper scroll, a list of Villefort's enemies from his ambitious rise. He reviewed the list again and again, satisfied by how many names could be written off as either dead or otherwise impotent, but still found no connection to Zaccone.

The earliest entries on the list conjured unsettling memories of his youth in Marseille. Pierre Morrel sat near the top, a shipowner and a thorn in his side in the delicate matter of Edmond Dantes. Both names were crossed out long ago, when time claimed the one-legged Bonapartist and the sea claimed Dantes.

Villefort also kept his white porcelain hunting mask in that compartment. His personal investigations on top of his official duties had kept him too busy to clean the whore's blood off of it. Weeks after drinking from her, the dry stains left stubborn maroon smears around the lower half to almost give the appearance of a beard. Villefort considered the possibility that only a fresh coat of white paint would cover them up.

That reminded him of the coverups being ruined by Caillat and his blasted articles. Villefort remembered his first victim, the Corsican soldier in Nimes. 1817 was a trying time for him; Valentine not quite a year old, Renee taken from him by illness, and Hermine de Nargonne three months pregnant from their affair. The stress of it proved more than his own blood could alleviate, and when he saw the Corsican wearing his Bonapartist uniform, inspiration had struck.

Since his induction as a Silver Brother of the Eternal Royalist League on his wedding night, Villefort had learned about many other League rituals calling for traitorous blood to be spilled. Bypassing the ritual was risky, but such an opportunity presenting itself was too appealing to resist with the Inquisition in full swing and certain factions of Royalists roaming the countryside conducting Inquisitions of their own. If Villefort's deputies even noticed the murder, Villefort could pin the blame on a faceless soldier who would never be found or brought to justice.

He had no mask then, and the pressure in his head had built to such a point that he had no time to find a Gold or Diamond member of the League to ask if his idea would be heresy. Villefort improvised a disguise with a hooded cloak, found the Corsican soldier at a tavern, and followed him when he went to relieve himself in an alley.

Villefort remembered the cold excitement of the hunt and the deep fervour of knowing that a traitor would be removed from the world. He recalled the names of angels he had learned during League meetings and settled on making his offering to Jegudiel, who brought reward and punishment on God's behalf to the righteous and the sinners.

Villefort whispered the angel's name as he lunged. Being quite drunk, the Corsican was easy to overpower while Villefort fumbled to find enough purchase with his teeth to open an artery. The brutal chorus of angels seemed to grant him strength and patience when he drank his own blood for them; he hoped the traitor's blood would garner an even greater reward. A powerful gush of hot blood filled his mouth when he hit his mark. He had drunk greedily, but much of the blood sprayed onto his face and clothes. There was much more of it than he had expected, and every movement of his head seemed to create some gap that the flow could escape from.

Throughout it all, Villefort maintained the image of Jegudiel in his mind: an upright figure of human perfection, a crown in his right hand and a whip of many thongs in his left. When he drank as much as he could and the Corsican was undeniably dead, he had let the body fall before pulling his black cloak around himself and running off to avoid discovery.

Unfortunately, his sacrifice was discovered too soon, and not by Villefort's officers. The Corsican's brother had arrived in Nimes, and the same soldiers Villefort planned as scapegoats had found the body and dumped it in a more public place to scare other Bonapartists. With the other Corsican standing in front of Villefort and demanding an inquiry, Villefort had forgotten his plan in a panic and insulted the man instead. That had driven the grieving Corsican to declare one of their savage blood feuds, leading to the attack in Auteuil.

Remembering all this in his study, Villefort chastised himself over how simple avoiding that misery could have been. He could have agreed to investigate, then hidden, delayed, or "misplaced" the required paperwork. Anyone who asked would learn that the trail had gone cold; he perfected this very method with future sacrifices. There would have been no attack, no discovery of his son's body, no need to drink from the servant to restore himself, and nothing for Jordan Caillat to expose. Instead, not only did his activities sit on the verge of discovery, but also, his possible heresy risked being exposed to the League.

Villefort glanced again at the mortite shard. Danglars' plan ran counter to his vow to protect the realm, but Bonaparte still held the posthumous advantage of having ended the Dead Plague. Balancing that score would push the usurper's memory further into obscurity and elevate the monarchy to its proper historical standing. Once Villefort ascended to Diamond status in the League from his role in ending Danglars' second Plague, and the enormous donation he could make of his profits, it wouldn't matter if the League learned of his heresy. With high enough rank to make his case, he could perhaps even persuade the League to promote his personal rituals to official practice.

A knock at the door startled Villefort out of his thoughts.

"Sir, Baron d'Epinay has arrived," a servant said from outside. Villefort heard a quiver in the girl's voice; his servants feared him, and the Caillat articles with their insinuations did nothing to alleviate the matter. "Viscount de Morcerf and Baron de Chateau-Renaud are with him, as is Mlle. Danglars."

Franz's arrival provided a slim ray of hope, as the marriage would allow Villefort to induct Valentine into the Silver level of the League. Regardless of how the Caillat scandal turned out, the Villefort name must be strengthened in Royalist circles. He put his mask back into the compartment and swung the panel closed.

"Serve Baron d'Epinay and his friends refreshments in the parlour. Valentine is home from work, summon her at once," Villefort shouted through the door. "I'll be there right away."

Villefort rushed to his mirror to ensure his clothing sat in proper array, and no recent cuts were visible. In his haste, he failed to notice that the green glow of the mortite still seeped through the compartment door, sitting ajar by not even half an inch.

CHAPTER 76
A SIGNED STATEMENT

Valentine's heart sank when she entered the parlour to see Franz seated by the window with a glass of wine in his hand. The presence of Albert and Raoul worsened her mood. None of them had ever treated her poorly, but their presence could only mean one thing. Her fears were confirmed when M. Deschamps, a small round notary with a receding hairline well-known to the Villefort family, entered the parlour as well.

Albert and Raoul had come there to sign the contract as Franz's two witnesses, and Eugenie as one of Valentine's; the other would be her father. Eugenie gave her a sympathetic look while ignoring Albert's attempts at conversation. She had no more power than Valentine did to stop the arrangements but her attendance was a small comfort. Villefort arrived all too soon.

"Valentine, the time has come," Villefort said. As always, he sounded as though he were proclaiming a prison sentence. "You are to become a married woman, joining the Villefort bloodline to the illustrious house of d'Epinay. There will be a ceremony tonight to bind you in the eyes of God, but first we must join you in the eyes of the king."

Deschamps produced a sheaf of papers from his briefcase along with quills and ink, and arranged them on a bureau. Franz read over the document and dipped one of the quills to sign his name.

"Valentine, I realize that we hardly know each other, but this is how things have always been done for families like ours," Franz said with a gentle smile as Albert and Raoul added their marks. "Don't be afraid; I will honour you, and be kind to you, and with luck we'll come to care for each other quite deeply."

Valentine stood frozen where she was, staring at her father and hoping he could read the desperate fear in her eyes. She wished that for once he would show the instincts of a loving parent and shield her from a fate she wanted more than anything to avoid. He left her wish ungranted; no mercy or understanding could be seen in his ice-blue eyes, nor any patience in his yellow face.

Villefort cleared his throat, urging Valentine onward. What possible consequences could she face if she just refused to move or sign? Her father could send her to rot and be forgotten in some far-off prison or somehow find Max and do the same to him; would he do so, was the only question.

Before she could find out, the grating flutter of stone wings entered the room and the gargoyle Barrois landed on a perch.

"M. Noirtier," Barrois croaked, "requests you all. Urgent. Regards the wedding. Bring the witnesses."

Valentine ran out of the parlour and up the stairs, starving for anything to delay her fate. Eugenie followed, and Franz saw no reason not to go along with Albert and Raoul behind him. Only Villefort and a very confused Deschamps remained in the parlour.

A cold sweat broke out on Villefort's neck. In the confusion of investigating the Count of Monte Cristo, he had forgotten about the plot he had overheard from his father's room. Valentine had some secret suitor, and Noirtier had cooked up some scheme to break the engagement.

"Father!" Villefort shouted as he made his way to the stairs, with Deschamps following. "Whatever you're plotting, don't you dare!"

By the time Villefort reached the mirror-lined bedroom, Barrois had a rusted key in hand to open the middle drawer of an ancient and battered desk. Barrois extracted bundles of papers one at a time, stacking them on the desk as Noirtier fluttered his eyelids at each one to refuse them.

"Father, stop this at once. Whatever you're doing, it's childish and will not be tolerated," Villefort said.

Noirtier rolled his eyes, then raised them to the ceiling and looked at the bookshelf. Valentine retrieved the dictionary, and proceeded through their letter system to pick out S, E, and C.

"Secret? Is that the word?" Valentine asked. Noirtier responded with a slow blink.

"Secret compartment," Barrois grunted.

"What a remarkable system," Franz said. "Valentine, I hope you'll teach me the intricacies of it. I would enjoy learning some of M. Noirtier's stories."

Noirtier stared at Franz for a moment with a peculiar expression that even Valentine could not read. Meanwhile, Barrois reached into the drawer and pressed an unseen spring. It click and raised a false bottom on a hinge. Villefort's anxiety mounted as Barrois held up a final bundle of papers tied with black string.

"That's enough!" Villefort said, stepping forward to snatch the papers from Barrois' claws. "The only document we're concerned with tonight is the marriage contract!"

The gargoyle's stone grip could not be overcome. Barrois hissed at Villefort and flew to the top of the bookshelf with the papers. Noirtier stared at the dictionary in Valentine's hand and together they selected the letters O, B, and J.

"Objection?" Valentine asked, hopeful. Noirtier gave a slow blink to confirm it.

"Pardon me," Deschamps said from the doorway, "but is M. Noirtier invoking his right to formally object to the marriage?"

Noirtier blinked yes, which Valentine relayed. To be certain, Deschamps pushed forward to where he could better see Noirtier and repeated the question. Deschamps had a basic understanding of how Noirtier communicated, having drafted Noirtier's will and notarized various medical forms on his behalf.

"M. de Villefort, I'm afraid we have to hear him out," Deschamps said after Noirtier blinked again. "The law is very clear that he gets to say his piece before any further signatures can be applied to the contract."

"Yes, let M. Noirtier speak!" Eugenie said, receiving a grateful look from Valentine. "Well, speak in the figurative sense. You know what I mean."

"And you thought this would be dull," Albert whispered to Raoul.

"Fine!" Villefort said, rubbing his forehead. "Valentine, read the damned documents."

Noirtier fluttered his eyelids and stared at Franz again.

"That was a 'no', correct?" Franz asked. "You want me to read the papers, not Valentine?"

Noirtier gave a slow blink for yes, even as Valentine retrieved the papers from Barrois and handed them to Franz. He untied the black string but soon stopped reading when a flush rose to his cheeks.

"These are minutes from the Bonapartist club in the Rue Saint-Jacques, on the same night in 1815 when my father was killed," Franz said. "He left to attend that meeting and was dead before he could return home. When the Hundred Days began, the imperial government settled his death as a suicide and tried to cover up his murder."

Valentine's eyes widened, and the blood drained from her face. Franz's words bridged a gap in her mind between a previously disconnected set of facts, spawning a horrible theory. She glanced at her father, but averted her eyes at once to not reveal her fear.

Franz continued to read aloud. The document confirmed that General Flavien de Quesnel, Baron d'Epinay, was recommended to the club in a letter from Bonaparte's secretary on the island of Elba. The club president had then brought Quesnel to the secret location of the meeting.

"My aunt told me about this," Franz said. "Father was a Royalist, but under orders from the king to infiltrate the Bonapartists as a potential turncoat."

The minutes revealed how Quesnel had been told at the meeting about the letter recommending him and the expectation of another letter to arrive aboard a ship called the Pharaon when it made port in Marseille. This second letter would bring details of the emperor's pending return from exile.

Although Quesnel had reacted well to that news and promised to help however he could, the club president suspected Quesnel of lying to them. They sent Quesnel to the lobby so the convened members could discuss other business; they then decided that Quesnel was a double-agent and must be eliminated to safeguard their plans. Franz rubbed his eyes.

"We always suspected that his murder and this assignment from the King were connected. Still, having proof after all these years brings a sense of closure," Franz said.

Noirtier gave a sign with his eyes, and Valentine urged Franz to continue reading. Both she and Villefort could start to see Noirtier's aim in sharing this document, though they accepted this realization with very different outlooks.

Quesnel was given a carriage to bring him home and told that further instructions would be delivered. They blindfolded him again to safeguard the club's location; that entry in the minutes was marked at midnight.

The carriage had carried Quesnel away from the Rue Saint-Jacques. Quesnel stepped down from the carriage when it stopped and removed his blindfold, and expressed his surprise to find himself standing on a bridge above the Seine. The club president, who had accompanied him and sat in silence throughout the drive, plunged a dagger into Quesnel's heart and waited for his struggles to cease.

Without ceremony, the club president pushed the corpse into the river and returned alone to the club. There he reported the deed in full for the secretary to record, in the very minutes Franz read in a shaking voice.

"Really, father," Villefort interjected while mopping his brow. "I knew you opposed the marriage, but this is a heartless wedding gift. Franz had agreed for you to live with them, to keep you from being separated from Valentine. After this, I would hardly be surprised if he barred you from ever crossing his doorstep!"

Noirtier looked with contempt and pride at his son, and Valentine guessed the words he would say if he could: "I never wanted to do this. You have forced my hand."

"There's more yet," Franz said with tears in his eyes. "It says, 'We have recorded these details against the eventuality that the Emperor or his staff may enquire as to the fate of General du Quesnel after retaking the throne, that it may be known they were deceived by him and he met a traitor's end.' And then it is signed—"

Franz's eyes widened, and the flush of rage replaced his pallor.

"It is signed by the secretary, Maxime Poilievre, and by the club president himself," Franz said. "The club president who murdered my father like a coward and left his body to bloat in the Seine: Jules Noirtier."

Furious, Franz spun to face Villefort.

"Has this been your idea of a joke, sir? Did you intend to make me the grandson-in-law to the man who orphaned me, or are you so ignorant to the history of your own family that you were unaware?" Franz said. He took the contract from Deschamps and tore it to pieces. "Needless to say, I'm cancelling our agreement. Albert, be so kind as to burn these."

Franz dropped the shreds of the marriage contract into Albert's hands. Albert looked to Raoul for guidance, then clasped his two hands together and ignited them for a moment. He brushed the ashes into a wastebasket.

"And you," Franz continued, his voice thick with grief while he advanced a step toward Noirtier. "You're lucky that your pitiful condition prevents me from challenging you to a duel. Nothing would give me greater pleasure than to put a bullet through your skull as revenge for my father; I'll have to content myself with the living death you already endure."

Noirtier's eyes did not gloat or even show satisfaction as Franz stormed from the room. Albert and Raoul followed silently, though Eugenie remained. With no contract to notarize, Deschamps said a meek goodbye and left. Valentine, who knew the subtleties of Noirtier's look like no other, read only a resigned sadness or some melancholy relief.

Villefort escaped the room, unnoticed by the remaining occupants. Part of him wanted to retreat to his study, lock the door, and drink his own blood until the angel Barachiel deigned to bless him with sleep. Another part of him roared to sink his teeth into Noirtier's throat and put an end to his meddling permanently.

Panicking, he ran to his carriage and yelled at his driver to drive and not stop until instructed to do so. As he drank from his arm in the privacy of the carriage, Villefort had an epiphany. He couldn't kill his father, but he could find and kill the young man who had captured Valentine's heart and spurred her to push Noirtier to ruin the engagement. He only needed a name.

Back in Noirtier's room, Valentine wrapped her grandfather in a grateful hug while murmuring a thousand thanks in his ear. Her joy was short-lived, as the insidious idea that Franz's remarks had planted in her mind demanded her attention. She turned to Eugenie.

"I need to investigate something in Father's study," Valentine said. "If I'm right, it's connected to Marie. Will you help me?"

"Of course," Eugenie said without hesitation, a confident smirk on her face. "What do you need?"

CHAPTER 77
THE STUDY

Eugenie stood watch from the staircase, where she could see and call out if Villefort returned, while Valentine made her way to her father's study. She possessed the only key besides Villefort's own, given to her so long ago that she doubted he even remembered.

At Marie's last Club meeting, she had given the girls a list of the missing or murdered people she knew about. Since Marie's death, Valentine had spent long hours staying late at work in the legal archives trying to find the official investigation records. She justified the extra time at the office to her father by claiming to study Dubois & Renard's past cases.

Research was one of the few parts of her job that she truly enjoyed, and she had soon found the details of when and where each person on Marie's list had gone missing or been found dead. With a piece of tracing paper over a map of Paris, she had plotted out each of those locations and marked the respective dates. Every case had gone cold, the officers involved lacking the resources or evidence to continue.

When the Jordan Caillat articles started to emerge, they vindicated Valentine's efforts. Caillat named victims from Marie's list one at a time and drew attention to the pattern of people vanishing from the slums and being found drained of their blood. The notion that one of the other girls in the Club may know Caillat and had given him Marie's list crossed her mind, but a more important one supplanted it.

In the archives, Valentine had begun searching for any other murders with the same unusual manner of death. She found a dozen more victims throughout Paris and added them to her map as well. Again, every murder was marked as a cold case. Unfortunately, her research gave no further insight into why these people had been killed or by whom; not until Franz's reading of Noirtier's meeting minutes, when he pointed out that the government of the day had covered up his father's death as a suicide. Valentine realized that there may be a pattern to the vampire murders which the legal records wouldn't show. Someone within the system, someone powerful, had suppressed the investigations.

Valentine rushed into her father's study with her notebook, tracing paper, and map. She marked the Palais de Justice on the tracing paper, and with a shaking hand, marked the Villefort home. Sure enough, both marks sat in worrying proximity to large clusters of victims. The other Caillat articles, the ones asking so many questions about the attempt on her father's life, took on a new light.

Her father had grown more distant and irritable every year of her life. On the Sunday that Marie had been killed, he had broken his usual routine to go into the office and returned home quite late. Valentine felt certain her father could use his position to make up an excuse and throw an inconvenient person into a cell if he had to, but never before had she suspected him capable of murder.

Still, she only had supposition. Without hard evidence of some kind, accusing Villefort of anything would be irresponsible. With that in mind, Valentine combed through her father's study to find any clue to prove or rule out her theory.

The last rays of evening sunlight illuminated the sombre room, and Valentine hurried inside without giving the fireplace a second look. She rifled through the papers on his desk, but found only ordinary legal documents. She gave up on them, realizing she was unlikely to find a confession letter in plain view.

The drawers provided no incriminating evidence either, no vials of blood or gruesome trophies. Valentine even toyed with the curtains, thinking in some vague way they may hold secrets of their own. Finally she slumped into her father's chair, uncertain whether to be relieved or even more concerned about the lack of proof she had found.

It took Valentine's eyes a moment to adjust to the change in the light with the sun at her back. As she prepared to admit her idea was mistaken, a green glow attracted her attention. The strange light came from a crack in the carved fireplace mantle; closer inspection revealed it was not a crack but a seam. Valentine levered it further open with a pencil.

The source of the glow was a green crystal about the size of a carrot. It could have been beautiful, but it produced a revulsion from deep in Valentine's bones. Something was wrong with that stone, although she could not articulate what it was. Next to the stone was a loosely curled piece of paper covered in miniscule coded writing.

The last item in the compartment gave her pause. A white porcelain mask sat on a velvet-lined tray, with no decoration but an abstract design in rust-coloured streaks. Valentine held it up to the light, observing its shape. If her father wore this mask, only his mouth and eyes would be visible while the rest of his distinctive yellow face appeared dead and white, just like Louise had described the vampire. Holding the mask in the dying sunlight, Valentine got a better look at the abstract brown design. A sob erupted from her throat when she realized the formless splotches were actually dried blood.

Valentine still wore her office jacket; when she had started working at Dubois & Renard, she had added a large pocket to the inside to carry a book whenever she wanted. She forced back her tears and slipped the mask into this pocket, then closed the compartment again and re-locked the study door from the hall.

"Father is the vampire," Valentine said to Eugenie in Noirtier's room, disbelieving the words even as they came out of her mouth. She showed them the mask, as well as her map of the murder victims. "Or he thinks he is, or he's pretending to be one, it doesn't matter. What am I going to do?"

"Get out," Eugenie said at once. "Go someplace safe. Don't take this the wrong way, but you're the worst liar I know. Your father will take one look at you and know something's wrong."

"But I can't leave Grandpapa here defenseless!" Valentine said. "Help me get his chair down the steps, we'll have to try and get him into a cab."

"No," Barrois croaked and pointed at Noirtier, who fluttered his eyelids with emphasis.

Noirtier stared at the dictionary again. As Valentine helped him spell out what he wanted to say, it became apparent that his goal wasn't a specific word but to dictate a message the only way he could. It took minutes to spell out what a healthy man could have said in a moment, but at last he blinked no to each letter she suggested, indicating that it was complete. She added punctuation to the message in likely places and read what Noirtier had dictated.

"Son will not harm me," Valentine read. "Neglect, insult, forget. But not harm."

"M. Noirtier, are you sure?" Eugenie asked. He met her eyes and gave a slow affirmative blink. "Alright Valentine, it's settled. You need to leave."

"Where would be safe?" Valentine asked. "I have no other family to run to. Grand-père Saint-Meran is in Belgium and would only send me back to Father anyway."

"My house would be no good," Eugenie said. "Your father knows we're friends, and mine is such a spineless twit that he would hand you over in a heartbeat. What about your mystery suitor, that dashing young man you love to talk about at the Club?"

"Max?" Valentine said, forgetting her promise to never say his name aloud in the house. "He lives with his family, if Father came after me they would all be in danger. But his friend, the Count of Monte Cristo, he might help."

"Perfect! If he needs any convincing, I'm sure Haydee will help you," Eugenie said. "Now get out of here, and go to the count's house as quick as you can!"

Valentine hesitated and looked at Noirtier for approval. He blinked and stared at the reflection of the door in one of his mirrors. Heavy tears rolled down Valentine's cheeks as she laid a tender kiss on Noirtier's forehead.

"I promise I'll come back for you," she said. "I love you."

Valentine stuffed a change of clothes into a sack and ran. The Champs-Elysees was only a few streets away and she arrived sooner than if she had waited for a cab. The concierge stopped her at the gate with an upheld hand.

"Is the Count of Monte Cristo expecting you, mademoiselle?" he said.

"No, he wouldn't be," Valentine said, her words coming in gasps. "It's something of an emergency. My name is Valentine de Villefort? I'm a friend of Haydee's?"

"I see," the concierge said. His dark eyes took in Valentine's condition after her run and softened with pity. "Mademoiselle, please sit and catch your breath while I check my orders."

"*Merci beaucoup*," Valentine said, accepting a seat in the concierge's chair while he consulted some paperwork. "What's your name?"

"My name is Carlo, Mlle. de Villefort," he said. "What is the nature of your business with the count today?"

Valentine considered her answer with care. "I'm caught in the middle of some family trouble," she said at last. "I was hoping to spend some time with Haydee to clear my head."

"She is very good company," Carlo said. "Ah, here we are. Mistress Haydee has requested that you be let in if you ever arrive at the gate. Which you plainly have. When you're ready, I'll admit you."

"Thank you again, Carlo," Valentine said, mopping her face with a handkerchief. "That isn't a very French-sounding name. Are you Spanish?"

"Distantly," Carlo said. "I come from the Catalan village in Marseille, mademoiselle."

"Oh, I've always wanted to visit Marseille!" Valentine said. "My parents were married there, but my father has never allowed us to go."

"It is a beautiful city," Carlo agreed. "Shall we?"

"Of course. Thank you for your hospitality, Carlo," Valentine said. Their brief chat had been a welcome diversion from the evening's horror.

Inside, Haydee greeted Valentine with a warm embrace. "Valentine, what's the matter?"

Valentine closed her eyes and allowed her discovery to spill out in a torrent that allowed precious few pauses for breath. She handed Haydee the mask and map, and showed pages from her notebook.

"And now Grandpapa is in that house with him alone, with only Barrois and the servants to look after him!" Valentine said. "I know he thinks Father would never hurt him, but how can any of us think we know what Father would or wouldn't do?"

"It's alright Valentine, it's alright," Haydee said with her hand on Valentine's shoulder. "We can wait for your father to leave the house and Max can go rescue M. Noirtier."

Valentine sighed with relief. "Yes, of course, why didn't I think of that," she said, but then her eyes snapped wide. "Wait, how do you know about Max?"

Haydee smiled and led Valentine into the parlour, where Max lay asleep on the settee with the count watching over him.

"Mlle. de Villefort," the count said, rising from his chair in a bow. "Don't be angry with Max for sharing your secret; he's been under a great deal of stress. I promise, I will give whatever help I can to putting a stop to your wedding to Baron d'Epinay."

"Actually my love," Haydee said, "that has already been taken care of. But now we have a larger problem."

With the count informed of recent events, he invited Valentine to take a spare bedroom on the second floor until her safety could be assured.

Villefort returned home after midnight, climbed the stairs in a daze, and fell asleep still wearing his coat. He didn't notice that both his daughter and his hunting mask were gone.

The Parisian Ladies' Vampire-Hunting Club met the following day. Eugenie read the girls a letter from Valentine explaining the situation.

"Ladies, we have genuine proof that M. de Villefort killed our dear Marie," Eugenie said, the news met with gasps from her friends. "Valentine thinks he's pretending to be a vampire; I think we shouldn't take chances."

Louise brought over a bag, and she and Eugenie gave each of the girls a bundle of garlic blossoms and a small silver crucifix on a chain.

"Wear the cross at all times, and always keep garlic on your person," Eugenie said.

"So we'll repel vampires, but attract Italians?" one of the girls said, snickering. "That hardly seems a worthwhile trade."

"Jessica, this is serious," Eugenie said, scowling at her. "We need to stay alive long enough to think of a plan."

"A plan to do what, Eugenie?" Jessica asked with her arms crossed.

"To kill the crown attorney of France and get away with it," Eugenie replied.

CHAPTER 78
PROGRESS OF
CAVALCANTI THE YOUNGER

When his father, the major, left France, Andrea Cavalcanti received from him a bundle of documents detailing Andrea's identity and lineage. Those papers served as his step-stool to enter the elegant carriage of Parisian society.

Andrea found himself in a fine position. As a viscount with a prestigious name and a comfortable income, he could enjoy the relative patience which the French extended to handsome and wealthy foreigners. Furthermore, he had the Count of Monte Cristo to guide him in making his first society connections.

Major Cavalcanti left his son behind with great regret, which weighed on him until his coach passed over the border of Switzerland. A flash of red light passed over his vision and the events of his adventure in Paris—impersonating a major of the Italian army, dining with bankers and counts, and meeting a long-lost son who he had never fathered—took on the qualities of a dream. He wasn't clear on how he had come to be in such a fine coach, but that worry didn't survive long once he found the gold and banknotes in his pockets. He proceeded with a smile onward to the taverns and gambling houses of home.

In the spirit of forging connections, Monte Cristo brought Andrea with him to visit Danglars. Despite it being a Sunday, Danglars worked in his study drafting a law which he said could not wait, but Hermine extended her own invitation to Andrea and the count.

Hermine Danglars hoped that by meeting the count again she could take the measure of the mind behind his unsettling red eyes. Her rational mind knew the count was taunting her with her own past, but the seat of her emotions rebelled at the idea of someone causing such harm just for sport. The count must, therefore, have some reason for his behaviour, Hermine decided.

The footman admitted the count and Andrea to Hermine's boudoir, that elegant oasis in the midst of the baron's garish décor, where she sat examining some papers with Eugenie. Andrea ran a hand through his fair hair as soon as he saw Eugenie, showing off a diamond which he had bought for his little finger against the count's advice.

"Mlle. Danglars, an unexpected pleasure," Andrea said. "May I ask what has so captivated your attention?"

"Certainly," Eugenie replied. "I belong to a small social club, dedicated to the hunting of vampires. It so happens that one of my friends witnessed one feeding not so long ago. This is a sketch that she made of the creature and these are lists of known characteristics and weaknesses of vampires."

It was a credit to either Andrea's imagination or his like for Eugenie that this bizarre assertion gave him only a moment's pause.

"A vampire, you say? I have to admit I've never believed they were real," Andrea said. "Then again, I never believed I would be reunited with my long-lost father! We do live in a strange world."

Andrea went to stand by the chaise longue where Eugenie sat. She held Louise's drawing of the brutal attack on Marie. The villain's suit and the blood smears around his face were painted with watercolours, but the face remained white as bone.

"Count, this fellow rather looks like you!" Andrea said. "Do you have a brother, or some dark secret we should know?"

Hermine coughed and fanned herself. The count only raised one corner of his mouth.

"When I started the Club, I didn't believe they were real either. But Louise saw this attack with her own eyes, and I trust her judgement completely," Eugenie said. "As you say, we live in a strange world. Men can become wolves at the full moon, the dead can wage war on the living, and a colony of wizards lives on the Marseille coast. The idea of another monster walking among us undetected and hunting us for food is not so far-fetched."

"Indeed it isn't," Andrea said with a peculiar glint in his eye. Only the count noticed, and only from the corner of his eye, that Andrea rubbed a thumb against one of his large white teeth.

A servant entered to announce both Baron Danglars and Louise d'Armilly, arriving by accident at the same time. Eugenie sprang to her feet with an enthusiasm seldom seen outside of Club meetings and raced to her room to receive Louise. The music of the piano and their voices combined in song soon drifted through the closed door, and Andrea stood by it listening thoughtfully. Danglars gave Andrea a long look as he passed through into the boudoir.

"Viscount Cavalcanti, didn't my daughter invite you to join her?" Danglars asked.

Without waiting for a reply, Danglars opened Eugenie's door and ushered Andrea inside. The count soon heard him singing a dignified Corsican song about fathers and sons. Monte Cristo noticed a certain decline in the music's vigour after that point, but Danglars and Hermine remained oblivious to it. If anything, Danglars puffed his chest up, quite pleased with himself.

"Baron, you're in high spirits," the count said. "I heard about some bad business in Milan and came over to see if you needed friendly company."

"It was nothing; a tempest in a teapot, which will soon blow over." Danglars waved his hand, never taking his eyes off his daughter's door. "Even in the worst case, I'm taking steps to recover the half-million or so of income which is at risk."

"Very good," Monte Cristo said. "It warms my heart to see such confidence."

His face presented a look of amiable concern, but triumph lurked behind the leathery white mask. Danglars would soon find the men in Milan he planned to blackmail were already financially secure, and the men he planned to threaten were quite safe from his goons.

"Let's leave aside the subject of money, it's all we ever talk about in this house," Hermine said. "How much do we have, how much do others have, how much should anyone be allowed to have; it's all so tiresome. Count, have you heard about the tragedy that has visited M. de Villefort?"

"I hadn't, but go on," Monte Cristo replied.

"I'm sure you heard that his daughter Valentine was engaged to marry that lovely Franz d'Epinay; your companion goes to Eugenie's club with Valentine," Hermine said. The count's face betrayed no twitch or even a blink to reveal his inner feelings. "Well, it seems that M. de Villefort's crippled old father killed d'Epinay's father nearly thirty years ago, and young Franz was so upset he called the whole thing off!"

"That would be quite a surprise to receive from one's in-laws," the count said. "I can't say I'd behave any differently in Franz's place."

"Yes, it's quite an understandable reaction. But still, it will be quite a scandal for the Villefort family," Hermine said. "He was so looking forward to having Franz as a son-in-law."

The count's lack of a reaction frustrated Hermine, certain as she was that mentioning Villefort and family matters would provoke one.

"How is Villefort taking this development?" the count asked, furrowing his dark eyebrows in a suitable mimicry of concern.

"Villefort's a moody fellow at the best of times," Danglars offered. "I imagine he'll cheer up after he gets the chance to crucify some poor miscreant in the courtroom again. Never mind Villefort, I would rather ask you about Cavalcanti. Is he really a prince?"

Monte Cristo shrugged and hid his satisfaction at the greedy gleam in Danglars' beady eyes, amplified by his thick spectacles.

"As far as I know, he is a viscount until his father's death," the count said. "Speaking of viscounts, what would Albert think if he found Andrea unsupervised in Eugenie's room?"

"He visits so seldom, it would be a true stroke of chance if he came here now," Danglars said. "As for his displeasure, at his mother's ball he danced with Eugenie once. Andrea danced with her three times, and his joy was matched only by Morcerf's indifference. Besides, my agents have uncovered certain rumours—"

"Viscount Albert de Morcerf," a servant announced, interrupting Danglars.

The colour drained from the folds of Danglars jowls at the cruel luck. Of course, the count had calculated Albert's visit as much as his own appearance with Andrea; he had planted the seed of an idea in Albert's head a week earlier. Hermine rose to correct the situation in Eugenie's room, but Danglars made it clear that Eugenie was not to be disturbed.

Albert entered the room with a deferential bow for his future in-laws and a wide smile for the unexpected presence of the count. Not wanting to singe his new gloves, Albert leaned towards a candle to light his cigar.

"Morcerf!" Danglars barked from his chair, not having bothered to rise when Albert entered the room. "Are you trying to kill some unsuspecting sailor? Don't you dare light that on a candle in my house."

Albert's eyes widened, still unused to Danglars' many superstitions, but he stopped himself from replying and instead removed a glove to light his cigar in his usual showy fashion.

Danglars then treated Monte Cristo to a marvelous display of passive aggression, as he met every one of Albert's conversational offerings with a polite rebuff. Albert did a credible job of hiding his annoyance, both at this treatment and at the presence of another suitor in Eugenie's bedroom. Finally, Albert took the hint that his visit came at a poor time.

"Might I pay my respects to Mlle. Danglars before I leave?" Albert asked.

"Just a moment, let's not disturb her quite yet. Listen." Danglars raised his finger to the ceiling.

In the quiet which followed, Eugenie's soprano and Andrea's baritone could be heard harmonizing well, if not with much joy, as their song drew to a close. Danglars applauded it wildly.

"What wonderful music Eugenie and Prince Cavalcanti make!" Danglars exclaimed.

"Quite," Albert said tersely. "One would almost think they were engaged to be married."

"I promised to give my daughter to a man who would love her," Danglars said, meeting Albert's eyes. "I think that a suitor who stands cold as marble around her without an ounce of affection would be failing to live up to his side of such a contract."

"I may be biased, but I promise that Albert is a charming young man," Monte Cristo said. "Sooner or later he would make your daughter happy, and his name is at least as good as Cavalcanti's."

"Is it, though?" Danglars asked, forgetting or ignoring Albert standing only a few metres away from him. "The Cavalcanti name is far older, and the stories of their fortune dwarf that of the Morcerfs. Even the prince's income is fifty thousand livres, sure to increase when he is the sole beneficiary of their mining interests."

"Is their money in mining? I wasn't aware," Monte Cristo said. He turned to Albert. "I fear I must apologize for throwing Andrea in the path of your marital bliss. I was only trying to make connections for him like you've done for me; I had no idea it would interfere so much in your fortunes."

"Count, you're new to Paris, but this sort of thing happens every day," Danglars said with a laugh. "Weren't we just speaking about the rapid change in Valentine de Villefort's prospects? Still, if it bothers you so much, go speak to General Morcerf. You're so friendly with his son, and enjoyed a private walk with his wife at their ball; I'm sure you can find his ear."

From Eugenie's room, another piece of music came to an end. Parodying Danglars, Albert applauded and cheered with poorly-disguised sarcasm. A servant whispered in Danglars' ear before he could react to the outburst. Danglars excused himself.

When Eugenie opened the door, Andrea reacted with a start to seeing Albert present, and Louise stifled a laugh. Eugenie and Louise went with Hermine to the study for tea, Eugenie ignoring Albert's compliments on her voice and talents. Monte Cristo remained seated, enjoying the efforts Albert and Andrea made to avoid meeting each other's gaze.

After a long and awkward silence, Danglars returned. His bald spot was damp with sweat and his remaining hair stuck out more than normal.

"I've just had a courier from Greece," Danglars said, offering no more explanation but staring at Albert with a curious expression.

"Count, I must be leaving. Shall we depart together?" Albert asked with a meaningful look.

"If you like," Monte Cristo replied with a shrug.

Andrea had the wisdom not to invite himself to join them. Albert went to have the carriages prepared, and Danglars approached the count as soon as he left.

"Your advice to conduct my due diligence was excellent," Danglars hissed into Monte Cristo's ear. To the count's sharp hearing, it was as if Danglars were yelling from the rooftops. "There's a whole sordid history of Fernand Mondego's time at Yanina. I'll tell you everything another time."

"Perhaps you should discuss this with General Morcerf yourself," Monte Cristo said. "When I see him, I'll suggest for him to come see you as soon as possible."

Monte Cristo left Danglars to consider the implications of the news from Greece, news which the count himself had known for over five years.

CHAPTER 79
HAYDEE

"Did you see how he glared at me?" Albert asked the count in the carriage. "It must have something to do with the news from Greece, but I can't imagine what that could be."

"Nor can I," Monte Cristo said. "I noticed that you seemed perturbed by Andrea's intrusion into your prospects with Eugenie. I didn't want to say anything in front of Danglars, but I would have thought that development would please you."

Albert burst into laughter.

"Are you joking? I knew I could play my part well enough to convince Danglars, but I never suspected I would trick you!" Albert said. He tossed the nub of his cigar from the carriage window and lit a fresh one. "Thank you for so ably throwing your protege into the mix, by the way."

"I offer no patronage to Andrea Cavalcanti; I'm doing his father a favour, nothing more," Monte Cristo said, declining Albert's offer of a cigar. "You did a very skillful job of pretending to be jealous of him; I had no idea you were such a thespian."

Albert fidgeted in his seat. "Don't mistake me, I'm very happy for the marriage to be called off," he said, smoking and looking out the carriage window. "I was just hoping it would happen without a public rejection to make me look like a fool. And there are the ramifications to my family name to think about."

The count nodded, a savage delight hidden behind his implacable face.

"Still, it seems as though you'll soon be free to pursue a wife more suitable to your tastes," Monte Cristo said. "You know, it has just occurred to me that something was missing from Baroness Danglars' boudoir."

"You picked up on Lucien's absence?" Albert said with a chuckle. "Yes, he's been giving the baroness a very wide berth lately. He won't talk about why, but his bandaged hand speaks volumes. I think Danglars gave him a demonstration of his knife-throwing skills."

"Really? I was of the understanding that Lucien and Danglars had, well, an understanding," Monte Cristo said.

"Apparently, Debray misunderstood," Albert said, snickering.

The count invited Albert in when they reached his house and commanded Baptistan to make tea. Within five minutes Baptistan reappeared with a fully-laid service, including a multi-tiered tray stacked with finger sandwiches and biscuits.

"You must introduce me to your inventor friend who built Baptistan," Albert said with his mouth full. "I'd be comfortable indeed with just one servant as attentive as that."

"You don't consider yourself comfortable already?" the count asked.

"Oh, compared to some unfortunate soul living through the collapse of Greece or in deepest China, I'm certainly comfortable," Albert said. "But I mean comfort in the Parisian sense, you understand."

"Quite," Monte Cristo said.

The count rang his gong, and Ali emerged in seconds from another room with two magnificent pipes. The tobacco packed into the engraved smoking pieces smelled sweet and earthy with a hint of herbs all at once.

"Good heavens, it seems your entire staff is as attentive as your wooden man!" Albert said. He conjured a small flame and took great care in lighting his pipe. "Is there some special note you can hit on that gong which declares 'I wish to smoke with a guest'?"

"Not at all," Monte Cristo said with a smile. "Ali knows my habits and knows his job. I generally smoke when having tea or coffee, and he keeps a close eye on who enters the house with me. Since I came home today at teatime with one of the foremost tobacco connoisseurs in Paris, here we are."

The music of a guitar drifting from above distracted Albert. His eyes found a second-floor balcony in the high-ceilinged sitting room and a half-open door beyond.

"Fate has decided this will be a musical day for you," Monte Cristo said. "You've escaped a performance at the Danglars household, only to find yourself assaulted by Haydee's practise of the Spanish guitar."

"Practise? She sounds like an old master of the instrument," Albert said.

Albert closed his eyes and listened to the chords, which mourned of loss and speculated with excitement about rebirth. Such a thoughtful expression was uncommon on Albert's face. When the piece came to an end, he opened his eyes as if waking from a rejuvenating meditation.

"Count, would it be untoward to ask to meet your mysterious slave princess?" Albert said. "It would be a relief for my soul after enduring Baron Danglars' company."

"Certainly, although I must remind you again that she is no slave," Monte Cristo said. "I purchased her from a slave trader, but returned her freedom to her immediately. She comes and goes as she pleases, sets her own schedule, and is free to go her own way if she ever chooses to."

"Of course, of course," Albert said. "You told me all that before, but I must have forgotten."

"I do insist on one thing when you meet her," Monte Cristo said, leaning forward. "Her father was Pasha Ali Tepelini, the ruler of the Greek state of Yanina in their war for independence against Sultan Mahmud of the Ottoman Empire. She grew up in luxury that dwarfs what my meagre fortune can provide."

"Not just a princess, but one from the Thousand and One Nights!" Albert said. "How did she come to be a slave?"

"How else can one's life change so drastically? War," Monte Cristo said. "I'll find out if she would like to meet you, but first promise one thing. You know that your father was sent to serve Pasha Ali?"

"Yes, with some other officers," Albert said. "Pasha Ali was so pleased with his service that he granted my father a generous bonus, helping him to re-establish the family fortune."

"Then you also know that one of those men betrayed his duty and sold the pasha to the sultan," Monte Cristo said, his red eyes focused on Albert's.

Albert's smile faded and he took a solemn draw from his pipe. "My father had been reassigned by the pasha to supervise troops in the field," he said. "He never knew which of his comrades did the deed."

"Of course," Monte Cristo said, already aware that Fernand was only reassigned after Pasha Ali's death. He knew also that the other officers had died or vanished in the years since. "Under no circumstances are you to tell Haydee that your father served hers. I worry that she would become quite emotional. While you and I know your father was blameless, she may become fixated on him as a suspect in her father's downfall."

"I understand completely," Albert said at once.

Monte Cristo nodded and rang his gong to summon Ali.

"Tell Haydee that I would like to visit her and that I ask permission to introduce a friend," he said.

Ali nodded and vanished again. Ali knocked at the door Albert could see on the second floor and entered, remained inside for perhaps a minute, and returned. He nodded again to the count, then led them up the stairs to Haydee's apartment.

Haydee rested on an overstuffed silk cushion with her legs curled under herself to support the Spanish guitar she held. Her thick, tantalizing hair cascaded in a dark tail behind her head, and she wore a red kimono from the Far East cut to allow movement. It also bared a significant expanse of her delicate olive-toned leg and a sliver of bare hip.

Albert swallowed hard and fought a losing battle not to stare. To him, Haydee looked just as remote as Eugenie Danglars. But for all the ways that Eugenie was a snow-capped mountain above the horizon, Haydee was a lush island paradise in an uncharted corner of the Pacific Ocean.

"Master, you've brought a visitor," Haydee said in Greek.

She extended her hand to Albert, who stood dumbfounded at the door. Though Albert did not understand a word of Greek, he understood the gesture and approached to raise her knuckles toward his lips. He didn't dare kiss her hand, but breathed in the jasmine perfume of her skin.

"You know that you don't need to call me that," the count replied, also in Greek and shaking his head with a chuckle.

"And you know that it amuses me to do so," Haydee said with a playful smile. "Who is it?"

Without knowing what she said, Albert knew he would lose his senses if such a smile were directed his way, from imagining the mischief that lurked behind it.

"My dear, don't let him see you react. This is Albert de Morcerf," the count said.

Haydee's eyes widened by a fraction, but she maintained the same smile.

"Why have you brought the traitor's whelp here to see me?" Haydee asked.

"You knew this was coming sometime," the count said. "Events are falling into place. It's time for him to learn what his father did, the way we discussed."

"Can't I just cut his throat and feed his body to your beetles?" Haydee asked, patting the divan to her left to invite Albert to sit.

"I'm afraid not," the count said.

"In that case, welcome to our humble home, viscount," Haydee said, turning to face Albert and switching to Italian so he could understand her.

As they made small talk about the theatre and Haydee's time in Paris, Albert found himself transported. Like at the count's rooms at the hotel in Rome, Albert could believe that some giant had plucked him from Europe and deposited him into a parlour anywhere between Constantinople and Tokyo. Handmaidens dressed in flowing transparent fabrics which he could not name brought trays of sorbet and shaved ice.

Haydee kept her guitar in her hands, and throughout their conversation she played; no specific piece or melody, but an improvised tune which Albert hoped would never end.

Albert found Haydee's perspective on the recent operas and plays quite refreshing. While those shows had circled through the same venues all Albert's life, Haydee's main exposure to theatre was the kabuki plays and Oriental dramas of the East during her travels with the count.

"What about the theatres in Greece?" Albert asked without thinking. "I would imagine the homeland of the great philosophers would produce magnificent actors as well."

Haydee's hand froze while bringing a cup of chilled coffee to her lips, and she looked at the count.

"Go ahead and tell him," Monte Cristo said, in Greek.

Haydee drank her coffee, then turned back to Albert.

"If I saw any plays in Greece, then I was too young to remember them," she said. "I was taken from my home when I was eight years old."

Albert's face fell as his faux pas occurred to him.

"I am sorry, I didn't mean to...do you remember anything of Greece?" Albert asked, blushing.

"I remember the palace," Haydee said with a fond smile. "I remember running through the halls, hiding from my maids and Father's servants. I remember my father as a fat, joyful man, and sitting on his lap playing with his long white beard. I remember a happy home."

A single tear gathered at the corner of her eye. "I also remember how it ended."

Haydee explained to Albert that the war to be free of the Ottoman Empire was going badly, although being only a child she did not understand that at the time. Pasha Ali sent the French officers away, most to the front lines, but dispatched one to Sultan Mahmud to negotiate surrender and a pardon.

"Do you remember that officer's name?" Albert asked, hoping to tell his father which of his former comrades was the culprit.

Haydee's eyes flicked towards the count. "I was always getting their names mixed up as a child," she said. "I cannot say who had been responsible for going to the Sultan."

A night came when a great clamour in the palace awakened her, and her mother had rushed into her bedroom. Together with their servants and maids, they went to a boat which waited for them in the palace grotto. Pasha Ali joined them there, and they escaped out into the lake as Sultan Mahmud's forces swarmed the palace.

The boat took them to an island stronghold where Pasha Ali could make his final stand. The caves there were stocked with the pasha's gold, and hundreds of barrels of gunpowder lined every wall. Selim, the pasha's chief bodyguard, stood constant watch with a lit match and orders to ignite the gunpowder if the sultan's men came before a pardon did.

"Good lord!" Albert exclaimed. "Your father was ready to kill you all and destroy his fortune?"

"If it meant keeping us out of the hands of the enemy, yes," Haydee said. "Terrible things happen to innocent people in war, and Father believed that there were worse things than a swift death. He also wished to safeguard the greatest treasure of Yanina: the Eye of Asclepius."

"What was the Eye?" Albert asked, wondering what sort of artifact could be worth self-immolation to protect.

"It was a silver amulet set with a white sapphire the size of a walnut," Haydee explained. "It had great power, and was named for the demigod son of Apollo who first taught mankind about medicine."

"Forgive me for saying so, but while silver and sapphires are valuable, this seems an odd piece to be your greatest treasure," Albert said.

"The value of the Eye was its role in healing the sick. Anyone who wielded it could draw off life force from another person, and royal physicians since antiquity had used it to diagnose ailments by sharing in a sufferer's symptoms," Haydee said. "It could also be used to share the essence of a healthy person so that a patient may have a better chance of recovering."

The days bled together as Haydee and her family waited in the caves. Pasha Ali kept an eye on the horizon at all times for approaching boats, boats which would mean either their doom or their salvation. If the sultan sent a pardon, they could return home. If he did not, they would attempt to flee. If the sultan prevented them from fleeing, Selim would light the powder and spare them from being tortured and executed by the Ottomans.

A boat approached from the mainland late one night, visible only by the lantern on the bow. Pasha Ali went to the mouth of the cave to meet his fate while Selim lit a fresh match. The boat docked in darkness, and a man emerged bringing the lantern with him. It was the French officer who had gone to Sultan Mahmud to discuss surrender.

He said he came bearing good news, and told Pasha Ali with a smile that the merciful sultan would not punish him. Pasha Ali laughed with relief and ordered Selim to stand down. Selim was all too happy to obey and extinguish his match. Then the French officer drew his pistol and shot Selim through the neck.

"His blood sprayed across my face, and I'll never forget the hot stench of it," Haydee said, then paused and took a deep breath. "The sultan's men, dressed in black, emerged from the shadows and restrained my father. Everyone else was swiftly captured or killed."

"What a fiend!" Albert exclaimed.

"The traitor had Father stripped naked and searched his clothes for the Eye of Asclepius. He used—" Haydee stopped to wipe a tear from her eye. "He used the Eye against Father. The Eye was meant to borrow or share life force in the service of medicine, but he used it to drain Father's energy until Father was nearly dead. Then he put the chain around his own neck and commanded the sultan's men to cut off my dear father's head and preserve it in a barrel of tar."

Monte Cristo savoured the sight of Albert grappling both with that story of depravity and his own guilt for bringing up the topic. The count reminisced about Fernand Mondego, thin and scrawny until his military service took him to Greece. As Caderousse had told Abbe Busoni, Fernand went to war as a walking stick and returned as Hercules. The Eye of Asclepius was never seen again after that bloody night in Yanina, not even in the black markets where such stolen treasures could often be found.

Albert stood up into a deep bow to Haydee. "Your Highness, I am deeply sorry," he said. "Both for your loss, and for my thoughtlessness in having you retell the tale. Please forgive me."

Haydee sniffled, dried her eyes on the count's handkerchief, and smiled.

"It's alright, Albert. You didn't force me to say anything, after all," she said. "Every time I share my story, I feel it losing its power to hurt me. Besides, remembering my sorrow provides perspective to the charmed life I lead today."

She reached out and placed her hand with familiarity on the count's knee.

"Sultan Mahmoud had promised the traitor he could keep a share of any gold and women he found in my father's stronghold," Haydee continued. "But the traitor lost his nerve once we were his possessions. My mother and I were sold to an Arab slaver who took us to Constantinople, and I never saw the traitor again. We were trained for the duties which would be expected of us, and when I was ten my mother was sold without me. Eventually I was sold as well, to the very same sultan who my father had rebelled against."

"That is where I found her," Monte Cristo said. "You recall at breakfast the day I arrived in Paris, I said I had bought a woman's freedom with an emerald? That was Haydee. I tried to find her mother as well, but by the time I could find her newest owner, she had died."

"It seems as though we each owe the count our lives," Albert said. "If you'll have me, I would greatly enjoy spending time with you again; at the moment though, I must depart."

Albert made his exit and returned home in his coupe. His father sat smoking in the garden, but Albert didn't go to join him. He felt it wouldn't be appropriate to share what he had learned about Yanina, although he wasn't certain why.

CHAPTER 80
THE SAUNA

After Albert left, the count removed his mask and spent time in Haydee's company without the pressure of their public personae. Having recovered from his time spent with one Morcerf, Monte Cristo prepared to visit another. The count paid an after-dinner call to Fernand and relayed Baron Danglars' wish to speak to Fernand about the coming marriage.

Morcerf dressed in his formal uniform at once to visit the baron. With his medals and ribbons arranged in just the right way, he ordered his fastest horses to take him to the gaudy house in the Rue de la Chaussee d'Antin.

"General Morcerf," the doorman said with a bow. "Baron Danglars is in the sauna, please follow me."

Confused, Morcerf followed the servant through the garish corridors to the rear of the house. The servant directed him outside to a small outbuilding clad in marble. Inside, Morcerf shed his uniform with reluctance in a tiled dressing room and proceeded wearing a plush towel made of fine Egyptian cotton. At last, he found Danglars in the sauna itself.

The cedar-lined room, lined with three levels of benches along each wall, possessed enough seating for fifty men. A pit piled with steaming black rocks dominated the centre of the sauna. The humidity gripped Morcerf's nose and mouth like soaked cheesecloth. It reminded him of humid summer days in Marseille, but far worse.

Danglars sat in the centre of the highest bench looking down on his visitor. Morcerf tried to find a seat on the upper level but found himself too tall to fit in the space between the bench and ceiling. His large frame forced him to settle for a space beneath Danglars' eyeline.

"Baron Danglars," Morcerf said. "I received your invitation, but I did not realize it was to be so...informal an audience."

"Why should two old friends such as we stand on ceremony?" Danglars asked with a grin.

Sweat ran down from Danglar's bare scalp and along the rolls of his stomach. His previous life as a ship's supercargo required a certain level of physical fitness, but luxury and idleness had allowed him to let himself go. A similar sheen of sweat already coated Morcerf's sculpted musculature as well.

"True enough, I suppose," Morcerf said. He took a deep breath; sauna air had that peculiar way of making it feel like a voluntary action. "I spoke to M. de Monte Cristo today, and he said you wanted to see me to discuss the wedding."

"I do indeed," Danglars said.

Danglars rang a large bell at his side and the doorman reappeared. The young man added more water to the pile of rocks using a ladle and bucket. This produced so much steam that Morcerf had trouble seeing Danglars sitting two feet from him. He felt as though he could push off from his seat and swim through the air, the vapour was so thick.

"I'll be blunt: another suitor is courting Eugenie, one more suitable than your son," Danglars said. The doorman still stood sweating in his livery by the door.

"Who could be more suitable than Albert? Has some witch hexed the d'Armilly girl and turned her into a man?" Morcerf asked. His laughter subsided when Danglars did not join in. "You're serious? After all the times we've helped each other, you're breaking off our arrangement? Who is this suitor?"

"Prince Andrea de Cavalcanti," Danglars said. "His fortune is vast, and his manners are impeccable; at least, once you allow for the eccentricities of a foreigner. When I see him with Eugenie, I see a man ready to dote upon her and make her a happy wife, which is more than I can say for Albert. And the Cavalcanti reputation is impeccable, which is more than I can say for yours."

"How dare you!" Morcerf growled. He rose to his feet with his hands outstretched, ready to burn Danglars alive in his own home.

However, no flames arrived. Instead Morcerf felt a strange

dissatisfaction in his fingers like a phantom limb. He stared at his empty hands in surprise, and then his eyes returned to the basin of rocks.

"I find that bad news is more palatable in a sauna," Danglars said casually. "Particularly when one is delivering it to a Catalan Flamekeeper."

"I don't need my gift to choke the life from you, you slack-jowled weasel!" Morcerf growled.

He reached out to wrap his hands around Danglars' neck, but the point of steel stopped him. The overheated doorman held the tip of a sword against a pulsing vein in Morcerf's neck.

"What is the meaning of this?" Morcerf said, still as a statue.

"I remember your temper well, Fernand," Danglars said. "It seemed wise to take precautions when I cancelled the marriage between our children. I reached my current station in life by examining developments in the world and adjusting my plans accordingly, and developments in the past fortnight have made this adjustment necessary."

"And what development has convinced you to tie your family name to some Italian vagabond?" Morcerf asked.

"Nothing which you can rectify," Danglars said. "I've simply learned new information, and that has resulted in the end of this arrangement."

Morcerf ground his teeth as his blood pounded in his temples. Violence roared through his mind and demanded to be vented upon the baron, but the moisture in the air and the steel at his neck prevented it.

"I think we understand each other," Danglars said. "My servant will see you out."

The tip of the sword moved just enough to allow Morcerf to step down from the bench. The servant never wavered, holding the point within striking distance as Morcerf dressed and returned to his coach. The humidity seeped into Morcerf's every pore and blocked him from summoning any flame. He couldn't conjure even enough fire to light a cigarette until after he got home.

The next day, a stack of the morning newspapers appeared on Danglars' doorstop. As usual, he skimmed the political and financial pages for items of interest to him; many of his finest deals began with him spotting an article about some new situation he could invest in and then legislate a tidy profit for himself.

Deviating from that routine, he set aside the largest journals and focused on The Independent. Towards the back he found Beauchamp Fournier's byline at the head of a paragraph titled "We hear from Yanina." Danglars' thin lips stretched to the side in that expression he used in place of a smile.

CHAPTER 81
WE HEAR FROM YANINA

At around nine o'clock that Monday morning, pedestrians on the Champs Elysees were treated to the sight of Albert de Morcerf stomping towards the home of the Count of Monte Cristo. Albert's black coat was buttoned up to his chin, though he had misfastened one, and he held a crumpled piece of newsprint in his hand. Passers-by who knew Albert might have seen the rage in his eyes and heat-shimmer above his head and been surprised the little paper did not burst into flame.

Carlo the concierge admitted him at once and Bertuccio escorted him to the backyard. The count sat smoking at a garden table where several newspapers sat next to a magnificent pistol. The polished mahogany woodwork of the pistol was complemented by workings and ornaments made of shining brass. At the far end of the yard by a brick wall, playing cards hung from a string.

"Albert, has there been some trouble?" Monte Cristo said. "If I had less faith in your good nature, I would think that murder was written all over your face."

"Not murder, but certainly a killing. I'm going to kill him. I'll fight him and I'll kill him," Albert said. "It's slander! I'll sue Beauchamp if he survives my challenge!"

"Really, do settle down," Monte Cristo said.

The count rang his gong and Ali appeared with an assortment of cigars. Albert handed his piece of newsprint to the count and lit his tobacco off a fireball the size of a torch.

"Read it," Albert said as he exhaled smoke, the words coming out with the cotton tones that can be achieved no other way.

Monte Cristo could guess what it said before he even glanced at the page, having played no small part in orchestrating the article. Danglars' operatives in Yanina, sent at the count's suggestion, were no more likely to hold their tongues about what they learned than Danglars himself. Still, it was a pleasant surprise for the revelations to come from one of Albert's closest friends. The count read the paragraph aloud.

"A correspondent in the Greek province of Yanina informs us of a fact long thought lost to history. While we knew that a trusted French officer betrayed the grand Pasha Ali to Sultan Mahmud, the officer's name had remained in obscurity. By interviewing several Ottoman slaves, former servants to Pasha Ali, the officer's name has been discovered to be Fernand," the count read. "Several officers were sent to aid the pasha in his fight for independence... Albert, I don't see why this means you need to challenge Beauchamp to a duel."

"Are you blind? It flatly mentions my father by his Christian name!" Albert said.

"It says Fernand, but who would connect that to your father?" Monte Cristo said. "Fernand is a common enough name. I'm sure nobody would think that a man of your father's reputation would be the same Fernand who committed such a vile betrayal."

"You don't know Paris! That is the most scandalous conclusion people could draw, and thus it's exactly the one they will draw. I have to challenge Beauchamp for this assault on my family's honour," Albert said, pacing. "That's why I came here; I'd like you to be my second."

"It's funny that you should say that; I had just finished shooting perhaps a quarter hour before you arrived. You see my targets there?" Monte Cristo said.

"The cards?" Albert asked. The string held a pristine suit of spades lacking only the face cards. "I've been tempted to try that feat of marksmanship myself. Don't feel bad for not marking them, such a small area is incredibly difficult to hit even at closer range."

"Not marking them? Albert, those cards are all hearts," Monte Cristo said with a chuckle.

In spite of his rage, Albert laughed at the count's joke. When Monte Cristo invited him to go check, he was astonished to see red numbers on each card and neat holes shot clean through each painted heart.

"*Mon dieu*, with aim like this you should perform in the circus!"

Albert exclaimed. "If Beauchamp should best me, I have no doubt you could end him at twice this distance."

"Guns are fantastic little testaments to man's ingenuity," Monte Cristo said. "They can be anything from the crudest tool to the finest piece of craftsmanship and used as an instrument of leisure as easily as they can feed a man's family in the countryside."

"Don't forget their usefulness in ending the lives of men," Albert said with his eyes locked on Beauchamp's article.

"Yes, but anything can be used that way. Don't forget that the earliest weapons of war were simple stones; that doesn't overshadow their uses as a building material, as millstones, or a medium of art," Monte Cristo said. "Besides, a pistol allows even the feeblest cripple to defend himself against an attacker many times his own strength."

"We've trailed off into philosophy again," Albert said, finishing his cigar with a last long draw. "I intend to go to the offices of the Independent, demand that Beauchamp publicly retract this slander, and slap my glove across his face if he refuses."

"I wouldn't be a good friend if I didn't point out the flaws in your plan," Monte Cristo said. Although it pleased him to see the Yanina matter affecting Albert so deeply, he could not allow Albert to murder Beauchamp. "I've known Beauchamp a short time, but even I know he won't retract the story as long as he knows a man named Fernand truly did betray the pasha. That will leave you fighting a friend to the death, over something that nobody in the world is likely to connect to your father."

"You don't understand!" Albert cried. He held up his hand, which he wrapped in a glove of fire. "I have Catalan blood, and more than that I'm a Flamekeeper. Greatness is expected of me, and I cannot achieve that if any hint of this scandal clings to my name."

"Can't you?" Monte Cristo asked. "Men have pulled themselves up by their bootstraps throughout history. The fathers of the United States of America were colonial farmers and the British considered them criminals, and nobody will ever forget their names."

"Are you saying that you won't be my second?" Albert asked.

"I told you my feelings about duels back in Rome. For a serious injury—which I guarantee you this isn't—a slower revenge is more appropriate," the count said. "At least duel him only to first blood; it would be far more suitable for such a minor slight."

"This attack on my family name is anything but minor!" Albert said. "I'm surprised that you're so reluctant to participate, considering what you were just doing with that suit of hearts."

"One of the reasons I practice shooting is because I may be challenged to the death by any harebrained fool who has no real quarrel with me, like you plan to do with Beauchamp," Monte Cristo replied. "At that time, I'd be obligated to kill the man over nothing at all. But there's a world of difference between self-defence, avenging a grave error, and simply attacking a man. And what if the wild conclusion you've reached turns out to be true?"

"True?" Albert said.

"I don't think it is, but what if it were?" Monte Cristo said. "Then you'll have challenged your friend, and either killed him or died in the attempt, all to punish him for reporting the truth. What sort of man would that make you?"

"The sort who doesn't allow any stain on his family name, regardless of veracity," Albert said.

Monte Cristo sighed. "If you're determined to challenge Beauchamp, at least do it alone, without witnesses," he said. "Give him the chance to discuss this with you in private, where he would be more receptive to your request. If he agrees to retract the article, you get your satisfaction. If he doesn't, then find two strangers and admit them to your secret for the challenge."

Albert waved for Ali and took a second cigar from the tray. After several long puffs, his expression softened.

"Very well, I'll see Beauchamp alone," Albert said. "If it does come to a duel, will you be my second then?"

"As much as I'll always place myself at your disposal, I have to refuse," Monte Cristo said.

Albert rolled his eyes in frustration. "Very well. Franz will stand with me, and if not then Raoul or Max certainly would."

Annoyed at this lack of cooperation from Monte Cristo, Albert cut his visit short and left to find Beauchamp at his office.

The Independent was written and printed in a gloomy and dusty building, though Beauchamp did his best to brighten up his own corner of it. Beauchamp was surprised when the doorman announced Albert; he had never shown an interest in the paper except to tease Beauchamp about the subjects of his articles. If pressed, Beauchamp would have admitted surprise that Albert even knew where the newspaper office was.

"Albert, welcome to my humble abode!" Beauchamp said, clearing scraps of paper off of his other chair. "Please have a seat next to the geranium, the only thing in this room that reminds me that the world is more than newsprint."

"I'll stand," Albert said with a stiff and formal bow.

He then explained to the baffled Beauchamp the purpose of his visit: the article about Yanina, the mention of an officer named Fernand, his father's role in Pasha Ali's service and certain blamelessness in the pasha's downfall.

"Your father's name is Fernand?" Beauchamp said. "I had no idea."

"A likely story!" Albert scoffed. "You claim to be my friend, but don't know my father's name?"

"Do you know my father's name?" Beauchamp asked.

Albert's mouth opened and closed like a fish. "That isn't the point!" he said at last. "The point is, I demand you publicly retract this article in the next edition."

"I'm afraid I cannot. We verified the information beyond doubt," Beauchamp said. He leaned back in his chair with his fingers steepled. "The recent issue of false news which so wounded Baron Danglars has pushed us to be even more careful than usual. There is no doubt that a man named Fernand betrayed Pasha Ali. Albert, I cannot retract facts."

"Then you refuse!" Albert said. His hand jerked toward the glove hanging out of his pocket. Beauchamp frowned.

"I refuse to undermine the principles of journalism, but I'll promise you this: give me some more time, and I'll verify that your father had nothing to do with this. You say he was deployed elsewhere when the pasha fell; I'll gather all the relevant facts and publish them," Beauchamp offered, his tone cool since the realization that Albert hadn't come as a friend asking a favour, but as a potential combatant. "There will be no doubt in anyone's mind that your father, Count Fernand de Morcerf, is not the same man as this other Fernand. That is, if any of them had made the connection to begin with."

Albert mulled the matter over. His visit with Monte Cristo had allowed him to vent the worst of his anger before reaching the Independent. He weighed the delay of letting Beauchamp investigate the issue against the prospect of dueling with his own friend. Another thought occurred to him as well, that if he killed Beauchamp then no retraction or clarification would ever come.

"Fine," Albert said. "Do your fact-checking, and publish an article explaining that my father wasn't even in Yanina at the time of the betrayal. How long will you need?"

Beauchamp stroked his mustache as he calculated response time, distance, and a dozen other considerations peculiar to investigative reporting.

"Three weeks," Beauchamp said.

"Three!" Albert said. It was outrageous, but he saw no way to improve it. "Very well. Three weeks, and then you publish your article exonerating my father. But it must be no further in than the second page!"

"Three weeks, and I'll publish my findings," Beauchamp said.

Beauchamp decided not to clarify that he couldn't guarantee his findings would line up with what Albert wanted. Experience told him that even the most decorated war hero could have secrets and exaggerations hidden in their history.

"Very well," Albert said. He stood silently, trying to think of anything else to say to Beauchamp.

Beauchamp, irritated at coming so close to a duel, offered no help in soothing the awkwardness of the situation. He stared until Albert left without a goodbye.

CHAPTER 82
THE RESCUE

For the first time since returning from Africa, Max felt like a happy man. Noirtier's divine intervention had lifted from his shoulders the weight of possibly losing Valentine forever. Growing up as the son of a moderate Bonapartist supporter, Max knew many stories of Noirtier's daring adventures as a gentleman rogue and bon-vivant. His father's face would have lit up if he would have known what the famous Jules Noirtier had done for Valentine, and through her, for Max.

On top of that, the act of confessing his pain to the count had robbed his memories of some of their power. In the days after his drunken confession, telling the count everything about Hugo's death and seeing his apparition, his spells came fewer and farther between. He still saw Hugo, watching him from the corner of a room or laying broken in the street, but the ghost held less power over him. At last, Max thought he may be able to get better.

Valentine found her new situation less favourable. Although she had a safe haven in the count's home to hide from her father, she couldn't help but feel trapped. On the rare occasions that she ventured out even for a walk along the Champs-Elysees, she flinched at every passing patrolman for fear of him reporting her location to Villefort. She therefore placed herself under a sort of house arrest until something could be done about bringing her father to justice.

Little did Valentine know, she needn't have worried. The threat of career-ending scandals kept Villefort far too distracted to notice he hadn't seen his only child in days. An intolerable number of reporters stood on permanent stakeout at the Palais de Justice, forcing Villefort to rely on his secret entrance to get in and out of the building. The stream of inflammatory articles by Jordan Caillat continued unabated, and Caillat seemed hell-bent on exposing every sacrifice Villefort had ever offered to heaven. How Caillat could have got the names to begin with remained beyond Villefort's understanding.

Even staff at the Palais, curious after reading a month's worth of Caillat articles in the Nightly Assemblage, began to look into the cold cases of the victims Caillat named. Villefort considered forbidding the clerks from entering the archives except on official business, but that would only serve to draw more attention. Villefort found himself caught between allowing someone to uncover the pattern on their own, or announcing to everyone that a pattern existed to be found.

In the Tuesday edition, Villefort was furious to see that Caillat released yet another article. The newest installment once again drew attention to the attempt on his life in Auteuil in 1817, and the mysterious woman staying at the house. To make matters worse, this time Caillat revealed that neighbours claimed the mystery woman was very pregnant at the time of the attack, and that Villefort's father-in-law owned the house. As always, Caillat left his article open-ended to allow the reader to draw their own conclusions.

On Wednesday, Max went to the Rue de Faubourg Saint-Honore. Dressed as a gardener, he circled around the Villefort house to the laneway beyond the garden wall at the rear. He found the back gate to the Villefort garden, latched from the other side. Fortunately, his time on campaign had left him in fine physical shape and he could leap high enough to grasp the top of the wall. With a grunt of effort, he used his upper body strength to push himself up and over into the garden. He unlatched the gate and made his way closer to the house.

Max found the back door locked as well but gained entry through a window into the dining room. Valentine had told him they employed very few servants to begin with, and only one would be in the house at this hour to take care of Noirtier. Even then, that servant would only come if Barrois went to fetch her. Max listened for that servant's footsteps to avoid discovery on his way to the second floor.

After opening three wrong doors and finding one locked, multiple Maxes reflected in a series of mirrors told him he had found the correct room. Sure enough, Noirtier sat in his chair by the window. Rather than watching the outdoors, Noirtier stared at Max in the nearest looking-glass; Max realized that Noirtier must have been able to watch him enter by the garden.

"M. Noirtier? My name is Maximilien Morrel, I'm here to get you out of this house," Max said. Noirtier fluttered his eyelids, and Max was thankful that Valentine had taught him their code.

"Monsieur, I know Valentine told you about me. I love her more than anything, and would do anything to keep her happy," Max said. "She also told me about your son's terrible proclivities."

"Master safe here," Barrois croaked from his perch by the bookshelf.

"Even so, Valentine will feel much better when she knows you're not under M. de Villefort's thumb anymore," Max said.

Noirtier considered this for a moment, then looked at Barrois and blinked once.

"Agreed," Barrois said.

Max breathed a sigh of relief.

"Very good. I'll carry you down to the garden, then come back for your chair," Max said. "Then I can bring you and Barrois back to where Valentine is staying."

Noirtier blinked again, but heavy footfalls coming up the stairs cut the rescue attempt short.

"Hide," Barrois said, as if Max needed the advice.

Max dove into a wardrobe in the corner. No sooner had he closed the door than Villefort entered the room.

"You ungrateful wretch!" Villefort shouted at once, levelling a jaundiced finger at Noirtier. "You couldn't have just kept quiet, could you? You had to reveal your poisonous secrets and tell Franz that he'd not only be marrying into the stain of treason, but also the legacy of murder!"

Max held his breath and kept his eye to a gap in the wardrobe door. This late in the morning, Villefort's schedule should have placed him at the Palais.

"Will your treason ever stop haunting me, Father?" Villefort asked as he paced through the room, running his hands through his hair. "Will you ever for even one moment display a bit of gratitude to me, for keeping you out of the sanatorium and letting you live under my roof?"

"Gratitude," Barrois said. "Position. Emperor."

Villefort turned to face Barrois. "You dare throw the Hundred Days in my face? Nobody asked for your opinion, you semi-articulate doorstop!"

Villefort swung his walking stick at Barrois, knocking the surprised gargoyle off its perch. Barrois hissed and climbed with surprising speed along the stick, slashing at Villefort with its claws. Villefort caught a chance blow on his hand and Barrois flew upward to cling to the ceiling, out of reach. Instinctively, Villefort brought his bloodied hand to his mouth to suck at the wound, either not realizing or not caring that his father could see. He calmed down as he drank.

"Rest assured, Father. Despite your scheming, I will find Valentine a suitable Royalist husband. This time, he may not be so understanding as to allow you to live with them," Villefort said. "I want you to think about how lonely an existence it will be when there is nobody in this house but you, me, and the staff."

Villefort took his leave, not realizing that his threat of loneliness had already been fulfilled, and after several long minutes Max judged it safe to emerge from hiding.

"I'm afraid this isn't the right time to get you out of here undetected, monsieur," Max said. "But Valentine and I will think of something, I swear."

Noirtier blinked once, and Max snuck out into the hallway. With no sign of Villefort, Max retraced his steps back to the dining room and let himself out. He didn't notice Villefort's yellow face looming in an upper window as he made his way through the garden.

Villefort recognized Max on sight: the military doctor from the Count of Monte Cristo's dinner party in Auteuil. Captain Morrel, son of Pierre Morrel, the Bonapartist shipowner from Marseille.

"What were you doing in my house, Morrel?" Villefort muttered to the empty room.

In the clarity that he often experienced after a bleeding, the pieces fell into place easily. He knew Valentine had a secret lover, having overheard her confess it to Noirtier. If the suitor were an honest Royalist, Valentine would have taken the chance of introducing him to Villefort in the hopes of replacing one match with another. Instead, she feared introducing him or even saying his name under Villefort's roof.

Furthermore, she told Noirtier that the man she loved had returned from war; a soldier from a traitorous family was the logical explanation for his identity.

"You've made a grave mistake, Captain Morrel," Villefort muttered as Max opened the back gate and escaped into the laneway.

CHAPTER 83
THE RETIRED BAKER

Andrea Cavalcanti made an appearance on Friday at the Danglars house. With his fair hair curled and his red goatee trimmed down to a waxed mustache, he cut a rather dashing figure. Andrea and Danglars spent many minutes locked in conversation in the drawing-room, where Andrea poured his heart out about his mixed emotions regarding the reunion with and subsequent departure of his estranged father.

Andrea also expounded on the kindness of the Danglars family for treating him, a foreigner, like their own son. At length, he came about to his main point: how Eugenie's company soothed his soul during such a trying time. Danglars pretended to be uncertain despite expecting, encouraging, and hoping for this declaration. He was not at all surprised when Andrea concluded with an offer of marriage.

"Aren't you rather young to be considering marriage, Prince Cavalcanti?" Danglars said.

"The Italian nobility generally marry young," Andrea said, not knowing whether it was true or not. "Besides, being separated from my father for so long has taught me that I should seize the moment and spend as much time as I can with those I love."

Having made his token gesture of conscientious objection, Danglars maneuvered the conversation to more important matters. He asked who could handle the preliminary arrangements, with Major Cavalcanti already returned to Italy. Andrea produced a letter from his father, promising one hundred fifty thousand livres per annum as long as the Major approved of the bride. A second later he proclaimed how agreeable Major Cavalcanti found the possibility of marital union with the illustrious house of Danglars.

"My father left me this first document when he guessed that I may wish to settle in France. When I wrote to him about how kind your family has been to me, he replied with the second," Andrea explained. The first letter was genuine, the second a forgery. "It's also possible that I could persuade my father to send me the capital of my allowance instead of just the interest; that would amount to two or three million."

"Oh?" Danglars asked, hiding his joy admirably.

"Our mutual friend, the Count of Monte Cristo, who knows my father well, thinks that acquiring the capital would be simple," Andrea said. "With your talents, those millions could realize ten percent."

"I never give more than four percent, but for my son-in-law I would cut my own profit and give five," Danglars replied.

"Very good, father-in-law," Andrea said, baring his large white teeth in a smile.

Andrea and Danglars shook on the arrangement. Danglars felt a relief not experienced since his days aboard the Pharaon, at times when water and rations ran low on calm seas, and the wind rose at the eleventh hour to carry them the rest of the way to port. With the money from the marriage he could replace Villefort's and Morcerf's buy-in for the Dead Plague scheme, which he had embezzled to cover his investment losses. The threat of dealing with a scorned crown prosecutor or a cheated Flamekeeper would no longer loom over his head.

On the other side of the transaction, Andrea could smell the security and status of marrying into a banker's family. As a foreign bachelor with a checkered past, Andrea still felt subject to a certain level of suspicion. If he could tie himself to the Danglars barony, he fancied that a great deal of those questions would cease.

"Barring any obstacle on your part, I see no reason not to allow you to marry my dear Eugenie," Danglars said.

"Marvelous," Andrea replied. "Now, having concluded business with my father-in-law, I need to conduct business with my banker. I need to withdraw some funds beyond my allowance."

"Ah, my indulgence toward family goes only so far," Danglars said. "I can let you withdraw to your month's limit, but no further."

"I thought you might say that, so I spoke to Monte Cristo," Andrea said. "He gave me this letter to say that the twenty thousand francs I ask for can be taken from his unlimited credit with you."

"Very well!" Danglars croaked. "My cashier will send a check to your hotel for the sum."

Andrea returned to his hotel around evening, right about the same time Eugenie learned without fanfare that she would marry Andrea Cavalcanti rather than Albert de Morcerf. She accepted the news at dinner in silence before departing in her coach to visit Louise d'Armilly's boarding house for vocal practice. Meanwhile, at the lobby of the Hotel des Princes, the porter greeted Andrea.

"Sir, it's about that man you leave an income for," the porter said. Andrea cut him off with a boisterous laugh.

"Oh yes, my father's old servant!" Andrea said, a little too loudly. "An odd fellow, but he served my father well. The least I can do is help old Pailletin to stay comfortable. Did he come for his payment?"

"Yes, but he wouldn't take it, sir," the porter said. "And—"

"Viscount Andrea Cavalcanti!" an old man with a thick black beard hollered from the hotel bar. "As I live and breathe!"

"Sir, he refused to leave and insisted on waiting for you," the porter whispered before scurrying away.

"Pailletin!" Andrea said, throwing an arm around Caderousse's shoulder. "Please, come up to my room."

Once behind closed doors, the mask of Andrea Cavalcanti fell away and Benedetto dropped all pretenses of his assumed persona.

"What do you want, Caderousse?" Benedetto asked. "I thought we both understood our arrangement."

"I understand our arrangement perfectly," Caderousse said, helping himself to some fruit in the sitting room. "You, however, don't seem to grasp the extent of it. My income isn't enough; I require an increase."

"An increase?" Benedetto asked, eyes wide. "Two hundred francs per week isn't enough to carry on the pretense of a beloved retired servant, or retired baker, or whatever it is you pretend to be?"

"You know how the world works, Benedetto. One day two hundred francs is plenty, and then the House passes some law or another, and the grocer must drive up his prices for the cost of compliance. Then two hundred francs is a paltry sum," Caderousse said.

He wandered the suite in search of more to satisfy himself, finding a bottle of old red wine in the liquor cabinet and a selection of wax-sealed cheese on the sideboard.

"Besides, you can afford to pay me more," Caderousse said. "As I hear it, you're to marry the daughter of Baron Danglars and grant yourself unlimited access to his vaults!"

"How the devil could you know that so soon?" Benedetto asked.

"Servants drink and drunkards talk," Caderousse said. "You know, Danglars is an old friend of mine. How cruel fate is, that she bestows her rewards on one person so bountifully and yet scarcely touch the men on either side! He and the Count de Morcerf and I used to dine together, before they were so proud."

"Get to your point, Caderousse," Benedetto said, already irritated with the old man's mannerisms.

"I have a plan," Caderousse said. "You would do well to listen, since I know the truth behind Viscount Andrea Cavalcanti."

Benedetto sighed, pinching the bridge of his nose. "Go ahead, then. What is your plan?"

"I understand you have a patron here in Paris, some wealthy princeling they call the Count of Monte Cristo," Caderousse said. "The stories of his riches are legendary in the taverns, and they call his house a treasure cave out of the Thousand and One Nights."

Benedetto guessed the shape of Caderousse's plan. "In exchange for your continued silence, you want me to help you rob the Count's house for gold or some treasures for you to sell, so you can retire off the proceeds."

"As well as increasing my payments to five hundred francs," Caderousse said with a smile. He enjoyed seeing Benedetto dressed in such finery and humbled in front of him; he could almost imagine himself wielding this power over Danglars or Fernand.

Benedetto fumed, but relented. "Fine. But be careful what you take; you may be in the business of stealing my inheritance."

"Your inheritance?" Caderousse said.

"I'm nearly certain it's true, that the Count of Monte Cristo is my real father," Benedetto said with a grin. "I always knew it wasn't that Corsican smuggler, and of course Major Cavalcanti was only ever a fiction. But it all makes sense: why else would Monte Cristo take such an interest in me? And also—well, what have you heard of him?"

"Besides his money, the only things ever said about him are his odd habits and ghastly appearance," Caderousse said.

"If you get the chance to lay eyes on him, you won't believe it," Benedetto said. "His skin is chalk-white, with fine lines like the cracks in the highest quality porcelain, and his eyes are blood-red. He is the most otherworldly person I have ever met."

"And you think that, given your own otherworldly appetites, he may be your sire?" Caderousse said. "Congratulations!"

Together they refined Caderousse's plan. Benedetto sketched the layout of the count's house on the Champs-Elysees, including the gardens and courtyards as well as the eight-foot walls around the perimeter. The servants slept in the upper apartments of a coach-house separate from the main building. Whenever the count gave Andrea gold or banknotes, he did so from a mahogany secretary in his dressing room on the second floor which always had the key left in it. Benedetto outlined the positions of each large window in the building with fastidious detail.

"Any dogs?" Caderousse asked.

"One, but the count told me it has been taken to his country-house at Auteuil for security there. He goes there himself two or three times a week and plans to spend the night there tomorrow." Benedetto glanced at Caderousse. "He has invited me to join him and made it clear that I'm always welcome to spend the night as well."

"Magnificent; tomorrow night I shall pay the princeling's palace a visit," Caderousse said. "And you, dear little Benedetto, will have the perfect alibi. How could the count suspect his secret son of robbing him when Andrea Cavalcanti was with him in the country at the time of the theft?"

"Very well, the plan is set. You have your means and opportunity, will you now leave me alone?" Benedetto asked.

"Certainly, as soon as my increase has been paid. And also that diamond you wear on your finger," Caderousse said with his large white grin.

Caderousse left with a sack of silver coins and a roll of banknotes, along with the reluctantly-given ring, and returned to the humble rooms he rented above a paper shop. The tools of his old tailoring trade covered the rough wooden table in his sitting room, where the pieces of a navy blue waistcoat sat waiting to be assembled.

"A few finishing touches on this, I think," Caderousse muttered.

From squares of yellow felt he cut out ancient runes and arcane symbols, sigils of protection against all manner of beasts.

"I may not know what you are, Benedetto, but I know what you do," he said. He sewed a symbol to ward off ghouls next to a rune meant to repel the undead, and drew another one to turn away the loup-garou. "For every creature that feasts on human flesh, I know a sigil. One day you'll turn on old Caderousse, and old Caderousse will be prepared."

CHAPTER 84
THE BURGLARY

Haydee and the rest of the Count of Monte Cristo's household started their preparations to set out for Auteuil early Saturday morning, except for Ali who would remain behind. Bertuccio returned from Normandy with news that the count's house there stood ready whenever he wished to visit. Monte Cristo praised Bertuccio's work and rewarded him with two days off.

"Go out into the city, see an opera, visit the Louvre, do anything your heart desires besides waiting on this house," the count said. He knew Andrea could decide to visit at any time, and it was not yet time to bring Bertuccio face-to-face with his adopted son.

When Bertuccio left, Baptistan entered the count's sitting-room. Its wooden footsteps rang out against the floors, and it carried a single folded letter on a silver tray.

"Master, this one has received an urgent message for you," Baptistan said in its peculiar artificial voice.

Monte Cristo accepted the paper. It warned of an impending burglary that night, and the letter-writer appealed to the count's courage to convince him to take matters into his own hands rather than involving the police. The count chuckled to himself.

"So many people are so eager to burgle my home," the count said. "Is this warning meant to entrap the burglar or to entrap myself? What do you think, Baptistan?"

"This one cannot provide advice, Master," Baptistan replied.

"Of course," Monte Cristo said.

He sat weighing the possible outcomes. He had expected something like this since he first told Andrea about his travel habits, but it seemed Andrea had enlisted an accomplice to conduct the job. Why then set up the burglary for failure? The most obvious explanation was that the other man knew Andrea's secret, and Andrea hoped the count would do the dirty work of silencing him.

"Go ahead with Haydee and the other servants to Auteuil," the count told Baptistan. "I'll remain here with Ali and reunite with you at my convenience."

As the household made their way to the country, Monte Cristo and Ali made preparations and took up positions in the count's bedroom. From there, the count slid aside a panel allowing a view into his own dressing-room. The mahogany secretary sat in plain view.

Ali carried a carbine rifle and twin double-barreled pistols, while the count needed no weapons. He remained motionless until nightfall with his red eyes locked on the secretary and his keen ears alert to any sound in the empty house. Ali kept watch on the street from the window, blending in with the darkness.

When the church bells struck quarter past twelve in the morning, a much fainter sound reached the count's ear. He heard a delicate scratching against a window on the ground floor of the house, then a second, and two more. To Monte Cristo's surprise, a voice he knew too well congratulated itself at a whisper. The count signaled to Ali to assist him with a disguise. Before fetching the makeup and wig, Ali replied with signs of his own: he had spied a figure standing watch in the street.

Caderousse stuck a piece of glued paper to the square he cut into the window using Benedetto's diamond ring. With a tap of his fist, the glass came loose without falling to the floor inside, and he peeled it away to reveal a neat hole. He discarded it into the grass and put his arm through the hole to undo the window-latch. It swung open, and Caderousse stepped inside.

"Very good, very good indeed," Caderousse muttered.

He followed Benedetto's map up the stairs and into the dressing-room, taking no particular care for silence once inside the house and, he thought, alone. Caderousse made straight for the secretary and found it locked, but he carried a selection of skeleton keys.

As he tried the fifth key, a door opening behind him illuminated the dark room. Caderousse turned to see Abbe Busoni, who once gave him a magnificent diamond which tempted him to murder, standing backlit in the doorway.

"M. Caderousse, what a surprise," Busoni said. He wore tinted spectacles, which Caderousse did not remember him wearing before, but otherwise there could be no mistake.

"Abbe Busoni!" Caderousse cried, too shocked and dumbfounded to even move.

"Ah good, you remember me," Busoni said. "It has been, what, ten years since we saw each other last? I would ask if you made good use of the diamond which was bequeathed to you, but then I remember hearing about your trial. That man, Johannes, had already paid you forty thousand for the diamond, but you killed him out of greed."

"It was my wife!" Caderousse blurted. "She killed the jeweller, the evidence was all there! After all, I was only sentenced to the galleys rather than the gallows!"

"Yes, you were. And yet I find you here, free but not reformed," Busoni said. "How are you walking among civilized men again?"

"Do you have soldiers lying in wait for me, reverend sir?" Caderousse asked, clasping his hands.

"No, I'm alone. And despite my better judgement, I'm compelled by pity and Christian charity to let you leave freely if you tell me the truth," Busoni said.

Caderousse dropped to his knees in thanks. "There I was in my chains, bound to a young Corsican," he said. "Some benefactor knew where he was and had a metal file smuggled aboard the ship. While the other slaves had their hour of rest, we snuck away and sawed through our chains."

As Caderousse told his story, he inched closer to Busoni.

"We swam for freedom, parted ways for a time, and then found each other again here in Paris," Caderousse said.

"And who was this Corsican? Is he here tonight?" Busoni asked.

"His name is Benedetto. His benefactor connected him with another wealthy protector; tonight he sleeps in Auteuil," Caderousse said.

"Whereas you have chosen other nocturnal activities," Busoni said, pointing at the secretary. Behind his impassive expression, the count's mind raced. If the man outside stood guard, Caderousse was too much of a coward not to admit it if he knew.

"But I am in poverty!" Caderousse whined at Busoni's feet.

"Poverty is the default state of mankind and can only be escaped through honest work which benefits your fellow man," Busoni replied. "Many are in poverty; they don't all violate people's homes in search of plunder."

"It's hardly plunder; this man has enough wealth for seven lifetimes!" Caderousse said. "This is the house of Benedetto's protector and natural father, the Count of Monte Cristo."

The admission caught Busoni off-guard. "The count is Benedetto's father?" he asked. "How did you reach that conclusion?"

"Easily," Caderousse said, drawing a dagger from beneath his coat and plunging it between Busoni's ribs.

Caderousse hoped to incapacitate Busoni and escape, but instead Busoni grabbed him by the neck. Busoni ignored his wound, lifting Caderousse off his feet with one hand and pulling the knife from his side with the other. He showed the bloodless blade to Caderousse.

"The Lord is my armour and grants me strength," Busoni said. "You say this Benedetto, this criminal, is the young man who my friend the count has taken under his wing?"

"Andrea Cavalcanti, yes," Caderousse said, gasping for breath.

"Here is what you will do," Busoni said. "I'll provide ink and paper, and you will write a letter to Andrea's intended father-in-law Baron Danglars. You'll explain precisely who Andrea truly is, and what crime he committed to be sentenced to the galleys. Do you understand?"

Busoni loosened his grip just a fraction to allow Caderousse some air.

"Yes, yes, anything you say!" Caderousse said.

Busoni dropped him to the floor and clapped his gloved hands together. Ali emerged from the bedroom, still armed, and fetched the writing materials Busoni called for.

Under close watch and with a pistol aimed at the back of his head, Caderousse wrote what Busoni dictated and supplied those details which Busoni claimed not to know.

"Baron Danglars: the man whom you are receiving at your house and betrothed to your daughter, known as Andrea Cavalcanti, is a felon who escaped with me from the galleys at Toulon," Caderousse read aloud. "His name was Benedetto, and he is a foundling with no knowledge of his real parents. His prisoner number was 59, and mine was 58. Of his many crimes, the worst was the unnatural and cannibalistic maiming of a man who owed him money."

Caderousse added his signature and addressed it. Busoni turned to Ali and made some signs with his hands which Caderousse did not understand; the count silently asked Ali if the other man still stood in the street below. Ali nodded, and Busoni took the note.

"That will suffice. Now begone, and let God's judgement be upon you," Busoni said.

"I'm free to go?" Caderousse asked, staring at the dagger hole in Busoni's shirt.

"Leave, before I change my mind," Busoni said. "After all, I offered you freedom and comfort once, and you squandered it. Perhaps I shouldn't do so again."

Caderousse wasted no more time and hurried down the stairs; meanwhile, the count unlocked his secretary and tucked the sealed letter away for safekeeping. Caderousse ran for the rope he had thrown over the wall, but received a third great shock when he reached the crest of the wall to find Benedetto's face.

"Hello Caderousse," Benedetto said with a grin, his teeth shining in the moonlight. He had climbed the rope from the other side, and he gripped Caderousse's outstretched arm to help him over. "Did you get the money?"

"Benedetto!" Caderousse cried. "No, I was interrupted and only barely escaped. You're supposed to be in Auteuil!"

"Yes, but I got hungry," Benedetto said.

He pulled Caderousse towards him and bit his shoulder. Benedetto sunk his strong teeth through Caderousse's coat and shirt, tearing away a ragged chunk of the deltoid muscle beneath. Benedetto chewed this grisly morsel with the speed of a savannah predator, blood smeared across his lips and chin. Caderousse was too surprised even to cry out as more blood sprayed from the wound.

"But I was protected," he said, his voice weak with disbelief, pulling his lapel aside to show the symbols on his clothing. "I was protected from anything like you."

"There is nothing like me." Benedetto smiled with his mouth full and then swallowed. "And soon, there will be nobody capable of telling my secret."

Benedetto clamped his other hand on the back of Caderousse's head and pulled him close again to rip into Caderousse's cheek. His grip proved stronger than Caderousse's struggles. This time Caderousse screamed as the bite tore away his flesh and beard on that side.

"This would be better if you'd gotten the money, but you have no idea how long I've wanted to do this," Benedetto said through his half-chewed mouthful. "It's just a shame I can't stay to finish my meal."

Benedetto swallowed again, pushed back Caderousse's sleeve, and ripped enough flesh from the inside of Caderousse's forearm to expose the bone beneath. He ignored Caderousse's ineffectual swats with his uninjured arm, already weak from blood loss and pain. Arterial blood, black in the moonlight, spurted in arcs through the air as Caderousse fell back into Monte Cristo's garden.

Benedetto leapt down from the wall and wiped his face clean with a handkerchief. Glancing around, he sprinted along the back lane until he arrived at a more well-lit street. There he resumed a more sedate pace, allowing himself to whistle as only a content and well-fed man can.

CHAPTER 85
THE HAND OF GOD

S till wearing the disguise of Abbe Busoni, the count rushed across the lawn to answer the screams and found Caderousse in a pitiful condition. Blood gushed from his right forearm and shoulder, and on the side of his face his bare cheekbone and teeth could be plainly seen as he wailed in pain.

Tendrils of the count's bandages reached out from beneath his sleeve and cinched tight around Caderousse's bicep to staunch the flow from the fatal wound in his arm. Monte Cristo knew that the tourniquet, and indeed modern medicine, was insufficient to save Caderousse's life.

Still, Monte Cristo carried Caderousse into the house like an infant and laid him down on a velvet-upholstered settee. Ali administered a few drops of an obscure elixir to ease Caderousse's pain enough that his wails subsided and he could stare Monte Cristo in the face.

"Ali, send for M. de Villefort at once to report this murder. Send also for a surgeon," the count added, only to soothe Caderousse's fears.

Ali hurried to pen a letter summoning Villefort and departed to deliver it, leaving Monte Cristo and Caderousse alone.

"Reverend sir, Abbe Busoni, I've been betrayed," Caderousse said. "Benedetto, that damned Corsican foundling, laid in wait to ambush me. He's not human, he's some fiend from the depths of Hell come to torment the living."

"I know," Monte Cristo said. "I took the confession of another who was fooled by this man and who revealed the depravity of his appetites."

"I'm dying, I know it," Caderousse said. His words emerged muddled with half of his upper lip torn away. "Bring me the pen once more; the least I can do is to give testimony against my murderer from beyond the grave."

"I've summoned the prosecutor, you can tell him your story," Monte Cristo said.

"He may not arrive in time; I can feel the world slipping away," Caderousse said.

Monte Cristo nodded. As he walked away, the bandage holding back Caderousse's lifeblood remained constricted in place and tethered him to the count. The count soon returned with pen and ink, a sheet of paper, and a wooden tray to act as a desk.

"It's lucky that I'm left-handed," Caderousse said with a weak chuckle.

He wrote the story of how he and Benedetto met, what Benedetto did to be sentenced to the galleys, and how they escaped together.

"He sent me to rob the man he thinks is his father, likely hoping I would kill the count and hasten his inheritance or be killed myself in the attempt. Failing either outcome, he murdered me personally in a savage attack befitting the days of the Dead Plague," Caderousse read aloud as he signed it. "There. The rest is up to you, reverend sir. You'll see that this reaches the police?"

"Of course," Monte Cristo said. "Benedetto will get the guillotine, I reckon."

"Good, good," Caderousse said. "If the sum total of my miserable life is that it means the end of a creature like Benedetto, I may die peacefully. Abbe Busoni, will you do a dying wretch one final favour and say my last rites?"

Monte Cristo frowned and considered the state of Caderousse. No force on earth could save the man from death, and only the tourniquet slowed the bleeding enough to keep him alive this long. He reached a decision.

"I cannot," the count said, "for I am no abbe or reverend."

The count removed his tinted spectacles to reveal the red hue of his eyes, and wiped away his makeup to expose the bloodless white of his face.

"With those eyes, you can be only one man," Caderousse said. "But why is the Count of Monte Cristo disguised as Abbe Busoni? What has happened to Busoni?"

"There never was an Abbe Busoni, Caderousse," the count said. "He's as much a fiction as the Count of Monte Cristo. Look past my strange features, look past my wealth. Can you see who I once was? Can you see the man Danglars and Fernand ruined while you sat by in a drunken stupor?"

"Edmond Dantes!" Caderousse said in shock. "What happened to you? I heard that you died in prison; are you some revenant then, walking the earth to punish us who hurt you?"

"Precisely that," Monte Cristo said.

A feeling the count could not name swelled in the hollow recesses of his chest at revealing himself to one of the architects of his misery after so long. It was some strange cousin to satisfaction and a distant relative of relief.

"You knew, then; you knew Benedetto was waiting for me?" Caderousse asked. He touched his fingers to the bloody exposed bone of his cheek. "Why didn't you warn me? Look at what he has done!"

"You had a chance once to prove your character, when you allowed Danglars and Fernand to plot my doom. I gave you another chance when I brought you that diamond. You squandered that as well," Monte Cristo said. "You even wasted your third chance when you accompanied Benedetto in his escape, which I engineered for him. Instead of using your newfound freedom to start a new life, you returned immediately to crime, burglary, and attempted murder. Why, when you've thrown away so many opportunities, should I continue to hand them to you?"

"Then you're also the Lord Wilmore who freed Benedetto," Caderousse said. "Is your hatred of the world so total that you needed to release such a fiend to feast upon it?"

"Not the world; only the other architects of my death," Monte Cristo said. "Benedetto has his role to play, which is nearly finished. Your involvement was unforeseen, but you brought it upon yourself."

"Oh, fate! Fate has been so cruel to poor me!" Caderousse moaned.

"You could have abandoned the path that led you here a hundred times, but you didn't," Monte Cristo said. "You've been cruel to yourself."

"Then you think fate has given me just what I deserve?" Caderousse asked, his eyes beseeching the count.

When the count only stared in return, a strange calm came over Caderousse. He made himself more comfortable on the settee and allowed his breathing to slow.

"Edmond, I'm sorry about your father," Caderousse said at last. "I couldn't have saved him from the Inquisition, but I should have done more to help him before then."

"Yes, you should have," Monte Cristo agreed gently.

Caderousse was quiet again for a moment. "Danglars and Fernand, then. You'll be going after them, I expect?"

"I began doing so before I ever arrived in Paris," Monte Cristo said.

"Good," Caderousse said. "They've risen too far in life; they deserve to be knocked into the mud with the rest of mankind. I only regret that I won't live to see it."

Monte Cristo shook his head in silence at Caderousse's eternal lack of perspective. Without speaking and with care for Caderousse not to notice, he loosened the tourniquet.

"I want to go back," Caderousse muttered. "I want to undo it all. I want a fresh start. I want - I want - I want..."

His voice trailed off, and the flow of blood from his arm stopped. His eyes, staring up at the ceiling, no longer blinked. Caderousse was dead.

Half an hour later, Ali returned. Monte Cristo allowed him to admit Villefort and a doctor, who found Abbe Busoni praying beside Caderousse's corpse. Villefort took Busoni's statement and Caderousse's deposition, and left to organize the police to search for a man named Benedetto.

BOOK THREE

PROVIDENCE

CHAPTER 86
SCANDALS

For two weeks, the only topics of conversation in Paris were the daring attempt to rob the Count of Monte Cristo and the manhunt for the mysterious Benedetto. The gruesome nature of Caderousse's murder made the hunt a top priority for the police, but the search proved fruitless.

Between the manhunt and a fresh set of Caillat articles naming old victims, Villefort slept little. Reporters hounded him with questions whenever he came within two blocks of the Palais: about the unsolved vampiric murders, about the Benedetto affair, about Villefort's connection to the pregnant woman at his father-in-law's house.

Villefort took his work home to his study and finally noticed he had not seen Valentine in weeks. His first duty was always to the crown, and concerns of fatherhood could wait until he devised a way to stop these slanderous attacks against his authority as an agent of that crown, no matter how true they were.

In fleeting moments of rest, he asked himself if Valentine was living in sin with her Bonapartist soldier. Villefort tried to track Max down, but found no address in his name anywhere in the city. Of course, Villefort had no reason to direct his attention to the house at No. 7 in the Rue Meslay, or to know that the Emmanuel Herbault who owned it was Max's brother-in-law.

Regarding the burglary, the Count of Monte Cristo told everyone that he slept in Auteuil at the time of the break-in. The only inhabitants of the house at the time were Abbe Busoni and Ali; the abbe had visited to examine some rare books in the count's library. Nobody noticed that Bertuccio turned pale at any mention of Benedetto's name.

Andrea retreated from public life for a few days, claiming a bout of flu, but his health soon recovered when he realized nobody suspected a connection between himself and the criminal Benedetto. Caderousse's letter to Danglars exposing Andrea still sat in the count's secretary, and his dying deposition neglected to mention Benedetto's assumed name. Soon enough, Andreacould focus his energy on his approaching marriage.

Letters from Major Cavalcanti, who couldn't leave Italy for the happy occasion, promised a wedding gift of one hundred fifty thousand livres and confirmed that he would entrust Andrea's three million in capital for Danglars to invest. Some of Andrea's newfound friends warned him of Danglars' recent financial losses, but he wouldn't hear a word against his future father-in-law.

Eugenie, prepared to tolerate Andrea in order to rid herself of Albert, at once showed Andrea the same coolness when her previous betrothal was cancelled. Neither Danglars nor Andrea noticed or cared, each focusing on how the marriage would benefit their balance sheets.

The promise of three million francs from Major Cavalcanti soothed Danglars' nerves. His heavy investment into a Canadian riverboat venture in early June had been erased, with a dam destroying the business entirely. The situation in the vaults of the Danglars Bank grew desperate, even with Villefort's and Morcerf's buy-ins covered by Andrea's inheritance.

In order to profit off his weapons investments, Danglars needed to first survive the revived Plague. That required a fortified place to hide, supplies, and other expenses. The spectre of a run on his bank still dissuaded him from cashing in the Count of Monte Cristo's withdrawal receipts to provide the money he needed. Danglars still had one more card he could play and intended to do so at the next meeting of the House of Peers.

Meanwhile, Albert came to see the wisdom of Monte Cristo's advice to let his quarrel with Beauchamp cool off. As the count predicted, no gossip connected the Count de Morcerf to the Fernand in Yanina. Still, the existence of the article tormented Albert. He took comfort knowing Beauchamp was off somewhere proving his father's innocence. For that reason he was quite pleased when his valet woke him on the morning of July 16, 1838, not quite two months since the Count of Monte Cristo first came for breakfast, with the news of Beauchamp's arrival.

Albert dressed in a flash and took the stairs two at a time to reach the smoking room. Albert put a pipe in each corner of his mouth, packed them with fine Spanish tobacco, and lit them with flame from his fingertips.

"Come, Beauchamp! Smoke with me," Albert said, offering him one of the pipes. "Nothing but good news could bring you here at such an early hour!"

It was ten o'clock, but Beauchamp did not comment on that. "Albert, you should sit down," he said, accepting the pipe. The words deflated Albert's optimism.

"What are you talking about, man?" Albert asked, taking a seat in his favourite chair opposite Beauchamp.

"I want you to understand how seriously I took this, Albert," Beauchamp said. "You were ready for us to kill each other over this matter; I spared no expense, went personally to Yanina, tracked down former members of the pasha's court through slave markets and brothels. If we were to fight, I needed to be sure I had done everything I could to prevent it."

"You went to Yanina yourself?" Albert asked. For the first time he noticed Beauchamp's pronounced suntan.

Beauchamp took his passport from his waistcoat and showed Albert the stamps: Geneva, Milan, Venice, Yanina, other names unfamiliar to Albert. "It's been quite the journey, and your house is the first place I came since returning to Paris."

Albert could not think of a response and gestured for Beauchamp to continue while he pulled a deep draught of smoke from his pipe, his anxiety mounting.

"I would be very pleased to be able to tell you that I learned your father was blameless, but that would be a lie," Beauchamp said. "There's no doubt whatsoever: the man who betrayed the pasha was in fact Fernand Mondego who would go on to be made the Count of Morcerf."

"No," Albert said, remembering Haydee's terrible story of the pasha's downfall. "I don't doubt that you've gone above and beyond to verify this, but surely someone lied to you."

"I'm afraid that is impossible," Beauchamp said.

From the same pocket in his waistcoat, he took a series of signed attestations written by individuals who were present at the pasha's final stand; some had escaped, others held prisoner for many years, others enslaved. Each account made it clear that Colonel Fernand Mondego was sent to Sultan Mahmud to negotiate Pasha Ali's surrender and instead sold the pasha's life. It was clear beyond doubt that Fernand had lied about the source of his fortune; from Pasha Ali, yes, but as plunder rather than payment. Albert let his pipe fall from his fingers. His father was not only a traitor, but a monster as well.

"If this becomes public, my father is ruined," Albert muttered. "Mother would likely die of revulsion, or throw herself from some cliff into the sea, and I would follow her."

Shame, disgust, and all the deep pity of Haydee's story welled up in his heart until it overflowed in a gush of tears. Beauchamp waited for Albert's grief to subside, averting his eyes respectfully.

"Albert," Beauchamp said at last, "we were born into a difficult world. Revolutions and unholy creatures created such a great upheaval just before our time that hardly anyone could pass through it without some stain. Your father committed a terrible act before you were born, but why should that stain follow you?"

"What are you saying?" Albert asked, his voice hoarse.

"I'm saying that you're holding the only proof of what your father did," Beauchamp replied. "And as a gesture of good will, I leave that proof with you to do as you please."

"You would do that for me?" Albert asked.

"I would do that, I hope, for a friend," Beauchamp replied with a half-smile.

"Beauchamp, I'm truly sorry for the demands I made," Albert said. He focused on the papers in his hand, which blackened and crumbled to ash. "I was wrong, and I hope you'll forgive me."

"Of course," Beauchamp said.

Albert stamped out the embers of his discarded pipe and lit a cigarette to replace it, smoking with Beauchamp in the spirit of reconciliation. Albert doubted he could ever conduct a civil conversation with his father again, knowing what he knew.

"Does Mother have any idea of the blood that soaks our fortune?" he muttered.

Another idea occurred to him, which Albert dared not voice. Somebody revealed the name Fernand in the first place, to put this whole affair in motion. With the unceremonious breaking-off of his engagement to Eugenie, Baron Danglars was as likely a culprit as anyone.

"Let's get outside and take some fresh air," Beauchamp said, sensing the returning darkness in Albert's mood. "You've said how much visiting the count boosts your spirits. Perhaps he'll accept us for breakfast."

Albert agreed; the count had a way of not interrogating a person unless he thought their position was unfounded. It seemed like just the atmosphere Albert needed.

CHAPTER 87
THE JOURNEY

Monte Cristo smiled to see Beauchamp and Albert arrive together. "Your quarrel is mended, then! You see Albert, I told you it would blow over."

"Oh yes, all done with," Albert said. "Beauchamp proved himself to be a true friend, I apologized for my behaviour, and that's the end of it."

"Magnificent. Well, come in and sit," Monte Cristo said. "I've finished my breakfast already, but my servants will bring you something."

Before Albert or Beauchamp could speak, he rang his ever-present bell. Soon a tray of piping hot coffee and a selection of pastries appeared before them.

"You find me in the middle of an arduous chore," the count said. "I had no idea what introducing Andrea Cavalcanti would entail when I agreed to it, and now I'm stuck arranging paperwork for his wedding."

"Ah yes, his marriage to Mlle. Danglars. Oh cruel fate! How could you tear the love of my life away from me?" Albert declared, pretending to faint with distress. "Don't worry count, I'll continue to pretend that I don't have you to thank for this."

"Mind your tongue so near a reporter, Albert," the count said. "Today's idle joke is tomorrow's headline. I'm no matchmaker; this decision was down to Baron Danglars and Viscount Cavalcanti. If anything, I've warned the baron against it on the grounds of how little is known about the intended groom."

"Well, regardless of your true involvement, the end of my engagement is a welcome bit of good news," Albert said. "I've come down with an incredible headache and needed something to lift my spirits."

"I know an infallible remedy for a headache: travel," Monte Cristo said. "With M. de Villefort and his minions continually rummaging through my house, I plan to abandon Paris for a few days. They keep searching for evidence regarding the break-in, and clues about this mysterious Benedetto who murdered the burglar so brutally. It's becoming a nuisance."

"I've heard rumours of this ghastly murder. Who was that man Caderousse who died here?" Beauchamp asked.

"Some provincial, originally from Marseille. I understand Baron Danglars had met him before," Monte Cristo said. "He escaped from the galleys and was betrayed by his accomplice. What do you say, Albert? Keep me company in Normandy for a few days and let the sea air clear your head."

Albert jumped at the chance to put some distance between himself and his father until he could better come to terms with his newfound knowledge. Monte Cristo extended the invitation to Beauchamp as well, but Beauchamp was weary of travel and wanted to rest in his own bed.

"Will your mother approve?" the count said to Albert. "She may have something to say about you travelling with the mysterious Count of Monte Cristo."

"You have nothing to fear, count," Albert said, waving a hand. "Mother has taken such an interest in you that she hardly speaks of anything else when we're together. I've told you before, you have her trust and affection; once she gives those to someone, she never falters."

Monte Cristo answered the assertion with a half-smile.

"At any rate, she's often encouraged me to spend more time with you, ever since the ball," Albert said. "She's of the opinion that you have a noble nature."

That evening, Albert returned to Monte Cristo's house. The count's coach was a model prepared for long-distance travel, in which the occupants could recline their seats as beds, and they set out as soon as the servants finished loading Albert's luggage. Their only companions in the count's seaside Normandy estate were to be Ali and a few other servants, horses to ride, dogs to hunt with, and whatever fish they pulled from the water.

As with everything else he did, Monte Cristo spared no expense on the journey. They took on fresh horses every three hours to maintain the highest speed, and under Ali's adept control they made such rapid progress that the spectators they passed could only gawk at them. It was peculiar to hear Ali make any sound at all, the "hah" and "woah" he used to direct the horses among the few words he could create with no tongue.

Monte Cristo regaled Albert with tales of places he had travelled and things he had witnessed there, and to this lullaby Albert drifted off to sleep. The count dropped any expression from the white mask of his features and settled his red gaze on Albert as the countryside of France blurred past. Before their departure, the count gave Bertuccio certain envelopes to post as soon as the coach departed. Monte Cristo reflected that this trip may be the last peace Albert ever experienced in life, a token gesture of thanks to a pawn before taking it off the board.

Albert awoke in his rooms at the house in Normandy, having been carried to bed by Ali while he still slept. His bedroom opened onto a terrace which extended around the corner of the house, giving a view of the sea on one side and of a wooded park on the other. The sound of the surf soothed him and gave him hope that his father's past sins could be overcome. Albert and the count spent the next two days hunting, fishing, dining, and enjoying every other pursuit which the country afforded them.

On the third day, Albert enjoyed an afternoon nap in an armchair near an open window. The count never tired from the sports they engaged in, but the exertion had caught up to Albert. Hoofbeats thundering up the road to the house woke him from his pleasant slumber, and to his surprise his own valet stood at the door.

"What are you doing here?" Albert demanded. "Is Mother ill?"

"No, monsieur; at least, not when I left. Your friend M. Beauchamp gave me this and said it was urgent that you receive it," the valet said. "He gave me money for the journey and instructions not to stop for anything."

The valet handed Albert a parcel containing a newspaper, the Tribune, and a letter. Unlike the Nightly Assemblage, the Tribune was no sensationalist rag; it was as well-known for journalistic integrity as the Independent, which Beauchamp wrote for.

Terror gripped Albert's heart as he opened the letter, already guessing what could have prompted Beauchamp's actions. Still, the first line of the letter caused him to cry out in dismay, and he came near to fainting when he unfolded the newspaper.

Monte Cristo was in another room speaking to an architect about plans to build a greenhouse on his island, but he rushed in when he heard the commotion.

"What's happened here?" the count asked.

"Something dreadful has happened at home, and I must return at once," Albert said. He steadied himself and dropped the newspaper to the table. "That newspaper will explain it."

"By all means, leave if you must. Take the coach, and present my card wherever you need to change horses; I reserved the fastest horses for our trip back," the count said. "I'll find another vehicle and come back to Paris when I can."

Albert and his valet ran to the coach. When they left, Monte Cristo sent the architect away as well and allowed himself to smile once he was alone. He relished reading the newspaper article Albert found so agitating.

"Several weeks ago in our esteemed competitor the Independent, it was revealed that a French officer named Fernand played an instrumental role in the betrayal of Pasha Ali Tepelini of Yanina," Monte Cristo read aloud to the empty house. "That French officer, in the pasha's service until he sold his benefactor's head to the Turks, was accurately but incompletely named by that article. Documents are now available which prove that the officer in question has added a title of nobility to his name, and now ranks among the peers as Count Fernand de Morcerf."

Back in Paris, the news of Fernand's past misdeeds spread through the circles of upper society at a speed that nothing but gossip could achieve.

CHAPTER 88
THE TRIAL

Exhausted and dusty from the road, Albert arrived at Beauchamp's door at eight o'clock the next morning. The valet brought him at once to Beauchamp's study.

"I had nothing to do with this," Beauchamp said, concern written across his face. "I gave you all the proof I had, and you destroyed it yourself."

"I believe you," Albert said. "You wouldn't have sent for me if it were you. But how did this happen?"

"I have an inkling," Beauchamp said. He relayed what had happened, as far as he knew, since Albert left for Normandy.

Two days after Albert's departure, the Tribune article was published. The editor of the Tribune was a friend of Beauchamp's, and Beauchamp rushed to the Tribune office to learn what he could.

"I pretended concern that he'd left himself open to libel charges, to try and gauge what proof he had," Beauchamp said to Albert. "But his proof was solid."

The editor explained to Beauchamp that a man from Yanina arrived with documents detailing the entire affair. The visitor even provided the contract, taken from Sultan Mahmud's registrar, detailing the agreement with Fernand Mondego to betray Pasha Ali and the payment for services rendered.

As Beauchamp sent Albert's valet to retrieve him, the news threw the House of Peers into an uproar. Everyone but Morcerf arrived early, and everyone held a copy of the Tribune. The chamber buzzed with commentary on the article, along with stories of Morcerf's past behaviour to which the account from Yanina granted new perspective.

They discussed Morcerf's version of his history and his wartime career, bringing to light certain suspicious inconsistencies.

Morcerf arrived at the chamber, oblivious to the fact that he walked into a lion's den. His daily reading seldom included the Tribune, and his morning had been spent writing letters instead. He entered the semicircular chamber and took his customary seat in the middle tier of the room, which resembled a Roman auditorium. Nobody said a word about the article until Baron Givenchy, an upstart not quite thirty years old and a political opponent of Morcerf's, rose to speak.

A full transcript of Givenchy's speech appeared in all the major papers the following day, but most of it was mere preamble to his objective. He spoke at length about a dreadful corruption recently exposed to the house, and went on a tirade about the importance of maintaining the people's faith in the institutions and establishments of their government. At last he mentioned Yanina, and when Morcerf paled, his face was as good as a signed confession.

When Givenchy began to read the article from the Tribune, Morcerf rose from his seat with a fireball already at hand; whether he intended to incinerate the paper or the baron would remain a topic of speculation for years. Before Morcerf could hurl the flame, the peers sitting in the row above emptied buckets of water upon him, having planned ahead with Givenchy for such a development.

Even with his Catalan gift subdued, Morcerf could still rely on his considerable physical strength. It took twelve men to restrain him as he climbed across his desk with the goal to reach Givenchy and silence him, but Givenchy continued to read uninterrupted until he completed the article.

"With these facts in mind, I call for the immediate arrest of Fernand Mondego and for the title of Count to be stripped from him. The grounds are treachery, fraud, and conspiracy to commit murder," Baron Givenchy said as his concluding statement.

The chamber guards rushed forward to thunderous applause from the assembled members, and at last they placed the soaking wet Morcerf in shackles. Nothing could be heard in the chamber above his cursing as they dragged him away.

"Defense!" Morcerf howled to the chamber. "I demand the opportunity to present my defense!"

"You'll have that opportunity at the trial," Baron Givenchy said. "We'll set the date at two weeks hence."

Albert listened to Beauchamp's retelling of events in shock. "Two weeks!" he said. "My father is to sit in a cell for two weeks awaiting trial? Why didn't you mention this in the letter?"

"I only learned about it after I had already sent your valet to get you," Beauchamp said. "But your father isn't in any cell; there's more yet."

Fernand insisted on defending himself that very day, claiming that his innocence could speak for itself. A committee assembled to examine the proof on both sides, with the trial set for eight o'clock that evening; at the time, Albert was fishing with Monte Cristo on their second day in Normandy.

The House guards kept Fernand submerged to his neck in a bathtub under close watch until the trial, and allowed him to dictate letters to organize his defense. Hearing about this, Albert wondered what provisions his father could have made to shield himself against the revelation of the truth.

When Beauchamp heard about the trial, he used his press credentials to gain access to the House balcony to witness the proceedings firsthand. The Chamber was rearranged as a courtroom, with an upright lead water tank as the defendant's box. Fernand was allowed to keep the clothes he was arrested in, including the medals he had worn to the chamber that morning, as a courtesy. The uniform being drenched and the water level rising to his shoulders diminished the effect somewhat. Still, he stood with his head high and his back straight. A representative stood next to him with a sheaf of papers. After opening statements, the court gave Fernand the chance to speak.

"He spoke eloquently, and if I didn't already know the truth he might have convinced me," Beauchamp told Albert.

With help from his lawyer, Fernand presented his evidence: documents proving that he held the trust of Pasha Ali's vizier, the pasha's signet ring which provided Fernand entry to the sanctum any time day or night, statements from a dozen people stating that Fernand never once treated the pasha with anything but love and respect. He insisted that the negotiations with Sultan Mahmud were unsuccessful, and when he went to deliver the bad news the pasha was already dead.

"Your father said that the pasha's trust in him was so great, he requested in his will that his wife Vasiliki and daughter Haydee be entrusted to the care of Fernand Mondego," Beauchamp added. Albert's stomach sank as he recalled Haydee's version of events. "He presented the deed to an estate in America, bought in Vasiliki's name, and explained that he had sent the women there to live safely outside of the sultan's reach.

"This demonstrates conclusively that this alleged betrayal is simply not possible," Fernand had said at the trial. "Finally, the greatest proof of my innocence against this anonymous slander: the prosecution has not a single witness who can contradict my words."

Albert allowed himself a moment of hope. He still believed that Beauchamp's story would end with the judge swayed and his father a free man.

"If that had been it, I suspect the judge would have ruled in your father's favour," Beauchamp said, dashing Albert's hopes. "But Givenchy rose to tell the room that a witness was available and beckoned for them to enter the chamber."

"And who was it?" Albert asked, fearing he knew already.

"I think you've met her; the Greek goddess who accompanies the Count of Monte Cristo to the opera," Beauchamp said.

Albert's legs failed him, and he fell into Beauchamp's desk-chair.

She wore a traditional Grecian mourning dress, but no veil covered her face, leaving her determination and rage on display for all to see. Fernand's reaction to her entrance provided another testament to his guilt as she took the witness stand. He had to lean on the side of his enclosure to remain upright.

"Mademoiselle, you say you are a witness for the prosecution?" the judge asked her.

"Not only that," Haydee replied, "but an eyewitness to the betrayal and craven murder of Pasha Ali."

Haydee told the court the same story Albert had heard, but with no pretense of failing to remember the traitor. She gave great detail about Fernand Mondego, including a distinctive scar on his upper forearm which bailiffs forced him to reveal to the courtroom.

The audience listened in silent horror to her tale of how the pasha was deceived, restrained, and drained of his life-force using the same treasure he had sworn to protect. When Haydee recounted the particulars of how Fernand sold her and Vasiliki into slavery, and the hardships she was forced to endure, it became clear that most of the men present were willing to tear Fernand apart on her behalf if he were not under close guard.

"As for this supposed house in America," Haydee said, "I've certainly never seen it. And since my mother died as a house-slave in Turkey, I doubt she was ever given a chance to live there either."

After this scathing testimony, the judge asked if she could provide any other proof of her story. Knowing about a hidden scar was a start, but the charges were far too serious for a conviction to be based on mere accusations. To answer this, Haydee produced her birth certificate to prove her identity as well as the paperwork which sealed Fernand's fate: a bill with his signature for the sale of two female slaves, one adult and one child. The document was in Turkish, but the court had brought in several translators in preparation for the trial. They verified the bill's authenticity.

A dreadful silence filled the courtroom. All eyes rested on Fernand, who stared at Haydee with wrath in his face. She had returned his gaze without blinking, but flushed with emotion and with tears at the corner of her eye. The water in Fernand's tank steamed around him, as he tried to summon the flames which had marked him for greatness since his boyhood. Baron Givenchy, as the accusatory party, approached the judge's bench and waited there to hear the verdict.

"Fernand Mondego, Count de Morcerf, the evidence against you speaks volumes. It is clear that you stand guilty of treason and murder, as well as participation in the slave trade," the judge said. "You are fit neither to bear the title of count, nor to walk freely on this earth. I hereby sentence you to death by guillotine, to be carried out in one week's time."

Haydee listened to the verdict with no sign of joy, but only an immense satisfaction. Hearing this from Beauchamp, Albert wailed in disbelief.

"Execution! If the trial was Wednesday, then he has only five days left! Where are they keeping him?" Albert said.

"There lies the final piece of my story," Beauchamp said. He continued his account of the trial.

Fernand fainted at the pronouncement of the verdict, and two bailiffs rushed to prevent him from drowning before the crown could cut off his head. Each one grabbed him by a shoulder and heaved his bulk above the water. Baron Givenchy still stood by the judge, smirking at his rival's distress.

"The Eye! He has the Eye!" Haydee cried from the witness stand, pointing at the medals upon Fernand's jacket.

Fernand's eyes snapped open, and he brought his manacled hands up to touch a round silver medal. A hidden clasp caused the false front to spring open, and behind it gleamed a large clear gemstone set in silver. A wavering beam of cold blue light arced from the stone towards Givenchy's heart as Haydee ducked for cover behind the witness stand.

"I've witnessed executions for the paper, Albert," Beauchamp said. "I've watched the light disappear from the eyes of a severed head as the mouth tried to pronounce some final message to the world. But the death of Baron Givenchy may be the most uniquely horrifying spectacle I've ever witnessed."

When the beam touched Givenchy, his entire body jerked as if struck by galvanic current. His thick dark hair faded to grey and crumbled off of his head like dust. His eyes filmed over with yellow cataracts and decayed within their sockets. The flesh of his face sagged and grew dull, before taking on the texture of ancient paper. The entire frame of his body deflated within his clothing as his muscles atrophied. Within the span of ten seconds, the energetic young man was reduced to a limp sack of bones on the courtroom floor. When Givenchy fell, the beam connecting him to Fernand vanished.

"The worst isn't that he died instantly," Beauchamp said. "The worst is that he gasped for breath and tried to stand."

While Givenchy's life-force drained away across the beam, Fernand received the bounty of it. His silver hair returned to the black lustre of his youth, and he stood a few inches taller. He turned to his right and aimed the Eye's awful beam at one of the bailiffs who held him, subjecting the bailiff to the same fate as Baron Givenchy.

Fernand's jacket ripped as his chest and arms bulged large enough to burst the seams. He roared as his expanding wrists met the iron of his manacles, but the restraints could not withstand the pressure and split in two, freeing his arms. Fernand tore apart his water-tank with his bare hands.

"For as long as I've known you, your father has had the build of a strongman," Beauchamp told Albert. "But when he escaped from that tank, he was the equal of any gorilla from the depths of Africa."

Unfettered, Fernand grabbed the other bailiff by the neck and lifted him off his feet. He touched his medal again and once again dried a vital man to a lifeless husk while growing larger and stronger himself. A guard approached with a bayonet, but the hulking Fernand struck him down using his drained victim like a club.

"Spare me more details, my friend," Albert said weakly. "Just tell me, how much damage did my father cause?"

Beauchamp poured a glass of rum and handed it to Albert to fortify him for the answer.

"Before he escaped, he drained nine people and murdered a dozen more," Beauchamp said softly. "He had grown so large by then that his shoulders cracked the stone arch around the chamber door when he left. We were all fortunate that he was still too soaked to call up any fire."

Albert drained the rum in one swallow. "Does anyone know where he is now?"

"Your father escaped into the catacombs. Nobody has seen him since," Beauchamp said, shaking his head.

"And Haydee?" Albert asked.

"Monte Cristo's companion? Alive," Beauchamp said. "She was hit with some debris when your father hurled a desk toward the judge, but she was otherwise unhurt."

"If my father was no murderer before, he certainly is now," Albert said. "No matter where he is hiding, someday he'll be found, and they'll never pardon him."

CHAPTER 89
THE CHALLENGE

Albert languished in self-pity, slumped over Beauchamp's desk. He accepted a second glass of rum and requested a third, becoming more introspective all the while. He could expect only ridicule and ostracism as the son of a murderer and a monster, and his reputation may never recover.

Even if he relocated to London or Rome permanently, he could not escape the scandal. He would forever be Albert de Morcerf, son of the man who betrayed Pasha Ali and murdered twenty Frenchmen. He realized he may not be able to call himself Morcerf anymore; he had never considered the possibility of losing his title and never bothered learning the protocol for it. These moribund thoughts gave way to anger.

"Why should I lose my position for my father's mistakes?" Albert asked to his empty glass. "Why was this even brought out so publicly? Who did this to me?"

Beauchamp remained quiet, allowing Albert to grieve, but grew concerned as Albert's voice raised closer to a yell.

"Someone brought those documents from Yanina," Albert said. "Someone told the Tribune what my father did, and I must know who."

"Why?" Beauchamp asked, fearing he knew the answer.

"So I can challenge him to a duel, mortally wound him, and then burn him to cinders before he has the chance to die," Albert said, throwing the glass against the wall.

"Albert, take a second and think this through," Beauchamp said, holding up his hands. "Even if you knew who had exposed the truth, that's all they did: expose truth. Your father did horrible things, you can't blame the person who told the world about them."

"I can and I will!" Albert insisted. "They could have approached my father directly, allowed him to make amends and take his punishment privately, rather than turning my family into a public spectacle! And he'll answer for it!"

Fire danced in Albert's eyes and literal flame at his fingertips, and Beauchamp convinced Albert to walk with him rather than risk his home burning down. Albert settled down by a fraction out in the fresh air, but remained insistent on finding and challenging the person who exposed Fernand. Beauchamp decided to help Albert find closure while doing what he could to minimize collateral damage.

"Before you left for Normandy, I didn't tell you everything that happened in Yanina," Beauchamp said to Albert. "One of my first contacts there was a banker, and he guessed my purpose before I had finished speaking. I asked him how; he said someone else had made the same inquiries a few weeks prior."

"Did he tell you who?" Albert asked.

"He said the inquiries were on behalf of his colleague in Paris, Baron Danglars," Beauchamp said.

"Danglars!" Albert said. "It makes perfect sense! He's been jealous of my father's status for years, and this happens so soon after he breaks the engagement? That horrible old man will pay!"

"Albert, wait!" Beauchamp said, but Albert already ran with purpose towards the Rue Saint-Germain.

Beauchamp jogged to keep up, hoping Albert could show enough prudence to avoid meeting one of Danglars' knives. When they arrived, they found the coach and arms of Andrea Cavalcanti.

"Better and better!" Albert said. "Danglars may decline the challenge, but I can still kill Cavalcanti as his second."

A servant announced their arrival to Danglars in his study, and Danglars refused them. Danglars had only just escaped the trial unhurt and could guess why Albert had come. Unfortunately, Albert followed the servant. When the servant tried to close the door, Albert burned a hole through it and unlocked it himself. Danglars jumped up from his seat and hid around the back of it.

"Sir, you forget what little manners your disreputable father may have taught you!" Danglars said, a flush rising in his jowls. "Can't a man decide who to receive in his own home? What's the meaning of this?"

"The meaning is that I've come to invite you to a meeting. It will be brief, and one of us will return while the other remains on the ground," Albert said.

"A duel?" Andrea said. He stood by the fireplace behind Albert's shoulder. "On what grounds?"

"You can come if you like, monsieur; I'm as happy to kill two members of this cowardly family as one," Albert said without looking away from Danglars.

"Is this because of Eugenie? I understood you were agreeable to the new arrangement. Surely we can settle this peacefully," Andrea said, confused by the proceedings. He had no issue with killing Albert if he needed to, but preferred to avoid the attention.

"No, I can guess why Albert is here," Danglars said. "Is it really my fault that your father dishonoured himself so spectacularly and received his punishment so poorly? I didn't make him betray the pasha, nor did I urge him to slaughter half of the courtroom!"

"You instigated the whole spectacle, when you could have settled whatever quarrel you had with him personally!" Albert shouted. "Instead, you drag my name and Mother's through the dirt with him!"

"And what makes you think that I was responsible for these revelations?" Danglars said.

"You wrote to Yanina and stirred up the entire controversy," Albert said.

"Of course I wrote to Yanina; one doesn't marry off his only daughter without learning all he can about her new family," Danglars said. "I had no idea what would come of my inquiries; if I knew, I wouldn't have needed to make them."

"A likely story!" Albert said. "You're stalling, baron."

"Believe me or don't," Danglars said, the sweat on his bald head betraying his nervousness, "but my inquiries were entirely innocent. I was talking about your father's fortune, and my correspondent asked where your father acquired his wealth. I replied that it was in Yanina, and he suggested that I write to Yanina to learn more."

"Who was this that you were speaking to?" Beauchamp asked, ever the journalist.

"It was that dandy whom you young people are all so enamoured with: the Count of Monte Cristo," Danglars replied.

"Monte Cristo told you to write to Yanina?" Albert asked, his rage tempered by confusion.

In his mind, facts fell together which he had ignored in the hectic rush of new information. When Haydee told him her story, she'd claimed not to remember who betrayed them, yet she had proof at the trial to condemn Fernand Mondego. Monte Cristo must have known the entire story when he bought Haydee from her former owners. Albert recalled their brief conversation in a foreign tongue before Haydee's tale; an opportunity for the count to tell Haydee to conceal the truth, no doubt.

The entire affair contained too many coincidences: Albert had been allowed to learn the shape of the story, almost duel Beauchamp over the first hint of his father's involvement, and then have it exposed for all of Paris to gawk at. The count even whisked Albert away to Normandy to keep him out of the way when the full truth came out.

Albert recalled back further to the Carnival at Rome. The count just so happened to stay in the same hotel as Albert and Franz, and just so happened to be in the perfect position to call off the bandits who abducted Albert. For the first time, Albert suspected their entire friendship was a ruse to give the count access to Fernand Mondego.

Albert shook his head with shame, remembering his laughing dismissal of Franz's attempted warnings about the Count of Monte Cristo. In a rare moment of self-awareness, Albert took Beauchamp aside to ask his advice and avoid any chance of a mistake. When Albert laid out the facts as he knew them, Beauchamp agreed that they must demand an explanation from the count.

"Don't think that this is over between us," Albert said to Danglars as he left. "If I find any indication that you planned this after all, I'll be back."

"Do what you have to. But ask your friend Debray, killing me won't be as easy as you think," Danglars called after him.

Danglars remained leaning on the back of his chair until he heard his front door close behind Albert, then he half-collapsed with relief. Andrea asked what help he could offer, but Danglars waved him away.

"No, I'm fine. Matters are just becoming more complicated than I thought," Danglars said. "I think that it's time to get you married, my boy."

Behind his paternal smile, Danglars pictured the three million francs Andrea would bring under his control.

CHAPTER 90
THE INSULT

As they waited for a cab, Beauchamp encouraged Albert to use more caution with the count than with Danglars. Being obsessed with money, Danglars remained aware at all times of how much he stood to lose, which made him difficult to provoke into a fight.

"But the count is an enigma," Beauchamp said. "From what you've told me, he's far more likely to accept your challenge than talk his way out of it."

"I'm certain he will," Albert said. "I've seen his marksmanship, seen him watch a man die like it was an opera, and heard his philosophy of dueling from his own lips. I know he'll fight me, but I have the advantage of youth and righteousness. I'll win."

"And if not, then at least you won't bear your father's shame," Beauchamp muttered.

They rode to the Champs Elysees in silence. The gates to the count's house stood closed, and Albert approached the concierge's hut.

"Is your master home from Normandy yet? I must see him," Albert said.

"The count is not receiving visitors," Carlo the concierge replied in monotone.

"He'll receive me. Open this gate at once!" Albert commanded. Carlo said nothing. "I am the Viscount de Morcerf, now open this blasted gate!"

When Carlo still didn't move to comply, Albert growled and grasped the wrought iron gate in both hands. He gritted his teeth and forced flame down through his arms and into the metal, heating it until it glowed red and started to run.

A great thrumming shock slammed into his body and knocked him away from the gate as if pushed by a giant. He looked around to find the source of it; Carlo rested one hand on the far end of the gate. Sparks danced between Carlo's outstretched fingers, and he glared at Albert.

"Your family aren't the only Catalans in Paris, monsieur," Carlo said. "The count is not receiving visitors, and I'll thank you not to vandalize the gate. If you must speak to the Count of Monte Cristo, he will be at the opera tonight."

Albert shook his arms to restore sensation in them and left with only a single backward glare at Carlo.

"I expected better of a Flamekeeper!" Carlo shouted after him. "We all expected better!"

Albert didn't care to find out if Carlo referred to him or to his father. He also did not see the count watching him from an upstairs window with a smirk on his chalk-white face.

Albert and Beauchamp went to find Raoul, Franz, Lucien, and Max. He invited each man to the opera with instructions not to be late under any circumstances, as a challenge required their presence. They had all seen the article about Fernand, and heard the news about his trial and subsequent rampage. In the spirit of friendship and loyalty, they all agreed to make a stand with Albert despite none of them knowing who he planned to challenge.

Lastly, Albert went to see Mercedes. Since the story first broke she had hidden herself away in the house, and the sight of Albert produced the predictable effect. When he sat next to her on the chaise longue, her grief and shame overflowed as she hugged him tight.

"Mother, I have something important to ask you," Albert said. "Do you know if my father has any enemies?"

"Any man who rises to your father's station in life makes enemies along the way, whether from his own misdeeds or their envy of his success," Mercedes said, averting her eyes. "Who can tell which inspired this informant?"

"Perhaps I can help to narrow it down," Albert said. "Can you guess what would inspire the Count of Monte Cristo to hurt us?"

Mercedes sprang to her feet, pale and shaking. "Monte Cristo? Why would you suspect him?"

"Because he knew about my father's crimes in Yanina long before we met in Rome. Because, as you noticed at the summer ball, he refused to eat or drink anything while under our roof," Albert said. "I believe that he's to blame for all of this."

"Albert, think about what you're saying," Mercedes said. "He's shown you such kindness and was such a good friend to you that you agreed to present him to Paris in the first place. M. de Monte Cristo saved your life, Albert!"

"After orchestrating my kidnapping to secure my confidence, I think," Albert said, gritting his teeth. "Franz tried to warn me that there was something suspicious about our entire adventure with the count in Rome, but I wouldn't listen."

"Albert, you're making wild accusations. I understand that the stress of our current situation may be affecting you, but please stop whatever you've put into motion and retain his friendship," Mercedes said.

"What I've put into motion will only set right what the Count of Monte Cristo did to us!" Albert said, rising to his feet. "He exposed your husband, why are you so determined to protect him? What do you know about why he hates us so much?"

Mercedes stared at Albert, taking in the determination on his face. She realized fully what Albert intended to do.

"Albert, this has been a trying time for us both. I'm not feeling well. Please, stay and keep me company," she said.

Albert shook his head, and Mercedes' heart sank. "I have an urgent appointment tonight that can't be postponed," he said.

Mercedes tried every trick in her maternal arsenal to make Albert stay, but neither guilt nor bribery could sway him from going to the opera that night. She relented, but as soon as Albert shut the door, Mercedes commanded a servant to follow Albert and report everything to her. With that done, she called for a change of clothes to be prepared for anything.

The footman following Albert had a simple task. Albert returned to his little house on the grounds and dressed for the opera with special care to look his absolute best. Impatient to get on with it, he arrived at the opera fifteen minutes early.

Franz came in a coupe with Beauchamp in due time, Lucien arrived alone with a black velvet glove hiding the puckered scar on his left hand, and Raoul came on foot with Max. Franz gave Max a warm greeting as a new acquaintance, having heard Raoul's story about the *kishi* in Africa.

Max struggled to look Franz in the eye, knowing what he knew about Noirtier and Franz's father.

"This is a noble thing you're doing, Albert," Raoul said with his usual bluster. "The finest things a man can do for his father are give him a grandson, humour him in his golden years, and avenge him if needed."

Franz nodded, musing about how it was impossible for him to ever claim vengeance for his own father.

Albert waited in the lobby with Franz and Beauchamp, hoping to catch the count there. The others waited at the stairwells to alert Albert if the count appeared, but the theatre bell called them to their seats without any sign of him. Lucien went to the minister's box, Beauchamp to the press box, and the rest found seats in the orchestra level. Albert didn't see or hear one moment of the performance, instead spending the entire first act watching the box where Haydee had not missed a single show since arriving in Paris. The curtains there remained closed until the start of the second act.

The count's box opened as the second act began. Despite bruises and cuts on her face from the trial, Haydee looked resplendent as ever in a sparkling silver gown. Albert's eyes remained riveted to the count, who stood at the railing dressed all in black except for the white of his gloves and his unsettling face. Monte Cristo scanned the audience for several moments before taking a seat and raising his opera glasses.

Albert considered hurling a ball of flame into the count's box, and allowing the fire chief and hospitals to sort out the rest. Instead, he sat fuming until intermission. He caught the gazes of his friends, and to those who sat in boxes of their own he held up his fingers to show the number of the count's box.

Although Monte Cristo pretended not to notice Albert in the orchestra seats, he never lost sight of him during the second act. Though Haydee left the box to visit her friends from the Vampire Club, the count remained seated as the young men converged on his box. He did not even turn to face them when Albert barged inside. The count gave a signal to Ali, concealed in the shadows, to let Albert and his friends enter.

"Good evening, Albert," the count said with utmost cordiality. "You seemed so upset when you left Normandy. Is everything well?"

"You already know that nothing is well, monsieur," Albert said. "I'm here to demand an explanation for your behaviour."

Albert's tone surprised his friends; with the exception of Beauchamp, none of them knew who Albert quarreled with. They each assumed that Monte Cristo was to be recruited to stand with them when Albert challenged his foe.

"I have to claim ignorance on many Parisian opera customs," Monte Cristo said, still not even turning to face Albert, "but it's my understanding that this isn't the correct venue for such demands."

"When certain people sequester themselves away and accept no visitors, then the rest of us must take what opportunities we can," Albert said. "And you're in no position to talk about the correct venue for personal matters."

"Whatever do you mean?" the count asked.

"I mean your cowardly assault upon my father's reputation!" Albert roared. The occupants of other boxes halted their conversations and took notice.

Monte Cristo stood in a single smooth motion, and the box grew darker. He loomed over Albert, a resolute anger radiating from his red eyes.

"Monsieur, your tone is far too loud to stay in my box as a guest. Speak at a civilized volume, or leave," Monte Cristo said, his cordiality evaporating like dew.

"Is my voice too loud? Perhaps this will sound more agreeable," Albert said.

To the shock of his friends, he pulled the glove off his left hand and slapped the count across the face with it. A murmur of astonishment rippled outward from boxes which afforded a view of the confrontation. Monte Cristo never broke eye contact with Albert.

"You're young and exuberant," the count said, "and distressed over your father's crimes. Perhaps you've forgotten my philosophy of dueling or are mad with grief. Either way, you have one chance to act as if this challenge never happened and walk away."

Without blinking, Albert slapped the count once more.

"Very well," Monte Cristo said. "You've given me your challenge, and I will give you an early grave in return. Get out of my box before I have you removed. Max, remain here so we can arrange the details."

Out of his element, Max looked to Albert for approval. Albert nodded, and Max waited in the count's box as the others left and closed the door behind them.

"What in heaven's name just happened?" Max asked. "I thought you and Albert were friends?"

"He didn't tell you?" Monte Cristo asked. With Albert gone, pleasant manner returned in a blink. "Haydee informed the House of Peers about his father's treason in Yanina, and young Albert holds me responsible."

"Then Haydee really is the daughter of Pasha Ali? I heard the rumours but didn't credit them," Max said. "What will you do?"

"Kill Albert, likely before ten o'clock tomorrow morning," Monte Cristo said. "He wants to defend the ruined honour of the Morcerf name; instead it will end with him."

Max shuddered at the cool indifference in the count's words. "But his mother loves him so dearly," he said. "Couldn't you just duel to first blood instead of to the death?"

"I could," Monte Cristo said. "But perhaps they should have raised a more careful son if they didn't want to lose him in such a way. As it is, he'll die, and someday Fernand Mondego will learn that what he loves most in this world is gone."

"His son?" Max asked.

"His legacy," Monte Cristo replied.

The bell rang to warn of the end of intermission, and Haydee returned. She gave Max a dazzling smile.

"Good evening, Max," Haydee said. "I tried to convince Valentine to come tonight, but until her father has been dealt with, she refuses to leave the grounds."

"Don't worry, Max; I have a plan, it will just take some more time. These things cannot be rushed," Monte Cristo said. "Haydee, Max and I were just about to finalize an appointment."

"Oh? What kind of appointment?" Haydee asked.

"An appointment for me to duel the son of the man who betrayed your father," the count said. "Albert thinks I told you to testify at the trial and challenged me."

Haydee's smile widened. "By all means, don't let me delay such a happy event," she said with iron in her voice which did not match her expression.

Max thanked his guardian angel to be on good terms with the count, if only because it prevented the combined wills of Monte Cristo and Haydee Tepelini from having reason to direct themselves against him. He felt genuine worry for Albert's life.

"Max, go and tell Albert that I'll face him at a location of his choosing at eight o'clock tomorrow morning. I'll even uphold my reputation for eccentricity and let him choose the weapons," Monte Cristo said.

Max saw no hope to sway the count from his course and agreed to carry the message.

"One more thing, Max. I have no other friends in Paris, and custom dictates that I have a second. Will you do me that favour?" Monte Cristo asked.

Max considered it. "I'm as much your friend as Albert's, but he has other seconds to choose from; I don't think it will be a problem," Max said. "Yes, I'll stand up as your second."

Monte Cristo nodded his thanks, and Max waited, sweating through the third act, for his next opportunity to find Albert. The opera ended, the patrons left, and that night a messenger came to the count's house in the Champs Elysees. He brought a slip of paper which bore only one line.

"Pistols at eight, in the Bois de Vincennes. Morcerf," the count read, baring his teeth in a grin.

CHAPTER 91
A NOCTURNAL PLEA

Monte Cristo set the paper aside with a smirk. He took his pistols into his study, locked the door, and set them on a desk by the fireplace to clean and inspect them. He made himself more comfortable, taking off his gloves to expose his bandaged fingers and unfastening his mask. The breeze from the window was a relief against his true face through the thin layer of bandages.

The count saw no possibility of losing the duel. Unless he brought the canopic jar which contained his heart and gave Albert the opportunity to fire at it, he was unlikely to be killed. Albert's flames presented an unknown factor; the count still did not know if he could be hurt by fire, or how badly.

His chief concern was the remote possibility of Albert firing first. Monte Cristo knew that if someone noticed him take a bullet wound, questions would follow. The witnesses to the duel would ask why he was not injured or even bleeding. As with Villefort's interrogation on the night of the Morcerf ball, his endgame would suffer if someone discovered his true nature.

The greater plan had required this risk from the start, and the count considered mesmerizing Albert to ensure a clean victory. He discarded the idea; after manipulating Albert to this point, it seemed right to let him spend the last minutes of his life as a free man.

It also occurred to him to mesmerize the witnesses and to fight Albert on more equal footing: his own abilities versus Albert's fire, and to hell with the uncertainty. The count felt confident he could still triumph in such a duel and make the witnesses remember any story he told them to remember. Such a battle would be satisfying, but also too much of a risk in a public venue.

Monte Cristo allowed himself to enjoy the process of disassembling his pistols and cleaning each part with oils and solvents. Lacking any physical need for sleep, he found the ritual soothing on a fundamental level. A knock at the door jarred him out of this reverie.

"I am not to be disturbed!" he called.

"This one has been told it is urgent," replied Baptistan's odd voice. "A woman has arrived to speak to you, master."

"Wait a moment," Monte Cristo said.

When he unlocked the door, he wore his face and gloves once again. Baptistan waited silently; behind it stood a woman in a thick, dark veil. The count stood aside to admit her and locked the door behind her.

The woman stood facing the count's worktable and pistols for a long moment, then raised her veil. Countess Mercedes de Morcerf met the count's red gaze with tears welling in her dark eyes and sank to her knees in front of him.

"Edmond Dantes, I beg you, please don't kill my son," she said.

Her gambit was rewarded with a widening of the count's eyes as he took a step back.

"Madame de Morcerf," he said, "I think we discussed this before. I remind you of someone from your past, but I'm not that man. In fact, I recall hearing about a man named Edmond Dantes; he died trying to escape from the Chateau d'If. I cannot be him."

"It's not Madame de Morcerf who has come to you; just Mercedes," she said. "I may be the only person in the world who remembers the man you once were; even including yourself."

The count shook his head and returned to his pistols.

"You are quite mistaken, madame. My name is Gianmarco Zaccone, not Edmond Dantes. I was born in Malta, my father was a shipbuilder. You and I met for the first time on May 21 of this year," he said.

"Then why did I recognize Edmond's voice coming from your mouth with the first word you spoke to me?" Mercedes asked. "Years and suffering have changed the tone of it, but never enough to fool me. And no matter what colour your face is, or how lean and morose it becomes, I've spent too many long nights recalling it not to recognize you."

Mercedes stood and stepped closer to him, extending her hand to his cheek. The count flinched away from the touch without looking at her.

"My god, Edmond, what happened to you to cause such drastic changes?" Mercedes said. "Your eyes were once a handsome shade of hazel; how did they become blood red?"

"We live in a world of wonders and horrors, madame. Sometimes we find both in the same instant and it changes us," Monte Cristo said, glancing up from the pistols. "But the explanation for my colouring is simple. I was born an albino, a trait which can be traced back through the Zaccone line for generations."

Mercedes stood next to the count and examined his face in the light of the gas lamps. The count made a point to ignore her, focusing on his pistols until they sat clean and assembled and he had no more pretense to avoid her. Finally, he heaved a great sigh and faced her again, and the lack of any love or pity in his features chilled Mercedes to her core.

"I can see that my son was right about the misfortune which struck M. de Morcerf," Mercedes said with the first touch of fear in her voice.

"You call him M. de Morcerf; since you're so fond of using names from the past, do you mean Fernand Mondego?" Monte Cristo asked. The hatred in his voice when he pronounced the name carried such power that a thin film of frost covered the corner of the window nearest to him. "Any misfortune that finds him, he brought upon himself. He built a career as a traitor, a coward, and a liar. Now the world knows it."

"Edmond, why are you doing this? Whatever your quarrel with him, can't you see that he has been punished already?" Mercedes pleaded. "Is it because he coveted me when you and I were engaged?"

"Has he been punished? I understand that he is still at large. The police would have announced it if they'd caught him and taken his head," Monte Cristo said.

"No, they haven't found him. The prosecutor's office has searched the house with drakes a dozen times since the trial, in case he returned to hide," Mercedes said.

"As for the reason, tell me: why did you marry Fernand, and not this Edmond who you imagine me to be?" the count continued. "You told me at the ball how much you loved M. Dantes."

"You were gone, arrested, and I thought you had died in prison," Mercedes said. "Can you really fault me for thinking that you were gone forever?"

"Why was Edmond absent? Why was he arrested?" Monte Cristo said.

"I don't know," Mercedes replied. "No matter how often I begged the prosecutor to tell me, he never said."

"Then allow me to tell you. Edmond Dantes was arrested on his wedding day because three men gathered at La Reserve and condemned him to lose everything," Monte Cristo said, his red eyes locked on hers with such intensity she shrank away. "A remorseless scoundrel named Danglars wrote a letter denouncing Edmond as a spy, a drunkard named Caderousse had the power to stop him and did nothing, and a gangly self-important fisherman named Fernand posted the letter himself. It would have ended there, but a zealous young attorney named Villefort saw a chance to advance his political ambitions."

"That's impossible," Mercedes said. "Fernand was jealous of you, but it's impossible that he could be so cruel."

Monte Cristo did not reply but instead walked over to a bureau. He unlocked a small drawer, touched a hidden spring to expose a false bottom, and withdrew a piece of paper. Time had faded the ink and robbed the paper of its original colour, but the words remained as legible as when Edmond Dantes had taken it from the prison inspector's files in those dim and faraway days before his transformation.

"The crown prosecutor is informed by a friend of the throne, that one Edmond Dantes, first mate of the ship Pharaon, arrived this morning after stopping at the Island of Elba. There, he delivered a letter to the usurper and was given one to deliver to the Bonapartist faction in Paris," Mercedes read aloud. "Proof of this crime will be found on arresting him, for the letter will be found upon him, or at his father's, or in his cabin on board the Pharaon. Edmond, is this true?"

"Every word, but Edmond was no spy," Monte Cristo said. "The errand was the dying request of Edmond's captain, which he was duty-bound to fulfill. But note the breathless sensationalism and lack of context in the note, with no concerns for the long-term consequences of those words. Danglars wrote this letter with the same careless manner in which he proposes laws in the House. And for carrying out a man's last request, I—"

"Yes?" Mercedes said, hopeful the count would at last drop his façade.

"That is to say, Edmond Dantes was condemned to life in prison," the count corrected himself.

"Life!" Mercedes groaned. "How did you ever manage to escape?"

"Edmond Dantes didn't escape, madame," the count said. "He vowed revenge on Fernand and on everyone else who was responsible for his circumstances. He renewed that vow every day, and fourteen years later he left the Chateau d'If the only way that anyone ever could: as a dead man."

Mercedes set the letter on the mantelpiece. "And is that vow so ironclad that it extends to the family of your tormentor?"

"Family! A fitting topic," Monte Cristo said with a terrible smile. "Imagine how shocked Edmond Dantes would have been if he had escaped captivity and returned to Marseille, only to learn that Fernand stole not only his time but also his family. Imagine if he had learned that his beloved father had been tortured to death by the Inquisition for being the father of a spy, or that the love of his life had married one of his greatest enemies?"

"So you're punishing him for what he did to you, by ensuring he is punished for what he did to the pasha," Mercedes said. "Must that revenge extend to his son? Albert is only a boy!"

"Fernand is vain, and concerned only with making sure his name lives alongside the other Catalan Flamekeepers as a model of greatness," Monte Cristo replied. "Now his legacy is ruined, and if he doesn't kill himself with shame, he must hide in obscurity for the rest of his life. All that is left is to wipe out his name."

"For the love of God, Edmond!" Mercedes said. "How can you justify killing Albert in the name of vengeance, when he wasn't even conceived until after your arrest? He may be the blood of your enemy, but he's still a human being, and blameless for your pain."

The count inhaled sharply, and once again Mercedes felt a glimmer of hope that her words had reached the man he used to be. He still grappled with the contradiction of his agreement to help Max and Valentine. The inconsistency stared him in the face, filling him with revulsion; he could either spare both Villefort's daughter and Fernand's son, or destroy them. They shared the same level of responsibility for Edmond's fate, which is to say, none at all. He couldn't deny that Mercedes was correct. He could not, without discarding reason entirely, hold Albert accountable for his father's actions.

Mercedes considered her next words carefully, hoping not to break the spell of the count's reverie.

"Whatever you have become now, you were once Edmond Dantes, and Edmond Dantes was a man who kept his word. You said in my greenhouse that you had forgiven me; was that true?" she said.

The count frowned. "I told you that I had forgiven the young woman who broke Gianmarco Zaccone's heart in Malta. But yes, that is true."

Mercedes clasped her hands before her. "Imagine if that woman from Malta had a son and you were set to duel him to the death. Can't you see the terrible punishment this would be to her, who you already forgave for her ignorance?" she asked. "Believe her when she tells you that she still loves Edmond Dantes with all her heart, and has never stopped loving him, and that she is begging him to spare her son's life!"

"Madame de Morcerf," the count said, but Mercedes interrupted him.

"Put formality aside, Edmond. I'm groveling before you," she said.

The count closed his eyes. "Mercedes," he said slowly, as if learning the word for the first time. "That name was groaned in sorrow by a man lying on damp straw in a dungeon. It was wailed in despair by a man thrashing on the stone floor. It was called out in prayer by a man who plunged into the unforgiving sea."

"Edmond," Mercedes whispered, "a name that has been in my prayers for over twenty years, and which I've said aloud for the first times in over a decade when I see the man I loved, and love still, on the point of murdering my son."

The count stopped himself from saying any more. Mercedes observed his face, so familiar while still so alien, as the inscrutable force of his intellect processed the situation. She knew the man at the heart of the being before her, or the man he had once been, and she hoped that her instincts were correct.

"It's a matter of honour and of reputation. I will not forfeit the duel," the count said at last. "If Albert proposes to fight to first blood then I'll deal him a minor wound, just enough to leave a scar. That will allow him to say truthfully that he tried to avenge his father's honour."

Mercedes choked back a sob of relief. "Thank you, Edmond."

"Don't," the count said. "If you make me think I was too generous, I may still change my mind."

Mercedes stood before the count again, taking in every detail of his face with her gaze. Mercedes laid her gentle hands upon his chest and placed a hesitant kiss against his lips, but soon recoiled. His skin was cold as ice, she felt no heartbeat beneath his clothes, and no draft of breath brushed her face.

"Edmond," she said, gripped by a new sort of fear, "what have you become?"

"Nothing that has walked this earth for a thousand years," he replied softly.

Shaking, Mercedes withdrew from him. As she left the study, she turned back once more.

"I remember Caderousse, that tailor from Marseille," she said. "Your vengeance has claimed him already, and Fernand. Do you have the same in mind for Danglars and Villefort?"

"I do," the count replied.

"Good," Mercedes said. She turned to leave again, but this time the count stopped her.

"Mercedes," he asked. "Do you ever shine your light anymore?"

"I do; sometimes," Mercedes said with a wistful smile. She looked down at her hands, which glowed with a soft radiance that came so seldom to her lately. "I could always shine brightest when I was happy. You should have seen me shine when Albert was born. But I suppose my light has dulled over the years from lack of use."

Mercedes left the count alone with his memories and returned home. She found Albert in the gardens practising his marksmanship in the moonlight and signaled for him to stop. The intrusion frustrated him, but his mood softened when confronted with her distress. They spoke for hours, as sleepless as the count himself.

CHAPTER 92
THE DUEL

The Bois de Vincennes remains the largest expanse of greenery in the heart of Paris, and on the morning of the duel, sunrise found it shrouded in a cool morning mist despite the season. A cab trundled along one of the many paths which crisscrossed the Bois and deposited the Count of Monte Cristo and Max by a shaded grove where they wouldn't be bothered by picnickers or nature lovers.

Max looked around at the old apple trees and manicured gardens around them, breathing in the morning air. The constant noise of the city felt very distant, replaced by birdsong and the humming of insects.

"This is a peaceful place," Max said. "It's a shame to spill blood here."

"Nature is anything but peaceful," Monte Cristo replied. "You hear the birds singing, and the insects buzzing, and you interpret it as peace because you find it soothing. To the birds, that buzzing is the sound of food; to the insects, that birdsong signals their looming death. Imagine if we stood on this spot millions of years ago in prehistory. This wouldn't be some tame garden; it would be a dark and dangerous forest filled with predators who saw you as a meal."

"Then we shouldn't enjoy the birdsong?" Max asked. "That seems an odd position to take, given your fondness for creature comforts."

"To the contrary, by all means enjoy it," Monte Cristo said. "Enjoy it all the more knowing that man has tamed nature in this small corner of the world so that you, as a human, may experience a sense of peace here."

"Of course, we aren't here to be peaceful," Max said. "I wish there was some other way to settle this."

Monte Cristo only nodded. Another coach approached, this one bearing the arms of Morcerf. Beauchamp stepped down from the coach first, followed by Raoul carrying the pistol-case, then Albert himself. Albert's face wore an odd expression which Monte Cristo could not read. Also from the coach stepped Franz d'Epinay and a quiet Lucien Debray.

"Albert, you have not only brought a second for the duel but also a fourth and a fifth," Max said. He found reason to be thankful for the occasion's formality, as it meant he wouldn't be expected to make conversation with Franz.

"Beauchamp is the proper second," Franz said. "After the challenge was made, Albert asked us to be here to be witnesses."

Albert, silent and pale, stood watching the count. Albert wore a high white collar and his black jacket opened above a white waistcoat, unconventional clothes for a duel. He may as well have painted targets on his neck and his heart. He cleared his throat and waved his hand in the air, signaling for everyone to take appropriate positions. The witnesses gathered at a safe distance parallel to the avenue of fire, except for Raoul who approached the combatants with the pistol-case. Albert stopped him before he could open it.

"Gentlemen, thank you for coming. I consider it a mark of true friendship," Albert said without looking away from the count. Standing toe to toe with him, Monte Cristo noticed Albert's bloodshot and swollen eyes. "Before we proceed, I have something to say to the Count of Monte Cristo in front of you all."

"Do you wish to insult me further, monsieur?" Monte Cristo asked.

Instead of answering immediately, Albert took a deep breath.

"Sir, I reproached you publicly and petulantly for exposing my father's behaviour in Greece. I knew already that he was guilty, but thought you had no right to provoke his punishment," Albert said in a voice which trembled and cracked at first but grew steadier as he continued. "Since challenging you, I've learned that you had every right. Yourself and Haydee were the most justly qualified people in the world to do it. Therefore, I forfeit."

Monte Cristo ignored the murmurs of shock which rippled through the witnesses, no greater than if the duelists were struck by lightning. Instead he took careful measure of Albert's seriousness.

"And what has led you to this sudden change of heart?" Monte Cristo asked.

"Mother told me a story about a sailor and a fisherman from Marseille," Albert replied. "I understand we may never again be friends, but at least we may both walk away from this with a better sense of one another."

Monte Cristo nodded and extended his hand. Albert took it in his, and for the first time no shudder ran through the count's grip.

"You know of course that the newspapers will call you a coward," Lucien said.

"Let them," Albert replied. "I think it's time I left Paris for a while anyway."

The Count of Monte Cristo said his goodbyes to the assembled witnesses and departed alone. Beauchamp came forward to shake Albert's hand.

"I can't pretend to understand what changed your mind, but I'm beyond pleased that today could be resolved without bloodshed," Beauchamp said, beaming.

The five young men climbed aboard Albert's carriage.

"Do you have a destination in mind, once you leave Paris?" Franz asked. "I think I'll return to Italy soon, now that my marriage has been called off. Why not come with me?"

Albert shook his head, not noticing Max's shoulders relax when Franz revealed his plan to leave.

"Pleasure travel wasn't quite what I had in mind," Albert said. "My father dishonoured the names Morcerf and Mondego; I intend to leave them behind. Mother's maiden name was Herrera, and I'll use that name to build an honest life for myself."

"You're joining the priesthood, then?" Lucien asked with a shadow of his old smirk.

Albert chuckled. "I was planning something more like earning my own fortune, possibly starting a business," he said. "Mother told me that her first love, the most honourable man she ever knew, was a sailor. Perhaps I'll go to the coast and try to make my living on the sea."

Lucien guffawed. "A fop like you, toiling in sun and seaspray from dawn to dusk? I'd like to see that."

"Give Albert some credit," Raoul said. "I grew up in the same plush lifestyle as he did, and I've survived the military so far. Albert has steel at his core, gentlemen. He'll do just fine."

The coach arrived at Raoul's door and he rose to leave.

"One word of warning, Albert," Raoul said with a grin before he left. "If you leave France without seeing me again for one last smoke, I'll hunt you down and make you a sorry man indeed."

Raoul saluted Albert and stepped out into the street.

"If you prefer, I could write a recommendation for you to bring to any newspaper in Europe," Beauchamp said. "The life of a reporter or fact-checker would be considerably less dangerous than that of a sailor."

"I'll consider it," Albert said. "But part of the appeal of the sea is that it will keep me away from prying eyes and society gossip long enough for the affair to die off from public memory. After a few years, I expect to be a new man with a clean slate."

"Well, if you find yourself in Rome, let me know immediately," Franz said with a sad smile as they arrived at his destination. "I'll spoil you with all the comforts you're leaving behind and try to tempt you back into a life on land. *A bientot, mon ami!*"

At his apartments, Lucien departed without much fuss.

"If you don't drown, try to find your way back to Paris. You're an adequate sparring partner and always good for a laugh," Lucien said as he stepped down from the coach.

Max had not spoken since Albert's disclosure of his intentions. He took a card and pencil from his jacket once the carriage turned onto the street where his sister lived.

"This is the address of Morrel & Dimonte in Marseille; tell the manager that I referred you, and it may help you find a position on one of their ships," Max said. "There's a great deal to see in the world. Some of it is wonderful, a lot of it is mundane, some of it will scar your soul forever. Be careful out there, and don't lose your way."

Max rested his hand on Albert's shoulder then left him and Beauchamp alone.

"How about you, Beauchamp?" Albert said. "Any advice before I begin my adventure? It seems like you and I have been through a great deal together in a short span of time."

"Just what Max already said: be careful out there," Beauchamp replied. "If you change your mind about entering journalism, just write to me and I'll use what connections I have to help."

"I'll keep that in mind," Albert said, shaking Beauchamp's hand again before they parted ways.

A deep sadness settled into him as he rode in solitude back to his father's house, mingled with a building excitement. He knew that he ventured into the unknown, into chaos, but also that a potential dwelled in that chaos to create something he could be proud of.

While he busied himself in his rooms packing the bare essentials, Mercedes admitted herself. She had spent the morning deep in prayer, hoping that her words to Albert sunk in and that the count stayed true to his word, and wept with relief when she heard the carriage return.

Mercedes found Albert gazing at the implements of his many discarded hobbies. It drove her to remember her own upbringing, before Fernand returned from war with his first military wages and grand promises to keep her in comfort. She recalled the little hut in the Catalan village and the light she poured into every corner whenever Edmond returned from the sea.

"Mother," Albert said, catching sight of her. "What brings you here?"

"I came as soon as I knew you were home," Mercedes said, "especially since I couldn't be sure if you ever would return."

Albert gave a melancholy laugh and rubbed his eyes. "Well, here I am. I apologized to the count—that is, to M. Dantes—and he accepted it graciously. My friends were confused, but I told them it had to be this way."

"If it were only Edmond you had to deal with, I'm certain it would never have gone even this far," Mercedes said. "But the Count of Monte Cristo is a very different sort of being, and I couldn't be so sure."

"At any rate, it worked out. Now all that's left is to finish packing and leave Paris," Albert said.

"Yes, I suppose I should finish as well," Mercedes said.

"You? Where are you going?" Albert said, surprised.

"The same place as you: anywhere away from the tainted legacy your father built for us," Mercedes replied, looking out the window toward the main house. "I'm not certain what I'll do; perhaps I'll find a school in some country town in need of a teacher, or work as a seamstress somewhere. Perhaps I'll just abandon the world entirely and become a nun."

Albert walked over to his mother, bowed before her and kissed her hand.

"I would be honoured if you travelled with me as far as Marseille," Albert said. "And wherever you go, send word to Franz. I'll stay in touch with him, and he can tell me where to find you."

Mercedes smiled. "Of course, my dear son." She wrapped her arms around him.

Together they completed packing, a single trunk each, and servants loaded them into the carriage. Mercedes gave the steward instructions to dismiss all of the staff; she left them each a month's pay and warm letters of recommendation to help them find new positions. Albert offered his hand to help her enter the coach, and stood on the runner for a moment as it started to move.

"*Au revoir* to everything I know," Albert muttered, watching the only place he had ever called home recede behind him. "Onward to new opportunity."

Albert entered the coach and sat down as they reached the gate, and the house staff filed out in pairs and clusters after them. Hours passed with no sign of life anywhere on the grounds until evening fell. Foliage rustled in a secluded rear corner of the property. An enormous hand parted the branches, swollen and deformed with a palm the size of a dinner plate and fingers each as thick as a man's wrist.

Fernand Mondego, formerly the Count de Morcerf, emerged from hiding and loped across the grounds to his mansion where he could hide from prying eyes. On a neighbouring roof, Bertuccio collapsed his spyglass and made his way down to the street to inform his master.

CHAPTER 93
THE FUGITIVE

Fernand's body was distorted to the point of being grotesque after using the Eye of Asclepius to siphon life force from so many people at his trial. Like the great apes Beauchamp had compared him to, he had become so massive he could only walk hunched over. Otherwise he would have stood nine or ten feet tall.

Every muscle bulged, exaggerated and rippling beneath his stretch-marked skin. He needed to turn sideways to squeeze his shoulders through the rear door of the house. His uniform hung from him in tatters, filthy from his time hiding in the Catacombs. The gleaming Eye remained pinned to those scraps.

Fernand had kept careful watch on his house from hiding, minding when the prosecutor's men came and went. As their visits became less frequent, he reached the conclusion that they no longer thought he remained in Paris, and felt safe enough returning to the house. He needed supplies for his true escape.

His mind returned again to the shard of mortite hidden in his desk. He was no longer in any position to command an army and be credited with destroying the second Dead Plague, but the money would be a great help to him in exile. Besides, the chaos of another uprising could provide a useful distraction from the manhunt for Fernand Mondego. Fernand decided to bring the mortite with him, if he had time to retrieve it, and figure out how to rendezvous with Danglars later.

Fernand crept through the halls, gathering food from the pantries and clothes to travel in. Over time his body would burn through the excess life force coursing through him, and he needed to look presentable when he returned to ordinary proportions. Returning to his study to retrieve the money he kept hidden there for emergencies, he found a letter addressed to him in Mercedes' hand. He unsealed it with his oversized fingers.

"My husband, I don't know if you'll be foolish enough to return to this house, but if you do, know that you'll never find us here again," Fernand read with a frown, his voice much deeper and more guttural than usual. "Albert and I are leaving Paris, and possibly France, forever. We know everything about what you did to Pasha Ali, and—"

His eyes widened and his breath stopped when his eyes took in the next line.

"And also to Edmond Dantes, to confine him to prison for the rest of his life and remove your rival from your path," he continued. "We forsake your name and the blood money you brought home from Yanina. Goodbye."

He re-read the letter several times, growing angrier every time his eyes beheld the name of Edmond Dantes. He hadn't allowed himself to think of Edmond in twenty years, and yet the man reached from beyond the grave one final time to slap Fernand in the face. Fernand clenched the letter in his fist and wreathed it in flame, savouring the sensation of the paper crumbling to dry ash.

The fire strengthened Fernand's resolve. Going back generations, the gift of flame marked Catalans for greatness. He had risen to that greatness before, and he would do it again. This time it would be easier; he had money already and the Eye to help deal with any opposition. He kept more gold and false passports at a secret cottage in the countryside, enough for a new life and a new identity if he could reach it. He had time to reclaim what he deserved, including Mercedes once he found her. Possessing her love was his birthright as a Flamekeeper.

"Goodness Morcerf, your dress sense has suffered greatly in the past few days," said a voice like smoke and salt.

Fernand turned to see the Count of Monte Cristo at the study door, dressed in a long black coat buttoned to the neck. The count took in Fernand's dramatic stature without a care in the world.

"Pardon me; I was not expecting visitors," Fernand said. His own voice had become a gargling rumble thanks to the Eye, which he hoped was also temporary. He resumed his search for the hidden money in a bureau. "What brings you to my home?"

"Is it still your home? I thought you were wanted for treason and murder. They're planning to seize your assets and mount your head on a spike at the city gates," Monte Cristo replied.

"Yes, and thank you for that," Fernand said with a manic smile. "Your Greek princess was the Tepelini brat all along, after all. I should have recognized her at the opera, but keep in mind, she was a child the last time I saw her."

"And also in chains, rather than fine clothes," Monte Cristo said.

"Well, I'll just have to thank her personally before I put this city behind me," Fernand said with a vicious glint in his eye. "It's the least I can do for the cause of my ruin and misery. Chains might still suit her."

"If you want to kill the one responsible for your ruin, pick up a pistol and point it at your own head," Monte Cristo said. "You brought this on yourself, and it didn't start when you betrayed the pasha. It started the day you betrayed Edmond Dantes."

Fernand stopped still. "That name again!" he said. "How does the ghost of Dantes rise twice in one day after so long? How do you even know that name?"

Monte Cristo didn't speak, but unfastened the buttons of his coat and walked toward Fernand.

"You peculiar little gnat," Fernand said, "explain yourself. I've hated you since I met you. As soon as you sat down in my parlour, I had a hunch that you would be trouble. I've been polite to you for saving Albert's life in Rome, but right now you try my patience and walk dangerously close to death!"

"You walk closer to death than ever before," Monte Cristo said. "Even when you deserted your post at Waterloo, or betrayed the Spanish as a spy, or stole the vitality of the pasha."

The count threw his overcoat and gloves aside. Beneath he wore the navy jacket and trousers of a sailor, the jacket's open neck revealing the white linen wrappings which crisscrossed his chest. The uniform sparked a memory deep in Fernand's mind, of another hated enemy dressed in the same clothes.

"Who are you?" Fernand demanded.

"I could tell you a hundred names," the count said, his red eyes burning with fury. "Instead, I should use one of yours. The day we met, Mercedes introduced you as the man she loved most in the world after me."

"Dantes!" Fernand said. The blood drained from his face. "You're supposed to be dead!"

"I am!" Monte Cristo said. "And now I'm here, to tear apart your life as you did mine."

Fernand snorted with rage, and with animal savagery he picked up the bureau in one hand. He swung it down upon the count as if crushing a bug with a rock and knocked the count to the floor. The sturdy piece of furniture broke in half on impact and gouged a hole into the marble tiles of the study.

The single swing broke what little control Fernand maintained over his temper. All the jealous fury of that scorned young fisherman flooded out as Fernand slammed the pieces of the bureau down onto the count again and again, reducing it to splinters. He took a jagged wooden leg from the debris and drove it through the count's chest with a primal yell. Panting like a frenzied bear, he took a step back from the pile of fragmented wood and watched the stone dust settle onto it.

After a moment of quiet, the count stirred. He rolled over and pushed himself up from the wreckage of the bureau, brushing documents and banknotes from his shoulders as he rose. The count looked down at the wooden stake that impaled him, chuckled, and pulled it from his chest. When he dropped it to the floor, Fernand could see the wall behind the count through the bloodless hole.

"You said it yourself: I'm supposed to be dead," Monte Cristo said, and tore away his sailor's jacket.

The bandages wrapping his hands and his torso met along his arms, covering every inch of his body except for where Fernand's assault tore away ragged strips. Those strips exposed glimpses of desiccated grey flesh.

Before Fernand could make sense of it, Monte Cristo reached behind his own head and slipped his fingers into the hidden seam beneath his hair. He locked eyes with Fernand and pulled. The white mask with its fine leathery grain, once the face of Edmond Dantes after his escape from the Chateau d'If, came away in his hands.

"What creature from hell are you?" Fernand asked.

"The Arabs called them *mumya* when they first stumbled across ancient Egyptian tombs. The British Museum would call me a mummy," Monte Cristo said.

More bandages clung to the count's neck and covered his head. The skin around his exposed mouth and eyes had the colour and dry texture of silver tree bark.

"The Egyptians, when they saw that I persevered through their most torturous and arcane rituals, would have called me a god," he continued.

"No matter; if I'm too late to kill you, I can at least cremate you," Fernand growled.

He raised his hands above his head and conjured a boulder of flame. The count twisted at an unnatural angle to dodge the fireball, which splashed against the far wall of the study. The plush curtains started to smolder.

"Mercedes' love was my birthright, and twice you stole it from me!" Fernand yelled, pointing at the count. A lance of flame darted from his finger, which the count also dodged, setting fire to a large oak desk.

Monte Cristo extended his arm, and serpentine bandages reached out to wrap around Fernand's wrist. The wrinkled grey flesh of his abdomen and ribcage exposed itself as his bandages unwound for the attack. The count pulled and toppled Fernand to the ground, then leapt onto his back.

"I stole nothing from you," Monte Cristo said as more linen tendrils shackled Fernand's ankles and his other wrist. "You took it for granted that Mercedes would love you for your flames."

"She would have, without your interference!" Fernand said, struggling to right himself. The cloth strips gripped him like the iron manacles at his trial.

"The only interference came from your fundamental misunderstanding of the world," Monte Cristo said as he tied Fernand's legs and arms behind his back. "The great flame-wielders of your culture weren't destined for greatness because of their gifts. They achieved greatness by using their gifts to do good in the world. You assumed greatness would flock to you."

"It should have! Mercedes should have been mine!" Fernand said.

The curtains burned with enthusiasm at the far end of the study, and the flames licked at the ceiling.

"You never saw her as an individual, with goals and dreams of her own; only as a prize," Monte Cristo said. "You've been married to her for years; can you even tell me her favourite meal?"

Fernand roared with rage. He engulfed himself in fire to burn away the bandages that bound him, and grabbed Monte Cristo by the ankle to hurl him across the room. The count smashed into the burning desk, reducing it to flaming chunks which scattered across the room to spread that flame to paintings and tapestries on the wood-paneled walls.

Wearing his gift like a cloak made up as a flame elemental from Hell, Fernand ran hunched over to a suit of decorative armour and retrieved a jousting lance. He used to tell visitors that a former king gifted that lance to his grandfather, actually just a restored antique he bought in Spain. He pinned the count to the floor through the stomach like a researcher pinning a bug to a card.

"Ever since I first heard your name, I've wanted to burn you to ash!" Fernand said, smoke pouring from his mouth.

Fernand's outstretched hands became the jaws of a twin-headed dragon, filling every corner of the room with flame. He no longer cared if he burned the entire house down; no fire could touch him, thanks to his gift. As the count gripped the lance, Fernand backed up to the door and continued his onslaught, intending to burn away any trace of Edmond Dantes for the last time. He escaped into the hall and barricaded the door from the outside.

"Go back to the grave where you belong," Fernand said to the study door, dropping the suit of conjured flame from around himself and making an effort to steady his breathing.

Burning wood roared on the other side of the door, punctuated by pieces of the roof caving in to crash against the marble floor. Taking stock of his injuries, he noticed that the scraps of his uniform hung looser than before; the extreme use of his gift drained the excess life force absorbed at his trial faster than anticipated. He caught his reflection in a nearby window and could not deny that he had shrunk closer to his customary physique.

Fire had consumed the money hidden in his study, but Fernand could still check Mercedes' bedroom or Albert's house for gold and jewels they may have left behind. Halfway up the stairs, the study doors rattled.

Terror gripped Fernand's heart as he turned to look. The doors rattled again, and then a burning fist punched a hole through the dark wood. A second hand joined it and tore the hole wider as if the door were made of paper. The Count of Monte Cristo stepped through the gap, leaving the inferno of the study behind him. His bandages had burned away, and those scraps that remained were burning still. The desiccated flesh beneath was charred, and his red eyes locked onto Fernand.

For the first time, Fernand was unsure if it even fell within his power to defeat the count. He laid down a barrier of flame at the base of the stairs to deter the implacable count and rushed to Mercedes' bedroom. As he went, he dropped additional fireballs and ignited the walls and floors to slow Monte Cristo down. He needed to buy enough time to escape.

In Mercedes' room, Fernand tore open every drawer in search of forgotten jewels but found none. He growled in frustration, imagining too well his ungrateful wife selling them to some merchant and handing the money to some beggar or orphanage. With spite and rage he ignited the plush bed where she had refused more and more of his overtures, then crept to the door to see if he could exit.

As he bent to peer through the crack, the door was driven open with astounding force. The heavy mahogany cracked against Fernand's nose, breaking it with a double stream of blood. He howled and staggered backward, swinging his hand to spray fire in every direction. The count advanced, staggering and lurching but otherwise unperturbed.

Seeing the raw power of the revenant, Fernand touched the Eye of Asclepius and aimed it at the count. The cold blue beam of the amulet reached out, but Fernand felt no gratifying rush of new strength. Instead, the count bared his teeth in a triumphant leer.

A great sense of vertigo gripped Fernand. His heart skipped a beat with a wrenching pain in his chest, and it became hard to breathe. He was used to feeling rejuvenated when he used the Eye, but this felt as though he were a basin full of water and someone had pulled his plug; a horrible feeling of being drained away. His distorted muscles shrank back to their typical size as the beam from the Eye darkened to a deep violet and the count advanced on Fernand.

"Did you expect to drain lie from the dead, Fernand?" the count said with a terrible laugh. "You never learned Aristotle, I see. *Horror vacuui!*"

Fernand released the Eye of Asclepius, but the beam did not subside. He ran for the only other exit, the seldom-used door to his adjoining bedroom, hoping to keep away from the count. The beam from the Eye curved through the open door but did not break, and the draining sensation continued.

Fernand caught sight of himself in a large mirror in his bedroom. He was no longer even as muscular as before his trial. He threw more fire behind him, the action taking more effort than ever before. Terrified to his core, Fernand threw the Eye away in desperation. The beam broke at last and the awful feeling of ebbing away cut off. The count stepped into the room.

"Now you look more how I remember you," the count said. "A scrawny, envious coward shrinking away from a challenge."

Fernand glanced at the mirror again. Every physical gain he ever took with the Eye was gone. His thin and bony arms and legs reminded him of his youth, and his sunken chest was almost concave. Instead of the Adonis he had lived as for so many years, he was once again a sickly fisherman from a backwater village. His goatee and hair were yellow and brittle, and his face sagged to make him look older than his forty years. The sight was a gruesome echo of what he had done to Pasha Ali.

The count picked up the Eye and appraised it; the flames in the doorway behind him danced in the jewel's many facets. Cowering on the floor, Fernand forced more flame through his hand to try and destroy the Eye so the count couldn't keep it. The count dodged this outburst and pinned the Eye to his own burnt flesh. He laid his decayed fingers on the gem, and the violet light struck Fernand again.

When the wrenching pain of the beam subsided, it left behind an unfamiliar ache. It took Fernand a moment to realize what was wrong; even as the flames devoured the house and inched ever closer to him, he was cold. He summoned a fireball but nothing came, not even enough of a spark to light a cigarette. The well of power inside him which had always supplied that heat felt numb.

"What have you done?" Fernand gasped.

"You've always been so proud of your flames, Fernand," the count said, advancing with outstretched hands. "Let's find out what they have in store for you."

"Stay away!" Fernand said, his voice cracking.

He scrambled to his bed and reached under the mattress for a loaded pistol. He aimed first at the count, but then reconsidered how best to use the single bullet loaded in the gun. With a trembling hand he put it under his chin and pulled the trigger.

The hammer clicked, but no shot fired. Monte Cristo laughed like a vengeful demon, knocked the useless misfired pistol from Fernand's hand, and grabbed him by his brittle hair. Relishing Fernand's screams, the count dragged him back into Mercedes' bedroom where every inch was engulfed in flame.

Searing pain gnawed at Fernand's flesh as he experienced being burned for the first time in his life. The air was too dry and hot to breathe. The count lifted him from the ground by his hair and cupped a hand under Fernand's chin, forcing him to stare into the monstrous charred face of the thing that had brought justice home to his door. Fernand couldn't withstand the pain for long, and he shrieked until smoke and overuse left his voice nothing but a thin wail. His skin crackled like a roasting pig as the fire closed in, engulfing him and the count together, and in the last moments of his life he experienced the true meaning of Hell.

Outside, spectators gathered by the front gate to see the Morcerf mansion blazing in the gathering dusk. The east wing caved in as fire ate away at the structure, spreading rapidly through the house. Fire marshals arrived with water wagons but determined they could do nothing to save the building. There was nothing anyone could do but watch it burn.

Unnoticed, a dark form stepped out of the flames at the rear of the house. This figure stepped through the side gate into a dark laneway and admitted itself to the sewers by way of a manhole. Safe in the dark, the Count of Monte Cristo allowed himself to slump over. The battle had taken far more effort than he had allowed Fernand to see, and his burns were more severe than he had expected.

With a great effort of will, he melted into the shadows. They whisked him away through the sewers to the Catacombs, and through the Catacombs to a point where he could emerge behind his home on the Champs Elysees.

CHAPTER 94
RECOVERY

The count admitted himself to the back garden and struck five notes on a gong he kept there. His servants recognized the signal: the master of the house was home and desired not to see anybody but Haydee or Ali. Their strict instructions said to leave at once when they heard that signal and not return until the following day. The noise also woke Valentine, who rushed to her bedroom window; in the darkness, she could only see a dark form approaching the house.

Baptistan and Haydee greeted him at the door, but Haydee's hands flew to her mouth in shock at his condition.

"Master, you are badly burned. This one cautioned against prolonged exposure to fire," Baptistan said, stepping forward to support the count's weight.

"It was the only way, Baptistan," the count said, grateful for the rest.

"How do I help you?" Haydee asked. She fretted over the holes in the count's torso and the charred scraps of bandages which had fused to his flesh under the heat.

"The burned layer must be debrided with silver instruments. The open wounds must be packed with herbs," Baptistan recited. "Sacred oils must be applied to the flesh beneath, and a fresh layer of bandages tightly wound. Following that, master must rest and rejuvenate."

Haydee laid her hand on the count's blackened cheek, her warm brown eyes diving deep into his red gaze. Attuned to the count as she was, she could see the great pain hiding behind it.

"I'll do it," she said.

"That is unnecessary, mistress. This one is fully equipped for the task," Baptistan said.

"Haydee can do it," the count said. "Talk her through the process. My dear, I've brought you gifts from the Morcerf estate."

He held up a large sack which he had brought from the ruins of the Morcerf house. Haydee took it from him, but did not look inside as she helped Baptistan bring the count to his bedroom. A shriek from the hallway interrupted them.

"What's happening?" Valentine asked, horrified at the sight of the count. "Who is that, what happened to him?"

"Valentine, it's alright," Haydee said, the slight panic in her own voice robbing it of the reassuring tone she wanted. "This doesn't concern you."

"You're carrying a burnt corpse through the house!" Valentine screamed. "I think it's reasonable that I have questions!"

"You're quite right," the count said. Valentine jumped when she heard what she thought was a dead man speak. "However temporarily, you are a part of this house."

"M. de Monte Cristo?" Valentine whispered. "What happened?"

"I fought a duel," the count said. The blackened skin around his mouth cracked as he smiled. "You should see my opponent."

Baptistan guided Valentine back to her room, then returned to the count's bedchamber. Past the plush four-canopy bed with rich cushions and a fine duvet, lay a carved stone table; a twin of the one in the cave beneath the island of Monte Cristo. Haydee helped the count to lay on it.

Next to the table stood a tall cupboard decorated with flowing Egyptian motifs. This held the necessary ingredients and instruments for mummification, as well as a supply of fresh bandages. Four golden jars stood on the top shelf with carved heads from Egyptian mythology: a baboon, a falcon, a jackal, and a human. In the middle of them sat a fifth jar, made of black stone with an unadorned lid.

Haydee knew these were the canopic jars holding the organs removed from Edmond Dantes' body during his transformation. The first four were traditional jars, representing the four sons of Horus. The falcon was the god Qebehsenuef, with the count's intestines within. Hapy the baboon held the lungs, Duamutef the jackal held the stomach, and the jar with the head of a man was Imsety, containing the liver.

Curiosity overtook Haydee and she touched the black jar in the centre. She felt a deep pulsation inside it.

"The debridement must begin, mistress," Baptistan said next to her. It picked up a gleaming silver tool like a crescent moon with a blade on the inside curve.

Haydee nodded, and Baptistan showed her how to begin on the count's ankle. It took almost no pressure for the blade to part the charred outer layer from the dry grey flesh beneath. She stroked the smooth grey skin of the uncovered area, eliciting a deep sigh from the count.

"Does that hurt, my love?" Haydee asked, watching the count's ravaged face.

"Not precisely," Monte Cristo said. "Imagine a rusted iron shackle on your wrist, grinding against your bones and tearing your skin. The only way to remove it is to make it even tighter for a moment, but then comes relief."

"In that case, let's free you," Haydee said.

She bent to her task, removing the burnt flesh with as much care as she could and dropping the pieces into a wooden basin by her feet. Baptistan helped her to turn the count over when needed and coached her on new instruments to use on particular areas. Certain pieces of his anatomy required an even more delicate touch.

As she worked, the count relaxed more upon the table. He remained silent all through her careful work on his face, watching with pride as she concentrated on her task. Even for Haydee, to see the count's unwrapped face was unusual; even without his mask, he remained wrapped in his protective bandages. Despite the strange colour of his freshly-scraped skin, Haydee marvelled at how ordinary he looked.

"Baptistan, bring Haydee's gifts," the count commanded once Haydee's work on his face was complete and she proceeded to his scalp.

Baptistan hefted the sack onto a side table. The first item to come out was the count's mask, rescued from the flames and needing only some cleaning. Baptistan reached into the sack again.

"My love, your mother and father are avenged," Monte Cristo said with a smile.

Baptistan held up a severed human head. The hair and goatee had burned away, and the flesh had run like tallow under the intense heat, but to one for whom tragedy had etched that face into everlasting memory there was no trouble to recognize it.

"I present to you the head of the traitor Fernand Mondego," Monte Cristo said, "and my promise that he died in agony after losing everything he held dear."

Haydee wept with the relief of one who sees the greatest demon of their life exorcised at last. Standing at the count's head, she bent over to plant a grateful kiss. Her thick black hair brushed against his chest, and her tears of joy ran onto his chin and down across his jaw.

"Baptistan, what do I need to do next?" she asked, her lips inches from the count's.

"The master's wounds must be tightly packed with herbs from the green enameled box," Baptistan replied. "Next, his exposed skin must be anointed thoroughly with oil from the jug adorned with a cat's head. Finally, he must be tightly wound in fresh bandages and rest. At least two weeks would be ideal."

"I can handle that alone," Haydee said. "Leave us. Have the traitor's skull cleaned and bleached."

Baptistan bowed at the waist and obeyed. The cupboard contained rolled bundles of the required herbs, no larger than a cigar, making it simple to fill in the holes of the count's torso.

"How did these happen?" she asked.

"This one? He hit me with a bureau and stabbed me with the broken leg," the count said, gesturing at the wound in his chest. He chuckled at how absurd it sounded when he said it out loud. "The smaller one is from a lance."

"My poor master," Haydee said, trailing her fingers across Monte Cristo's skin between the two dressed wounds.

"I've told you, you don't need to call me that. You're free," the count said.

"And I've told you, I know that," Haydee said with her mischievous smile. She put away the herb box, reached for the oil bottle, and paused to look down at herself. "You know, it would be a shame to spill oil on these fine clothes."

The count propped himself up on his elbows as Haydee reached behind her neck to undo the single clasp which held up her flowing silk dress and allowed it to fall to the floor. The moon from the skylight reflected off her bare skin as she opened the bottle. She applied the oil to the count's legs and breathed in the exotic aromas of coriander, cumin, and cloves released by the heat of her palms. Haydee climbed onto the stone table with the count to apply the oil along his body, straddling him to anoint his chest and arms.

"I have another gift for you," Monte Cristo said. "I recovered the Eye of Asclepius, and we can return it to your homeland when our business in Paris is complete."

Haydee shushed him with an oiled finger against his lips, and kept him quiet with another kiss as she caressed the sides of his face to apply the oil there as well. She felt the count stir beneath her and smiled.

"I have a gift for you as well, my love," she murmured, shifting her hips and drawing another sigh from the count. Together, as was their way, they helped one another forget their pain.

The servants returned to the house in the morning to resume their posts. Haydee knocked on Valentine's bedroom door, dressed in a yellow silk dressing gown. After seeing the count in such a state, Valentine slept very little and the dark bags under her eyes attested to that.

"If you'd like to understand, come with me," Haydee said with a smile. "Just don't press him to tell you more than he chooses to; he's badly hurt, and needs to rest. And you can't tell anyone what you learn, not even Eugenie, until the count and I leave Paris for good."

Valentine considered whether she wanted to know what madness allowed a man to walk so close to death and survive the night, or if she would be happier to remain ignorant. It didn't take her long to decide; if she ever wanted to become a journalist, she couldn't begin shying away from uncomfortable stories.

Soon, she sat next to the count's bedside. The count sat propped up against a mound of cushions with the duvet pulled up to his chest. His arms lay above the covers, showcasing the fresh bandages that covered everything but his mouth and eyes. A folding Japanese room divider concealed the stone table and the sacred cupboard.

"Valentine, I can't tell you the entire truth right away," the count said with kindness in his strange gaze. "But what I can tell you began with a man named Cesare Spada in the fifteenth century."

CHAPTER 95
FATHER AND DAUGHTER

In his gaudy salon, Baron Danglars sat making calculations and recalculations. His grand design to reintroduce the Dead Plague to the world had devolved from a matter of multiplying his fortune to a matter of restoring it after his run of bad luck and the Count of Monte Cristo's damned unlimited credit account. As the final straw to convince him to alter the plan, Fernand had been arrested and subsequently disappeared.

The original plan called for Villefort to tell the king that his network of contacts had found the source of the Plague and for Fernand to volunteer to lead the expedition to destroy it. Danglars knew nobody else in the military he could trust to bring into the plan but another general, one ignorant of the situation, could lead the charge just as well. Without Fernand to give informed orders, more soldiers would lose their lives fighting before Danglars closed the box, but he wrote them off easily.

"What are a few more dead soldiers?" he muttered as he scribbled notes about his estimated returns. "Their corpses will lend authenticity to the enterprise."

In a recent letter, Villefort told him that he had a man in mind to become one of the first victims of the new Plague. If Villefort wanted to expend the effort and rid himself of an undesirable, there was no reason to stop him, saving Danglars the effort of providing Patient Zero himself.

Villefort could prove a weak link as well. The prosecutor seemed to be in the middle of a breakdown brought on by the Nightly Assemblage's continued questioning of his integrity and competence. Cutting him out entirely could be prudent; if he were to lose his position, he would lose all power to retaliate against Danglars.

Danglars chuckled, thinking of the demonstration he had subjected Villefort and Fernand to in his cellar two months previously. The shards of mortite he gave them as good-faith gestures meant nothing, of course. With or without them, Danglars' box held more than enough mortite to raise the dead. Giving away two insignificant fragments played a useful ruse to give the others a false sense of importance and encourage them to buy in.

On a fresh sheet of paper, Danglars scribbled a new set of calculations. If Villefort could not direct the king to a particular place, armies would need to search for the outbreak source in earnest themselves. That search, based on scouring the continent and hoping for good luck, was unlikely to stumble upon whatever apartment or rural chateau Danglars chose to hide in. The war effort to combat the new Plague could well drag on longer than the original plan called for, resulting in even greater profits for Danglars' portfolio; profits he no longer needed to share. So long as Danglars could find a safe place to wait, he could allow the undead to rampage for as long as he liked and end it when he pleased. The sum at the bottom of the page caused his eyes to grow wide, and his lips stretched in that ugly approximation of a smile.

Without knocking, Eugenie entered the salon. Danglars didn't bother to hide his papers; his notes, written in his own cipher, looked to anyone else like meaningless symbols around columns of digits. Eugenie approached the desk with her typical haughty expression.

"Father, I will not marry Andrea Cavalcanti," she said.

"Really," Danglars replied, raising his eyebrows. "And why is that?"

"Because he's an unpleasant sycophant, because he's more interested in access to your bank than in making me happy, and because I simply don't want to," Eugenie replied. "Andrea was a useful tool in getting rid of Albert, who didn't even bother pretending to like me, but now this has gone far enough and I'm saying no."

Danglars shook his head, wobbling his loose cheeks. "You misunderstood my question, dear," he said. "I didn't mean to ask why you don't want to marry Prince Cavalcanti. I meant to ask why you think you have any say in the matter."

Eugenie stepped back as if slapped. "You don't own me, Father."

"Don't I?" Danglars asked. "While other girls your age work, I've kept you comfortable so you can pursue your hobbies without the drab lifestyle of penniless artists like your friend Louise."

"And you think that gives you some claim on my life?" Eugenie said.

"Of course it does. You've eaten the food I provided, benefitted from the shelter I've provided, and only have this self-important attitude because of the security I've provided," Danglars said. "You owe me everything."

"In exchange for what? Things I was given as a child, when I couldn't understand the terms of this abhorrent deal you're describing?" Eugenie said, her cheeks flushing with frustration. "Am I supposed to be your indentured servant for life?"

"It's the social contract, my dear," Danglars said. "If you don't like it, you're free to leave. But keep in mind that while you've been dependent on me, you haven't learned a single useful skill with which to find steady employment. How much work do you expect to find in the country for an amateur musician?"

Eugenie had no reply and paced about the salon, fuming and venting her anger by kicking the garishly-carved furniture. Danglars allowed her tantrum to continue without comment until she returned to him.

"You'll really force me into marrying Andrea to repay you for the effort of raising me?" she asked.

"Considering the utter lack of gratitude you've shown me for doing so, I shouldn't be surprised that you're being so disagreeable now," Danglars said. "But yes, that's exactly the situation."

Eugenie balled her fists with a high-pitched growl. She took a deep breath, then another, and found her centre again after a third.

"Very well, Father. I'll marry Andrea," she said, her eyes closed. "But I suggest you don't spend one cent of the money his father gives you for me. Hold it in your vault, leave it safe somewhere, but don't use it. At least not for now."

"An unemployed artist dictating how I run my business? Will wonders never cease," Danglars said. "What are you playing at?"

Danglars worked hard not to let his new anxiety show on his face. Cavalcanti's payment for Eugenie had already been converted into shares of the weapons manufacturers required for his plans, and his vaults at the Danglars Bank may as well have been empty. If the marriage fell through, the news might be the last straw to prompt his creditors to call in their debts, which he did not have the money to pay. The same crisis of debt which came close to destroying Morrel & Sons in 1815 would destroy him just the same, before he ever stood a chance to profit from his Plague. The law he aimed to propose at the next session of the House of Peers was his sole insurance policy.

"Nothing at all, Father," Eugenie said. "I simply don't trust Andrea and wouldn't be surprised if he were some swindler aiming to take advantage of us somehow."

"No doubt you reach this conclusion from your vast experience of the human condition," Danglars said, cleaning his spectacles. "Leave the financial matters in my hands, dear. Yours are better suited to the piano and the paintbrush."

Eugenie glared at her father and departed. A few minutes later, Danglars heard her and Louise singing a duet in her bedroom.

"Ungrateful girl," Danglars muttered. "If she were anyone but my own blood, I would throw her to the undead myself."

CHAPTER 96
THE CONTRACT

To reassure Parisian society of his and his bank's financial security, Danglars spent a great deal on credit for the signing ceremony. Three days after discussing the facts of life with Eugenie, the guests gathered at the Danglars home.

According to French custom, the bride and groom would sign the marriage contract at the party in front of the assembled guests, then travel to the courthouse by carriage to have it notarized. With the paperwork filed to recognize them as husband and wife, the same carriage would carry them to some far-flung corner of France for their honeymoon. A well-fortified former castle had been arranged for that part of their journey under the guise of a romantic retreat but really to keep them safe from the Plague Danglars intended to unleash.

Andrea arrived at Danglars' house at half-past eight in the evening, dressed as if he intended to marry a princess. He came in a coach lent to him by the Count of Monte Cristo, who declined to attend due to illness.

Andrea walked on air up the steps to the house. From his beginnings as a foundling and a galley-slave, he had acquired money and a title as well as a suitable marriage to an adequate woman. The only person who knew the fraud of his identity was dead. He licked his lips at the memory of sinking his teeth at last into that aggravating Caderousse and how satisfying his peculiar hunger had found the tailor's flesh.

As Monte Cristo's coach pulled away, Andrea smiled all the wider. One other person did know that Andrea Cavalcanti was not who he claimed, but Andrea feared no danger from him. With all the count had done for him, Andrea had no worries that his situation would change. If the count really were his father, then Andrea expected at the very least to be acknowledged in the will and enriched even further in the long run when Monte Cristo died.

"That run may not even need to be so long, either," he muttered, tapping a thumbnail against his teeth.

The one sour note of the whole situation remained the cold distance the count put between them. He associated with Andrea little if at all beyond making introductions and occasional gifts of cash. Even the borrowed coach lacked the count's coat of arms. In Andrea's best guess, the count sought to wait until the marriage was official to acknowledge him, though he still could not think of why.

Entering the house banished any chance of considering the matter further. All of Paris seemed to be there, everyone who mattered at any rate, presenting many hands to shake and cheeks to kiss. Every few moments the doorman announced some well-known name from the upper echelons of banking or government—to the extent that those organizations differ. One thing Andrea never lacked was superficial charm, often the best sort of charm in such circles, and he was in his element.

Danglars' furniture and the guests' jewelry reflected the dazzling light of the crystal chandeliers, overwhelming the eye no matter where one looked. String quartets played in any room large enough to hold one, performing from the same list of songs but with no coordination with each other. Eugenie drifted through it all, dressed in an elegant white silk dress with a single white rose in her black hair, her face set in a look of confident indifference. In contrast, Louise lingered near her at all times in a state of agitation close to fits.

Beauchamp and Raoul came for the wedding, having joined Andrea at the races on several occasions since his arrival in Paris almost two months earlier; Franz had already left for Rome two days after the aborted duel. They brought a subdued Lucien, who swiveled his head to watch out for Danglars. Raoul had convinced Max to come for the spectacle of a society wedding, and both wore their dress uniforms. Like Lucien, Max was preoccupied and distant; Valentine still refused to leave the count's house for fear of seeing her father. The other Vampire Club girls were invited as well; besides Valentine, only Haydee declined.

The lawyers arrived to bureaucratize the sacred joining of two hearts in matrimony. A gilt table, with legs carved like lion claws and draped in velvet, sat ready for the signing of documents. The chief notary sat down while his colleagues remained standing and read the terms of the contract aloud, a dense fog of legalese. Nobody present understood the particulars of it, but everybody understood the intent. The ritual underscored the prestige of the fortune to come under the command of the young couple. Andrea still had trouble believing the entire affair was really happening.

"It is now time," the chief notary intoned as he flourished a silver pen above his head, "to sign the contract."

Protocol called for Baron Danglars to sign first, then a representative of Major Cavalcanti, followed by Andrea and Eugenie, and lastly their two witnesses: Louise for Eugenie and Raoul for Andrea.

Considering the solemnity of the contract, it may have surprised anyone not well-acquainted with Paris that the gossip resumed as soon as the chief notary fell silent. Hermine leaned on a friend's arm while Danglars spoke to the lawyer.

"It's a dreadful shame that Valentine de Villefort couldn't attend," Hermine said. "I heard it has something to do with that invasion of M. de Monte Cristo's home."

"Oh yes, her father has been so busy with that, and the rumour is that Valentine is too afraid of monsters to leave the house," said Hermine's friend, the wife of a member of the Royal Reserve's board. "You recall that poor burglar, who was so savagely killed by his own accomplice during the break-in?"

Andrea overheard this, and his ears pricked up.

"The devil who killed him took deep bites out of the poor man, in some sort of cannibalistic ravaging," the board member's wife continued. "The burglar was undressed so the coroner could examine his wounds, and the clothes were thrown into the corner. The clothes were recovered later as evidence, but the waistcoat had become separated from the other garments and went overlooked for some time."

"Indeed?" Hermine asked, with the rapt attention such people pay to dreadful things which happen to strangers. Meanwhile Danglars added the final embellishments to his signature and handed the pen off to Major Cavalcanti's proxy.

"The waistcoat was found by M. de Monte Cristo's cleaning staff and assumed to be an old rag, but then someone noticed the bloodstains. They searched the coat and found a letter addressed to your husband," Hermine's friend said.

As she spoke, Andrea moved through the crowd shaking hands and laughing at cliched jokes until he reached the door and slipped through it.

"A letter to me?" Danglars said, having caught the thread of the conversation. "Why should that concern M. de Villefort?"

"The letter was evidence, of course," Hermine's friend said. "Do you think they will give you the letter when the case is closed, or keep it forever?"

The time arrived for the couple to sign their marriage contract. Eugenie stepped forward with all the enthusiasm of a child receiving an inoculation, but Andrea did not appear. The chief notary called out for him by his title and several of his friends shouted his Christian name, but he could not be found.

With a great commotion, armed police officers burst into the grand salon. Guards with drakes posted themselves at each exit and throughout the house. They silenced the various string quartets. The guests screamed with alarm and huddled together in clumps, the most gallant men forming ranks around the women and their less courageous peers. A magistrate wearing his official scarf entered the room, scanning the crowd and walking straight to Danglars. Danglars broke into a sweat at once, assuming his plot had been uncovered. Instead of arresting him, the magistrate stood by the contract table and addressed the room.

"Which of you answers to the name Andrea Cavalcanti?" the magistrate asked, his voice resounding through the salon.

Astonished murmurs rippled through the crowd, but Andrea did not come forward.

"I ask again, where is Andrea Cavalcanti?" the magistrate said. "Andrea Cavalcanti, alias Benedetto, a galley-slave escaped from Toulon, hereby charged with the murder of Gaspard Caderousse."

The murmurs of astonishment turned to cries of alarm. Shock prevented Hermine from speaking, and Danglars collapsed into the nearest chair. Struggling for air, he loosened his necktie and unfastened his collar. Of the Danglars family, only Eugenie maintained her wits. She took Louise by the hand and led her to the hall. The guards let them pass, being on alert only for the fugitive.

CHAPTER 97
THE DEPARTURE

The officers escorted the guests to the exits, questioning the men to prevent Benedetto from escaping in disguise. They pieced together the facts and realized they were too late, Benedetto had fled before they arrived. None of the guests found it necessary or helpful to make their condolences to the Danglars family, but many speculated in whispers about tomorrow's newspapers.

Soon only the Danglars family remained in the house. Danglars gave his statement to the police while Hermine sat in terrified silence in her boudoir, and Eugenie retired to her bedroom with Louise. Louise, already stressed by the impending threat of the marriage, came close to hyperventilating.

"Pigeon, be still," Eugenie said, sitting on the bed and watching Louise pace. "You'll give yourself a nervous fit."

"How can I be still? You were so close to being bound to that oaf, and now we learn that he's a cannibal too!" Louise said, gesticulating wildly. "Where did he escape to? What if he comes back? What if he decides that he still wants you for dinner if he can't have you for a wife?"

"Don't worry about that," Eugenie said in a gentle tone which her father never heard. "Louise, come here."

Louise traded her pacing for fretting with her gloves and biting her lip, but walked over to Eugenie regardless. Eugenie took her hands and smiled with a warmth neither Albert or "Andrea Cavalcanti" suspected her capable of. She lifted Louise's fingers to her lips and kissed them, then stood and kissed Louise's forehead and the tip of her nose. As a smile grew on Louise's face, Eugenie placed a firmer kiss on her lips, holding it until Louise's breathing slowed down. Eugenie leaned back to look Louise in the eye.

"Better?" she asked.

"Better," Louise agreed, blushing. "But what will we do? Even if Andrea never comes back, sooner or later your father will marry you off again."

"Yes, his ridiculous idea of a social contract will continue to be a problem," Eugenie said, frowning as she opened a wardrobe. "This invisible contract is printed on immaterial paper, and yet somehow I signed it when I was first born. Imagine signing a contract you can never see, before you could read or write, let alone comprehend and consent to the terms."

She gathered up the dresses which hung in the wardrobe and flung them onto her bed, exposing the back panel and opening a secret compartment. Louise smiled when Eugenie took out a bundle wrapped in greaseproof paper.

"It's time for our plan?" Louise said.

"Get the scissors," Eugenie replied with a grin.

The bundle contained a complete men's suit, including collar and necktie, as well as a particular corset and a trimmed false beard as black as her hair. A second bundle included travelling clothes for Louise, more sensible for the road than her party dress.

In under a minute, Louise trimmed Eugenie's flowing locks to a shorter and more masculine style. Freed from the weight of length, the waves of her hair tightened into smaller curls. Eugenie discarded her wedding dress and laced up the corset, with Louise's help, to compress and conceal her breasts.

"Doesn't that hurt?" Louise asked, running a hand along her own bosom.

"It doesn't tickle," Eugenie said, testing a few deep breaths. "As long as I can avoid a fistfight, I'll be fine."

With the difficult work completed, Eugenie donned the rest of her assemblage of men's clothes, finishing off with the application of her fake beard. In the end, she cut a fine figure of a waifish young man in a plain brown coat, not likely to attract attention. She could have been any concierge or carriage-driver on his way to the country for a day off. From the inside pocket of her coat Eugenie produced a handful of papers.

"With these passports, we can get out of this sorry country and start a new life somewhere else; Rome, or Milan, or even Munich if we're so inclined," she said, affecting a deeper voice to complete her disguise. The passports bore the names of siblings Gilles and Adrienne Durand. "Are our other preparations in place?"

Louise counted on her fingers. "I hired a coach the day you spoke to your father," she said. "It's waiting for us at the Bell and Bottle hotel in Compiegne with the trunks we packed. I have the letters of introduction from Haydee and M. de Monte Cristo that will pave our way in any of the continent's artistic communities. We have enough money to live in reasonable comfort until we can establish ourselves; I think that was everything."

"Not quite everything," Eugenie said. She returned to the hidden compartment in her wardrobe a third time and held up a sharpened wooden stake. "We still have a vampire to kill."

The two young women made their way outdoors by way of a garden staircase in the parlour and slipped past the porter with the last group of stragglers to leave the party. They hurried to Louise's boarding-house in the slums, where the rooftop of the Palais de Justice stood in the distance between the outlines of other buildings.

"All we need to do is watch the Palais; sooner or later, he'll arrive," Eugenie said. "I have my disguise; you're not missing from anywhere you're supposed to be. When we find him, we need to catch him off-guard."

"And then what?" Louise asked.

"Then I drive this into his heart," Eugenie replied, holding up the stake. "Whether he's a monster or just a murderer, this will kill him all the same."

CHAPTER 98
THE ESCAPE

B enedetto walked the back streets for over an hour in a sorry state. After such an unexpected blow to his fortune, he moved with no goal in mind but to get away from the Danglars' house.

"Speed, speed!" he muttered. "All I need is to move away from here, and quickly!"

Before long, a cab trundled into view. Benedetto hailed the driver and told a lie about needing to travel to Belgium to see a sick relative.

"I can hardly get you all the way to Belgium, sir," the driver said. "I can get you as far as Compiegne, sure enough."

"Fine," Benedetto said. Compiegne lay to the northeast and on the way to Belgium, an easy border to cross from the French side. "I'll find another driver when I get there."

They agreed on a fare and Benedetto settled into the cab to consider his next move. It would be a simple matter for him to stay in Belgium, but the authorities could follow him just as easily. He needed to find a Belgian port and join the throng of emigration to America. Benedetto spoke passable English learned from his fellow galley-slaves and could disappear into the crowd of Europeans sailing from the continent to the east coast of England. From there they would cross to the west coast by train, and board another ship to cross the Atlantic.

Benedetto took stock of his cash and valuables, his own as well as some stolen during his escape from the Danglars mansion. If he was careful, and frugal, he reasoned he could afford the passage without arriving penniless in America. Once there, he could write to the Count of Monte Cristo and explain himself in hopes of the count taking pity on his unfortunate son and sending aid.

His grumbling stomach interrupted his plotting. Naturally, food presented a problem for a traveler evading the law on a tight budget. The driver flicked his reins, catching Benedetto's attention and bringing a smirk to his face.

Benedetto sat back and waited. Soon enough, the driver called to him that they were nearing Compiegne and a suitable hotel at the edge of town. Benedetto leaned out the side and asked the driver to stop.

"My nerves have me so anxious about my dear uncle, I simply must stretch my legs and walk a while or I'll never be able to sleep," Benedetto said.

"Sure enough, sir," the driver replied.

The cab slowed to a stop in the darkness. Trees lined either side of the road.

"Thank you, thank you," Benedetto said, standing on the rail of the cab to pay the driver.

When the driver reached out for the money, Benedetto grabbed his wrist instead and pulled himself up onto the driver's seat. He sank his teeth deep into the driver's throat with the speed of a wild cat, biting through the windpipe in one swift motion and extinguishing the driver's scream. Assured of enjoying his meal in peace, Benedetto threw the driver down from the cab and jumped after him, dragging the driver into the forest far enough to avoid undue attention.

"A free ride and a free meal. Well, hardly free for you," Benedetto said to the dying driver before taking another bite from the man's leg.

An hour later, he walked into the Bell and Bottle hotel at the edge of Compiegne. He bought a room for the night with the driver's money, also wearing the unlucky man's simple clothing over his own finery to avoid attention. The fashionable clothes could be sold once he reached a safer distance from Paris, for a little more money to aid his escape. Well-fed and pleased with himself for improvising such a good plan, he settled into bed with the intent of leaving before daybreak.

At about seven in the morning, a ray of sunlight crept across Benedetto's face. He stretched and smiled, waking from a deep sleep, but sat up with a start. A gendarme crossed the hotel's courtyard beneath Benedetto's window. His heart lurched in his throat, but he forced himself not to panic.

"He's alone; he wouldn't come alone to catch a murderer," Benedetto muttered. "He may be staying here himself or just on patrol."

Benedetto dressed himself in the driver's clothes again and gathered his Parisian suit into a sack. He hoped to wait for the gendarme to disappear from view, then find a coach to get closer to the border. When he looked again, his blood froze at the sight of a second gendarme guarding the stairway he needed, and a third officer on horseback waiting with a musket at the inn's main entrance.

That settled it; they knew or suspected Benedetto was there. Panic crept in, and with it an anxious hunger. He wanted nothing more than a hunk of meat to sink his teeth into and time to think as he chewed, but neither were available. The door or the window both led into the hands of the police.

His eyes landed on the room's writing desk, with pen and ink and paper provided for the discerning guest. Benedetto penned a hasty note pretending to be a shamefaced guest with no money to pay his bill. He unbolted the door and left it ajar, to make it appear that the fictional pauper had absconded in the night and neglected to close it completely. The ruse, he hoped, would throw the police off his trail.

Finally, he tied the sack to his ankle and stepped into the room's modest fireplace. He took a deep breath and climbed into the chimney; not the first time he had exited a room by such a manner. Only moments after he emerged onto the roof, a magistrate entered his room.

Benedetto didn't realize he owed this visit to simple bad luck. Someone better acquainted with the layout of France would have known that Compiegne hosted one of the many royal cottages. It thus also hosted a police force as formidable as that of Paris itself. They began sweeping the area's hotels in search of Benedetto the cannibal when the telegraphs first broadcast his name and description. Benedetto attracted their attention with his arrival at the Bell and Bottle so late in the night.

To their credit, these officers did not take his note at face value; they checked every possible hiding place in the room, the chimney included, before accepting that their target had already fled.

On the roof, too high to jump and without a drain-pipe to shimmy down, Benedetto considered his options. The roof provided no long-term refuge either, since many windows in the surrounding buildings would allow anyone to see him crouched there. He could only hope to enter another room through their chimney, and hide there until the gendarmes decided he no longer occupied the hotel.

Benedetto selected a nearby chimney with no smoke issuing from it and shimmied down into one of the hotel's upscale rooms with an ensuite bath. Benedetto smiled at this stroke of luck and settled into a chair by the window to watch the police in the courtyard. If he could just wait them out, he could continue his travels and find something or someone to eat.

A noise from the bathroom caught his attention and a maid with a scrub-brush and pail, a pretty young thing with chestnut hair, came into the main room. She cried out in alarm when she saw Benedetto.

"Don't be frightened!" Benedetto said, hoping to silence her. "I've just rented this room, I didn't mean to startle you."

The girl remained wary as Benedetto moved closer while continuing to speak reassuring lies. His gaze flitted between her wide brown eyes and her slender throat. When he stood within a few steps of her, his stomach burbled in protest of the morning's excitement. He lunged.

The girl, quick enough to see the change in Benedetto's eyes, reacted on instinct and swung the heavy pail of water as hard as she could. In a lucky shot, she struck him in the ribs and knocked him off-balance. Benedetto staggered and hit his head against the brick fireplace, dazing him and drawing a thin trickle of blood from his scalp.

The girl screamed in earnest. "Police! Murderer! Murderer in room number twelve!" she cried as loud as she could. "Help!"

Benedetto growled and bared his teeth, moving once more to sink them into her neck and shut her up, but his feet became tangled in the bag still tied to his ankle and he tumbled to the floor. The cleaning girl took the chance to run, slamming the door behind her and pounding at every door she passed on her way to the courtyard.

Benedetto was halfway up the chimney again when an officer burst into the room, grabbed him by the ankle, and yanked him down. Benedetto found himself on the floor again, staring up the barrel of a carbine.

"Alright, very well," he said with as much dignity as he could muster. "I surrender."

CHAPTER 99
THE DANGLARS HOUSEHOLD

While the Compiegne police put Benedetto in shackles, Danglars hid in his study and double-locked the door. After spending all night refactoring his balance sheet to stave off bankruptcy, the numbers still refused to cooperate.

By the end of the week, the gossip of "Andrea" being wanted for murder would be established fact and prompt an inevitable run on the Danglars bank with no time for him to produce a fresh run of banknotes from the Reserve to keep himself afloat. The money Major Cavalcanti had promised him was forfeit, if it ever existed, but he had already emptied his vaults on the expectation of it. Danglars had one last trick to play.

The House of Peers met at ten o'clock, and Danglars stood straight-backed before them. As a baron he could not vote on legislation, but he could debate bills and, more importantly, propose them.

Fernand's trial and subsequent rampage still left a fresh wound on the chamber, both in the structural scars of Fernand's physical and pyrotechnic might as well as the diminished attendance. Many of the survivors were either too injured or too afraid to appear at the House. Those of them who could vote but weren't there would be counted as abstaining, which worked in Danglars' favour; fewer people to convince suited him just fine.

Danglars launched into a masterful speech to the few assembled peers, one he had crafted for the past month as his swan song. He spoke at length about how many people made their livings employed by French banks and how many more businesses depended on the lending ability of those banks in order to function. He borrowed the Count of Monte Cristo's definition of a third-rate fortune, illustrating how the whims of chance could bring a major bank to its knees. Such a situation could not be sustainable, he insisted; he neglected to mention that the situation had sustained itself worldwide since the earliest banks appeared two thousand years before Christ.

As was his habit as a lobbyist in the House, Danglars wrapped a cloak of false concern around his true objective to paint the voting senators into a corner. He didn't need to convince them all that his proposals were factually accurate, or would have the stated effects; he needed only to convince some of them that his ideas were morally correct, thus implicitly branding anyone who spoke against them as a heartless monster.

Danglars concluded by insisting that the continued health of the French economy demanded the government vote to provide security to all of the country's largest commercial banks. He did not draw attention to how his definition of large ensured that the Danglars Bank would receive such protection. To allow a large bank to fail on the basis of a mere few months of bad luck was irresponsible, he insisted. His proposed law was necessary in order to provide those banks with a guarantee that if their loans went sour, the government would use tax revenue to repay them.

The peers debated the proposal, and the barons filed out of the chamber for the counts to deliberate. Danglars fought the impulse to pace the halls of the House, recognizing that he must appear calm and disinterested in the result of the vote. It seemed to take hours for the bailiffs to retrieve the barons and escort them back to the chamber.

"Baron Danglars, we have considered the merits of your bill," said the Count de Salvieux, standing to deliver the verdict.

"We agree with the points you have raised regarding the welfare of the country's banks," Salvieux continued.

Danglars' disused heart leapt with joy, and he made the effort not to sigh with relief. Victory lay within his grasp; if the government reimbursed his bank, it would erase the consequences of his recent bad luck and provide him the means to live like a prince while he hid from his revived Dead Plague.

"However, we do not agree that the issue is nearly as widespread nor nearly as dire as you say," Salvieux added, causing Danglars' blood to run cold. "We also cannot agree with your proposed remedy. Having the crown become an underwriter to every bank loan in the financial landscape is a recipe for disaster."

Danglars leaned on the desk in front of him, his eyes bulging behind his thick spectacles as he gawked at Salvieux. Danglars did not know it, but this was the son of the same Count de Salvieux who had attended Gerard de Villefort's wedding twenty-three years earlier and given Villefort a letter of introduction to the king's keeper of seals. He also was unaware that the current Count's nephew faced a five-year prison sentence for public intoxication as a result of Danglars' lobbying efforts for mandatory minimum sentencing.

"To say nothing of the cost to His Majesty's government, there are the other long-term effects to consider," Salvieux continued. "If there is no pain to a bank when they make a loan that can't be paid off, why have any due diligence at all? The incentive will be to loan every pauper enough money to buy a house, with the knowledge that if he defaults the bank will be no worse off than before."

Sweat erupted on Danglars' bald head as his hopes crumbled before him.

"We would effectively manufacture demand for bad loans which cannot be paid back," Salvieux said, enjoying the spectacle of Danglars squirming. "Simply put, Baron Danglars, a good bank doesn't need this guarantee, and a bad bank doesn't deserve it. This prompts me to wonder what kind of banker would propose such a bill. We have voted against your measure and put forward one of our own: to remove you as the chair of the Royal Bourbon Reserve."

"No!" Danglars shouted. "You cannot do that!"

"We already have, Baron Danglars. It passed unanimously," Salvieux replied.

The story of Danglars' disgrace found the front page of not only the Nightly Assemblage but also every other newspaper. Friday morning, a crowd of desperate account holders and creditors swarmed the doors of the Danglars Bank offices to withdraw their funds and cash in their debts. Every one of them knew that if the bank was as poor as rumours claimed, there would be no money to pay them with if they waited.

Danglars could see no other choice but to raise the dead; time had run out, and his fortune demanded it. He dispensed with his fine blue coat, dressed in a drab brown suit to avoid attention, and gathered up his lead-lined box containing the crucial shards of mortite. He would abscond for some far-off country and hope the world soon found itself too occupied with death and fear to care about the Danglars Bank.

While he fetched his mortite, he remembered one final financial instrument he could leverage. In a portfolio inside his desk drawer were the receipts from every withdrawal against the Count of Monte Cristo's unlimited credit, guaranteed by the bankers Thomson & French of Rome.

The receipts amounted to millions of francs. If Danglars brought the receipts to Rome, they meant more than enough money for a comfortable period of hiding during the coming apocalypse, until he decided to close the box, end the Plague, and reap the profits. The new Plague could begin in Rome as well as anywhere else.

Feeling far more confident about his state of affairs, Danglars called for his valet and gave him instructions to prepare for an immediate trip to Marseille. The last of his money would just cover passage on a ship headed to Civitavecchia and then a coach to Rome.

As Danglars proposed his doomed bill to the House, Hermine lay awake in her boudoir dreading the scandal descending upon their house. Socially, they were ruined; they could not possibly recover from being foolish enough to almost marry Eugenie to a cannibal. Hermine's cheeks burned when she recalled how little help she'd offered Mercedes when Fernand's crimes became public.

Hermine had grown used to turning to Lucien in a crisis, but he hadn't returned her letters since being maimed by her husband. Even if Lucien agreed to see her, this wasn't some financial matter his connections could help with. He could only give her advice; she needed someone with power and authority.

Her mind came to Villefort, who had, in a way, brought this misfortune into her life. Like some clockwork mechanism of justice, he could only proceed forward in the defined way once the wheels were in motion. Perhaps she could appeal to their shared past to get him to halt his progress. If she could convince him to let Benedetto escape into the wide world, then without the display of a trial the scandal may evaporate and be replaced in the public eye by some other occurrence.

"Absolutely not," Villefort said without looking up from his papers when she stood in his home study the next day.

For the past month, Villefort's papers were delivered to him at home as he avoided the Palais. His jaundiced face was a paler yellow than usual from the lack of sun and his frequent refuge in his ritual of bleeding.

"But Gerard—"

He cut her off with an upraised hand. "Madame, you came here today for a favour from the office of the crown prosecutor. You may address me in that capacity as M. de Villefort."

Hermine recoiled at the unsettling wildness she saw in his ice blue eyes.

"M. de Villefort," she said, "won't you reconsider your decision at all?"

"On what grounds? This man Benedetto, who called himself Andrea Cavalcanti, is one of the foulest murderers I have ever seen in my career," Villefort said. "And you hope that I should call off the search for him, for the sake of your social reputation? From a stranger, the request would be ridiculous; from you, who knows my devotion to the king and his law, it's insulting."

"I'm not asking you to break the law," Hermine insisted, "just to relax a degree in your pursuit of it. Andrea is cunning, I'm sure he intends to flee France and won't darken our country again."

"The law cannot relax. The lives of the French people belong to the crown, and Benedetto will not escape the consequences of stealing one," Villefort said. "Without the steel backbone of justice and paternal eye of the state, the common folk would degenerate to their base instincts and we would have the anarchy that the Count of Monte Cristo is so fond of."

Villefort allowed no room in his mind to consider how the base instincts of a commoner differ from those of a police officer or magistrate, considering that all came from the same species of human being.

"Monte Cristo!" Villefort spat. "Of all the people whose homes could have played host to this crime."

"Have you learned anything about why he taunted us with the ghost of our son?" Hermine asked, hoping to make the visit worthwhile in spite of her rejected plea.

"Not a thing. Nothing in the count's past which would indicate why he would want to torment us. It's as if he learned the truth by accident and orchestrated that dinner party for sport," Villefort said. "I have one final avenue to pursue. Monte Cristo has kept his bedroom locked every time my men have gone to collect evidence in Benedetto's crime. If he's hiding anything, it's there, and all I need is an appropriate warrant to find it."

A knock at the door interrupted them. Villefort commanded the visitor to enter, and his secretary brought an envelope sealed with the Justice Department's mark. Villefort broke the seal with his knife and scanned the document inside.

"Speak of the devil, and he shall appear," Villefort said. "Benedetto has been arrested in Compiegne, where a servant girl narrowly avoided becoming his next meal. There's only the trial left, and then the criminal shall meet the guillotine at the Place de l'Hotel de Ville!"

CHAPTER 100
THE LION'S DEN

In La Force, the most formidable prison in Paris and a true repository of lost souls, dwelled an area reserved for the worst of the worst. Behind walls and bars twice as thick as could be found elsewhere in the prison, murderers and rapists rubbed shoulders under the eyes of human and forged guards with ravenous drakes. The walls stood so high that the sun showed itself above the courtyard only at the very middle of the day. This place was called the Lion's Den.

Unlike the Chateau d'If, prosecutors did not send prisoners to the Lion's Den to be forgotten. The Lion's Den contained dangerous men who waited for trial, though many waited there for months or years. Often through ill fortune or the deliberate delay of their time in court, men in the Lion's Den met brutal deaths at the hands of their peers before ever facing a judge. The ragged occupants did their best to live up to the reputation of their home, a reputation known far and wide across France. Of the men who left the Lion's Den, most went either to the galleys or the grave.

Despite the danger, Benedetto carried himself in the Lion's Den courtyard with surprising nonchalance. He still wore the shabby clothes he stole from the cab driver, but kept them as clean as possible under the circumstances. With every speck of soot from his attempted chimney escape swept away, he walked the yard with the air of a man waiting for a holiday train.

Such an attitude might guarantee a violent end in the Lion's Den. However, like the Den itself, Benedetto's reputation preceded him. The other prisoners already knew the story of his crimes and wanted no trouble with a man who tore others to shreds with his own teeth and could fool a baron into thinking him a prince. Benedetto was aware of this effect on his new neighbours, and although he never admitted to anything, he took every opportunity to flash his large and even teeth if anyone gave him an odd look.

Benedetto felt quite at ease in the Lion's Den, certain that in a matter of days his benefactor, the count, would pay the appropriate bribes to set him free. After all, the count had gone to such expense on Benedetto's account already, only a fool would allow him to rot in prison.

He passed his time amusing himself, frightening the other inmates and asking the guards to lend him money for a nicer cell. They rebuffed him each time and ordered their forged companions to turn him away. Benedetto accepted this with a smile, wondering whether his wealth or his teeth would be the more rewarding way to ruin those guards after his release.

Benedetto knew the count possessed a flair for the dramatic and expected nothing less than an eleventh-hour rescue. When he received a summons to the visitor's room, it surprised him only because it came earlier than he thought.

The dismal visitor's room had whitewashed stone walls and straw covering the floor. Waist-high brick walls and bars extending to the ceiling split the room lengthwise into three sections. The section nearest the yard admitted prisoners while visitors stood in the opposite section. The middle section was six feet of no-man's land preventing any physical contact with visitors or the passing of contraband from the outside world. Though unpleasant, any admission to the visitor's room meant a break from the dangers of the yard, and thus the inmates saw it as a place of refuge.

A forged conducted the smiling Benedetto to the visitor's room. He had no doubt that his release was imminent, even when Bertuccio's dour face greeted him on the civilian side of the divide.

"How droll," Benedetto muttered. "My father has sent my step-father to be his agent."

"Benedetto," Bertuccio said, pronouncing the word like a curse.

Benedetto started and swung his head around, hoping nobody but the silent forged could hear.

"Keep your voice down, you old fool!" Benedetto hissed. "You'll ruin everything if the wrong person hears you say that name!"

"Is that any way to speak to your father, you ungrateful child?" Bertuccio asked.

"You're no father of mine!" Benedetto said. "My name is Andrea Cavalcanti, my father is Major Bartolomeo Cavalcanti of Italy, and you are a stranger to me. What are you doing here?"

Bertuccio sighed and shook his head, then held up a piece of paper for the forged guard to see.

"I've been sent to speak to you in private, Signor Cavalcanti," Bertuccio said.

The forged spun Benedetto around by the shoulders and shackled him hand and foot. It led him to a more comfortable room on an upper floor, furnished with a table and chairs, a small hearth, and a simple bed. Its common occupants were wealthy prisoners who could pay for the privilege of a conjugal visit. Inmates from the Lion's Den were seldom taken there.

Bertuccio already sat in one of the chairs when Benedetto arrived. Benedetto opted to recline on the bed, finding the straw mattress quite comfortable after sleeping on the stone floor of his cell. He knew enough about the workings of prisons to be satisfied that they were alone and away from hungry ears.

"I see you haven't changed at all, in spite of your fancy clothes," Bertuccio said. "You were a remorseless cannibal in Corsica, and evidently our time apart hasn't driven that compulsion out of you."

"Ah yes, my dear step-mother. What was her name again, Agrippa? Angiola? No, it was Assunta, wasn't it," Benedetto said, leering at Bertuccio. "Your dead brother's wife. Would you like to know how she tasted? With the way you always looked at her, you must have wondered."

"It warms my heart to see you in chains and behind bars, Benedetto. It's where you belong," Bertuccio said, flushed with anger and shame.

"Yes, it's always been very clear how you felt about me," Benedetto said, feigning a yawn. "Trying to press-gang me into a sailor's life with you, insisting on tiresome discipline even though you had to know it was beneath me. You've been sent here, yes?"

"I have," Bertuccio said.

"Then let's have it. When has my father—that is, my real father—arranged for me to be released?" Benedetto asked.

Bertuccio's eyes widened, then a small smirk touched the corner of his mouth.

"Why should your father do anything to have you released?" he asked.

"Why wouldn't he? This whole grand charade of arranging my escape from the galleys, forging documents for me under the Cavalcanti name, hiring some cripple to pretend to be my father, and giving me an allowance once I arrived in Paris; this all must have taken enormous effort," Benedetto said. "That effort would be wasted now if I went to the guillotine just for eating some commoners and fooling that banker."

"You think your birth father arranged all of this for you?" Bertuccio asked.

"Who else would go to the trouble?" Benedetto responded. "The Count of Monte Cristo clothed me, gave me a name, financed me; which is the simpler explanation, that he does this on behalf of someone else or that he does it because I'm his own son?"

"You keep his name out of your cursed mouth!" Bertuccio shouted, jumping to his feet. "The Count is an honourable man, who was... hoodwinked somehow into introducing you under false pretenses!"

"How could I have fooled him, when it was I who was brought to his house at the direction of some Lord Wilmore, who I assume to be one of his agents," Benedetto said. "You work for the count; haven't you noticed how otherworldly he is? Doesn't his supernatural superiority and disregard for the norms of men remind you of anyone; namely, me?"

"You flatter yourself, Benedetto," Bertuccio said. "But let me tell you something you never knew; I was there the night you were born. I heard your mother's agony at pushing you into the world. I saw your father abandon you to die in a box, where I should have left you. With God as my witness, the Count of Monte Cristo is not your father."

"Really," Benedetto drawled. He pretended to inspect his nails while keeping a close eye on Bertuccio's face. "If the count isn't my father, then who is?"

"Nobody who would arrange for the release of a murderer like yourself, even if he knew you were his son," Bertuccio said.

"This makes no sense," Benedetto said, his arrogance faltering. "If not my father, then who is arranging my release?"

"Nobody is, you wretched boy!" Bertuccio said. "You're finally getting the punishment you deserve. Your trial has been accelerated on the orders of the crown prosecutor; you face him tomorrow."

"Then why are you here?" Benedetto demanded, anger and fear finally showing on his face. "Just to gloat, is it?"

"No. I've come because for once, your instinct for mayhem will prove useful," Bertuccio said. "I have a vendetta against your father and have only recently learned that I failed in my quest the night you were born. I've come to tell you who he is and the details of that night, so at the right moment you can expose yourself as the bastard son he abandoned and get revenge for us both."

Benedetto considered the proposal. "What makes you think I'll play along? It might be more fun to frustrate your vendetta a second time."

"Because I know you, and I know your dark mind will obsess tonight over this: rather than raise you as his own, or send you to an orphanage, or even give you to a childless maid, your father decided it would be better to let you suffocate in a shallow grave when you were less than an hour old," Bertuccio replied, staring into Benedetto's eyes as he did so. He waited for Benedetto to process the revelation.

"I'll consider your offer, old man," Benedetto said at last. "Now tell me, who on this foul earth is the man who gave me life?"

"Remember to wait for an opportune public moment to disclose this; you're certain to find one," Bertuccio said. "Your father is the crown prosecutor Gerard de Villefort, who tomorrow will try you for murder, robbery, and fraud. And I hope his final act as prosecutor before your news destroys his career, is to sentence you to die."

With those words, Bertuccio stood. He handed a sealed letter to the dumbstruck Benedetto and left him to think about his parentage. Outside, he told the human guard that they had concluded their visit and Benedetto could go back to his cell.

CHAPTER 101
RELOCATION

On the same morning the run on the Danglars Bank began, Max received a letter from M. Noirtier, still a prisoner in Villefort's house. Max had made many more attempts to rescue Noirtier since his first a month earlier, but each was thwarted. With Villefort working from home and his movements growing more erratic every week, Max found it impossible to enter the house and extract Noirtier.

Max rushed to the Champs Elysees to show Valentine the letter, which Barrois must have written with painstaking dictation from Noirtier's eyes. She grew more and more anxious as long as Noirtier remained in that house, and she continued her self-imposed exile in the count's house. The count and Haydee continued to reassure her that they had a plan to deal with Villefort, and that the endgame was in motion, but refused to divulge any further details.

"This is the perfect pretext to enter the house," Max said. "Your grandfather has formally invited me to visit him, saying he read about my military career in the newspapers."

"What then, Max? Will you just carry him out of the house and down the road?" Valentine asked with dark bags beneath her large blue eyes.

"I've thought of that already," Max said. "I'll offer to bring him outdoors in his wheelchair for a stroll down the road; I can even pretend I don't know his language and need Barrois to translate for me."

"And once you're outside, you bring him here to safety," Valentine said, her face lighting up. "Max, that's a wonderful idea! But promise me you'll be careful. We can't guarantee that an invitation will keep you safe from my father."

"I'm certain it will be fine," Max said with a grin. "After all, he has no reason to suspect me of anything; to him, I'm nothing but a soldier he met once at a dinner party."

That afternoon, Max stood before the door of the Villefort house. The structure loomed above him like the walls of Constantine on the eve of the siege. He steeled his resolve and knocked, and presented his letter to the doorman.

"Captain Maximilien Morrel, visiting M. Noirtier," Max said, with what he hoped was a confident smile. "Please."

The doorman raised an eyebrow, unaccustomed to politeness from the dignitaries and legal professionals who often called on Villefort. He escorted Max to Noirtier's room, and Noirtier's eyes sprang to life at the sight of Max reflected in his many mirrors. The doorman left them, but did not return to his post. Instead, he crept to the study.

"Good afternoon, M. Noirtier," Max said. "I received your letter."

Noirtier blinked once for yes and glanced at Barrois, who hoisted a black leather bag.

"Medicines," Barrois said. "Belongings. Ready to go."

"Perfect; I was going to ask if you wanted me to bring you outside, but I see you've anticipated that," Max said. "Barrois, is there a wheelchair for him downstairs or should I carry this one down?"

"Behind you," Barrois said, as Noirtier's eyes widened.

Max looked at the mirrors in search of a second chair. Instead, behind his shoulder hung the yellow face of Villefort, his blue eyes radiating a malice beyond human reason. Before Max could react, Villefort clubbed him across the temple with a paperweight and locked his arm around Max's neck in a choke hold.

"You stole my daughter and now try to steal my father too?" Villefort said. "I'm sure you would make a picturesque Bonapartist family, raising my grandchildren with your poisonous ideals."

Max gasped and clawed at Villefort's arm, but he couldn't loosen the iron grip. Blood trickled from the blow to his head and his medical training brought trivia to his mind; the hold compressed the blood vessels in the sides of his neck, cutting off the blood flow to his brain while leaving his windpipe unobstructed. The choke was non-fatal, but he would lose consciousness in eight to fourteen seconds if he couldn't break free.

"I saw you sneak out of my house a month ago and have had my doorman waiting for your return ever since," Villefort said. From the corner of his eye, he caught Barrois move as if to intervene. "Do it, gargoyle. Give me an excuse to fetch a hammer and pummel you to rubble."

Max's struggles weakened until his arms fell limp. Ignoring Noirtier's astonished stare, Villefort dragged Max away. In his study, Villefort bound Max to a chair and gagged him with a handkerchief to stifle any cries when he awoke.

"Danglars needs victims for his plot," Villefort said, unaware that Danglars had already abandoned Paris. "You'll do nicely."

Villefort locked the door from the outside and returned to Noirtier's bedroom. He noticed for the first time that Max's blood clung to his cheek. Accompanied only by his mute father, he ran his finger through the blood and tasted it. He savoured both the iron tang of Bonapartist blood and the shock in Noirtier's eyes.

"A tax of blood, Father. A tax of blood to buy glory for the crown," Villefort said with a smirk and a glint of madness in his eye. "He's not dead, not yet. I'll deal with him after the Benedetto trial."

Noirtier's eyes bulged and his breath came in splutters. From long experience, Villefort could guess his meaning.

"Why should I care if you see me?" Villefort asked. "Valentine is gone, you mute fossil. Who will you tell?"

CHAPTER 102
THE COURTROOM

July 28, 1838; the morning of Benedetto's trial at last. The public waited with excitement for the outcome, less for concern about justice for Caderousse and more for the sake of seeing a real cannibal in the courtroom.

The younger generation grew up on tales of the dead walking the land and devouring human flesh and were curious to see the closest thing to a zombie they ever expected to see. The older people who lived through the uprising felt a morbid duty to know what happened to this living man who ate like the undead. It was common for the courtroom at the Palais de Justice to sell tickets of admission in advance of sensational murder trials; what was uncommon was for those tickets to sell out in under forty-eight hours, as this trial had.

In a way, Benedetto himself gave Villefort a gift. Until his arrest in Compiegne, the evidence against him was circumstantial. They had only the written account of Caderousse, himself an escaped convict. The attempted attack on the cleaning girl at the inn sealed his fate, along with the discovery of the cab driver's bones in the forest. Villefort felt confident he would see Benedetto's head in a basket.

While dressing for the day, Villefort caught sight of a stack of newspapers in the mirror behind him and snarled without thinking. Jordan Caillat had remained relatively quiet, contenting himself only with bringing up the names of dead men, but the latest Nightly Assemblage contained another direct attack.

The latest Caillat article reminded readers that Villefort was attacked at his father-in-law's house, with a pregnant mystery woman, and that a servant went missing after the attack, never to be heard from again. Then it took the scandal a step further: it claimed the baby was

Villefort's bastard and Caillat had proof. In keeping with the Assemblage's sensational style, the article never specified the nature of that proof.

Villefort could ill afford such a distraction. He knew from his contacts that the press already surrounded the Palais as usual, as eager to shout their endless questions at him as to see Benedetto and the verdict. Villefort resolved that if the Nightly Assemblage survived Danglars' undead plot, he would find any legal pretense to have them shut down, their presses destroyed, and their editors thrown into the Chateau d'If.

Benedetto's newfound infamy came with one silver lining which Villefort hoped to exploit. After proving himself capable of imitating an aristocrat, it was not beyond reason to think he may have powerful friends. Those friends could, perhaps, have protected him from the consequences of other actions thus far. Villefort could deflect suspicion of his own covered-up vampiric murders to Benedetto and his appetites.

The Benedetto Affair, as people called it, became a tremendous public spectacle. As "Andrea," he frequented all of the most fashionable places for young people and built a wide circle of acquaintances and hangers-on. He ignored the Count's advice about keeping a low profile and instead had done what so many do when given money for nothing and a promise of more: spend it lavishly.

The young men and women who called themselves his friends at the Cafe de Paris, Boulevard de Gand, and other places continued to meet there. They were happy before to benefit while "Andrea" bought rounds of coffee and wine and liquor to attract friends, and now instead, picked apart every interaction with him to figure out if there had been any opportunity to see through his lies.

As is common with cases of fraud, many claimed to have known from the start that Benedetto was a fake. They hoped to appear intelligent; their peers dashed those hopes by asking why they said nothing if they'd known. The women who Benedetto bedded received relentless teasing, their peers asking if he had taken any bites out of them. Through it all, a common joke was repeated in a variety of themes: how could the esteemed Baron Danglars be so blind as not to see through the disguise?

In addition to their primary function of reprinting gossip, several of the major newspapers returned to their roots and investigated

Benedetto's history. Thanks to them, Paris learned about the accusations of Benedetto murdering his step-mother and fleeing Corsica and his adventures as a petty burglar that resulted in his time at the galleys. The only thing they could not discover was the secret of Benedetto's escape from forced labour.

While the cannibalism aspect of the case captured the public's imagination, the aristocracy remained far more concerned with how a commoner could have impersonated a prince so capably. The Count of Monte Cristo went on record with Beauchamp's paper, the Independent, to reveal documents from Major Cavalcanti which had convinced him that Benedetto really was the major's son. None of the Danglars family could be reached for comment.

A small and loyal cadre of people still supported the good name of Andrea Cavalcanti. During his short time as part of Parisian society, Cavalcanti had made sure to latch onto the most popular causes and learn the correct things to say to ingratiate himself with their supporters. These people believed in their hearts that anyone who funded their operations and spoke out on their behalf could not possibly be evil. They referred to the entire Benedetto Affair as a conspiracy to discredit them, and held out that "Andrea" would either be found innocent by the impartial forces of justice or convicted in error by corrupt officials.

All of these factors taken together meant that tickets for admission to the courthouse sold out within two days. In response to the incredible demand, they printed additional tickets and on the day of the trial the spectators packed themselves in shoulder-to-shoulder. One clever gentleman brought in a small telegraph and ran the wire out the window, where a colleague waited with a receiver to announce trial updates to an impatient crowd outside.

Like so many people, Raoul and Lucien stood in the crowd trying to reckon how Benedetto had fooled them. Beauchamp stood in the balcony above them in his professional capacity. He spared his friends a wave, but remained focused on recording the events as they happened.

"Franz is going to be livid that he missed this," Lucien said.

The magistrates who were to judge the trial filed into the courtroom and took their seats along the bench at the head of the room. Villefort entered next, his unnatural colouring strengthening the impression that he left his humanity at the door to become nothing but an instrument of the law; he took his place at the prosecutor's stand. His assistants followed and laid out evidence of Benedetto's crimes: Caderousse's bloody waistcoat and the accusatory letter found within it, sketches of the cab driver's remains, the cleaning-girl's written testimony, and so on.

"You know, I don't see the Count of Monte Cristo anywhere," Raoul said, craning his neck to see above the crowd around him. "I'd think that his involvement in this case would guarantee his presence."

"He's probably embarrassed to be so deep in it," Lucien said, happy to spread more gossip. "General Cavalcanti is an old companion of his, and Benedetto tricked them both."

"Yes, I imagine I wouldn't want to be present either," Raoul said.

"As if that embarrassment wasn't enough, that old beggar who Benedetto ate was killed while robbing the count's house," Lucien continued. "The prevailing theory is that he and Benedetto knew each other already, conspired to murder and rob the count, and then Benedetto saw an opportunity to silence his accomplice."

"It's good luck he wasn't at home that night," Raoul said. "You know, I recall now that Max said the count has been bedridden for several days. Come to think of it, can you see Max anywhere? I sent word for him to meet us."

The heavy clatter of chains interrupted their conversation as guards brought Benedetto into the courtroom.

CHAPTER 103
THE INDICTMENT

B enedetto came in from the holding cells with his wrists shackled at waist-height and connected by another chain to his leg-irons; he would need to sit on his haunches for enough slack to scratch his nose. A half-mask of narrow iron bars covered his mouth, held in place with leather straps around the back and top of his head. He grinned at the assembled crowd, his large white teeth still quite visible in the gaps of the mask. Benedetto's lawyer, a thin young man appointed to him by the court, took his position at the defense desk.

"That fellow has a long row to hoe!" Lucien whispered to Raoul.

The guards led Benedetto to the witness stand to hear the charges read against him and have an opportunity to speak before the trial proper commenced. He stood at ease and unconcerned with the impending risk to his life, an attitude Villefort was glad to see. He always enjoyed watching a condemned man's eyes shift from pompousness to despair when the verdict came down and the defendant realized he was going to die for his crimes. For just a moment, Benedetto and Villefort's blue eyes locked together. Something in them triggered a moment of unease in Villefort's gut.

"Is the prosecution ready to begin?" asked the head magistrate from the bench. He would direct the proceedings, deliberate on the evidence with his peers on either side of him, and announce their verdict at the close of the trial.

"I am, your honour," Villefort said.

His voice rang out through the courtroom with his prepared remarks, elaborating on the crimes which Benedetto stood accused of. The charges of murder, attempted murder, and desecration of corpses would each be enough on their own for Benedetto to lose his head, but

Villefort also included fraud, impersonating an aristocrat, jailbreaking, and accomplice to breaking and entering. Benedetto remained calm during the reading and the subsequent recounting of the burglaries and muggings which had sent him to the galleys in the first place.

Villefort's reputation as an orator was well-deserved. By the end of his indictment, none but the most diehard Cavalcanti supporters could doubt the danger that Benedetto presented to society, and that he must be dealt with. True to Lucien's assessment, a sheen of sweat covered the young defense lawyer's face and his protruding Adam's apple bobbed continually.

"Does the accused have any opening remarks to make?" the head magistrate asked.

"My client has no remarks at this time," the lawyer said with a slight crack to his voice.

"M. de Villefort, please proceed," the magistrate said.

Villefort approached the witness stand, glared at Benedetto, then turned to face the crowd.

"You the accused, state your name and surname," Villefort said.

Benedetto cleared his throat. "We reach a problem already, M. de Prosecutor," he said in a calm voice which carried as much as Villefort's. "I know that you have a series of opening questions for me, which you never stray from: my name, my age, my place of birth, and my profession. I must insist on a deviation, that you not ask me my name quite yet."

"This is absurd," Villefort said, annoyed by the excited murmur which moved through the crowd. He confronted uncooperative defendants as a matter of routine, but never one who tried to rearrange trial procedure.

"It certainly is, but I must insist, or I won't answer any questions at all. And wouldn't that spoil your fun?" Benedetto said.

"You will not dictate terms in my courtroom. Your name and surname, monsieur," Villefort said.

Benedetto did not reply or even look at Villefort. Instead he took the opportunity to observe the high ceilings and the size of his audience, several of whom chuckled at the display.

The head magistrate banged his gavel. "If the defendant will not answer questions, I will have to declare a recess."

Villefort scanned the room; hands came to mouths stifling yawns, and some people even shuffled to the exit out of boredom. He needed the spectacle of a dramatic win to restore his standing in the public eye and couldn't afford to lose more of the audience to a recess.

"Very well. Will you tell the court your age, at least?" Villefort asked.

Benedetto smirked behind his mouthguard. "Of course. I'm nearly twenty-one years old. My birthday is the 17th of September, and the year was 1817."

The date buzzed in Villefort's ear, repeated too often in the Nightly Assemblage for him or the audience to fail to notice it's significance.

"And where were you born?" Villefort asked.

"I was born in Auteuil," Benedetto said.

The crowd murmured louder, and a deep frown settled onto Villefort's face. All of the information available to both the police and the public claimed Corsica as Benedetto's birthplace. Villefort, of course, found the location concerning for other reasons.

"What is your profession?" Villefort asked, using his command of his voice to disguise his growing anxiety. He wanted nothing more than the taste of blood to settle his nerves.

"Let's see, I began with forgery, and then I was a thief," Benedetto said, counting his misdemeanours on his fingers. "I was engaged as an oarsman for a while on His Majesty's large boats, which didn't agree with me at all, so I decided to try my hand at being a dandy."

This provoked a boisterous laugh from the crowd, which the judge silenced with his gavel.

"M. de Prosecutor, are you alright? You look quite pale, although it can be hard to tell when you began at a sort of pea soup colour," Benedetto remarked.

"Hold your tongue!" Villefort snapped. His face and hands grew clammy with worry over the defendant's command of the courtroom.

"But didn't you want me to answer another question?" Benedetto asked with eyes wide, prompting another laugh from the gallery. "I think you wanted to know my name."

"You will speak respectfully or be charged with contempt of court," Villefort said, wiping his hands against his jacket. "You've had your fun; I imagine you're so proud of your criminal resume, your list of flagrant violations of morality and decency, that you wanted a chance to recite it as a list of titles prior to your name."

"Remarkable, you've guessed my thinking exactly," Benedetto said. "It's as if you knew me."

He dropped his bravado, answering the accusation with a sincerity which brought a hush to the murmuring crowd.

"Very well, now, tell the court your name," Villefort said with the last shred of his patience.

"Simply, I cannot. I never knew it. But I know my father's name, and I can tell you right now," Benedetto said.

The announcement, coupled with the dreadful seriousness in Benedetto's gaze, caused the bottom to drop out of Villefort's stomach.

"Go on then, what is your father's name," Villefort said, dreading the answer. Not a breath could be heard in the courtroom.

"My father is the king's attorney, Gerard de Villefort, son of that famous Bonapartist Jules Noirtier," Benedetto said. "I've waited a long time to meet you, Father; if only I'd known at the count's dinner that I already had!"

Nothing could stop the explosion of noise in the audience. The head magistrate slammed his gavel to no avail and called on the gendarmes to enforce silence. The delay provided a welcome break for Villefort, who needed to lean against the evidence table until his legs could support him again.

"The defendant will refrain from sensational slander in this courtroom!" the head magistrate declared. "You're facing serious charges, young man. You won't escape them by besmirching M. de Villefort without proof! Your arrest records list your name as Benedetto and your place of origin as Corsica. Explain these contradictions at once."

"I've always known that I was a foundling, and it's true that my adoptive father gave me that name and raised me on that dreary island. But it was only after my arrest that I learned the truth," Benedetto said. Villefort's head ached in anticipation. "I was born in Auteuil, at No. 28 Rue de la Fontaine, in a room hung with red curtains. It was the night of September 17, 1817. As soon as I was born, M. de Villefort wrapped me in a handkerchief marked with my mother's initials, stuffed me into a wooden box, and buried me in the garden behind the house."

"How can you possibly know that? You were minutes old, I thought you were dead!" Villefort demanded.

The head magistrate lifted his gavel in preparation, but the crowd stood stunned. Every one of them compared Benedetto's composure to Villefort's visible terror as he realized what he had just said. The accusation of attempted infanticide loomed heavy in the air. Nobody noticed a young bearded man with dark shoulder-length hair, who had watched Villefort with great intensity, push through the audience and slip out of the courtroom.

"What kind of son would I be if I refused to answer my dear father?" Benedetto said. "The Corsican who raised me is the same one who stabbed you in the chest for refusing to investigate his brother's murder. He dug up my box hoping it was treasure and found me instead. Before that, he laid in wait and heard everything."

Villefort's lack of rebuttal was a damning confirmation of Benedetto's words.

"Speaking of the attempt on my father's life, I've figured out how he survived. It will also help to prove my story," Benedetto said. He nodded to his lawyer, who gave a signal to the bailiff, who escorted a physician into the room. "This doctor's stethoscope will confirm, and the magistrates can listen for themselves, that my heart beats on the right-hand side of my chest. An extremely rare condition, and one passed down to me by my father, who shares it."

Benedetto unbuttoned his shirt with as much dignity as his shackles allowed. The wary physician pressed the cup of his instrument to the left side with a puzzled expression; his eyes widened when he moved the cup to the right.

"This is most irregular, but we must follow procedure," the magistrate said. "Swear this man in on a Bible, and let's hear his testimony."

"Get out of my way!" Villefort shouted.

He rushed forward and snatched the stethoscope, put on the earpieces, and bent to listen to Benedetto's chest. Sure enough, like his own and like Noirtier's, the heartbeat was found on the right.

"M. de Villefort!" the magistrate said, banging his gavel yet again. "I have never seen such disruptive behaviour from a crown prosecutor. You will follow proper decorum!"

"It's no use!" Villefort moaned, tugging at his hair until clumps of it tore away. "It's him, it's him, a revenant back from the grave to haunt me!"

"Compose yourself, M. de Villefort!" the magistrate demanded. "We will launch a full investigation into this man's claims, but you must behave as befits your station!"

"There's something I'd love to know, Father," Benedetto asked, smiling to show his large even teeth. "Do you feel the same hunger I do? Did I inherit that from you as well as my strange heartbeat? Is that why you needed to drink the blood of my step-uncle Cristofano, or the servant Gaston Piaget, or the whore Marie Brouillard?"

Villefort did not reply as Benedetto continued to recite names of his past victims, memorized from the list given to him by Bertuccio at the Lion's Den. The crowd once again clamoured about these revelations and Villefort's guilty responses to them. Villefort heard the magistrates on the bench murmuring to each other. He could guess their topic: whether to lay criminal charges against him. He needed to escape, but with the courtroom packed to bursting there was no clear path to an exit.

"Your Honour, I apologize for my outbursts," Villefort said. He smoothed his remaining hair as best he could and wiped the sweat from his sallow face. "At this time, I request a brief recess; perhaps it would be best if the deputy prosecutor took first chair when we return."

"Agreed, a recess would serve this court quite well. Bailiff, escort M. de Villefort to his office," the magistrate replied.

The stone-faced bailiff approached Villefort with a pair of gendarmes. It became clear he would remain in his office until such time as the magistrates were ready to deal with him. Villefort nodded to the bailiff and followed him without argument.

CHAPTER 104
EPIPHANY

Villefort said nothing to the guards as they directed him to his second-story office and locked the door from the outside, leaving him alone but under supervision. He stood in the centre of the room, listening to what happened on the other side of the door. The bailiff and the guards took the opportunity for a break and some gossip before returning to the courtroom for further instructions. Villefort nodded and moved to the far corner of the office.

On the long walk from the courtroom, he struggled coming to terms with his sins being exposed in such a public forum. The similarities to the scandal of the former Count de Morcerf struck him as suspicious. One day, business as usual for Fernand; the next, the count's opera companion publicly marks him as a criminal. Fernand was forced to flee, as Villefort himself prepared to do.

Villefort examined the corner bookcase, moved a particular volume, and pressed a small switch concealed behind it. It revealed his hidden staircase, where no guard waited at the bottom. Villefort smiled at the confirmation that his personal exit remained as secret as he hoped, and stood as a free man in the alley behind the Palais du Justice.

He took a deep breath to steady himself, and considered his options. He needed to find Danglars and initiate the plan, not only to bestow glory onto the crown, but also to bolster his reputation in the face of Benedetto's claims. As an instrumental figure in ending a second zombie invasion, certainly his sins would be forgiven.

"Pardon me, monsieur. Have you the time?" a woman asked from behind him.

"I have no time to answer you, madame," Villefort said without looking.

"Are you certain, M. de Villefort? Do you have an appointment to drink a defenseless young lady's blood today?" the woman said, much closer than before.

Villefort turned but only saw a dark-haired young man. Ever the lawman, Villefort identified the beard as a fake in the moment before the young man lunged. A sharpened stake the width of a walking stick plunged into the left side of Villefort's chest, driving the breath out of the prosecutor.

"That was for Marie, monsieur. I hope your torment in hell brings her spirit some peace," Eugenie Danglars said, her voice full of cold rage. She pushed Villefort to the ground and stood over him as he gasped for breath.

"What's happening down there?" called a voice from above.

Eugenie looked up; the bailiff from the courtroom looked out from Villefort's study window. She wasted no time with words and ran to the end of the alley, jumping into the coach where Louise waited, and together they rode away at speed.

Meanwhile, Villefort lurched to his feet. For the second time in his life, his condition prevented an assassin from striking his heart. He could still breathe with great effort, and even after pulling the stake from his chest he felt a tight gripping sensation within himself. Villefort was no doctor but had cross-examined enough coroners to realize the stake had hit his lung.

Still, he determined the risk of recapture to be worse than his risk of death, so he lurched down the alley in the opposite direction as his attacker. His black coat hid the blood well enough. Every breath pained him, a reminder that for some reason God and the archangels had forsaken him. Had he not given them enough blood? Were they displeased, or simply bored of him? His hobbling progress brought him to the street, where he stepped out in front of a cab to force it to stop.

"Where do you want to go, monsieur?" the driver asked.

Villefort licked his own blood from his hand, pretending to stifle a cough. The tang of it sharpened his thoughts, and he realized he had other business to attend to in Paris before visiting Danglars.

"I need something from my home, and then take me to the Champs-Elysees," he said, and gave the driver the number.

Villefort chastised himself for not connecting the facts sooner, blaming his recent distractions. The taste of blood and pain of his wound grounded him, just as his rituals always had. Benedetto could not have escaped the galleys without help. Someone must have bankrolled him before he even arrived in Paris. The Count of Monte Cristo claimed Major Cavalcanti had presented Benedetto as his son without reason to question the claim, but the count had no evidence besides documents to support his story. Forged documents were trivial for wealthy men like the count to acquire.

Another link connected the count to Benedetto as well: at his dinner party in Auteuil, he made the impossible claim to have found Benedetto's infant skeleton in the garden. With a lurch in his stomach, Villefort realized that Monte Cristo could be Jordan Caillat's source for his damning articles in the Nightly Assemblage. Nobody knew the truth of that horrible night besides the Corsican assassin. The Corsican could have shared his story with the count or his agents, or the count could have put him in touch with Caillat. He recalled the accusatory article Caillat had written after the count's arrest, saying that Villefort had abused his authority. It fit the pattern.

After a brief stop at the Rue de Faubourg Saint-Honore, they arrived at the count's mansion. Villefort stood at the gate looking up at the house for a long moment, then approached the concierge's hut.

"The count is accepting no visitors, monsieur," Carlo said, but Villefort did not stop.

Seeing the impassive malice on Villefort's face, Carlo raised his hand and summoned his Catalan gift of lightning. As a warning, he allowed sparks to dance across his glove.

"Monsieur, I must insist you find another cab and leave," Carlo said.

Villefort did not answer. Instead, he reached into his jacket and withdrew the pistol he had retrieved from home. In one smooth motion he aimed and fired, the bullet passing through Carlo's outstretched palm, into his eye socket, and out the back of his head. Villefort reloaded the pistol, found Carlo's keys, and admitted himself through the gate. He crossed the grounds with the pistol at the ready, but met no further resistance as he entered the house.

"M. de Villefort, may I help you?" asked a familiar voice.

Villefort turned to find the Corsican assassin from Auteuil,

Benedetto's rescuer, wearing a servant's uniform and shocked at the sight of Villefort.

"You serve the count?" Villefort asked, raising the pistol. He barked out a laugh, the sound rusted from misuse in such a humourless throat. "Of course you do; why wouldn't you? I'm looking for your master."

"I'm afraid that's impossible," the Corsican said. His trembling lip betrayed his steady voice. "The count is accepting no visitors."

"Bertuccio? Who is it?" a woman asked.

A young woman entered the foyer at another door, and Villefort recognized her as the beautiful Greek who had ruined Mondego. She wore simple trousers and an artist's smock, it and her fingers dark with charcoal.

Villefort swung the pistol in her direction and sprinted forward. Haydee was too stunned to react and Bertuccio too slow to save her as Villefort grabbed her by the hair and held the barrel to her head.

"Take me to your master, you Corsican scum, or the girl dies," Villefort said.

The pain in his chest grew worse, but was still manageable. He resolved to see this through without succumbing to his injury.

Bertuccio met Haydee's gaze as she nodded. "Very well, monsieur. The count is resting in his bedchamber. This way," he said.

Villefort never loosened his grip on Haydee or lowered the pistol, keeping his hostage close and secure while Bertuccio led the way. Finally, Bertuccio stopped at a door and lifted his hand.

"Don't knock. Just open it," Villefort said.

Bertuccio grimaced and did as commanded. As soon as Bertuccio turned the knob, Villefort raised his foot and kicked the door open, throwing Haydee before him into the room. She struck her head against the bedpost and lay dazed on the floor, and Bertuccio darted forward to assess her condition.

Villefort expected a more opulent bedroom for such a dandy as the count. A four-post bed sat with the curtains open, but almost no other furniture occupied the room. Daylight streamed in through the skylight, illuminating the bed but leaving the corners of the room in dimness. The only other items were a strange stone table and a tall cupboard like something from a museum. Villefort stalked around the room, ending near the stone table, and found no other exits.

"Come out, Monte Cristo! Face me, Zaccone!" Villefort called, waving his pistol.

When nobody answered his challenge, Villefort threw open the Egyptian cupboard. The oils and rolls of linen inside did not interest him, though his eyes did linger on the silver instruments. He found the idea of using one to open the Greek woman's jugular very appealing, to replenish his strength with her blood when his business was done.

Villefort's eye wandered across the jars stored in the cupboard. He couldn't guess the purpose behind the four golden jars, but felt drawn to the centre jar made of black stone. Villefort grasped it with his free hand. He felt a deep thrum within the jar, as if the contents pulsated in rhythm.

Villefort felt a chill behind him and turned to see Monte Cristo on the opposite side of the stone table. His bizarre appearance stood out even by the count's standards. Instead of his usual finery, he wore nothing but tightly-wound bandages from the neck down, with some Oriental sash as a loincloth.

"Good grief, Zaccone. Does your degeneracy have no limits?" Villefort said, taking in the strange costume.

Monte Cristo did not answer, or even move. He held his head cocked at an odd angle and his unblinking red eyes locked on the jar in Villefort's hand, following it as the prosecutor moved his arm.

"What the hell is wrong with you? Why are you staring like that?" Villefort asked.

"You hold the jar," Monte Cristo said, with something like surprise.

Villefort took a second inquisitive look at the black jar. He used the barrel of the pistol to nudge the lid, which cracked on the floor when it landed but remained undamaged. Bile rose in his throat at the sight of the heart inside, immersed in scented oil and beating an unholy rhythm.

"What is the meaning of this?" Villefort croaked, feeling a pressure building up behind his eyes. He pointed his pistol first at Monte Cristo, but then some instinct told him to aim it into the jar instead.

"Revenge," the count answered. Despite the desperation on his chalky face, he made no move to rescue the heart.

"Revenge? Is that why you dragged Benedetto from whatever pit he rotted in, and published the names of the vermin I exterminated?" Villefort asked.

"Yes, that is why," the count said. His voice came out in a monotone very unlike his ordinary cadence.

"How did you learn so much?" Villefort asked, his instincts as a prosecutor driving him to know the truth.

"I have many faces, and much wealth," the count said. "One can buy one's way into a great deal of information, even information which powerful men wish to keep hidden. A galley slave's escape is trivial to arrange; acquiring police documents is no effort at all."

"What reason could you possibly have for revenge on me?" Villefort asked. Sweat broke out on his forehead and his headache intensified. The air stifled him and the count's face blurred for a brief moment. "Did your brother commit some crime and you feel that ruining a servant of the law is justified in response? Tell me, or by the crown and all it stands for I will pull the trigger and destroy this infernal heart!"

"In 1815, you condemned a young man to be forgotten in the Chateau d'If for the crime of carrying a letter," the count said. "You sentenced him to death by tedium. You robbed him of liberty, love, and happiness. You left his innocent father to die hungry and humiliated as a public spectacle."

A dizzy spell passed over Villefort, and his pistol wavered as his arm grew weak.

"That man spent fourteen years in prison, nearly died in his escape, and was reborn in darkness. His name was Edmond Dantes," the count said. "I stand before you as his wraith, his revenant, cloaked in diamonds and armed with power you can't understand."

The name struck Villefort like an axe between the eyes, transporting him back in time to Marseille and his triumph in warning the king about Bonaparte's return; the first time he had ever abused his position to his personal advantage.

Dantes, one of the earliest names on his list of enemies and the first to be crossed out. The first life he sacrificed for a reason other than the good of the realm; the event that first compelled him to drink his own blood as a distraction from the shame of hypocrisy.

"Father?" someone asked.

Villefort stared with mouth agape at the bedroom door, where Valentine stood watching the scene with horror written across her face.

"How did you find me?" Valentine asked, half-hiding behind the door frame. "Have you come to kill me too, like you killed Max?"

More so than the name of Edmond Dantes, the revelation that his daughter, who he had always worked so hard to protect, was afraid of him shocked Villefort to his core. This time, the entire room blurred and he smelled a sudden odour of charred bread. Villefort tried to reply, to tell Valentine that everything he did was to ensure she could live in service to a safe and stable monarchy, but his lips and tongue struggled against his attempts to form the words. The pistol fell from his numb hand and he released the canopic jar as his legs buckled beneath him and he tumbled to the floor.

In the same instant the jar left Villefort's grasp, the count moved around the table in a blink. He caught the jar before a drop of oil could spill, and stared for a long reverent moment at his beating heart before replacing the lid and returning the jar to its place.

Monte Cristo looked down at Villefort. Villefort's eyes swung about in an otherwise immobile face, the yellow flesh sagging on one side. The count lowered himself on his haunches to reach a closer level with Villefort and gripped Villefort's chin to force him to meet his own red eyes.

"M. de Villefort, you appear to have had an attack of apoplexy. Months of increased stress, courtesy of my actions and articles," the count said, "have raised your blood pressure to the point that a vein or artery somewhere in your head has burst. Vital parts of your brain are starved of oxygen without that blood flow, leaving you unable to move or speak. But I don't need to tell you the symptoms; you've seen them clearly enough in your father, M. Noirtier."

Monte Cristo relished the panic in Villefort's eyes giving way to a dawning sense of deep and genuine fear. It brought a thin smile of satisfaction to his bloodless lips.

"I'll have you know, this was never my plan. I intended you to be publicly humiliated for your connection to Benedetto, then imprisoned and likely executed for your unusual drinking habits," the count continued. "But I think this is better. The crown would never execute an invalid, and now you will spend the rest of your miserable life trapped as you trapped me for fourteen years. You quoted Scripture to me when we met in May, do you recall? Here I have some verses for you. 'The nations have fallen into a pit of their making; their feet are snared in the net they have hidden.' Psalm 9, lines 15 and 16."

The count stood, and Bertuccio helped Haydee to her feet. Bertuccio did an admirable job of hiding his surprise and confusion, but not enough to hide it from the count's keen eyes.

"Bertuccio, how much did you see?" the count asked.

Bertuccio took a deep breath. "I saw enough, my lord. A heart in a jar, a man wrapped in bandages, confessions and magic and things I don't understand," he said, looking the count in the eye.

"Do you have any questions?" Monte Cristo asked. "Now would be the time to ask."

"Just one, excellency," he said. "What will you have me do?"

Monte Cristo smiled, touched by the man's loyalty.

"Have him taken to a hospital. He has some wound to his chest, not of my doing." The count glanced to Valentine. "Nothing will reverse his condition now."

Bertuccio nodded, helped Haydee to sit on the bed, and motioned for Valentine to come attend to her. He picked Villefort up like a bundle of firewood, eyeing the stake wound and noticing that someone else had made the same mistake he once had.

"Wait! Max never returned yesterday. I need to know what happened to him," Valentine said before Bertuccio could leave. She ran to her father's side and looked him in the eye. "Father, if you ever loved me, tell me where to find Maximilien. I'll find a dictionary, you can tell me the way Grandpapa would."

Rage filled Villefort's eyes. He blinked slowly, giving Valentine a moment of encouragement, but then he blinked again and again, faster each time. Soon he fluttered his eyelids in as emphatic a response as Noirtier himself could give: "I will not."

"Allow me," the count said.

His bandaged fingers grasped either side of Villefort's head, forcing their eyes to meet again, and a baleful light illuminated the count's stare. It reminded her of a jack o'lantern on Halloween night, and an immense discomfort grew on the living side of her father's face. After a moment, the light dimmed and the count stepped away. He said nothing, but gave Bertuccio a signal to continue his task.

"What did you do?" Valentine asked.

"Our minds met," the count said, distracted. "He was...*mon dieu...*"

Valentine took his cold hand in both of hers.

"Please, monsieur. Is Max alright?" she asked.

The count shook his head to clear it. "Yes, yes, I know where Max is, and we can rescue him if we hurry," he said. "Go and pack anything you brought to this house; we need to leave tonight."

Tears of joy leapt to her eyes as Valentine ran from the room. Haydee stood with the aid of the bedpost before chancing her weight on her own two feet.

"My love, you're worried," Haydee said. "In all the time we've spent together, even after your duel with Mondego, I've never seen you worried."

"When I was in Villefort's mind, when I forced him to tell me where Max is, I saw something else. Something terrible," Monte Cristo said, stroking Haydee's thick dark hair. "We need to find Danglars right away. No longer just my revenge, but the lives of millions depend on it."

"Danglars surely fled Paris when the run on his bank started; he is too cowardly to do otherwise," Haydee said. "How can you hope to find him?"

"There's only one place that a man of such greed would go, after all I did to drain his accounts," Monte Cristo said. He went to find paper, to leave a note for Bertuccio. "Gather Ali and Baptistan. Pack everything you care about. First we find Max. Then, we return to Rome."

CHAPTER 105
A FAREWELL TO PARIS

B ack at the Palais, Benedetto's trial continued with the deputy prosecutor presiding. With no further theatrics over the next few hours, the facts of the case produced a straightforward conclusion: Benedetto was found guilty on all counts and sentenced to the guillotine. When Beauchamp published his article about the trial, he noted that the gravity of the sentence seemed to escape Benedetto even after the head magistrate's gavel proclaimed it final.

Benedetto continued to smile with confidence all the way back to his cell. He held one certainty in his mind: whoever Lord Wilmore was, his hatred for M. de Villefort must run deep to pull both Benedetto and the count into his game. For his success in publicly exposing and humiliating Villefort, Benedetto expected to be rewarded for a job well done with a second escape. He found a letter addressed to him when he returned to his cell at the Lion's Den.

"M. Benedetto, you performed your part admirably. However, I regret to inform you," he read aloud, his smile fading for the first time, "that murdering the tailor and the cab driver were deviations from the plan which cannot be tolerated. Your services are no longer required, and the consequences of your actions will not be avoided. Sincerely, and may God have mercy on your soul, Lord Wilmore."

The trial audience was also treated to surprising news as soon as they left the courthouse. Since being escorted to his office for the recess, Villefort had since appeared in a minor hospital with extreme paralysis from apoplexy and a collapsed lung. The doctors expected him to live, but never move or speak again.

As Haydee directed the evacuation of the house in the Champs-Elysees, the Count of Monte Cristo descended into the Catacombs via the sewers and traversed the shadows to reach the Villefort home. He covered his bandages with his simplest travelling-clothes, a plain shirt and jacket with his ever-present gloves and a light scarf to hide the line of his mask at his throat. No servants minded the entrance, and Monte Cristo used his strength to force the front door open.

The lack of staff persisted inside; most of them had resigned when they realized Valentine had disappeared, and the rest abandoned the house when news of the trial reached them. Monte Cristo stalked the halls, checking every room. Villefort had told him across the mental link that Max was somewhere in the house, as well as the dreadful purpose he was to be put to. Though his body was ruined, Villefort's will remained strong enough to fight back before the count could learn Max's precise location.

The count would not have imagined it possible to hate Danglars more than he already did, but this despicable plot shocked him to his core. Dim memories from Edmond's childhood bubbled to the surface, of the constant gnawing fear that came from knowing the hungry dead roamed the earth and there was no guarantee of safety anywhere. Danglars grew up in that same environment, immersed in that same fear, and yet he prepared to plunge Europe into that darkness again. The count could not banish the notion that if Danglars took half the effort he spent on deceit and used it on entrepreneurship instead, he could have earned all the riches he desired honestly.

The count did not find Max anywhere on the ground floor or in the cellar, so he moved on to the second story. He found M. Noirtier's bedroom, where the old man himself sat in his wheelchair. Barrois the gargoyle helped him drink a glass of water, but concern filled Noirtier's eyes. When he saw the count in one of the many mirrors lining the room, he winked his right eye frantically; his signal to fetch Valentine, though the count didn't know it.

Valentine had told Haydee about her methods to translate her grandfather's eye movements into spoken language, but Monte Cristo had a faster way to communicate. He rushed to Noirtier's side and locked eyes with him, probing into Noirtier's mind with as much care and gentleness as he could.

"Valentine! Valentine! Where is Valentine?" Noirtier screamed inside the count's head.

"Listen, monsieur! We have no time to lose. I can hear you, monsieur. I can hear you!" Monte Cristo projected across their link.

Immediate surprise flooded into Noirtier's face. "You...you can hear me? I can speak?"

"Your voice is still imprisoned, M. Noirtier," the count said, "but at this moment I can hear your thoughts."

Noirtier closed his eyes as tears rolled down his creased cheeks, the simple relief of knowing someone could hear his words again overriding the urgency of the situation.

"Valentine is safe, Noirtier," the count continued. "She's with my companion Haydee, and I've come to find Maximilien Morrel. Do you know what your son did with him?"

"Morrel! Gerard attacked him right in front of me! I didn't think it possible, but my son has gone utterly mad," Noirtier said. "If he's not dead already, Gerard must have put him in his study. The servants aren't allowed to enter, if any of them are still here, and he has the only key."

"Locks will not be a problem, monsieur," the count said. "Now, I have to go."

"Wait!" Noirtier said. "You can't leave me here. Barrois can bring me food, but the pantry will run out someday."

"Don't worry, monsieur. I've left word with my steward to come find you and take you away. We'll reunite you with Valentine soon," the count promised. He gave Noirtier's shoulder a firm squeeze and broke the mental connection.

Max sat slumped in his chair, parched from thirst, delirium setting in from two days without food. Cords bound his arms and legs, and an old necktie held a cloth gag in his mouth.

His mind reeled over what Villefort meant to do with him. Was he to be shot? Tried on some fabricated charge and executed, or forgotten in the study to die of thirst? He tried to remember if Villefort had really said they were going on a trip, and something about Baron Danglars, or if that was a fiction from the blow to his head.

A sound caused Max to raise his head a fraction. He thought he saw the doorjamb splintering under the force of the Count of Monte Cristo pushing his way into the study. The count hurried to Max's side and tore away the gag and restraints. Too tired to hold himself up anymore, Max slithered to the floor and lost consciousness.

Max returned to awareness in fits broken by long hours of darkness. He experienced the world in fragmented moments of Barrois holding a water glass to his lips or the count giving him a mix of brandy and chicken broth. Gradually, his lapses out of the world felt less like sickness and more like sleep.

Finally, he awoke feeling much more human, and found himself in a carriage on a country road. He sat up and stretched, opened a window for the sensation of moving air on his face, and turned to see the count watching him. Baptistan also sat in the carriage, neither moving nor speaking.

"Welcome back," the count said with a warm smile.

"Where are we?" Max asked, his voice hoarse after his captivity.

"On the road to Marseille, where we will board my yacht," Monte Cristo said, handing Max a canteen. "Haydee and Valentine will meet us at the port, and I'll leave you with them at my island."

Max took a grateful drink of the cool, sweet water. "What about you, aren't you coming with us?"

"In time," Monte Cristo said, "but there's something important I have to take care of in Rome first."

"Whatever it is, let me help you," Max said. "You've done so much for me, including saving my life twice directly and indirectly. I was a shell of a man, not worthy of Valentine's affection when I came back from war. You helped me return to myself."

The count's smile did not falter. "I suppose this is as good a time as any to correct you; I've saved you three times."

"Impossible!" Max said. "I have no doubt you'd be capable of it, but I'd remember such a thing."

"Well, you never knew I did it," Monte Cristo said. "You remember the story of the man who saved your father's business?"

"Of course, how could I forget?" Max laughed.

"You recall that Thomson & French denied ever sending the clerk who bought and forgave your father's debts? That's because they never did send one," Monte Cristo said. "Saving your father was one of the first things I did when I found my fortune, before being reborn as the man you see. I also left the red purse for your sister to find in my old home."

"I always thought that they denied sending a clerk because the clerk was really Signor Dimonte, disguising himself as a..." Max trailed off, realization dawning on his face. "Signor Dimonte. Monte Cristo. Egad, have I really been that blind for months?"

Monte Cristo only smiled.

"Wait, you said that Julie found the money in your old home? She took me to that address many years ago, and I remember a sailor lived there once who worked for my father," Max said. "His name was..."

"Edmond Dantes," the count answered. "Yes, that was my name once. In fact, I remember you as an infant; I was about eleven years old when you were born, and our fathers knew each other. How would your new society friends react to know that you once bounced on the Count of Monte Cristo's knee and even spit up on him once!"

Max laughed at the revelation, a deep belly laugh that shook him until it moved him to tears. When he composed himself again, his eyes widened.

"My word, Julie! Emanuel! Raoul! They'll be worried sick, I have to tell them what's happened!" Max said.

"Settle yourself, Max," the count said. "You'll have plenty of time to write on my island. I have friends who carry any mail I wish to send to the mainland."

"The island! You changed the subject so deftly, you almost avoided answering me," Max said. "What do you plan to do in Rome, and what can I do to help?"

Monte Cristo stared at Max for a while before answering. "I need to find Baron Danglars, who has fled to Rome," he said at last, watching Max's reaction. "I've manipulated his fortunes for months to ruin him financially, as payment for his part in destroying Edmond Dantes' life. Now I need to stop him before he can carry out the foulest deed you could possibly imagine, which would cause the deaths of millions."

"Then I can do nothing less than help you," Max said, straightening his spine and squaring his shoulders.

"It could be dangerous. It could be bloody," the count said.

"All the more reason that you may need the help," Max replied.

Monte Cristo nodded. "Get some rest, then. I need to think, and plan. There won't be much time once we arrive, and we must be prepared."

As Max made himself more comfortable, the count opened a compartment by his seat and retrieved the hollowed-out emerald which held his wondrous preparation of hashish pills. He swallowed one and allowed the effects to expand his mind, focusing on his goal of stopping Danglars.

Monte Cristo and Max left Paris on July 28 and arrived in Marseille on July 30. By then, the count had crafted the beginnings of a plan. When Max asked him about it, the count told him they could discuss it aboard the yacht. As usual, the count preferred to pilot the vessel himself as they pulled out of the harbour.

Though the storefronts and people had changed, the streets of Marseille remained all too familiar to the count. Unexpected memories of Edmond Dantes, which the count had assumed to be buried, lurched to the surface. He had last come to Marseille in another life and as another man; in spite of that, he felt a certain degree of lingering fear that the past would swell up and swallow him like a whale.

The count watched in silence as the yacht passed the Catalan village and the stony heap of the Chateau d'If.

CHAPTER 106
A NEW PLAGUE

Five days later, Monte Cristo and Max arrived just outside Rome. They came to *la foro prigione* of San Sebastian, one of the many defensive pits built around Rome during the Dead Plague and in particular the one where Albert had been held hostage. They came in the count's own carriage, transported in a custom compartment aboard the count's yacht. Baptistan followed behind them to the trap door which allowed access to the underground structure. No sentinel stood guard this time, and the count led Max to find Luigi Vampa.

"Signor Vampa, I've come to check in on the task I assigned you," the count said, catching the assembled bandits by surprise. "The matter has become even more important than before. Is our guest secure in *la foro?*"

Luigi Vampa jumped to his feet and bent into a deep bow, taking off his wide-brimmed hat as he went.

"Your excellency, we failed you; I failed you," Vampa said. "As soon as we received your telegraph that the banker would be coming this way, we set out our sentries to capture him. Somehow, he slipped through our perimeter. And then, well, you see what has become of the city."

"I haven't come from the city," Monte Cristo said.

"Excellency, you should see for yourself," Vampa said. He motioned for a dozen of his men to join him and escorted the count and Max back outside and up a nearby hill.

The hill offered a vantage point on the city of Rome. Smoke rose above the walls from dozens of burning buildings, and panicked screams carried across the plain. Towering over it all, a diseased green beacon of light lanced into the sky. As repulsive as the light was, the count felt it calling to something within him.

"Vampa, what is that light?" Monte Cristo asked.

"Light? I don't see a light, but perhaps it is a building on fire," Vampa said. "The panic in the city is like nothing I've ever heard of."

"Are you blind? That column of green light, right there!" Monte Cristo said, pointing at the glowing shaft.

"Count, I see no green light," Max said. "There's nothing there."

Monte Cristo looked around at Vampa and his men, all of whom nodded in agreement.

"Never mind," Monte Cristo said. "Perhaps I'm overtired from the journey. What has caused this panic in the city?"

"The walking dead, excellency," Vampa said. "The first sighting that I know of came two days ago, when dozens of zombies poured forth into the streets from the Hospital of Saint Cosmas, attacking and infecting anyone they found. I don't know yet if this has spread beyond Rome."

Monte Cristo considered the situation in silence. In eight days they had travelled from Paris to Marseille, to the island, to where they stood just outside Rome. The port of Civitavecchia was closed for quarantine, forcing them to make landfall elsewhere and losing yet more time. Between Danglars' head start and their delays, Danglars could have been in Italy and free to wreak havoc for two full days. It seemed he had used the time well.

Carriages trying to flee the carnage choked the roads out of Rome, so many panicked people attempting the same course of action caused an impassible traffic jam. As Monte Cristo watched, a coachman veered off the road to risk the uncertain ground of the plain.

A trio of zombies approached his carriage as he struggled to maneuver off the paving. The driver's seat offered no protection; one of them closed a hand on his ankle, biting his leg. His screams carried to the hill where the count stood, and the carriage toppled over on the uneven ground. One of the wooden arms broke off, freeing a panicked horse to run from the zombies at a full gallop. The horse remained attached to the reins, wrapped around the driver's forearm at the other end, and it dragged him across the dirt and rocks into the forest. With their intended meal pulled away from them, the zombies climbed onto the carriage in search of a way to eat the passengers trapped inside.

The driver had not escaped, however. A single bite transferred the taint and if he survived being dragged by the horse, a terrible fever from the infection would set in to boil his brain and kill him. His corpse was doomed to stand up and search out more victims.

"We're too late," Max said, staring in horror. "Danglars has already done it."

"All is not lost, Max," Monte Cristo said. "We saw no undead on our road here, meaning the Plague cannot have spread far. And we know how to destroy it at the root."

"The crystal?" Max said. "But how will we find it? Danglars could be anywhere."

The shaft of green light rising out of the city called to the count again. He recognized the feeling it stirred in him; it was similar to the song he heard from the jar which held his heart, but like a piece of music with every note played out of key.

"The music of death," he muttered, then continued loud enough for his companions to hear. "I think I can find it. Baptistan, to the carriage!"

Max followed the count back to the road, where Baptistan unlatched hidden panels and compartments on the sides of the carriage. By the time Max reached it, hidden drawers and cabinets blossomed across the carriage to display pistols, rifles, sabres, hatchets, maces, and other weaponry. Monte Cristo laughed at the look on Max's face.

"Max, don't be so surprised!" he said. "Didn't I tell you at Albert's breakfast that I always travel prepared? Arm yourselves, gentlemen."

Vampa and many of his men already carried armaments, and those who did not helped themselves to guns and knives from the carriage. Max selected a rifle, pistols, and a sword similar to his army-issued equipment from Africa. Monte Cristo sprang to the top of a nearby rock, standing head and shoulders above the others.

"Gentlemen, we walk into the mouth of Hell," Monte Cristo said, as he tightened a double bandolier of prepared pistols. "We'll be surrounded at all times by an evil which hasn't been seen on this earth in over thirty years. Some of you were fortunate enough to never know it. The rest of us are haunted every day by the memories of it."

The oldest among Vampa's men nodded. Several of them still bore the scars of those dark days.

"I cannot command you to follow me. I cannot guarantee your safety. I can't even predict what we'll find. What I can promise is the satisfaction of saving the world and vanquishing the darkness ahead of us," Monte Cristo continued. He grinned. "And also a million francs to anyone who survives to the end."

A cheer went up from Vampa's men, every one of them intimately familiar with violence and gold.

"When your guns run dry, hand them to Baptistan," Monte Cristo said. Baptistan pulled on a bulging rucksack and a belt of rattling pouches. "It's hands are faster than they look; it will reload for you. Now, we march on Rome!"

CHAPTER 107
NERO

S everal nights before the count and Max witnessed the devastation of Rome, Danglars arrived in Civitavecchia by ship. His French accent and his utter lack of Italian vocabulary outed him as a foreigner; "less," "cheaper," "discount," and whatever musical terms he happened to recall made up the extent of his command of the language.

He carried almost no luggage with him. In one hand he carried a single suitcase with some essentials, and in the other he carried the lead-lined wooden case containing the mortite crystals. Beneath his coat he wore a double brace of throwing knives.

His original plan called for him to get passage from Civitavecchia into Rome, but the midnight arrival put a sinister idea into his head. Knowing the working of ships from personal experience, he snuck below decks during disembarkation and waited. Sure enough, he found a pair of sailors working down in the hold unsupervised.

Concealed behind a crate, Danglars opened the box of mortite. He emptied one brace of his knives and tucked the crystals into the loops, freeing them from the lead and exposing their power. The knives from that brace went into the box in their place, save for two, and he closed his jacket to conceal the glow.

Remaining unseen by the sailors, Danglars took aim and threw his knives. Each one hit true in the sailors' necks from the far end of the hold. Danglars pushed additional crates into place to conceal their corpses and soon heard shuffling movements from the other side of this barricade. His lips stretched wide with satisfaction, knowing that his fortune was assured.

Danglars reached the gangplank just as the ship prepared to pull away, claiming to have overslept. He watched them leave, still smiling, imagining the crew's surprise when one returned to the hold and found his undead comrades. With a little luck, they could kill most of the crew by the time the ship next drifted ashore and create a small horde to spread the Plague to new lands.

As Danglars looked for a coach to take him to Rome, he found more opportunities on the dark streets of Civitavecchia to hurl his blades into random passers-by. Each one of them felt the unnatural touch of the mortite crystals and rose soon after, fueled by their hunger for flesh. By the time Danglars found a driver and departed, his first wave of zombies found a half-dozen new victims between them. Four of those could only lie in place like revenant bear-traps due to the maiming they received, but two remained mobile enough to hunt.

The authorities quarantined the port while they investigated these strange murders, and when the truth came out, the town echoed with wails of despair. Some older residents remembered the days of the first Dead Plague well enough to know they never wanted to experience it again and took their own lives. The alleys teemed so thick with the undead by that point that their group influence proved as effective as mortite itself, and the suicides reanimated without being bitten.

In Rome Danglars ignored the magnificent dome of St Peter's Cathedral, which is visible long before any other landmark can be seen and has inspired many travelers to tell their coachmen to slow down and let them take it in. Instead, he made his way to the branch office of Thomson & French without distractions.

He arrived on Thursday during a morning lull at the bank. He presented his receipts from the Count of Monte Cristo to a clerk and expressed his wish to be repaid for his extended credit. The clerk examined the receipts and excused himself to speak to the manager, then returned after several minutes. Danglars left his suitcase and wooden box in the waiting room under the eye of a receptionist and followed the clerk into a small office in the back of the bank.

"*Bonjour*, Baron Danglars," the bank manager said in French, always ready to accommodate his customers. He was an older man wearing a simple brown suit and a neat grey mustache. "I understand you wish to make a withdrawal."

"Yes, from the account of the Count of Monte Cristo," Danglars said, having prepared a passable cover story. "I'm afraid the count came to me in Paris at the start of the summer, borrowed millions of francs against the unlimited credit you gave him, and then vanished without a trace."

"I see," the manager said. He motioned to the papers arranged on his desk. "And you say that these are the receipts given to you by the Count of Monte Cristo for these withdrawals?"

"Yes, those are the documents," Danglars said.

"I see," the manager said again. He paused for a moment, considering his words carefully. "Baron Danglars, I am loathe to bring you this information, but I'm afraid you have been duped. We have no record of any account under the name Monte Cristo, and this bank has never extended unlimited credit to any individual, no matter how wealthy."

"That's impossible," Danglars said, his head swimming. "No, that can't be. You must be mistaken."

"There is no mistake, monsieur. Did you not perform your due diligence when this man came to you?" the manager asked.

Danglars recalled his first meeting with the count, when the matter of unlimited credit was first broached. The odd request had somehow begun to sound reasonable once he met the count's eyes, and the rest of their conversation existed in a red haze. When he attempted to recall any more details, his only reward was an awful headache like metal tools scraping the inside of his skull.

"Baron Danglars, I am sorry for your misfortune," the manager continued. "If you like, I can send someone to fetch a police officer to take your report of this fraud. Perhaps they may be able to catch this man and recover your funds."

Danglars shook his head. Drawing police attention to himself was not an option. Even if they didn't connect him to the murders in Civitavecchia, he could be extradited back to France to serve time in a debtor's prison. Besides, he did not even know the count's true name to give to the police. He had no option but to see his plan through. Danglars stood.

"That won't be necessary. I am a successful banker, after all; losing such a sum is a trifle, part of doing business." He extended his hand to the manager. "By the beginning of next quarter, my projected gains will have already wiped this loss from the books."

"If you're certain, monsieur," the bank manager said.

He rose from his seat and leaned across the desk to shake Danglars' offered hand. Danglars clamped the manager's hand in his right and drew a knife with his left. He slashed the blade across the manager's wrist, severing the arteries to spray blood across the opposite wall. Before the shocked manager could cry for help, Danglars lunged forward and stabbed him in the neck as well.

Danglars left the office with the unconcerned air of a satisfied customer. Without a fuss, he killed several clerks and secretaries with his throwing knives as he made his way back to the entrance, ensuring the creation of more zombies thanks to the exposed mortite in his coat. A single guard stood watch in the main vestibule and received a knife through his eye for his trouble before another took him in the throat. Danglars retrieved them, his suitcase, and his box; with a wink at the terrified receptionist, he left.

The receptionist, Laura, remained where she was, too frightened to move or do anything but stare at the dead guard. She knew him, ate lunch with him every day, and for weeks harboured a secret hope for him to ask her to dinner. The sight of his abrupt death in front of her was too much to process.

A twitching in his limbs brought Laura hope that his injuries were less severe than they looked. Her paralysis broke and she moved to his side, already thinking of ways to reassure him he could still live a happy life with one eye. As she cradled his head in her lap, his remaining eye pointed towards her.

"Stefano, it's alright," she said, smiling for his sake. "You're okay."

Stefano did not answer. Instead he bared his teeth and rolled towards Laura, sinking a deep bite into her thigh. As she screamed, he bit down harder to tear away a chunk of her leg. He chewed it and swallowed the fabric of her dress and all.

Laura flung herself backwards and scuttled away on her hands and knees in panic as Stefano pursued her in a half-crawl. She could not reach the exit without passing him and risking another bite, but she could barricade a corner office and call for help from the window. As she made her way through the bank, ignoring the agony in her leg as much as she could, movement ahead of her caught her attention. She sobbed with relief when she recognized the bank manager facing away from her, forced herself to stand and tapped him on the shoulder. His teeth were the last thing she ever saw as he attacked her.

Danglars proceeded to the Hotel de Londres. Signor Pastrini agreed to waive the deposit on a room when Danglars introduced himself as a foreign baron, hoping to nurture a repeat customer. Danglars left his suitcase in his room, replenished the empty spaces in his brace of knives, and ventured back out into the streets of Rome.

Inspiration struck him in front of the Hospital of Saint Cosmas. Danglars lurked nearby until one of the doctors stepped outside into a back alley for a breath of fresh air. The doctor gave up his white coat when confronted with a knife, but Danglars murdered him anyway and entered the hospital with his new disguise.

Though he understood it no better than anyone else, Danglars knew about the proximity theory of the undead. With enough zombies in an area, as few as a dozen, bodies already dead would rise on their own. The effect had proved devastating during the first Dead Plague, when peaceful corpses rose from their graves to meet and join the hordes roaming the landscape.

Danglars could lurk near the hospital with his mortite and have the desired effect without any effort on his part. With a thrill of excitement, he realized that someone may have died of disease or old age anywhere in the building and be turning at that very moment. Still, he decided to help nature take its course.

He prowled the halls watching for an opportunity, which presented itself with a sign directing him to the Comatose Care Unit. Danglars found wards full of docile, bedridden patients who made no sound or struggle as he cut each of their throats. Nobody disturbed him in his repulsive work until a nurse, returning from her break, held up a hand to stop him in the hall outside the wards.

"Excuse me, but only Doctor Dufour is on this service today," she asked. "Are you new here?"

"Nurse, thank God you're here," Danglars said, allowing his excitement to bubble through his words. He pointed to a ward he had just left. "One of the patients has begun speaking, you must come at once!"

Her sense of duty overrode her caution, and the nurse followed Danglars. The dead men inside stirred and rose from their beds. Before the nurse could remark on the situation, Danglars grabbed her by the hair. He slammed her head twice into the doorframe to stun her, then pushed her into the room as prey for the zombies. As with the other wards, he left the doors ajar to allow them to exit when they finished with her.

With his task complete, Danglars walked out the front door of the hospital. He wanted to run, but could not risk drawing attention to himself. The concentration of undead in the hospital touched patients recently dead of injuries or illness throughout the building. They sat up and attacked their mourners and nurses, and the occupants of the morgue kicked loose of their winding sheets. The first screams echoed through the halls as Danglars returned to the street.

To his credit, Danglars did spare a thought for the faithless wife and ungrateful daughter he left behind. He wondered, more from curiosity than from concern, about their chances for survival once the coming terror reached Paris. Eugenie stood a much better chance than Hermine did, he thought; in Hermine's case a better question was if her corpse remained intact enough to rise again.

Zombies overran the hospital by nightfall and spilled into the street to prey on the public. The doctor Danglars murdered for a disguise roamed the back alleys, biting vagrants and winos who slept beneath sheets of newspaper. The unlucky staff of Thomson & French were likewise all turned or too torn apart to reanimate and began to terrorize the Via de Banchi. The second Dead Plague was underway.

CHAPTER 108
THE CONQUEST OF ROME

On the afternoon of Saturday August 4, the Count of Monte Cristo and his makeshift army made the descent into Rome in search of Danglars and his mortite. The count took the lead with a pistol in each hand. A dozen living snares of bandages extended from his arms and from beneath his coat, exposing swathes of furrowed grey flesh. The bandages lashed out under the count's control, pushing zombies from his path or tossing them away like leaves in the wind.

His red eyes kept watch for any zombies which penetrated the movements of his linen tendrils and drew closer to the group, and his pistols responded with lead. Another pair of tendrils handled the task of passing his empty guns back to Baptistan, and returning freshly-loaded guns to his hands. Vampa and his men followed behind the count, spread out in a loose line as they crossed the plain, and fired on anyone who got too close.

"Anyone bleeding could be bitten!" Vampa cried. He shot a zombie with his rifle and stabbed a second through the head with the bayonet before trading it with Baptistan for a fresh gun. "Take no chances, take no prisoners!"

Their tactics worked in the open field, but in the tighter confines of the city streets they found themselves exposed. The stench of dead flesh under the summer sun was an overpowering distraction. Men on each end of the line strayed too close to the mouths of alleys, and a hungrier sort of mouth ravaged them for it. Another zombie creeping behind the line brought down one of the bandits from behind.

"Move closer together!" Max said, unsure if anyone could hear him above the screams and gunfire. "We need to coordinate!"

"Max, what's happening back there?" the count shouted, still ahead of the rest of the group and dispatching the undead with apparent ease. He risked a moment's lapse of concentration to glance back.

"Never mind us, watch out!" Max yelled, pointing forward.

A zombie slipped through the count's guard and came within a foot of him, still shambling forward. To the count's surprise, it ignored him and instead lunged for one of Vampa's men. Max raised his rifle to blow the zombie's head apart, too late to prevent the bandit from being bitten.

"Circle up!" Max yelled, surprised at the authority in his own voice. He fell back to parroting orders given to him while on campaign. "Formation, formation!"

With Max's military direction, Vampa and his men formed a circle around Baptistan. This protected their flanks and allowed men in the rear to watch for threats behind them. A disbelieving laugh rose to Max's lips as he realized that battle-hardened bandits and lifelong criminals were following the orders of a medic prone to mood swings and hallucinations. Movement caught his eye and he swung his gun to respond, but then he realized the person moving toward him came at a run rather than a shambling plod. Furthermore, he recognized the man's face.

"Franz!" Max cried. He rushed out of the circle to grab Franz and bring him to safety. "Are you alive or undead?"

"Alive, dammit, alive!" Franz yelled in response, his eyes wide with fright. He wore shirtsleeves with no jacket or waistcoat. "Alive, but who knows how much longer? What the hell is happening?"

"Armageddon," Vampa replied, punctuating his statement with two pistol shots to put down zombies which approached behind Franz.

"Do you have a weapon?" Max asked, not wasting time on pleasantries. Franz shook his head. "Then get in the circle and help the wooden man reload."

Franz nodded and took up his position, accepting guns from the bandits around him along with powder and shot from Baptistan's supplies. As he worked, he noticed the count in all his glory for the first time. The bandages danced through the air, his pistols blazed, and he even kicked a zombie into a stone wall with enough force to crumble the masonry. The astounding display of the count's powers brought Franz a small degree of satisfaction. If he survived long enough to see Albert again, he could gloat about the count not being all that he appeared.

"I heard the shots and came as fast as I could," Franz said, talking just to stave off panic. "Any company with a gun is good company at a time like this!"

The group fought their way through the streets, Monte Cristo leading the way to the towering green light which only he could see. It called to him with such force that he hardly needed to see it, but they reached familiar avenues soon enough.

Franz recognized the area as well; they approached the Hotel de Londres, where he and Albert stayed for the Carnival and had their first official introduction to the count. While reloading a pistol for Vampa, he hoped Signor Pastrini had found somewhere safe to take refuge.

"This is madness! Where are we going?" cried one of Vampa's men. "The count leads us deeper into a pit of demons, and we don't even know where we're going!"

"Hold your tongue!" Vampa answered above the din. "I trust him, and that'll be good enough for you!"

The man cursed in Italian and broke away from the circle. Some of the others followed him. They retreated in the hopes of escaping the city again, but did not make it far before being overwhelmed by the dead.

"Excellency, I trust that you know where you're going," Vampa shouted, "but I hope it's not far!"

"It's here," the count replied.

They stood in front of the Hotel de Londres itself. To everyone else it appeared to be an ordinary building, but to the count it stood as the epicentre of a pulsing green illumination. The aura surrounding the building crept outward, growing larger by inches as the count watched.

"Everyone, inside now," the count said. "We can barricade the door, and this Plague will be over soon enough."

Max stood guard at the door, firing into the undead to keep them at bay while Vampa and his few remaining bandits filed into the hotel. Franz was one of the last to enter, with only the count and Max still outside.

"Behind you!" Franz shouted as Max mounted the steps.

Lunging forward with an empty rifle, Franz swung the bayonet at a zombie creeping around the corner. He stabbed it through the head before it could bite Max, but while he struggled to pull the bayonet free, another zombie stepped forward and sunk its teeth into Franz's shoulder.

An instant too late, a bandage darted forward and tore the zombie's head off. Max rushed to bring Franz inside, and Monte Cristo shut the doors after following them. Vampa and his men carried the lobby furniture over to barricade the door. All they could hear was Franz's rapid breathing and the pounding of rotting fists from outside.

CHAPTER 109
ROOM SERVICE

To Monte Cristo's eyes, a distracting green haze flooded the hotel and made it difficult to see or focus. He could make out Vampa rummaging behind the front desk and Max cutting away Franz's sleeve to examine his wound, but it seemed to come to him in a series of photographs.

"It's not deep," Max said to reassure Franz. He sent a bandit to the hotel bar for a bottle of liquor, and poured the rum onto the wound to clean it as best he could. "The teeth grazed the bony part of your shoulder, where the humerus meets the clavicle."

A simple bandage torn from the discarded sleeve managed the bleeding, but blood loss was not the main concern. With the infection already in his blood, he turned pale and began to sweat. The location of the bite made a battlefield amputation impossible, even if Max had access to a proper medical tent.

"Max, be a friend," Franz said, his voice shaking. To his credit, he met the prospect ahead of him without tears. "Be a friend and don't let me become one of those things."

"Never mind that," Max said, putting on a brave face. He recalled with shame his fervent prayers from only a few weeks before, that something would remove Franz from his and Valentine's lives. "The count knows how to stop all of this. Just be strong and hold on."

The call of the mortite echoed from every angle around the count, surrounding him and making it impossible to follow the song to Danglars. The count felt like a blind man standing in an orchestra pit, trying to single out a particular clarinet.

"I've found him!" Vampa said from the desk. He held up the guest ledger. "The fool took a room under his own name. Fourth floor, suite 405."

Monte Cristo led the way up the stairs, with Max supporting Franz. The count used his strength to force open the locked door to suite 405. Immediately, a knife slammed into the count's chest. Danglars stood at the far end of the room, another knife at the ready and his smile fading when the count ignored the attack.

The count held out his hands and bandages leapt forward from beneath his sleeves. They wrapped Danglars in linen from shoulders to waist, immobilizing him. Vampa ordered his men to ransack the room in search of glowing green crystals.

"Where is the mortite?" Monte Cristo demanded.

"The what?" Danglars asked, hiding his fear as he glanced at the grey skin of the count's hands exposed by his living bandages.

"Don't toy with me, baron. Villefort told me everything," the count said.

"Really, M. de Monte Cristo, I haven't any idea what you're talking about," Danglars said. "By the way, I will have to cancel your unlimited credit."

The count growled deep in his throat, frustrated by the very sound of Danglars' voice against the background noise of the mortite itself. He focused his power to compel Danglars to tell him what he wanted, but Danglars did something unexpected: he closed his eyes.

"It's a funny thing; when I went to Thomson & French, they told me they had never heard of you. The bank manager did remind me of something before he died, though," Danglars said. "When we first met, the last thing I can remember before agreeing to your insane request is meeting your red eyes. So you'll forgive me if I don't look at them again."

"Count, Franz doesn't have time for this," Max said. Franz sat shivering violently against the wall, nearly as pale as the count himself.

"Oh dear, is that Franz d'Epinay? Was he bitten? What a shame," Danglars said with an exaggerated frown. "You'd better put him down, and quickly, before he turns."

"Putting people down? What a capital idea, baron," Monte Cristo said.

With a flick of his wrists, he hurled Danglars across the room and through the nearest window. Only the count's will channeled through his bandages kept him aloft, four storeys above the ground. Danglars shrieked with fright, a high-pitched keening very unlike his ordinary voice.

"Alright, alright! The mortite is in the bedroom, stuffed into the blue pillow on the left!" Danglars screamed. "Just don't kill me, please!"

Vampa barked orders to his men and they soon returned with every pillow from the bed, tearing them open with daggers until the glowing shards scattered to the floor. Monte Cristo grinned his fearsome grin.

"I'll make you a deal, Danglars," he said. "If you can figure out who I am, who I really am, I won't kill you."

Danglars worked in his mind to compose a list of everyone who could mean him ill, but soon gave up. So many abandoned creditors, spurned business partners, and political rivals accumulated through the years made it a useless exercise.

"You're responsible for my bank losing everything," Danglars said, making an educated guess. "You put the fraud Andrea Cavalcanti into my path to humiliate me."

"Both true, but not the answer I wanted," Monte Cristo said. "I'll give you a hint. You once wrote a letter denouncing me, twisting a dying man's request into an act of treason. Do you remember now?"

The words rang familiar to Danglars, and he remembered an evening in Marseille with a lovesick Catalan and a drunken tailor. He had wanted to get someone out of his way, someone he couldn't bear to deal with anymore, and it had all seemed very important at the time. That time, however, had been over twenty years ago.

"I remember the letter," Danglars admitted, his voice very thin. "But as for your name, I can't recall."

"Edmond Dantes!" the count roared, and tore away his mask. As he spoke, all light drained from the confines of the hotel room for a moment. "My name was Edmond Dantes, and your letter took everything from me!"

Danglars' blood chilled and his heart skipped a beat, as much from the brunt of such unbridled fury as from seeing the count's true face.

"Well, I certainly remember you now," Danglars said, hoping to placate the count. "You seem to have done well for yourself since going to prison. How did you find me?"

"I spent six years alone in a dungeon before learning what you did,"

Monte Cristo said, hate burning in his red eyes. "You'll go the rest of your life without learning how I tracked you down. *Au revoir*, Baron Danglars."

"Wait, wait!" Danglars screamed. "You said you wouldn't kill me!"

Rather than drop him, the count lowered Danglars and set him on the ground with all the care of handling a china teacup. The nearest group of zombies milled at least a hundred feet away. Danglars looked up as the bandages released him to see the count leaning out the window and watching him. In a rare moment of gratitude, Danglars waved.

"Thank you, monsieur! Thank you!" he said, and turned to avoid the slow-moving zombies who had taken notice of his voice.

Danglars walked away at a brisk pace, conserving his energy in case he needed to run later. He could still find a safe place to hide, he reasoned, and even if the count put a premature stop to the Plague it may not ruin him. After all, the sudden reappearance of zombies could still drive the demand he relied on. Uncertainty might serve him as well as actual danger.

A sharp pain in his ankle interrupted his thoughts before he lost sight of the Hotel de Londres. Danglars felt something crawling beneath his trousers; when he raised his cuffs to look, shining black beetles covered his lower legs and bit his flesh. He couldn't shake them off, nor take the time to remove them one by one with the undead shambling towards him. Instead he held his cuffs up like a lady raising her skirts to run through mud, hoping they would fall away on their own.

The beetles clung on and continued biting, their mandibles like razor blades. The pain spread to both of his ankles and worsened until he heard a small pop in his right leg, coupled with a sensation like a horse kicking him in his calf. He yelped, attracting the attention of more zombies, and found he could no longer hold his considerable weight on that foot.

He cast a desperate look over his shoulder, hobbling as his former employer, Pierre Morrel, had hobbled on his wooden leg so long ago. The zombies grew closer, and the count's bandaged face still watched him from the upper floor of the hotel. Danglars' only choice was to keep going, but he hardly made any progress at all with his severe limp. He sobbed with panic as pain exploded in his left ankle as well. His leg buckled beneath him, sending him to the ground. From there, he could see the cause of his agony: the beetles had eaten through the tendons on the backs of his calves.

Danglars still tried to crawl away, his whimpers and sniffling reaching the count's keen ears as if they were face to face, but the zombies at last caught up to him. He cried out for his mother when the first hand closed around his ankle, and cursed the name of God when the first set of teeth tore flesh from his calf. More zombies took hold of his useless legs and pulled him backward into the mob, where they feasted on his thighs.

From the hotel window, the count took in the spectacle without blinking and smiled as the hungry dead found the fat rolls of Danglars' stomach. After four or five zombies bit into Danglars' abdomen, another reached into the wound and pulled out a loop of intestine to gnaw on. The howls of agony from the street sang to the count's ears sweeter than any opera or symphony, but all symphonies come to an end, and the cries faltered. When the group of zombies moved on, Danglars' reanimated corpse crawled after them with one of his legs torn away and the other stripped to the bone.

Monte Cristo turned and picked up a piece of mortite in each hand. The pulsating light within the crystals spoke promises to him, temptations of letting them continue their work. The undead had ignored him during the battle through the streets, in favour of attacking and feasting on his living companions. He could allow the new Plague to claim the entire world, even use his powers to help it, and rule a planet of the dead; not a count, but a king.

"Count!" Max yelled, breaking Monte Cristo's reverie. "We need to hurry!"

Through the green haze, Franz indeed appeared to be at death's door. More than that, the concern and compassion in Max's eyes spoke to the count. If he allowed the Plague to burn through the world, he would undo Max and Valentine's struggle for their love. He could grant immortality to Haydee, but would she want to take it knowing what he'd done? All of human history would be for naught, terminating the moment he succumbed to the mortite's call. With a shudder, he realized he would be no better than Danglars himself.

The count clenched his fists, and the mortite crystals crumbled to lightless sand beneath the pressure. He discarded the sand and picked up another pair of shards, crushing them as well and grinding another beneath his heel. The ambient green light that only he could see filling the room dimmed bit by bit as Vampa and Baptistan handed the count more and more mortite to be destroyed, until the job was done.

Out in the street, Danglars' shambling corpse laid still, cut off from the dark energy which sustained it. The rest of the horde followed suit, the effect rippling outwards from the Hotel de Londres and across the city. The driver who the count had seen dragged into the forest, fell before he could reach a sleeping vagrant resting beneath a tree.

The ship of zombies Danglars had sent off from Civitavecchia ran aground in Tunis, where the undead sailors were freed by well-meaning rescue efforts and began to spread the Plague there. They and all of their reanimated victims fell minutes after the mortite was destroyed in Rome.

In the hotel, Franz stopped shivering. He breathed easier for a moment, then ran across the room and vomited a black oily substance into the wastebasket. Max felt Franz's forehead and announced the fever had broken.

"I do feel much better," Franz said, colour returning to his face. He shook Max's hand. "Thank you for not being too hasty with a bullet."

"You should thank the count," Max said with a smile. "He did all the work."

Franz stood before the count with hand extended, then changed his mind and bent in a deep bow to him instead.

"Your excellency, my sincere thanks," Franz said. "And also my apologies. When we first met, I was half-convinced you were some nefarious creature of the night. While you're clearly something more than human, humanity should be thankful that you walk among us."

"You flatter me too much, Franz," the count replied as he put his mask back on. He hadn't expected such a heartfelt display of gratitude. "It was trivial. My goal was to wipe out everything Danglars held dear, up to and including his undead horde."

Vampa's men cleared the room of Danglars' few valuables and returned to *la foro prigione*. Monte Cristo took Vampa aside and reminded him to supply the names of the men who had survived the attack, and any family of the men who did not, to receive the promised reward.

The walk back to Vampa's hideout was peaceful, but gruesome. They and any other survivors brave enough to venture outside found the streets littered with corpses and the gutters running deep with blood. Max swallowed hard and walked beside the count, resolute not to look down and risk seeing Hugo's face again among the dead.

"Count, you said that you destroyed the crystals only to spite Danglars," Max said in a low voice. "Did you really mean that?"

"Of course," the count said. After a moment, he caught Max's worried eye and smiled. "Although, I suppose that it did occur to me that I would leave you and Valentine with a dreadful mess to deal with if I didn't."

Max laughed, surprised that he even could among so much death. The bystanders must think him crazy for it, and he sympathized with them completely. When they reached the bandit lair, Vampa's wife Teresa waited for them wearing a simple violet dress.

"The man with no future," she said with a smile, reaching out to embrace Monte Cristo. "It's not often someone manages to surprise me."

"It was nothing," the count said. "A detour at the end of a road I've been travelling for twenty-three years."

"And now that the road is ended?" Teresa asked.

Monte Cristo considered his answer, staring down at his bandaged hands where spatters of Danglars' blood stained the linen. The single aim of his transformation had been revenge, revenge had now been carried out in full. Fernand died by his own flames, knowing his precious legacy was permanently erased. Villefort had been publicly disgraced and crippled past the point of ever orating or drinking blood again. Danglars had been bankrupted and subjected to the same horrific fate he had been willing to inflict on the entire world. Even Caderousse was dead, after squandering every opportunity God and the count gave him to atone for his misdeeds.

He left Teresa without answering her question, and continued pondering it in silence on his yacht as he sailed back to his island with Max and Baptistan. Haydee waited for him there with Ali, and reuniting with her was as good a short-term goal as any.

"After that, then what?" Monte Cristo muttered, gazing at the setting sun. "What do I do with eternity?"

CHAPTER 110
FAITH

The count's island came into view at about six o'clock in the evening on August 5, with the setting sun casting a few final rays across the water. A soft rose hue suffused the sky and the mountain for which both the island and the count were named stood half illuminated, half in darkness.

Dusk settled across the island as the yacht approached, with the count standing unmasked at the prow. He wore a simple blue pea jacket, open to expose his bandaged chest, and canvas trousers. The sea breeze passed through his bandages as through a delicate nightshirt, caressing his embalmed flesh and stirring murky memories of Edmond Dantes savouring the fresh air and toil of life as a sailor.

"Master, we approach the island," Baptistan said from behind him. "We must drop anchor soon."

"Yes, of course," the count replied.

He returned to his cabin intending to put on the mask of his old face, but reconsidered. It watched him with hollow eyes from the mannequin bust where it rested, taunting him. Valentine and Bertuccio had accepted his true nature admirably, and Max had limited himself to a few medical questions on the journey to Rome. Haydee, of course, knew and loved his true face. He decided to leave the mask where it was, but stood staring at it for a long moment.

Although it was the face he wore at the time of his mummification beneath Monte Cristo, the count did not recognize it as the face Edmond Dantes was born with and grew into. Edmond's face was full of life and wonder; the nameless man who escaped from the Chateau d'If wore the harder, narrow-eyed and suspicious face which now stared at the count.

Not for the first time, the count doubted who he was. A continuity existed from Edmond Dantes to him, he knew that, but did he have any right to the name? The events of Edmond's life felt like memories cut out of someone else and implanted into his own head. The count's pursuit of vengeance had driven him to lengths which would have horrified Edmond, but at the same time, he did it all for the sake of achieving justice for Edmond.

The count felt a certain peace when he set foot on the solid rock of his island again. The island and its secrets were the final gift from his teacher and friend Gianmarco Faria, where Edmond died and the count was reborn with fresh purpose.

Returning with that purpose fulfilled was an interesting feeling. If he chose, he could climb to the top of the mountain and sit there satisfied with his revenge for the next hundred years or more. For the first time in almost twenty years, there was no next step in his plan. He could climb into a sarcophagus and sleep for millennia, or open the black stone jar and put a knife through his own heart to grant himself the repose which every other human being takes for granted. People throughout history have grappled with a lack of purpose, but none had faced the prospect of eternity without direction.

Instead, he walked off into the darkness of the island's interior. Baptistan and Max followed behind with a torch, but fourteen years of darkness bought the count excellent night vision. He followed the old signs carved by Cardinal Spada centuries ago, and found the door to the cave.

After his transformation, he ordered the construction of a hidden door to mask the entrance. A boulder still blocked the entrance, but this hollow boulder could be moved aside after pressing a secret latch.

As soon as the count lifted the trapdoor, he heard music and laughter from his grotto beneath the earth. An enticing aroma of stewing goat reached his nose; his arrival coincided with Haydee and Valentine sitting down to their evening meal. The count descended the stairs into the room where he had first received Franz d'Epinay, still decorated with the lavish silks and tapestries which had so impressed Franz and distracted him from the strangeness of their meeting.

The count realized his eccentric persona as a millionaire infatuated with the Far East, the peacocking and superficial theatre intended to keep the Parisian elites gossiping about trivialities while he did his work, was no longer required. Without the need of it, he could be truer to himself, whoever that self was.

When Max heard Valentine speaking to Haydee, as Haydee played idle chords on her gusle, he did not wait for the count. He pushed aside the tapestry which led to the dining-room, and the count heard the clatter of a teacup against a saucer as well as Valentine's squeal of delight.

The count moved the tapestry aside just far enough to see within. Max recounted the horror in Rome and their actions to combat it, spellbinding Valentine. Haydee's eyes stayed riveted to the tapestry in anticipation of the count's entry, and she met his gaze with a smile. Noirtier sat in a comfortable chair, Bertuccio having delivered him to the island.

That smile, and Valentine's gasps of surprise as Max told the story of their battle, made the count realize that Edmond need not be horrified by everything he'd done. Edmond would have taken pride to know some of what the man using his body had done, such as rescuing a slave from bondage or helping a war-damaged young man and a prisoner of an overbearing father find love and freedom. Indeed, as Max's story reminded him, he saved the entire world from darkness in pursuit of his own personal agenda. The legacy of the Count of Monte Cristo not only told of revenge, but also of hope and restoration.

As if to underscore his thoughts, Haydee took off her necklace on which the Eye of Asclepius hung as a pendant. She laid it in Max's hand and spoke a few low words to him, educating him on the Eye's purpose as a tool for medicine and healing. Under her coaching, Max extended the Eye towards Noirtier and closed his eyes. Warm white light touched Noirtier's heart for a moment.

The count remembered Faria imploring to Edmond that he hold onto the light within himself. Comforted by the thought of that light being reflected in the happy souls before him, he moved the tapestry aside and stepped forward. Noirtier's eyes widened at the count's bandaged form, but he recognized the red eyes at once.

"Hrm," Noirtier said. He coughed in a spasm as Valentine covered her mouth in shock, and his fingers twitched as he did so. "Hngh. Hello ag-again, m-monsieur."

"Take it slowly, M. Noirtier," Haydee said as she refastened her necklace. "Your voice has gone unused for six years."

She stepped up to the count and placed a warm kiss against his cold grey lips, then leaned back to meet his gaze.

"Is it done?" she asked.

"It's done," the count replied. "The mortite is destroyed, but not before Danglars experienced the horror of it firsthand."

"Then sit and enjoy some wine, my love," Haydee said. "You've earned your rest."

She guided the count to the head of the table and poured him a glass of Bordeaux, the light bringing out a ruby hue similar to his own eyes. He stared at it in silence without drinking.

"Count?" Max asked. "Are you alright?"

"Of course I am; I have everything I could want," the count said. "My enemies are vanquished, I'm wealthy beyond most men's imaginations, and I have no fear of death. I have absolutely nothing left to pursue."

"My love, take a moment to savour your victory," Haydee said, standing behind him and running her fingers along his bandaged scalp. "You've finished a monumental project, it's natural to wonder what to do next. Don't focus on forever; forever will come."

"But what am I, without a goal?" Monte Cristo asked.

"What you have been for as long as I've known you: a man of learning, power, resources, and patience," Haydee said. "The world is a troubled place; you could do much good with those traits."

Max swallowed a mouthful of stew and dabbed his mouth with a napkin. "On campaign, I saw the local warlords doing terrible things which we were powerless to stop. And who's to say what happens elsewhere in the world?" he said. "With all your abilities, I can't help but think you could change things for the better."

"And what about that crystal?" Valentine asked. "If Danglars was able to find that much of it, couldn't there be more of it scattered around, waiting for other evil men to find?"

The count sat gazing at his wine. His reflection floated in the depths of the glass, and for a moment he could see beneath his wrappings to the face of Edmond Dantes. The truth which had been teasing him began to dawn.

Edmond died within the walls of the Chateau d'If, and was reborn through Faria's friendship and tutoring. Likewise, that reborn man found the grotto beneath Monte Cristo but never emerged; instead, the count walked the earth from that point forward. For all their dissimilarities, they still shared a core of experiences that bound them together; one thread of identity that led from Edmond's birth through to that very moment of staring into a glass of deep red wine. Though they had distinctions more dramatic than those between an ordinary man's childhood, adolescence, and adulthood, none of them could deny that they were likewise parts of the same man.

Slowly, Edmond Dantes raised the glass to his lips and savoured the sharp tang of the grapes. For the first time since his mummification, he considered what advice his first incarnation would have given.

"I lack a purpose," he said after emptying his glass, "and my loving family offers me one. One day, if I exhaust the world's supply of petty and harmful men, I may come back here and stop the beating of my heart. But until then, it seems I have more work to do."

Max grinned wide and reached for another helping, and Valentine applauded Edmond's resolve. Even Noirtier smiled, his face twitching as the unpracticed muscles moved for the first time in years. Haydee bent over to plant another kiss on Edmond's cheek.

"And perhaps one day we'll both return," she whispered in his ear, "and place my heart next to yours, to better do your work with you."

"I suppose we'll all need to pack, first thing in the morning," Max said. "There's an awful lot of world to cover if we're going to start searching for mortite."

"I think not," Edmond said with a gentle smile. "Maximilien, Valentine, you have been through so much already. Your love for each other helped me recover a part of myself I thought had been destroyed. You deserve to start your lives together, normal lives, and I want to help you begin them."

"What are you saying, count?" Valentine asked.

"I'm saying that I grant you full use of my island, for as long as you wish to stay and as often as you'd like to return," Edmond said. "I have a second yacht, moored on the far side of the island; I had been planning to give it to Max to enjoy with his family, but now it's plain that this includes yourself and M. Noirtier. See the world. Experience it, write about it, learn to love it. The means are yours."

Valentine stumbled over her own words in a rush to thank Edmond for his kindness, and knelt in front of Noirtier to learn his opinion about the news. Too overcome to try and speak, Noirtier made the great effort to move his hand on top of hers and squeeze as hard as he could manage. Edmond stood and walked around to Max's side.

"When the time comes," he whispered in Max's ear, "leave word here at the island and I'll find out. The county of Monte Cristo is very real, and very much mine; I can officiate the wedding whenever you like."

Max blushed and did not answer, but gave Edmond a single pat on the shoulder. After enjoying the remainder of their meal together, everybody retired to the various furnished sleeping chambers within the grotto.

At daybreak the next morning, Max and Valentine awoke to the songs of the island's birds and the aroma of breakfast from the dining room. Near a pot of fresh coffee, they found an envelope addressed to them in Edmond's hand. Valentine read it aloud.

"My son, my daughter, dear Max and Valentine. I hope the morning dawns clear and bright, with all the promise of hopeful seas," she read. "By the time you find this, Haydee and I will have left. We have brought Ali and Baptistan; Bertuccio has remained behind to be your steward for as long as you'll have him. Your yacht awaits you when you are ready to go."

"They're gone?" Max said with disbelief. "How could they leave without saying goodbye?"

"I think this is their goodbye; there's more," Valentine said, continuing with the letter. "Remain on the island as long as you wish, and return as often as you like. You know the secret of the door, and Bertuccio can help you find it if you forget. Perhaps we'll all meet again here someday. I also leave you half of my fortune and treasure; use it well, invest it wisely, and it will help you to build a life with all the comfort you deserve. You'll find it in the farthest angle of the second opening to the west in the grotto."

Max spilled coffee over his hand in the midst of pouring a cup.

"Does it really say half? That's madness! We could travel the breadth of the world twice and still settle down on a farm outside Marseille!"

"Shush, I'm nearly finished," Valentine said, bringing the last part of the letter over to Max to read with him. "Haydee and I have taken your suggestions to heart and intend to make sure there is no possible way for the world to be troubled by the undead again. If we find evil amongst the living in our travels, we'll put a stop to it as it comes. That is our task, but yours is a simpler one: live well, love each other, and be the light that you want to see shining in the world. And if your mettle is tested again, just remember that all human wisdom can be summed up in two words: adapt and overcome."

Valentine set the letter on the table, tears in her eyes from the generosity of the mysterious stranger who had upended their lives and freed them to finally be together. Max stepped forward to hold her in his arms, where he could feel her heartbeat against his.

"So, what should we do now?" he asked.

"Now? Breakfast would be a good start," Valentine replied, smiling against his neck. "After that, I suppose we do what the count hoped we would: we live."

ACKNOWLEDGMENTS

First of all, of course, this book wouldn't be what it is without the foundation of Alexandre Dumas' classic revenge tale *The Count of Monte Cristo*. I first opened it on a family trip to British Columbia in 2009, as something to read on the plane and in the hotel, and could hardly put it down. It would be another 6 very eventful years before I thought of taking on the challenge to expand on some of Dumas' themes against a backdrop of monsters and a looming apocalypse.

I've also got to thank my brother Shawn. When I was 11 or 12, he brought a big stack of hand-me-down paperbacks, including the first Stephen King books I ever read. Those books introduced me to horror and crystallized my desire to be a published author myself someday; which seems odd, considering what tends to happen to authors in Stephen King stories.

A big thank you to the people behind Pitch Wars and #PitMad; it was during my second or third pitch event that I caught the attention of Immortal Works, which of course led to *The Mummy of Monte Cristo* being published! If you're trying to get published, don't discount the power of a social media event like that.

Lastly, I'd like to acknowledge the sources of many of the philosophical and economic ideas put forward by Faria, the count, the smuggler captain, and other characters. Many of those ideas have their roots in the school of Austrian economics, and the work of men like Frederic Bastiat, Murray Rothbard, Ludwig von Mises, and Hans Herman Hoppe. To learn more about Austrian economics and liberty in general, visit the Mises Institute at www.mises.org or listen to the Tom Woods Show podcast.

ABOUT THE AUTHOR

When J Trevor was young, he received a well-worn stack of mystery and horror novels from his older brother, and it instilled in him a lifelong desire to be an author. Heavily influenced by Stephen King's scares, Jim Butcher's action scenes, and the larger-than-life characters in Ayn Rand's books, he blended those influences with classic literature and pulp horror to write his Immortal Works debut THE MUMMY OF MONTE CRISTO.

He has also self-published a young-adult horror novel THE GOOD FIGHT, and was published in the Amazon #1 bestselling horror anthology SECRET STAIRS as the sole romance story in the collection.

He lives in Toronto Canada keeping the redhead gene alive with his wife and newborn daughter, born Friday the 13th.

This has been an
Immortal Production